GOTHIC

SPIRITS & GHOULS SHORT STORIES

ANTHOLOGY OF NEW & CLASSIC TALES

Foreword by Dr. Ahmed Al-Rawi

FLAME TREE PUBLISHING

FANTASY

This is a FLAME TREE Book

Publisher & Creative Director: Nick Wells
Project Editor: Taylor Bentley

Publisher's Note: Due to the historical nature of the classic text, we're aware that there may be some language used which has the potential to cause offence to the modern reader. However, wishing overall to preserve the integrity of the text, rather than imposing contemporary sensibilities, we have left it unaltered.

FLAME TREE PUBLISHING
6 Melbray Mews, Fulham,
London SW6 3NS, United Kingdom
www.flametreepublishing.com

First published 2023

23 25 27 26 24
1 3 5 7 9 10 8 6 4 2

ISBN: 978-1-80417-586-6
Special ISBN: 978-1-80417-339-8

The cover image is created by Flame Tree Studio based on artwork by Slava Gerj and Gabor Ruszkai.

A copy of the CIP data for this book is available from the British Library.

Printed and bound in China

GOTHIC

SPIRITS & GHOULS SHORT STORIES

ANTHOLOGY OF NEW & CLASSIC TALES

Foreword by Dr. Ahmed Al-Rawi

FLAME TREE PUBLISHING

FANTASY

Contents

GOTHIC

SPIRITS & GHOULS SHORT STORIES

ANTHOLOGY OF NEW & CLASSIC TALES

Foreword by Dr. Ahmed Al-Rawi

FLAME TREE PUBLISHING

FANTASY

Foreword: Spirits & Ghouls Short Stories

THE BELIEF IN SPIRITS and legendary creatures like ghouls has certainly existed since the beginning of time, when humans gathered in caves to tell oral stories to each other about the meaning and purpose of life. In Irving Finkel's *The First Ghosts* (2019), a study of Mesopotamian early beliefs, the historian stresses how the earliest known human civilization took the issue of ghosts and mythical beasts for granted, considering it as part of their existence. Since then, we seem to have maintained such a belief despite our scattered geographical locations and different religions, cultures and ethnicities.

There is no doubt, however, that different cultures have made minor and sometimes major changes to the representation of these supernatural creatures in a way that fit their own original beliefs and desires. I studied, for example, the way pre-Islamic Arabian ghouls were transformed in the West to better fit the West's conception of the East and its sensual and imaginative desire in such creatures. In other words, these creatures function as an exotic sensual escape into the mysteries of the past and faraway lands. Hence, they represent an escape into imaginative, emotional and often scary worlds away from the rigid intellectualism that has mostly shaped the West since the Renaissance.

The main reason behind this kind of fascination with the supernatural belief in mythical creatures is certainly related to the nature of human self or our psychological makeup. These beliefs suggest a sense of fear of the unknown especially when it comes to the issue of the unpredictability of death and danger to human life. Indeed, this is ingrained in our DNA, for we are programmed to survive by protecting ourselves from external threats, diseases and other types of physical danger, but most of them, especially death, cannot be conquered. Since our natural surroundings and available knowledge do not offer enough answers, we seek imaginative interpretations to explain the world around us, including the belief in the supernatural. Anything and everything could denote the existence of mythical powers and creatures, such as the stars above us and the movements of winds and birds, giving us false assurances and comfort that we can peek into the unknown and avoid danger, disaster or even death.

When it comes to ghosts and ghouls, they seem to be used in literature mostly side by side with humans either to scare or deter some from achieving their goals or assist others in exploring and navigating their own worlds. Hence, it is never about the metaphysical world of the dead, but it is about the physical world of the living. These creatures and beasts represent archetypes or actual types of people whom we sometimes love, abhor or fear, and their often ethereal existence enhances their power and sense of fear or danger associated with them. Regardless of how we view them, they retain their function as different types of humans, and we seem to remain fixated by them by allowing them to have a permanent state of existence in our minds.

In the future, I think we will continue embracing these ghost and ghoul stories, and they will never fade away from our collective memory. This is because they both entertain and scare us even though they seem absurd to some people who view them using a scientific lens. These stories remain exciting by offering us a thrilling way to express physiological and emotional reactions while actively engaging us to avoid tedious living experiences. More importantly, they reflect who we are as humans by shedding light onto our inner desires, beliefs and, more importantly, our vulnerabilities.

Dr. Ahmed Al-Rawi
School of Communication
Simon Fraser University

Publisher's Note

THE DARK ALLURE of creatures connected to decay, death and a world beyond our own has persisted through the ages and continues to enthral us still – even as the stories and legends this fascination has given rise to fill us with feelings of terror, dread, and even revulsion.

The short stories ahead are teeming with ghosts, ghouls, elemental spirits and other ghastly and mysterious entities and creatures. Among the classic tales are two translated stories from the *One Thousand and One Nights*, which depict the ghūls of Arabian folklore, which would go on to inspire many of the Western authors also featured within, perhaps most notably H.P. Lovecraft. Other stories, such as J. Sheridan Le Fanu's 'Squire Toby's Will', are ghoulish in theme, as characters are haunted by grotesque visions from those beyond the grave, or stumble into uncanny graveyard encounters.

As ever, it was a rewarding challenge to select the modern stories featured in this book. We received over seven hundred stories, which offered a thrilling range of interpretations on the theme, from gothic horror and murder mysteries to science fiction, while other tales drew on folklore and legends from across the globe. In and amongst the creeping chills, many of these stories also have moments of humour and stark beauty. We hope that our readers enjoy the stories in this collection as much as we have, and that they stir and absorb the senses as they delve into the darker recesses of the mind.

The Mother of Sands

Stewart C. Baker

SMILŠU MĀTE, mother of sands – how I wish I had never heard that name, that I had never learned what waits on the far shore of that river we cross upon dying. But I have, and I did, and I must share what I witnessed with you, my closest friends.

It began last September, at the end of that hot, dry summer. I received a letter from the Countess of —, whom I had known as a girl through my mother, who had been her lady's maid. Although as children we had often played together, I had not heard from her in fifteen years, and was much amazed that she remembered me – let alone that she had thought to send me a letter.

My dearest Clara, the letter began, and went on at some length about the rigours of life amidst the landed gentry which I in my rented room in gloomy Stepney cared little to read. Towards the end, though, was a section that riveted my eyes:

> *In short, my dearest Clara, I find myself quite bereft of the friendship we shared in our youth, and should like nothing more than to renew it. It would grant my fondest hope should you accompany me to my native Riga to visit my mother, who has taken ill.*

The letter was signed with my old friend's given name of Ilze. At this I laughed and shook my head, quite certain that I was the recipient of a passing aristocratic fancy, and nothing more.

So it was that I set the affair from my mind and went back to my writing.

* * *

The days wound on until a full month passed and I was surprised by a knocking at my door. I opened it, steeling myself to be set upon by some creditor or unhappy patron, and was met instead with Ilze's smiling face.

"You did not return my letter," she admonished, "but it does not matter. I have everything prepared."

I sputtered my protests – I had work still to do; my creditors would never let me rest – but they fell on deaf ears. Ilze spirited me down the stairs to a waiting carriage, where she plied me with stories of her life. Such was her enthusiasm that I could not so much as speak, let alone request that she return me to my home. Truth be told, I did not try too hard, for while I still felt my old friend would discard me as soon as she grew bored, I had resolved to enjoy the unexpected respite from my worries for as long as it lasted.

We passed the day in a pleasant enough fashion, and stopped for the evening in the seaside town of Southend, where Ilze insisted on a shared room at a common inn. I considered it odd that we had not departed by boat from London, and that she had no servants with her; her insistence on sharing a room was doubly strange. But I did not speak of it: who was I to question the Countess of —?

It was here that the first strange event of our journey occurred. That evening as the sun set, Ilze suddenly paled and rushed me from the inn's dining hall to the room we were to share. I asked what was wrong, but she would say only *Smilšu māte* – the words croaked out from between her lips like a curse and a prayer all at once.

In our quarters, she walked all around with a candle, thrusting it here and there until the shadows danced with movement. After some minutes of this, she placed the candle on the sill, locked the door, and collapsed into bed, sobbing.

I tried to get some sensible response from her, but it was futile. Growing weary myself, I at last reached for the candle myself and blew it out, thinking to sleep. But just as the light guttered away into night's inky blackness, I saw as clear as day a woman standing over my companion, her eyes pooled shadows in her pinched, drawn face.

My heart hammered in my ears; I scarcely dared breathe, so fearful was I. At length, enough moonlight filtered through the window for me to see the woman was gone. Nonetheless I could not calm myself, and lay wakeful all through the long night, with only Ilze's hiccoughing sobs to distract me.

* * *

Though Ilze and I did not speak of it, the first thing we did that morning was search our quarters thoroughly. We found no sign of the woman, only a small heap of dull, brownish-grey sand. Ilze quaked when she saw this, and quickly scattered it about, muttering something in her native tongue, though she would not say why or what.

"It is bad luck to speak of such things," she told me.

"Smilšu māte?" I asked. "Who is she? What does it mean?"

But Ilze only shook her head, and would say no more.

* * *

The rest of our trip passed slowly but uneventfully, and I need spend no time here in recounting it. We went by ship to Amsterdam, and from that squat, bustling port travelled again by carriage. Neither in our cabin nor in any of the inns where we stayed did I again see the woman, though on occasion we found a small heap of sand, which Ilze dealt with in the manner of the first.

We arrived in Riga, the heart of old Livonia, on the first day of November, more than a month after setting out. You who have never visited that distant place will know nothing of its cobbled streets. It will mean nothing to you if I speak of the way the stately Daugava flows past the city's many spires, its frigid waters surprisingly strong.

Ilze's mother lived in a narrow three-storey house painted in a delicate green. Huddled amidst more expansive buildings, it seemed to cling to the edge of the cobblestones, afraid of losing its place. Ilze knocked at the door and entered without waiting for a response, and I followed her reluctantly, for the building birthed in me a nameless unease.

Inside, the walls pressed in on me. They reminded me of our worries. If Ilze felt anything of what I did, however, she did not show it; indeed, compared to the pale, nervous woman I had known on our journey, here in the rooms of her earliest moments she was a different person entirely. She strode from room to room on the ground floor, calling out in her native language, and did not seem to mind when there was no response.

"Mama must be out," she said with a smile. "Come; I shall show you the sights of the town."

But no sooner had we set out than her face took on its familiar melancholy cast. She became listless, and offered no commentary as we strolled from sight to sight, across age-worn bridges and along the banks of the Daugava. I saw a pleasure steamer plying the waters, festooned with flags and filled with travellers. Marvelling at its existence in this antique place, I mentioned that I should like to try it. But, as ever, Ilze would not be drawn out, and I heard no word from her until we returned to her mother's home with the sun pinking the sky.

A light was on in the ground floor window, and my earlier unease returned. I found myself looking for sand as Ilze led me inside, and my heart's blood thrummed in my ears as it had that night when I saw the shadow-pool woman.

My fears proved unfounded. Reclining in a chaise longue was a woman I had never seen before, but who was clearly Ilze's mother: she had the same rich brown hair, the same slightly square face, and the set of her eyes somehow spoke to me, pulling me along despite myself.

"You are late," she said, in slightly accented English. "I had started to fear you would not arrive."

"Oh, mother," Ilze said, reproachful. "Of course I had to come when I heard you were sick."

"Ha! A year ago and more I sent that letter. A strange form of concern you show me, daughter, when you tarry for so long, and bring an uninvited guest when at last you arrive."

Even behind Ilze, I could see her skin flush. "I had pressing business to attend to," she said. "After you sold me to the Count in marriage, my life has not been my own. And it is so remote here that travel alone is—"

"Remote! You speak this way of the land where you were born? I should never have sent you to England, no matter the prize. You—"

Ilze snapped out in her native tongue, and her mother responded in kind. Their voices grew louder as they argued, and not wanting to intrude further than I already had, I stepped into the next room, where tables were laid out with an astounding feast. There were rolls, cheese, and butter by the bowlful; fine cuts of roast and fowl; and delicacies I could not name. Balls of dough adorned with hemp seed filled a plate next to pastries overflowing with a thick, white cream.

Where had it all come from?, I wondered. Who was it for? I had seen no servants in the house, nor any other guests. At a loss for what I might do to pass the time, I popped a pastry into my mouth. Almond paste in the cream, I thought, or something like it – sweet almost to bitterness. Still, I had not eaten in some time and it was good enough. I took another.

At length the shouting in the next room subsided, and Ilze and her mother entered, their arms entwined for all the world as though they had not just been engaged in a fight of the most intimate sort.

"Your pardon, Clara, dearest," Ilze said to me, breaking away from her mother. "In this part of the world we believe it better to air out our emotions."

"It is true," her mother said, as she ushered me to one of the chairs, "no matter what part of the world you find yourself in. You English would be more agreeable did you not bottle up your feelings so. Now sit, and we will show you another of our customs: the feast of the dead."

"All this is for the dead?" The pastries in my stomach heavy as rocks.

Ilze laughed. "Of course not. But it is tradition to give them the first morsel, and the first draught of mead."

"Especially tonight," her mother added, "for on the night after Simjudas, the dead can return to the living, to take back for those who have offended them." And with a light, tinkling laughter, she poured a splash of alcohol into the fireplace, following it with one of the dough balls.

My tongue burned; I only hoped the colour did not spread to my cheeks. Neither Ilze nor her mother seemed to notice. Each piled her plate high with food and filled her cup with mead. Reluctantly, I did the same, although I supposed there was no harm in my inadvertent breaking of their pagan custom so long as they did not know it.

We ate in an uncomfortable silence for a time, until, casting around for some topic of conversation, I said to Ilze's mother: "I am glad to see, Mrs. —, that you have at least regained your health."

The older woman's eyes darkened, and I cursed myself. Why had I brought up the very thing which had caused her and Ilze to erupt earlier?

But I had no need for concern, it seemed; after a moment, the older woman smiled and said, "I will tell you how it came about."

And with that she launched into a story that I myself would not believe, were it not for what happened after.

* * *

Last year (Ilze's mother said), I caught a coughing sickness that would not leave me. The doctors could not cure me, and the prayers of a local priest rumoured to perform miracles failed as well. On the 29th of September, I began to cough blood. ("The day is Saint Michael's," Ilze whispered, "and the start of the month of the dead.")

Despairing, I walked to the shores of the Daugava, certain that I had not long in this life. As I crossed one of the river's bridges, a cold wind overtook me and I fell into a coughing fit so violent that my knees went weak. When I recovered, so much black, clotted blood covered my handkerchief that I resolved to end my life there and then. I leapt into the river, which drew me down into its cold, smothering embrace.

I awoke on a shore I had never before seen: in place of the city were trees of oak and linden, flanked in the distance by rolling hills of a sandy, yellow-grey soil. I was bone wet and shivering, and next to me stood a woman with eyes the colour of shadow.

"You have forsaken the traditions," she said to me. "You sent your only daughter to an uncaring land, and your ancestors go hungry each year. That is why you suffer."

Her voice was like grit: fine and sharp and hard, impossible to shake free.

"What should I do then, Mother?" I asked, shivering from more than damp – for I knew then who she was, and where I had found myself. "How can I gain your forgiveness?"

"Bring her back," she said. "I will take care of the rest."

With that she was gone, and I was alone. I staggered to my feet and walked upstream, thinking to return to Riga. When at last I came upon a town, however, it was not my home, but a clump of simple dwellings surrounded by a wall of stakes as thick as trees.

The townspeople seemed unable to hear me, and would not meet my eyes. I returned to the river, to gaze on its tranquil waters…

* * *

At this, Ilze's mother stopped talking, lost, it seemed, in reminiscence. Ilze, who had grown progressively paler throughout the recounting, gave no sign of talking. My own throat being dry as parchment, I took a swallow of mead and spoke.

"What then?"

Ilze's mother looked at me and smiled, but not pleasantly. Her face melted away, replaced by that of the woman I had seen over Ilze's bed that first night of our journey.

"Why, then, of course," she said, "she died." Her voice was just as Ilze's mother had described it.

She stood in one fluid motion; the candles guttered out, and the dark swarmed in with an inhuman shriek.

The rest of that night is a blur, all shadow and terror and ash. When I woke in the morning I found I had fallen asleep in a chair in the banquet room, and Ilze as well. The tables were empty save a patina of dust, and, search as we might, the two of us could find no evidence whatsoever that anyone lived in the house. All we found was a heap of yellow-grey sand in the front waiting room, where Ilze's mother had greeted us.

We passed some time huddled together, unsure and uncertain. I was of the opinion that the night's events had been a hallucination, brought on perhaps by the fatigue of our journey, or by some ailment we had gathered to ourselves along the way. Ilze, contrarily, believed that we had seen her mother's ghost – that all she had spoken was true, and that Smilšu māte, the mother of sands, had granted her passage on the night of the feast so she might visit her absent daughter and (this in a darkening tone) take her to that other land by force.

"At least, then," I said, "you escaped the last. For you are here with me, alive."

Ilze only shook her head, and sank once more into gloom.

"Come," I said, "and I will show us both the truth of life." For I myself felt a need to be among people.

Ilze protested, but not with any heart, as I dragged her to the offices of the steamer I had seen the day before. Looking back, I cannot recall what moved me to think that a visit to the river – whence her mother claimed to have visited the other side of death – would take Ilze's mind off the previous night's occurrence. Perhaps it was the steamer itself, the only thing in that city which looked to the future instead of the past. Perhaps some stronger, stranger power was at work.

Whatever the reason, we had no trouble booking passage on the afternoon's cruise, and in short order were aboard the little ship's deck. The steamer was just as I had imagined it: a modern marvel, bursting with the energy of a new era, fuelled by the powers of men turned to gods. Gliding past the banks of that provincial land suffused me with optimistic health, but all Ilze cared to do was stand and look into the waters of the river. I am afraid I must tell you I left her there, determined that I, at least, would find pleasure in the day's outing.

But we had been out barely half an hour when the boat began to shudder, and the deck pitched to one side with a crack and roaring boom. A mid-channel collision, I thought, or a fault in the hull. There was another jolt, the air filled with screams, and then the water hit me with a slap of icy cold.

As I sputtered, the truth came to me: it was Smilšu māte, come to claim her own. No sooner had I thought this than the power faded from my limbs and I resigned myself to death, but just before blackness took me, a surge of strength burst through in my limbs; a sudden passion rose in my heart. I would not die here, I resolved – not today! I broke the surface of the water and pushed to the river's edge with surprising ease, shivering in my thin travelling clothes. There was no sign of the steamer, the river's surface crowded with boats and men and ropes – a rescue, I thought, but too late, too late for poor Ilze and the rest.

I watched until evening, cold though I was. Hoping they would stumble across some miraculous survivor – that they would pull my old friend from the water still pink and full of breath, like me.

They found no one. As the rescuers returned to the shore, I asked what had happened, but none answered, lost perhaps in melancholy thoughts of their own. And though I waited by that shore until the moon came full in the sky, I never again saw any sign of Ilze.

Shuddering to think that I had nearly shared her fate, and eschewing any thoughts of Smilšu māte, or of the dead woman who had returned from the river to claim her only child, I left the city of Riga behind me, and set off for England.

* * *

It was a long, cold journey home, my friends. Without Ilze, I could not afford a carriage or an inn; I dragged myself along the continent's highways, snatching fitful bouts of sleep under trees, in bushes – anywhere I might lie unseen until morning. At first I attempted to beg for alms, but it was as though none could see me. My lack of any language save English, I thought, or the misery writ in my eyes.

I do not remember what I ate, nor where or how I drank, but I crossed that whole lonely land, and the choppy seas which make England an isle. I did these things for you, my dearest friends, for I could not rest easy until I had told you of what happened.

But now I can delude myself no longer – Smilšu māte is calling me, and I must go. For I can admit at last, to myself as well as you, that I did not in fact survive the steamer's wreck, but drowned in the cold, stately waters of the Daugava along with the Countess of —, all those many miles from home.

But do not despair. Though I am leaving you, whom I have just rejoined, we shall surely meet again. All those who live must cross that river's waters, to die and live again on its most distant shore. And if you ever should see sand in your chambers, or the face of a woman whose eyes are shadow-shrouded, know that I shall see you soon.

Good Lady Ducayne

Mary Elizabeth Braddon

Chapter I

BELLA ROLLESTON HAD made up her mind that her only chance of earning her bread and helping her mother to an occasional crust was by going out into the great unknown world as companion to a lady. She was willing to go to any lady rich enough to pay her a salary and so eccentric as to wish for a hired companion. Five shillings told off reluctantly from one of those sovereigns which were so rare with the mother and daughter, and which melted away so quickly, five solid shillings, had been handed to a smartly-dressed lady in an office in Harbeck Street, W., in the hope that this very Superior Person would find a situation and a salary for Miss Rolleston.

The Superior Person glanced at the two half-crowns as they lay on the table where Bella's hand had placed them, to make sure they were neither of them forms, before she wrote a description of Bella's qualifications and requirements in a formidable-looking ledger.

'Age?' she asked curtly.

'Eighteen, last July.'

'Any accomplishments?'

'No; I am not at all accomplished. If I were I should want to be a governess – a companion seems the lowest stage.'

'We have some highly accomplished ladies on our books as companions, or chaperon companions.'

'Oh, I know!' babbled Bella, loquacious in her youthful candour. 'But that is quite a different thing. Mother hasn't been able to afford a piano since I was twelve years old, so I'm afraid I've forgotten how to play. And I have had to help mother with her needlework, so there hasn't been much time to study.'

'Please don't waste time upon explaining what you can't do, but kindly tell me anything you can do,' said the Superior Person, crushingly, with her pen poised between delicate fingers waiting to write. 'Can you read aloud for two or three hours at a stretch? Are you active and handy, an early riser, a good walker, sweet tempered, and obliging?'

'I can say yes to all those questions except about the sweetness. I think I have a pretty good temper, and I should be anxious to oblige anybody who paid for my services. I should want them to feel that I was really earning my salary.'

'The kind of ladies who come to me would not care for a talkative companion,' said the Person, severely, having finished writing in her book. 'My connection lies chiefly among the aristocracy, and in that class considerable deference is expected.'

'Oh, of course,' said Bella; 'but it's quite different when I'm talking to you. I want to tell you all about myself once and for ever.'

'I am glad it is to be only once!' said the Person, with the edges of her lips.

The Person was of uncertain age, tightly laced in a black silk gown. She had a powdery complexion and a handsome clump of somebody else's hair on the top of her head. It may be that Bella's girlish freshness and vivacity had an irritating effect upon nerves weakened by an eight hours day in that over-heated second floor in Harbeck Street. To Bella the official apartment, with its Brussels carpet, velvet curtains and velvet chairs, and French clock, ticking loud on the marble chimney-piece, suggested the luxury of a palace, as compared with another second floor in Walworth where Mrs. Rolleston and her daughter had managed to exist for the last six years.

'Do you think you have anything on your books that would suit me?' faltered Bella, after a pause.

'Oh, dear, no; I have nothing in view at present,' answered the Person, who had swept Bella's half-crowns into a drawer, absentmindedly, with the tips of her fingers. 'You see, you are so very unformed – so much too young to be companion to a lady of position. It is a pity you have not enough education for a nursery governess; that would be more in your line.'

'And do you think it will be very long before you can get me a situation?' asked Bella, doubtfully.

'I really cannot say. Have you any particular reason for being so impatient – not a love affair, I hope?'

'A love affair!' cried Bella, with flaming cheeks. 'What utter nonsense. I want a situation because mother is poor, and I hate being a burden to her. I want a salary that I can share with her.'

'There won't be much margin for sharing in the salary you are likely to get at your age – and with your – very – unformed manners,' said the Person, who found Bella's peony cheeks, bright eyes, and unbridled vivacity more and more oppressive.

'Perhaps if you'd be kind enough to give me back the fee I could take it to an agency where the connection isn't quite so aristocratic,' said Bella, who – as she told her mother in her recital of the interview – was determined not to be sat upon.

'You will find no agency that can do more for you than mine,' replied the Person, whose harpy fingers never relinquished coin. 'You will have to wait for your opportunity. Yours is an exceptional case: but I will bear you in mind, and if anything suitable offers I will write to you. I cannot say more than that.'

The half-contemptuous bend of the stately head, weighted with borrowed hair, indicated the end of the interview. Bella went back to Walworth – tramped sturdily every inch of the way in the September afternoon – and 'took off' the Superior Person for the amusement of her mother and the landlady, who lingered in the shabby litle sitting – room after bringing in the tea-tray, to applaud Miss Rolleston's 'taking off'.

'Dear, dear, what a mimic she is!' said the landlady. 'You ought to have let her go on the stage, mum. She might have made her fortune as a hactress.'

Chapter II

BELLA WAITED AND hoped, and listened for the postman's knocks which brought such store of letters for the parlours and the first floor, and so few for that humble second floor, where mother and daughter sat sewing with hand and with wheel and treadle, for the greater part of the day.

Mrs Rolleston was a lady by birth and education; but it had been her bad fortune to marry a scoundrel; for the last half – dozen years she had been that worst of widows, a wife whose husband had deserted her. Happily, she was courageous, industrious, and a clever needlewoman; and she had been able just to earn a living for herself and her only child, by making mantles and cloaks for a West-end house. It was not a luxurious living. Cheap lodgings in a shabby street off the Walworth Road, scanty dinners, homely food, well-worn raiment, had been the portion of mother and daughter; but they loved each other so dearly, and Nature had made them both so light-hearted, that they had contrived somehow to be happy… But now this idea of going out into the world as companion to some fine lady had rooted itself into Bella's mind, and although she idolized her mother, and although the parting of mother and daughter must needs tear two loving hearts into shreds, the girl longed for enterprise and change and excitement, as the pages of old longed to be knights, and to start for the Holy Land to break a lance with the infidel.

She grew tired of racing downstairs every time the postman knocked, only to be told 'nothing for you, miss,' by the smudgy-faced drudge who picked up the letters from the passage floor.

'Nothing for you, miss,' grinned the lodging-house drudge, till at last Bella took heart of grace and walked up to Harbeck Street, and asked the Superior Person how it was that no situation had been found for her.

'You are too young,' said the Person, 'and you want a salary.'

'Of course I do,' answered Bella; 'don't other people want salaries?'

'Young ladies of your age generally want a comfortable home.

'I don't,' snapped Bella; 'I want to help mother.'

'You can call again this day week,' said the Person; 'or, if I hear of anything in the meantime, I will write to you.

No letter came from the Person, and in exactly a week Bella put on her neatest hat, the one that had been seldomest caught in the rain, and trudged off to Harbeck Street.

It was a dull October afternoon, and there was a greyness in the air which might turn to fog before night. The Walworth Road shops gleamed brightly through that grey atmosphere, and though to a young lady reared in Mayfair or Belgravia such shop-windows would have been unworthy of a glance, they were a snare and temptation for Bella. There were so many things that she longed for, and would never be able to buy.

Harbeck Street is apt to be empty at this dead season of the year, a long, long street, an endless perspective of eminently respectable houses. The Person's office was at the further end, and Bella looked down that long, grey vista almost despairingly, more tired than usual with the trudge from Walworth. As she looked, a carriage passed her, an old-fashioned, yellow chariot, on cee springs, drawn by a pair of high grey horses, with the stateliest of coachmen driving them, and a tall footman sitting by his side.

'It looks like the fairy god-mother's coach,' thought Bella. 'I shouldn't wonder if it began by being a pumpkin.'

It was a surprise when she reached the Person's door to find the yellow chariot standing before it, and the tall footman waiting near the doorstep. She was almost afraid to go in and meet the owner of that splendid carriage. She had caught only a glimpse of its occupant as the chariot rolled by, a plumed bonnet, a patch of ermine.

The Person's smart page ushered her upstairs and knocked at the official door. 'Miss Rolleston,' he announced, apologetically, while Bella waited outside.

'Show her in,' said the Person, quickly; and then Bella heard her murmuring something in a low voice to her client.

Bella went in fresh, blooming, a living image of youth and hope, and before she looked at the Person her gaze was riveted by the owner of the chariot.

Never had she seen anyone as old as the old lady sitting by the Person's fire: a little old figure, wrapped from chin to feet in an ermine mantle; a withered, old face under a plumed bonnet – a face so wasted by age that it seemed only a pair of eyes and a peaked chin. The nose was peaked, too, but between the sharply pointed chin and the great, shining eyes, the small, aquiline nose was hardly visible..'This is Miss Rolleston, Lady Ducayne.'

Claw-like fingers, flashing with jewels, lifted a double eyeglass to Lady Ducayne's shining black eyes, and through the glasses Bella saw those unnaturally bright eyes magnified to a gigantic size, and glaring at her awfully.

'Miss Torpinter has told me all about you,' said the old voice that belonged to the eyes. 'Have you good health? Are you strong and active, able to eat well, sleep well, walk well, able to enjoy all that there is good in life?'

'I have never known what it is to be ill, or idle,' answered Bella.

'Then I think you will do for me.'

'Of course, in the event of references being perfectly satisfactory,' put in the Person.

'I don't want references. The young woman looks frank and innocent. I'll take her on trust.'

'So like you, dear Lady Ducayne,' murmured Miss Torpinter.

'I want a strong young woman whose health will give me no trouble.'

'You have been so unfortunate in that respect,' cooed the Person, whose voice and manner were subdued to a melting sweetness by the old woman's presence.

'Yes, I've been rather unlucky,' grunted Lady Ducayne.

'But I am sure Miss Rolleston will not disappoint you, though certainly after your unpleasant experience with Miss Tomson, who looked the picture of health – and Miss Blandy, who said she had never seen a doctor since she was vaccinated—'

'Lies, no doubt,' muttered Lady Ducayne, and then turning to Bella, she asked, curtly, 'You don't mind spending the winter in Italy, I suppose?'

In Italy! The very word was magical. Bella's fair young face flushed crimson.

'It has been the dream of my life to see Italy,' she gasped.

From Walworth to Italy! How far, how impossible such a journey had seemed to that romantic dreamer.

'Well, your dream will be realized. Get yourself ready to leave Charing Cross by the train deluxe this day week at eleven. Be sure you are at the station a quarter before the hour. My people will look after you and your luggage.'

Lady Ducayne rose from her chair, assisted by her crutch-stick, and Miss Torpinter escorted her to the door.

'And with regard to salary?' questioned the Person on the way.

'Salary, oh, the same as usual – and if the young woman wants a quarter's pay in advance you can write to me for a cheque,' Lady Ducayne answered, carelessly.

Miss Torpinter went all the way downstairs with her client, and waited to see her seated in the yellow chariot. When she came upstairs again she was slightly out of breath, and she had resumed that superior manner which Bella had found so crushing.

'You may think yourself uncommonly lucky, Miss Rolleston,' she said. 'I have dozens of young ladies on my books whom I might have recommended for this situation – but I remembered having told you to call this afternoon – and I thought I would give you a chance.

Old Lady Ducayne is one of the best people on my books. She gives her companion a hundred a year, and pays all travelling expenses. You will live in the lap of luxury.'

'A hundred a year! How too lovely! Shall I have to dress very grandly? Does Lady Ducayne keep much company?'

'At her age! No, she lives in seclusion – in her own apartments – her French maid, her footman, her medical attendant, her courier.'

'Why did those other companions leave her?' asked Bella..'Their health broke down!'

'Poor things, and so they had to leave?'

'Yes, they had to leave. I suppose you would like a quarter's salary in advance?'

'Oh, yes, please. I shall have things to buy.'

'Very well, I will write for Lady Ducayne's cheque, and I will send you the balance – after deducting my commission for the year.'

'To be sure, I had forgotten the commission.'

'You don't suppose I keep this office for pleasure.'

'Of course not,' murmured Bella, remembering the five shillings entrance fee; but nobody could expect a hundred a year and a winter in Italy for five shillings.

Chapter III

From Miss Rolleston, at Cap Ferrino, to Mrs. Rolleston, in Beresford Street, Walworth.

'How I wish you could see this place, dearest; the blue sky, the olive woods, the orange and lemon orchards between the cliffs and the sea – sheltering in the hollow of the great hills – and with summer waves dancing up to the narrow ridge of pebbles and weeds which is the Italian idea of a beach! Oh, how I wish you could see it all, mother dear, and bask in this sunshine, that makes it so difficult to believe the date at the head of this paper. November! The air is like an English June-the sun is so hot that I can't walk a few yards without an umbrella. And to think of you at Walworth while I am here! I could cry at the thought that perhaps you will never see this lovely coast, this wonderful sea, these summer flowers that bloom in winter. There is a hedge of pink geraniums under my window, mother – a thick, rank hedge, as if the flowers grew wild – and there are Dijon roses climbing over arches and palisades all along the terrace-a rose garden full of bloom in November! Just picture it all! You could never imagine the luxury of this hotel.

It is nearly new, and has been built and decorated regardless of expense. Our rooms are upholstered in pale blue satin, which shows up Lady Ducayne's parchment complexion; but as she sits all day in a corner of the balcony basking in the sun, except when she is in her carriage, and all the evening in her armchair close to the fire, and never sees anyone but her own people, her complexion matters very little.

'She has the handsomest suite of rooms in the hotel. My bedroom is inside hers, the sweetest room – all blue satin and white lace – white enamelled furniture, looking-glasses on every wall, till I know my pert little profile as I never knew it before. The room was really meant for Lady Ducayne's dressing-room, but she ordered one of the blue satin couches to be arranged as a bed for me-the prettiest little bed, which I can wheel near the window on sunny mornings, as it is on castors and easily moved about. I feel as if Lady Ducayne were a funny old grandmother, who had suddenly appeared in my life, very, very rich, and very, very kind.

'She is not at all exacting. I read aloud to her a good deal, and she dozes and nods while I read.

Sometimes I hear her moaning in her sleep – as if she had troublesome dreams. When she is tired of my reading she orders Francine, her maid, to read a French novel to her, and I hear her chuckle and groan now and then, as if she were more interested in those books than in Dickens or Scott. My French is not good enough to follow Francine, who reads very quickly. I have a great deal of liberty, for Lady Ducayne often tells me to run away and amuse myself; I roam about the hills for hours. Everything is so lovely. I lose myself in olive woods, always climbing up and up towards the pine woods above – and above the pines there are the snow mountains that just show their white peaks above the dark hills. Oh, you poor dear, how can I ever make you understand what this place is like – you, whose poor, tired eyes have only the opposite side of Beresford Street? Sometimes I go no farther than the terrace in front of the hotel, which is a favourite lounging-place with everybody. The gardens lie below, and the tennis courts where I sometimes play with a very nice girl, the only person in the hotel with whom I have made friends. She is a year older than I, and has come to Cap Ferrino with her brother, a doctor – or a medical student, who is going to be a doctor. He passed his M.B. exam at Edinburgh just before they left home, Lotta told me. He came to Italy entirely on his sister's account. She had a troublesome chest attack last summer and was ordered to winter abroad. They are orphans, quite alone in the world, and so fond of each other. It is very nice for me to have such a friend as Lotta. She is so thoroughly respectable. I can't help using that word, for some of the girls in this hotel go on in a way that I know you would shudder at. Lotta was brought up by an aunt, deep down in the country, and knows hardly anything about life. Her brother won't allow her to read a novel, French or English, that he has not read and approved.

'"He treats me like a child," she told me, "but I don't mind, for it's nice to know somebody loves me, and cares about what I do, and even about my thoughts."'

'Perhaps this is what makes some girls so eager to marry – the want of someone strong and brave and honest and true to care for them and order them about. I want no one, mother darling, for I have you, and you are all the world to me. No husband could ever come between us two. If I ever were to marry he would have only the second place in my heart. But I don't suppose I ever shall marry, or even know what it is like to have an offer of marriage. No young man can afford to marry a penniless girl nowadays. Life is too expensive.'

'Mr Stafford, Lotta's brother, is very clever, and very kind. He thinks it is rather hard for me to have to live with such an old woman as Lady Ducayne, but then he does not know how poor we are-you and I – and what a wonderful life this seems to me in this lovely place. I feel a selfish wretch for enjoying all my luxuries, while you, who want them so much more than I, have none of them – hardly know what they are like – do you, dearest? – for my scamp of a father began to go to the dogs soon after you were married, and since then life has been all trouble and care and struggle for you.'

This letter was written when Bella had been less than a month at Cap Ferrino, before the novelty had worn off the landscape, and before the pleasure of luxurious surroundings had begun to cloy. She wrote to her mother every week, such long letters as girls who have lived in closest companionship with a mother alone can write; letters that are like a diary of heart and mind. She wrote gaily always; but when the new year began Mrs. Rolleston thought she detected a note of melancholy under all those lively details about the place and the people.

'My poor girl is getting homesick,' she thought. 'Her heart is in Beresford Street.'

It might be that she missed her new friend and companion, Lotta Stafford, who had gone with her brother for a little tour to Genoa and Spezzia, and as far as Pisa. They were to return before February; but in the meantime Bella might naturally feel very solitary among all those strangers, whose manners and doings she described so well.

The mother's instinct had been true. Bella was not so happy as she had been in that first flush of wonder and delight which followed the change from Walworth to the Riviera. Somehow, she knew not how, lassitude had crept upon her. She no longer loved to climb the hills, no longer flourished her orange stick in sheer gladness of heart as her light feet skipped over the rough ground and the coarse grass on the mountain side. The odour of rosemary and thyme, the fresh breath of the sea, no longer filled her with rapture. She thought of Beresford Street and her mother's face with a sick longing. They were so far – so far away! And then she thought of Lady Ducayne, sitting by the heaped-up olive logs in the over-heated salon – thought of that wizened-nut – cracker profile, and those gleaming eyes, with an invincible horror.

Visitors at the hotel had told her that the air of Cap Ferrino was relaxing – better suited to age than to youth, to sickness than to health. No doubt it was so. She was not so well as she had been at Walworth; but she told herself that she was suffering only from the pain of separation from the dear companion of her girlhood, the mother who had been nurse, sister, friend, flatterer, all things in this world to her. She had shed many tears over that parting, had spent many a melancholy hour on the marble terrace with yearning eyes looking westward, and with her heart's desire a thousand miles away.

She was sitting in her favourite spot, an angle at the eastern end of the terrace, a quiet little nook sheltered by orange trees, when she heard a couple of Riviera habitués talking in the garden below. They were sitting on a bench against the terrace wall.

She had no idea of listening to their talk, till the sound of Lady Ducayne's name attracted her, and then she listened without any thought of wrong-doing. They were talking no secrets – just casually discussing an hotel acquaintance.

They were two elderly people whom Bella only knew by sight. An English clergyman who had wintered abroad for half his lifetime; a stout, comfortable, well-to-do spinster, whose chronic bronchitis obliged her to migrate annually.

'I have met her about Italy for the last ten years,' said the lady; 'but have never found out her real age.

'I put her down at a hundred – not a year less,' replied the parson. 'Her reminiscences all go back to the Regency. She was evidently then in her zenith; and I have heard her say things that showed she was in Parisian society when the First Empire was at its best – before Josephine was divorced.'

'She doesn't talk much now.'

'No; there's not much life left in her. She is wise in keeping herself secluded. I only wonder that wicked old quack, her Italian doctor, didn't finish her off years ago.'

'I should think it must be the other way, and that he keeps her alive.'

'My dear Miss Manders, do you think foreign quackery ever kept anybody alive?'

'Well, there she is – and she never goes anywhere without him. He certainly has an unpleasant countenance.'

'Unpleasant,' echoed the parson, 'I don't believe the foul fiend himself can beat him in ugliness. I pity that poor young woman who has to live between old Lady Ducayne and Dr. Parravicini.'

'But the old lady is very good to her companions.'

'No doubt. She is very free with her cash; the servants call her good Lady Ducayne. She is a withered old female Croesus, and knows she'll never be able to get through her money, and doesn't relish the idea of other people enjoying it when she's in her coffin. People who live to be as old as she is become slavishly attached to life. I daresay she's generous to those poor girls – but she can't make them happy. They die in her service.'

'Don't say they, Mr. Carton; I know that one poor girl died at Mentone last spring.'

'Yes, and another poor girl died in Rome three years ago. I was there at the time. Good Lady Ducayne left her there in an English family. The girl had every comfort. The old woman was very liberal to her – but she died. I tell you, Miss Manders, it is not good for any young woman to live with two such horrors as Lady Ducayne and Parravicini..They talked of other things – but Bella hardly heard them. She sat motionless, and a cold wind seemed to come down upon her from the mountains and to creep up to her from the sea, till she shivered as she sat there in the sunshine, in the shelter of the orange trees in the midst of all that beauty and brightness.

Yes, they were uncanny, certainly, the pair of them – she so like an aristocratic witch in her withered old age; he of no particular age, with a face that was more like a waxen mask than any human countenance Bella had ever seen. What did it matter? Old age is venerable, and worthy of all reverence; and Lady Ducayne had been very kind to her. Dr. Parravicini was a harmless, inoffensive student, who seldom looked up from the book he was reading. He had his private sitting-room, where he made experiments in chemistry and natural science-perhaps in alchemy.

What could it matter to Bella? He had always been polite to her, in his far-off way. She could not be more happily placed than she was – in this palatial hotel, with this rich old lady.

No doubt she missed the young English girl who had been so friendly, and it might be that she missed the girl's brother, for Mr. Stafford had talked to her a good deal – had interested himself in the books she was reading, and her manner of amusing herself when she was not on duty.

You must come to our little salon when you are "off," as the hospital nurses call it, and we can have some music. No doubt you play and sing?' upon which Bella had to own with a blush of shame that she had forgotten how to play the piano ages ago.

Mother and I used to sing duets sometimes between the lights, without accompaniment,' she said, and the tears came into her eyes as she thought of the humble room, the half-hour's respite from work, the sewing-machine standing where a piano ought to have been, and her mother's plaintive voice, so sweet, so true, so dear.

Sometimes she found herself wondering whether she would ever see that beloved mother again. Strange forebodings came into her mind. She was angry with herself for giving way to melancholy thoughts.

One day she questioned Lady Ducayne's French maid about those two companions who had died within three years.

'They were poor, feeble creatures,' Francine told her. 'They looked fresh and bright enough when they came to Miladi; but they ate too much and they were lazy. They died of luxury and idleness. Miladi was too kind to them. They had nothing to do; and so they took to fancying things; fancying the air didn't suit them, that they couldn't sleep.'

'I sleep well enough, but I have had a strange dream several times since I have been in Italy.'

'Ah, you had better not begin to think about dreams, or you will be like those other girls. They were dreamers – and they dreamt themselves into the cemetery.'

The dream troubled her a little, not because it was a ghastly or frightening dream, but on account of sensations which she had never felt before in sleep – a whirring of wheels that went round in her brain, a great noise like a whirlwind, but rhythmical like the ticking of a gigantic clock: and then in the midst of this uproar as of winds and waves she seemed to sink into a gulf of unconsciousness, out of sleep into far deeper sleep – total extinction. And then, after that blank interval, there had come the sound of voices, and then again the whirr of wheels, louder and louder – and again the blank – and then she knew no more till morning, when she awoke, feeling languid and oppressed.

She told Dr. Parravicini of her dream one day, on the only occasion when she wanted his professional advice. She had suffered rather severely from the mosquitoes before Christmas – and had been almost frightened at finding a wound upon her arm which she could only attribute to the venomous sting of one of these torturers. Parravicini put on his glasses, and scrutinized the angry mark on the round, white arm, as Bella stood before him and Lady Ducayne with her sleeve rolled up above her elbow.

'Yes, that's rather more than a joke,' he said, 'he has caught you on the top of a vein. What a vampire! But there's no harm done, signorina, nothing that a little dressing of mine won't heal.

You must always show me any bite of this nature. It might be dangerous if neglected. These creatures feed on poison and disseminate it.'

'And to think that such tiny creatures can bite like this,' said Bella; 'my arm looks as if it had been cut by a knife.'

'If I were to show you a mosquito's sting under my microscope you wouldn't be surprised at that,' replied Parravicini.

Bella had to put up with the mosquito bites, even when they came on the top of a vein, and produced that ugly wound. The wound recurred now and then at longish intervals, and Bella found Dr. Parravicini's dressing a speedy cure. If he were the quack his enemies called him, he had at least a light hand and a delicate touch in performing this small operation.

Bella Rolleston to Mrs. Rolleston – April 14th.

'Ever Dearest, – Behold the cheque for my second quarter's salary – five and twenty pounds.

There is no one to pinch off a whole tenner for a year's commission as there was last time, so it is all for you, mother, dear. I have plenty of pocket-money in hand from the cash I brought away with me, when you insisted on my keeping more than I wanted. It isn't possible to spend money here – except on occasional tips to servants, or sous to beggars and children – unless one had lots to spend, for everything one would like to buy – tortoise-shell, coral, lace-is so ridiculously dear that only a millionaire ought to look at it. Italy is a dream of beauty: but for shopping, give me Newington Causeway.

'You ask me so earnestly if I am quite well that I fear my letters must have been very dull lately. Yes, dear, I am well – but I am not quite so strong as I was when I used to trudge to the West-end to buy half a pound of tea – just for a constitutional walk – or to Dulwich to look at the pictures. Italy is relaxing; and I feel what the people here call "slack". But I fancy I can see your dear face looking worried as you read this. Indeed, and indeed, I am not ill. I am only a little tired of this lovely scene – as I suppose one might get tired of looking at one of Turner's pictures if it hung on a wall that was always opposite one. I think of you every hour in every day – think of you and our homely little room – our dear little shabby parlour, with the armchairs from the wreck of your old home, and Dick singing in his cage over the sewing-machine. Dear, shrill, maddening Dick, who, we flattered ourselves, was so passionately fond of us. Do tell me in your next that he is well.

'My friend Lotta and her brother never came back after all. They went from Pisa to Rome.

Happy mortals! And they are to be on the Italian lakes in May; which lake was not decided when Lotta last wrote to me. She has been a charming correspondent, and has confided all her little flirtations to me. We are all to go to Bellaggio next week – by Genoa and Milan. Isn't that lovely? Lady Ducayne travels by the easiest stages – except when she is bottled up in the train de luxe. We shall stop two days at Genoa and one at Milan. What a bore I shall be to you with my talk about Italy when I come home.

'Love and love-and ever more love from your adoring, Bella.'

Chapter IV

HERBERT STAFFORD and his sister had often talked of the pretty English girl with her fresh complexion, which made such a pleasant touch of rosy colour among all those sallow faces at the Grand Hotel. The young doctor thought of her with a compassionate tenderness – her utter loneliness in that great hotel where there were so many people, her bondage to that old, old woman, where everybody else was free to think of nothing but enjoying life. It was a hard fate; and the poor child was evidently devoted to her mother, and felt the pain of separation-only two of them, and very poor, and all the world to each other,' he thought.

Lotta told him one morning that they were to meet again at Bellaggio. 'The old thing and her court are to be there before we are,' she said. 'I shall be charmed to have Bella again. She is so bright and gay – in spite of an occasional touch of homesickness. I never took to a girl on a short acquaintance as I did to her.'

'I like her best when she is homesick,' said Herbert; 'for then I am sure she has a heart.'

'What have you to do with hearts, except for dissection? Don't forget that Bella is an absolute pauper. She told me in confidence that her mother makes mantles for a West-end shop. You can hardly have a lower depth than that.'

'I shouldn't think any less of her if her mother made match-boxes.'

'Not in the abstract – of course not. Match-boxes are honest labour. But you couldn't marry a girl whose mother makes mantles.'

'We haven't come to the consideration of that question yet,' answered Herbert, who liked to provoke his sister.

In two years' hospital practice he had seen too much of the grim realities of life to retain any prejudices about rank. Cancer, phthisis, gangrene, leave a man with little respect for the outward differences which vary the husk of humanity. The kernel is always the same – fearfully and wonderfully made – a subject for pity and terror.

Mr Stafford and his sister arrived at Bellaggio in a fair May evening. The sun was going down as the steamer approached the pier; and all that glory of purple bloom which curtains every wall at this season of the year flushed and deepened in the glowing light. A group of ladies were standing on the pier watching the arrivals, and among them Herbert saw a pale face that startled him out of his wonted composure.

'There she is,' murmured Lotta, at his elbow, 'but how dreadfully changed. She looks a wreck.'

They were shaking hands with her a few minutes later, and a flush had lighted up her poor pinched face in the pleasure of meeting.

'I thought you might come this evening,' she said. 'We have been here a week.'

She did not add that she had been there every evening to watch the boat in, and a good many times during the day. The Grand Bretagne was close by, and it had been easy for her to creep to the pier when the boat bell rang. She felt a joy in meeting these people again; a sense of being with friends; a confidence which Lady Ducayne's goodness had never inspired in her.

'Oh, you poor darling, how awfully ill you must have been, exclaimed Lotta, as the two girls embraced.

Bella tried to answer, but her voice was choked with tears.

'What has been the matter, dear? That horrid influenza, I suppose?'

'No, no, I have not been ill – I have only felt a little weaker than I used to be. I don't think the air of Cap Ferrino quite agreed with me.'

'It must have disagreed with you abominably. I never saw such a change in anyone. Do let Herbert doctor you. He is fully qualified, you know. He prescribed for ever so many influenza patients at the Londres. They were glad to get advice from an English doctor in a friendly way.'

'I am sure he must be very clever!' faltered Bella, 'but there is really nothing the matter. I am not ill, and if I were ill, Lady Ducayne's physician—'

'That dreadful man with the yellow face? I would as soon one of the Borgias prescribed for me. I hope you haven't been taking any of his medicines.'

'No, dear, I have taken nothing. I have never complained of being ill.'

This was said while they were all three walking to the hotel. The Staffords' rooms had been secured in advance, pretty ground-floor rooms, opening into the garden. Lady Ducayne's statelier apartments were on the floor above.

'I believe these rooms are just under ours,' said Bella.

'Then it will be all the easier for you to run down to us,' replied Lotta, which was not really the case, as the grand staircase was in the centre of the hotel.

'Oh, I shall find it easy enough,' said Bella. 'I'm afraid you'll have too much of my society.

Lady Ducayne sleeps away half the day in this warm weather, so I have a good deal of idle time; and I get awfully moped thinking of mother and home.'

Her voice broke upon the last word. She could not have thought of that poor lodging which went by the name of home more tenderly had it been the most beautiful that art and wealth ever created. She moped and pined in this lovely garden, with the sunlit lake and the romantic hills spreading out their beauty before her. She was homesick and she had dreams: or, rather, an occasional recurrence of that one bad dream with all its strange sensations – it was more like a hallucination than dreaming – the whirring of wheels; the sinking into an abyss; the struggling back to consciousness. She had the dream shortly before she left Cap Ferrino, but not since she had come to Bellaggio, and she began to hope the air in this lake district suited her better, and that those strange sensations would never return.

Mr Stafford wrote a prescription and had it made up at the chemist's near the hotel. It was a powerful tonic, and after two bottles, and a row or two on the lake, and some rambling over the hills and in the meadows where the spring flowers made earth seem paradise, Bella's spirits and looks improved as if by magic.

'It is a wonderful tonic,' she said, but perhaps in her heart of hearts she knew that the doctor's kind voice and the friendly hand that helped her in and out of the boat, and the watchful care that went with her by land and lake, had something to do with her cure.

'I hope you don't forget that her mother makes mantles,' Lotta said, warningly.

'Or match-boxes: it is just the same thing, so far as I am concerned.'

'You mean that in no circumstances could you think of marrying her?'

'I mean that if ever I love a woman well enough to think of marrying her, riches or rank will count for nothing with me. But I fear – I fear your poor friend may not live to be any man's wife.'

'Do you think her so very ill?'

He sighed, and left the question unanswered.

One day, while they were gathering wild hyacinths in an upland meadow, Bella told Mr. Stafford about her bad dream.

'It is curious only because it is hardly like a dream,' she said. 'I daresay you could find some common-sense reason for it. The position of my head on my pillow, or the atmosphere, or something.'

And then she described her sensations; how in the midst of sleep there came a sudden sense of suffocation; and then those whirring wheels, so loud, so terrible; and then a blank, and then a coming back to waking consciousness.

'Have you ever had chloroform given you – by a dentist, for instance?'

'Never – Dr. Parravicini asked me that question one day.

'Lately?'

'No, long ago, when we were in the train de luxe.'

'Has Dr. Parravicini prescribed for you since you began to feel weak and ill?'

'Oh, he has given me a tonic from time to time, but I hate medicine, and took very little of the stuff. And then I am not ill, only weaker than I used to be. I was ridiculously strong and well when I lived at Walworth, and used to take long walks every day. Mother made me take those tramps to Dulwich or Norwood, for fear I should suffer from too much sewing-machine; sometimes – but very seldom – she went with me. She was generally toiling at home while I was enjoying fresh air and exercise. And she was very careful about our food – that, however plain it was, it should be always nourishing and ample. I owe at to her care that I grew up such a great, strong creature.'

'You don't look great or strong now, you poor dear,' said Lotta.

'I'm afraid Italy doesn't agree with me.'

'Perhaps it is not Italy, but being cooped up with Lady Ducayne that has made you ill.'

'But I am never cooped up. Lady Ducayne is absurdly kind, and lets me roam about or sit in the balcony all day if I like. I have read more novels since I have been with her than in all the rest of my life.'

'Then she is very different from the average old lady, who is usually a slave-driver,' said Stafford. 'I wonder why she carries a companion about with her if she has so little need of society.'

'Oh, I am only part of her state. She is inordinately rich – and the salary she gives me doesn't count. Apropos of Dr. Parravicini, I know he is a clever doctor, for he cures my horrid mosquito bites.'

'A little ammonia would do that, in the early stage of the mischief. But there are no mosquitoes to trouble you now.'

'Oh, yes, there are, I had a bite just before we left Cap Ferrino.

She pushed up her loose lawn sleeve, and exhibited a scar, which he scrutinized intently, with a surprised and puzzled look.

'This is no mosquito bite,' he said.

'Oh, yes it is – unless there are snakes or adders at Cap Ferrino.'

'It is not a bite at all. You are trifling with me. Miss Rolleston – you have allowed that wretched Italian quack to bleed you. They killed the greatest man in modern Europe that way, remember. How very foolish of you.'

'I was never bled in my life, Mr. Stafford.'

'Nonsense! Let me look at your other arm. Are there any more mosquito bites?'

'Yes; Dr. Parravicini says I have a bad skin for healing, and that the poison acts more virulently with me than with most people.'

Stafford examined both her arms in the broad sunlight, scars new and old.

'You have been very badly bitten, Miss Rolleston,' he said, 'and if ever I find the mosquito I shall make him smart. But, now tell me, my dear girl, on your word of honour, tell me as you would tell a friend who is sincerely anxious for your health and happiness – as you would tell your mother if she were here to question you – have you no knowledge of any cause for these scars except mosquito bites – no suspicion even?'

'No, indeed! No, upon my honour! I have never seen a mosquito biting my arm. One never does see the horrid little fiends. But I have heard them trumpeting under the curtains, and I know that I have often had one of the pestilent wretches buzzing about me.

Later in the day Bella and her friends were sitting at tea in the garden, while Lady Ducayne took her afternoon drive with her doctor.

'How long do you mean to stop with Lady Ducayne, Miss Rolleston?' Herbert Stafford asked, after a thoughtful silence, breaking suddenly upon the trivial talk of the two girls.

'As long as she will go on paying me twenty-five pounds a quarter.'

'Even if you feel your health breaking down in her service?'

'It is not the service that has injured my health. You can see that I have really nothing to do – to read aloud for an hour or so once or twice a week; to write a letter once in a way to a London tradesman. I shall never have such an easy time with anybody else. And nobody else would give me a hundred a year.'

'Then you mean to go on till you break down; to die at your post?'

'Like the other two companions? No! If ever I feel seriously ill – really ill – I shall put myself in a train and go back to Walworth without stopping.'

'What about the other two companions?'

'They both died. It was very unlucky for Lady Ducayne. That's why she engaged me; she chose me because I was ruddy and robust. She must feel rather disgusted at my having grown white and weak. By-the-bye, when I told her about the good your tonic had done me, she said she would like to see you and have a little talk with you about her own case.

'And I should like to see Lady Ducayne. When did she say this?'

'The day before yesterday.'

'Will you ask her if she will see me this evening?'

'With pleasure I wonder what you will think of her? She looks rather terrible to a stranger; but Dr. Parravicini says she was once a famous beauty.'

It was nearly ten o'clock when Mr. Stafford was summoned by message from Lady Ducayne, whose courier came to conduct him to her ladyship's salon. Bella was reading aloud when the visitor was admitted; and he noticed the languor in the low, sweet tones, the evident effort.

'Shut up the book,' said the querulous old voice. 'You are beginning to drawl like Miss Blandy.'

Stafford saw a small, bent figure crouching over the piled-up olive logs; a shrunken old figure in a gorgeous garment of black and crimson brocade, a skinny throat emerging from a mass of old Venetian lace, clasped with diamonds that flashed like fire-flies as the trembling old head turned towards him.

The eyes that looked at him out of the face were almost as bright as the diamonds – the only living feature in that narrow parchment mask. He had seen terrible faces in the hospital – faces on which disease had set dreadful marks – but he had never seen a face that impressed him so painfully as this withered countenance, with its indescribable horror of death outlived, a face that should have been hidden under a coffin-lid years and years ago.

The Italian physician was standing on the other side of the fireplace, smoking a cigarette, and looking down at the little old woman brooding over the hearth as if he were proud of her.

'Good evening, Mr. Stafford; you can go to your room, Bella, and write your everlasting letter to your mother at Walworth,' said Lady Ducayne. 'I believe she writes a page about every wild flower she discovers in the woods and meadows. I don't know what else she can find to write about,' she added, as Bella quietly withdrew to the pretty little bedroom opening out of Lady Ducayne's spacious apartment. Here, as at Cap Ferrino, she slept in a room adjoining the old lady's.

'You are a medical man, I understand, Mr. Stafford.'

'I am a qualified practitioner, but I have not begun to practise.'

'You have begun upon my companion, she tells me.'

'I have prescribed for her, certainly, and I am happy to find my prescription has done her good; but I look upon that improvement as temporary. Her case will require more drastic treatment.

'Never mind her case. There is nothing the matter with the girl – absolutely nothing – except girlish nonsense; too much liberty and not enough work.'

'I understand that two of your ladyship's previous companions died of the same disease,' said Stafford, looking first at Lady Ducayne, who gave her tremulous old head an impatient jerk, and then at Parravicini, whose yellow complexion had paled a little under Stafford's scrutiny.

'Don't bother me about my companions, sir,' said Lady Ducayne. 'I sent for you to consult you about myself – not about a parcel of anaemic girls. You are young, and medicine is a progressive science, the newspapers tell me. Where have you studied?'

'In Edinburgh – and in Paris.'

'Two good schools. And you know all the new-fangled theories, the modern discoveries – that remind one of the mediaeval witchcraft, of Albertus Magnus, and George Ripley; you have studied hypnotism – electricity?'

'And the transfusion of blood,' said Stafford, very slowly, looking at Parravicini.

'Have you made any discovery that teaches you to prolong human life – any elixir – any mode of treatment? I want my life prolonged, young man. That man there has been my physician for thirty years. He does all he can to keep me alive – after his lights. He studies all the new theories of all the scientists – but he is old; he gets older every day – his brain-power is going – he is bigoted – prejudiced – can't receive new ideas – can't grapple with new systems. He will let me die if I am not on my guard against him.'

'You are of an unbelievable ingratitude, Ecclenza,' said Parravicini.

'Oh, you needn't complain. I have paid you thousands to keep me alive. Every year of my life has swollen your hoards; you know there is nothing to come to you when I am gone. My whole fortune is left to endow a home for indigent women of quality who have reached their ninetieth year. Come, Mr. Stafford, I am a rich woman. Give me a few years more in the sunshine, a few years more above ground, and I will give you the price of a fashionable London practice – I will set you up at the West-end.'

'How old are you, Lady Ducayne?'

'I was born the day Louis XVI was guillotined.'

'Then I think you have had your share of the sunshine and the pleasures of the earth, and that you should spend your few remaining days in repenting your sins and trying to make atonement for the young lives that have been sacrificed to your love of life.'

'What do you mean by that, sir?'

'Oh, Lady Ducayne, need I put your wickedness and your physician's still greater wickedness in plain words? The poor girl who is now in your employment has been reduced from robust health to a condition of absolute danger by Dr. Parravicini's experimental surgery; and I have no doubt those other two young women who broke down in your service were treated by him in the same manner. I could take upon myself to demonstrate – by most convincing evidence, to a jury of medical men – that Dr. Parravicini has been bleeding Miss Rolleston, after putting her under chloroform, at intervals, ever since she has been in your service. The deterioration in the girl's health speaks for itself; the lancet marks upon the girl's arms are unmistakable; and her description of a series of sensations, which she calls a dream, points unmistakably to the administration of chloroform while she was sleeping. A practice so nefarious, so murderous, must, if exposed, result in a sentence only less severe than the punishment of murder.'

'I laugh,' said Parravicini, with an airy motion of his skinny fingers; 'I laugh at once at your theories and at your threats. I, Parravicini Leopold, have no fear that the law can question anything I have done.'

'Take the girl away, and let me hear no more of her,' cried Lady Ducayne, in the thin, old voice, which so poorly matched the energy and fire of the wicked old brain that guided its utterances. 'Let her go back to her mother – I want no more girls to die in my service. There are girls enough and to spare in the world, God knows.'

'If you ever engage another companion – or take another English girl into your service, Lady Ducayne, I will make all England ring with the story of your wickedness.'

'I want no more girls. I don't believe in his experiments. They have been full of danger for me as well as for the girl – an air bubble, and I should be gone. I'll have no more of his dangerous quackery. I'll find some new man – a better man than you, sir, a discoverer like Pasteur, or Virchow, a genius – to keep me alive. Take your girl away, young man. Marry her if you like.

I'll write her a cheque for a thousand pounds, and let her go and live on beef and beer, and get strong and plump again. I'll have no more such experiments. Do you hear, Parravicini?' she screamed, vindictively, the yellow, wrinkled face distorted with fury, the eyes glaring at him.

The Staffords carried Bella Rolleston off to Varese next day, she very loth to leave Lady Ducayne, whose liberal salary afforded such help for the dear mother. Herbert Stafford insisted, however, treating Bella as coolly as if he had been the family physician, and she had been given over wholly to his care.

'Do you suppose your mother would let you stop here to die?' he asked. 'If Mrs. Rolleston knew how ill you are, she would come post haste to fetch you.

'I shall never be well again till I get back to Walworth,' answered Bella, who was low-spirited and inclined to tears this morning, a reaction after her good spirits of yesterday.

'We'll try a week or two at Varese first,' said Stafford. 'When you can walk half-way up Monte Generoso without palpitation of the heart, you shall go back to Walworth.'

'Poor mother, how glad she will be to see me, and how sorry that I've lost such a good place.'

This conversation took place on the boat when they were leaving Bellaggio. Lotta had gone to her friend's room at seven o'clock that morning, long before Lady Ducayne's withered eyelids had opened to the daylight, before even Francine, the French maid, was astir, and had helped to pack a Gladstone bag with essentials, and hustled Bella downstairs and out of doors before she could make any strenuous resistance.

'It's all right.' Lotta assured her. 'Herbert had a good talk with Lady Ducayne last night and it was settled for you to leave this morning. She doesn't like invalids, you see.'

'No,' sighed Bella, 'she doesn't like invalids. It was very unlucky that I should break down, just like Miss Tomson and Miss Blandy.'

'At any rate, you are not dead, like them,' answered Lotta, 'and my brother says you are not going to die.'

It seemed rather a dreadful thing to be dismissed in that off-hand way, without a word of farewell from her employer.

'I wonder what Miss Torpinter will say when I go to her for another situation,' Bella speculated, ruefully, while she and her friends were breakfasting on board the steamer.

'Perhaps you may never want another situation,' said Stafford.

'You mean that I may never be well enough to be useful to anybody?'

'No, I don't mean anything of the kind.'

It was after dinner at Varese, when Bella had been induced to take a whole glass of Chianti, and quite sparkled after that unaccustomed stimulant, that Mr. Stafford produced a letter from his pocket.

'I forgot to give you Lady Ducayne's letter of adieu,' he said.

'What, did she write to me? I am so glad – I hated to leave her in such a cool way; for after all she was very kind to me, and if I didn't like her it was only because she was too dreadfully old.'

She tore open the envelope. The letter was short and to the point:

'Goodbye, child. Go and marry your doctor. I enclose a farewell gift for your trousseau. – Adeline Ducayne.'

'A hundred pounds, a whole year's salary – no – why, it's for a – A cheque for a thousand!' cried Bella. 'What a generous old soul! She really is the dearest old thing.'

'She just missed being very dear to you, Bella,' said Stafford.

He had dropped into the use of her Christian name while they were on board the boat. It seemed natural now that she was to be in his charge till they all three went back to England.

'I shall take upon myself the privileges of an elder brother till we land at Dover,' he said; 'after that – well, it must be as you please.'

The question of their future relations must have been satisfactorily settled before they crossed the Channel, for Bella's next letter to her mother communicated three startling facts.

First, that the enclosed cheque for £1,000 was to be invested in debenture stock in Mrs. Rolleston's name, and was to be her very own, income and principal, for the rest of her life.

Next, that Bella was going home to Walworth immediately.

And last, that she was going to be married to Mr. Herbert Stafford in the following autumn.

'And I am sure you will adore him, mother, as much as I do,' wrote Bella. 'It is all good Lady Ducayne's doing. I never could have married if I had not secured that little nest-egg for you.

Herbert says we shall be able to add to it as the years go by, and that wherever we live there shall be always a room in our house for you. The word "mother-in-law" has no terrors for him.'

The Widow Watcher of Wooten Creek

Rebecca Brothers

THE MIST DEEP in the hollers of Leslie County, Kentucky clings. You cannot shake it off or blow it away. It creeps into your mouth and coats your throat; screaming will not free you. It is best to swallow it down, to let it sit in your belly and make you part of the landscape.

I was not from those Appalachian mountains of Eastern Kentucky. I grew up 130 miles away in Lexington, the horsey part of the state. But my father was born in the mountains. Our Scottish and Irish ancestors had populated the hollers and glens. By the time I came to visit, the old families were mostly gone; abandoned homes and lonely rock chimneys were all that was left, and those were falling back into the soil and slate. But I was still kin, so I was welcomed.

My father's great-grandparents had built a sturdy white frame farmhouse at the base of three mountains, snugly nestled on a triangle of land bordered by branches of Wooten Creek. The mountains still guarded the house a hundred and ten years later from the worst of the wind. The creek still ran pure, rarely escaping its banks. The land was coated in green moss and sweet grass, carpeted with laurel hells, hung with wild honeysuckle. Big boulders slid down the mountains ages ago. Those rocks and the giant tulip poplar trees stood guard over the old farm as ancient sentries.

My granny still lived in the house alone when I was a kid. White siding, gingerbread trim. Her porch was hung heavily with windchimes and little mirrors strung on twine around the whole thing like a garland.

Dad would walk me from her place around the old farm and he'd narrate its past into being. "This is where Thumb George lived. Drove a team of mules with the reins wrapped around the stump of his hand and that one big thumb. Lost the rest of his fingers in the sawmill. Great-grandad sewed him up. He was always grateful to keep that thumb…" A dozen tales of gruesome mangling from farm equipment or in the mines would follow, each with old Dr. Hamilton coming to stitch men back together with his big needle and thick thread.

We climbed the ruins of a grist mill, dug around for rusty nails and ox shoes near the old forge, and sifted through the sandy dirt at the base of the Indian Cliffs, looking for arrowheads and stone ax blades. My dad loved watching his little girl explore his childhood memories.

I had thought about seeing a ghost there, imagining it would be something friendly. Maybe I expected to see a flash of my grandfather as a boy, he and his brothers sporting summer buzz cuts, dangling from wild grape vines or splashing in the creek. I thought I might find the shadow of my great-grandfather walking the old barbed-wire fence line, counting his cattle.

But the spirit who haunted that holler turned out to be a woman.

We had come to visit my granny again at her farmhouse, to help her get the green bean crop in. Dad had let me go out to explore, but he shouted loudly as I left, "Stay near the house! Watch out for snakes!"

Though most of the old houses and stores nearby were crumbled, the one-room schoolhouse my father had attended still stood straight and strong: a white clapboard building with a little bell tower. I couldn't resist; I headed straight for the school, fifty yards from Granny's front porch.

I knew the front door was nailed shut. I scrambled up the sagging steps anyway, clinging to kudzu vines instead of the rotted railing. I leaned over to a window, trying my best to peek inside.

The chalkboard still clung to the back wall with dusty outlines of old sums still faint on its surface. A green banner hung above it, the curly cursive alphabet marching along its length. Golden afternoon light filtered in through the broken windows, little clouds of dust swirling. Instead of desks, the floor was filled with old wooden radio cabinets: Zenith, RCA, Edison, models spanning the twentieth century. One of my great uncles took these old machines in the way some people collected stray cats; he repaired what he could and used the schoolhouse as a warehouse for the rest.

The front window was cracked like a spiderweb. When I pressed my hand to the surface, the glass gave way, cutting my fingers deeply. I watched with detached fascination as my bright blood trickled down the white wall.

Suddenly, the friendly afternoon sunlight disappeared and a gust of icy wind blew through the trees and straight down my back. The poplar leaves turned silver and shook. A streak of terrible lightning cut the sky. I broke from my trance at the window and ran back down the schoolhouse steps.

The creek lay between me and the house. I knew to run from a storm, to find shelter, to hide from the lightning. The house seemed close enough, but another loud crack of lightning and thunder rang out, bringing one of the boney white sycamore trees crashing down onto the bridge, blocking my way. I turned all around, desperate for a safe place.

The school would have to do.

I ran back up the steps and shoved all my sixty pounds against the door. It splintered, the wood more rotten than I'd thought. I landed hard on the floor and clouds of ancient chalk and coal dust swirled around my head. Sneezing, I sat up carefully, sizing up my injuries. But another loud BOOM scared me deeper inside, and I hid behind the bulk of a Sylvania console.

I closed my eyes against the bright lightning, counting between the flash and the thunder, trying to guess how far away the storm was: one second for each mile. The storm tumbled on top of me, and I couldn't hear the numbers leave my mouth.

Another sound started up: a long, high-pitched wail. At first I thought it must be the wind, singing through the old windows that hung like broken teeth in the east wall of the schoolhouse. But the sound got louder and more human. I opened my eyes and crawled to the door, looking for funnel clouds. The sky was the sickly green we'd been warned about at school.

I huddled behind the biggest radio I could find, my back to the wall of broken windows. As the storm grew, the wind picked up more swirls of the dirt from the floor – I felt the grit of it enter my mouth before I could think to keep it closed. I buried my face in my arms.

The whine turned to a scream that filled my ears. I tried to block the sound, but there was no getting away from it. Pain filled my head and I thought I would puke with the intensity.

I suddenly felt a cold hand on the back of my neck.

I popped up, expecting to see my father. But there was no one. The storm was completely gone, as if it had never started. I sat there on the dirty floor, stunned.

I looked down to see a shiny red puddle at my feet, growing as my hand bled. I could see my face reflected back at me as if in a red mirror, my pigtails and plastic glasses unmistakable. And there, over my left shoulder, was a woman's broad white face, her eyes wide and her mouth flung open. I whirled around.

I was alone.

I ran back down the steps and tore up the road. I stared at my pink sneakers, willing myself not to stumble. I made it to the bridge over the creek, ready to scramble through the fallen sycamore's limbs, only to find my way clear. The white tree still stood with its arms raised to a now cloudless sky.

I pounded the gravel pathway up to the house, tore up the steps, and found my dad and Granny sitting on the covered porch, breaking green beans into a dishpan. Granny's windchimes and mirrored decorations swayed gently in the soft breeze, not a hint of the storm left.

"You look a sight, Little Rabbit," Dad said.

"Scared to death!" Granny added. "What's happened to you, Rachel? See a snake?"

Adults always think kids are ready to tell their trauma, ready to tattle on the forces that have terrorized them. They forget that agonizing fear a child has of not being believed. And rather than being laughed at, many kids choose to keep these fears buried.

That's what I did that day. I felt immense guilt at breaking the door, of invading the old school. I stumbled towards Granny, my hand dripping.

"What happened here?" she asked. She squeezed my hand and squinted at the cuts.

"I fell in the weeds," I stammered. I remember the intense sting of iodine from an ancient bottle in her bathroom and longed for the gentler Bactine my mother kept at home.

We went inside and Granny dressed my wound and scolded me for being careless. I nodded sheepishly, but I couldn't bring myself to say anything about the terrifying reflection I'd seen in the schoolhouse.

A few hours later we ate our supper, just as the sun was setting. It was the usual spread: home canned green beans and cornbread; steaming hot fried potatoes and onions; chicken crispy and still stinging with the heat of the skillet. I was uncharacteristically quiet, and Dad asked more than once if I was all right. I just nodded and tried to eat.

Bedtime found me tucked up under three of Granny's quilts, the weight of them pinning me to the mattress. The adults sat up and talked by the fireplace. Their soft laughter lulled me to sleep.

I woke to darkness and lay silently for a while, trying to gauge the time and listening for the sounds of anyone stirring. I let my feet dangle over the side of the bed and winced as they met the freezing floor. I wrapped one of the smaller blankets tight around my shoulders and crept to the front room.

I peered through the front window into the darkness. Granny had one intense spotlight that lit up the whole front yard. I could see no movement or sunlight and decided it was too early to be up. I was just about to tiptoe back to bed when I heard the wailing begin again.

There was no wind or open window to explain the sound this time. The cry was faint, but steady, and very human: a woman's cry. I squinted into the dark.

Thick fog swirled slowly around our car tires and the porch steps. I crouched down low, just the tip of my nose and eyes peeking over the windowsill.

I heard a soft scuffling behind me. A moment later, Granny was there in the doorway. She had on a terrycloth robe and rubber-soled house shoes. Her hair was up in rollers and covered with a gauzy scarf. She shuffled right past me, never looking my way, and went right out the front door. I wanted to call after her, to warn her of the screams, but I choked on my words.

I finally found my courage and scrambled to my feet, running down the steps after her.

The spotlight made a bright pool of the yard but hit a wall of darkness at the gravel drive. The mist soaked my feet and ankles. I felt the dampness climb up my body. I swam through the white fog, keeping the dim outline of Granny's shape just barely in sight.

She crossed the bridge over the creek and I lost her in the thick fog. It swirled up to meet my face. I tried to fight it, but the urge to open my mouth was stronger than my will. I gulped down big mouthfuls of the wet, cold mist. I pushed forward, blind, worried I'd tumble off the road and down the mountain on the other side.

The wailing was louder now, filling my head. I looked around wildly, no longer thinking to save Granny, just longing for her company. I saw a blur ahead and realized she was climbing the schoolhouse steps. I broke into a run.

Just as I got to the school, I saw the white glow of Granny's fuzzy robe disappear inside. I scrambled up the steps after her, trying to call out the whole time, choking on the mist.

The wailing stopped.

When I finally made it to the top step, I gasped. Granny was sitting on top of one of the old radio cabinets, her slippered feet dangling. A beautiful woman with long silvery hair knelt next to her, holding my granny's wrist to her mouth, sucking away. I could hear her smacking her lips.

I stepped backwards, lost my footing, and tumbled down the whole flight. I landed in a tangled pile at the bottom, the wind knocked out of me.

I lay there, gasping like a beached trout, cold fog rolling all around. After a few moments, I felt warm hands on my face and warm breath on my cheek, pushing the mist away. I was lifted to my feet and guided to a big boulder and made to sit. I looked up and saw not Granny, but the white woman. Her hair shone bright as silver, skin pale as milk. And her mouth was a red hole.

A sight like that should have sent me screaming through the woods. But I sat enchanted. I felt no fear, only warmth and safety. She smiled at me and stroked my hair. She pulled my wrist towards her face.

"Not her, Banshee."

Granny stood at the top of the schoolhouse steps, her feet planted wide and her fists balled up on her hips.

"You've had your fill for tonight. No more. Be gone with you," she scolded.

The white woman smiled down at me again and patted my head one last time. Then she danced off into the foggy woods and vanished.

Granny took the steps one at a time, grunting with the effort. "These knees!" she huffed.

I couldn't move. I had forgotten to breathe. I sucked in a big gulp of fog, coughing at the unexpected heaviness of the wet air.

"Take it easy, Rachel," Granny warned. She walked slowly towards me. "You're all right. Let's get back to the house."

She pulled me up. We shuffled slowly through the dark, our feet loud on the gravel. I kept my eyes wide, afraid of meeting the white woman again.

When we got back to the house, Granny pushed me into an overstuffed chair. She bent down to the hearth and built up the fire again, its gentle glow filling the room with orange light.

"Hot chocolate," she announced. She shuffled into the kitchen.

I strained to hear the wailing, but all I heard was the gentle tinkling of a spoon in a mug.

Granny appeared back in the doorway, a cup in each hand. I took mine and let the warmth seep into my cold hands. I suddenly realized I was freezing and shook with the surprise of it.

"Now what you saw tonight… You need to promise me you won't go telling tales if I let you in on the secret," she started. "You're not from here, but you're *of here*, which is the next best thing. Your kinfolk have lived here for almost two hundred years. And in that time, we've had to learn to make our peace with all kinds of creatures. Your grandpa farmed these fields for sixty years with the skunks and the copperheads all around. You just have to walk carefully and carry a good stick with you. And the deer we used to have, and the raccoons. Why, they'd eat two whole rows of sweetcorn every summer. Grandpa just planted two extra rows, knowing that was the price you had to pay to get your own share. This creature you saw tonight, she's not so different."

Granny paused and motioned for me to drink. I took a tiny sip, coughing as the steam filled my mouth.

"The fog," I said in a whisper.

"Yes, the fog is her pet. It searches the dark places for her. Looks for the black lung inside you. Some say it even cures you. But let me tell you about the lady; she's just another thing that clings to these hills. She's always been with us."

Granny wrapped her crocheted afghan around her lap. She stared hard at me. "I am going to tell you about the lady the same way my granny told me." She yanked at her robe sleeve, covering her bitten wrist. "My Granny said the White Lady is the Banshee, the woman of the fairies. She keens when death is near. She also keens when she's hungry."

"Keens…" I tried the word.

"A long, shrill wailing. Now some say she followed us from the old world. Our Irish and Scottish kin knew her well, the white lady with long silver hair. The stories from the old ways, passed down from granny to granddaughter, say she comes to comfort us when the men cannot. When they've died before us, as they so often do. She is a reflection of our sorrow. She appears to those who will soon know death. She warns us of our fate."

"But she…She was…" I stammered. I shivered and gulped my drink, desperate to get warm.

"Hush, Rachel. I know you saw something shocking. I'll get to that. But let me tell you what I know. Here about sixteen years ago we had a bad mining disaster down on Hurricane Creek. An explosion caused a collapse, killing thirty-eight men. Now those boys were trapped, some of them for a few days, before we got them all out. And when all that rock gives way, it's not a pretty thing." She stopped, studying my face. "You all right to hear this, Little Rabbit?"

I nodded.

"All right. Now. They laid them out in the high school gym and the women and children came to go through their pockets and study their boots, trying to find daddies and husbands and sons. You understand, their faces were… they weren't what you'd call recognizable. Women started wailing then, their cries filling up the holler and echoing off every mountain from Hyden to Hell-For-Certain. The Banshee, she always comes around death. All this noise drew her out. She feeds on those mourning cries, gets fat with their grief. And there was plenty to be had that day.

"Three of the men were from here at the head of Wooten Creek. They were brought up here and were laid out in the old schoolhouse. Martin Cotrell, Morris Mullins, Timothy Shauncey. Their women were there, washing the dead, wailing and crying. They sat up with the bodies all night, waiting for morning to come and bring the preacher with it.

"In the night, the women heard the Banshee keening and it grew so loud, they ran out into the woods. When the cries stopped, they came back to find the bodies all white as sheets. Rumors spread that the Banshee had drained them of their blood. The preacher scoffed, but we knew what we'd seen. Bite marks on the men's arms. Their color too pale, even for death."

The cold I'd been feeling gripped me. I shook so hard I dropped my empty mug. It rolled over the rag rug to Granny's foot. She bent down and picked it up. "Can't read cocoa like tea leaves," she giggled. "Come over here."

I scrambled into her lap, my long legs dangling. She wrapped her afghan around me and I sank into her body, searching for her heat. She rocked me a little.

"Baby girl, I tell you this to calm your fears, not to feed them. You have to know this about the Banshee: she is ours."

I didn't like that idea much. The broad, white face had been angry and terrifying. Who would want something like that hanging around?

"Can't you send her away? Say a spell or ask the preacher to bless the schoolhouse?"

Granny squeezed my shoulders. "Now listen to the rest, and you'll see why we claim her and ask her to stay.

"After the miners were buried, one of the widows, Bonnie Mullins, she was taking it harder than the others. She about grieved herself to death. Wouldn't eat. Wouldn't wash. Took to wandering around barefoot at night. We were all fearful for her."

I pictured a young woman crying, walking the woods, the rocks and sticks making her feet bleed.

"She had nearly wasted away, when one night we all heard the keening again, loud as a freight train. I thought at first it was a tornado, finally come to Wooten Creek. But I knew it for what it was as soon as I stepped off our porch. I could see the Banshee, standing in the road. She was beckoning me with her long, pale hand. I had no choice but to follow."

I buried my face in the scratchy front of Granny's white nightgown. She took my chin in her hand and tilted it up with her soft warm hand. "You ready? You're going to like this part."

I had my doubts. My heart was racing.

"I followed her up the road and into the woods. We walked down a path towards the creek bottom. And soon I saw Bonnie there, lying by a big fallen tree. I ran to her. She was half-dead, starved and cold. I found her just in time. The Banshee had saved Bonnie. After that night, Bonnie started to take to her food again, started to have some interest in the land of the living. So you see, our Banshee, she doesn't just come at a killing. She comes to warn us, too."

I did like that part. I felt my heartbeat slow. I sighed and laid my head on Granny's soft shoulder.

"I've been alone up here in this holler since your grandpa left me, ten years ago. She came on the night before he died. I heard her keening out in his watermelon patch. I asked Grandpa if he could hear it, but he told me it was coyotes. He got up the next day and went to hoe the corn. He didn't come home for his noon dinner and I went out to look for him. Found him between the rows, his hat next to him and his hands folded on his chest. They said it was his heart. I know my Banshee was with him because I know she laid him out like that for me, all peaceful and calm, as a comfort to me."

Granny stood up slowly, pouring me from her lap. She walked over to the mantel and took down a black and white photo. "Here we are, on our wedding day. He was just home from the war. Look how handsome he was in his uniform."

I could hear the tears in her voice. I studied their impossibly young faces, their smiles shy. She placed the frame back on the mantel and sat down, pulling me onto her lap again.

"I would've had to move to town long ago if it weren't for my Banshee. I was all alone after Grandpa was gone, all by myself here on this farm. All the neighbors had moved away by then. The whole holler was closing in on itself, the woods taking it back. Oh, the boys come to help. Your daddy is here every spring to plant. Your cousins come every summer to weed and work. We get the crop in. But the nights are long and lonesome. My Banshee comes to visit, right here on the porch."

I glanced quickly out the front windows, terrified of seeing her there. But the rocking chairs were empty.

"She doesn't chat. But she sits with me while I sew or shuck corn. That's why I have all those mirrors hanging around out there. You can't see her unless she wants you to. But a mirror reveals her, every time."

"When I saw her the first time, yesterday, there was a storm. I thought there was a storm... and I ran into the schoolhouse for shelter. I had cut my hand and there was a pool of my blood on the floor. I saw her reflection there..."

"And then you came out and there hadn't been a storm at all, right? She does things like that. Makes me feel half-crazy sometimes. But she was trying to show herself to you. I take comfort in her. She saw my mother safely to the other side. And all my sisters and brothers who died up here long ago. Of course, Grandpa, too."

But I still wasn't so sure about this creature. "Granny, she was... biting you..."

"Oh, honey. There's no one dying up here anymore and I'm taking too long to do it. My Banshee, she's hungry. She feeds on death. So I give her what I can to pay my dues."

I grasped her arm and pushed up her sleeve. Two pinpricks of bright red blood stood out on her white wrist.

"I've got high blood pressure anyway. I let her have a little drink from time to time and it calms her down. And my pressure comes right down, too. Not much of a price to pay for her company and protection."

I stared up at her. I thought of her lonely there, no one to talk to for weeks. I thought of all those acres of woods, growing up around her, thicker every year.

"What will happen to the Banshee when you're gone? You're the last one here," I said softly.

"I think she'll find her way down out of this holler. I hope she does. Now that you've met her, maybe she'll follow you home the day they put me in the ground. Do not fear her. Pay her little price. She'll watch over you, too."

I was too stunned to speak.

Granny patted my head. "Going on daylight soon. Let's go fry up some eggs. I'm starved, myself. All that work tonight." She winked at me and shuffled into her yellow kitchen.

I peered back out the front window, searching all the little mirrors for a glimpse of the Banshee's ghostly white face. The windchimes and mirrors just swung in the morning breeze, reflecting glints of the rising sun.

But the fog was behaving strangely. It was curling up the steps, rising like floodwater. Swirls of mist rose up in front of the window and turned into a curvy silhouette. All the little hairs on my arm stood straight up and I leaned forward, ready to run.

The mist solidified. The Banshee was there, her red mouth and flashing eyes coming into focus. I winced, expecting awful keening, but she stayed quiet and smiled. She was beautiful.

I nodded. My heart pounded. I took big gulps of air and willed myself to calm down, to not bolt. The Banshee's long hair blew behind her. She wasn't as ghostly white now and looked more human. More alive.

"Oh no," I whispered. "You're not here to tell me Granny's dying, are you?"

The Banshee shook her head from side to side. The mist curled up around her feet like a cat before climbing up her skirt, then her shoulders, and then her face. She waved and faded into the foggy morning light.

My shivers returned. "See you later."

Holding the Light

Ramsey Campbell

AS HIS COUSIN followed him into the Frugoplex lobby Tom saw two girls from school. Out of uniform and in startlingly short skirts they looked several years older. He hoped his leather jacket performed that trick for him, in contrast to the duffle coat Lucas was wearing. Since the girls were giggling at the cinema staff dressed as Halloween characters, he let them see him laugh too. "Hey, Lezly," he said in his deepest voice. "Hey, Dianne."

"Don't come near us if you've got a cold," Lezly protested, waving a hand that was bony with rings in front of her face.

"It's just how boys his age talk," Dianne said far too much like a sympathetic adult and blinked her sparkly purple eyelids. "Who's your friend, Tom?"

"It's my cousin Lucas."

"Hey, Luke."

Lezly said it too and held out her skull-ringed hand, at which Lucas stared as if it were an inappropriate present. "He's like that," Tom mumbled but refrained from pointing at his own head. "Don't mind him."

"Maybe he doesn't want to give you his germs, Lezly." To the boys Dianne said "What are you going to see?"

"*Vampire Dating Agency*," Lucas said before Tom could make a choice.

"That's for kids," Lezly objected. "We're not seeing any films with them."

"We don't have to either, do we, Lucas?" Tom said in a bid to stop his face from growing hotter. "What are you two seeing?"

"*Cheerleaders with Guts*," Dianne said with another quick glittery blink.

"We can't," Lucas informed everyone. "Nobody under fifteen's allowed."

Tom glared at him as the girls did. At least none of the staff dealing with the noisy queues appeared to have heard the remark. Until that moment Tom had been able to prefer visiting the cinema to any of the other activities their parents had arranged for the boys over the years – begging for sweets at neighbours' houses, ducking for apples and a noseful of water, carving pumpkins when Lucas's received most of the praise despite being so grotesque only out of clumsiness. Now that the parents had reluctantly let them outgrow all this Tom seemed to be expected to take even more care of his cousin. Perhaps Lucas sensed his resentment for once, because he said "We don't have to go to a film."

"Who doesn't?" said Dianne.

Tom wanted to say her and Lezly too, but first he had to learn "Where, then?"

"The haunted place." When nobody admitted to recognising it Lucas said "Grinfields."

"Where the boy and girl killed themselves together, you mean," Lezly said.

"No, he did first," Dianne said, "and she couldn't live without him."

It was clear that Lucas wasn't interested in these details, and he barely let her finish. "My mum and dad say they did it because they watched films you aren't supposed to watch."

"My parents heard they were always shopping," Tom made haste to contribute. "Them and their families spent lots of money they didn't have and all it did was leave them thinking nothing was worth anything."

That was his father's version. Perhaps it sounded more like a gibe at the girls than he was afraid Lucas's comment had. "Why do you want us to go there, Luke?" Dianne said.

"Who's Luke?"

"I told you," Tom said in some desperation, "he's like that."

"No I'm not, I'm like Lucas."

At such times Tom understood all too well why his cousin was bullied at school. There was also the way Lucas stared at anybody unfamiliar as if they had to wait for him to make up his mind about them, and just now his pasty face – far spottier than Tom's and topped with unruly red hair – was a further drawback. Nevertheless Dianne said "Are you sure you don't want to see our film?"

She was speaking to Tom, but Lucas responded. "We can't. We've been told."

"I haven't," Tom muttered. He watched the girls join the queue for the ticket desk manned by a tastefully drooling vampire in a cloak, and then he turned on Lucas. "We need to switch our phones off. We're in the cinema."

Accuracy mattered most to Lucas. Once he'd done as he was told Tom said "Let's go, and not to the kids' film either."

A frown creased Lucas's pudgy forehead. "Which one, then?"

"None of them. We'll go where you wanted," Tom said, leading the way out into the Frugall retail park.

More vehicles than he thought he could count in a weekend were lined up beneath towering lamps as white as the moon. In that light people's faces looked as pallid as Lucas's, but took on colour once they reached the shops, half a mile of which surrounded the perimeter. As Tom came abreast of a Frugelectric store he said "We'll need a light."

Lucas peered at the lanky lamps, and yet again Tom wondered what went on inside his cousin's head. "A torch," he resented having to elucidate.

"There's one at home."

"That's too far." Before Lucas could suspect he didn't want their parents learning where the boys would be Tom said "You'll have to buy one."

He was determined his cousin would pay, not least for putting the girls off. He watched Lucas select the cheapest flashlight and load it with batteries, then drop a ten-pound note beside the till so as to avoid touching the checkout girl's hand. He made her place his change there for him to scoop up while Tom took the flashlight wrapped in a flimsy plastic bag. "That's mine. I bought it," Lucas said at once.

"You hold it then, baby." Tom stopped just short of uttering the last word, though his face was hot again. "Look after it," he said and stalked out of the shop.

They were on the far side of Frugall from their houses and the school. An alley between a Frugranary baker's and a Frugolé tapas bar led to a path around the perimeter. A twelve-foot wall behind the shops and restaurants cut off most of the light and the blurred vague clamour of the retail park. The path was deserted apart from a few misshapen skeletal loiterers nuzzling the wall or propped against the chain-link fence alongside Grinfields Woods. They were abandoned shopping trolleys, and the only sound apart from the boys' padded footsteps was the rustle of the plastic bag.

Tom thought they might have to follow the path all the way to the housing estate between Grinfields and the retail park, but soon they came to a gap in the fence. Lucas dodged through it so fast that he might have forgotten he wasn't alone. As Tom followed he saw his own shadow emerge from a block of darkness fringed with outlines of wire mesh. The elongated shadows of trees were reaching for the larger dark. By the time the boys found the official path through the woods they were almost beyond the glare from the retail park, and Lucas switched on the flashlight. "That isn't scary," he declared as Tom's shadow brandished its arms.

Tom was simply frustrated that Lucas hadn't bothered to remove the flashlight from the bag. He watched his cousin peer both ways along the dim path like a child showing how much care he took about crossing a road, and then head along the stretch that vanished into darkness. The sight of Lucas swaggering off as though he didn't care whether he was followed did away with any qualms Tom might have over scaring him more than he would like. He tramped after Lucas through the woods that looked as if the dark had formed itself into a cage, and almost collided with him as the blurred jerky light swerved off the path to flutter across the trees to the left. "What's pulling something along?" Lucas seemed to feel entitled to be told.

"It's got a rope," Tom said, but didn't want to scare Lucas too much too soon. "No, it's only water."

He'd located it in the dried-up channel out of sight below the slope beyond the trees. It must be a lingering trickle of rain, which had stopped before dark, unless it was an animal or bird among the fallen leaves. "Make your mind up," Lucas complained and swung the light back to the path.

The noise ceased as Tom tramped after him. Perhaps it had gone underground through the abandoned irrigation channel. Without warning – certainly with none from Lucas – the flashlight beam sprang off the ragged stony path and flew into the treetops. "Is it laughing at us?" Lucas said.

Tom gave the harsh shrill sound somewhere ahead time to make itself heard. "What do you think?"

"Of course it's not," Lucas said as if his cousin needed to be put right. "Birds can't laugh."

Once more Tom suspected Lucas wasn't quite as odd as he liked everyone to think, although that was odd in itself. When the darkness creaked again he said "That's not a bird, it's a tree."

Lucas might have been challenging someone by striding up the path to jab the beam at the treetops. As he disappeared over a ridge the creaking of the solitary branch fell silent. Though he'd taken the light with him, Tom wasn't about to be driven to chase it. He hadn't quite reached the top of the path when he said "No wonder aunt and uncle say you can't make any friends."

He hadn't necessarily intended his cousin to hear, but Lucas retorted "I've got one."

Tom was tempted to suggest that Lucas should have brought this unlikely person instead of him. His cousin was taking the light away as though to punish Tom for his remark. Having left the path, he halted under an outstretched branch. "You can see where they did it," he said.

The flashlight beam plunged into the earth – into a circular shaft that led down to the middle of the irrigation tunnel. At some point the entrance had been boarded over, but now the rotten wood was strewn among the trees. Tom peered into the opening, from which a rusty ladder descended into utter darkness. "You can't see if you don't take the bag off."

As darkness raced up the ladder, chasing the light out of the shaft, Lucas said "What do you think is laughing now?"

"Maybe you should go down and find out."

Another hollow liquid giggle rose out of the unlit depths, and Tom thought of convincing his cousin it wasn't water they were hearing. Lucas crumpled the bag in his hand and sent the light down the shaft again. The beam just reached the foot of the ladder, below which Tom seemed to glimpse a dim sinuous movement before Lucas snatched the beam out of the shaft and aimed it at the branch overhead. "He hung himself on that, didn't he, and then she threw herself down there."

He sounded little more than distantly interested, which wasn't enough for Tom. "Aren't you going down, then? I thought you wanted a Halloween adventure."

The glowing leafless branch went out as Lucas swung the light back to the path. "All right," he said and made for the opposite side of the ridge.

Did he really need absolute precision or just demand it? As Tom trudged after him he heard a rustling somewhere near the open shaft. “I thought you never left litter,” he called. “How about that bag?”

“It’s here,” Lucas said and tugged it half out of his trouser pocket before stuffing it back in.

When Tom glanced behind him the Frugall floodlights glared in his eyes, and he couldn’t locate what he’d heard – perhaps leaves stirring in a wind, although he hadn’t felt one. Of course there must be wildlife in the woods, even if he’d yet to see any. He followed Lucas down the increasingly steep path and saw the flashlight beam snag on the curve of a stone arch protruding from the earth beside the track. It was the end of the tunnel, which had once helped irrigate the fields beyond the ridge. Now the fields were overgrown and the tunnel was barricaded, or rather it had been until somebody tore the boards down. As Lucas poked the flashlight beam into the entrance he said “Where’s the bell?”

Tom thought the slow dull metallic notes came from a car radio in the distance, but said “Is it in the tunnel?”

Lucas stooped under the arch, which wasn’t quite as tall as either of the boys. “Listen,” he said. “That’s where.”

Tom heard a last reverberation as he stepped off the path. Surely it was just his cousin’s gaze that made him wonder if the noise had indeed come from the tunnel, unless someone was playing a Halloween joke. Suppose the girls had followed them from the cinema and were sending the sound down from the ridge? In his hopelessly limited experience this didn’t seem the kind of thing girls did, especially while keeping quiet as well. The thought of them revived his discontent, and he said “Better go and see.”

Lucas advanced into the tunnel at once. His silhouette blotted out most of the way ahead, the stone floor scattered with sodden leaves, the walls and curved roof glistening with moss, a few weeds drooping out of cracks. The low passage was barely wider than his elbows as he held them at his sides – so narrow that the flashlight bumped against one wall with a soft moist thud as he turned to point the beam at Tom. “What are you doing?”

“Get that out of my face, can you?” As the light sank into the cramped space between them Tom said “I’m coming too.”

“I don’t want you to.”

Tom backed out, almost scraping his scalp on the arch. “Now you’ve got what you want as usual. Just you remember you did.”

“It won’t be scary if we both go in.” This might have been an effort to placate his cousin – as much of one as Lucas was likely to make – but Tom suspected it was just a stubborn statement of fact. “I’m not scared yet,” Lucas complained. “It’s Halloween.”

“Want me to make sure?”

“I know it is.” Before Tom could explain, if simply out of frustration, Lucas said “You’ve got nothing to do.”

He sounded intolerably like a teacher rebuking an idle pupil. As Tom vowed to prove him wrong in ways his cousin wouldn’t care for, Lucas ducked out of the tunnel and thrust the flashlight at him. “You can hold this while I’m in there.”

Tom sent the beam along the tunnel. It fell short of the ladder, which was a couple of hundred yards in. Once Lucas returned to the tunnel the light wouldn’t even reach past him. Tom was waiting to watch his reaction to this when Lucas said “I don’t mean here.”

He might have been criticising Tom’s ability to understand, a notion that was close to more than Tom could take. “Where?” he demanded without at all wanting to know.

“Go up and shine it down the hole, then I can see where halfway is. Shout when you get to the hole.”

"And you answer." In case this wasn't plain enough Tom added "So I can hear."

"Course I will."

Tom could have done without the haughtiness. He made off with the flashlight, swinging it from side to side of the deserted woods. As he reached the top of the path the lights above the distant retail park glared in his eyes, and he had a momentary impression that a rounded object was protruding just above the shaft at the midpoint of the tunnel. He squeezed his eyes shut, widening them as he stepped onto the ridge. Perhaps he'd seen an exposed root beyond the shaft, but he couldn't see it now. He marched to the opening and sent the beam down to the tunnel, where he seemed to glimpse movement – a dim shape like a scrawny limb or an even thinner item retreating at speed into the dark. It must have been a shadow cast by the ladder. "Come on," he called. "I'm here."

"I'm coming."

Tom was disconcerted to hear his cousin's shout resound along the tunnel while it also came from beyond the ridge. Despite straining his eyes he couldn't judge how far the flashlight beam reached; the glare from the retail park was still hindering his vision. He dodged around the shaft to turn his back on the problem, and saw that the beam of the cheap flashlight fell short of illuminating the tunnel itself. "Can you see the light?" he called.

"I see something."

Tom found this wilfully vague. "What?" he yelled.

"Must be you."

This was vaguer still, particularly for Lucas. Was he trying to unnerve his cousin? Tom peered into the shaft, waiting for Lucas to dart into view in a feeble attempt to alarm him. Or did Lucas mean to worry him by staying out of sight? Tom vowed not to call out again, but he was on the edge of yielding to the compulsion when an ill-defined figure appeared at the bottom of the shaft. He didn't really need it to turn its dim face upwards to show it was Lucas. "What am I doing now?" Tom grudged having to ask.

"Holding the light."

"I'm saying," Tom said more bitterly still, "what do you want me to do?"

"Stay there till I say," Lucas told him and stooped into the other section of the tunnel.

Tom tried to listen to his receding footsteps but soon could hear nothing at all – or rather, just the sound he'd previously ascribed to plastic. Perhaps the bag in his cousin's pocket was brushing against the wall, except that Tom seemed to hear the noise behind him. Had Lucas sneaked out of the far end of the tunnel to creep up and pounce on him? Surely his shadow would give him away, and when Tom swung around, only the trees were silhouetted against the glare from the retail park. He'd kept the flashlight beam trained down the shaft on the basis that he might have misjudged Lucas, but how long would he have to wait to hear from him? He had a sudden furious idea that, having left the tunnel, Lucas was on his way home. "Where are you now?" he shouted.

"Here," Lucas declared, appearing at the foot of the shaft.

So he'd been playing a different trick – staying out of sight until Tom grew nervous. "Finished with the light?" Tom only just bothered to ask.

"Go and meet me at the end," Lucas said before ducking into the dark.

Tom felt juvenile for using the flashlight to search among the trees around him – he wasn't the one who was meant to be scared – and switched it off as he hurried down the path. He was waiting at the mouth of the tunnel by the time his cousin emerged. Lucas looked dully untroubled, unless the darkness was obscuring his expression, and Tom wished he'd hidden long enough to make his cousin nervous. "What's it like?" he tried asking.

"Like I wasn't alone."

"You weren't."

"That's scary."

Tom thought he'd been more than sufficiently clear. He was feeling heavy with resentment when Lucas said "Now it's your turn."

As Tom switched on the flashlight, darkness shrank into the tunnel. "You can't do that," Lucas protested. "I'm supposed to go on top with it so you'll be in the dark."

Was he planning some trick of the kind Tom had spared him? When Tom hesitated while the unsteady shadows of weeds fingered the moss on the walls of the tunnel, Lucas said "I have to say what we do with it. It's mine."

Tom was so disgusted that he almost dropped the flashlight because of his haste to be rid of it. "I'll have to shout," Lucas told him. "You won't see."

He hadn't extinguished the light, which scrambled up the path ahead of him, leaving Tom to wonder if Lucas was uneasy after all. Suppose that distracted him from keeping the beam down the shaft? Once his cousin vanished over the ridge Tom peered along the tunnel, but it might as well have been stuffed with earth. He hadn't distinguished even a hint of light when Lucas called "It's waiting."

His voice was in more than one place again – somewhere down the tunnel and on the ridge as well. It occurred to Tom that he should have extracted a promise, and he cupped his hands around his mouth to yell "Say you'll wait there for me."

"That's what I'm doing."

Tom could have fancied he was hearing another voice imitate Lucas. "Say you will," he insisted, "as long as I want the light."

"I will as long as you want the light."

This had to be precise enough, and surely Lucas was incapable of acting other than he'd said he would. Wasn't his saying it in more than one voice like a double promise? Tom had no reason to hesitate, even if he wished Dianne were with him to be scared and then comforted. He wouldn't be comforting Lucas, and he ducked into the tunnel.

The darkness fastened on his eyes at once. They felt coated with it, a substance like the blackest paint. It hindered his feet too, as if they had to wade through it, shuffling forward an inch at a time, which was all he felt able to risk. He extended his arms in front of him to avoid touching the slimy walls, though he could have imagined his fingertips were about to bump into the dark. Of course there was nothing solid in front of him. Lucas hadn't switched off the flashlight and sneaked down the ladder to stand in the blackness until Tom's outstretched fingers found him. Just the same, the thought made Tom bring his hands back and lower his arms. "Are you really up there?" he shouted.

"You'll see."

His cousin's voice was somewhere ahead and above the tunnel. Otherwise the exchange didn't reassure Tom as much as he would have hoped if he'd needed reassurance. It wasn't simply that his shout had been boxed in by the walls and the roof that forced his head down; his voice had seemed muffled by some obstacle in front of him. Was he about to see it? There appeared to be a hint of pallor in the blackness, if that wasn't just an effect of straining his eyes or of hoping to locate the flashlight beam. When he edged forward the impression didn't shift, and he kept his gaze fixed on the promise of light until his foot nudged an object on the floor of the tunnel.

He heard it stir and then subside. He had no room to sidle around it, and he didn't care to turn his back. By resting his foot on it and trampling on it he deduced that it was a mass of twigs and dead leaves. He trod hard on it on his way past, and worked out that the material must have fallen down the shaft, which was just visible ahead by the light that nearly reached down to the tunnel roof. He could scarcely believe how long he'd taken to walk halfway; it felt as if the darkness had weighed down the passing of time. A few waterlogged leaves slithered underfoot as he reached the shaft and was able to raise his head. "See me?" he called.

Lucas was an indefinite silhouette against the night sky beyond the flashlight, which almost blinded Tom even though the beam on the wall opposite the ladder was so dim. "You were a long time," Lucas protested.

An acoustic quirk made versions of his voice mutter in both sections of the tunnel. Before Tom could reply, less irately than the complaint deserved, Lucas said "When you've been through the rest you have to come back this way."

That he had needn't mean Tom should. Lucas wasn't frightened yet, which was among the reasons why Tom intended to leave the tunnel by the far end so as to tiptoe up behind him. He shut his eyes to ready them for the darkness as far as he could. He hadn't opened them when Lucas enraged him by calling "Are you scared to go in?"

Tom lowered his head as if he meant to butt the dark and advanced into the tunnel. He wouldn't have believed the blackness could grow thicker, but now it didn't just smother his eyes – it filled them to the limit. He'd taken a very few steps, which felt shackled by his wariness, when his foot collided with another heap of leaves. He heard twigs if not small branches snap as he trod several times on the yielding heap, which must be almost as long as he was tall. Once he was past it the floor seemed clear, but how far did he have to shuffle to catch his first glimpse of the night outside? It couldn't be so dark out there that it was indistinguishable from the underground passage. He was stretching his eyes wide, which only served to let more of the darkness into them, when his foot struck a hindrance more solid than leaves – an object that his groping fingers found to be as high and wide as the tunnel. The entrance was boarded up.

So Lucas hadn't just been setting out the rules of the game. Perhaps he'd believed he was making it plain that Tom couldn't leave the tunnel at this end. Tom thumped the boards with his fists and tried a few kicks as well, but the barrier didn't give. When he turned away at last he had to touch the cold fur of the wall with his knuckles to be certain he was facing down the tunnel. He shuffled forward as if he were being dragged by his bent head, and his blacked-out eyes were straining to find the light when his toe poked the mass of leaves and wood on the floor. If he was so close to the shaft, why couldn't he make out even a hint of the flashlight beam? "What are you playing at?" he shouted.

There was no response of any kind. Perhaps Lucas had decided to alarm him. He dealt the supine heap a kick, but it held more or less together. He tramped on it a number of times while edging forward. It was behind him, though not far, when something moved under his feet – a large worm, he thought, or a snake. As he stumbled clear of it he heard scattered leaves rustle with its movement, and recognised the sound he'd attributed to plastic on his way to the tunnel. He needn't think about it further – he only wanted to reach the light. That still wasn't visible, and he wasn't eager to shout into the dark again, surely just because Lucas might think he was scared. He had no idea how many timid paces he'd taken before he was able to lift his head.

For a moment this felt like nothing but relief, and then he saw that the top of the shaft was deserted. "Lucas," he yelled. "Lucas." He was trying just to feel furious, but the repetition unnerved him – it seemed too close to doing his best to ensure that only his cousin would respond. He was about to call once more when Lucas appeared above him, at least fifty feet away, and sent the flashlight beam down the highest rungs of the ladder. Tom would have shouted at him except for being assailed by a sudden unwelcome thought. He knew why he'd seemed to take too long to return to the shaft: because the supine mass on which he'd trodden was further from it than before. While he'd been trying to find his way out, it had crawled after him in the dark.

He twisted around to peer behind him, but the blackness was impenetrable. Although he was afraid to see, not seeing might be worse. "Lucas," he blurted, and then forced himself to raise his voice. "Send the light down here."

The response was a noise very much like one he'd previously heard – a clang like the note of a dull bell. Now he realised it had been the sound of an object swinging against the ladder, repeatedly colliding with the upper rungs. This time the flashlight was making the noise, and struck another rung as it plummeted down the shaft. The lens smashed on the tunnel floor, and the light went out at once.

"What have you done now," Tom almost screamed, "you stupid useless retard?" He dropped into a crouch that felt as if a pain in his guts had doubled him over. His fingers groped over the cold wet stone and eventually closed around the flashlight. He pushed the switch back and forth, but the bulb must be broken too. When he jerked his head back to yell at Lucas he saw that the dim round hole at the top of the shaft was empty once more. He staggered to his feet and threw out a hand to help him keep his balance, and clutched an object that was dangling beside him in the tunnel. It was the rope he'd wanted to think was a worm or a snake.

A mindless panic made him haul at the bedraggled rope, and an object nuzzled the back of his hand. It was a face, though not much of one, and as he recoiled with a cry he felt it sag away from the bone. He was backing away so fast he almost overbalanced when he heard sounds in the other section of the tunnel. Between him and the way out, someone was running through the absolute blackness as if they had no need of light – as if they welcomed its absence.

For a moment that seemed endless Tom felt the darkness claim him, and then he shied the flashlight in the direction of the sodden flopping footsteps. He clutched at the ladder and hauled himself desperately upwards. He mustn't think about climbing towards the outstretched branch that had creaked as the boys made for the ridge. Perhaps nobody had killed themselves – perhaps that was just a story made up by adults to scare children away from any danger. He could no longer hear the loose footsteps for all the noise he was making on the shaky ladder. Lucas must be waiting by the shaft – he'd promised to – and of course he'd turned the light away when he'd heard Tom thumping the boards that blocked the tunnel. The thought gave Tom the chance to realise who the friend Lucas said he had must be. "I'm still your friend," he called, surely not too late, as he clambered up the rusty ladder. He didn't dare to look down, and he was just a few rungs from the top when he lost his footing. His foot flailed in the air and then trod on the head of whatever was climbing after him.

It moved under his foot – moved more than any scalp ought to be able – as he kicked it away. He was terrified what else he might tread on, but he only found the rung again. His head was nearly level with the exit from the shaft before a pulpy grasp closed around his ankle. However soft they were, the swollen fingers felt capable of dragging him down into the blackness to share it with its residents. He thrust his free hand above the shaft in a desperate appeal. Surely Lucas hadn't felt so insulted that he'd abandoned his cousin – surely only he was out there. "Get hold of me," Tom pleaded, and at once he had his answer.

They Come At Night

Georgia Cook

THE HYENAS were back.

Malik peered through his binoculars, watching the heavy brown shapes slink along the edges of the compound, their eyes glinting like fireflies under the spotlights. They were nothing to worry about – even brown hyenas were famously timid around humans – and yet their presence was disconcerting nonetheless. Hyenas were nature's rag-and-bone men; the spirits haunting the killing grounds of larger, more vicious predators. And the way this particular pack moved…

"—How're the readings?" asked a voice, jolting Malik from his trace. Aashif had appeared in the doorway of the observation shack, his dark hair ruffled with sweat and sleep. He suppressed a yawn.

"Normal," grunted Malik, watching another shadow slip out of sight.

Aashif snorted, batting away a mosquito. "Great, thanks."

"There are more of them today." Malik handed him the binoculars.

Aashif took them with a show of surprise. "Pretty rare out here, aren't they?" he said.

"That's what I thought."

Aashif peered through the binoculars, letting out a low whistle. "God, that's gotta be… what? Thirty? Forty?"

"Thirty-five, I think." Malik had counted.

"Well," Aashif clapped Malik on the shoulder and grinned. "Last I checked they're not herbivores, and they can't get past the fence, so whatever they're up to, it's not professional sabotage."

"Hm," Malik tried to smile. He was peering through the binoculars again, watching one of the muscular brown shapes slip between the spotlights in the morning gloom, nearly black against the desert landscape.

"Malik," Aashif snapped his fingers in front of Malik's face. "Earth to Malik. Come on, we're not paid to watch the wildlife. How are the babies doing?"

Malik rolled his eyes and heaved himself upright out of his plastic chair. "Same as always," he said, following Aashif from the sweltering gloom of the observation shack out into the blazing sunlight. "You can check for yourself."

A neat line of specimen tables sat in the middle of the compound yard, facing the shack. A further three occupied one of the tall white tents by the perimeter fence, basking in its sweltering gloom. Each table held five identical plastic boxes, each in turn containing a bloom of greyish-purple fungi.

God, thought Malik. *All this way for a crate of bloody mushrooms.*

"How's Sandra?" he asked, as Aashif bent to examine the nearest box.

"Sleeping sound as a baby when I passed her tent," Aashif grinned. Sandra Roberts rounded out their secluded team of three; a skeleton crew just large enough to maintain a consistent watch pattern, each hand-picked from Oxford's latest batch of Master's degree graduates.

"Come on," Aashif clapped Malik on the shoulder. "Big trek in the morning. Get a few hours shut-eye, yeah? It's my turn to babysit the mushrooms."

Malik wasn't about to argue. Even the cramped confines of his tent, with its swaddling mosquito blankets and sweltering sleeping bag, seemed a luxury after a gruelling nighttime watch.

As he turned to go, he caught the outline of a dark brown shape, slinking away from the fence and off into the shadows.

All around the compound, the hyenas lingered.

* * *

The Calico research compound encompassed a scattering of tents, out-buildings, and tall wire fencing in the middle north of the Namib Desert, at least two days' drive from Gobabeb. Cold air off the Hadley Cell created a fog belt which enveloped the tents in the morning, sweeping across the sand in clumps and drifts, turning the desert into a drifting ocean, through which the dunes rose like islands.

It was beautiful, and it was strange, and it was isolating.

They'd driven there in convoy, dragging their equipment through the evening heat, with the intention of staying upwards of three months. Three months among the rocks and endless blue skies. Three months of staring bleary-eyed at boxes and boxes of mushrooms – taking readings and making meticulous notes, working diligently to answer the riveting question of whether this particular breed thrived in extreme desert conditions. The pay was decent – probably because the lab back in Oxford could only convince the most foolhardy or desperate to go – but not, Malik often thought, quite decent enough.

* * *

They set off at dawn towards the first encampment, lugging backpacks of water, hiking equipment, and Aashif's camera equipment between them, following a carefully marked path through the rock.

As well as the tables up in the compound, there were three designated areas of natural habitat out in the brush, each with its own box of fungi to monitor. The team visited them every two days, documenting the progress of each sample, taking photos. This wouldn't have been too awful if the locations weren't spread in a ten-mile triangle around the compound, forcing them to trek the full distance. Not for the first time, Malik wondered if the spots had been chosen specifically to torture them.

They'd been walking twenty minutes, the outpost shrinking to a hazy blot on the horizon, when they came across the campsite. It lay scattered across a ten-foot radius down the side of a dune; pots and pans glimmered red-hot in the sunlight. A shred of fabric, bleached almost white, fluttered feebly in the raw breeze. The unmistakable bones of a tent stuck haphazardly out of the sand, gleaming bright like the ribs of some strange animal.

The group stood for a moment, staring in shock.

"Animals?" suggested Sandra, breaking the silence. "Coyotes, maybe?"

"Teenagers," Aashif shrugged, hefting his backpack. "Hunters."

Sandra's eyebrows rose sceptically. "All the way out here?"

"Why not?"

Sandra frowned. "It looks old," she said. "Have we passed it before?"

Malik nudged a scrap of metal with his foot. "The desert buries things quickly out here," he said. "The wind probably just unearthed it."

She was right though; they'd passed this way several times in the last few weeks. Why hadn't they spotted these remains earlier? It couldn't be a new campsite, not in such a state…

"Come on," said Malik, forcing the thought away. "It's bloody boiling."

The heat swirled as they set off again, rising around their ankles in a haze of sand and debris, rippling back across the settlement and its strange metal bones.

* * *

The first encampment lay in a round basin of rock six miles from the research station. The basin floor was a sheer scramble down merciless yellow rocks, searing hot in the afternoon sun. Shadows were fleeting and saturated, slinking pitch black beneath stones and into tight little corners.

Even before they approached the lip of the basin, it was clear something was wrong. Metal flashed on the rock below, making the sunlight blinding. The specimen box lay on its side in the dirt, scraps of fungi flung haphazardly amongst the rocks.

"*Fuck*," Sandra hissed.

"We knew it was going to happen eventually," sighed Aashif. "We'll just set up again. Making a note in the files…"

Sandra knelt to peer into the hole, her eyes narrowed. "But what could have *done* that?" she whispered. Malik knelt beside her. Finally he saw what she was looking at: the heavy square box, built to withstand the desert elements, was covered in scratches. The worst of them gouged through the metal, warping the sides, as if something had dragged it across the rock.

Despite the heat, Malik shivered. An image of the abandoned campsite flashed through his mind. "…Animals?" he suggested. "Plenty of things eat vegetation."

"But mushrooms? *These* mushrooms? They aren't even native!" Sandra sounded strained.

Aashif placed a reassuring hand on her shoulder. "Scavengers will eat anything," he said. "They don't know any better."

Sandra nodded, raking a handful of hair out of her eyes.

Nobody spoke as they gathered the necessary evidence for the university files. Nobody made the perilous scramble down the rocks to retrieve the specimen box. By unspoken agreement they left it where it lay.

* * *

To everyone's relief, the final two specimen boxes – one wedged between a thin chasm of rock a mile from the basin, the other inside the welcome coolness of a small sandstone cave – remained untouched. Still, conversation was infrequent and brief, as if the desert might swallow it whole. The morning's strange discoveries had left an odd tension in the air, and Malik was glad when they finally turned and headed back to base.

He busied himself in his tent with a write up of their findings, glad of the time alone, carefully documenting the fungi's progress. The spores were responding well to the drier, damper areas of desert, but reacted badly in open sun. *Like any of us couldn't have said that already*, Malik thought, irritably.

When he wandered outside at noon to stretch his legs, he found Sandra sitting in the dirt by the fence, staring out across the desert.

"Hey." He sat beside her, noting with unease that her skin was slick with sweat.

Sandra nodded her acknowledgement without looking up, her gaze fixed on the horizon.

"…It's the oldest desert in the world, did you know that?" she murmured. "Sand and rocks older than human civilization."

Malik shifted uncomfortably. "Guess so," he said. Perhaps the trek this morning had affected Sandra worse than he'd thought. He considered leading her inside, gently coaxing a bottle of water into her hands. They'd all been trained on how to spot and treat encroaching heatstroke…

Sandra took a deep breath. "I've been thinking," she said suddenly. "About the site we found earlier."

"What about it?" Malik asked.

Sandrda finally shot him a look. "Didn't it seem strange to you?"

"Well… yeah," Malik laughed. "It was a camp in the middle of nowhere, of course it seemed strange." He paused. Sandra's expression was pleading. "Probably just poachers, Sandra," he added with a sigh. "Plenty of things get abandoned in the desert."

"I didn't see any animal droppings," Sandra argued.

"So?"

"So it's *strange*."

Malik struggled to uphold reason. "So… what? Exactly? Some campers arrived in the middle of nowhere, set up between our last trek and today, then just… vanished?"

Sandra rummaged in her pocket. "I went back." she said.

Malik blanched. "*You went back?* On your own?"

Sandra fixed him with a look. "I wanted to see if there were any correlations with the monitor site – if what attacked the camp attacked the crate. If we knew what caused that damage, we could prepare accordingly."

This made sense to Malik, but something about Sandra's intensity unnerved him. "So?"

"So I found this." Sandra held out a little slip of plastic, scratched, and scorched by the sun. Malik recognised it instantly; it was an ID card, identical to the kind owned and worn by everyone at the Calico Research Station. The text was too faded to read, but the photo appeared to show a dark middle-aged man, peering out from a mist of scratches.

"It's one of ours," Sandra confirmed. "From this compound. Another research team."

Malik stared at it for a long moment, uncertainty rising in this throat, then fumbled in his pocket and drew out his own ID. It glinted in the sunlight, unmistakable. "How on earth…?"

"I want to go back there, Malik. Just to check. Just to *see*. There's something we're missing!"

Malik gaped at her. "Sandra—"

"I know it sounds mad…" Sandra stared past the fence at the desolate landscape. The sun had begun to sink below the horizon, spreading deep blue shadows across the sand. Stars dotted the sky overhead. A light breeze sent waves of dust rustling around Malik's ankles. He shivered.

"I've seen…creatures…out there…" admitted Sandra in a small, soft voice. "Late at night, when I'm on watch. Big black eyes, staring at me through the dark…"

"Hyenas," said Malik. "I've seen them too."

Sandra dragged a finger through the dirt, making a tight swirl. "There are… creatures… " she whispered. "In African mythology. Scavengers that eat every scrap of living flesh; human, animal, it doesn't matter. They look like large dogs, but when you get close…" She trailed off, staring up at Malik with her wide, wide eyes. "Ghouls, they're called," she said.

Despite himself, Malik laughed. "Oh, come off it, Sandra. *Ghouls?*"

Sandra reddened. "Then how do you explain what happened?" she snapped.

"Animals!" Malik protested. "Just normal animals, doing normal animal things!"

"And the ID card?" Sandra fumbled in her pocket again.

Malik put out a hand to stop her, not wanting to see it again. "The site was near this compound," he said. "Someone probably dropped it on another research mission. Sandra, *please*."

Sandra's shoulders slumped. She turned away from him, staring back out across the horizon. "...I wonder sometimes," she said, so softly Malik almost didn't hear. "If we were really sent all this way just to study fungi..."

* * *

There was a hole in the compound fence. It was about the size of a small child, positioned where the wire met the firm sandy ground. Aashif let out a low whistle as he knelt to inspect it. "Christ, what do you think made that?"

"No idea," said Malik. He'd spotted it earlier that morning, padding across the compound in search of coffee. Fence maintenance was just one of the many intricate little parts of living in the desert. "I checked the tents," he added. "Nothing's missing."

"And none of our supplies have been touched." Aashif prodded the wire with a finger. "Looks like something tore a piece right off," he mused. "Look at that..." He stood, a clump of brownish fur held between thumb and forefinger. "Definitely an animal."

Malik's brow furrowed. "But it didn't take anything?"

"Probably deterred by the spotlights." Aashif brushed himself down, flicking a curl out of his eyes. "I'll grab the bolt cutters later and see what I can patch up."

"Thanks." Malik wasn't sure why, but the hole unnerved him. It wasn't uncommon to get the odd night creature skittering across the compound, and no fence in hell could keep out the bugs. But even so...

Aashif must have caught his expression, because his brow furrowed. "Has Sandra been talking to you?" he asked.

Malik's spine prickled. "Talking about what?" he asked.

Aashif sighed. "I think the heat's getting to her."

Malik shifted. "She thinks... something happened with the campsite we found the other day," he admitted. "Something connected to the specimen box. It really spooked her."

Aashif nodded, his expression grave. When he finally spoke, it was in a low, uncomfortable voice, as if admitting a dark and terrible secret: "She asked me about ghouls this morning."

Malik stifled an uncomfortable laugh. "God, you too?"

Aashif shrugged. "My family's from this region. She wanted to know about our legends."

Malik paused. Aashif's expression had begun to unnerve him. "And what did you tell her?" he asked.

"That it's an old myth: Ghouls are said to wander the desolate wastes out in the desert, screaming across the dunes, luring travellers to their deaths and feasting on their corpses."

Despite himself, Malik shivered. "I thought ghouls were a Romanian thing," he said. "You know, like vampires."

Aashif flashed him a humourless little smile. "Everywhere has monsters, Malik." he said.

Malik shifted uncomfortably. "You realise she actually thinks they're *real*, right?" he asked.

He expected Aashif to laugh, or at least reassure him; even chide him, like an adult to a naive child. Instead, Aashif stared out across the landscape. A band of sunlight spread across the horizon, stretched thin as an antique necklace, flashing gold and crimson into the growing night. The air hung dry and relentless, thick with heat. Sitting here, it was easy to believe they were the last two people alive in the whole world.

"In a place like this," said Aashif, softly, "you can believe almost anything."

* * *

Malik sat bolt upright, fighting back the mosquito nets draped around his cot. For a moment he didn't know what had awoken him, sweat-drenched and uncomfortable in the middle of the night, then the screams came again. They echoed across the compound, strangled and animal; closer than they'd ever been before. Too close.

Malik struggled into his sand shoes and ran to the tent opening, peering out into the floodlit night.

Screams and laughter bounced across the dunes, impossible to pinpoint. Shapes slunk through the darkness on the other side of the fence, too many to count. Eyes flashed pearl-white, like stars fallen from the pitch-black sky.

The hyenas were back.

Aashif appeared around the corner, barefoot, stumbling in his nightclothes. "Christ, do you hear that?" he hissed

"Of course I bloody hear it!" Malik snapped.

"What are they *doing?*" Aashif turned. "Where's Sandra?"

"She should be on watch," said Malik.

They turned in the direction of the specimen tables. Both the chair and observation tent were empty.

Aashif cursed. "I'll go check her tent," he said, stumbling off into the darkness.

Malik went to follow, but something along the fence caught his attention; the holes in the wire had grown larger and more frequent, dotted across the wire in haphazard bursts, as if something had been working diligently to expand them.

Something with sharp sharp teeth.

Aashif reappeared at a run. "She's not there!" he gasped, his forehead dripping with sweat.

I want to go back there, Malik. Just to check. Just to see.

Malik's heart jolted. "She went back to the campsite…" he whispered.

Aashif paused. "The what – how do you know?"

Because we didn't listen to her. Because she's convinced of monsters.

Aashif didn't wait for the reply. "I'll go," he said. "One of us has to stay here. Keep the generator going, okay? Make sure the lights stay on."

Malik nodded, his heart pounding. "Call me on the radio when you find her."

"I will."

As Aashif vanished into the night, Malik wondered why he hadn't offered to go instead, why he hadn't suggested they go in the morning. It had been his idea, after all. But something about the darkness outside, enclosing the compound on all sides, spilling to the edges of the spotlights like the water in a pitch black sea…

The hairs on the back of Malik's neck rose. Something stood just beyond the spotlight overlooking the gate. It looked like a hyena, with its crest of bristling brown fur and snubbed snout, but there was something about its eyes – small and bright in the darkness, like fireflies – something about its stance, its sureness of footing. Too human, too precise, too certain.

A thought rose in Malik's mind, kicked loose by Sandra's feverish words the previous afternoon. Perhaps a thought he'd been suppressing for as long as they'd been here:

Why *had* they been sent to the Calico base? Just the three of them, all alone out here, made to trail a long looping circle across the desert, day after day, chasing a pointless task, marking their camp with bright white floodlights, drawing the animals to their scent…

Baiting the monsters.

Shapes shifted in the shadows between the tents. Malik turned. A cluster of muscular silhouettes slunk towards the generator shack, their coats slick and glimmering. Malik caught a flash of yellow teeth, a glittering human eye, then a crash rang out across the compound. At once, every spotlight around the perimeter flicked out, plunging the world into blackness.

Malik staggered, blinded by the sudden dark. Shapes whispered all around him; the gentle patter of paws. Ragged breathing filled the night, sharp and victorious. A smell like spoiled meat rose in the air.

The abandoned campsite flashed across Malik's mind; tents and utensils strewn across the sand, no sign of life; not even bones. Picked clean.

How many other research teams had been here before them? Offered up to the rolling sands and blistering heat. Sent into the night to expose the beating heart of desert mythology. Would someone come across the research station eventually? What would they find when they did?

Ghouls ate everything, Sandra had said. Every last scrap.

Malik staggered, his eyes finally adjusting enough to carve shape from shadow.

The gate lay ahead of him, open to the endless sky. Holes littered the boundary fence, filled with struggling shapes and glittering, slavering jaws; the night come alive, the night arriving to feast.

Malik ran.

He plunged into the darkness, stumbling over rocks and vegetation, his heart pounding, his breath misting the air. At night, desert temperatures dropped to below freezing, but Malik had blundered out of his tent without a protective layer. The cold prickled his skin, promising far worse to come. How long could he possibly hope to survive out here?

Longer than Sandra. Longer than Aashif. Maybe if he kept running…

A cry went up across the dunes. A second rose from the left, then another from the right, until the night filled with screams.

No. Not screams. Laughter.

They were hunting him, and they knew the desert so much better than he did. They'd be on him soon. They'd finish the job. They were hungry, after all, so hungry, and they'd been waiting all this time.

Then there would be nothing left; nothing but sand and heat and the circling vultures. The bones of the desert, picked clean beneath the blazing sun.

Once Upon a Graveyard

Gina Easton

AMARETTA STARED at the corpse sprawled on the floor and waited for it to speak.

Not to literally speak, of course, but communicate with her, show her images of who, or what, had killed it.

Detective Inspector Rutherford eyed her keenly. "Anything to tell me, Miss Fontaine?"

Amaretta stood very still, not replying. Her gaze was fixated on the dead woman lying in a pool of blood, torso slashed open, exposing entrails and other organs. The light from the full moon shining through the window highlighted the wet glistening mess.

She swallowed back the rising nausea and bile. "Are those bite marks?" She gestured at some wounds on the victim's thighs. The woman, clad in a nightgown which had been ripped and shredded, had apparently gotten out of bed. Had she perhaps been awakened by a noise, gone to investigate and stumbled upon an intruder who had savagely attacked and killed her?

Rutherford lifted his lantern, bending down to peer closely at the body. "Yes," he nodded. "They appear to be human, albeit odd in contour and rather large. But we shall have to wait for the coroner's verdict on that."

"Is there anyone else in the house?"

The detective shook his head. "Mrs. Carrington was alone. Her husband is away on business in Brussels, due back in two days."

"Who alerted the constabulary?"

"A neighbour who was awake and heard a commotion coming from the Carrington's house. He arrived with his blunderbuss to find the lady deceased, and the perpetrator fled."

Amaretta closed her eyes. An image unfolded slowly in her mind as the petals of a rose might open to reveal its secret centre. Alice Carrington in her boudoir, seated at her dressing-table, brushing her chestnut-coloured tresses. Suddenly a frown creases her brow. Does she hear something? Her nose crinkles in distaste. No, not a noise, but a *smell*. She smells something unpleasant, something disturbing.

Rising from her chair she grabs her lamp, turning up the light before leaving the room. The smell is stronger in the corridor. Gamy, slightly tangy, with an undertone of something dark and foul. Despite her growing apprehension Alice forces herself to descend the staircase as quietly as possible so as not to disturb whatever might be in her house.

Could a wild animal, a coyote or fox, perhaps even a badger, have somehow gained entry? Had she carelessly left a window unlatched?

She wishes she'd thought to bring a weapon, perhaps the brass candelabra on the fireplace mantel. At the very least a handkerchief to cover her mouth and nose. The smell, no *reek,* is intensifying, causing her stomach to roil with a sickening sensation. As she approaches the front parlour she can almost *taste* the stench. It seems to coat her tongue and the back of her throat with a noxious oily film. She pauses, stifling an urge to retch.

With her trepidation escalating to outright fear Alice reaches the threshold of the parlour. Holding the lamp in front of her she swings it in an arc to illuminate the room and its shadowed corners. She quickly ascertains that the room is empty.

Relieved but perplexed she thinks, there is nothing here, yet the smell is so strong. *Something* has been in this room, maybe is still lurking elsewhere in the house. But what could it—

Her thoughts are brutally cut short by a vice-like grip that grabs her by the throat.

Amaretta gasped, doubling over and clutching her stomach.

"Miss Fontaine?" Rutherford hurried to her side.

Amaretta lifted a hand as she slowly straightened up. "I'm alright, Inspector."

"You saw something, didn't you?"

Amaretta nodded. "Yes, but I didn't see who or *what* killed Alice Carrington."

* * *

At the police station, Amaretta reviewed the details of her vision with the detective. She frowned as a thought occurred to her. "I didn't notice any unusual smell in the house. Did you, Inspector?"

Rutherford shook his head. "Aside from the odour of blood and viscera, no. I understand Mrs. Carrington thought it could be an animal, but she was mistaken. This was no animal, unless one has mastered the ability to use a knife, for those wounds were caused by a blade of some sort."

Amaretta sipped her cup of tea. "I realize that. However, there is no doubt about the smell, or should I say, stench. It is what prompted Alice to leave the safety of her bedchamber and venture downstairs. And she definitely thought an animal had invaded her house. Until..."

"Until it grabbed her and slashed her throat." Rutherford's tone was laced with irony.

Amaretta sighed. "Obviously it was a man. But what sort of man?"

"What indeed?" Rutherford echoed. Since the Jack the Ripper murders two years ago in 1888, London, in particular the notoriously crime-infested East End, had continued to experience an inordinate number of heinous murders. Prostitutes, criminals, those who were indigent, often alcohol-or-drug-addicted, were easy prey. Some were killed in pub fights, some in dark alleys. Many bodies were fished out of the River Thames, most with significant parts missing. But this was central London and Alice Carrington a respectable woman brutally murdered in her own home, not some filthy, vermin-laden alleyway.

And yet... the murder bore more than a passing resemblance to the Ripper killings. In those, like this one, the unfortunate women had their throats slit and their bodies severely mutilated. And in one memorable incident, a kidney was removed by the killer and sent to the police, along with a taunting letter.

Jack the Ripper had never been caught. He had simply disappeared after the last murder in November of 1888. What if he'd started killing again?

"You're thinking it's him," Amaretta said quietly. "The Ripper."

"I'd wager you don't have to be clairvoyant to know that," Rutherford said ruefully.

Amaretta Fontaine *was* a clairvoyant and a spiritualist with a thriving practice. She had a regular clientele who consulted her for readings, predictions about the future, communication with the dead, and other issues pertaining to the realm of spirit. Occasionally she was asked by the constabulary to assist with an investigation. Or rather, her assistance was requested, albeit in an unofficial capacity, by one particular detective.

James Rutherford was not the average London Metropolitan police detective. He had been raised by a mother who was a spiritualist of some renown. Her skills as a clairvoyant were celebrated in the spiritualist circles of London, Paris, Milan and other European cities.

As a child James had been exposed to the intricacies of the spiritualist movement. His father had died when he was quite young and he spent his childhood travelling with his mother to and from the Continent. His mother had warned him that many frauds and mountebanks existed within the profession, swindlers intent on cheating gullible clients and getting rich in the process. Lillian Rutherford was genuinely gifted and devoted her time and energy to those who sought communion with loved ones who had passed from this existence into the next.

Thus, Rutherford had always had a belief in and respect for the abilities of his mother and others like her. Though many of his fellow detectives mocked those who professed belief in the supernatural, he knew that the brutality of the Ripper murders had caused even some of the most hardened and sceptical policemen to question whether such a murderer was entirely human. There had been widespread speculation in Whitechapel, including amongst the constabulary, that perhaps Jack the Ripper was no ordinary man, but a being with occult abilities. The fact that he had managed to elude the authorities and seemingly vanish into thin air reinforced this belief for many.

The detective had met Amaretta Fontaine through his mother, who had accepted the young woman as her protégé. Rutherford was impressed by the clairvoyant's self-possession, thoughtfulness and intelligence. She expressed an interest in police work and asked him insightful questions about crime and criminals. He discovered that Amaretta's abilities included receiving messages from the dead, not in words, but in images and sensations.

At the time he had been in charge of a murder investigation in which the killer was still at large, with no concrete clues as to his or her identity. He asked Amaretta if she would be willing to visit the crime scene to see if she could sense any information that could aid in solving the case.

To his surprise, the young woman agreed. Walking through the scene of the murder, which had occurred in an alley behind a brothel, she was able to piece together images of what had transpired. Her description of the killer and his relationship to the victim were revealed to her by the deceased. Rutherford and his men were able to track the man and apprehend him. Once in police custody the suspect had tearfully admitted his guilt. Since that case a year ago the inspector sometimes consulted with the clairvoyant, who had succeeded where regular police detection had failed.

Now, as he watched Amaretta finish her tea, he said, "You know that I believe the Ripper is out there somewhere. Killers like that don't just 'disappear', nor do their heinous impulses dissipate. It is possible he has once again embarked on a murderous spree."

Amaretta nodded. "It is unfortunate that I could not get a sense from Alice as to who grabbed her. It was all too sudden an attack from behind. She could see nothing."

"Well, Miss Fontaine, I am appreciative of your time and effort. Now I shall find a hansom to drive you home."

* * *

When Amaretta arrived home she knew by the smell that Bertram was there. Sure enough, when she entered the small sitting-room there was movement in the corner. A shape detached itself from the shadows and shuffled into the patch of carpet illuminated by a beam of moonlight.

"Did your inspector call you out again?" he asked in his raspy voice.

"He is not 'my' inspector," Amaretta said mildly. She lit a lamp and carried it over to her chair, careful to shield the light from Bertram's sensitive eyes. "And yes, there was a particularly gruesome murder tonight. I think it may have been committed by one of *your* brethren." She told him the details of her vision.

Bertram stared at her, curiosity piqued. He was a ghoul and Amaretta was his only human contact. "Really?" he inquired laconically. "It would be unusual for one of my 'brethren' to commit murder. As you know, we much prefer a diet of *dead* flesh."

"Yes, but ghouls have been known to kill and feed off live victims, too."

Bertram regarded her thoughtfully. "It does happen," he conceded, "albeit rarely. And these incidents occur in or near graveyards. I have never heard of a ghoul intruding into someone's house to kill them." The moon's rays highlighted his gaunt, grey features. He was clad in a long black robe, much like a monk's attire, complete with cowl and corded sash at the waist. The robe concealed his mottled ashen skin, the cowl the sparse tufts of lifeless hair that clung to his misshapen head.

The hands which emerged from the voluminous folds of his sleeves had long slender fingers, fingers which, back in the eighteenth century, had entertained many in the great music houses of Europe. In that life he had been Bertram Marceau, a highly gifted concert pianist. Now those fingers were curved into talons sharp as scimitars, perfect for the tearing and rendering of flesh. When he smiled, which was seldom, it was a truly ghastly sight, for a set of crooked, jagged teeth were exposed, ideal for sinking into rotted, decaying tissue.

"Why do you think it was a ghoul?"

"Obviously there is the smell to consider. I couldn't detect it myself, but when I was in communication with the dead woman she allowed me to experience it. It was a familiar stench." Amaretta stared pointedly at Bertram. "It smelled of excavated tombs, putrid corpses, corruption. A singular, unique *reek*." Her expression was troubled. "What I don't understand, however, is why a ghoul would use a knife to kill. Why not use its claws? They are just as lethal."

"Hmm." Bertram began to pace around the room, busy in thought. "It would not be a pure blood, ancient ghoul. A ghoul who was not born of the womb would never deliberately seek out a living being. But it might be a young ghoul. By that I mean a ghoul that has been newly 'transformed'. Having recently been human it may not yet have developed a taste for decomposed flesh, but may prefer its meat a little… ah… fresher. As for the knife… if the ghoul is still undergoing a transition phase it may lack confidence in its skills and feel that a weapon is necessary to kill its prey.

"Or, and this does occur also, it may have gone mad. Some humans do not adapt to the transition and end up lapsing into lunacy. These ghouls are highly erratic and unpredictable in their behaviour and are generally shunned by other ghouls. I am not aware of any such creatures in this vicinity. But for you, my dear, I shall be alert for any indications of this aberration."

Bertram then left the house, as always, through the secret tunnel in Amaretta's cellar.

* * *

Amaretta had met Bertram quite by accident one night two years ago when she happened to be walking through a local church graveyard. Though some might find it a strange pastime, Amaretta, because of her familiarity and ease with the dead, actually found the environment peaceful. Walking in the dark meant she was less likely to meet other people, and it afforded her the opportunity to think through whatever issues required her attention.

On this occasion, however, the small cemetery was far from peaceful. She became aware of a strange noise, a combination of chomping, smacking and gurgling sounds which drew her attention towards one of the graves. As she approached her nostrils were assaulted by an overpowering, noxious stench. She paused, footsteps faltering, and almost turned around. But her inquisitive nature propelled her forward.

She came upon a figure hunched on the ground. The horrible smell emanated both from him and the desecrated grave over which he crouched.

Amaretta gasped in horror and revulsion as her mind registered what she was seeing. She was familiar with the folklore of ghouls – creatures loathed for their predilection for consuming dead flesh. Caught somewhere between the living and the dead, belonging to neither, they lived a clandestine existence; in abandoned mausoleums, disused tunnels, cellars, crypts and caverns, any subterranean structures which afforded shelter and a hiding place. They eschewed the daylight, emerging only in the dark of night to feed, when there was little chance of discovery.

She'd heard whispers recently in spiritualist circles of incidents at London burial sites. Graves had been disturbed, corpses found with evidence of predation. It was rumoured that a company of ghouls were secreted in the city, and followers were warned not to venture into graveyards alone and never at night.

Amaretta had dismissed such concerns, not wishing to curtail the walks she enjoyed so much. Now she had unwittingly stumbled upon a ghoul at feeding time. She meant to turn around and quietly retrace her steps, but her foot crunched on a small twig that cracked loudly as her weight descended upon it.

Amaretta held her breath as the ghoul's head snapped up from its gustatory experience. The cowl of its robe fell back to reveal its lurid, blotchy features; the sunken eyes, the flattened nose… and the mouth, slightly agape, from which dangled shreds of decomposed corpse.

The deformed head swivelled around until its gaze fixed on the clairvoyant. Amaretta, rooted to the spot, felt shivers of fear coursing up and down her spine. The eyes of the ghoul burned a dark red, and it snarled as it rose from the ground, poised to flee.

Some wild impulse caused Amaretta to raise her hand. Despite her fear her voice was strong. "No. Wait," she said urgently.

She didn't understand what prompted her to take a step forward, but later, when she reviewed the incident in her mind, she realized what had happened. Somehow she had intuited the sadness, the despair that gripped the gnarled creature before her. It was not content with its present state, but suffered acute misery and sorrow because of its existence.

In spite of her misgivings and revulsion Amaretta felt a stirring of pity for the monster.

"I don't mean you any harm," she said. "What is your name?"

The ghoul started and stared at her, its expression inscrutable. "It has been a long time since I spoke my name, since anyone cared to ask." The voice was definitely male, sounding raspy and rusty as an old hinge creaking.

"My name is Amaretta," she offered. "Retta, for short."

The ghoul nodded warily. "Bertram."

"Bertram, I am sorry that I interrupted your… er… meal… but I have never met a ghoul before. Would you mind if I sat here? Perhaps we could chat."

And so began the unlikely friendship between the clairvoyant and the ghoul.

* * *

Bertram had been returning home one night after another stellar performance in his native Paris. He was thirty-five years old, at the pinnacle of his musical career, a master pianist of international acclaim. After a celebration with friends at which he had imbibed too much good wine, he made a decision which would end up costing his life. The shortcut through the graveyard was something he normally avoided, as rumours abounded that the site was cursed, perhaps even haunted by ghouls. However, the wine had gone to his head, clouding his normally sound judgement.

He was proceeding nonchalantly through the graveyard when something pounced upon him from behind, knocking him to the ground. He was almost overcome by the foetid odour assaulting his senses and instinctively rolled away from his attacker. Inebriated though he was Bertram managed to regain his footing. He could barely discern the dark shape a few metres away. Flailing his arms wildly he yelled at the assailant, who then turned and fled into the shadows of the tombstones.

Bertram laughed with relief and stumbled his way home. It was only after arriving indoors, shedding his coat, that he noticed the tear in the left arm of the fabric. Sure enough, his shirtsleeve was also ripped and stained with blood. In mounting trepidation he wiped away the blood. An ugly, festering wound was revealed.

A bite mark. A dizzying terror gripped Bertram. Being attacked and bitten in a graveyard after midnight meant only one thing. He had been set upon by a ghoul. And now his fate was sealed, for it was common knowledge that if one was attacked by such a monster one was doomed to become a ghoul as well.

Bertram ranted and raved through the night. He was helpless to fight his doom. He cursed the folly and recklessness which had led to this horrific fate. He felt the poison from the ghoul's bite course through his body, contaminating and transforming every fibre of his being. Eventually he collapsed, no longer alive, yet not truly dead, to the floor.

When he emerged from this state it was to his new existence as a creature of the night, a monster reviled by all. A ghoul.

* * *

Two nights after the murder of Alice Carrington, Amaretta heard a discreet knock at her door. She opened it to find Detective Rutherford on her front step.

"Another one?" she asked.

"I'm afraid so." He looked at her curiously. "It is long past midnight, yet once again you are wide awake. Don't you ever sleep?"

"Probably about as much as you do," Amaretta replied. "Let me fetch my coat."

Rutherford supplied the details of the latest murder as they rode in the carriage. "Another woman, Margaret Harris. Killed earlier in the evening on her way home from the London Hospital. She was a nurse employed there."

The hansom cab deposited them at the scene.

"Here? " Amaretta asked. "In the graveyard?"

"No, just outside the gates. Her route home apparently took her past the graveyard."

They walked over to where a shape lay on the ground, covered by a tarpaulin.

Rutherford, his face grim in the moonlight, stooped down to remove it.

The body of Margaret Harris bore wounds identical to those sustained by Alice Carrington. Throat slashed, torso opened, organs exposed.

Rutherford cleared his throat. "There is something different about this murder. It is not readily apparent, with all the blood and devastation, but the coroner examined the corpse in situ. Some of the organs are missing their parts... And the remaining portions show evidence of..."

"Of being eaten," Amaretta said quietly.

Rutherford started in surprise. "How do you know? Are you receiving images?"

The clairvoyant shook her head. "Not yet, Inspector. But after the first murder I had my suspicions as to who, or what, may have been responsible." She moved closer to the body, mindful to avoid stepping in the blood. She bent down and sniffed the air beside the corpse.

"Do you smell it, Inspector? It is difficult to detect because of the other odours, but it is underneath. A foul reek."

Rutherford approached and inhaled a few deep breaths. He nodded. "You are right, Miss Fontaine. I do smell something… extremely unpleasant."

"Like rotting meat?" Amaretta inquired.

"Precisely," Rutherford agreed. Perplexed, he stared at his companion. "But what does it mean?"

Amaretta reached for the detective's extended hand as he assisted her to her feet. "I believe I have the answer to that, Inspector. I trust that you will give credence to what I have to say, although your policeman instincts may dictate otherwise."

* * *

They sat in Amaretta's front parlour, sipping cups of tea. The inspector was silent, digesting the details of the theory the clairvoyant had offered.

"A *ghoul*? " he finally asked. "You're telling me that such creatures actually exist?"

"Without a doubt, Inspector. I have irrefutable proof of their existence."

Rutherford's interest quickened. "What sort of proof?"

Amaretta shook her head. "I cannot disclose this information, but I ask you to trust what I am saying."

Rutherford looked uncertain. "I know you to be a person of honesty and integrity, Miss Fontaine. Nevertheless, I am sure you can appreciate my scepticism. I don't profess to know a lot about the folklore, but I understood that ghouls did not attack the living, instead desecrating graves to satisfy their appalling appetites."

"Yes, that is true. However there are ghouls who apparently may suffer from a form of madness that compels them to attack live humans."

"But Alice Carrington's body did not show signs of being…"

"Consumed?" Amaretta offered helpfully. "That is most likely due to the intervention by the neighbour, don't you think? His presence would have frightened away the ghoul before it had a chance to feed."

Rutherford nodded his agreement. "But if your theory is correct, Miss Fontaine, how are we to stop this monster from killing again? I can't very well tell my men to search graveyards for a ghoul. They would think me mad."

Amaretta smiled. "I have a plan I should like to propose, Inspector."

* * *

Against his better judgement James Rutherford reluctantly agreed to Amaretta's plan. It was very risky to be sure, and he was loath to involve any civilian in a dangerous endeavour, particularly the young clairvoyant. However the detective recognized the logic of it. Plus he really didn't have any other viable options.

Bertram also expressed his concerns when Amaretta apprised him of the details. "You shall be putting yourself in great peril," he remonstrated. "This type of ghoul is plagued by a lunacy which makes it unpredictable and savage. It may not behave as you foresee. Why can you not leave this to your inspector and his police force, Retta?"

"Because the police are useless in this case. They would laugh Inspector Rutherford out of a job if he told them the truth. My plan is solid and has every chance of succeeding, especially if you are correct about this ghoul. He will not be able to resist the lure of a live victim. And I have confidence in the inspector's ability to keep me safe."

Bertram scowled. "But why you, Retta? Why must *you* place yourself in such danger?"

Amaretta's expression was sober. "I saw the terror those women experienced. I *felt* it, Bertram. It resonated throughout my entire being. Not just my body, but my soul as well. I do not want any more people to suffer that fate. This fiend must be stopped."

Bertram regarded the young clairvoyant, recognizing the earnestness and depth of her conviction. He knew there would be no dissuading her from this course of action. "And your detective knows what to do?"

Amaretta nodded. "I gave him the knowledge you supplied. He now has the means to dispatch the monster once and for all."

* * *

Dead of night. An unearthly silence enshrouded the graveyard. Nothing in sight. Except for a solitary figure slowly walking among the tombstones.

Amaretta's steps were steady and sure. Her movements did not betray the unease she felt. Despite knowing that Inspector Rutherford was close by, albeit hidden, a fearful anticipation was making her mouth dry and causing her heart to pound uncomfortably. Nevertheless she continued on, hoping they would not have long to wait, that the prospect of a convenient victim would prove too tempting for the ghoul to resist.

A furtive rustling behind her. Amaretta pretended to ignore it. Underneath her overcoat she wore a thick leather apron which covered her from neck to toe, plus leather coverings on her arms. These measures were to protect her from being bitten by the ghoul. Her face, however, was exposed. They had gambled that the fiend would most likely attack her torso, wherein the juiciest morsels of meat could be found. Unfortunately the extra weight meant that Amaretta's movements were slow and her ability to evade an attack significantly compromised.

She walked on, feigning obliviousness as the stealthy noises kept pace behind her. The familiar stench enveloped her. She felt the monster's presence closing in, sensed it preparing to launch itself at her.

At the last possible moment Amaretta turned around to confront her would-be assailant.

The ghoul leered at her, thick saliva drooling from its gaping mouth. Its eyes blazed maniacally with a voracious hunger. Grey skin the colour of lifelessness hung in loose folds from its naked body. It raised a hand in which the talons had been bitten down, gnawed to mere stubs, now useless as weapons. In the hand was a large knife, the blade of which gleamed a lethal silver as the monster lunged at her.

Unable to dodge the blow, Amaretta raised her arms to protect her face. She tumbled to the ground, the ghoul atop her, its gnashing teeth mere inches from her face. She tried, but failed, to hold her breath against the overwhelming stink of charnel houses. She struggled as best she could to avoid a fatal bite, but she was tiring, the weight of the fiend's body threatening to crush the life from her…

The sword slash was swift and sure, slicing the ghoul's head from its shoulders. Amaretta rolled from underneath the body and crawled away from the decapitated head lying close by. Inspector Rutherford dropped the sword and rushed to her side.

"Are you hurt, Miss Fontaine?" he inquired urgently, helping her to her feet.

Amaretta, recovering her breath, shook her head. "No, Inspector. I am quite fine." She smiled at the detective. "And our plan worked. I had no idea you were so skilled with a sword."

"Believe it or not, I used to fence. A while ago, to be sure, but some skills one doesn't forget." He looked at the clairvoyant, admiration in his eyes. "Well done, Miss Fontaine. You did not falter at all. "

"And your timing was impeccable. I think we make rather a good team, Inspector."

He smiled back. "Indeed we do."

* * *

Ensconced in her favourite armchair Amaretta relaxed in front of the fire.

"You know, I think I am finally becoming accustomed to your smell."

Bertram regarded her sardonically. "You are fortunate that I do not actually live here, but merely visit on occasion. But you did take an inordinate risk. One bite from that ghoul…"

"Yes, I know. Then I, too, would be like you."

His expression was wistful and sad. "It is not a fate I would wish on anyone, Retta. When I think of all that is lost to me forever I would give my very soul, if indeed I still possess one, to be human again. To not be obliged to shun the daylight. To not have to live in shadows and darkness. To be able feel the warmth of the sun's rays or the touch of a woman. At least with mortality comes the certainty of an ending to the pain of such an existence."

She leaned forward in her chair, a serious look on her face. "I realize that you have suffered colossal loss, Bertram. Believe me, I am not insensitive to your plight. And I *was* frightened in that graveyard. But I had faith in Rutherford. He understood that he would have only the one chance to destroy the monster. And I knew that, should he fail in dispatching the fiend, you were lurking in the shadows to deliver the fatal blow."

The ghoul raised one hairless eyebrow. "Indeed? So you were aware of my presence?"

Amaretta smiled. "Of course, Bertram. I knew you would not let me face such peril alone. I had no doubt that you would be there for me.

"When all is said and done, that is what friendship is about. And despite your present circumstances, you *do* retain much of your humanity, though your appearance might be fearful to behold. I quite find that it is no longer of concern to me.

"I see *you*, Bertram. I see that you are a kind and compassionate being. I see my friend. And I *foresee* that our adventures together are only just beginning."

Sister Johanna's Story

Amelia B. Edwards

IF YOU HAVE ever heard of the Grödner Thal, then you will also have heard of the village of St. Ulrich, of which I, Johanna Rœderer, am a native. And if, as is more likely, you have never heard of either, then still, though without knowing it, many of you have, even from your earliest childhood, been familiar with the work by which, for many generations, we have lived and prospered. Your rocking-horse, your Noah's ark, your first doll, came from St. Ulrich – for the Grödner Thal is the children's paradise, and supplies the little ones of all Europe with toys. In every house throughout the village – I might almost say in every house throughout the valley – you will find wood-carving, painting, or gilding perpetually going on; except only in the hay-making and harvest-time, when all the world goes up to the hills to mow and reap, and breathe the mountain air. Nor do our carvers carve only grotesque toys. All the crucifixes that you see by the wayside, all the carved stalls and tabernacles, all the painted and gilded saints decorating screens and side altars in our Tyrolean churches, are the work of their hands.

After what I have said, you will no doubt have guessed that ours was a family of wood-carvers. My father, who died when my sister and I were quite little children, was a wood-carver. My mother was also a wood-carver, as were her mother and grandmother before her; and Katrine and I were of course brought up by her to the same calling. But, as it was necessary that one should look after the home duties, and as Katrine was always more delicate than myself, I gradually came to work less and less at the business; till at last, what with cooking, washing, mending, making, spinning, gardening, and so forth, I almost left it off altogether. Nor did Katrine work very hard at it, either; for, being so delicate, and so pretty, and so much younger than myself, she came, of course, to be a great deal spoiled and to have her own way in everything. Besides, she grew tired, naturally, of cutting nothing but cocks, hens, dogs, cats, cows, and goats; which were all our mother had been taught to make, and, consequently, all she could teach to her children.

"If I could carve saints and angels, like Ulrich, next door," Katrine used sometimes to say; "or if I might invent new beasts out of my own head, or if I might cut caricature nutcrackers of the Herr Pürger and Don Wian, I shouldn't care if I worked hard all day; but I hate the cocks and hens, and I hate the dogs and cats, and I hate all the birds and beasts that ever went into the ark – and I only wish they had all been drowned in the Deluge, and not one left for a pattern!"

And then she would fling her tools away, and dance about the room like a wild creature, and mimic the Herr Pürger, who was the great wholesale buyer of all our St. Ulrich ware, till even our mother, grave and sober woman as she was, could not help laughing, till the tears ran down her cheeks.

Now the Ulrich next door, of whom our little Katrine used to speak, was the elder of two brothers named Finazzer, and he lived in the house adjoining our own; for at St. Ulrich, as in some of the neighbouring villages, one frequently sees two houses built together under one roof, with gardens and orchards surrounded by a common fence. Such a house was the Finazzer's and ours; or I should rather say both houses were theirs, for they were our landlords, and we rented our cottage from them by the year.

Ulrich, named after the patron saint of our village, was a tall, brown, stalwart man, very grave, very reserved, very religious, and the finest wood-sculptor in all the Grödner Thal. No Madonnas, no angels, could compare with his for heavenly grace and tenderness; and as for his Christs, a great foreign critic who came to St. Ulrich some ten or twelve years ago said that no other modern artist with whose works he was acquainted could treat that subject with anything like the same dignity and pathos. But then, perhaps, no other modern artist went to his work in the same spirit, or threw into it, not only the whole force of a very noble and upright character, but all the loftiest aspirations of a profoundly religious nature.

His younger brother, Alois, was a painter – fairhaired, light-hearted, pleasure-loving; as unlike Ulrich, both in appearance and disposition, as it is possible to conceive. At the time of which I am telling you, he was a student in Venice and had already been three years away from home. I used to dream dreams, and weave foolish romances about Alois and my little Katrine, picturing to myself how he would some day come home, in the flush, perhaps, of his first success, and finding her so beautiful and a woman grown, fall in love with her at first sight, and she with him; and the thought of this possibility became at last such a happy certainty in my mind, that when things began to work round in quite the other way, I could not bring myself to believe it. Yet so it was, and, much as I loved my darling, and quick-sighted as I had always been in everything that could possibly concern her, there was not a gossip in St. Ulrich who did not see what was coming before I even suspected it.

When, therefore, my little Katrine came to me one evening in the orchard and told me, half laughing, half crying, that Ulrich Finazzer had that day asked her to be his wife, I was utterly taken by surprise.

"I never dreamed that he would think of me, dear," she said, with her head upon my bosom. "He is so much too good and too clever for such a foolish birdie as poor little Katrine."

"But – but my birdie loves him?" I said, kissing her bright hair.

She half lifted her head, half laughed through her tears, and said with some hesitation: –

"Oh, yes, I love him. I – I think I love him – and then I am quite sure he loves me, and that is more than enough."

"But, Katrine—"

She kissed me, to stop the words upon my lips.

"But you know quite well, dear, that I never could love any lover half as much as I love you; and he knows it, too, for I told him so just now, and now please don't look grave, for I want to be very happy tonight, and I can't bear it."

And I also wanted her to be very happy, so I said all the loving things I could think of, and when we went in to supper we found Ulrich Finazzer waiting for us.

"Dear Johanna," he said, taking me by both hands, "you are to be my sister now."

And then he kissed me on the forehead. The words were few; but he had never spoken to me or looked at me so kindly before, and somehow my heart seemed to come into my throat, and I could not answer a word.

It was now the early summer time, and they were to be married in the autumn. Ulrich, meanwhile, had his hands full of work, as usual, and there was, besides, one important task which he wanted to complete before his wedding. This task was a Christ, larger than life, which he designed as a gift to our parish church, then undergoing complete restoration. The committee of management had invited him in the first instance to undertake the work as an order, but Ulrich would not accept a price for it. He preferred to give it as a freewill offering, and he meant it to be the best piece of wood-sculpture that had ever yet left his hand. He had made innumerable designs for it both in clay and on paper, and separate studies from life for the limbs, hands, and feet. In short, it was to be no ordinary piece of mere conventional Grödner Thal work, but a work of art in the true sense of the word. In the meanwhile, he allowed no one to see the figure in progress – not even Katrine; but worked upon it with closed doors, and kept it covered with a linen cloth whenever his workshop was open.

So the Summer time wore on, and the roses bloomed abundantly in our little garden, and the corn yellowed slowly on the hillsides, and the wild white strawberry-blossoms turned to tiny strawberries, ruby-red, on every mossy bank among the fir-forests of the Seisser Alp. And still Ulrich laboured on at his great work, and sculptured many a gracious saint besides; and still the one object of his earthly worship was our little laughing Katrine.

Whether it was that, being so grave himself, and she so gay, he loved her the better for the contrast, I cannot tell; but his affection for her seemed to deepen daily. I watched it as one might watch the growth of some rare flower, and I wondered sometimes if she prized it as she ought. Yet I scarcely know how, child that she was, she should ever have risen to the heights or sounded the depths of such a nature as his. That she could not appreciate him, however, would have mattered little, if she had loved him more. There was the pity of it. She had accepted him, as many a very young girl accepts her first lover, simply because he was her first. She was proud of his genius – proud of his preference – proud of the house, and the lands, and the worldly goods that were soon to be hers; but for that far greater wealth of love, she held it all too lightly.

Seeing this day after day, with the knowledge that nothing I could say would make things better, I fell, without being conscious of it, into a sad and silent way that arose solely out of my deep love for them both, and had no root of selfishness in it, as my own heart told me then, and tells me to this day.

In the midst of this time, so full of happiness for Ulrich, so full of anxiety for me, Alois Finazzer came home suddenly. We had been expecting him in a vague way ever since the Spring, but the surprise when he walked in unannounced was as great as if we had not expected him at all.

He kissed us all on both cheeks, and sat down as if he had not been away for a day.

"What a rich fellow I am!" he said, joyously. "I left only a grave elder brother behind when I went to Venice, and I come back finding two dear little sisters to welcome me home again."

And then he told us that he had just taken the gold medal at the Academy, that he had sold his prize-picture for two hundred florins, and that he had a pocketful of presents for us all – a necklace for Katrine, a spectacle-case for our mother, and a housewife for myself. When he put the necklace round my darling's neck he kissed her again, and praised her eyes, and said he should some day put his pretty little sister into one of his pictures.

He was greatly changed. He went away a curly-headed lad of eighteen; he came back a man, bearded and self-confident.

Three years, at certain turning-points on the road of life, work with us more powerfully, whether for better or worse, than would ten years at any other period. I thought I liked Alois Finazzer better when he was those three years younger.

Not so Katrine, however – not so our mother – not so the St. Ulrich folk, all of whom were loud in his praise. Handsome, successful, gay, generous, he treated the men, laughed with the girls, and carried all before him.

As for Ulrich, he put his work aside, and cleared his brow, and made holiday for two whole days, going round with his brother from house to house, and telling everyone how Alois had taken the great gold medal in Venice. Proud and happy as he was, however, he was prouder and happier still when, some three or four days later, at a meeting of the Church Committee of management, the Commune formally invited Alois to paint an altar-piece for the altar of San Marco at the price of three hundred florins.

That evening Ulrich invited us to supper, and we drank Alois's health in a bottle of good Barbera wine. He was to stay at home now, instead of going back to Venice, and he was to have a large room at the back of Ulrich's workshop for a studio.

"I'll bring your patron saint into my picture if you will sit for her portrait, Katrine," said Alois, laughingly.

And Katrine blushed and said, "Yes;" and Ulrich was delighted; and Alois pulled out his pocket-book, and began sketching her head on the spot.

"Only you must try to think of serious things, and not laugh when you are sitting for a saint, my little Mädchen," said Ulrich, tenderly; whereupon Katrine blushed still more deeply, and Alois, without looking up from his drawing, promised that they would both be as grave as judges whenever the sittings were going on.

And now there began for me a period of such misery that even at this distance of time I can scarcely bear to speak or think of it. There, day after day, was Alois painting in his new studio, and Katrine sitting to him for Santa Catarina, while Ulrich, unselfish, faithful, trustful, worked on in the next room, absorbed in his art, and not only unconscious of treachery, but incapable of conceiving it as a possibility. How I tried to watch over her, and would fain have watched over her still more closely if I could, is known to myself alone. My object was to be with her throughout all those fatal sittings; Alois's object was to make the appointments for hours when my household duties compelled me to remain at home. He soon found out that my eyes were opened. From that moment it was a silent, unacknowledged fight between us, and we were always fighting it.

And now, as his work drew nearer to completion, Ulrich seemed every day to live less for the people and things about him, and more for his art. Always somewhat over-silent and reserved, he now seemed scarcely conscious, at times, of even the presence of others. He spoke and moved as in a dream; went to early mass every morning at four; fasted three days out of seven; and, having wrought himself up to a certain pitch of religious and artistic excitement, lived in a world of his own creation, from which even Katrine was for the time excluded. Things being thus, what could I do but hold my peace? To speak to Ulrich would have been impossible at any time; to speak to my darling (she being, perhaps, wholly unconscious) might be to create the very peril I dreaded; to appeal to Alois, I felt beforehand, would be worse than useless. So I kept my trouble to myself, and prayed that the weeks might pass quickly, and bring their wedding-day.

Now, just about this time of which I am telling (that is towards the middle of August) came round the great annual fête, or Sagro, as we call it, at Botzen; and to this fête Katrine and I had for some years been in the habit of going – walking to Atzwang the first day by way of Castelruth; sleeping near Atzwang in the house of our aunt, Maria Bernhard, whose husband kept the Gasthaus called the Schwarze Adler; taking the railway next morning from Atzwang to Botzen, and there spending the day of the Sagro; and returning in the same order as we came. This year, however, having the dread of Alois before my eyes, and knowing that Ulrich would not leave his work, I set my face against the Botzen expedition, and begged my little sister, since she could not have the protection of her betrothed husband, to give it up. And so I think she would have done at first, but that Alois was resolute to have us go; and at last even Ulrich urged it upon us, saying that he would not have his little Mädchen balked of her festa simply because he was too busy to take her there himself. Would not Johanna be there to take care of her, Alois to take care of them both? So my protest was silenced, and we went.

It is a long day's walk from St. Ulrich to Atzwang, and we did not reach our aunt's house till nearly supper-time; so that it was quite late before we went up to our room. And now my darling, after being in wild spirits all day, became suddenly silent, and instead of going to bed, stayed by the window, looking at the moon.

"What is my birdie thinking of?" I said, putting my arm about her waist.

"I am thinking," she said, softly, "how the moon is shining now at St. Ulrich on our mother's bedroom window, and on our father's grave."

And with this she laid her head down upon my shoulder, and cried as if her heart would break.

I have reproached myself since for letting that moment pass as I did. I believe I might have had her confidence if I had tried, and then what a world of sorrow might have been averted from us all!

We reached Botzen next morning in time for the six o'clock mass; went to high mass again at nine; and strolled among the booths between the services. Here Alois, us usual, was very free with his money, buying ribbons and trinkets for Katrine, and behaving in every way as if he, and not Ulrich, were her acknowledged lover. At eleven, having met some of our St. Ulrich neighbours, we made a party and dined all together at a Gasthaus in the Silbergasse; and after dinner the young men proposed to take us to see an exhibition of rope-dancers and tumblers. Now I knew that Ulrich would not approve of this, and I entreated my darling for his sake, if not for mine, to stay away. But she would not listen to me.

"Ulrich, Ulrich!" she repeated, pettishly. "Don't tease me about Ulrich; I am tired of his very name!"

The next moment she had taken Alois's arm, and we were in the midst of the crowd.

Finding she would go, I of course went also, though sorely against my inclination; and one of our St. Ulrich friends gave me his arm, and got me through. The crowd, however, was so great that I lost sight somehow of Alois and Katrine, and found myself landed presently inside the booth and sitting on a front seat next to the orchestra, alone with the St. Ulrich people. We kept seats for them as long as we could, and stood upon the bench to look for them, till at last the curtain rose, and we had to sit down without them.

I saw nothing of the performance. To this day I have no idea how long it lasted, or what it consisted of. I remember nothing but the anxiety with which I kept looking towards the door, and the deadly sinking at my heart as the minutes dragged by. To go in search of them was impossible, for the entrance was choked, and there was no standing-room in any part of the booth, so that even when the curtain fell we were fully another ten minutes getting out.

You have guessed it, perhaps, before I tell you. They were not in the market-place; they were not at the Gasthaus; they were not in the Cathedral.

"The tall young man in a grey and green coat, and the pretty girl with a white rose in her hair?" said a bystander. "Tush, my dear, don't be uneasy. They are gone home; I saw them running towards the station more than half an hour ago."

So we flew to the station, and there one of the porters, who was an Atzwang man and knew us both, confirmed the dreadful truth. They were gone indeed, but they were not gone home. Just in time to catch the Express, they had taken their tickets through to Venice, and were at this moment speeding southwards.

How I got home – not stopping at all at Atzwang, but going straight away on foot in the broiling afternoon sun – never resting till I reached Castelruth, a little after dusk – lying down outside my bed and sobbing all the night – getting up at the first glimmer of grey dawn and going on again before the sun was up – how I did all this, faint for want of food, yet unable to eat; weary for want of rest, yet unable to sleep – I know not. But I did it, and was home again at St. Ulrich, kneeling beside our mother's chair, and comforting her as best I could, by seven.

"How is Ulrich to be told?"

It was her first question. It was the question I had been asking myself all the way home. I knew well, however, that I must be the one to break it to him. It was a terrible task, and I put it from me as long as possible.

When at last I did go, it was past mid-day. The workshop door stood open – the Christ, just showing a vague outline through the folds, was covered with a sheet, and standing up against the wall – and Ulrich was working on the drapery of a St. Francis, the splinters from which were flying off rapidly in every direction.

Seeing me on the threshold, he looked up and smiled.

"So soon back, liebe Johanna?" he said. "We did not expect you till evening."

Then, finding I made no answer, he paused in his work, and said, quickly: –

"What is the matter? Is she ill?"

I shook my head.

"No," I said, "she is not ill."

"Where is she, then?"

"She is not ill," I said, again, "but – she is not here."

And then I told him.

He heard me out in dead silence, never moving so much as a finger, only growing whiter as I went on. Then, when I had done, he went over to the window, and remained standing with his back towards me for some minutes.

"And you?" he said, presently, still without turning his head. "And you – through all these weeks – you never saw or suspected anything?"

"I feared – I was not sure—"

He turned upon me with a terrible pale anger in his face.

"You feared – you were not sure!" he said, slowly. "That is to say, you saw it going on, and let it go on, and would not put out your hand to save us all! False! false! false! – all false together – false love, false brother, false friend!"

"You are not just to me, Ulrich," I said; for to be called false by him was more than I could bear.

"Am I not just? Then I pray that God will be more just to you, and to them, than I can ever be; and that His justice may be the justice of vengeance – swift, and terrible, and without mercy."

And saying this he laid his hand on the veiled Christ, and cursed us all three with a terrible, passionate curse, like the curse of a prophet of old.

For one moment my heart stood still, and I felt as if there was nothing left for me but to die – but it was only for that one moment; for I knew, even before he had done speaking, that no words of his could harm either my poor little erring Katrine or myself. And then, having said so as gently as I could, I formally forgave him in her name and mine, and went away.

That night Ulrich Finazzer shut up his house and disappeared, no one knew whither. When I questioned the old woman who lived with him as servant, she said that he had paid and dismissed her a little before dusk; that she then thought he was looking very ill, and that she had observed how, instead of being as usual hard at work all day in the workshop, he had fetched his gun out of the kitchen about two o'clock, and carried it up to his bedroom, where, she believed, he had spent nearly all the afternoon cleaning it. This was all she had to tell; but it was more than enough to add to the burden of my terrors.

Oh, the weary, weary time that followed – the long, sad, solitary days – the days that became weeks – the weeks that became months – the Autumn that chilled and paled as it wore on towards Winter – the changing wood – the withering leaves – the snow that whitened daily on the great peaks round about! Thus September and October passed away, and the last of the harvest was gathered in, and November came with bitter winds and rain; and save a few hurried lines from Katrine, posted in Perugia, I knew nothing of the fate of all whom I had loved and lost.

"We were married," she wrote, "in Venice, and Alois talks of spending the Winter in Rome. I should be perfectly happy if I knew that you and Ulrich had forgiven us."

This was all. She gave me no address; but I wrote to her at the Poste Restante Perugia, and again to the Poste Restante, Rome; both of which letters, I presume, lay unclaimed till destroyed by the authorities, for she never replied to either.

And now the Winter came on in earnest, as Winter always comes in our high valleys, and Christmas-time drew round again; and on the eve of St. Thomas, Ulrich Finazzer returned to his house as suddenly and silently as he had left it.

Next door neighbours as we were, we should not have known of his return but for the trampled snow upon the path, and the smoke going up from the workshop chimney. No other sign of life or occupation was to be seen. The shutters remained unopened. The doors, both front and back, remained fast locked. If any neighbour knocked, he was left to knock unanswered. Even the old woman who used to be his servant, was turned away by a stern voice from within, bidding her begone and leave him at peace.

That he was at work was certain; for we could hear him in the workshop by night as well as by day. But he could work there as in a tomb, for the room was lighted by a window in the roof.

Thus St. Thomas's Day, and the next day which was the fourth Sunday in Advent, went by; and still he who had ever been so constant at mass showed no sign of coming out amongst us. On Monday our good curé walked down, all through the fresh snow (for there had been a heavy fall in the night), on purpose to ask if we were sure that Ulrich was really in his house; if we had yet seen him; and if we knew what he did for food, being shut in there quite alone. But to these questions we could give no satisfactory reply.

That day when we had dined, I put some bread and meat in a basket and left it at his door; but it lay there untouched all through the day and night, and in the morning I fetched it back again, with the food still in it.

This was the fourth day since his return. It was very dreadful – I cannot tell you how dreadful – to know that he was so near, yet never even to see his shadow on a blind. As the day wore on my suspense became intolerable. Tonight, I told myself, would be Christmas Eve; tomorrow Christmas Day. Was it possible that his heart would not soften if he remembered our Happy Christmas of only last year, when he and Katrine were not yet betrothed; how he supped with us, and how we all roasted nuts upon the hearth and sang part-songs after supper? Then, again, it seemed incredible that he should not go to church on Christmas Day.

Thus the day went by, and the evening dusk came on, and the village choir came round singing carols from house to house, and still he made no sign.

Now what with the suspense of knowing him to be so near, and the thought of my little Katrine far away in Rome, and the remembrance of how he – he whom I had honoured and admired above all the world my whole life long – had called down curses on us both the very last time that he and I stood face to face – what with all this, I say, and what with the season and its associations, I had such a great restlessness and anguish upon me that I sat up trying to read my Bible long after mother had gone to bed. But my thoughts wandered continually from the text, and at last the restlessness so gained upon me that I could sit still no longer, and so got up and walked about the room.

And now suddenly, while I was pacing to and fro, I heard, or fancied I heard, a voice in the garden calling to me by name. I stopped – I listened – I trembled. My very heart stood still!

Then, hearing no more, I opened the window and outer shutters, and instantly there rushed in a torrent of icy cold air and a flood of brilliant moonlight, and there, on the shining snow below, stood Ulrich Finazzer.

Himself, and yet so changed! Worn, haggard, grey.

I saw him, I tell you, as plainly as I see my own hand at this moment. He was standing close, quite close, under the window, with the moonlight full upon him.

"Ulrich!" I said, and my own voice sounded strange to me, somehow, in the dead waste and silence of the night—"Ulrich, are you come to tell me we are friends again?"

But instead of answering me he pointed to a mark on his forehead – a small dark mark, that looked at this distance and by this light like a bruise – cried aloud with a strange wild cry, less like a human voice than a far-off echo, "The brand of Cain! The brand of Cain!" and so flung up his arms with a despairing gesture, and fled away into the night.

The rest of my story may be told in a few words – the fewer the better. Insane with the desire of vengeance, Ulrich Finazzer had tracked the fugitives from place to place, and slain his brother at mid-day in the streets of Rome. He escaped unmolested, and was well nigh over the Austrian border before the authorities began to inquire into the particulars of the murder. He then, as was proved by a comparison of dates, must have come straight home by way of Mantua, Verona, and Botzen, with no other object, apparently, than to finish the statue that he had designed for an offering to the church. He worked upon it, accordingly, as I have said, for four days and nights incessantly, completed it to the last degree of finish, and then, being in who can tell how terrible a condition of remorse, and horror, and despair, sought to expiate his crime with his blood. They found him shot through the head by his own hand, lying quite dead at the feet of the statue upon which he had been working, probably, up to the last moment; his tools lying close by; the pistol still fast in his clenched hand, and the divine pitying face of the Redeemer whose law he had outraged, bending over him as if in sorrow and forgiveness.

Our mother has now been dead some years; strangers occupy the house in which Ulrich Finazzer came to his dreadful death, and already the double tragedy is almost forgotten. In the sad, faded woman, prematurely grey, who lives with me, ever working silently, steadily, patiently, from morning till night at our hereditary trade, few who had known her in the freshness of her youth would now recognise my beautiful Katrine. Thus from day to day, from year to year, we journey on together, nearing the end.

Did I indeed see Ulrich Finazzer that night of his self-murder? If I did so with my bodily eyes and it was no illusion of the senses, then most surely I saw him not in life, for that dark mark which looked to me in the moonlight like a bruise was the bullet-hole in his brow.

But did I see him? It is a question I ask myself again and again, and have asked myself for years. Ah! who can answer it?

The Story of Salome

Amelia B. Edwards

A FEW YEARS ago, no matter how many, I, Harcourt Blunt, was travelling with my friend Coventry Turnour, and it was on the steps of our hotel that I received from him the announcement that he was again in love.

"I tell you, Blunt," said my fellow-traveller, "she's the loveliest creature I ever beheld in my life."

I laughed outright.

"My dear fellow," I replied, "you've so often seen the loveliest creature you ever beheld in your life."

"Ay, but I am in earnest now for the first time."

"And you have so often been in earnest for the first time! Remember the innkeeper's daughter at Cologne."

"A pretty housemaid, whom no training could have made presentable."

"Then there was the beautiful American at Interlaken."

"Yes; but—"

"And the bella Marchesa at Prince Torlonia's ball."

"Not one of them worthy to be named in the same breath with my imperial Venetian. Come with me to the Merceria and be convinced. By taking a gondola to St. Mark's Place we shall be there in a quarter of an hour."

I went, and he raved of his new flame all the way. She was a Jewess – he would convert her. Her father kept a shop in the Merceria – what of that? He dealt only in costliest Oriental merchandise, and was as rich as a Rothschild. As for any probable injury to his own prospects, why need he hesitate on that account? What were "prospects" when weighed against the happiness of one's whole life? Besides, he was not ambitious. He didn't care to go into Parliament. If his uncle, Sir Geoffrey, cut him off with a shilling, what then? He had a moderate independence of which no one living could deprive him, and what more could any reasonable man desire?

I listened, smiled, and was silent. I knew Coventry Turnour too well to attach the smallest degree of importance to anything that he might say or do in a matter of this kind. To be distractedly in love was his normal condition. We had been friends from boyhood; and since the time when he used to cherish a hopeless attachment to the young lady behind the counter of the tart-shop at Harrow, I had never known him "fancy-free" for more than a few weeks at a time. He had gone through every phase of no less than three *grandes passions* during the five months that we had now been travelling together; and having left Rome about eleven weeks before with every hope laid waste, and a heart so broken that it could never by any possibility be put together again, he was now, according to the natural course of events, just ready to fall in love again.

We landed at the traghetto San Marco. It was a cloudless morning towards the middle of April, just ten years ago. The Ducal Palace glowed in the hot sunshine; the boatmen were clustered, gossiping, about the quay; the orange-vendors were busy under the arches of the piazzetta; the *flâneurs* were already eating ices and smoking cigarettes outside the cafés. There was an Austrian military band, strapped, buckled, moustachioed, and white-coated, playing just in front of St. Mark's; and the shadow of the great bell-tower slept all across the square.

Passing under the low round archway leading to the Merceria, we plunged at once into that cool labyrinth of narrow, intricate, and picturesque streets, where the sun never penetrates – where no wheels are heard, and no beast of burden is seen – where every house is a shop, and every shop-front is open to the ground, as in an Oriental bazaar – where the upper balconies seem almost to meet overhead, and are separated by only a strip of burning sky – and where more than three people cannot march abreast in any part. Pushing our way as best we might through the motley crowd that here chatters, cheapens, buys, sells, and perpetually jostles to and fro, we came presently to a shop for the sale of Eastern goods. A few glass jars, filled with spices and some pieces of stuff, untidily strewed the counter next the street; but within, dark and narrow though it seemed, the place was crammed with costliest merchandise. Cases of gorgeous Oriental jewelry; embroideries and fringes of massive gold and silver bullion; precious drugs and spices; exquisite toys in filigree; miracles of carving in ivory, sandal-wood, and amber; jewelled yataghans; scimitars of state, rich with "barbaric pearl and gold," bales of Cashmere shawls, China silks, India muslins, gauzes, and the like, filled every inch of available space from floor to ceiling, leaving only a narrow lane from the door to the counter, and a still narrower passage to the rooms beyond the shop.

We went in. A young woman who was sitting reading on a low seat behind the counter, laid aside her book, and rose slowly. She was dressed wholly in black. I cannot describe the fashion of her garments. I only know that they fell about her in long, soft, trailing folds, leaving a narrow band Of fine cambric visible at the throat and wrists; and that, however graceful and unusual this dress may have been, I scarcely observed it, so entirely was I taken up with admiration of her beauty.

For she was indeed very beautiful – beautiful in a way I had not anticipated Coventry Turnour, with all his enthusiasm, had failed to do her justice. He had raved of her eyes – her large, lustrous, melancholy eyes, – of the transparent paleness of her complexion, of the faultless delicacy of her features; but he had not prepared me for the unconscious dignity, the perfect nobleness and refinement, that informed her every look and gesture. My friend requested to see a bracelet at which he had been looking the day before. Proud, stately, silent, she unlocked the case in which it was kept, and laid it before him on the counter. He asked permission to take it over to the light. She bent her head, but answered not a word. It was like being waited upon by a young Empress.

Turnour took the bracelet to the door and affected to examine it. It consisted of a double row of gold coins linked together at intervals by a bean-shaped ornament studded with pink coral and diamonds. Coming back into the shop he asked me if I thought it would please his sister, to whom he had promised a remembrance of Venice.

"It is a pretty trifle," I replied; "but surely a remembrance of Venice should be of Venetian manufacture. This, I suppose, is Turkish."

The beautiful Jewess looked up. We spoke in English; but she understood, and replied.

"*E Greco, signore*," she said coldly.

At this moment an old man came suddenly forward from some dark counting-house at the back – a grizzled, bearded, eager-eyed Shylock, with a pen behind his ear.

"Go in, Salome – go in, my daughter," he said hurriedly. "I will serve these gentlemen."

She lifted her eyes to his for one moment – then moved silently away, and vanished in the gloom of the room beyond.

We saw her no more. We lingered awhile looking over the contents of the jewel-cases; but in vain. Then Turnour bought his bracelet, and we went out again into the narrow streets, and back to the open daylight of the Gran' Piazza.

"Well," he said breathlessly, "what do you think of her?"

"She is very lovely."

"Lovelier than you expected?"

"Much lovelier. But—"

"But what?"

"The sooner you succeed in forgetting her the better."

He vowed, of course, that he never would and never could forget her. He would hear of no incompatibilities, listen to no objections, believe in no obstacles. That the beautiful Salome was herself not only unconscious of his passion and indifferent to his person, but ignorant of his very name and station, were facts not even to be admitted on the list of difficulties. Finding him thus deaf to reason, I said no more.

It was all over, however, before the week was out.

"Look here, Blunt," he said, coming up to me one morning in the coffee-room of our hotel just as I was sitting down to answer a pile of home-letters; "would you like to go on to Trieste tomorrow? There, don't look at me like that – you can guess how it is with me. I was a fool ever to suppose she would care for me – a stranger, a foreigner, a Christian. Well, I'm horribly out of sorts, anyhow – and – and I wish I was a thousand miles off at this moment!"

* * *

We travelled on together to Athens, and there parted, Turnour being bound for England, and I for the East. My own tour lasted many months longer. I went first to Egypt and the Holy Land; then joined an exploring party on the Euphrates; and at length, after just twelve months of Oriental life, found myself back again at Trieste about the middle of April in the year following that during which occurred the events I have just narrated. There I found that batch of letters and papers to which I had been looking forward for many weeks past; and amongst the former, one from Coventry Turnour. This time he was not only irrecoverably in love, but on the eve of matrimony. The letter was rapturous and extravagant enough. The writer was the happiest of men; his destined bride the loveliest and most amiable of her sex; the future a paradise; the past a melancholy series of mistakes. As for love, he had never, of course, known what it was till now.

And what of the beautiful Salome?

Not one word of her from beginning to end. He had forgotten her as utterly as if she had never existed. And yet how desperately in love and how desperately in despair he was "one little year ago!" Ah, yes; but then it *was* "one little year ago;" and who that had ever known Coventry Turnour would expect him to remember *la plus grande des grandes passions* for even half that time?

I slept that night at Trieste and went on next day to Venice. Somehow I could not get Turnour and his love-affairs out of my head. I remembered our visit to the Merceria. I was haunted by the image of the beautiful Jewess. Was she still so lovely? Did she still sit reading in her wonted seat by the open counter, with the gloomy shop reaching away behind, and the cases of rich robes and jewels all around?

An irresistible impulse prompted me to go to the Merceria and see her once again. I went. It had been a busy morning with me, and I did not get there till between three and four o'clock in the afternoon. The place was crowded. I passed up the well-remembered street, looking out on both sides for the gloomy little shop with its unattractive counter; but in vain. When I had gone so far that I thought I must have passed it, I turned back. House by house I retraced my steps to the very entrance, and still could not find it. Then, concluding I had not gone far enough at first, I turned back again till I reached a spot where several streets diverged. Here I came to a stand-still, for beyond this point I knew I had not passed before.

It was now evident that the Jew no longer occupied his former shop in the Merceria, and that my chance of discovering his whereabouts was exceedingly slender. I could not inquire of his successor, because I could not identify the house. I found it impossible even to remember what trades were carried on by his neighbours on either side. I was ignorant of his very name. Convinced, therefore, of the inutility of making any further effort, I gave up the search, and comforted myself by reflecting that my own heart was not made of adamant, and that it was, perhaps, better for my peace not to see the beautiful Salome again. I was destined to see her again, however, and that ere many days had passed over my head.

A year of more than ordinarily fatiguing Eastern travel had left me in need of rest, and I had resolved to allow myself a month's sketching in Venice and its neighbourhood before turning my face homeward.

As, therefore, it is manifestly the first object of a sketcher to select his points of view, and as no more luxurious machine than a Venetian gondola was ever invented for the use of man, I proceeded to employ the first days of my stay in endless boatings to and fro; now exploring all manner of canals and canaletti; now rowing out in the direction of Murano; now making for the islands beyond San Pietro Castello, and in the course of these pilgrimages noting down an infinite number of picturesque sites, and smoking an infinite number of cigarettes.

It was, I think, about the fourth or fifth day of this pleasant work, when my gondolier proposed to take me as far as the Lido. It wanted about two hours to sunset, and the great sandbank lay not more than three or four miles away; so I gave the word, and in another moment we had changed our route and were gliding farther and farther from Venice at each dip of the oar.

Then the long, dull, distant ridge that had all day bounded the shallow horizon rose gradually above the placid level of the Lagune; assumed a more broken outline; resolved itself into hillocks and hollows of tawny sand; showed here and there a patch of parched grass and tangled brake; and looked like the coasts of some inhospitable desert beyond which no traveller might penetrate. My boatman made straight for a spot where some stakes at the water's edge gave token of a landing-place; and here, though with some difficulty, for the tide was low, ran the gondola aground. I landed. My first step was among graves.

"*E'l Cimiterio Giudaico, signore*," said my gondolier, with a touch of his cap.

The Jewish cemetery! The *ghetto* of the dead! I remembered now to have read or heard long since how the Venetian Jews, cut off in death as in life from the neighbourhood of their Christian rulers, had been buried from immemorial time upon this desolate waste. I stooped to examine the headstone at my feet. It was but a shattered fragment, crusted over with yellow lichens, and eaten away by the salt sea air. I passed on to the next, and the next.

Some were completely matted over with weeds and brambles; some were half-buried in the drifting sand; of some only a corner remained above the surface. Here and there a name, a date, a fragment of emblematic carving or part of a Hebrew inscription, was yet legible; but all were more or less broken and effaced.

Wandering on thus among graves and hillocks, ascending at every step, and passing some three or four glassy pools overgrown with gaunt-looking reeds, I presently found that I had reached the central and most elevated part of the Lido, and that I commanded an uninterrupted view on every side. On the one hand lay the broad, silent Lagune bounded by Venice and the Euganean hills – on the other, stealing up in long, lazy folds, and breaking noiselessly against the endless shore, the blue Adriatic. An old man gathering shells on the seaward side, a distant gondola on the Lagune, were the only signs of life for miles around.

Standing on the upper ridge of this narrow barrier, looking upon both waters, and watching the gradual approach of what promised to be a gorgeous sunset, I fell into one of those wandering trains of thought in which the real and unreal succeed each other as capriciously as in a dream.

I remembered how Goethe here conceived his vertebral theory of the skull – how Byron, too lame to walk, kept his horse on the Lido, and here rode daily to and fro – how Shelley loved the wild solitude of the place, wrote of it in *Julian and Maddalo*, and listened perhaps from this very spot, to the mad-house bell on the island of San Giorgio. Then I wondered if Titian used sometimes to come hither from his gloomy house on the other side of Venice, to study the gold and purple of these western skies – if Othello had walked here with Desdemona – if Shylock was buried yonder, and Leah whom he loved "when he was a bachelor."

And then in the midst of my reverie, I came suddenly upon another Jewish cemetery.

Was it indeed another, or but an outlying portion of the first? It was evidently another, and a more modern one. The ground was better kept. The monuments were newer. Such dates as I had succeeded in deciphering on the broken sepulchres lower down were all of the fourteenth and fifteenth centuries; but the inscriptions upon these bore reference to quite recent interments.

I went on a few steps farther. I stopped to copy a quaint Italian couplet on one tomb – to gather a wild forget-me-not from the foot of another – to put aside a bramble that trailed across a third – and then I became aware for the first time of a lady sitting beside a grave not a dozen yards from the spot on which I stood.

I had believed myself so utterly alone, and was so taken by surprise, that for the first moment I could almost have persuaded myself that she also was "of the stuff that dreams are made of." She was dressed from head to foot in deepest mourning; her face turned from me, looking towards the sunset; her cheek resting in the palm of her hand. The grave by which she sat was obviously recent. The scant herbage round about had been lately disturbed, and the marble headstone looked as if it had not yet undergone a week's exposure to wind and weather.

Persuaded that she had not observed me, I lingered for an instant looking at her. Something in the grace and sorrow of her attitude, something in the turn of her head and the flow of her sable draperies, arrested my attention. Was she young? I fancied so. Did she mourn a husband? – a lover? – a parent? I glanced towards the headstone. It was covered with Hebrew characters; so that, had I even been nearer, it could have told me nothing.

But I felt that I had no right to stand there, a spectator of her sorrow, an intruder on her privacy. I proceeded to move noiselessly away. At that moment she turned and looked at me.

It was Salome.

Salome, pale and worn as from some deep and wasting grief, but more beautiful, if that could be, than ever. Beautiful, with a still more spiritual beauty than of old; with cheeks so wan, and eyes so unutterably bright and solemn, that my very heart seemed to stand still as I looked upon them. For one second I paused, half fancying, half hoping that there was recognition in her glance; then, not daring to look or linger longer, turned away. When I had gone far enough to do so without discourtesy, I stopped and looked back. She had resumed her former attitude, and was gazing over towards Venice and the setting sun. The stone by which she watched was not more motionless.

The sun went down in glory. The last flush faded from the domes and bell-towers of Venice; the northward peaks changed from rose to purple, from gold to grey; a scarcely perceptible film of mist became all at once visible upon the surface of the Lagune; and overhead, the first star trembled into light. I waited and watched till the shadows had so deepened that I could no longer distinguish one distant object from another. Was that the spot? Was she still there? Was she moving? Was she gone? I could not tell. The more I looked, the more uncertain I became. Then, fearing to miss my way in the fast-gathering twilight, I struck down towards the water's edge and made for the point at which I had landed.

I found my gondolier fast asleep, with his head on a cushion and his bit of gondola-carpet thrown over him for a counterpane. I asked if he had seen any other boat put off from the Lido since I left? He rubbed his eyes, started up, and was awake in a moment.

"*Per Bacco, signore*, I have been asleep," he said apologetically; "I have seen nothing."

"Did you observe any other boat moored hereabouts when we landed?"

"None, signore."

"And you have seen nothing of a lady in black?"

He laughed and shook his head.

"*Consolatevi, signore*," he said, archly; "she will come tomorrow."

Then, seeing me look grave, he touched his cap, and with a gentle "*Scusate, signore*," took his place at the stern, and there waited. I bade him row to my hotel; and then, leaning dreamily back, folded my arms, closed my eyes, and thought of Salome.

How lovely she was! How infinitely more lovely than even my first remembrance of her! How was it that I had not admired her more that day in the Merceria? Was I blind, or had she become indeed more beautiful? It was a sad and strange place in which to meet her again. By whose grave was she watching? By her father's? Yes, surely by her father's. He was an old man when I saw him, and in the course of nature had not long to live. He was dead: hence my unavailing search in the Merceria. He was dead. His shop was let to another occupant. His stock-in-trade was sold and dispersed.

And Salome – was she left alone? Had she no mother? – no brother? – no lover? Would her eyes have had that look of speechless woe in them if she had any very near or dear tie left on earth? Then I thought of Coventry Turnour, and his approaching marriage. Had he ever really loved her? I doubted it. "True love," saith an old song, "can ne'er forget;" but he had forgotten, as though the past had been a dream. And yet he was in earnest while it lasted – would have risked all for her sake, if she would have listened to him. Ah, if she *had* listened to him!

And then I remembered that he had never told me the particulars of that affair. Did she herself reject him, or did he lay his suit before her father? And was he rejected only because he was a Christian? I had never cared to ask these things while we were together; but now I would have given the best hunter in my stables to know every minute detail connected with the matter.

Pondering thus, travelling over the same ground again and again, wondering whether she remembered me, whether she was poor, whether she was, indeed, alone in the world, how long the old man had been dead, and a hundred other things of the same kind, – I scarcely noticed how the watery miles glided past, or how the night closed in. One question, however, recurred oftener than any other: How was I to see her again?

I arrived at my hotel; I dined at the *table d'hôte*; I strolled out after dinner to my favourite café in the piazza; I dropped in for half an hour at the Fenice, and heard one act of an extremely poor opera; I came home restless, uneasy, wakeful; and sitting for hours before my bedroom fire, asked myself the same perpetual question – How was I to see her again?

Fairly tired out at last, I fell asleep in my chair, and when I awoke the sun was shining upon my window.

I started to my feet. I had it now. It flashed upon me, as if it came with the sunlight. I had but to go again to the cemetery, copy the inscription upon the old man's tomb, ask my learned friend, Professor Nicolai of Padua, to translate it for me, and then, once in possession of names and dates, the rest would be easy.

In less than an hour, I was once more on my way to the Lido.

I took a rubbing of the stone. It was the quickest way, and the surest; for I knew that in Hebrew everything depended on the pointing of the characters, and I feared to trust my own untutored skill.

This done, I hastened back, wrote my letter to the professor, and despatched both letter and rubbing by the mid-day train.

The professor was not a prompt man. On the contrary, he was a pre-eminently slow man; dreamy, indolent, buried in Oriental lore. From any other correspondent one might have looked for a reply in the course of the morrow, but from Nicolai of Padua it would have been folly to expect one under two or three days. And in the meanwhile? Well, in the meanwhile there were churches and palaces to be seen, sketches to be made, letters of introduction to be delivered. It was, at all events, of no use to be impatient.

And yet I was impatient – so impatient that I could neither sketch, nor read, nor sit still for ten minutes together. Possessed by an uncontrollable restlessness, I wandered from gallery to gallery, from palace to palace, from church to church. The imprisonment of even a gondola was irksome to me. I was, as it were, impelled to be moving and doing; and even so, the day seemed endless.

The next was even worse. There was just the possibility of a reply from Padua, and the knowledge of that possibility unsettled me for the day. Having watched and waited for every post from eight to four, I went down to the traghetto of St. Mark's, and was there hailed by my accustomed gondolier.

He touched his cap and waited for orders.

"Where to, signore?" he asked, finding that I remained silent.

"To the Lido."

It was an irresistible temptation, and I yielded to it; but I yielded in opposition to my judgment. I knew that I ought not to haunt the place. I had resolved that I would not. And yet I went.

Going along, I told myself that I had only come to reconnoitre. It was not unlikely that she might be going to the same spot about the same hour as before; and in that case I might overtake her gondola by the way, or find it moored somewhere along the shore. At all events, I was determined not to land. But we met no gondola beyond San Pietro Castello; saw no sign of one along the shore. The afternoon was far advanced; the sun was near going down; we had the Lagune and the Lido to ourselves.

My boatman made for the same landing-place, and moored his gondola to the same stake as before. He took it for granted that I meant to land; and I landed. After all, however, it was evident that Salome could not be there, in which case I was guilty of no intrusion. I might stroll in the direction of the cemetery, taking care to avoid her, if she were anywhere about, and keeping well away from that part where I had last seen her. So I broke another resolve, and went up towards the top of the Lido. Again I came to the salt pools and the reeds; again stood with the sea upon my left hand and the Lagune upon my right, and the endless sandbank reaching on for miles between the two. Yonder lay the new cemetery. Standing thus I overlooked every foot of the ground. I could even distinguish the headstone of which I had taken a rubbing the morning before. There was no living thing in sight. I was, to all appearance, as utterly alone as Enoch Arden on his desert island.

Then I strolled on a little nearer and a little nearer still; and then, contrary to all my determinations, I found myself standing upon the very spot, beside the very grave, which I had made up my mind on no account to approach.

The sun was now just going down – had gone down, indeed, behind a bank of golden-edged cumuli – and was flooding earth, sea, and sky with crimson. It was at this hour that I saw her. It was upon this spot that she was sitting. A few scant blades of grass had sprung up here and there upon the grave. Her dress must have touched them as she sat there – her dress – perhaps her hand. I gathered one, and laid it carefully between the leaves of my note-book.

At last I turned to go, and, turning, met her face to face!

She was distant about six yards, and advancing slowly towards the spot on which I was standing. Her head drooped slightly forward; her hands were clasped together; her eyes were fixed upon the ground. It was the attitude of a nun. Startled, confused, scarcely knowing what I did, I took off my hat, and drew aside to let her pass.

She looked up – hesitated – stood still – gazed at me with a strange, steadfast, mournful expression – then dropped her eyes again, passed me without another glance, and resumed her former place and attitude beside her father's grave.

I turned away. I would have given worlds to speak to her; but I had not dared, and the opportunity was gone. Yet I might have spoken. She looked at me – looked at me with so strange and piteous an expression in her eyes – continued looking at me as long as one might have counted five… I might have spoken. I surely might have spoken! And now – ah! now it was impossible. She had fallen into the old thoughtful attitude, with her cheek resting on her hand. Her thoughts were far away. She had forgotten my very presence.

I went back to the shore, more disturbed and uneasy than ever. I spent all the remaining daylight in rowing up and down the margin of the Lido, looking for her gondola – hoping, at all events, to see her put off – to follow her, perhaps, across the waste of waters. But the dusk came quickly on, and then darkness; and I left at last without having seen any farther sign or token of her presence.

Lying awake that night, tossing uneasily upon my bed, and thinking over the incidents of the last few days, I found myself perpetually recurring to that long, steady, sorrowful gaze which she fixed upon me in the cemetery. The more I thought of it, the more I seemed to feel that there was in it some deeper meaning than I, in my confusion, had observed at the time. It was such a strange look – a look almost of entreaty, of asking for help or sympathy; like the dumb appeal in the eyes of a sick animal. Could this really be? What, after all, more possible than that, left alone in the world – with, perhaps, not a single male relation to advise her – she found herself in some position of present difficulty, and knew not where to turn for help? All this might well be. She had even, perhaps, some instinctive feeling that she might trust me. Ah! if she would indeed trust me…

I had hoped to receive my Paduan letter by the morning delivery; but morning and afternoon went by as before, and still no letter came. As the day began to decline, I was again on my way to the Lido; this time for the purpose, and with the intention, of speaking to her. I landed, and went direct to the cemetery. It had been a dull day. Lagune and sky were both one uniform leaden grey, and a mist hung over Venice.

I saw her from the moment I reached the upper ridge. She was walking to and fro among the graves, like a stately shadow. I had felt confident, somehow, that she would be there; and now, for some reason that I could not have defined for my life, I felt equally confident that she expected me.

Trembling and eager, yet half dreading the moment when she should discover my presence, I hastened on, printing the loose sand at every noiseless step. A few moments more, and I should overtake her, speak to her, hear the music of her voice – that music which I remembered so well, though a year had gone by since I last heard it. But how should I address her? What had I to say? I knew not. I had no time to think. I could only hurry on till within some ten feet of her trailing garments; stand still when she turned, and uncover before her as if she were a queen.

She paused and looked at me, just as she had paused and looked at me the evening before. With the same sorrowful meaning in her eyes; with even more than the same entreating expression. But she waited for me to speak.

I did speak. I cannot recall what I said; I only know that I faltered something of an apology – mentioned that I had had the honour of meeting her before, many months ago; and, trying to say more – trying to express how thankfully and proudly I would devote myself to any service however humble, however laborious, I failed both in voice and words, and broke down utterly.

Having come to a stop, I looked up and found her eyes still fixed upon me.

"You are a Christian?" she said.

A trembling came upon me at the first sound of her voice. It was the same voice; distinct, melodious, scarce louder than a whisper – and yet it was not quite the same. There was a melancholy in the music, and if I may use a word which, after all, fails to express my meaning, a *remoteness*, that fell upon my ear like the plaintive cadence in an autumnal wind.

I bent my head, and answered that I was.

She pointed to the headstone of which I had taken a rubbing a day or two before.

"A Christian soul lies there," she said, "laid in earth without one Christian prayer – with Hebrew rites – in a Hebrew sanctuary. Will you, stranger, perform an act of piety towards the dead?"

"The Signora has but to speak," I said. "All that she wishes shall be done."

"Read one prayer over this grave; and trace a cross upon this stone."

"I will."

She thanked me with a gesture, slightly bowed her head, drew her outer garment more closely round her, and moved away to a rising ground at some little distance. I was dismissed. I had no excuse for lingering – no right to prolong the interview – no business to remain there one moment longer. So I left her there, nor once looked back till I had reached the last point from which I knew I should be able to see her. But when I turned for that last look, she was no longer in sight.

I had resolved to speak to her, and this was the result. A stranger interview never, surely, fell to the lot of man! I had said nothing that I meant to say – had learnt nothing that I sought to know. With regard to her circumstances, her place of residence, her very name, I was no wiser than before. And yet I had, perhaps, no reason to be dissatisfied. She had honoured me with her confidence, and entrusted to me a task of some difficulty and importance. It now only remained for me to execute that task as thoroughly and as quickly as possible. That done, I might fairly hope to win some place in her remembrance – by and by, perhaps, in her esteem.

Meanwhile, the old question rose again – whose grave could it be? I had settled this matter so conclusively in my own mind from the first, that I could scarcely believe even now that it was not her father's. Yet that he should have died a secret convert to Christianity was incredible. Whose grave could it be? A lover's? A Christian lover's? Alas! it might be. Or a sister's? In either of these cases, it was more than probable that Salome was herself a convert. But I had no time to waste in conjecture. I must act, and act promptly.

I hastened back to Venice as fast as my gondolier could row me; and as we went along I promised myself that all her wishes should be carried out before she visited the spot again. To secure at once the services of a clergyman who would go with me to the Lido at early dawn and there read some portion, at least, of the burial service; and at the same time to engage a stonemason to cut the cross; – to have all done before she, or anyone, should have approached the place next day, was my especial object. And that object I was resolved to carry out, though I had to search Venice through before I laid my head upon my pillow.

I found a clergyman without difficulty. He was a young man occupying rooms in the same hotel, and on the same floor as myself. I had met him each day at the *table d'hôte*, and conversed with him once or twice in the reading-room. He was a North-countryman, had not long since taken orders, and was both gentlemanly and obliging. He promised in the readiest manner to do all that I required, and to breakfast with me at six next morning, in order that we might reach the cemetery by eight.

To find my stonemason, however, was not so easy; and yet I went to work methodically enough. I began with the Venetian Directory; then copied a list of stonemasons' names and addresses; then took a gondola *a due remi* and started upon my voyage of discovery.

But a night's voyage of discovery among the intricate back *canaletti* of Venice is no very easy and no very safe enterprise. Narrow, tortuous, densely populated, often blocked by huge hay, wood, and provision barges, almost wholly unlighted, and so perplexingly alike that no mere novice in Venetian topography need ever hope to distinguish one from another, they baffle the very gondoliers, and are a *terra incognita* to all but the dwellers therein.

I succeeded, however, in finding three of the places entered on my list. At the first I was told that the workman of whom I was in quest was working by the week somewhere over by Murano, and would not be back again till Saturday night. At the second and third, I found the men at home, supping with their wives and children at the end of the day's work; but neither would consent to undertake my commission. One, after a whispered consultation with his son, declined reluctantly. The other told me plainly that he dared not do it, and that he did not believe I should find a stonemason in Venice who would be bolder than himself.

The Jews, he said, were rich and powerful; no longer an oppressed people; no longer to be insulted even in Venice with impunity. To cut a Christian cross upon a Jewish headstone in the Jewish Cemetery, would be "a sort of sacrilege," and punishable, no doubt, by the law. This sounded like truth; so, finding that my rowers were by no means confident of their way, and that the *canaletti* were dark as the catacombs, I prevailed upon the stonemason to sell me a small mallet and a couple of chisels, and made up my mind to commit the sacrilege myself.

With this single exception, all was done next morning as I had planned to do it. My new acquaintance breakfasted with me, accompanied me to the Lido, read such portions of the burial service as seemed proper to him, and then, having business in Venice, left me to my task. It was by no means an easy one. To a skilled hand it would have been, perhaps, the work of half-an-hour; but it was my first effort, and rude as the thing was – a mere grooved attempt at a Latin cross, about two inches and a half in length, cut close down at the bottom of the stone, where it could be easily concealed by a little piling of the sand – it took me nearly four hours to complete. While I was at work, the dull grey morning grew duller and greyer; a thick sea-fog drove up from the Adriatic; and a low moaning wind came and went like the echo of a distant requiem. More than once I started, believing that she had surprised me there – fancying I saw the passing of a shadow – heard the rustling of a garment – the breathing of a sigh. But no. The mists and the moaning wind deceived me. I was alone.

When at length I got back to my hotel, it was just two o'clock. The hall-porter put a letter into my hand as I passed through. One glance at that crabbed superscription was enough. It was from Padua. I hastened to my room, tore open the envelope, and read these words:–

"CARO SIGNORE, – The rubbing you send is neither ancient nor curious, as I fear you suppose it to be. It is a thing of yesterday. It merely records that one Salome, the only

and beloved child of a certain Isaac Da Costa, died last Autumn on the eighteenth of October, aged twenty-one years, and that by the said Isaac Da Costa this monument is erected to the memory of her virtues and his grief.

"I pray you, caro signore, to receive the assurance of my sincere esteem.

"NICOLO NICOLAI."

The letter dropped from my hand. I seemed to have read without understanding it. I picked it up; went through it again, word by word; sat down; rose up; took a turn across the room; felt confused, bewildered, incredulous.

Could there, then, be two Salomes? or was there some radical and extraordinary mistake?

I hesitated; I knew not what to do. Should I go down to the Merceria, and see whether the name of Da Costa was known in the *quartier*? Or find out the registrar of births and deaths for the Jewish district? Or call upon the principal rabbi, and learn from him who this second Salome had been, and in what degree of relationship she stood towards the Salome whom I knew? I decided upon the last course. The chief rabbi's address was easily obtained. He lived in an ancient house on the Giudecca, and there I found him – a grave, stately old man, with a grizzled beard reaching nearly to his waist.

I introduced myself and stated my business. I came to ask if he could give me any information respecting the late Salome da Costa who died on the 18th of October last, and was buried on the Lido.

The rabbi replied that he had no doubt he could give me any information I desired, for he had known the lady personally, and was the intimate friend of her father.

"Can you tell me," I asked, "whether she had any dear friend or female relative of the same name – Salome?"

The rabbi shook his head.

"I think not," he said. "I remember no other maiden of that name."

"Pardon me, but I know there was another," I replied. "There was a very beautiful Salome living in the Merceria when I was last in Venice, just this time last year."

"Salome da Costa was very fair," said the rabbi; "and she dwelt with her father in the Merceria. Since her death, he hath removed to the neighbourhood of the Rialto."

"This Salome's father was a dealer in Oriental goods," I said, hastily.

"Isaac da Costa is a dealer in Oriental goods," replied the old man very gently. "We are speaking, my son, of the same persons."

"Impossible!"

He shook his head again.

"But she lives!" I exclaimed, becoming greatly agitated. "She lives. I have seen her. I have spoken to her. I saw her only last evening."

"Nay," he said, compassionately, "this is some dream. She of whom you speak is indeed no more."

"I saw her only last evening," I repeated.

"Where did you suppose you beheld her?"

"On the Lido."

"On the Lido?"

"And she spoke to me. I heard her voice – heard it as distinctly as I hear my own at this moment."

The rabbi stroked his beard thoughtfully, and looked at me. "You think you heard her voice!" he ejaculated. "That is strange. What said she?"

I was about to answer. I checked myself – a sudden thought flashed upon me – I trembled from head to foot.

"Have you – have you any reason for supposing that she died a Christian?" I faltered.

The old man started and changed colour.

"I—I—that is a strange question," he stammered. "Why do you ask it?"

"Yes or no?" I cried wildly. "Yes or no?"

He frowned, looked down, hesitated.

"I admit," he said, after a moment or two, – "I admit that I may have heard something tending that way. It may be that the maiden cherished some secret doubt. Yet she was no professed Christian."

"Laid in earth without one Christian prayer; with Hebrew rites; in a Hebrew sanctuary!" I repeated to myself.

"But I marvel how you come to have heard of this," continued the rabbi. "It was known only to her father and myself."

"Sir," I said solemnly, "I know now that Salome da Costa is dead; I have seen her spirit thrice, haunting the spot where…"

My voice broke. I could not utter the words.

"Last evening at sunset," I resumed, "was the third time. Never doubting that – that I indeed beheld her in the flesh, I spoke to her. She answered me. She – she told me this."

The rabbi covered his face with his hands, and so remained for some time, lost in meditation. "Young man," he said at length, "your story is strange, and you bring strange evidence to bear upon it. It may be as you say; it may be that you are the dupe of some waking dream – I know not."

He knew not; but I… Ah! I knew only too well. I knew now why she had appeared to me clothed with such unearthly beauty. I understood now that look of dumb entreaty in her eyes – that tone of strange remoteness in her voice. The sweet soul could not rest amid the dust of its kinsfolk, "unhousel'd, unanointed, unanealed," lacking even "one Christian prayer" above its grave. And now – was it all over? Should I never see her more?

Never – ah! never. How I haunted the Lido at sunset for many a month, till Spring had blossomed into Autumn, and Autumn had ripened into Summer; how I wandered back to Venice year after year at the same season, while yet any vestige of that wild hope remained alive; how my heart has never throbbed, my pulse never leaped, for love of mortal woman since that time – are details into which I need not enter here. Enough that I watched and waited; but that her gracious spirit appeared to me no more. I wait still, but I watch no longer. I know now that our place of meeting will not be here.

The Poor Clare

Elizabeth Gaskell

Chapter I

DECEMBER 12TH, 1747. – My life has been strangely bound up with extraordinary incidents, some of which occurred before I had any connection with the principal actors in them, or indeed, before I even knew of their existence. I suppose, most old men are, like me, more given to looking back upon their own career with a kind of fond interest and affectionate remembrance, than to watching the events – though these may have far more interest for the multitude – immediately passing before their eyes. If this should be the case with the generality of old people, how much more so with me!... If I am to enter upon that strange story connected with poor Lucy, I must begin a long way back. I myself only came to the knowledge of her family history after I knew her; but, to make the tale clear to any one else, I must arrange events in the order in which they occurred – not that in which I became acquainted with them.

There is a great old hall in the north-east of Lancashire, in a part they called the Trough of Bolland, adjoining that other district named Craven. Starkey Manor-house is rather like a number of rooms clustered round a gray, massive, old keep than a regularly-built hall. Indeed, I suppose that the house only consisted of a great tower in the centre, in the days when the Scots made their raids terrible as far south as this; and that after the Stuarts came in, and there was a little more security of property in those parts, the Starkeys of that time added the lower building, which runs, two stories high, all round the base of the keep. There has been a grand garden laid out in my days, on the southern slope near the house; but when I first knew the place, the kitchen-garden at the farm was the only piece of cultivated ground belonging to it. The deer used to come within sight of the drawing-room windows, and might have browsed quite close up to the house if they had not been too wild and shy. Starkey Manor-house itself stood on a projection or peninsula of high land, jutting out from the abrupt hills that form the sides of the Trough of Bolland. These hills were rocky and bleak enough towards their summit; lower down they were clothed with tangled copsewood and green depths of fern, out of which a gray giant of an ancient forest-tree would tower here and there, throwing up its ghastly white branches, as if in imprecation, to the sky. These trees, they told me, were the remnants of that forest which existed in the days of the Heptarchy, and were even then noted as landmarks. No wonder that their upper and more exposed branches were leafless, and that the dead bark had peeled away, from sapless old age.

Not far from the house there were a few cottages, apparently, of the same date as the keep; probably built for some retainers of the family, who sought shelter – they and their families and their small flocks and herds – at the hands of their feudal lord. Some of them had pretty much fallen to decay. They were built in a strange fashion. Strong beams had been sunk firm in the ground at the requisite distance, and their other ends had been fastened together, two and two, so as to form the shape of one of those rounded waggon-headed gipsy-tents, only very much larger. The spaces between were filled with mud, stones, osiers, rubbish, mortar – anything to keep out the weather. The fires were made in the centre of these rude dwellings, a hole in the roof forming the only chimney. No Highland hut or Irish cabin could be of rougher construction.

The owner of this property, at the beginning of the present century, was a Mr. Patrick Byrne Starkey. His family had kept to the old faith, and were stanch Roman Catholics, esteeming it even a sin to marry any one of Protestant descent, however willing he or she might have been to embrace the Romish religion. Mr. Patrick Starkey's father had been a follower of James the Second; and, during the disastrous Irish campaign of that monarch he had fallen in love with an Irish beauty, a Miss Byrne, as zealous for her religion and for the Stuarts as himself. He had returned to Ireland after his escape to France, and married her, bearing her back to the court at St. Germains. But some licence on the part of the disorderly gentlemen who surrounded King James in his exile, had insulted his beautiful wife, and disgusted him; so he removed from St. Germains to Antwerp, whence, in a few years' time, he quietly returned to Starkey Manor-house – some of his Lancashire neighbours having lent their good offices to reconcile him to the powers that were. He was as firm a Catholic as ever, and as stanch an advocate for the Stuarts and the divine rights of kings; but his religion almost amounted to asceticism, and the conduct of these with whom he had been brought in such close contact at St. Germains would little bear the inspection of a stern moralist. So he gave his allegiance where he could not give his esteem, and learned to respect sincerely the upright and moral character of one whom he yet regarded as an usurper. King William's government had little need to fear such a one. So he returned, as I have said, with a sobered heart and impoverished fortunes, to his ancestral house, which had fallen sadly to ruin while the owner had been a courtier, a soldier, and an exile. The roads into the Trough of Bolland were little more than cart-ruts; indeed, the way up to the house lay along a ploughed field before you came to the deer-park. Madam, as the country-folk used to call Mrs. Starkey, rode on a pillion behind her husband, holding on to him with a light hand by his leather riding-belt. Little master (he that was afterwards Squire Patrick Byrne Starkey) was held on to his pony by a serving-man. A woman past middle age walked, with a firm and strong step, by the cart that held much of the baggage; and high up on the mails and boxes, sat a girl of dazzling beauty, perched lightly on the topmost trunk, and swaying herself fearlessly to and fro, as the cart rocked and shook in the heavy roads of late autumn. The girl wore the Antwerp faille, or black Spanish mantle over her head, and altogether her appearance was such that the old cottager, who described the possession to me many years after, said that all the country-folk took her for a foreigner. Some dogs, and the boy who held them in charge, made up the company. They rode silently along, looking with grave, serious eyes at the people, who came out of the scattered cottages to bow or curtsy to the real Squire, "come back at last," and gazed after the little procession with gaping wonder, not deadened by the sound of the foreign language in which the few necessary words that passed among them were spoken. One lad, called from his staring by the Squire to come and help about the cart, accompanied them to the Manor-house. He said that when the lady had descended from her pillion, the middle-aged woman whom I have described as walking while the others rode, stepped quickly forward, and taking Madam Starkey (who was of a slight and delicate figure) in her arms, she lifted her over the threshold, and set her down in her husband's house, at the same time uttering a passionate and outlandish blessing. The Squire stood by, smiling gravely at first; but when the words of blessing were pronounced, he took off his fine feathered hat, and bent his head. The girl with the black mantle stepped onward into the shadow of the dark hall, and kissed the lady's hand; and that was all the lad could tell to the group that gathered round him on his return, eager to hear everything, and to know how much the Squire had given him for his services.

From all I could gather, the Manor-house, at the time of the Squire's return, was in the most dilapidated state. The stout gray walls remained firm and entire; but the inner chambers had been used for all kinds of purposes. The great withdrawing-room had been a barn; the state tapestry-chamber had held wool, and so on. But, by-and-by, they were cleared out; and if the Squire had no money to spend on new furniture, he and his wife had the knack of making the best of the old. He was no despicable joiner; she had a kind of grace in whatever she did, and imparted an air of elegant picturesqueness to whatever she touched. Besides, they had brought many rare things from the Continent; perhaps I should rather say, things that were rare in that part of England – carvings, and crosses, and beautiful pictures. And then, again, wood was plentiful in the Trough of Bolland, and great log-fires danced and glittered in all the dark, old rooms, and gave a look of home and comfort to everything.

Why do I tell you all this? I have little to do with the Squire and Madame Starkey; and yet I dwell upon them, as if I were unwilling to come to the real people with whom my life was so strangely mixed up. Madam had been nursed in Ireland by the very woman who lifted her in her arms, and welcomed her to her husband's home in Lancashire. Excepting for the short period of her own married life, Bridget Fitzgerald had never left her nursling. Her marriage – to one above her in rank – had been unhappy. Her husband had died, and left her in even greater poverty than that in which she was when he had first met with her. She had one child, the beautiful daughter who came riding on the waggon-load of furniture that was brought to the Manor-house. Madame Starkey had taken her again into her service when she became a widow. She and her daughter had followed "the mistress" in all her fortunes; they had lived at St. Germains and at Antwerp, and were now come to her home in Lancashire. As soon as Bridget had arrived there, the Squire gave her a cottage of her own, and took more pains in furnishing it for her than he did in anything else out of his own house. It was only nominally her residence. She was constantly up at the great house; indeed, it was but a short cut across the woods from her own home to the home of her nursling. Her daughter Mary, in like manner, moved from one house to the other at her own will. Madam loved both mother and child dearly. They had great influence over her, and, through her, over her husband. Whatever Bridget or Mary willed was sure to come to pass. They were not disliked; for, though wild and passionate, they were also generous by nature. But the other servants were afraid of them, as being in secret the ruling spirits of the household. The Squire had lost his interest in all secular things; Madam was gentle, affectionate, and yielding. Both husband and wife were tenderly attached to each other and to their boy; but they grew more and more to shun the trouble of decision on any point; and hence it was that Bridget could exert such despotic power. But if everyone else yielded to her "magic of a superior mind," her daughter not unfrequently rebelled. She and her mother were too much alike to agree. There were wild quarrels between them, and wilder reconciliations. There were times when, in the heat of passion, they could have stabbed each other. At all other times they both – Bridget especially – would have willingly laid down their lives for one another. Bridget's love for her child lay very deep – deeper than that daughter ever knew; or I should think she would never have wearied of home as she did, and prayed her mistress to obtain for her some situation – as waiting maid – beyond the seas, in that more cheerful continental life, among the scenes of which so many of her happiest years had been spent. She thought, as youth thinks, that life would last for ever, and that two or three years were but a small portion of it to pass away from her mother, whose only child she was. Bridget thought differently, but was too proud ever to show what she felt. If her child wished to leave her, why – she should go. But people said Bridget became ten years older in the course of two months at this time. She took it that Mary wanted to leave her. The truth was, that Mary wanted for a time to leave the place, and to seek some change, and would thankfully have taken her mother with her. Indeed when Madam Starkey had gotten her a situation with some grand lady abroad, and the time drew near for her to go, it was Mary who clung to her mother with passionate embrace, and, with floods of tears, declared that she would never leave her; and it was Bridget, who at last loosened her arms, and, grave and tearless herself, bade her keep her word, and go forth into the wide world. Sobbing aloud, and looking back continually, Mary went away. Bridget was still as death, scarcely drawing her breath, or closing her stony eyes; till at last she turned back into her cottage, and heaved a ponderous old settle against the door. There she sat, motionless, over the gray ashes of her extinguished fire, deaf to Madam's sweet voice, as she begged leave to enter and comfort her nurse. Deaf, stony, and motionless, she sat for more than twenty hours; till, for the third time, Madam came across the snowy path from the great house, carrying with her a young spaniel, which had been Mary's pet up at the hall; and which had not ceased all night long to seek for its absent mistress, and to whine and moan after her. With tears Madam told this story, through the closed door – tears excited by the terrible look of anguish, so steady, so immovable – so the same today as it was yesterday – on her nurse's face. The little creature in her arms began to utter its piteous cry, as it shivered with the cold. Bridget stirred; she moved – she listened. Again that long whine; she thought it was for her daughter; and what she had denied to her nursling and mistress she granted to the dumb creature that Mary had cherished. She opened the door, and took the dog from Madam's arms. Then Madam came in, and kissed and comforted the old woman, who took but little notice of her or anything. And sending up Master Patrick to the hall for fire and food, the sweet young lady never left her nurse all that night. Next day, the Squire himself came down, carrying a beautiful foreign picture – Our Lady of the Holy Heart, the Papists call it. It is a picture of the Virgin, her heart pierced with arrows, each arrow representing one of her great woes. That picture hung in Bridget's cottage when I first saw her; I have that picture now.

Years went on. Mary was still abroad. Bridget was still and stern, instead of active and passionate. The little dog, Mignon, was indeed her darling. I have heard that she talked to it continually; although, to most people, she was so silent. The Squire and Madam treated her with the greatest consideration, and well they might; for to them she was as devoted and faithful as ever. Mary wrote pretty often, and seemed satisfied with her life. But at length the letters ceased – I hardly know whether before or after a great and terrible sorrow came upon the house of the Starkeys. The Squire sickened of a putrid fever; and Madam caught it in nursing him, and died. You may be sure, Bridget let no other woman tend her but herself; and in the very arms that had received her at her birth, that sweet young woman laid her head down, and gave up her breath. The Squire recovered, in a fashion. He was never strong – he had never the heart to smile again. He fasted and prayed more than ever; and people did say that he tried to cut off the entail, and leave all the property away to found a monastery abroad, of which he prayed that some day little Squire Patrick might be the reverend father. But he could not do this, for the strictness of the entail and the laws against the Papists. So he could only appoint gentlemen of his own faith as guardians to his son, with many charges about the lad's soul, and a few about the land, and the way it was to be held while he was a minor. Of course, Bridget was not forgotten. He sent for her as he lay on his death-bed, and asked her if she would rather have a sum down, or have a small annuity settled upon her. She said at once she would have a sum down; for she thought of her daughter, and how she could bequeath the money to her, whereas an annuity would have died with her. So the Squire left her her cottage for life, and a fair sum of money. And then he died, with as ready and willing a heart as, I suppose, ever any gentleman took out of this world with him. The young Squire was carried off by his guardians, and Bridget was left alone.

I have said that she had not heard from Mary for some time. In her last letter, she had told of travelling about with her mistress, who was the English wife of some great foreign officer, and had spoken of her chances of making a good marriage, without naming the gentleman's name, keeping it rather back as a pleasant surprise to her mother; his station and fortune being, as I had afterwards reason to know, far superior to anything she had a right to expect. Then came a long silence; and Madam was dead, and the Squire was dead; and Bridget's heart was gnawed by anxiety, and she knew not whom to ask for news of her child. She could not write, and the Squire had managed her communication with her daughter. She walked off to Hurst; and got a good priest there – one whom she had known at Antwerp – to write for her. But no answer came. It was like crying into the' awful stillness of night.

One day, Bridget was missed by those neighbours who had been accustomed to mark her goings-out and comings-in. She had never been sociable with any of them; but the sight of her had become a part of their daily lives, and slow wonder arose in their minds, as morning after morning came, and her house-door remained closed, her window dead from any glitter, or light of fire within. At length, some one tried the door; it was locked. Two or three laid their heads together, before daring to look in through the blank unshuttered window. But, at last, they summoned up courage; and then saw that Bridget's absence from their little world was not the result of accident or death, but of premeditation. Such small articles of furniture as could be secured from the effects of time and damp by being packed up, were stowed away in boxes. The picture of the Madonna was taken down, and gone. In a word, Bridget had stolen away from her home, and left no trace whither she was departed. I knew afterwards, that she and her little dog had wandered off on the long search for her lost daughter. She was too illiterate to have faith in letters, even had she had the means of writing and sending many. But she had faith in her own strong love, and believed that her passionate instinct would guide her to her child. Besides, foreign travel was no new thing to her, and she could speak enough of French to explain the object of her journey, and had, moreover, the advantage of being, from her faith, a welcome object of charitable hospitality at many a distant convent. But the country people round Starkey Manor-house knew nothing of all this. They wondered what had become of her, in a torpid, lazy fashion, and then left off thinking of her altogether. Several years passed. Both Manor-house and cottage were deserted. The young Squire lived far away under the direction of his guardians. There were inroads of wool and corn into the sitting-rooms of the Hall; and there was some low talk, from time to time, among the hinds and country people whether it would not be as well to break into old Bridget's cottage, and save such of her goods as were left from the moth and rust which must be making sad havoc. But this idea was always quenched by the recollection of her strong character and passionate anger; and tales of her masterful spirit, and vehement force of will, were whispered about, till the very thought of offending her, by touching any article of hers, became invested with a kind of horror: it was believed that, dead or alive, she would not fail to avenge it.

Suddenly she came home; with as little noise or note of preparation as she had departed. One day some one noticed a thin, blue curl of smoke ascending from her chimney. Her door stood open to the noonday sun; and, ere many hours had elapsed, some one had seen an old travel-and-sorrow-stained woman dipping her pitcher in the well; and said, that the dark, solemn eyes that looked up at him were more like Bridget Fitzgerald's than any one else's in this world; and yet, if it were she, she looked as if she had been scorched in the flames of hell, so brown, and scared, and fierce a creature did she seem. By-and-by many saw her; and those who met her eye once cared not to be caught looking at her again. She had got into the habit of perpetually talking to herself; nay, more, answering herself, and varying her tones according to the side she took at the moment. It was no wonder that those who dared to listen outside her door at night believed that she held converse with some spirit; in short, she was unconsciously earning for herself the dreadful reputation of a witch.

Her little dog, which had wandered half over the Continent with her, was her only companion; a dumb remembrancer of happier days. Once he was ill; and she carried him more than three miles, to ask about his management from one who had been groom to the last Squire, and had then been noted for his skill in all diseases of animals. Whatever this man did, the dog recovered; and they who heard her thanks, intermingled with blessings (that were rather promises of good fortune than prayers), looked grave at his good luck when, next year, his ewes twinned, and his meadow-grass was heavy and thick.

Now it so happened that, about the year seventeen hundred and eleven, one of the guardians of the young squire, a certain Sir Philip Tempest, bethought him of the good shooting there must be on his ward's property; and in consequence he brought down four or five gentlemen, of his friends, to stay for a week or two at the Hall. From all accounts, they roystered and spent pretty freely. I never heard any of their names but one, and that was Squire Gisborne's. He was hardly a middle-aged man then; he had been much abroad, and there, I believe, he had known Sir Philip Tempest, and done him some service. He was a daring and dissolute fellow in those days: careless and fearless, and one who would rather be in a quarrel than out of it. He had his fits of ill-temper besides, when he would spare neither man nor beast. Otherwise, those who knew him well, used to say he had a good heart, when he was neither drunk, nor angry, nor in any way vexed. He had altered much when I came to know him.

One day, the gentlemen had all been out shooting, and with but little success, I believe; anyhow, Mr. Gisborne had none, and was in a black humour accordingly. He was coming home, having his gun loaded, sportsman-like, when little Mignon crossed his path, just as he turned out of the wood by Bridget's cottage. Partly for wantonness, partly to vent his spleen upon some living creature. Mr. Gisborne took his gun, and fired – he had better have never fired gun again, than aimed that unlucky shot, he hit Mignon, and at the creature's sudden cry, Bridget came out, and saw at a glance what had been done. She took Mignon up in her arms, and looked hard at the wound; the poor dog looked at her with his glazing eyes, and tried to wag his tail and lick her hand, all covered with blood. Mr. Gisborne spoke in a kind of sullen penitence:

"You should have kept the dog out of my way – a little poaching varmint."

At this very moment, Mignon stretched out his legs, and stiffened in her arms – her lost Mary's dog, who had wandered and sorrowed with her for years. She walked right into Mr. Gisborne's path, and fixed his unwilling, sullen look, with her dark and terrible eye.

"Those never throve that did me harm," said she. "I'm alone in the world, and helpless; the more do the saints in heaven hear my prayers. Hear me, ye blessed ones! hear me while I ask for sorrow on this bad, cruel man. He has killed the only creature that loved me – the dumb beast that I loved. Bring down heavy sorrow on his head for it, O ye saints! He thought that I was helpless, because he saw me lonely and poor; but are not the armies of heaven for the like of me?"

"Come, come," said he, half remorseful, but not one whit afraid. "Here's a crown to buy thee another dog. Take it, and leave off cursing! I care none for thy threats."

"Don't you?" said she, coming a step closer, and changing her imprecatory cry for a whisper which made the gamekeeper's lad, following Mr. Gisborne, creep all over. "You shall live to see the creature you love best, and who alone loves you – ay, a human creature, but as innocent and fond as my poor, dead darling – you shall see this creature, for whom death would be too happy, become a terror and a loathing to all, for this blood's sake. Hear me, O holy saints, who never fail them that have no other help!"

She threw up her right hand, filled with poor Mignon's life-drops; they spirted, one or two of them, on his shooting-dress, – an ominous sight to the follower. But the master only laughed a little, forced, scornful laugh, and went on to the Hall. Before he got there, however, he took out a gold piece, and bade the boy carry it to the old woman on his return to the village. The lad was "afeared," as he told me in after years; he came to the cottage, and hovered about, not daring to enter. He peeped through the window at last; and by the flickering wood-flame, he saw Bridget kneeling before the picture of Our Lady of the Holy Heart, with dead Mignon lying between her and the Madonna. She was praying wildly, as her outstretched arms betokened. The lad shrunk away in redoubled terror; and contented himself with slipping the gold piece under the ill-fitting door. The next day it was thrown out upon the midden; and there it lay, no one daring to touch it.

Meanwhile Mr. Gisborne, half curious, half uneasy, thought to lessen his uncomfortable feelings by asking Sir Philip who Bridget was? He could only describe her – he did not know her name. Sir Philip was equally at a loss. But an old servant of the Starkeys, who had resumed his livery at the Hall on this occasion – a scoundrel whom Bridget had saved from dismissal more than once during her palmy days – said:

"It will be the old witch, that his worship means. She needs a ducking, if ever a woman did, does that Bridget Fitzgerald."

"Fitzgerald!" said both the gentlemen at once. But Sir Philip was the first to continue:

"I must have no talk of ducking her, Dickon. Why, she must be the very woman poor Starkey bade me have a care of; but when I came here last she was gone, no one knew where. I'll go and see her tomorrow. But mind you, sirrah, if any harm comes to her, or any more talk of her being a witch – I've a pack of hounds at home, who can follow the scent of a lying knave as well as ever they followed a dog-fox; so take care how you talk about ducking a faithful old servant of your dead master's."

"Had she ever a daughter?" asked Mr. Gisborne, after a while.

"I don't know – yes! I've a notion she had; a kind of waiting woman to Madam Starkey."

"Please your worship," said humbled Dickon, "Mistress Bridget had a daughter – one Mistress Mary – who went abroad, and has never been heard on since; and folk do say that has crazed her mother."

Mr. Gisborne shaded his eyes with his hand.

"I could wish she had not cursed me," he muttered. "She may have power – no one else could." After a while, he said aloud, no one understanding rightly what he meant, "Tush! it is impossible!" – and called for claret; and he and the other gentlemen set-to to a drinking-bout.

Chapter II

I NOW COME to the time in which I myself was mixed up with the people that I have been writing about. And to make you understand how I became connected with them, I must give you some little account of myself. My father was the younger son of a Devonshire gentleman of moderate property; my eldest uncle succeeded to the estate of his forefathers, my second became an eminent attorney in London, and my father took orders. Like most poor clergymen, he had a large family; and I have no doubt was glad enough when my London uncle, who was a bachelor, offered to take charge of me, and bring me up to be his successor in business.

In this way I came to live in London, in my uncle's house, not far from Gray's Inn, and to be treated and esteemed as his son, and to labour with him in his office. I was very fond of the old gentleman. He was the confidential agent of many country squires, and had attained to his present position as much by knowledge of human nature as by knowledge of law; though he was learned enough in the latter. He used to say his business was law, his pleasure heraldry. From his intimate acquaintance with family history, and all the tragic courses of life therein involved, to hear him talk, at leisure times, about any coat of arms that came across his path was as good as a play or a romance. Many cases of disputed property, dependent on a love of genealogy, were brought to him, as to a great authority on such points. If the lawyer who came to consult him was young, he would take no fee, only give him a long lecture on the importance of attending to heraldry; if the lawyer was of mature age and good standing, he would mulct him pretty well, and abuse him to me afterwards as negligent of one great branch of the profession. His house was in a stately new street called Ormond Street, and in it he had a handsome library; but all the books treated of things that were past; none of them planned or looked forward into the future. I worked away – partly for the sake of my family at home, partly because my uncle had really taught me to enjoy the kind of practice in which he himself took such delight. I suspect I worked too hard; at any rate, in seventeen hundred and eighteen I was far from well, and my good uncle was disturbed by my ill looks.

One day, he rang the bell twice into the clerk's room at the dingy office in Grey's Inn Lane. It was the summons for me, and I went into his private room just as a gentleman – whom I knew well enough by sight as an Irish lawyer of more reputation than he deserved – was leaving.

My uncle was slowly rubbing his hands together and considering. I was there two or three minutes before he spoke. Then he told me that I must pack up my portmanteau that very afternoon, and start that night by post-horse for West Chester. I should get there, if all went well, at the end of five days' time, and must then wait for a packet to cross over to Dublin; from thence I must proceed to a certain town named Kildoon, and in that neighbourhood I was to remain, making certain inquiries as to the existence of any descendants of the younger branch of a family to whom some valuable estates had descended in the female line. The Irish lawyer whom I had seen was weary of the case, and would willingly have given up the property, without further ado, to a man who appeared to claim them; but on laying his tables and trees before my uncle, the latter had foreseen so many possible prior claimants, that the lawyer had begged him to undertake the management of the whole business. In his youth, my uncle would have liked nothing better than going over to Ireland himself, and ferreting out every scrap of paper or parchment, and every word of tradition respecting the family. As it was, old and gouty, he deputed me.

Accordingly, I went to Kildoon. I suspect I had something of my uncle's delight in following up a genealogical scent, for I very soon found out, when on the spot, that Mr. Rooney, the Irish lawyer, would have got both himself and the first claimant into a terrible scrape, if he had pronounced his opinion that the estates ought to be given up to him. There were three poor Irish fellows, each nearer of kin to the last possessor; but, a generation before, there was a still nearer relation, who had never been accounted for, nor his existence ever discovered by the lawyers, I venture to think, till I routed him out from the memory of some of the old dependants of the family. What had become of him? I travelled backwards and forwards; I crossed over to France, and came back again with a slight clue, which ended in my discovering that, wild and dissipated himself, he had left one child, a son, of yet worse character than his father; that this same Hugh Fitzgerald had married a very beautiful serving-woman of the Byrnes – a person below him in hereditary rank, but above him in character; that he had died soon after his marriage, leaving one child, whether a boy or a girl I could not learn, and that the mother had returned to live in the family of the Byrnes. Now, the chief of this latter family was serving in the Duke of Berwick's regiment, and it was long before I could hear from him; it was more than a year before I got a short, haughty letter – I fancy he had a soldier's contempt for a civilian, an Irishman's hatred for an Englishman, an exiled Jacobite's jealousy of one who prospered and lived tranquilly under the government he looked upon as an usurpation. "Bridget Fitzgerald," he said, "had been faithful to the fortunes of his sister – had followed her abroad, and to England when Mrs. Starkey had thought fit to return. Both his sister and her husband were dead, he knew nothing of Bridget Fitzgerald at the present time: probably Sir Philip Tempest, his nephew's guardian, might be able to give me some information." I have not given the little contemptuous terms; the way in which faithful service was meant to imply more than it said – all that has nothing to do with my story. Sir Philip, when applied to, told me that he paid an annuity regularly to an old woman named Fitzgerald, living at Coldholme (the village near Starkey Manor-house). Whether she had any descendants he could not say.

One bleak March evening, I came in sight of the places described at the beginning of my story. I could hardly understand the rude dialect in which the direction to old Bridget's house was given.

"Yo' see yon furleets," all run together, gave me no idea that I was to guide myself by the distant lights that shone in the windows of the Hall, occupied for the time by a farmer who held the post of steward, while the Squire, now four or five and twenty, was making the grand tour. However, at last, I reached Bridget's cottage – a low, moss-grown place: the palings that had once surrounded it were broken and gone; and the underwood of the forest came up to the walls, and must have darkened the windows. It was about seven o'clock – not late to my London notions – but, after knocking for some time at the door and receiving no reply, I was driven to conjecture that the occupant of the house was gone to bed. So I betook myself to the nearest church I had seen, three miles back on the road I had come, sure that close to that I should find an inn of some kind; and early the next morning I set off back to Coldholme, by a field-path which my host assured me I should find a shorter cut than the road I had taken the night before. It was a cold, sharp morning; my feet left prints in the sprinkling of hoar-frost that covered the ground; nevertheless, I saw an old woman, whom I instinctively suspected to be the object of my search, in a sheltered covert on one side of my path. I lingered and watched her. She must have been considerably above the middle size in her prime, for when she raised herself from the stooping position in which I first saw her, there was something fine and commanding in the erectness of her figure. She drooped again in a minute or two, and seemed looking for something on the ground, as, with bent head, she turned off from the spot where I gazed upon her, and was lost to my sight. I fancy I missed my way, and made a round in spite of the landlord's directions; for by the time I had reached Bridget's cottage she was there, with no semblance of hurried walk or discomposure of any kind. The door was slightly ajar. I knocked, and the majestic figure stood before me, silently awaiting the explanation of my errand. Her teeth were all gone, so the nose and chin were brought near together; the gray eyebrows were straight, and almost hung over her deep, cavernous eyes, and the thick white hair lay in silvery masses over the low, wide, wrinkled forehead. For a moment, I stood uncertain how to shape my answer to the solemn questioning of her silence.

"Your name is Bridget Fitzgerald, I believe?"

She bowed her head in assent.

"I have something to say to you. May I come in? I am unwilling to keep you standing."

"You cannot tire me," she said, and at first she seemed inclined to deny me the shelter of her roof. But the next moment – she had searched the very soul in me with her eyes during that instant – she led me in, and dropped the shadowing hood of her gray, draping cloak, which had previously hid part of the character of her countenance. The cottage was rude and bare enough.

But before the picture of the Virgin, of which I have made mention, there stood a little cup filled with fresh primroses. While she paid her reverence to the Madonna, I understood why she had been out seeking through the clumps of green in the sheltered copse. Then she turned round, and bade me be seated. The expression of her face, which all this time I was studying, was not bad, as the stories of my last night's landlord had led me to expect; it was a wild, stern, fierce, indomitable countenance, seamed and scarred by agonies of solitary weeping; but it was neither cunning nor malignant.

"My name is Bridget Fitzgerald," said she, by way of opening our conversation.

"And your husband was Hugh Fitzgerald, of Knock Mahon, near Kildoon, in Ireland?"

A faint light came into the dark gloom of her eyes.

"He was."

"May I ask if you had any children by him?"

The light in her eyes grew quick and red. She tried to speak, I could see; but something rose in her throat, and choked her, and until she could speak calmly, she would fain not speak at all before a stranger. In a minute or so she said – "I had a daughter – one Mary Fitzgerald," – then her strong nature mastered her strong will, and she cried out, with a trembling wailing cry: "Oh, man! what of her? – what of her?"

She rose from her seat, and came and clutched at my arm, and looked in my eyes. There she read, as I suppose, my utter ignorance of what had become of her child; for she went blindly back to her chair, and sat rocking herself and softly moaning, as if I were not there; I not daring to speak to the lone and awful woman. After a little pause, she knelt down before the picture of Our Lady of the Holy Heart, and spoke to her by all the fanciful and poetic names of the Litany.

"O Rose of Sharon! O Tower of David! O Star of the Sea! have ye no comfort for my sore heart? Am I for ever to hope? Grant me at least despair!" – and so on she went, heedless of my presence. Her prayers grew wilder and wilder, till they seemed to me to touch on the borders of madness and blasphemy. Almost involuntarily, I spoke as if to stop her.

"Have you any reason to think that your daughter is dead?"

She rose from her knees, and came and stood before me.

"Mary Fitzgerald is dead," said she. "I shall never see her again in the flesh. No tongue ever told me; but I know she is dead. I have yearned so to see her, and my heart's will is fearful and strong: it would have drawn her to me before now, if she had been a wanderer on the other side of the world. I wonder often it has not drawn her out of the grave to come and stand before me, and hear me tell her how I loved her. For, sir, we parted unfriends."

I knew nothing but the dry particulars needed for my lawyer's quest, but I could not help feeling for the desolate woman; and she must have read the unusual sympathy with her wistful eyes.

"Yes, sir, we did. She never knew how I loved her; and we parted unfriends; and I fear me that I wished her voyage might not turn out well, only meaning, – O, blessed Virgin! you know I only meant that she should come home to her mother's arms as to the happiest place on earth; but my wishes are terrible – their power goes beyond my thought – and there is no hope for me, if my words brought Mary harm."

"But," I said, "you do not know that she is dead. Even now, you hoped she might be alive. Listen to me," and I told her the tale I have already told you, giving it all in the driest manner, for I wanted to recall the clear sense that I felt almost sure she had possessed in her younger days, and by keeping up her attention to details, restrain the vague wildness of her grief.

She listened with deep attention, putting from time to time such questions as convinced me I had to do with no common intelligence, however dimmed and shorn by solitude and mysterious sorrow. Then she took up her tale; and in few brief words, told me of her wanderings abroad in vain search after her daughter; sometimes in the wake of armies, sometimes in camp, sometimes in city. The lady, whose waiting-woman Mary had gone to be, had died soon after the date of her last letter home; her husband, the foreign officer, had been serving in Hungary, whither Bridget had followed him, but too late to find him. Vague rumours reached her that Mary had made a great marriage: and this sting of doubt was added, – whether the mother might not be close to her child under her new name, and even hearing of her every day; and yet never recognizing the lost one under the appellation she then bore. At length the thought took possession of her, that it was possible that all this time Mary might be at home at Coldholme, in the Trough of Bolland, in Lancashire, in England; and home came Bridget, in that vain hope, to her desolate hearth, and empty cottage. Here she had thought it safest to remain; if Mary was in life, it was here she would seek for her mother.

I noted down one or two particulars out of Bridget's narrative that I thought might be of use to me: for I was stimulated to further search in a strange and extraordinary manner. It seemed as if it were impressed upon me, that I must take up the quest where Bridget had laid it down; and this for no reason that had previously influenced me (such as my uncle's anxiety on the subject, my own reputation as a lawyer, and so on), but from some strange power which had taken possession of my will only that very morning, and which forced it in the direction it chose.

"I will go," said I. "I will spare nothing in the search. Trust to me. I will learn all that can be learnt. You shall know all that money, or pains, or wit can discover. It is true she may be long dead: but she may have left a child."

"A child!" she cried, as if for the first time this idea had struck her mind. "Hear him, Blessed Virgin! he says she may have left a child. And you have never told me, though I have prayed so for a sign, waking or sleeping!"

"Nay," said I, "I know nothing but what you tell me. You say you heard of her marriage."

But she caught nothing of what I said. She was praying to the Virgin in a kind of ecstasy, which seemed to render her unconscious of my very presence.

From Coldholme I went to Sir Philip Tempest's. The wife of the foreign officer had been a cousin of his father's, and from him I thought I might gain some particulars as to the existence of the Count de la Tour d'Auvergne, and where I could find him; for I knew questions *de vive voix* aid the flagging recollection, and I was determined to lose no chance for want of trouble. But Sir Philip had gone abroad, and it would be some time before I could receive an answer. So I followed my uncle's advice, to whom I had mentioned how wearied I felt, both in body and mind, by my will-o'-the-wisp search. He immediately told me to go to Harrogate, there to await Sir Philip's reply. I should be near to one of the places connected with my search, Coldholme; not far from Sir Philip Tempest, in case he returned, and I wished to ask him any further questions; and, in conclusion, my uncle bade me try to forget all about my business for a time.

This was far easier said than done. I have seen a child on a common blown along by a high wind, without power of standing still and resisting the tempestuous force. I was somewhat in the same predicament as regarded my mental state. Something resistless seemed to urge my thoughts on, through every possible course by which there was a chance of attaining to my object. I did not see the sweeping moors when I walked out: when I held a book in my hand, and read the words, their sense did not penetrate to my brain. If I slept, I went on with the same ideas, always flowing in the same direction. This could not last long without having a bad effect on the body. I had an illness, which, although I was racked with pain, was a positive relief to me, as it compelled me to live in the present suffering, and not in the visionary researches I had been continually making before. My kind uncle came to nurse me; and after the immediate danger was over, my life seemed to slip away in delicious languor for two or three months. I did not ask – so much did I dread falling into the old channel of thought – whether any reply had been received to my letter to Sir Philip. I turned my whole imagination right away from all that subject. My uncle remained with me until nigh midsummer, and then returned to his business in London; leaving me perfectly well, although not completely strong. I was to follow him in a fortnight; when, as he said, "we would look over letters, and talk about several things." I knew what this little speech alluded to, and shrank from the train of thought it suggested, which was so intimately connected with my first feelings of illness. However, I had a fortnight more to roam on those invigorating Yorkshire moors.

In those days, there was one large, rambling inn, at Harrogate, close to the Medicinal Spring; but it was already becoming too small for the accommodation of the influx of visitors, and many lodged round about, in the farm-houses of the district. It was so early in the season, that I had the inn pretty much to myself; and, indeed, felt rather like a visitor in a private house, so intimate had the landlord and landlady become with me during my long illness. She would chide me for being out so late on the moors, or for having been too long without food, quite in a motherly way; while he consulted me about vintages and wines, and taught me many a Yorkshire wrinkle about horses. In my walks I met other strangers from time to time. Even before my uncle had left me, I had noticed, with half-torpid curiosity, a young lady of very striking appearance, who went about always accompanied by an elderly companion, – hardly a gentlewoman, but with something in her look that prepossessed me in her favour. The younger lady always put her veil down when any one approached; so it had been only once or twice, when I had come upon her at a sudden turn in the path, that I had even had a glimpse at her face. I am not sure if it was beautiful, though in after-life I grew to think it so. But it was at this time overshadowed by a sadness that never varied: a pale, quiet, resigned look of intense suffering, that irresistibly attracted me, – not with love, but with a sense of infinite compassion for one so young yet so hopelessly unhappy. The companion wore something of the same look: quiet melancholy, hopeless, yet resigned. I asked my landlord who they were. He said they were called Clarke, and wished to be considered as mother and daughter; but that, for his part, he did not believe that to be their right name, or that there was any such relationship between them. They had been in the neighbourhood of Harrogate for some time, lodging in a remote farm-house. The people there would tell nothing about them; saying that they paid handsomely, and never did any harm; so why should they be speaking of any strange things that might happen? That, as the landlord shrewdly observed, showed there was something out of the common way he had heard that the elderly woman was a cousin of the farmer's where they lodged, and so the regard existing between relations might help to keep them quiet.

"What did he think, then, was the reason for their extreme seclusion?" asked I.

"Nay, he could not tell, – not he. He had heard that the young lady, for all as quiet as she seemed, played strange pranks at times." He shook his head when I asked him for more particulars, and refused to give them, which made me doubt if he knew any, for he was in general a talkative and communicative man. In default of other interests, after my uncle left, I set myself to watch these two people. I hovered about their walks drawn towards them with a strange fascination, which was not diminished by their evident annoyance at so frequently meeting me. One day, I had the sudden good fortune to be at hand when they were alarmed by the attack of a bull, which, in those unenclosed grazing districts, was a particularly dangerous occurrence. I have other and more important things to relate, than to tell of the accident which gave me an opportunity of rescuing them, it is enough to say, that this event was the beginning of an acquaintance, reluctantly acquiesced in by them, but eagerly prosecuted by me. I can hardly tell when intense curiosity became merged in love, but in less than ten days after my uncle's departure I was passionately enamoured of Mistress Lucy, as her attendant called her; carefully – for this I noted well – avoiding any address which appeared as if there was an equality of station between them. I noticed also that Mrs. Clarke, the elderly woman, after her first reluctance to allow me to pay them any attentions had been overcome, was cheered by my evident attachment to the young girl; it seemed to lighten her heavy burden of care, and she evidently favoured my visits to the farmhouse where they lodged. It was not so with Lucy. A more attractive person I never saw, in spite of her depression of manner, and shrinking avoidance of me. I felt sure at once, that whatever was the source of her grief, it rose from no fault of her own. It was difficult to draw her into conversation; but when at times, for a moment or two, I beguiled her into talk, I could see a rare intelligence in her face, and a grave, trusting look in the soft, gray eyes that were raised for a minute to mine. I made every excuse I possibly could for going there. I sought wild flowers for Lucy's sake; I planned walks for Lucy's sake; I watched the heavens by night, in hopes that some unusual beauty of sky would justify me in tempting Mrs. Clarke and Lucy forth upon the moors, to gaze at the great purple dome above.

It seemed to me that Lucy was aware of my love; but that, for some motive which I could not guess, she would fain have repelled me; but then again I saw, or fancied I saw, that her heart spoke in my favour, and that there was a struggle going on in her mind, which at times (I loved so dearly) I could have begged her to spare herself, even though the happiness of my whole life should have been the sacrifice; for her complexion grew paler, her aspect of sorrow more hopeless, her delicate frame yet slighter. During this period I had written, I should say, to my uncle, to beg to be allowed to prolong my stay at Harrogate, not giving any reason; but such was his tenderness towards me, that in a few days I heard from him, giving me a willing permission, and only charging me to take care of myself, and not use too much exertion during the hot weather.

One sultry evening I drew near the farm. The windows of their parlour were open, and I heard voices when I turned the corner of the house, as I passed the first window (there were two windows in their little ground-floor room). I saw Lucy distinctly; but when I had knocked at their door – the house-door stood always ajar – she was gone, and I saw only Mrs. Clarke, turning over the work-things lying on the table, in a nervous and purposeless manner. I felt by instinct that a conversation of some importance was coming on, in which I should be expected to say what was my object in paying these frequent visits. I was glad of the opportunity. My uncle had several times alluded to the pleasant possibility of my bringing home a young wife, to cheer and adorn the old house in Ormond Street. He was rich, and I was to succeed him, and had, as I knew, a fair reputation for so young a lawyer. So on my side I saw no obstacle. It was true that Lucy was shrouded in mystery; her name (I was convinced it was not Clarke), birth, parentage, and previous life were unknown to me. But I was sure of her goodness and sweet innocence, and although I knew that there must be something painful to be told, to account for her mournful sadness, yet I was willing to bear my share in her grief, whatever it might be.

Mrs. Clarke began, as if it was a relief to her to plunge into the subject.

"We have thought, sir – at least I have thought – that you knew very little of us, nor we of you, indeed; not enough to warrant the intimate acquaintance we have fallen into. I beg your pardon, sir," she went on, nervously; "I am but a plain kind of woman, and I mean to use no rudeness; but I must say straight out that I – we – think it would be better for you not to come so often to see us. She is very unprotected, and—"

"Why should I not come to see you, dear madam?" asked I, eagerly, glad of the opportunity of explaining myself. "I come, I own, because I have learnt to love Mistress Lucy, and wish to teach her to love me."

Mistress Clarke shook her head, and sighed.

"Don't, sir – neither love her, nor, for the sake of all you hold sacred, teach her to love you! If I am too late, and you love her already, forget her, – forget these last few weeks. O! I should never have allowed you to come!" she went on passionately; "but what am I to do? We are forsaken by all, except the great God, and even He permits a strange and evil power to afflict us – what am I to do! Where is it to end?" She wrung her hands in her distress; then she turned to me: "Go away, sir! go away, before you learn to care any more for her. I ask it for your own sake – I implore! You have been good and kind to us, and we shall always recollect you with gratitude; but go away now, and never come back to cross our fatal path!"

"Indeed, madam," said I, "I shall do no such thing. You urge it for my own sake. I have no fear, so urged – nor wish, except to hear more – all. I cannot have seen Mistress Lucy in all the intimacy of this last fortnight, without acknowledging her goodness and innocence; and without seeing – pardon me, madam – that for some reason you are two very lonely women, in some mysterious sorrow and distress. Now, though I am not powerful myself, yet I have friends who are so wise and kind that they may be said to possess power. Tell me some particulars. Why are you in grief – what is your secret – why are you here? I declare solemnly that nothing you have said has daunted me in my wish to become Lucy's husband; nor will I shrink from any difficulty that, as such an aspirant, I may have to encounter. You say you are friendless – why cast away an honest friend? I will tell you of people to whom you may write, and who will answer any questions as to my character and prospects. I do not shun inquiry."

She shook her head again. "You had better go away, sir. You know nothing about us."

"I know your names," said I, "and I have heard you allude to the part of the country from which you came, which I happen to know as a wild and lonely place. There are so few people living in it that, if I chose to go there, I could easily ascertain all about you; but I would rather hear it from yourself." You see I wanted to pique her into telling me something definite.

"You do not know our true names, sir," said she, hastily.

"Well, I may have conjectured as much. But tell me, then, I conjure you. Give me your reasons for distrusting my willingness to stand by what I have said with regard to Mistress Lucy."

"Oh, what can I do?" exclaimed she. "If I am turning away a true friend, as he says? – Stay!" coming to a sudden decision – "I will tell you something – I cannot tell you all – you would not believe it. But, perhaps, I can tell you enough to prevent your going on in your hopeless attachment. I am not Lucy's mother."

"So I conjectured," I said. "Go on."

"I do not even know whether she is the legitimate or illegitimate child of her father. But he is cruelly turned against her; and her mother is long dead; and for a terrible reason, she has no other creature to keep constant to her but me. She – only two years ago – such a darling and such a pride in her father's house! Why, sir, there is a mystery that might happen in connection with her any moment; and then you would go away like all the rest; and, when you next heard her name, you would loathe her. Others, who have loved her longer, have done so before now. My poor child! whom neither God nor man has mercy upon – or, surely, she would die!"

The good woman was stopped by her crying. I confess, I was a little stunned by her last words; but only for a moment. At any rate, till I knew definitely what was this mysterious stain upon one so simple and pure, as Lucy seemed, I would not desert her, and so I said; and she made me answer:

"If you are daring in your heart to think harm of my child, sir, after knowing her as you have done, you are no good man yourself; but I am so foolish and helpless in my great sorrow, that I would fain hope to find a friend in you. I cannot help trusting that, although you may no longer feel toward her as a lover, you will have pity upon us; and perhaps, by your learning you can tell us where to go for aid."

"I implore you to tell me what this mystery is," I cried, almost maddened by this suspense.

"I cannot," said she, solemnly. "I am under a deep vow of secrecy. If you are to be told, it must be by her." She left the room, and I remained to ponder over this strange interview. I mechanically turned over the few books, and with eyes that saw nothing at the time, examined the tokens of Lucy's frequent presence in that room.

When I got home at night, I remembered how all these trifles spoke of a pure and tender heart and innocent life. Mistress Clarke returned; she had been crying sadly.

"Yes," said she, "it is as I feared: she loves you so much that she is willing to run the fearful risk of telling you all herself – she acknowledges it is but a poor chance; but your sympathy will be a balm, if you give it. Tomorrow, come here at ten in the morning; and, as you hope for pity in your hour of agony, repress all show of fear or repugnance you may feel towards one so grievously afflicted."

I half smiled. "Have no fear," I said. It seemed too absurd to imagine my feeling dislike to Lucy.

"Her father loved her well," said she, gravely, "yet he drove her out like some monstrous thing."

Just at this moment came a peal of ringing laughter from the garden. It was Lucy's voice; it sounded as if she were standing just on one side of the open casement – and as though she were suddenly stirred to merriment – merriment verging on boisterousness, by the doings or sayings of some other person. I can scarcely say why, but the sound jarred on me inexpressibly. She knew the subject of our conversation, and must have been at least aware of the state of agitation her friend was in; she herself usually so gentle and quiet. I half rose to go to the window, and satisfy my instinctive curiosity as to what had provoked this burst of, ill-timed laughter; but Mrs. Clarke threw her whole weight and power upon the hand with which she pressed and kept me down.

"For God's sake!" she said, white and trembling all over, "sit still; be quiet. Oh! be patient. Tomorrow you will know all. Leave us, for we are all sorely afflicted. Do not seek to know more about us."

Again that laugh – so musical in sound, yet so discordant to my heart. She held me tight – tighter; without positive violence I could not have risen. I was sitting with my back to the window, but I felt a shadow pass between the sun's warmth and me, and a strange shudder ran through my frame. In a minute or two she released me.

"Go," repeated she. "Be warned, I ask you once more. I do not think you can stand this knowledge that you seek. If I had had my own way, Lucy should never have yielded, and promised to tell you all. Who knows what may come of it?"

"I am firm in my wish to know all. I return at ten tomorrow morning, and then expect to see Mistress Lucy herself."

I turned away; having my own suspicions, I confess, as to Mistress Clarke's sanity.

Conjectures as to the meaning of her hints, and uncomfortable thoughts connected with that strange laughter, filled my mind. I could hardly sleep. I rose early; and long before the hour I had appointed, I was on the path over the common that led to the old farm-house where they lodged. I suppose that Lucy had passed no better a night than I; for there she was also, slowly pacing with her even step, her eyes bent down, her whole look most saintly and pure. She started when I came close to her, and grew paler as I reminded her of my appointment, and spoke with something of the impatience of obstacles that, seeing her once more, had called up afresh in my mind. All strange and terrible hints, and giddy merriment were forgotten. My heart gave forth words of fire, and my tongue uttered them. Her colour went and came, as she listened; but, when I had ended my passionate speeches, she lifted her soft eyes to me, and said:

"But you know that you have something to learn about me yet. I only want to say this: I shall not think less of you – less well of you, I mean – if you, too, fall away from me when you know all. Stop!" said she, as if fearing another burst of mad words. "Listen to me. My father is a man of great wealth. I never knew my mother; she must have died when I was very young. When first I remember anything, I was living in a great, lonely house, with my dear and faithful Mistress Clarke. My father, even, was not there; he was – he is – a soldier, and his duties lie aboard. But he came from time to time, and every time I think he loved me more and more. He brought me rarities from foreign lands, which prove to me now how much he must have thought of me during his absences. I can sit down and measure the depth of his lost love now, by such standards as these. I never thought whether he loved me or not, then; it was so natural, that it was like the air I breathed. Yet he was an angry man at times, even then; but never with me. He was very reckless, too; and, once or twice, I heard a whisper among the servants that a doom was over him, and that he knew it, and tried to drown his knowledge in wild activity, and even sometimes, sir, in wine. So I grew up in this grand mansion, in that lonely place. Everything around me seemed at my disposal, and I think every one loved me; I am sure I loved them. Till about two years ago – I remember it well – my father had come to England, to us; and he seemed so proud and so pleased with me and all I had done. And one day his tongue seemed loosened with wine, and he told me much that I had not known till then, – how dearly he had loved my mother, yet how his wilful usage had caused her death; and then he went on to say how he loved me better than any creature on earth, and how, some day, he hoped to take me to foreign places, for that he could hardly bear these long absences from his only child. Then he seemed to change suddenly, and said, in a strange, wild way, that I was not to believe what he said; that there was many a thing he loved better – his horse – his dog – I know not what.

"And 'twas only the next morning that, when I came into his room to ask his blessing as was my wont, he received me with fierce and angry words. 'Why had I,' so he asked, 'been delighting myself in such wanton mischief – dancing over the tender plants in the flower-beds, all set with the famous Dutch bulbs he had brought from Holland?' I had never been out of doors that morning, sir, and I could not conceive what he meant, and so I said; and then he swore at me for a liar, and said I was of no true blood, for he had seen me doing all that mischief himself – with his own eyes. What could I say? He would not listen to me, and even my tears seemed only to irritate him. That day was the beginning of my great sorrows. Not long after, he reproached me for my undue familiarity – all unbecoming a gentlewoman – with his grooms. I had been in the stable-yard, laughing and talking, he said. Now, sir, I am something of a coward by nature, and I had always dreaded horses; be-sides that, my father's servants – those whom he brought with him from foreign parts – were wild fellows, whom I had always avoided, and to whom I had never spoken, except as a lady must needs from time to time speak to her father's people. Yet my father called me by names of which I hardly know the meaning, but my heart told me they were such as shame any modest woman; and from that day he turned quite against me; – nay, sir, not many weeks after that, he came in with a riding-whip in his hand; and, accusing me harshly of evil doings, of which I knew no more than you, sir, he was about to strike me, and I, all in bewildering tears, was ready to take his stripes as great kindness compared to his harder words, when suddenly he stopped his arm mid-way, gasped and staggered, crying out, 'The curse – the curse!' I looked up in terror. In the great mirror opposite I saw myself, and right behind, another wicked, fearful self, so like me that my soul seemed to quiver within me, as though not knowing to which similitude of body it belonged. My father saw my double at the same moment, either in its dreadful reality, whatever that might be, or in the scarcely less terrible reflection in the mirror; but what came of it at that moment I cannot say, for I suddenly swooned away; and when I came to myself I was lying in my bed, and my faithful Clarke sitting by me. I was in my bed for days; and even while I lay there my double was seen by all, flitting about the house and gardens, always about some mischievous or detestable work. What wonder that every one shrank from me in dread – that my father drove me forth at length, when the disgrace of which I was the cause was past his patience to bear. Mistress Clarke came with me; and here we try to live such a life of piety and prayer as may in time set me free from the curse."

All the time she had been speaking, I had been weighing her story in my mind. I had hitherto put cases of witchcraft on one side, as mere superstitions; and my uncle and I had had many an argument, he supporting himself by the opinion of his good friend Sir Matthew Hale. Yet this sounded like the tale of one bewitched; or was it merely the effect of a life of extreme seclusion telling on the nerves of a sensitive girl? My scepticism inclined me to the latter belief, and when she paused I said:

"I fancy that some physician could have disabused your father of his belief in visions—"

Just at that instant, standing as I was opposite to her in the full and perfect morning light, I saw behind her another figure – a ghastly resemblance, complete in likeness, so far as form and feature and minutest touch of dress could go, but with a loathsome demon soul looking out of the gray eyes, that were in turns mocking and voluptuous. My heart stood still within me; every hair rose up erect; my flesh crept with horror. I could not see the grave and tender Lucy – my eyes were fascinated by the creature beyond. I know not why, but I put out my hand to clutch it; I grasped nothing but empty air, and my whole blood curdled to ice. For a moment I could not see; then my sight came back, and I saw Lucy standing before me, alone, deathly pale, and, I could have fancied, almost, shrunk in size.

"IT has been near me?" she said, as if asking a question.

The sound seemed taken out of her voice; it was husky as the notes on an old harpsichord when the strings have ceased to vibrate. She read her answer in my face, I suppose, for I could not speak. Her look was one of intense fear, but that died away into an aspect of most humble patience. At length she seemed to force herself to face behind and around her: she saw the purple moors, the blue distant hills, quivering in the sunlight, but nothing else.

"Will you take me home?" she said, meekly.

I took her by the hand, and led her silently through the budding heather – we dared not speak; for we could not tell but that the dread creature was listening, although unseen, – but that IT might appear and push us asunder. I never loved her more fondly than now when – and that was the unspeakable misery – the idea of her was becoming so inextricably blended with the shuddering thought of IT. She seemed to understand what I must be feeling. She let go my hand, which she had kept clasped until then, when we reached the garden gate, and went forwards to meet her anxious friend, who was standing by the window looking for her. I could not enter the house: I needed silence, society, leisure, change – I knew not what – to shake off the sensation of that creature's presence. Yet I lingered about the garden – I hardly know why; I partly suppose, because I feared to encounter the resemblance again on the solitary common, where it had vanished, and partly from a feeling of inexpressible compassion for Lucy. In a few minutes Mistress Clarke came forth and joined me. We walked some paces in silence.

"You know all now," said she, solemnly.

"I saw IT," said I, below my breath.

"And you shrink from us, now," she said, with a hopelessness which stirred up all that was brave or good in me.

"Not a whit," said I. "Human flesh shrinks from encounter with the powers of darkness: and, for some reason unknown to me, the pure and holy Lucy is their victim."

"The sins of the fathers shall be visited upon the children," she said.

"Who is her father?" asked I. "Knowing as much as I do, I may surely know more – know all. Tell me, I entreat you, madam, all that you can conjecture respecting this demoniac persecution of one so good."

"I will; but not now. I must go to Lucy now. Come this afternoon, I will see you alone; and oh, sir! I will trust that you may yet find some way to help us in our sore trouble!"

I was miserably exhausted by the swooning affright which had taken possession of me. When I reached the inn, I staggered in like one overcome by wine. I went to my own private room. It was some time before I saw that the weekly post had come in, and brought me my letters. There was one from my uncle, one from my home in Devonshire, and one, re-directed over the first address, sealed with a great coat of arms, It was from Sir Philip Tempest: my letter of inquiry respecting Mary Fitzgerald had reached him at Liége, where it so happened that the Count de la Tour d'Auvergne was quartered at the very time. He remembered his wife's beautiful attendant; she had had high words with the deceased countess, respecting her intercourse with an English gentleman of good standing, who was also in the foreign service. The countess augured evil of his intentions; while Mary, proud and vehement, asserted that he would soon marry her, and resented her mistress's warnings as an insult. The consequence was, that she had left Madame de la Tour d'Auvergne's service, and, as the Count believed, had gone to live with the Englishman; whether he had married her, or not, he could not say. "But," added Sir Philip Tempest, "you may easily hear what particulars you wish to know respecting Mary Fitzgerald from the Englishman himself, if, as I suspect, he is no other than my neighbour and former acquaintance, Mr. Gisborne, of Skipford Hall, in the West Riding. I am led to the belief that he is no other, by several small particulars, none of which are in themselves conclusive, but which, taken together, furnish a mass of presumptive evidence. As far as I could make out from the Count's foreign pronunciation, Gisborne was the name of the Englishman: I know that Gisborne of Skipford was abroad and in the foreign service at that time – he was a likely fellow enough for such an exploit, and, above all, certain expressions recur to my mind which he used in reference to old Bridget Fitzgerald, of Coldholme, whom he once encountered while staying with me at Starkey Manor-house. I remember that the meeting seemed to have produced some extraordinary effect upon his mind, as though he had suddenly discovered some connection which she might have had with his previous life. I beg you to let me know if I can be of any further service to you. Your uncle once rendered me a good turn, and I will gladly repay it, so far as in me lies, to his nephew."

I was now apparently close on the discovery which I had striven so many months to attain. But success had lost its zest. I put my letters down, and seemed to forget them all in thinking of the morning I had passed that very day. Nothing was real but the unreal presence, which had come like an evil blast across my bodily eyes, and burnt itself down upon my brain. Dinner came, and went away untouched. Early in the afternoon I walked to the farm-house. I found Mistress Clarke alone, and I was glad and relieved. She was evidently prepared to tell me all I might wish to hear.

"You asked me for Mistress Lucy's true name; it is Gisborne," she began.

"Not Gisborne of Skipford?" I exclaimed, breathless with anticipation.

"The same," said she, quietly, not regarding my manner. "Her father is a man of note; although, being a Roman Catholic, he cannot take that rank in this country to which his station entitles him. The consequence is that he lives much abroad – has been a soldier, I am told."

"And Lucy's mother?" I asked.

She shook her head. "I never knew her," said she. "Lucy was about three years old when I was engaged to take charge of her. Her mother was dead."

"But you know her name? – you can tell if it was Mary Fitzgerald?"

She looked astonished. "That was her name. But, sir, how came you to be so well acquainted with it? It was a mystery to the whole household at Skipford Court. She was some beautiful young woman whom he lured away from her protectors while he was abroad. I have heard said he practised some terrible deceit upon her, and when she came to know it, she was neither to have nor to hold, but rushed off from his very arms, and threw herself into a rapid stream and was drowned. It stung him deep with remorse, but I used to think the remembrance of the mother's cruel death made him love the child yet dearer."

I told her, as briefly as might be, of my researches after the descendant and heir of the Fitzgeralds of Kildoon, and added – something of my old lawyer spirit returning into me for the moment – that I had no doubt but that we should prove Lucy to be by right possessed of large estates in Ireland.

No flush came over her gray face; no light into her eyes. "And what is all the wealth in the whole world to that poor girl?" she said. "It will not free her from the ghastly bewitchment which persecutes her. As for money, what a pitiful thing it is! it cannot touch her."

"No more can the Evil Creature harm her," I said. "Her holy nature dwells apart, and cannot be defiled or stained by all the devilish arts in the whole world."

"True! but it is a cruel fate to know that all shrink from her, sooner or later, as from one possessed – accursed."

"How came it to pass?" I asked.

"Nay, I know not. Old rumours there are, that were bruited through the household at Skipford."

"Tell me," I demanded.

"They came from servants, who would fain account for every thing. They say that, many years ago, Mr. Gisborne killed a dog belonging to an old witch at Coldholme; that she cursed, with a dreadful and mysterious curse, the creature, whatever it might be, that he should love best; and that it struck so deeply into his heart that for years he kept himself aloof from any temptation to love aught. But who could help loving Lucy?"

"You never heard the witch's name?" I gasped.

"Yes – they called her Bridget: they said he would never go near the spot again for terror of her. Yet he was a brave man!"

"Listen," said I, taking hold of her arm, the better to arrest her full attention: "if what I suspect holds true, that man stole Bridget's only child – the very Mary Fitzgerald who was Lucy's mother; if so, Bridget cursed him in ignorance of the deeper wrong he had done her. To this hour she yearns after her lost child, and questions the saints whether she be living or not. The roots of that curse lie deeper than she knows: she unwittingly banned him for a deeper guilt than that of killing a dumb beast. The sins of the fathers are indeed visited upon the children."

"But," said Mistress Clarke, eagerly, "she would never let evil rest on her own grandchild? Surely, sir, if what you say be true, there are hopes for Lucy. Let us go – go at once, and tell this fearful woman all that you suspect, and beseech her to take off the spell she has put upon her innocent grandchild."

It seemed to me, indeed, that something like this was the best course we could pursue. But first it was necessary to ascertain more than what mere rumour or careless hearsay could tell. My thoughts turned to my uncle – he could advise me wisely – he ought to know all. I resolved to go to him without delay; but I did not choose to tell Mistress Clarke of all the visionary plans that flitted through my mind. I simply declared my intention of proceeding straight to London on Lucy's affairs. I bade her believe that my interest on the young lady's behalf was greater than ever, and that my whole time should be given up to her cause. I saw that Mistress Clarke distrusted me, because my mind was too full of thoughts for my words to flow freely. She sighed and shook her head, and said, "Well, it is all right!" in such a tone that it was an implied reproach. But I was firm and constant in my heart, and I took confidence from that.

I rode to London. I rode long days drawn out into the lovely summer nights: I could not rest. I reached London. I told my uncle all, though in the stir of the great city the horror had faded away, and I could hardly imagine that he would believe the account I gave him of the fearful double of Lucy which I had seen on the lonely moor-side. But my uncle had lived many years, and learnt many things; and, in the deep secrets of family history that had been confided to him, he had heard of cases of innocent people bewitched and taken possession of by evil spirits yet more fearful than Lucy's. For, as he said, to judge from all I told him, that resemblance had no power over her – she was too pure and good to be tainted by its evil, haunting presence. It had, in all probability, so my uncle conceived, tried to suggest wicked thoughts and to tempt to wicked actions but she, in her saintly maidenhood, had passed on undefiled by evil thought or deed. It could not touch her soul: but true, it set her apart from all sweet love or common human intercourse. My uncle threw himself with an energy more like six-and-twenty than sixty into the consideration of the whole case. He undertook the proving Lucy's descent, and volunteered to go and find out Mr. Gisborne, and obtain, firstly, the legal proofs of her descent from the Fitzgeralds of Kildoon, and, secondly, to try and hear all that he could respecting the working of the curse, and whether any and what means had been taken to exorcise that terrible appearance. For he told me of instances where, by prayers and long fasting, the evil possessor had been driven forth with howling and many cries from the body which it had come to inhabit; he spoke of those strange New England cases which had happened not so long before; of Mr. Defoe, who had written a book, wherein he had named many modes of subduing apparitions, and sending them back whence they came; and, lastly, he spoke low of dreadful ways of compelling witches to undo their witchcraft. But I could not endure to hear of those tortures and burnings. I said that Bridget was rather a wild and savage woman than a malignant witch; and, above all, that Lucy was of her kith and kin; and that, in putting her to the trial, by water or by fire, we should be torturing – it might be to the death – the ancestress of her we sought to redeem.

My uncle thought awhile, and then said, that in this last matter I was right – at any rate, it should not be tried, with his consent, till all other modes of remedy had failed; and he assented to my proposal that I should go myself and see Bridget, and tell her all.

In accordance with this, I went down once more to the wayside inn near Coldholme. It was late at night when I arrived there; and, while I supped, I inquired of the landlord more particulars as to Bridget's ways. Solitary and savage had been her life for many years. Wild and despotic were her words and manner to those few people who came across her path. The country-folk did her imperious bidding, because they feared to disobey. If they pleased her, they prospered; if, on the contrary, they neglected or traversed her behests, misfortune, small or great, fell on them and theirs. It was not detestation so much as an indefinable terror that she excited.

In the morning I went to see her. She was standing on the green outside her cottage, and received me with the sullen grandeur of a throneless queen. I read in her face that she recognized me, and that I was not unwelcome; but she stood silent till I had opened my errand.

"I have news of your daughter," said I, resolved to speak straight to all that I knew she felt of love, and not to spare her. "She is dead!"

The stern figure scarcely trembled, but her hand sought the support of the door-post.

"I knew that she was dead," said she, deep and low, and then was silent for an instant. "My tears that should have flowed for her were burnt up long years ago. Young man, tell me about her."

"Not yet," said I, having a strange power given me of confronting one, whom, nevertheless, in my secret soul I dreaded.

"You had once a little dog," I continued. The words called out in her more show of emotion than the intelligence of her daughter's death. She broke in upon my speech:

"I had! It was hers – the last thing I had of hers – and it was shot for wantonness! It died in my arms. The man who killed that dog rues it to this day. For that dumb beast's blood, his best-beloved stands accursed."

Her eyes distended, as if she were in a trance and saw the working of her curse. Again I spoke:

"O, woman!" I said, "that best-beloved, standing accursed before men, is your dead daughter's child."

The life, the energy, the passion, came back to the eyes with which she pierced through me, to see if I spoke truth; then, without another question or word, she threw herself on the ground with fearful vehemence, and clutched at the innocent daisies with convulsed hands.

"Bone of my bone! flesh of my flesh! have I cursed thee – and art thou accursed?"

So she moaned, as she lay prostrate in her great agony. I stood aghast at my own work. She did not hear my broken sentences; she asked no more, but the dumb confirmation which my sad looks had given that one fact, that her curse rested on her own daughter's child. The fear grew on me lest she should die in her strife of body and soul; and then might not Lucy remain under the spell as long as she lived?

Even at this moment, I saw Lucy coming through the woodland path that led to Bridget's cottage; Mistress Clarke was with her: I felt at my heart that it was she, by the balmy peace which the look of her sent over me, as she slowly advanced, a glad surprise shining out of her soft quiet eyes. That was as her gaze met mine. As her looks fell on the woman lying stiff, convulsed on the earth, they became full of tender pity; and she came forward to try and lift her up. Seating herself on the turf, she took Bridget's head into her lap; and, with gentle touches, she arranged the dishevelled gray hair streaming thick and wild from beneath her mutch.

"God help her!" murmured Lucy. "How she suffers!"

At her desire we sought for water; but when we returned, Bridget had recovered her wandering senses, and was kneeling with clasped hands before Lucy, gazing at that sweet sad face as though her troubled nature drank in health and peace from every moment's contemplation. A faint tinge on Lucy's pale cheeks showed me that she was aware of our return; otherwise it appeared as if she was conscious of her influence for good over the passionate and troubled woman kneeling before her, and would not willingly avert her grave and loving eyes from that wrinkled and careworn countenance.

Suddenly – in the twinkling of an eye – the creature appeared, there, behind Lucy; fearfully the same as to outward semblance, but kneeling exactly as Bridget knelt, and clasping her hands in jesting mimicry as Bridget clasped hers in her ecstasy that was deepening into a prayer. Mistress Clarke cried out – Bridget arose slowly, her gaze fixed on the creature beyond: drawing her breath with a hissing sound, never moving her terrible eyes, that were steady as stone, she made a dart at the phantom, and caught, as I had done, a mere handful of empty air. We saw no more of the creature – it vanished as suddenly as it came, but Bridget looked slowly on, as if watching some receding form. Lucy sat still, white, trembling, drooping – I think she would have swooned if I had not been there to uphold her. While I was attending to her, Bridget passed us, without a word to any one, and, entering her cottage, she barred herself in, and left us without.

All our endeavours were now directed to get Lucy back to the house where she had tarried the night before. Mistress Clarke told me that, not hearing from me (some letter must have miscarried), she had grown impatient and despairing, and had urged Lucy to the enterprise of coming to seek her grandmother; not telling her, indeed, of the dread reputation she possessed, or how we suspected her of having so fearfully blighted that innocent girl; but, at the same time, hoping much from the mysterious stirring of blood, which Mistress Clarke trusted in for the removal of the curse. They had come, by a different route from that which I had taken, to a village inn not far from Coldholme, only the night before. This was the first interview between ancestress and descendant.

All through the sultry noon I wandered along the tangled brush-wood of the old neglected forest, thinking where to turn for remedy in a matter so complicated and mysterious. Meeting a countryman, I asked my way to the nearest clergyman, and went, hoping to obtain some counsel from him. But he proved to be a coarse and common-minded man, giving no time or attention to the intricacies of a case, but dashing out a strong opinion involving immediate action. For instance, as soon as I named Bridget Fitzgerald, he exclaimed:

"The Coldholme witch! the Irish papist! I'd have had her ducked long since but for that other papist, Sir Philip Tempest. He has had to threaten honest folk about here over and over again, or they'd have had her up before the justices for her black doings. And it's the law of the land that witches should be burnt! Ay, and of Scripture, too, sir! Yet you see a papist, if he's a rich squire, can overrule both law and Scripture. I'd carry a faggot myself to rid the country of her!"

Such a one could give me no help. I rather drew back what I had already said; and tried to make the parson forget it, by treating him to several pots of beer, in the village inn, to which we had adjourned for our conference at his suggestion. I left him as soon as I could, and returned to Coldholme, shaping my way past deserted Starkey Manor-house, and coming upon it by the back. At that side were the oblong remains of the old moat, the waters of which lay placid and motionless under the crimson rays of the setting sun; with the forest-trees lying straight along each side, and their deep-green foliage mirrored to blackness in the burnished surface of the moat below – and the broken sun-dial at the end nearest the hall – and the heron, standing on one leg at the water's edge, lazily looking down for fish – the lonely and desolate house scarce needed the broken windows, the weeds on the door-sill, the broken shutter softly flapping to and fro in the twilight breeze, to fill up the picture of desertion and decay. I lingered about the place until the growing darkness warned me on. And then I passed along the path, cut by the orders of the last lady of Starkey Manor-House, that led me to Bridget's cottage. I resolved at once to see her; and, in spite of closed doors – it might be of resolved will – she should see me. So I knocked at her door, gently, loudly, fiercely. I shook it so vehemently that a length the old hinges gave way, and with a crash it fell inwards, leaving me suddenly face to face with Bridget – I, red, heated, agitated with my so long baffled efforts – she, stiff as any stone, standing right facing me, her eyes dilated with terror, her ashen lips trembling, but her body motionless. In her hands she held her crucifix, as if by that holy symbol she sought to oppose my entrance. At sight of me, her whole frame relaxed, and she sank back upon a chair. Some mighty tension had given way. Still her eyes looked fearfully into the gloom of the outer air, made more opaque by the glimmer of the lamp inside, which she had placed before the picture of the Virgin.

"Is she there?" asked Bridget, hoarsely.

"No! Who? I am alone. You remember me."

"Yes," replied she, still terror stricken. "But she – that creature – has been looking in upon me through that window all day long. I closed it up with my shawl; and then I saw her feet below the door, as long as it was light, and I knew she heard my very breathing – nay, worse, my very prayers; and I could not pray, for her listening choked the words ere they rose to my lips. Tell me, who is she? – what means that double girl I saw this morning? One had a look of my dead Mary; but the other curdled my blood, and yet it was the same!"

She had taken hold of my arm, as if to secure herself some human companionship. She shook all over with the slight, never-ceasing tremor of intense terror. I told her my tale as I have told it you, sparing none of the details.

How Mistress Clarke had informed me that the resemblance had driven Lucy forth from her father's house – how I had disbelieved, until, with mine own eyes, I had seen another Lucy standing behind my Lucy, the same in form and feature, but with the demon-soul looking out of the eyes. I told her all, I say, believing that she – whose curse was working so upon the life of her innocent grandchild – was the only person who could find the remedy and the redemption. When I had done, she sat silent for many minutes.

"You love Mary's child?" she asked.

"I do, in spite of the fearful working of the curse – I love her. Yet I shrink from her ever since that day on the moor-side. And men must shrink from one so accompanied; friends and lovers must stand afar off. Oh, Bridget Fitzgerald! loosen the curse! Set her free!"

"Where is she?"

I eagerly caught at the idea that her presence was needed, in order that, by some strange prayer or exorcism, the spell might be reversed.

"I will go and bring her to you," I exclaimed. Bridget tightened her hold upon my arm.

"Not so," said she, in a low, hoarse voice. "It would kill me to see her again as I saw her this morning. And I must live till I have worked my work. Leave me!" said she, suddenly, and again taking up the cross. "I defy the demon I have called up. Leave me to wrestle with it!"

She stood up, as if in an ecstasy of inspiration, from which all fear was banished. I lingered – why I can hardly tell – until once more she bade me begone. As I went along the forest way, I looked back, and saw her planting the cross in the empty threshold, where the door had been.

The next morning Lucy and I went to seek her, to bid her join her prayers with ours. The cottage stood open and wide to our gaze. No human being was there: the cross remained on the threshold, but Bridget was gone.

Chapter III

WHAT WAS TO be done next? was the question that I asked myself. As for Lucy, she would fain have submitted to the doom that lay upon her. Her gentleness and piety, under the pressure of so horrible a life, seemed over-passive to me. She never complained. Mrs. Clarke complained more than ever. As for me, I was more in love with the real Lucy than ever; but I shrunk from the false similitude with an intensity proportioned to my love. I found out by instinct that Mrs. Clarke had occasional temptations to leave Lucy. The good lady's nerves were shaken, and, from what she said, I could almost have concluded that the object of the Double was to drive away from Lucy this last, and almost earliest friend. At times, I could scarcely bear to own it, but I myself felt inclined to turn recreant; and I would accuse Lucy of being too patient – too resigned. One after another, she won the little children of Coldholme. (Mrs. Clarke and she had resolved to stay there, for was it not as good a place as any other, to such as they? and did not all our faint hopes rest on Bridget – never seen or heard of now, but still we trusted to come back, or give some token?) So, as I say, one after another, the little children came about my Lucy, won by her soft tones, and her gentle smiles, and kind actions. Alas! one after another they fell away, and shrunk from her path with blanching terror; and we too surely guessed the reason why. It was the last drop. I could bear it no longer. I resolved no more to linger around the spot, but to go back to my uncle, and among the learned divines of the city of London, seek for some power whereby to annul the curse.

My uncle, meanwhile, had obtained all the requisite testimonials relating to Lucy's descent and birth, from the Irish lawyers, and from Mr. Gisborne. The latter gentleman had written from abroad (he was again serving in the Austrian army), a letter alternately passionately self-reproachful and stoically repellant. It was evident that when he thought of Mary – her short life – how he had wronged her, and of her violent death, he could hardly find words severe enough for his own conduct; and from this point of view, the curse that Bridget had laid upon him and his, was regarded by him as a prophetic doom, to the utterance of which she was moved by a Higher Power, working for the fulfilment of a deeper vengeance than for the death of the poor dog. But then, again, when he came to speak of his daughter, the repugnance which the conduct of the demoniac creature had produced in his mind, was but ill-disguised under a show of profound indifference as to Lucy's fate. One almost felt as if he would have been as content to put her out of existence, as he would have been to destroy some disgusting reptile that had invaded his chamber or his couch.

The great Fitzgerald property was Lucy's; and that was all – was nothing.

My uncle and I sat in the gloom of a London November evening, in our house in Ormond Street. I was out of health, and felt as if I were in an inextricable coil of misery. Lucy and I wrote to each other, but that was little; and we dared not see each other for dread of the fearful Third, who had more than once taken her place at our meetings. My uncle had, on the day I speak of, bidden prayers to be put up on the ensuing Sabbath in many a church and meeting-house in London, for one grievously tormented by an evil spirit. He had faith in prayers – I had none; I was fast losing faith in all things. So we sat, he trying to interest me in the old talk of other days, I oppressed by one thought – when our old servant, Anthony, opened the door, and, without speaking, showed in a very gentlemanly and prepossessing man, who had something remarkable about his dress, betraying his profession to be that of the Roman Catholic priesthood. He glanced at my uncle first, then at me. It was to me he bowed.

"I did not give my name," said he, "because you would hardly have recognised it; unless, sir, when, in the north, you heard of Father Bernard, the chaplain at Stoney Hurst?"

I remembered afterwards that I had heard of him, but at the time I had utterly forgotten it; so I professed myself a complete stranger to him; while my ever-hospitable uncle, although hating a papist as much as it was in his nature to hate anything, placed a chair for the visitor, and bade Anthony bring glasses, and a fresh jug of claret.

Father Bernard received this courtesy with the graceful ease and pleasant acknowledgement which belongs to a man of the world. Then he turned to scan me with his keen glance. After some alight conversation, entered into on his part, I am certain, with an intention of discovering on what terms of confidence I stood with my uncle, he paused, and said gravely –

"I am sent here with a message to you, sir, from a woman to whom you have shown kindness, and who is one of my penitents, in Antwerp – one Bridget Fitzgerald."

"Bridget Fitzgerald!" exclaimed I. "In Antwerp? Tell me, sir, all that you can about her."

"There is much to be said," he replied. "But may I inquire if this gentleman – if your uncle is acquainted with the particulars of which you and I stand informed?"

"All that I know, he knows," said I, eagerly laying my hand on my uncle's arm, as he made a motion as if to quit the room.

"Then I have to speak before two gentlemen who, however they may differ from me in faith, are yet fully impressed with the fact that there are evil powers going about continually to take cognizance of our evil thoughts: and, if their Master gives them power, to bring them into overt action. Such is my theory of the nature of that sin, which I dare not disbelieve – as some sceptics would have us do – the sin of witchcraft. Of this deadly sin, you and I are aware, Bridget Fitzgerald has been guilty. Since you saw her last, many prayers have been offered in our churches, many masses sung, many penances undergone, in order that, if God and the holy saints so willed it, her sin might be blotted out. But it has not been so willed."

"Explain to me," said I, "who you are, and how you come connected with Bridget. Why is she at Antwerp? I pray you, sir, tell me more. If I am impatient, excuse me; I am ill and feverish, and in consequence bewildered."

There was something to me inexpressibly soothing in the tone of voice with which he began to narrate, as it were from the beginning, his acquaintance with Bridget.

"I had known Mr. and Mrs. Starkey during their residence abroad, and so it fell out naturally that, when I came as chaplain to the Sherburnes at Stoney Hurst, our acquaintance was renewed; and thus I became the confessor of the whole family, isolated as they were from the offices of the Church, Sherburne being their nearest neighbour who professed the true faith. Of course, you are aware that facts revealed in confession are sealed as in the grave; but I learnt enough of Bridget's character to be convinced that I had to do with no common woman; one powerful for good as for evil. I believe that I was able to give her spiritual assistance from time to time, and that she looked upon me as a servant of that Holy Church, which has such wonderful power of moving men's hearts, and relieving them of the burden of their sins. I have known her cross the moors on the wildest nights of storm, to confess and be absolved; and then she would return, calmed and subdued, to her daily work about her mistress, no one witting where she had been during the hours that most passed in sleep upon their beds. After her daughter's departure – after Mary's mysterious disappearance – I had to impose many a long penance, in order to wash away the sin of impatient repining that was fast leading her into the deeper guilt of blasphemy. She set out on that long journey of which you have possibly heard – that fruitless journey in search of Mary – and during her absence, my superiors ordered my return to my former duties at Antwerp, and for many years I heard no more of Bridget.

"Not many months ago, as I was passing homewards in the evening, along one of the streets near St. Jacques, leading into the Meer Straet, I saw a woman sitting crouched up under the shrine of the Holy Mother of Sorrows. Her hood was drawn over her head, so that the shadow caused by the light of the lamp above fell deep over her face; her hands were clasped round her knees. It was evident that she was some one in hopeless trouble, and as such it was my duty to stop and speak. I naturally addressed her first in Flemish, believing her to be one of the lower class of inhabitants. She shook her head, but did not look up. Then I tried French, and she replied in that language, but speaking it so indifferently, that I was sure she was either English or Irish, and consequently spoke to her in my own native tongue. She recognized my voice; and, starting up, caught at my robes, dragging me before the blessed shrine, and throwing herself down, and forcing me, as much by her evident desire as by her action, to kneel beside her, she exclaimed:

"'O Holy Virgin! you will never hearken to me again, but hear him; for you know him of old, that he does your bidding, and strives to heal broken hearts. Hear him!'

"She turned to me.

"'She will hear you, if you will only pray. She never hears *me*: she and all the saints in heaven cannot hear my prayers, for the Evil One carries them off, as he carried that first away. O, Father Bernard, pray for me!'

"I prayed for one in sore distress, of what nature I could not say; but the Holy Virgin would know. Bridget held me fast, gasping with eagerness at the sound of my words. When I had ended, I rose, and, making the sign of the Cross over her, I was going to bless her in the name of the Holy Church, when she shrank away like some terrified creature, and said—

"'I am guilty of deadly sin, and am not shriven.'

"'Arise, my daughter,' said I, 'and come with me.' And I led the way into one of the confessionals of St. Jaques.

"She knelt; I listened. No words came. The evil powers had stricken her dumb, as I heard afterwards they had many a time before, when she approached confession.

"She was too poor to pay for the necessary forms of exorcism; and hitherto those priests to whom she had addressed herself were either so ignorant of the meaning of her broken French, or her Irish-English, or else esteemed her to be one crazed – as, indeed, her wild and excited manner might easily have led any one to think – that they had neglected the sole means of loosening her tongue, so that she might confess her deadly sin, and, after due penance, obtain absolution. But I knew Bridget of old, and felt that she was a penitent sent to me. I went through those holy offices appointed by our Church for the relief of such a case. I was the more bound to do this, as I found that she had come to Antwerp for the sole purpose of discovering me, and making confession to me. Of the nature of that fearful confession I am forbidden to speak. Much of it you know; possibly all.

"It now remains for her to free herself from mortal guilt, and to set others free from the consequences thereof. No prayers, no masses, will ever do it, although they may strengthen her with that strength by which alone acts of deepest love and purest self-devotion may be performed. Her words of passion, and cries for revenge – her unholy prayers could never reach the ears of the holy saints! Other powers intercepted them, and wrought so that the curses thrown up to heaven have fallen on her own flesh and blood; and so, through her very strength of love, have brused and crushed her heart. Henceforward her former self must be buried, – yea, buried quick, if need be, – but never more to make sign, or utter cry on earth! She has become a Poor Clare, in order that, by perpetual penance and constant service of others, she may at length so act as to obtain final absolution and rest for her soul. Until then, the innocent must suffer. It is to plead for the innocent that I come to you; not in the name of the witch, Bridget Fitzgerald, but of the penitent and servant of all men, the Poor Clare, Sister Magdalen."

"Sir," said I, "I listen to your request with respect; only I may tell you it is not needed to urge me to do all that I can on behalf of one, love for whom is part of my very life. If for a time I have absented myself from her, it is to think and work for her redemption. I, a member of the English Church – my uncle, a Puritan – pray morning and night for her by name: the congregations of London, on the next Sabbath, will pray for one unknown, that she may be set free from the Powers of Darkness. Moreover, I must tell you, sir, that those evil ones touch not the great calm of her soul. She lives her own pure and loving life, unharmed and untainted, though all men fall off from her. I would I could have her faith!"

My uncle now spoke.

"Nephew," said he, "it seems to me that this gentleman, although professing what I consider an erroneous creed, has touched upon the right point in exhorting Bridget to acts of love and mercy, whereby to wipe out her sin of hate and vengeance. Let us strive after our fashion, by almsgiving and visiting of the needy and fatherless, to make our prayers acceptable. Meanwhile, I myself will go down into the north, and take charge of the maiden. I am too old to be daunted by man or demon. I will bring her to this house as to a home; and let the Double come if it will! A company of godly divines shall give it the meeting, and we will try issue."

The kindly, brave old man! But Father Bernard sat on musing.

"All hate," said he, "cannot be quenched in her heart; all Christian forgiveness cannot have entered into her soul, or the demon would have lost its power. You said, I think, that her grandchild was still tormented?"

"Still tormented!" I replied, sadly, thinking of Mistress Clarke's last letter – He rose to go. We afterwards heard that the occasion of his coming to London was a secret political mission on behalf of the Jacobites. Nevertheless, he was a good and a wise man.

Months and months passed away without any change. Lucy entreated my uncle to leave her where she was, – dreading, as I learnt, lest if she came, with her fearful companion, to dwell in the same house with me, that my love could not stand the repeated shocks to which I should be doomed. And this she thought from no distrust of the strength of my affection, but from a kind of pitying sympathy for the terror to the nerves which she clearly observed that the demoniac visitation caused in all.

I was restless and miserable. I devoted myself to good works; but I performed them from no spirit of love, but solely from the hope of reward and payment, and so the reward was never granted. At length, I asked my uncle's leave to travel; and I went forth, a wanderer, with no distincter end than that of many another wanderer – to get away from myself. A strange impulse led me to Antwerp, in spite of the wars and commotions then raging in the Low Countries – or rather, perhaps, the very craving to become interested in something external, led me into the thick of the struggle then going on with the Austrians. The cities of Flanders were all full at that time of civil disturbances and rebellions, only kept down by force, and the presence of an Austrian garrison in every place.

I arrived in Antwerp, and made inquiry for Father Bernard. He was away in the country for a day or two. Then I asked my way to the Convent of Poor Clares; but, being healthy and prosperous, I could only see the dim, pent-up, gray walls, shut closely in by narrow streets, in the lowest part of the town. My landlord told me, that had I been stricken by some loathsome disease, or in desperate case of any kind, the Poor Clares would have taken me, and tended me. He spoke of them as an order of mercy of the strictest kind, dressing scantily in the coarsest materials, going barefoot, living on what the inhabitants of Antwerp chose to bestow, and sharing even those fragments and crumbs with the poor and helpless that swarmed all around; receiving no letters or communication with the outer world; utterly dead to everything but the alleviation of suffering. He smiled at my inquiring whether I could get speech of one of them; and told me that they were even forbidden to speak for the purposes of begging their daily food; while yet they lived, and fed others upon what was given in charity.

"But," exclaimed I, "supposing all men forgot them! Would they quietly lie down and die, without making sign of their extremity?"

"If such were the rule the Poor Clares would willingly do it; but their founder appointed a remedy for such extreme cases as you suggest. They have a bell – 'tis but a small one, as I have heard, and has yet never been rung in the memory man: when the Poor Clares have been without food for twenty-four hours, they may ring this bell, and then trust to our good people of Antwerp for rushing to the rescue of the Poor Clares, who have taken such blessed care of us in all our straits."

It seemed to me that such rescue would be late in the day; but I did not say what I thought. I rather turned the conversation, by asking my landlord if he knew, or had ever heard, anything of a certain Sister Magdalen.

"Yes," said he, rather under his breath, "news will creep out, even from a convent of Poor Clares. Sister Magdalen is either a great sinner or a great saint. She does more, as I have heard, than all the other nuns put together; yet, when last month they would fain have made her mother-superior, she begged rather that they would place her below all the rest, and make her the meanest servant of all."

"You never saw her?" asked I.

"Never," he replied.

I was weary of waiting for Father Bernard, and yet I lingered in Antwerp. The political state of things became worse than ever, increased to its height by the scarcity of food consequent on many deficient harvests. I saw groups of fierce, squalid men, at every corner of the street, glaring out with wolfish eyes at my sleek skin and handsome clothes.

At last Father Bernard returned. We had a long conversation, in which he told me that, curiously enough, Mr. Gisborne, Lucy's father, was serving in one of the Austrian regiments, then in garrison at Antwerp. I asked Father Bernard if he would make us acquainted; which he consented to do. But, a day or two afterwards, he told me that, on hearing my name, Mr. Gisborne had declined responding to any advances on my part, saying he had adjured his country, and hated his countrymen.

Probably he recollected my name in connection with that of his daughter Lucy. Anyhow, it was clear enough that I had no chance of making his acquaintance. Father Bernard confirmed me in my suspicions of the hidden fermentation, for some coming evil, working among the "blouses" of Antwerp, and he would fain have had me depart from out the city; but I rather craved the excitement of danger, and stubbornly refused to leave.

One day, when I was walking with him in the Place Verte, he bowed to an Austrian officer, who was crossing towards the cathedral.

"That is Mr. Gisborne," said he, as soon as the gentleman was past.

I turned to look at the tall, slight figure of the officer. He carried himself in a stately manner, although he was past middle age, and from his years might have had some excuse for a slight stoop. As I looked at the man, he turned round, his eyes met mine, and I saw his face. Deeply lined, sallow, and scathed was that countenance; scarred by passion as well as by the fortunes of war. 'Twas but a moment our eyes met. We each turned round, and went on our separate way.

But his whole appearance was not one to be easily forgotten; the thorough appointment of the dress, and evident thought bestowed on it, made but an incongruous whole with the dark, gloomy expression of his countenance. Because he was Lucy's father, I sought instinctively to meet him everywhere. At last he must have become aware of my pertinacity, for he gave me a haughty scowl whenever I passed him. In one of these encounters, however, I chanced to be of some service to him. He was turning the corner of a street, and came suddenly on one of the groups of discontented Flemings of whom I have spoken. Some words were exchanged, when my gentleman out with his sword, and with a slight but skilful cut drew blood from one of those who had insulted him, as he fancied, though I was too far off to hear the words. They would all have fallen upon him had I not rushed forwards and raised the cry, then well known in Antwerp, of rally, to the Austrian soldiers who were perpetually patrolling the streets, and who came in numbers to the rescue. I think that neither Mr. Gisborne nor the mutinous group of plebeians owed me much gratitude for my interference. He had planted himself against a wall, in a skilful attitude of fence, ready with his bright glancing rapier to do battle with all the heavy, fierce, unarmed men, some six or seven in number. But when his own soldiers came up, he sheathed his sword; and, giving some careless word of command, sent them away again, and continued his saunter all alone down the street, the workmen snarling in his rear, and more than half-inclined to fall on me for my cry for rescue. I cared not if they did, my life seemed so dreary a burden just then; and, perhaps, it was this daring loitering among them that prevented their attacking me. Instead, they suffered me to fall into conversation with them; and I heard some of their grievances. Sore and heavy to be borne were they, and no wonder the sufferers were savage and desperate.

The man whom Gisborne had wounded across his face would fain have got out of me the name of his aggressor, but I refused to tell it. Another of the group heard his inquiry, and made answer – "I know the man. He is one Gisborne, aide-de-camp to the General-Commandant. I know him well."

He began to tell some story in connection with Gisborne in a low and muttering voice; and while he was relating a tale, which I saw excited their evil blood, and which they evidently wished me not to hear, I sauntered away and back to my lodgings.

That night Antwerp was in open revolt. The inhabitants rose in rebellion against their Austrian masters. The Austrians, holding the gates of the city, remained at first pretty quiet in the citadel; only, from time to time, the boom of the great cannon swept sullenly over the town. But if they expected the disturbance to die away, and spend itself in a few hours' fury, they were mistaken. In a day or two, the rioters held possession of the principal municipal buildings. Then the Austrians poured forth in bright flaming array, calm and smiling, as they marched to the posts assigned, as if the fierce mob were no more to them then the swarms of buzzing summer flies. Their practised manœuvres, their well-aimed shot, told with terrible effect; but in the place of one slain rioter, three sprang up of his blood to avenge his loss. But a deadly foe, a ghastly ally of the Austrians, was at work. Food, scarce and dear for months, was now hardly to be obtained at any price. Desperate efforts were being made to bring provisions into the city, for the rioters had friends without. Close to the city port, nearest to the Scheldt, a great struggle took place. I was there, helping the rioters, whose cause I had adopted. We had a savage encounter with the Austrians. Numbers fell on both sides: I saw them lie bleeding for a moment: then a volley of smoke obscured them; and when it cleared away, they were dead – trampled upon or smothered, pressed down and hidden by the freshly-wounded whom those last guns had brought low. And then a gray-robed and grey-veiled figure came right across the flashing guns and stooped over some one, whose life-blood was ebbing away; sometimes it was to give him drink from cans which they carried slung at their sides; sometimes I saw the cross held above a dying man, and rapid prayers were being uttered, unheard by men in that hellish din and clangour, but listened to by One above. I saw all this as in a dream: the reality of that stern time was battle and carnage. But I knew that these gray figures, their bare feet all wet with blood, and their faces hidden by their veils, were the Poor Clares – sent forth now because dire agony was abroad and imminent danger at hand. Therefore, they left their cloistered shelter, and came into that thick and evil mêlée.

Close to me – driven past me by the struggle of many fighters – came the Antwerp burgess with the scarce-healed scar upon his face; and in an instant more, he was thrown by the press upon the Austrian officer Gisborne, and ere either had recovered the shock, the burgess had recognized his opponent.

"Ha! the Englishman Gisborne!" he cried, and threw himself upon him with redoubled fury. He had struck him hard – the Englishman was down; when out of the smoke came a dark-gray figure, and threw herself right under the uplifted flashing sword. The burgess's arm stood arrested. Neither Austrians nor Anversois willingly harmed the Poor Clares.

"Leave him to me!" said a low stern voice. "He is mine enemy – mine for many years."

Those words were the last I heard. I myself was struck down by a bullet. I remember nothing more for days. When I came to myself, I was at the extremity of weakness, and was craving for food to recruit my strength. My landlord sat watching me. He, too, looked pinched and shrunken;

he had heard of my wounded state, and sought me out. Yes! the struggle still continued, but the famine was sore: and some, he had heard, had died for lack of food. The tears stood in his eyes as he spoke. But soon he shook off his weakness, and his natural cheerfulness returned. Father Bernard had been to see me – no one else. (Who should, indeed?) Father Bernard would come back that afternoon – he had promised. But Father Bernard never came, although I was up and dressed, and looking eagerly for him.

My landlord brought me a meal which he had cooked himself: of what it was composed he would not say, but it was most excellent, and with every mouthful I seemed to gain strength. The good man sat looking at my evident enjoyment with a happy smile of sympathy; but, as my appetite became satisfied, I began to detect a certain wistfulness in his eyes, as if craving for the food I had so nearly devoured – for, indeed, at that time I was hardly aware of the extent of the famine. Suddenly, there was a sound of many rushing feet past our window. My landlord opened one of the sides of it, the better to learn what was going on. Then we heard a faint, cracked, tinkling bell, coming shrill upon the air, clear and distinct from all other sounds. "Holy Mother!" exclaimed my landlord, "the Poor Clares!"

He snatched up the fragments of my meal, and crammed them into my hands, bidding me follow. Down stairs he ran, clutching at more food, as the women of his house eagerly held it out to him; and in a moment we were in the street, moving along with the great current, all tending towards the Convent of the Poor Clares. And still, as if piercing our ears with its inarticulate cry, came the shrill tinkle of the bell. In that strange crowd were old men trembling and sobbing, as they carried their little pittance of food; women with tears running down their cheeks, who had snatched up what provisions they had in the vessels in which they stood, so that the burden of these was in many cases much greater than that which they contained; children, with flushed faces, grasping tight the morsel of bitten cake or bread, in their eagerness to carry it safe to the help of the Poor Clares; strong men – yea, both Anversois and Austrians – pressing onward with set teeth, and no word spoken; and over all, and through all, came that sharp tinkle – that cry for help in extremity.

We met the first torrent of people returning with blanched and piteous faces: they were issuing out of the convent to make way for the offerings of others. "Haste, haste!" said they. "A Poor Clare is dying! A Poor Clare is dead for hunger! God forgive us and our city!"

We pressed on. The stream bore us along where it would. We were carried through refectories, bare and crumbless; into cells over whose doors the conventual name of the occupant was written. Thus it was that I, with others, was forced into Sister Magdalen's cell. On her couch lay Gisborne, pale unto death, but not dead. By his side was a cup of water, and a small morsel of mouldy bread, which he had pushed out of his reach, and could not move to obtain. Over against his bed were these words, copied in the English version "Therefore, if thine enemy hunger, feed him; if he thirst, give him drink."

Some of us gave him of our food, and left him eating greedily, like some famished wild animal. For now it was no longer the sharp tinkle, but that one solemn toll, which in all Christian countries tells of the passing of the spirit out of earthly life into eternity; and again a murmur gathered and grew, as of many people speaking with awed breath, "A Poor Clare is dying! a Poor Clare is dead!"

Borne along once more by the motion of the crowd, we were carried into the chapel belonging to the Poor Clares. On a bier before the high altar, lay a woman – lay Sister Magdalen – lay Bridget Fitzgerald. By her side stood Father Bernard, in his robes of office, and holding the crucifix on high while he pronounced the solemn absolution of the Church, as to one who had newly confessed herself of deadly sin. I pushed on with passionate force, till I stood close to the dying woman, as she received extreme unction amid the breathless and awed hush of the multitude around. Her eyes were glazing, her limbs were stiffening; but when the rite was over and finished, she raised her gaunt figure slowly up, and her eyes brightened to a strange intensity of joy, as, with the gesture of her finger and the trance-like gleam of her eye, she seemed like one who watched the disappearance of some loathed and fearful creature.

"She is freed from the curse!" said she, as she fell back dead.

The Devil of Avalon

Bruce Golden

HIS INTEREST IN the New World was more than just financial. As of yet, his investment in the Virginia Company's Jamestown colony had not yielded a penny of profit, unlike his more lucrative investment in the East India Company. But this unexplored continent to the west was full of promise and mystery, and that intrigued Calvert more than coin – though he was certain, in time, there was plenty to be gained monetarily.

As part of his duties as secretary of state, he'd read all the reports sent to the king from John Guy, governor of the first English settlement of what they called "Newfoundland" – a very unimaginative name he thought. There were hardships, as there were with any new colony, but Calvert never let that deter him. He was more interested in long-term potential.

He'd invited William Vaughan to Whitehall, having heard he was looking to sell his investment in this new land. He knew Vaughan from his days at Oxford, where they were fellow students. Vaughan had been a year ahead of him, and a chance meeting had led to the Welshman shepherding Calvert around the school his first few weeks.

Vaughan had been very scholarly, but a bit of a dreamer whose dreams were not always practical. He often complained bitterly about the poverty in his homeland, and Calvert got the sense from his writings that he felt it was his duty to, one day, do something about it. Being from Wales was not something most students bragged about. But, despite the penury of his countrymen, Vaughan had always been a proud Welshman, and Calvert admired him for it. He'd even named his colony in Newfoundland "New Cambriol," from the ancient name for Wales. From what he knew of the man, Calvert speculated Vaughan saw himself as the Welsh Moses, who would lead his people from poverty and oppression to the promised land of the New World.

Vaughan had always had a literary bent as well – a good writer who'd helped Calvert with his papers. Two decades earlier, not long after he'd left Oxford, he'd published a book that Calvert had made a point to read. *The Golden Grove* was a general guide to the morals, politics and literature of the time, being highly critical of each. It praised poetry, but denounced current plays, even those of master Shakespeare, as folly and wickedness.

Despite his success as a scholar, a lawyer, a writer and investor, Vaughan had known much tragedy. In tracking the man down, Calvert had learned Vaughan's son had died as a toddler, and soon after that his wife was struck and killed by a bolt of lightning. Yet he'd persevered. That's the way Calvert remembered him from their days at Oxford. As a fellow who always persevered, no matter the obstacles.

That's why he wondered what had influenced the man to part with his interests in the New World. Calvert was as curious as he was anxious to purchase a piece of Newfoundland for himself.

"Your lordship, William Vaughan Esquire awaits an audience," announced Calvert's secretary.

"Show him in, show him in."

The William Vaughan who walked apprehensively into his office was not the one he remembered from Oxford. He was not only decades older, he'd grown paper-thin, his clothes rumpled and threadbare for a man of his station. A doleful look clouded his eyes, and his posture spoke of apathy, as if there were no fight left in him. The tenacious Welshman Calvert had known was gone.

"Thou summoned me, your lordship?"

"Come, come, my good man. Call me George as thee used to. None of this lordship nonsense," said Calvert, coming forward to grasp Vaughan's hand. "And I did not 'summon' thee. I requested thy presence on a matter of business."

"What business could I have with the king's secretary of state?" asked Vaughan, concern coloring his voice.

"Come – sit down and we will discuss it. Would thee like a glass of sherry?"

"I beg pardon?"

"I say sherry – would thee like a glass of sherry?"

"My apologies. I hear not as well as I used to. Yes, yes, sherry would be nice."

Calvert wondered why his old acquaintance seemed so ill at ease. Possibly he'd had problems with government officials in the past. Or he was simply suspicious of the motives behind this belated reunion. Calvert intended to promptly alleviate any misconceptions he might have.

He handed the sherry to Vaughan.

"I'll get right to it. I understand thou art looking to sell thy interests in Newfoundland. Is that true?"

"'Tis true, though, to be honest, I cannot, in good conscience, recommend it as a promising investment."

"Not a very strong stance for a negotiation, my friend," said Calvert. "Why would thee say such?"

Vaughan cleared his throat and took a sip of the sherry. "Because we are old friends and I want to be honest with thee."

"I appreciate that, William. But, pray tell, why would thee discourage such an investment? I believe the New World to be full of auspicious opportunities."

"I believed the same… until I actually visited my colony of New Cambriol."

"Oh? I was not aware thee had actually set foot there."

"Yes, I have been there… much to my regret," replied Vaughan. His eyes darkened as if haunted by the memory. "That is why I speak naught of it, and few know of my journey… my ordeal."

"I know establishing a new settlement can be fraught with hazards, but surely it could not have been all that bad."

Vaughan let out a laugh that was part cackle, part cough. "I thought the same thing when I got the initial reports from Captain Richard Whitbourne, whom I sent there to take charge after the first settlers reported problems. Then, ere I left for the colony myself, I went to visit John Guy, whom the London and Bristol Company had lead their first attempts at colonization."

"Yes, I know of him."

"Well, his wife would not let me in to see him, because he had taken ill. But as I was leaving she ventured out her door, and in a curious whisper told me that for many years after his return to England, Guy would wake up screaming in the middle of the night. And each time she would have to convince him he was no longer in Newfoundland.

"Of course I dismissed her words as the prattling of an old woman, but now I know different. I know what incites the nightmares of John Guy. I experience them myself, from time to time."

Calvert was more intrigued than ever to learn what had happened to the man. He didn't remember his old school chum being so dramatic, but time had a way of changing people.

"Come, come. Enough preamble. Tell me why I should not invest in Newfoundland."

"Well, first, there are the pirate raids. Spanish pirates, French pirates, even deserters from Sir Walter Raleigh's Guiana fleet. Mongrels all, they harry our coasts, steal our livestock, raid our fishing vessels."

"I am aware of these brigands and have spoken to King James about dealing with them," said Calvert.

"The weather is also a major problem. The winters are longer and more harsh than thee can believe. What crops will grow in the rocky soil are stunted by the late spring and short summer. Fishing is the only industry which could thrive there, but..."

Vaughan shrugged and took another sip of his sherry.

"Tell me about the natives," said Calvert, encouraging him to continue. "What about these 'red Indians' I have heard of? Is it true their skin is the color of blood?"

Vaughan hesitated, then shook his head. "No, but it might as well be."

Calvert wondered what he meant by that remark.

"'Tis not their skin which is red," continued Vaughan, "but a combination of a powdered red ochre mixed with fish oil or animal grease they cover themselves with. I believe the coloring began as an insect repellant, but among the Beothuk the red color hath become sacred, with much cultural significance. They paint their canoes with it, their weapons, even their newborn children as a way of welcoming them to the tribe."

"How are relations with these Beothuk?"

"Not cordial. The language barrier is a problem. There have been attacks... thefts."

"Jamestown hath dealt with similar issues," said Calvert. "But they have been able to establish friendly relations with their natives, and even trade."

"In the beginning there was a bit of trade, but relations soured when one of the settlers occupied himself with a native girl. Whether 'twas consensual or forced mattered not to the Beothuk. They attacked the settlement. They were rebuffed, but after that incident relations were all but severed."

Calvert stood and paced behind his desk. Vaughan took another drink and Calvert refilled his glass.

"I understand why thee would warn me, and I appreciate thy candor, William. But all that thou hath relayed to me is simply the cost of doing business. The normal hazards of exploration and colonization. I see no reason why thee and I should not be able to agree upon a fair price, and—"

"There's something else," said Vaughan, then looked as if he regretted his words.

"Well, what is it, man?"

"Thou will not believe me. Thou will think I am mad." He laughed. "Indeed I would be mad if I expected thy belief. At first I rejected the evidence of my own senses. Then I doubted my sanity, as thee will. I even considered that I had been dreaming. But I was awake, my senses were sharp, and I am as sane as the next man, if now more wary."

"Tell me," said Calvert, intrigued more than ever. "I'll believe thee."

Vaughan hesitated, took another sip of sherry, and began his tale.

"'Twas my third night in New Cambriol. I was staying in the settlement I had named Vaughan's Cove. 'Twas only late autumn, but the weather had already turned bitterly cold. The wind upon that hill was like shards of ice cutting into our skin, and the stone structures in which we slept were as dank as tombs.

"We were settling for the night when we heard a scream so awful from outside it sent even greater chills through us. We looked at each other, then heard another, more muddled shriek.

The men grabbed their muskets, I clutched a torch, and we rushed outside in search of the poor soul whose cry we had heard. We did not have to go far.

"One of the men, who had likely gone outside to relieve himself, lay across a hillock, his torso in bloody shreds. At first I could not see it, but I sensed the darkness around him was alive. Then the torchlight struck it and we all caught a glimmer of what would beset our nightmares from then on.

"Crouched over the fellow, who was surely dead, was this… this thing. Vaguely human in shape, emaciated but larger than any man I had ever seen. I watched as it tore the flesh from its victim and devoured it.

"Transfixed by the sight, each of us stood as frozen as the ground beneath our feet. Until it turned and saw us. With an ear-shattering roar it stood, growing larger as it did. It must have been at least ten feet tall, with enormous fangs. Mangy strands of silver-gray hair sprouted here and there from its body, but the rest of its skin was lathered with ice crystals."

Vaughan paused, glancing at his host.

"I see the look on thy face, George. I recognize the expression of disbelief. But I swear to thee we all witnessed this monster."

Incredulous though he might have been, Calvert was entranced by the tale.

"Go on. What happened next?"

"The men opened fire with their muskets. Having been struck by at least a half dozen balls, the thing fell to the earth. The men began to reload, but ere they could, this demon from hell stood as if fully resurrected and gave voice to a wail so potent we fell to our knees, covering our ears. Even dulled by our hands, the sound created such pain as thee cannot imagine.

"Though we were at its mercy, it did not attack. Instead it scooped up the remains of its victim and vanished into the night. Reloaded, we gave pursuit, but found no sign of the creature. We climbed a ridge and came upon a large pond where a group of Beothuk had gathered. By their fearful expressions, I knew they had seen the demon as well. Using hand signs we tried to ask them about the creature, but their replies were beyond our grasp. They were so agitated I knew not whether they were warning us about the monster, or threatening us with its return. The one word they kept repeating was Chenoo – Chenoo. I gathered that was what they called the thing.

"We returned to our shelter, shaken from the experience as thee might guess. Most of the men, including myself, were still plagued by a ringing in our ears. We posted guards, but I doubt anyone slept very well that night. The next day I went directly to see Oubee, the Beothuk girl who had been staying with the settlers. After her assignation with one of the men, she had become an outcast from her tribe. She had learned a few words of English, so I was able to question her to some degree. She told me that, indeed, the monster was called Chenoo. Her people believed it had once been a human being – someone who had committed a terrible act and become possessed by evil spirits. Its heart had turned to ice, and 'twas cursed to forever roam the land as the behemoth we had seen. What she could not tell me, was why it had appeared now, at this time. She did not say the words, but I think she believed 'twas because of my own arrival in New Cambriol."

Calvert's first thought, as Vaughan paused his story to take another drink, was his memory of how good a writer his old friend always was. A yarn such as this was certainly within his capacity. And yet the way he told it was so authentic. Calvert heard the dread in his voice, the trepidation with which he relayed it.

"The next night it came again. This time neither musket nor arquebus slowed it. It howled until our ears felt as if they would burst. Men scattered to reload despite their weapons' ineffectiveness. Then, for some reason, the Chenoo focused on me. I saw the malevolent hunger in its eyes, but was immobile with fear. It came at me. In that moment I resigned myself to a gruesome death.

"From my left, someone doused the monster with whale oil. A torch was tossed and flames erupted from its back. The Chenoo screeched as though 'twas dying. It was not. It turned hence from me and fled into the night. Yet on its way it seized another man who tried to brain it with his musket.

"We never found the fellow, nor any remnants of his existence."

Vaughan looked at Calvert, gauging his reaction. The king's secretary was both terrified and enthralled. He spoke not, only waited for Vaughan to continue.

"It took not long afterwards for me to realize 'twas the end of New Cambriol. Even if the ice creature had burned to ash – and many amongst us doubted it – I knew no one who had seen it would ever rest easy anywhere in Newfoundland. If I had not declared we were returning to England, I am certain Captain Whitbourne and his men would have marooned me there.

"We spent the next day making preparations to leave. As night began to fall, I sensed the fear amongst us growing. 'Twas a tangible thing, oppressive in its weight. Come dark we gathered inside the largest shelter, barricading the door as well we might. 'Twas for naught. The Chenoo came once more.

"It pounded and clawed at the door, soon ripping it from its posts, sending stones from the wall flying like round shot. There was not a burn mark upon it. If indeed it had ever burned, it had healed all but its anger, for it came with a vengeance. Ignoring the musket shots which must have stung it, it waded through us like a scythe through wheat. Men were flung like dolls. Those who could escape through the portal that had been the door ran for their lives. Others tried to hide or play dead. The Chenoo roared and I fell to the ground in pain, covering my ears. When I looked up I saw the monster had grabbed hold of Oubee. She screamed but I heard it not. I had gone deaf."

Vaughan paused, looked down at the floor, then up into the eyes of his old friend. "I swear to thee, George, if thee doth not already think me mad, what happened next was even more preposterous than the monster itself. Whether 'twas the Chenoo's abduction of the girl Oubee or God's own hand I cannot say. But there appeared before the Chenoo, blocking its path, a scarlet specter. I say specter because this apparition, this ghost, though it seemed substantial in every way, drifted more than walked as it moved. It revealed itself, in every aspect of its features, to be a native of the land. Its face, its costume, its hair, even its red coloring rendered it one of the Beothuk tribe. Yet the red tint was not simply ochre grease spread along its skin. The crimson hue was complete, coloring everything from its bare feet to its clothing to its eyes. I knew immediately 'twas no mortal man.

"When it blocked the Chenoo's way, the monster tossed aside its captive. The girl fell, stunned but alive. She stared up in horror as the new player on this otherworldly stage grappled with the much larger Chenoo. Their strength seemed evenly matched until the red man, in the blink of an eye, swung round, attached itself to the monster's back, wrapping its forearm under the Chenoo's neck. The ice creature's wail was cut short as the apparition jerked its head, apparently breaking its neck. The Chenoo fell to ground. Its slayer floated back to the earth.

"I stood there, as thee might imagine, unable to reconcile what I had seen, let alone speak. The apparition looked at me, and the gaze was not a welcoming one. Then it vanished. Dissipated like red smoke in the wind.

"We left the next day. Oubee came with us, though she was silent for days. When the terror lifted from her soul I was finally able to question her about the scarlet ghost. She told me he was Kluskap, the legendary hero of her people, sworn to protect them, even in death.

"I doubt not 'twas Oubee this Kluskap was protecting – not I nor my men. Just as I am certain the Chenoo would have returned, despite its apparent demise, had we not departed New Cambriol in all haste."

Vaughan paused, took a breath that was part sigh, sipped his sherry and set down his glass. He stood to leave.

"So thee can see, my old friend, why neither thee nor anyone should want to purchase New Cambriol from me. Thou hath already done well for thyself. Thou hath been knighted, made secretary of state to the king, and 'tis said thou art one of the most powerful men in England. Is that not enough? If thou must, seek fortune and adventure at Jamestown, for I have heard of no monsters there."

It was a harrowing tale, and Calvert had no doubt Vaughan believed every word of it. The dispirited gloom in his eyes was no literary fabrication. The horror which had touched his soul was no lie.

Nonetheless, the essence of it had to be a figment of the man's imagination – a dark figment to be sure. Whether it was the death of his child, or that of his wife, or something even more grievous that had befallen him, Calvert knew not. But he knew the man's psyche had been damaged by something. He also knew Vaughan's finances were in dire straits. He needed to sell at least a portion of his Newfoundland investment in order to return to Wales with some modicum of stability.

"Old friend, I understand and appreciate thy reluctance to sell me thy interests in Newfoundland, but I am determined to gain a foothold in the New World, Chenoo or Kluskap be damned. Now I need not acquire thy entire holdings, but surely we can come to some arrangement regarding a portion of it."

Vaughan did not reply. He simply shook his head slowly side to side as if he'd done all he could. Then he sat back down, waiting for Sir Calvert to begin the negotiations.

Historical Epilogue

In that year, 1621, Sir George Calvert did purchase a portion of William Vaughan's interests in Newfoundland, and gave the peninsula its current name – Avalon. Yet his two attempts to colonize Newfoundland also failed, due to what he described as "a winter which lasts from October to May," as well as pirates, a war with France, and his policy of religious tolerance for all colonists – which did not sit well with the protestant majority. Eventually giving up on Newfoundland, Calvert did as Vaughan suggested in this tale, turning his attention to Jamestown, and later to colonizing the territory that would become known as Maryland.

Word of the Beothuk tribe's use of red ochre to color their bodies spread to Europe, where they began to call all Native Americans "Red Indians," a designation which would last for centuries.

There is no official record of a Kluskap or Chenoo. They are folk legends of the native peoples of Newfoundland. However, there is a ridge with a pond near Vaughan's failed colony which still carries the name today of Hell Hill.

In Bleak December

Caye Gowyn

WINTER COMES HARD in Ohio. Thanksgiving slipped past almost unnoticed at the farm but not in the rest of the country. It was 1945. The war had ended. Soon our boys, the ones who had survived the long fight, would be coming home. My fiancé Albert was in that number. He'd written a few weeks back that he was returning to me earlier than I'd dared hope, he should be here before Christmas. Maybe that would bring some cheer, some warmth, to our home. Albert was what we needed, who I was waiting for. He was my reason for holding on. Him, and my little sister, Opal. They were the only two people who meant anything to me anymore.

Mama died when I was twelve and Opal was eight, leaving us and Daddy to carry on the best we could. Then, just after harvest, he got the flu, then the pneumonia, then I was washing his body and we were laying him in a grave. Then there were two, just us girls. Two girls and Albert's letters, the ones that made him seem so close it pushed out the lonely of quiet, empty rooms. Opal had all but stopped talking, taking the losses as hard as the ground outside, her eyes as empty as our winter resting fields. She used to be a summer child, bright, chatty, but she was barely eighteen and she was finding the wide world full of war and loss a difficult way to come into her womanhood. In so many ways she was still a child but now she was a winter child and it broke my heart.

"I'm still here for you," I reassured her when she stared into the fire late at night. She never answered, never gave any acknowledgement she heard me at all. Sometimes she would pace, walking lightly across our wooden floors, her steps making almost no noise. She never cried, she rarely spoke, and when she did it was to herself and not to me. Sometimes it seemed the way the windows would fog when she stood staring out of them was the only indication she was even there. For a time, Albert's letters remained a bright spot but they'd stopped coming. He'd warned me to expect that, it just meant he was traveling on his way back to the States, crossing that big ocean, but it left a gap, adding more silence.

Opal didn't falter in her duties though. Every morning she got up with the sun, stepping out into the cold pale light of just after dawn to go out to the barn to milk our two cows, named Milk and Butter. That was who she used to be, a girl who cheekily named our pigs Bacon, Ham, and Chops, who cried when we had to kill a chicken for dinner, who stood outside in the wind to watch the crows dance across the sky in the late evenings. She still watched the crows, standing still as stone as they filled the sky with their black wings and the air with their relentless caws, but she no longer shed tears over dead chickens and she no longer chitchatted to the cows as she sat on the milking stool. I worried but it was all I could do to hold on. Fixing Opal's mind was beyond my capabilities.

The trees were bare, everything green had already died away and was sleeping until spring. A cold white sky hovered over our weather-beaten little farm in the center of all that empty. It was so hard not to let myself fade into the grayness of the landscape, but Opal seemed to crave the open air. She would slip on her rather threadbare jacket late each evening, put on Daddy's heavy coat over it, even though it nearly dragged the ground on her small frame. She wrapped a scarf around her head and across her nose the way I taught her when we were little, because nothing stings the lungs like air filled with ice, and she'd walk for an hour or more all alone, never minding the bitter wind or the vacant landscape that greeted her. I stayed indoors while she faced her own solitude in the deepening dusk. I wanted as little part of outdoors as I could manage. I wanted to escape the barren trees, the icicles that sparkled lifelessly from the eaves, the desolate look of our wintering fields. Especially the fields. Those fields lay heavy on my mind. We were lucky Daddy waited 'til after harvest to get the sickness but he was gone and we couldn't do all he did to keep this place running. There was money for the winter but what about afterwards? That's where I pinned all my longing hopes on Albert, whether that was fair or not. If only he'd decide to take on the farm, but I fretted he might come back from Europe with all kinds of newfangled ideas. What if he wanted to try living in a city and turn his back on everything we'd ever known? The farm that had been in my family for generations would be lost. I couldn't abide that. He'd have to stay. It was on him now to make the wrongs right, if for no other reason than for Opal. She simply couldn't bear up under another grief.

* * *

She was gentle, my sweet summer sister. The unyielding life on a Midwestern farm during what the newspapers called The Great Depression didn't seem to touch her, didn't stop her from cooing and giggling almost from birth. My mother suffered through several stillbirths and miscarriages to be able to bring Opal and myself into the world and our family was made up of us four. Then we lost Mama. Daddy damn near went crazy and it was up to me to look after my baby sister, and when he came close to losing the farm he got his mind right and things got marginally better. Then came the war and while it was terrible it was also exciting. Especially for a girl stuck out in the sticks. I was old enough to go into town and attend the USO dances, meet the young men going off to fight, have a fine time away from planting and cows and endless chores. Opal was too small and Daddy was too protective so she had to stay home, which to be honest didn't bother me a bit. Those nights were mine, my time, my adventures, my opportunities to get all decked out in my best dress and have a gas. Finally though Daddy relented and gave in to her pleas. He let her go to one of the dances with me despite her only being just barely fifteen and that was the night Albert Miller walked into our lives.

It was Opal who saw him first but seeing as how she was a kid and I was near his age it was me he took to. Me and him cut a rug 'til they shooed us all out of the hall, telling us to go home. He was a dreamboat with dark hair and brown eyes, a line of freckles across his cheeks and nose that made him look full of wholesome mischief. The kinda mischief that make daddies laugh and shake their heads, not the kind that make them reach for their shotguns.

"I'll write you Sarah," he promised with breath that smelled of Coca-Cola and a borrowed cigarette. I pressed a scrap of paper with my address into his hand and never again looked at another fellow. It didn't take but a few weeks of writing and we were in love, making promises and saying all those sweet words that were all the more urgent when there's a war on. At first I'd read his letters to Opal but I started to suspect she was falling in love with him too, so I started keeping them to myself. Then Daddy died. Afterwards I often found my unmentionables drawer open where I kept the stack of letters hid. I knew she was reading them but I couldn't be troubled over it. I was willing to share his words. Lord knows she needed the comfort.

* * *

She was out again, walking across the fields, wearing a pair of Daddy's old trousers cinched up around her too-small waist so her legs wouldn't freeze. She looked like a specter, a waif come to haunt our farm, not that she'd be good at haunting seeing as how she's always so silent. I caught her staring at the one picture we have of us as a family of four, the one that's propped on the mantel. That night she stood so close to the fire, as if she couldn't get warm, as if the cold of the room was pushing the heat back into the fireplace instead of letting it radiate into the house. As she studied the photograph, I asked her what she was thinking and for a long minute she didn't answer. Finally, she said, "What's dead is dead," then walked from the room, turning in for the night. The sound of her voice was like a gash through the quiet. All I'd heard for hours was snow against the windows and howling wind. Her feather-light voice gave me chills and I almost wished she hadn't spoken at all.

* * *

A fresh layer of snow lay glittering as far as I could see the day Albert returned. I was outdoors by the clothesline trying to feel the sun but no warmth was able to break through the bitter air. The sky was a cloudless cobalt blue over a world too bright and too dark all at the same time. I squinted trying to make out the figure coming up the rutted drive to our place. I wondered who was walking and why at first, then realized the mud and recent storms had made the path unpassable for cars or even trucks. Then suddenly I knew I was seeing Albert. With a glance back at the house where Opal had disappeared indoors, I ran. I ran as fast as I could to him, to the man I loved and who had come back to me. I let myself have that joy, the first joy in so long. I determined to let happiness be mine at least for a little while.

I barely reached him before he had me in his arms, crushing me against his chest, his breath hot against my neck.

"I missed you so much," I said even though it was absurd, we'd only spent one evening in person together.

"You're so cold," he said, trying to warm my hands between his own. He was as handsome as I remembered and he told me I was beautiful, words tumbling out of him like music. My ears could hardly hold the sound of his voice after Opal's long weeks of near silence. It was a balm and yet underneath was pain. His eyes veered towards the house and its warmth but that's where Opal was, and I wasn't ready to share him yet. Not when I had so much to say.

"Walk with me," I urged him and though I saw the disappointment in the back of his eyes of having to stay out longer in the cold, he agreed.

He let me lead him, my arm through his, as he talked about coming home and seeing his mother, how he'd taken the first train here, about the plans he had for our wedding, a home, future children. I knew I should talk to him about the farm, about Opal, but the words were dry as husks in my mouth so first I just listened, enjoying the feel of him next to me and the sound of his voice. Nothing he was saying was going to matter, it was a future that couldn't be mine, and when he paused I pulled my arm free and turned to face him. It was time. This is what I had been waiting for.

"It sounds lovely, and impossible Albert," I said, my heart straining with all the tears I wanted to cry but couldn't. "But I'm hoping, I have been hoping, that your life can be here, at the farm. With my sister."

"With you and your sister, you mean? At least until she finds her own fellow, or maybe if we do well we'll send her to college, girls are going now, it's not that unusual."

"No Albert. I need you to stay here and I need you to marry Opal."

"Marry Opal...? Have you gone crazy?" Surprise and hurt filled his eyes and my chest was so tight, like it had been that night when it was so hard to breathe. "Or, or did something happen?" he asked, shades of anger creeping in. "Is there someone else, Sarah, did you promise yourself to some other fellow and not tell me?"

"There's no one else," I assured him, longing to reach out to enjoy his warmth one last time. "I loved you until the day I died." I nodded my head towards the homemade wooden marker next to my father's grave. My mother and her two stillborn babies were on the other side. There was my name, Sarah Violet Sutton. Opal had painted the words, taking great care to make them uniform and straight. Her hands had been chapped raw, an angry wind ending autumn early and ushering in the unrelenting winter.

She had written Albert telling him of my passing, choosing as gentle words as she was able, pausing to collect herself every sentence or two. Yet every evening, on her long walks to our mailbox up on the main road, the letter tucked into Daddy's coat pocket, she was never able to make herself post it. I don't know why, I only had guesses, but whatever her reasoning it worked in my favor. He was none the wiser so he came to the farm just as we'd planned when the war first ended, giving me my chance to make my plea. I could not go to him so Opal, without realizing what she was doing, had made sure he would still come to me.

I saw the confusion on his face but I had no words for him to make the world make sense. It was plain that he wanted to think it was some kind of cruel prank. That it was mischief. And perhaps it was but not the laughing kind, it was the bad kind of mischief, the kind where the worst of everything wins. But I had done what I set out to do and now it was time for me to fade. I let myself go just a little, just enough for him to see. It had been so hard to hold on, to wait for him to come back, but how could I leave my baby sister all alone? I was so tired, so very tired. I wanted rest but I had to see this through first. Please, I thought, I begged, please take care of my sister and her farm.

"She loves you," I said and my voice was a gust of wind through bare branches, "and I can't rest knowing she's all alone. I waited for you."

His tears fell, crossing his line of freckles, and I knew if I touched them they would turn to ice. He wasn't mine. Not anymore. Grief and shock covered his face like a mask and then, with the eyes of a man who has seen so much death already, a grim acceptance. I couldn't hold my form any longer and the last thing I remember was his squared shoulders walking away from me, up the hill, towards the house, to Opal.

The Smoke Market

John Linwood Grant

Morocco, 1977

I CONSIDER MYSELF, in fanciful moments, to be akin to a fine wine, or even a vintage port. That is to say, I improve with age, but I do not travel well, and if I must be moved far, I need time to settle and recover.

That latter point was much on my mind after a long train journey from Casablanca. The carriages were awash with Moroccan soldiers in transit; there was war in the Western Sahara, now that the Spanish were gone, and we civilians crouched out of the way as rifle butts jabbed – by accident, I hoped – into innocent ribcages. Already feeling harassed when I stepped outside the railway station, I descended like Lucifer into more chaos and heat, a Pandemonium of croaking beggars – 'Baksheesh! Baksheesh!' – steaming taxi radiators, and tourist guides… endless guides to the reputedly endless pleasures that awaited any foreign visitor.

Fortunately, I had been here before.

"Je ne suis pas américain!" I yelled, and the herd thinned, for the dollar was a sacred animal in these parts. Of the remaining candidates, I picked out a rather plain Arab boy in djellaba and scuffed baseball boots, a teenager scratching at pockmarks on his face. He appeared charmless and practical, which was all I required.

"Tu parles anglais?" I asked.

"Bialtabe," he replied in Arabic, then kicked his own ankle in annoyance. "Of course. I am Salim."

"Excellent. I am Margrave." I drew out a wad of dirham and handed him what would be two week's pay for the typical guide. He took the notes, squinting at them.

"This is much money, father of generosity," he said.

I noticed his suddenly averted gaze, and I knew what he suspected, for there were many types of white men who visited countries like Morocco.

"Jeune, I am an old man, with a small bed."

Reassured, he asked where I needed to go, instead of launching into a torrent of advice on the bargains which his myriad 'uncles and cousins' had to offer. And there was no mention of what his 'sister' might do for me.

I decided that Salim would do.

* * *

I was in Marrakesh to assess a range of local sculpture and ceramics on behalf of my wealthy friend David Causton. David's interest was in importing unusual pieces to give inspiration to artists in the various studios he ran. To bring vitality to tired European styles. Put that way, it sounded close to intellectual theft – which is common enough in the art world, of course. Personally, I preferred the idea of finding Moroccan-born artists who would consent to doing a guest circuit in England, but

I would have to sell that little scheme to David after the fact.

The city was awash with history, with a scent, a feeling, a mood. Here you were open to both Arabic and Berber influences, intertwined with French and Spanish colonial history. And the Berbers, who I should properly call the Imazighen – for the B-word was imposed upon them – were here first, long before the Arabs.

Salim knew his city. He found the less-frequented galleries, the right people at local museums and innocuous-looking carpet stalls which were only fronts for more expensive goods; he calmed bad-tempered gendarmes and suspicious dealers. In the first couple of days I was eased into bars where the artistic and political gathered, with few other Europeans in sight. It went well; a tall, dark-skinned painter even offered a much larger bed than the one in my hotel, but I declined his offer, tempting though it was. The indulgent pleasures of the flesh and the acid eye of art criticism do not mix – that's how my colleagues in London so often end up praising absolute stinkers made by pretty people.

It was whilst seeking out sustenance one afternoon that I noticed an iron-studded door in a mud-brick alley wall, not that far from the Medina. It reminded me of monasteries and castle sally ports, of hidden places; it spoke under my skin.

"Do you know what's behind there, Salim?"

"You do not go," said Salim, tugging at my sleeve.

"No?" I raised my eyebrows. "Why not, dear boy? Is it illegal, or forbidden?"

"It is… strange place. Not safe."

This was Marrakesh, not always the safest of places itself, yet 'strange' was such a delectable word.

"What is it called?"

Salim shuffled, picking at his spots, until I offered him a few dirham notes.

"It is called Souk al-Dkhaan, the Smoke Market," he muttered. "A place of the Berber women, who make pots. Only women."

The twitch of his eyelids showed fear… and fear has been an altar boy to me for many years (not that I was ever High Church, mind you). It has brought me many rare moments. I knew that, somehow, I was meant to see this door.

That feeling was amplified later that day, on the edge of the Djemaa el-Fna, when I spotted a woman squatting behind a wealth of interesting pottery – starkly-decorated urns with bold black geometric patterns, plates with cunningly intertwined threads of red and blue.

"This is Berber – I mean Amazigh – work, yes?" I asked.

She nodded, but made no sale pitch.

"And you are the potter?"

Again a nod, but her henna-tattooed finger pointed at a particular group of platters, wide enough to hold a family meal. The outsides were plain, but the glazed interiors were rich with blue and grey geometries which confused the eye. I was impressed, and bought a smaller example of her work.

"Do you have a workshop I might visit?"

Her eyes narrowed, and she turned away. I was dismissed.

* * *

It was inevitable that in my hotel that evening I thought of the Souk al-Dkhaan and the Amazigh women. Holding the plate I bought, I was reminded of an occasional market outside a Welsh town (I will not name it) where women from the hill farms come to sell their weaving – blankets and cloaks which last for lifetimes. The women are short, dour, and slightly darker hued than the townsfolk, a strand of the Celtic past in a larger tapestry. And they rarely speak, except to state their prices.

I had felt something of that here, under the commercial bustle of Marrakesh.

I needed to know more.

Salim had the night off (I believe that he had family on the edge of the city), so I made my own way into the alleys around the Medina, taking many wrong turnings until, shadowed by the late sun, I saw at last the scarred, studded door again. It had a small iron grille, a wooden hatch obscuring any view inside.

I rapped on the door. Twice, three times. After a few seconds, the hatch slid back, and brilliant blue eyes met mine.

"I believe… I believe I am meant to be here," I said, struggling with the Arabic.

The eyes blinked, puzzled wrinkles forming around them. What I said must not have been expected, for although the hatch slammed shut, a moment later hinges creaked and the door opened, revealing a short, robed woman with those blue eyes set in a dark, weathered face.

"Come," she said, gesturing with a crooked finger.

I followed.

Inside was an open square which seemed to serve as both souk and workshops, surrounded by thick walls which rose ten, eleven feet from the ground; pungent smoke drifted from large kilns at the far end (perhaps why it had its name?). A colonnaded two-storey building rose behind these, a place such as a rich official might once have owned, hinting at former splendour. Eight or nine people, all women, worked under drooping date trees, and the doorkeeper pointed to the oldest potter, who had those faded blue tattoos you rarely saw in Morocco any more, running from her lower lip to the tip of her whiskered chin. She was grinding pigment, and looked up at my approach. I felt the lowered gazes of the others were quite deliberate, so I walked over to her, hands held out, open.

"As-salaam alykum," I said, and then in French: "Forgive my presence. I believe I saw your ceramics, your pottery, laid out by the Djemaa el-Fna. My name is Margrave. Justin Margrave."

Her deep-set eyes appraised me, and she replied in the same tongue, heavily-accented. "English. You are a merchant?"

"Not exactly." I couldn't think of a suitable word for a critic and valuer. "I travel, and I look. Sometimes I see."

That seemed to please her.

"Wa alaikum salaam. I am Dihya." Her voice was sand-dry, almost a whisper. "Margrave. A good name, not unlike al-maghrib – 'the West'. Nadia," she gestured to a younger woman, "you shall show al-Maghrib here what we do."

Nadia, it turned out, was the woman from the Djemaa el-Fna. Dihya shrilled something to the others – in Amazigh, I thought – and so it came about that I was allowed to explore their small souk.

This time Nadia was willing to talk – a little. In her thirties, she spoke some English, but we continued in French. I was told that women could come here to buy directly from them, but men were not welcome. She offered no explanation as to why I had been allowed in, and I decided not to ask, just in case doing so had me ejected. I tried to confine myself to the art – for art it was.

"How is it," I asked her, "that you produce such incredibly fine, fired pieces? I am told that such work was done by men, that women in this area usually confine themselves to domestic ware, pots for the home."

The spouted jar I held was a masterpiece, heavily glazed, with dots and lines in black and red, patterns which drew the eye back to them again and again.

As Nadia took it back from me, I saw that, underneath the henna pattern on her left hand, the skin was scarred, as if by acid.

"We are not the same as others," she said. "We are unwelcome in our homes, and so we work as we choose." She lifted up a broad plate. "This may please you, al-Maghrib. It is one of mine."

It pleased me greatly – a rich green glaze with intricate black lines intertwining along the rim, and in the centre, a symbol that I knew from across North Africa, one to avert the Evil Eye.

"The khamsa."

"The Hand of Fatima," she agreed.

"To protect you from… what? The evil that drove you from your homes?"

Nadia's brows tightened. "From men. Most evil comes from men, al-Maghrib."

Perhaps I had been too direct, for I was soon handed over to another woman, Ghanima, who was content to discuss pigment-grinding and kiln temperatures at length, but would say nothing about the souk. When my 'tour' was done, I knew only that there was much more I wanted to discover about this closed community.

"May I return?" I asked Dihya.

"With others?"

"Alone."

She put down her mortar and pestle, and closed both her hands over one of mine. Callouses rasped against my soft skin.

"You have seen darkness, al-Maghrib," she said at last. "More than most of your kind."

Well, yes, maybe I had… but what was a fellow to do if such things kept coming his way?

"I am only what I am, mother." I shrugged. "And half the world is dark, however many lights we carry."

That brought forth a thin smile.

"You may come again."

* * *

Salim was disappointed that I had no need of him for a few days, though I paid him a bonus and said I would use his services again before I left. I didn't mention my visit to the Souk al-Dkhaan. I went in the evenings, when the street was either quiet, or too busy for anyone to notice me.

Trust came slowly, but over the grind of pestles, and whilst I watched strong fingers shaping pots for the kiln, I learned more from Dihya, Ghanima, and eventually from Nadia.

The souk was an unofficial refuge. These were women who had been mistreated or abandoned by husbands – or had incurred the anger of their families, their communities. Some were Arab, most Amazigh. Nadia had refused sex with a police captain, the cost of protection for her village, and been shown what her lack of 'respect' meant.

"My father did this," she said, holding up her scarred hand. "To him, I had failed to do my duty. My family was weak… and I heard of the Smoke Market…"

Some tales were of physical violence, others of mental cruelty. Dihya, who had been there many years, would not speak of what had happened to her, but she did arouse my curiosity when I asked why she didn't fear the women being found by those who had abused them.

We were drinking mint tea in the courtyard, away from the bags of pigment and the half-finished goods.

"This was a palace, once," she said. "It saw lords come, and lords go. One day, however, in the time when France chose to punish us and bombard our coasts, a French column came to

Marrakesh. They sought one of the 'Alawi chieftains who had interfered in their wars in Algeria, and they found him here, in this place."

"Was there violence?" I added more sugar to my already sweet tea.

"There is always violence. The French troops broke down the door through which you come, and let their guns speak for them; as men lay dying, the Amazigh women who served in this place turned on the French using whatever tools or weapons they could find...

"The women did not win. Some were killed, others made captive. And afterwards, the French officer let his men do what they would with the survivors – mothers and daughters. The tearing away of undergarments... you understand?" She saw that I did. "Those women, al-Maghrib, they are still here."

"Their spirit of defiance, you mean?"

Reaching down, she picked up a broken tile, which might have been from the eighteenth or even seventeenth century. Deep red and polished by so many feet, it shone in the lamplight.

"In the clay, in the tiles beneath our feet."

She bade me press my hands to the mud-brick outer wall, and I humoured her. The wall held the warmth of the day, and... something else.

I am not, to the best of my knowledge, a psychic or sensitive, yet when I touched the rough material, a mixture of clay, straw and dried camel dung, I had the oddest sensation, that of fierce, embracing maternalism, of anger and nurture which swirled in and out of each other...

"They are still here," she repeated.

Perhaps she was right. It could always have been my imagination, though, after the power of her words.

On other nights, one of the potters played a two-stringed rebab, and I listened to her songs – some Arabic, some from the Imazighen. The women occasionally smoked hashish, though I refused it; it always gave me indigestion, which in your fifties becomes a constant obsession.

There was a hypnotic tranquillity to these times at the souk, especially compared to my work during the day, which consisted mostly of arguing over figurines and artisanal work in cramped backrooms or offices.

"You have no heat for women, al-Maghrib," Dihya stated as she threaded a last few silver beads onto a wire.

"Mother, I barely have enough heat for men these days."

She laughed, and gave me the slender necklace she had made.

* * *

Returning from the Smoke Market on the fifth evening, I saw Salim outside my hotel. The hood of his djellaba was up, and he gestured to me.

"Some men wish to meet you." He sounded rather awkward. "They have much art, and an offer they wish to propose," he added. "But not... not where others might see, yes?"

Ah. Well, we had already been to many dubious nooks of the city. Short of a kidnapping, I should be safe at least until I arranged for money to change hands. Robbing me of what little cash I carried seemed unlikely. And as my grandmother used to say, a cow that will deliver buckets of milk for a month is better than a stolen cupful.

He led me back towards the Medina, and I started to lose track of where we were.

"Salim—"

"Almost there, Margrave."

Around the next corner, a group of men were smoking cigarettes under a street-light. My heart sank (as they say), for they didn't look like patrons of the arts, or the usual middle-men. They looked like rather more like peasant farmers, about to beat up a passing traveller.

I turned, but there was another man there, a curved blade in his sash belt.

"You are a friend of the Souk al-Dkhaan," he stated in guttural French. "We have heard how you come and go among... them." His dismissive tone left little doubt as to where he stood.

I looked to Salim, but he was cowering across the street; his djellaba hood had fallen down, and I could see the ugly bruises across one side of his face, the left eye almost closed.

"Whatever your argument here, it doesn't involve Salim or me." I tried to get my muddled brain to work. "Let us alone, let the women alone, and I won't report this."

"Oh, I know you will not. You will speak at the souk door, and they will open it for you. After that... you will know to stay silent."

"Please, afak, I cannot do this. It's their place, not yours, and—"

A dirty hand clamped over my mouth from behind; the man in front of me slid his knife from his belt.

"You prefer we find some woman who can be persuaded? Someone who is even less of a man than you?" He moved the knifepoint close to my crotch, and mimed the act of procreation.

Another men, who had only one eye, came closer. His breath smelled of neat alcohol.

"My daughter is in there, English, but their door is barred against me. It seems that you are the key."

My protests were ignored; with a blade at my back, I was bundled down the alleyways, and into the passage at the side of the Souk al-Dkhaan.

"Go, say your words," hissed the knife-man.

There were seven of them in all, and there was nowhere to run – not that I could have outpaced any of them.

I stepped up to that scarred door. One knock.

"It is al-Mahgrib," I said, and then, with a sudden courage which surprised me, I added more loudly: "But do not let me in – evil follows!"

Despite my warning, the door fell open. There was no sign of the doorkeeper.

I turned to try and block the way, perhaps slow my abductors, but my resolve had come too late. They thrust me ahead of them into the souk, with knives, cudgels and unlit torches in their hands.

Dihya was standing in a circle of lantern-light, the other women behind her. My attempt to grab the djellaba of the nearest man was met with a blow which sent me crashing into a stack of unfired pottery; I tried to rise, but Dihya called out that I should be still.

"This is not a place of men," she said to the one-eyed intruder.

He laughed, humourless. "All places belong to men, as do all women, to treat as we will. To use or cast aside. God made it so."

"Then you have not met God," she responded.

She sat down, settling herself cross-legged on the cracked tiles, followed by a rustle of robes and clink of jewellery as the other women did likewise.

And this is the point where you stop believing my story – of which, after all, I have no proof. For the moonlight dimmed, and I caught a scent of blood on the air, blood and ancient perfumes, the smell of fresh henna...

They came from the earth walls, from the ground beneath us; they were smoke, dkhaan, and glints of fire. Some had obvious wounds, and some had not. The main door to the souk slammed shut, though no one was near it, and the courtyard filled with these wraiths, these women from another time.

The dead of Souk al-Dkhaan.

Terrified men cried out 'Ghūl!" and "'Afārīt!" They yelled for Allah, even for the police – ironic, given their original intent. No aid came. As mist and smoke, the women were among us, brushing past Dihya and her sisters, and a rebab which was not there played an angry tune upon the night air.

The spirits of the souk were upon the men in a heartbeat.

I saw One-Eye fall, his face contorted, a mask of bloody gashes as if clawed by an animal, and I saw him drawn, impossibly, into the wall of the souk, half flesh, half shadow now. The smoke-wraiths surrounded, enveloped, each man in turn – their bodies were insubstantial, and yet their nails were iron, hot iron which slashed and seared mere flesh – and dragged them to, no, into, the fabric of this place. Flesh met clay, and flesh was overwhelmed.

The screaming did not last long, lost in a swirl of dust which obscured my view. I rose to my feet, trembling, as vague figures closed on me…

Dihya spoke out, gentle words in Amazigh, caresses between mothers, daughters, sisters – women's words – and the figures slowed. Hands, insubstantial hands, plucked at my hair, my clothes, but did no harm, and at a further word from the old woman, something again in her own language, they withdrew.

"God is merciful to fools, and to those whose eyes are open," she said. I wondered into which category she placed me.

By the light of torches and lanterns, I could see only the residents of the refuge. Those sturdy walls had perhaps more cracks and buckled places in them than before, but of the men who had forced me here, there was no sign, save scuff marks in the dust.

"Souk al-Dkhaan remembers," said Dihya. "And that is why we do not fear. So, you look – and sometimes you see. What did you see this night, al-Mahgrib?"

If I had been younger, if I myself had never suffered scorn and abuse simply because of what I was… maybe then I would have demanded answers. But I was not that man.

"I saw nothing," I said. "Nothing of worth came here this night, and nothing of worth has left."

I spoke in fractured Arabic, and my words drew a soft ululation from those around me.

"Margrave," said Nadia. "It was willed."

Generous words, since it was through my weakness that the men had come here. Or perhaps not – perhaps Nadia knew better than I did.

With that – and the blessings of Allah – I took my leave of Souk al-Dkhaan.

I never saw Salim again, though I held no rancour, and would have paid him recompense for what the men had done to him.

Nor did I forget why I was supposed to be in Marrakesh. Making a few telephone calls, and further hurried visits to certain local artists and dealers I had already met, I gathered together enough over the next day to earn my fee from David when I returned to England.

* * *

I have been back to Marrakesh since then, but never to that particular alley, however tempting. The Smoke Market needs little from men, and men do not belong within it, whatever those scarred mud-brick walls may hold.

I do still have Dihya's necklace, though.

Nine Rings of Silver and One of Bronze

Rayne Hall

THE SKY FLARED in hues of magenta and purple, and behind the tethered camels, the mountains seemed to grow darker and taller. On those slopes waited Mourad's redemption – or his death.

Tonight, he must visit the accursed ruin town.

Despite the lingering afternoon heat, his fingers stiffened with cold. He could still walk away from the danger, keep his attention on the living people of the caravan, and leave the past buried on those slopes.

He splintered a juniper branch across his thigh and fed it to the red blush of the flames. The wood snapped and popped. As if on cue, the two dozen travellers shifted closer to the crackling fire, hands clutching earthenware mugs, woollen shawls pulled around heads.

"Ghuls don't prey on travellers in groups." One of the matrons waved her arm authoritatively, clanking bronze bangles. "Not normally, anyway."

Others contributed ghul lore, tragedies which had happened to ancestors, hearsay events and superstitions. Mourad half-listened. He knew about the ghuls. They lived mostly in the desert and ruined places. As shapeshifters they took animal form, and even the form of the people they had eaten. The gods marred their form with one imperfection – a missing eye, a hideous ear – to reveal their depravity.

As a caravan master, Mourad encouraged the telling of scary stories around the campfire, because frightened travellers were easier to shepherd. Fear made them docile, and they wouldn't go exploring or wander from the camp in the dark. But tonight Mourad had to confront his own, very real, fear.

"Well, this is the desert," the matron said with more clinks of her bangle-covered arm. "But there's nothing here besides sand and rocks and mountains. No deserted places, so probably no ghuls."

Mourad's gaze went to the mountain. Behind that dark outcrop stood the accursed town, crushed in an earthquake many years ago. Dread constricted his throat. He crossed his legs and fed more wood to the fire.

"You're mistaken, lady," the spice merchant Adishir said. He was a brooding man whose big turban shadowed his face and dark moustache. "Our caravan master doesn't want to alarm us with this fact – but we are in the centre of a ghul haunt."

Hands flew to mouths.

Mourad donned his authoritative caravan master voice. "There are old stories about ghul attacks—"

"Not just stories," Adishir interrupted.

"Ghul attacks that happened in this stretch of the desert long ago." Mourad balanced his words to keep his flock nervous but not panicking. "We're reasonably safe here, as long as we take precautions. Don't leave camp, wear your amulets, and keep a sprig of basil on you at all times."

"I lost my bride to the ghuls." Adishir's voice was grave. "It happened not long ago, and not far from here."

His listeners shuddered, pressed for details, and leant forward so they wouldn't miss a word.

Mourad's stomach grew heavy with dread. He dug his nails into his palms, hoping that Adishir's story was not about last year's tragedy.

Adishir combed his fingers through his moustache. "It happened a year ago, on this remote route betwen Ain Zigat and Djildit, in the vicinity of these mountains. My bride was travelling across the desert to wed me. Her name was Talitha."

The name seared across Mourad's chest like the lash of a whip. He stared straight ahead into the fire, careful not to betray himself with a movement of his limbs or a flicker on his face.

Adishir pulled at the headcloth where it wound around his neck, as if struggling to breathe. "The caravan leader was young, lacking the sense and the experience to fear the ghuls, and neglected the basic precautions – not like our conscientious Master Mourad here."

Mourad forced a swallow through his tight throat and touched the new beard which gave him a look of maturity. Through the veil of woodsmoke, he darted a glance at Adishir, but the merchant was not looking at him.

Silence hung like a cloud over the group. Travellers fidgeted, unsure if they should express sympathy or if that would be insensitive.

A change of subject revived the talk, but Mourad's mind circled around the memory of a young woman who had wandered off into those mountains alone.

The sun vanished, leaving a red, gashing wound on the horizon. The time had come for Mourad to face his fear and atone for his guilt.

He set a sentry rota, reminded everyone to keep basil in their blankets and wear their amulets so the metal touched the skin, and urged them to alert one another should the slightest disturbance occur.

"I have already put a ward on this place which will keep ghuls and other demons away. For added protection, I will ride sunwise around the camp, draw sigils with my cedar wand and incant the protection rite."

His charges nodded, clearly impressed with his knowledge and reassured by his responsible attitude.

But he had to desert them for tonight.

* * *

After spiralling around the camp for a while, withdrawing further and further from the sight of its fire, he rode to the foot of the mountain.

He hobbled his camel and lit a torch from the embers he had brought. The wisewoman in Ain Zigat had told him there was only one way to rip out the guilt that gnawed at his heart. He must go to where he had failed through cowardice, right into the heart of the place, and bury an offering under the light of the gibbous moon: nine rings of silver and one of bronze.

He had planned this caravan trek to lead past this spot at the right time. Now he had to follow his planning with action.

A canyon cut a black slash into the mountain, and from there the overgrown trail threaded its way in zigzags up the slope, between a tangled mass of gnarled junipers, rocks and thorny vines. With every step, the weight of his guilt and the dread pressed heavier on him, but he forced himself onward.

A year ago he had seen a young woman labour up this path, hampered by overlong skirts. He had followed her, because as the caravan master he wanted to admonish her for leaving the camp – but also because she was young and pretty, and whatever her reason for climbing the mountain alone, she might wish for company during the night. The thought of a dalliance on the slopes had stirred his lusts. How foolish he had been, how thoughtless!

The broken town lay on the mountain outcrop and clung to its downward slopes, tier after tier of walled enclosures with jagged edges. Vines clustered in the walls' creases, skeleton-white in the moonlight. The gatehouse had crumbled, only its arch still stood like a sentinel of death.

Last year he had paused here, listening to the whispers and cackles of the wind, and peeked through the entrance at the bodies which lay crushed beneath the weight of falling rocks, their bones gnawed bare by scavengers, their skulls grinning their challenge up at him. In this creepy place, he was suddenly less certain of his disbelief in demons, and the prospect of a brief dalliance no longer seemed worth the risk.

Eventually, his responsibility as caravan master had asserted itself, and he took a few trembling steps into the ruins to call Talitha back to the camp. Then she had screamed. Her echoing scream was answered by what could only be demonic laughter. Mourad had fled while the ghuls feasted on their victim.

Tonight, he needed to be braver, and atone for his cowardice. He carried every possible shield – twigs of basil, amulets of obsidian and black hematite, known to deter demons – although nothing could entirely safeguard a human against a determined ghul's attack.

With his feet planted wide and one fist clutched around his torch, the other around the rings, he encouraged himself to step into the accursed town. He had to reach its centre not looking right or left, not dithering anywhere, not let anything deflect his purpose. The faster he accomplished his quest, the sooner he could leave.

He marched into the ruined town. The air grew thicker, colder. The near-blackness of the night lay like a weight on his shoulders. Eerie silence wrapped around him, and his own sandals slapping on the stones sounded like an intrusion. He entered the first of the chambers where he had heard Talitha's scream, and shone his torch on silhouettes and shadows of cracked walls and shattered furniture. Rats scurried from the light, flipping their long tails.

His heartbeat fluttered like a nightbird but he refused to let fear undermine his resolve.

Smells of dust, decay and animal excrement filled the air.

His foot hit an obstacle, he stumbled. The torch slipped from his hand, rolled into a floor crack, went out. Darkness became absolute, and terror squeezed his throat.

Mourad groped his way onwards. His fingers slid along cold stone, crumbling brick, and tangles of thorny weeds.

Some chambers lay submerged in water, the result of underground lakes pocking most mountains in this land. The walls were slimy with algae and stank of mould, rodent droppings and rotten eggs.

At last, he reached what must have been the courtyard of a rich person's home, colonnaded with arches and mosaic floors. Moonlight poured from above, showing fractured statues, silhouetted lemon trees and remnants of a private well. It was good to see light again, however sparse.

This courtyard, Mourad reckoned, was the place where he had to carry out his mission in the centre of the ruined town.

To calm his thudding heart, he breathed deeply of the cool night air.

He knelt, ripped a tuft of grass from the ground, and dug his fingers into the soil where the roots had been. Scraping with his nails, he created a small hollow for his offering. One by one he placed the rings, the way the wisewoman had instructed, first the nine silver, then the bronze.

"Forgive me, Talitha," he murmured. "Forgive my cowardice."

The pale moon crept behind scattered clouds, robbing the place of all but a shred of light.

Behind his back, something rustled. Something moaned. The sound came from the colonnade. An animal? A predator?

Then, "Help! Help!" A weak voice, more a whisper than a shout – a woman's.

He leaped up. Fighting his urge to bolt, he clutched the hematite amulet on his chest and advanced towards the source of the sound.

Aided by a sliver of moonlight, he found a person cowering in an alcove. He bent over the body.

"Mourad," she croaked.

His knees buckled, and he stumbled back a step and sagged against the wall.

"Talitha!" he gasped. "Talitha, is that you?"

She moaned.

He fell on his knees by her side and shifted to allow the moonlight to fall on her features. It was the face that had haunted his conscience for so long.

Wrapped in a tattered blanket, she stank of sickness and filth. Her hair was a tangled mess of plaits, her once-pretty face gaunt, her eyes dulled, but she clasped his hand.

"You've come back!" Her voice was weak and raw. "You've come at last, you've come!"

"Yes," he managed, groping for reason.

He felt her cold bony wrist and found a pulse.

"You're alive!" he said. "You really are alive."

The gods must have seen his remorse and rewarded his courage. Tears welled up behind his eyelids. "When I heard you scream that day, I thought the ghuls had got you. But you're alive!"

"Slipped," she croaked. "Sprained ankle. So much pain."

"Talitha, I didn't know. I'm so sorry!"

"Thank you, thank you. You've come," she repeated.

"I have a camel waiting below, and a caravan is on the plain. You're safe now. But tell me, how did you survive?"

She turned her face towards the courtyard. "Pomegranates grow there. Lemons. The cellars held pickled olives – but none left, now."

"You shall have food," he promised. "And good care." Warmth spread throughout his body, and his heartbeat raced. He tried to order his scattered thoughts. "I'll take you to the caravan first for a meal and a good rest, and tomorrow, I'll take you to a healer who will make you well. Can you walk?"

"Thank you." She struggled to rise.

He lifted her into his arms. Emaciated, she weighed less than a child.

He carried her into the courtyard. In the light of the moon, her eyes looked feverish, and her skin had an unhealthy glow.

He wrapped his arms tightly around her, lifted her higher – and saw her bare feet.

One foot twisted inwards, with toes like bulbs.

Coldness slammed his core. Was this Talitha – or was it a ghul in her shape?

Ghuls could take on the form of the people they had devoured – with a single deformity giving them away.

Thoughts churned, and hot sweat drenched Mourad's chest. Had the demons really killed Talitha, and now impersonated her?

Her face – the eyes protruded, glazed with silver. The lips pulled back, bared teeth – this was a ghul.

With all his might, he pushed the ghul from him.

But the monster held him in his demonic grip. It clung and clawed, hissed and screeched. Sharp nails raked his flesh.

With the writhing burden, Mourad staggered towards the well. While the ghul's howls echoed through the ruins, he managed to pry a bony finger off his elbow, then the whole hand. He bent and shoved the flailing form towards the dark hole.

But the ghul still clung to the well head, its fingers bony and pale, its demonic eyes glaring up at Mourad. He stomped hard on the head, heard the skull crack, and at last forced the monster down the shaft.

With a sharp cry, the ghul fell. The body landed with a faraway thudding splash.

Mourad recoiled and heaved.

An unearthly scream tore from the depth. The demon was still not dead!

Mourad could not recall if ghuls could be killed. He knew they could be trapped, and of that he would make sure. He grabbed rocks, bricks, whole sections of broken wall, and slammed them down the well, not resting until the shaft was filled to the brim.

At last, the screams stopped. Now the only sound was the thud of his own heart, racing from effort and fear. He rubbed his hands down his tunic.

Then he ran, through the echoing chambers which now seemed to compress to crush him between their walls, through the gatehouse arch, to the safety of the moonlit slope. The mocking laughter of a thousand ghuls seemed to follow him down the rock-strewn path.

His heart thudded in his ears as he slithered down the slope, releasing stones, stumbling, falling, scrambling back up, finally reaching his camel.

What a fool he had been! How nearly had he fallen for the ghul's ruse! How narrowly he had escaped!

* * *

By the time he neared the familiar yellow glow of the campfire, his heartbeat had almost slowed to normal. He had fought a ghul – and won!

A tall silhouette swayed towards him: the merchant Adishir riding his camel away from the camp.

"I've been looking for you," the merchant said gravely, one hand on the saddle pommel, the other holding the camel's reins. "Don't worry – all is well in the camp. But I have to leave on a quest tonight. I must ride to that mountain yonder."

"Don't!" Mourad croaked. "There's an abandoned town, and it's infested with ghuls."

"I know, my friend, I know. That's why I must go there."

"The ghuls – they're shapeshifters! They appear as someone you think you know, and devour your living flesh."

"I know, my friend, and I must take this risk to atone for what I have done. Earlier, I told how my bride had travelled to wed me, and was stolen on the way by ghuls. This was not the full truth."

He rubbed a hand across his eyes. "Talitha was the daughter of a trading partner in Ain Zigat. I coveted her dowry, warehouses in a prime location in Djildit. Her father sent her with a caravan, like I told you – but what I didn't tell you was that she arrived. On disrobing in the bridal chamber, I discovered that her father had foisted off a deformed person on me."

Mourad's throat tightened. He stared at Adishir's hands clutching the camel reigns.

"Outraged, I did not consummate the marriage, but repudiated her on her wedding night. I sent her back to her father with the first available caravan, and in my anger, did not see to her safety or arrange a proper escort. Later I heard that in her despair she had walked into those ruins infested by flesh-eating ghuls.

"So you see, it was all my fault. The guilt has gnawed at my soul ever since. I asked a wisewoman's advice. She said I must go to the place where Talitha died, as close as I can ascertain it, and place an offering in her memory."

Bile burned at the back of Mourad's throat. Talitha.

Adishir's lips curved in a sad smile, and his eyes remained dark. "I may not come back alive, and my body may be fodder for the ghuls. If that is so, it is just punishment for the heartless way I treated a woman in my care. The poor girl: detested from childhood, traded by her father, rejected by her husband, eaten by ghuls… all because she had a club foot."

Mourad stared at the merchant. Cold pain thudded where his heart should be.

Adishir clasped his forearm. "Farewell, my friend. Don't look so horrified. Should I not return, I have made arrangements that you will be held free from all blame."

Two Trees

Vanessa C. Hawkins

Taking place in St. Andrews, New Brunswick

A LOT OF people don't know the significance of the two trees. Nowadays they walk on by during a hot day, take a rest beneath their shade while having a drink from a canteen, and look over the cemetery beyond. No one realizes that my Mama and Daddy, long since festered away, are beneath their feet.

Most folks don't know the *importance* of the two trees.

From the inside the cemetery, I see them every night, my calloused hands bracing the iron bars of the boneyard. People don't see me watching them, but sometimes when the day ends they do. I never thought I'd be left to guard them for an eternity.

Mama named me Margaret. She used to tell me it meant pearl, and Daddy said I was as pretty as one but I didn't believe him. We lived in Shantytown where if pearls were found, they were given to the richer folk who came down in the summers to enjoy the fresh breeze blown off from the Bay of Fundy. When I was younger, I would watch the tide. You could throw a rock a kilometer and depending on the time of day it may or may not hit the water. I heard Daddy say once that we had the highest tides in the whole wide world.

* * *

"Get away from there, Margaret. You wanna be mauled by the merfolk?"

I looked up from the between the boats moored at the wharf, listening to Daddy chuckle as the vessels bobbed up and down behind him. He had been collecting old ropes to use for netting, anything that could be salvaged and reused. Beads of sweat formed on his forehead.

"Merfolk aren't real," I protested, stepping back anyway. The sun was brilliant in my eyes, and I squinted to see. My daddy was nothing but a silhouette on the St. Andrews wharf.

"Sure are," he said without the amused hitch in his voice that usually accompanied his candor. "S'why we gotta feed 'em." He passed me the ropes, then bent down to look between the boats. I was supposed to be watching out for the Wharfinger, making sure he didn't notice what we were doing. Instead I found myself preoccupied.

"What if we don't feed them?" I had taken more than a few steps away from the edge of the wharf now.

"Then they gets *really* hungry."

I looked over my shoulder as Daddy bent to retrieve another piece of rope. Though the sea was ebbing away into low tide, I could see the waves rolling into white foam on the horizon, making it look like there were creatures in the water. With the sun behind me I was sure I saw the great tails of merfolk sparkling in the Bay of Fundy, open maws slobbering and hungry for little girls like me.

I squeezed the sea-sodden ropes in my hands until the rockweed bladders entwined within popped and oozed over my fingers. The salty breeze whipping at my soiled linen shift stung my eyes and so I closed them, forgetting my duty as watchman.

"You aren't paying any attention, Margaret," I heard my Daddy grumble before he tossed a bunch of rope over my shoulders. I almost collapsed from the weight of them, imagining a great big sea snake hissing in my ears as it squeezed me to death and drug me down under.

"Let's get goin' home before Mama gets irate."

The seawater soaked through my clothes and ran in rivulets down my sides to the back of my knees. Still, I nodded. I was leaving footprints in the dirt the whole way home, smelling the pungent odor of the Bay. An old bundle of potato cloth was tangled within the ropes, and I vaguely wondered if merfolk shed their scales like snakes did.

We walked back to Shantytown, the Bay disappearing behind the ramshackle homes where all the living poor resided. Mama had a chowder ready for us when we arrived. She was all excited to have had the milk to make it, saying how the lady at the house she cleaned had given it to her for getting the wine stain out of her good handkerchief. I didn't listen much as she prattled on. Instead I'd been thinking of what Daddy had said, and the severity with which he'd said it.

"Margaret Stewart, look at you! You look like a bundle of sea trash," she said, finally taking notice of me.

"Leave 'er be, Maria. She was helpin' me at the docks." I watched as Daddy hung his hat next to the basin Mama washed the dishes in. We had set the ropes outside. Flies were already buzzing around them, sometimes finding their way into the house to bother our dinner.

"She can wash up after supper. We're both hungrier than spring bears."

It may have been true for Daddy, but it sure wasn't for me. Despite the long day of walking and heaving old wet ropes, I didn't want any of Mama's fish chowder. Not after smelling the burst rockweed and dank slime of the Bay all day.

I couldn't say that though, else I was bound to get a hidin'. So instead I sat at the table in my soiled linen shift and said my prayers, contemplating monsters as I forced down Mama's well-earned seafood chowder.

I had heard of mermaids before. On the really nice boats, they were there at the prow with their bare chests, sweating with seawater. Mama had told me that they gave the sailors good luck, but now I wondered why. Was it a disguise? A trick to tame the rage of the real sea monsters?

No, I thought, spooning at another chunk of mackerel floating in my bowl. Daddy was putting me on. I was twelve, too old to be believing in fairy tales and nightmares.

Still, when Daddy asked me to come outside with him to toss the garbage, I didn't wanna. He did it every night. Right beside our house down a narrow path through a garble of trees was a cliff side. Daddy would pitch the trash over the side of the rocks by our house and I'd watch the hungry tide sweep it into the Bay until he'd yell back to me to get going.

Though I usually liked getting out the house for a walk before bedtime, I made extra sure my feet were planted on the ground as I made my way to the cliff. The moon was big and swollen, so it was easy to see my Daddy's back as he hauled the heft of trash over one shoulder. Everyone always pitched their trash in the Bay. The high tides swept it away nice and clean, though sometimes I saw bundles of old potato cloth when the tide was out.

We could hear the waves hushing the night to be silent as they crashed against the cliffs. I could still taste Mama's chowder in my mouth, and the briny flavor of mackerel lingered on my tongue.

"Gotta feed the tide," Daddy said, stopping just short of where the bank collapsed. I skulked up behind him, wringing my hands together as he hurled the burlap sack over the side.

We didn't have much for trash. We didn't have much to begin with so what we threw away was limited. But still, I watched as it was swallowed up by the Bay tide, swore that I heard growls between the crash of waves.

"Daddy, wait for me!" I called, horrified that he'd left without me.

Normally I would watch as the Bay of Fundy carried away our trash. After then, I didn't anymore. Not even when the other kids went down to the shore to go beach-combing. Instead I sat on the old red rocks, watching as they'd pick up debris and stomp the crabs that would come running out from underneath. Unlike the other kids, I knew that just hours before when the tide was high, there might have been monsters waiting beneath the bundles of seaweed and the old discarded potato cloth, instead of ten-legged crustaceans.

* * *

"Stay in your room, child."

My Daddy's voice. In the kitchen, our paraffin lamp glowed dimly among the shadows. The moon itself had hidden behind the clouds. The air smelled of the sea, curiously mingled with copper.

I didn't remember getting up, but thought I must have gotten out of bed to relieve myself. The vague shapes from inside our shack were forming in the corners of my eyes, and as I tried to peer past the shadows in the kitchen to the front door, I heard a painful scream from Mama and gasped.

"Get back to bed!" she screamed, drawing out the last vowel in a squeal of manic pain. I didn't dare protest. Instead, I leapt over the threshold that separated the kitchen from where I slept and closed the door.

We lived in a small shack, nothing but the bare necessities. Usually Mama and Daddy and myself slept in the same room off the kitchen. When I jumped into the homey mattress that was my bed, I could hear Daddy out in the kitchen, the muffled sounds of furniture scraping along the dirt floor as stifled moans and groans resounded in our little house.

Beneath the covers I was immediately terrified. I tucked the blankets up over my head, trying to block the sounds out. Mama was breathing hard, Daddy grumbling. After a few short moments I finally managed the courage to defy Mama's orders and peer over the headboard of my slight little bed and into a chink in the wall.

Blood pooled on our dirt floor. I stifled a scream, ducking back down to cram my head into my pillow.

Daddy would butcher pigs, sometimes chickens. I've seen things die up at the farms when he had to go to work there. Curious, I had wanted to watch as those animals had their heads cut off. Sick fascination had led to disgust; disgust, eventually to disappointment. This reminded me of those times, and despite my Mama's warning that I mind my own and stay inside the room, my morbid interest drew me back to that slit in the wall.

Something squirmed in Daddy's hands right before it began to wail.

"Daddy? Is something the matter?" I asked, playing dumb.

Daddy didn't know it, but I saw him look towards the door to our bedroom. He had his hand over a babe's mouth, and the sound of crying stopped.

"Ain't nothing, Margaret. Your Mama's just sick. Go back to bed."

Mama was lying on the kitchen table with her legs apart. There was a leather strap in her mouth, her teeth clenching down hard on it as she struggled to breathe.

"Is she alright?" The blood on the table and the floor gleamed in the lamplight.

"S'fine. I gotta take the trash out. Forgot to at supper. Go to bed, Margaret."

I didn't know till much later, but back then, when there were unwanted children, it wasn't uncommon for them to be wrapped up in potato cloth and thrown into the sea. It wasn't just our house that had done it.

At the time I didn't understand what I was seeing.

Daddy left our house, the babe in his hands swaddled carefully in that old potato cloth. His thick, calloused palm muffled the babe's cries. He shut the door behind him.

I turned back around, settled beneath the blankets, and fell asleep to the sound of her blood dripping on the kitchen floor.

* * *

In the morning, they told me it had all been a dream. That there hadn't been a babe at all.

"But you said Mama was sick. I heard crying!"

Daddy spooned at the bowl of beans Mama had heated for breakfast. He shook his head, looking up at me from beneath the severe slope of his forehead. Beyond the window, a pall of gray clouds cloaked the sky. The air was chilly.

Mama said, "I ain't gonna tell you anymore stories, Margaret, if they're givin' you nightmares."

Her face was gaunt and pale, her body deflated like a dried up cucumber. She sat at the stove by the fire, boiling Daddy's old socks clean. The entire shack smelled of beans, mackerel, and damp feet. The faint smell of copper, too. The blood on the floor was gone, though.

"If it was all just a dream, then why you so tired? You look like you were up all night, Mama. You look *sick*."

"You best take her to church on the way to the docks," she told Daddy, then narrowed her eyes at me. "Pray away that sinful imagination."

Mama looked back to the fire. The cool wind was coming from off the water this morning, but she was wrapped up in her winter blanket *and* her summer shawl.

I didn't believe I could have imagined it all up, but Mama and Daddy got angry when I mentioned it again, and Daddy took me to church later in the day, just like Mama said he should.

Days after, I started coming back out to the sea when Daddy took the trash out, started believin' that my mind had some evil in it. Even when I continued seein' the merfolk in the water, snarling under the waves, I'd say to myself: *They aren't real. A figment of my vile imagination.*

Every day, the continuous roar of the sea against the cliff side worked upon my imagination so that I heard snarls, malevolent sighs, hissing. Soon, I was certain I heard a babe's cries echoing among them from the Bay.

I fancied the babe as my little sister. *Pearl,* I called her, because she ought to be as pretty as one.

Mama and Daddy, you drowned her in the Bay of Fundy.

Mama's voice protested in my mind: *No, we did not. How could you even dare think we'd do such a thing? After all we do to take care of you?*

I stared at the water, listening to my baby sister's wails, hoping that mermaids had found her, taken her to some underwater kingdom away from all the garbage we used to throw in the sea. There, she could live out her days in happiness. I wanted to join her, throw myself from the wharf and see where the sea took me. I understood, however, that I'd only sink, become some waterlogged body buried under seaweed, under garbage and potato cloth, an anchor hold for some rich man's boat.

Or meat for the merfolk.

There are no merfolk!

I heard Pearl crying.

There is no Pearl. It was a dream!

When Daddy went to throw out the trash, I saw her ghost, trapped within the waves every night. The merfolk taunted her, dragged her beneath the sea to drown her again and again.

"Hurry along, Margaret," my Daddy said as he began walking back to Shantytown, hands empty of the haul of nightly trash. He must have thought my fears of the Bay were quelled since I rejoined him on his walk to the cliff side. Instead they were only growing.

Why couldn't he see it too? Was my mind ripe with wicked fascinations? Or was he hiding from the murder he and Mama had committed?

Was I crazy? Did no one else hear the babe screaming from the sea?

* * *

At the end of the summer I got a job at the Kennedy House. Small work, and not a bad job for a girl with a sturdy set of shoulders. Mostly I cleaned and laundered the soiled clothes of the richer folks vacationing for the season. It was away from the seaside – as much as anything could be in St. Andrews – and enough of a distraction to keep me from thinking of Pearl.

"Did you hear what happened, Margaret?" Delilah, my co-worker, asked as she scrubbed at the stains on some bedclothes. We were both down in the basement of the Kennedy House, old cobwebs and the squeak of mice keeping us company. "The Wharfinger's closed the wharf."

I looked up, staring into Delilah's dark brown eyes. She was taller than me, prettier, with a round face and sunshine in her eyes. She was older than me by two whole years, but I was certain that most of the Kennedy guests thought she was younger.

"Why?" I asked, feeling phantom fingers poking down my spine.

Delilah smiled, looking around conspiratorially. I could tell she was pleased to be the first one to relay this piece of gossip. "They found a body in the water. All mauled up and half eaten. Now everyone's sayin' the sea's haunted."

I dropped the tablecloth I was scrubbing into the basin. Water splashed over the side and onto Delilah's apron. She grimaced, tutting that I should watch what I was doing.

"What kind of body, Delilah? Tell me. Tell me now." I asked, eyes as wide as dinner plates. I held myself back from saying, *Was it a babe? A child?*

Delilah stared at me with guarded curiosity, taken aback by my sudden outburst. Bending to her work, she resumed her task with the laundry. "It was a sailor," she said after a while, stopping to wipe her forehead. "But I guess the body looked pretty bad."

She regarded me. I was staring down into the washbasin, watching the tablecloth settle into the water until only a small section of it bobbed on the surface.

It reminded me of a baby's head.

"I have heard people sayin' they've heard cries though," Delilah continued, "babes in the water."

"Since when?" My voice was barely a whisper.

I watched her bite the inside of her cheek, no longer pleased to spread such gossip.

"Just heard about it, is all," Delilah continued. "In either case the wharf is closed. All the rich folks'll be disappointed and so I imagine they'll be taking it out on us."

I watched as she hauled her laundry from the water into a basket. "Better get this done quick," she said, walking away with the load in her arms.

I'm not crazy! Pearl really was out on the water. Thrown to the ravenous tide by my Mama and Daddy! Crying out for someone to save her. The merfolk were the ones that had killed the sailor! Who else?

* * *

I went to the sea that night. Defying the Wharfinger's orders, I cut the ropes of a small skiff and went out as far as I could in hopes to save my sister. At the worst case, I thought, Pearl's ghost would rise up to drown me too for not saving her, and then perhaps I could be there with her at least, and stave off the merfolk that tortured her.

The tide was high, and the gibbous moon kissed the surface as my paddle split the waves. All around me I saw them, the domes of their skulls decorated with knotted rockweed.

"I hear you, Pearl!" I screamed, watching as they crowded the skiff and tossed it teetering on the surf. From underneath I could hear the merfolk's fists pounding at the keel. They had limbs like drywood, shards of sea-glass in their eyes. As they rose up from the water the Bay exhaled, and fierce winds sent the skiff hurtling backwards, dropping down into the valleys of the sea.

"Pearl!" I saw her. She was bundled in the potato cloth, her forehead dry from where Daddy had kissed her. She drifted through the moonlight, cradled within the sweeping arc of the tidal waves. Serpentine tails with scabby black fins and missing scales sloshed around her. Bones stuck out from the merfolk's torsos. Barnacles burst from their thick skin, meandering around mouths crowded with shark teeth and tentacles.

"No! Leave her alone!"

The Bay inhaled, and floating upon the lung of the sea, I pierced the rushing water with my paddle. The salt on my face stung my eyes. The wind whipped at my hair and clothes. I couldn't reach her, was too far away, and in my desperation the wave transformed, moonlight illuminating its malformation.

Foam frothed at the edge of the water. Serpent eyes breached the surface. I fell back into the skiff as the Bay of Fundy reared back and closed its maw around Pearl. Her cries pierced my brain and left me feeling helpless as the surface began to equalize and the skiff settled back into place, right overtop where her body had been. The boat marked her grave like a tombstone.

I whimpered, holding my knees. The sodden ropes littering the bottom of the boat floated around me. The wind pushed the water over the edge. I heard the monsters. Was I going to be eaten alive too? Like the sailor on the wharf?

"Leave us alone. Leave her, me alone." I offered Pearl so many tears, and the Bay answered with the sounds of waves and merfolk voices.

At high tide when the belly of the Bay was pregnant with monsters, and the moon was full and farthest from the sun, I said my prayers and dove into its depths. I knew she was there, prisoner of the surf, and as I sunk down deep, my limbs filling with water, I swore I would find her.

But the rockweed swept over me and all the discarded potato cloth and trash of the sea wrapped about my legs. Trapped, I began to drown as the seabed buried me beneath its debris. As my lungs slowly began to fill with water I panicked, kicking as I closed my eyes, fearful that I had failed to help her. But when I opened them again I could see the sun piercing through the Bay. Pearl was there, above the surface, giggling from the prow of my skiff and haloed in the morning light. I reached out to her and smiled, glad that she had been freed from the merfolk, from the sea monsters that had invaded my nightmares and hers. Leaving my body behind, I swam to the surface to join her.

* * *

August 29th 1826 was the day they hung my parents. It cost eight shillings to build the gallows. Though the ordeal surrounding my parents was to remain quiet, the bells always tolled with every hanging, and it did so then without prejudice. Mama and Daddy hung until 2pm in the hot afternoon. They had been there since nine in the morning. Potato cloth hoods were placed over their heads, a suitable end even though they didn't hang for Pearl.

Some wealthy old man had found my body curled up inside his anchor. I stayed in the sea fighting for Pearl until they pulled me out. Authorities deduced that I had been strangled about the neck with an old rope, the same kind Daddy used to fetch from the sea when he thought the Wharfinger wasn't looking. It had been the Wharfinger's testimony that had truly sent my folks to the gallows. If only I had been a better lookout.

Mama and Daddy hung for my death. The community of St. Andrews drug my body from the sea and buried it in the St. Andrews boneyard, right alongside the cemetery gate. Just outside its iron bars stood the two trees.

Criminals could not be buried in the cemetery. Only the righteous and just could lay their souls to rest in sanctified church soil. I am sure there were many who had fled the courts and were buried six feet under and went straight to hell, but Mama and Daddy were not allowed to be among those in the St. Andrews Catholic cemetery. Instead they were buried alongside it, just outside the gate and beside my headstone.

They are close by us always: Pearl and I. We walk along the cemetery together, my soul with hers who will never see her body at rest. We don't hate them for what they did, but they suffer now beneath the ground, eternally drowning as we stand sentinel.

I wish I knew why they did it, why they threw Pearl to the Bay like trash. They had both loved me, provided for me and nurtured me like loving parents were wont to do. I remember Mama singing hymns to me, telling me tales of kings and queens. I remember Daddy telling me how someday I'd go to school and get out of Shantytown. Earn enough money to take care of them when they were old and gray.

Was our family too poor to provide love and care for Pearl as well?

Don't worry. We'll never be apart again.

Two trees. There are two trees outside the graveyard. You can see them still if you're walking down the Prince of Wales towards the shore, away from Shantytown where the poor had laboured. Those trees are the headstones of my Mama and Daddy. In the space between them the spouses touch, feet to feet, their bones wound between the roots, hoods still over their heads. I lay within the boneyard, not very far away from them. My gravestone fell down a while ago and the grass has hidden it from those who come to pay the dead respect, but I'm still there, forever with Pearl whose body will never be put to rest.

I don't think it's fair that we were all buried side by side, brown bones knit between the tree roots, separated by a boneyard gate while my sister lies beneath the Bay.

But I'll stay with her forever, until Pearl's body is fetched from the sea.

Atticat

Jennifer Hudak

THE CAT IS the only one who can see us.

His name is Jekyll, and he's half gray and half white. Sometimes he ignores us but sometimes he stares at us, unblinking, until we give up and melt back into the walls. Jekyll isn't afraid of ghosts, but sometimes, when he stares at us like that, we are a little afraid of Jekyll.

Every ghost has a place, and this house is ours. We don't know why. None of us died here; none of us even stepped foot in this house when we were alive. And yet here we are. We're not complaining. This house suits us. We hide inside cupboards and look out the mirrors and take turns bouncing on the bed. We haunt every room and closet and alcove.

Everywhere but the attic. No one goes into the attic.

The hallway beneath the attic is where we first appear when we arrive in the house upon our death. It's where we always return when we're not paying attention. Some of us are drawn here more often than others, but none of us can stay away forever. Over and over again we find ourselves huddled in the hallway, disoriented and disconsolate, aware only of the trap door looming overhead, getting larger by the second, air whistling through the cracks, a strange suction. If we were alone, we'd be drawn straight upwards like smoke.

But here, in our house, we're not alone.

We surround each other, linking arms, reminding ourselves that we had arms, that we have them still, even if no one but Jekyll can see them. The energy of our collective presence allows us to remember ourselves: our names, our personalities. We cast nervous eyes at the trap door and coax ourselves away from it. We watch out for each other; we keep each other grounded. We remain.

* * *

Callie, a living woman, owns both Jekyll and this house. She doesn't seem to care that the house is haunted. At least, she's never said anything about it, not even when Giles rattles his chains or Francis knocks a painting off the wall. Francis cheerfully tells us that he was always loud and impulsive and destructive, even when he was alive, so it's no wonder he became a poltergeist when he died. But Callie doesn't seem to mind even Francis. She just hangs the paintings back up, making sure they're level, and checks to make sure he didn't do anything really stupid like blow out the pilot light on the stove.

We're not sure if Callie knows the attic exists. She walks underneath the trap door every day as she moves between the bedroom and the stairs, and never looks up. Still, every time she passes beneath it, we cringe. Rose thinks that's why this house is our place; she thinks we're guardians sent to keep Callie and Jekyll from ever going into the attic. She thinks that's why we can't stay away from it, no matter how much we try.

Giles, with a pompous shake of his chains, says that Callie is unaware of us, as most living people are. Susan disagrees. She believes that Callie is simply unafraid of death, and, being unafraid, is particularly suited to owning a haunted house. Kenneth can never decide whether Callie is unaware or unafraid, but he insists that whichever it is, it's Jekyll who keeps her that way. Kenneth has always had a soft spot for Jekyll.

Kenneth is our most recent arrival. He appeared in the hallway beneath the attic two years ago. By the time we found him, Jekyll was already there, giving Kenneth a slow blink as he began to lose cohesion and float, mist-like, toward the trap door. None of this was unusual. Jekyll always gets to the new arrivals before we do, and the call of the attic is strongest when we first appear. But even when we gathered around Kenneth, even when we whispered our names and showed him our true faces, he resisted awakening. Giles tried to loop his chains around Kenneth's waist but they slipped right through. Francis threw himself at the mist but only scattered it further. Susan's mouth widened into a panicked oval. We'd never lost anyone to the attic, not once. But the longer Kenneth held out, the more he decohered; and the longer we stayed to help, the more we risked decohering with him. Even now, the crowns of our heads flickered like candles, pulling and stretching and narrowing toward the trap door. Only when Rose let out a banshee wail did Kenneth shudder and gather himself back together, settling onto the floor in a terrified, weeping ball.

We huddled around him, coaxing him out of the hallway with parlor tricks and soothing songs. Even though we still hummed with the frequency of the attic's greedy pull, none of us begrudged Kenneth's slow transition. Dying is frightening. It takes time to become used to insubstantiality, to bodilessness. In this house, we have each other to ground us. While we might be something less than human, together, we are more than we once were.

* * *

When Callie sleeps at night, we try to be quiet. Giles stills his chains; Susan and Rose tuck themselves into a closet where they can whisper among the coats. Even Kenneth, who's itching to have a chase with Jekyll, resists waking him. But Francis just can't help himself. He's found himself beneath the trap door again, rope dangling above. And because he's Francis, he reaches for it. The first two times, the rope swishes right through his hand. But the third time, he catches it.

The creak as the trap door opens takes even Francis by surprise. A skeletal staircase slides downward, landing at the end of its track with a sound like the clapping of hands. We can't believe the noise doesn't wake Callie, but she's so used to Francis's periodic disruptions that she simply flips over and buries her head beneath the blankets.

We gather in the hallway. We can't not.

The air that wafts downward is thick; it settles on us in a mist of unease. We feel dizzy and disoriented. We feel as though we are stuffed full of cotton. We *feel*, and we are unused to feeling.

Francis reaches a shaking, insignificant hand to close the door, but before he solidifies enough to make contact, Jekyll runs past in a flash of black and white, darting up the stairs and into the shadows of the attic.

Susan's mouth opens so wide her face elongates like pulled taffy. Giles trembles, his chains skittering on the floor. Francis's hand hovers halfway through the staircase. For a moment, we wonder if he'll simply push the stairs back up and shut the door, leaving Jekyll to his fate. But even Francis isn't that terrible. Like the house, Jekyll is *ours*. Losing him would be like losing part of our own scaffolding. It is a fate none of us want to contemplate. We have to bring him back down.

Floating up into the trap door is as easy as releasing a clenched fist. Once inside the attic, our dizziness intensifies, but it's different for each of us. For Giles, it brings back the heat and dehydration of his jail cell. For Rose, it's the sensation of the airplane in free-fall, just before the crash. It reminds Kenneth of sitting in his car, hose running from the tailpipe to the cracked passenger window, swigging vodka while the fumes did their work. All of us silently scream, holding heads we don't have. All of us search for Jekyll.

He finds us before we find him. His eyes, round as marbles, stare at us from a pitch-dark alcove. Rose reaches out a wispy hand, beckons with transparent fingers, as she's seen Callie do countless times. But Jekyll doesn't blink, and he doesn't move. He's waiting for us to come to him. We edge closer, fighting the increasing feeling of dislocation. With each step, we worry our legs will simply pull free of our feet, that our heads will float like balloons toward the rafters. We huddle together, to keep ourselves from dissipating into nothingness.

And then we see it. The opening behind Jekyll.

We can't decide if it's full of a deeper darkness, or a strange light. Possibly it's both, half and half, like Jekyll's fur. The closer we get to the opening, the more dizzy we feel. As if we are trapped in the crushing weight of our nonexistent bodies, but also as if our bodies are flying apart – as if we're losing the very thing that holds us together.

Jekyll curls his tail around his paws and gives us a slow blink.

Giles steps forward. He's been dead the longest of us, and whether that makes him brave or simply tired we don't know. The rest of us cling together, watching his chains sway in the darkness. But as he approaches Jekyll, Giles grows less distinct. His edges soften and blend into shadow; we can see right through his torso into the opening that widens in front of him. It's as if the opening is swallowing Giles. It's as if Giles is dissolving into the opening. And we, we begin to lose our sense of Giles. We forget the weight of his chains bumping against us, the sound of their rattle. We forget the cupboard he most liked to haunt. We cannot call to mind the contours of his face, the feeling of his presence in the house. He is becoming something different – something *not us.*

Francis knocks against the walls in warning. Susan's horrified face has stretched so that she is all mouth, her chin brushing against her feet, and she makes a sound of distress like floors settling. But Giles walks straight past Jekyll. He doesn't stop. His hair, the hem of his pants, even the tips of his fingers become gossamer and fog-like, drifting toward the opening like a candle flame toward an open window. He is a ball of yarn unwinding. The opening is unraveling him, strand by strand, and we can't stop it. Rose shrieks like a tree breaking in the wind, and Francis tumbles a set of boxes in the far corner. And still, Jekyll sits with wide, placid eyes, as if nothing at all is wrong.

And then the chains Giles has worn since he died – an echo of the chains that shackled him in his jail cell when he was a young, living man – fall away and clatter silently to the floor. Giles lifts and turns his wrists, smooth and bare for the first time in centuries. And even as his body grows more and more transparent, even as he breaks apart entirely, he turns to us with an expression like an indrawn breath. He's bathed in darkness and light for a shining moment, and then he's gone.

* * *

Later, after we've fled the attic, after we've hidden behind mirrors and inside closets and beneath beds, we'll debate whether Jekyll is an angel or a demon. We'll avoid him when he yawns and stretches and laps water from his dish. Even Kenneth will try not to catch Jekyll's eye. We'll watch Callie close the trap door the next morning, and wonder what she's thinking. We'll wonder if Giles's chains are still lying on the attic floor, or if they've faded away. We'll wonder if Giles is still Giles, somewhere.

We'll stay here, in our house. Some of us will forgive Jekyll. Some of us will even forgive Francis. We'll remain *us*. We'll remain.

Giles will grow less and less distinct in our memory, like a long-ago story we used to tell. But we'll always remember his chains falling. We'll remember how he seemed to shed himself like an old skin; how, even after the opening erased him, it yawned wider, an insatiable gullet. We'll never stop wondering what it meant.

We'll look nervously at the trap door, and wonder when it will be our turn to follow.

Apartment 3G

Brianna Ishii-McFaull

I WAKE TO the sound of a child crying, loud and insistent. Even before I'm fully conscious, I know it's coming from 3G. I run my hand over my face with a groan. Exhaustion covers me like a heavy blanket, weighing down my limbs and making my movements clumsy. *I'm so tired! I just want to rest.* But once again, my youngest neighbour is making too much noise.

While many of the other tenants are known to be loud, none are as consistently disruptive as whoever lives in the last apartment on my floor. Maybe it's because I'd had children of my own once, but there's something about a baby's cries that cuts right through me. It can't be ignored, unlike the yelling, loud music and occasional bout of breaking dishes that emanates from the other units.

I'm sure it'll stop soon. It always does, I think to myself as I lie there filled with restless tension. I close my eyes and try to go back to sleep but the pitiful sobs keep me tethered to consciousness. *Any second now…* I am keenly aware of the passage of time as the minutes tick by, my cognizance of it seeming to amplify the sound. The cries fill the room like water in a bathtub, submerging me in the child's distress. Two minutes becomes five, then ten, then fifteen as I fidget anxiously, twisting my hands together over my stomach.

The wails reach a screeching crescendo and I realize rest isn't coming so long as the baby is crying. With a resigned sigh, I give up on sleep and rise. *Just a quick look,* I promise myself as I step out into the fluorescent brightness of the hallway and make my way towards the source of the sobbing.

I shouldn't be doing this – it's none of my business. I'm so weak already… My own tired objections run through my mind as I traverse the long, narrow hallway connecting the elevator to the units. Three doors bearing rusted brass markers for 3B, 3C and 3D line the wall across from the elevator, with 3E and 3F on either side of the ancient, sluggish contraption. My own apartment, 3A, is on the far-left wall. 3G is directly across, at the opposite end of the corridor.

The building has looked the same for years, since long before I moved in. The carpet is a sickly shade of yellow-beige that may have once had a pattern, now faded and stained brown in certain spots. Dust and dirt collect in the corners and water stains decorate walls covered in outdated, peeling wallpaper that had probably been hideous even in its prime. Mismatched lightbulbs cast the hall in varying shades of white and blue, the glow doing nothing to hide the many deficiencies. The complex is a run-down mess but the people who live here are past caring about cosmetic offenses.

I reach the last apartment and pause, surprised to see that the door is ajar. Hesitantly, I approach, peering through the crack to the dwelling within. What I can see of the living room is filthy. Trash covers the coffee table and floor – a mix of pill containers, empty liquor bottles and food waste. An old grey couch sits with its back to the kitchen, its surface covered in stains. A hole in the lower-right side spills crumbling mustard-yellow foam into the ocean of waste around it. Muted sunlight forces its way through the threadbare fabric of the curtains, casting the room in a soft glow.

The baby's cries are coming from the bedroom at the back of the unit. They're filled with the anger and distress only an upset child can manage. *I wonder where the mother is.* I don't see anyone in the front room and aside from the wailing, the apartment is dark and silent.

I push my way through the door and silently navigate a short hallway carpeted with more empties and fast-food wrappers. The layout is identical to my own unit: a kitchen on the left that opens into the living room, and a bathroom and small second bedroom on the right. All the rooms are in a similar state. Apparently, no one has been taking care of this apartment for a very long time.

As I get closer to the master bedroom at the end of the hall, the volume of the child's cries increases. The door is open wide and hanging askew – the upper hinge broken and the wooden surface dented around face level. The sight summons memories of my own life I would have rather left in the past. A terrible sense of premonition fills me as I approach the doorway, accompanied by fear that is ultimately unfounded. *It's not as though anything can hurt me,* I tell myself as the room comes into view.

A woman lies sideways on the bed, wiry limbs sprawled haphazardly over the rumpled blue linens. Dark bruises mar the pale skin of her face and arms and her light brown hair spreads across the comforter in greasy, limp strands. My stomach does a slow flip as I spy the belt around her upper arm and a needle on the bed by her elbow. She's alive but clearly unconscious, floating in a drug-induced haze. She doesn't even stir as her daughter continues to scream from the playpen set up next to the bed.

Horrified pity swells as I look at the child, standing up in the pen. She grips the edge as she wails for her mother, chubby hand grasping and reaching for the prone figure only six feet away. She has her mom's hair, hanging in a tangled mess around her tear-streaked face, red with exertion. She's wearing nothing but a diaper that I can see from here is soiled. Her pen is bare, only a ragged blanket and a small stuffed giraffe to occupy her as she waits for her caretaker to return from her trip. Evidence of what her mother prefers to spend her money and time on surrounds the child – a sea of multi-colored glass, discarded clothes and pill bottles cover the floor between us. Only a few bare spots of beige carpet remain, creating a path between the bed, the pen, and the door.

When she sees me, her cries quiet slightly, soft sobs escaping her tiny body. Though my first instinct is to go to her, I hesitate, knowing I have not fully recovered since my last outing. But one glance at her mother, still passed out and unresponsive, decides the matter.

Resolved, I make my way over the piles of detritus to reach the baby, thankful the broken glass and needles hiding in the mounds pose no threat to me. She stretches her arms out, obviously having decided an unknown adult is better than nothing, and I lift her up. She feels warm and solid against me but far too thin. Based off the state of her home and how often I'd heard her crying before this, it's clear this is not the first time her needs have gone unattended. Guilt assails me at the realization. *I should have come sooner!*

I croon to her as I walk back out to the hall, snagging a pale pink baby bag from the floor on my way. It lifts off the ground with a clatter. I clear the kitchen table off with a sweep of my arm and pull a faded changing mat out of the side pocket of the bag. It seems dirty but it's certainly better than exposing her to whatever sticky substance coats the cracked linoleum. I spread it out across the table's worn surface and lay her down, tucking a soft yellow blanket around her so she won't roll off the edge. There are barely any supplies left, but I manage to find just enough to change her diaper. Laying the items on the edge of the mat, I get to work, thankful my sense of smell is practically nonexistent. I begin to feel weak but I ignore it, concentrating on the task at hand.

The child is quiet as I toil, with only an occasional sniffle to break her silence. I talk to her softly, telling her that she'll be alright. I don't know that it's true but I can't bring myself to say anything else. Anger fills me at how completely her mother has failed her. I had made mistakes with my own children but even in my darkest moments I had never allowed my desire to escape to overpower my need to provide for them. I would have never abandoned them – I only left because I had to.

As I smooth down the last tab of the diaper, her stomach grumbles loudly. She whimpers again, sniffles threatening to become sobs, and I shush her soothingly. I check the fridge for a bottle and to my relief, find one already made. Pushing through the looming fatigue, I set about warming it up. The little one lies on the table silently, watching me with eyes far too old for someone so young.

As I stand in the middle of the room trying to conserve my strength, I contemplate adding the dirty diaper to the mound of garbage in the corner of the kitchen. Somewhere beneath the heap was a trashcan, now completely obscured. A shudder of disgust runs through me at the thought of how long it would take to grow a pile that large. Wearily, I discard the idea and leave the makeshift changing table as it is. I've already expended too much of my energy and I still have to feed her.

Worry gnaws at me as I think about the little girl. Clearly no one but her inept caretaker lives here and from the state I'd found them in, it's unlikely that she'll be receiving proper care going forward. *What am I going to do?* My options are very limited but I know I have to do something. *I can't leave her like this!* I'm filled with guilt at the thought of what she's already suffered through. *How much of that is on my hands?* I wonder, remembering how often I'd heard her crying before this. *How much of her pain could I have prevented?*

A soft beep indicates the bottle is ready. I test it against my wrist, judging it cool enough for the fussing baby. Summoning my strength, I lift her back into my arms and tilt the bottle down towards her. She latches on, sucking greedily as I stroke her leg with my thumb, urging her to drink slower. I cast a look back into the hallway but there's no movement – her mother has slept through the entire process.

I burp her when she's drained the bottle and leave it on the table with the rest of her supplies. *What's one more empty?* I think wryly as I rock her. Happy little coos emanate from her as she drifts off into sleep, needs finally sated. I press my lips to her head and whisper my apologies to her. Apologies for the cards she's been dealt, for the life she's been born into. Apologies for the mother she has been entrusted to and what I must do to give her any hope of a future.

Though I'm no fan of the foster system, having grown up in it myself, I know a child as young as her has a good chance of being adopted. So, I use my waning strength to call the police from the landline in the kitchen, cradling the neglected baby against my chest as we wait.

It doesn't take long. Flashing blue and red lights cast a strobe-like pattern across dingy cupboards as I stare out the grimy kitchen window to the police cruiser below. Two officers – a blond man in his mid-thirties and a younger man with dark hair. The older one seems familiar to me but he's too far away to be sure. As they begin to ascend the stairs into the building, I quietly make my way back into the bedroom with the sleeping child.

With the last of my energy, I lay her down in the pen. She stirs, blinking up at me sleepily, then reaches for me as I tuck the worn blanket around her and place the stuffed giraffe at her side. Sadly, I shake my head and stroke the soft skin of her cheek.

"I'm sorry, little one. It's time for us to part ways."

"Police! Is anyone here?"

The officer's voice, coming from the front door, confirms my initial suspicion. I remember him coming to pay my own home a visit once, long ago. It's a good thing – I recall his kindness as he carried my girls from the building when I could no longer look after them.

I hear the noises of disgust from the cops as they enter the filthy apartment. Clinking bottles and the crunching of wrappers signal their progression through the front room and down the hall. I step behind the playpen and up against the far wall as they finally reach the master bedroom.

The horror and sadness on their faces as they take in the scene before them is an echo of my own. The dark-haired officer immediately goes to the baby as his partner kneels on the bed next to the mother, feeling for a pulse. I stand in the darkest corner of the room, an invisible witness.

The next few minutes are a flurry of activity as they radio for an ambulance and social services. The younger officer carries the quietly-fussing baby out into the living room while the blond remains with the mother. My exhaustion urges me to return to my own home but I'm determined to see this through.

At some point before the paramedics arrive, the mother wakes, immediately becoming belligerent. Rage fills me at her lack of remorse, her slurred insistence that they give her the baby and leave. Despite how weak helping her daughter has left me, I feel myself becoming more solid as my anger grows.

Feeling seeps into my numb limbs, the sensations stark in comparison to the cold nothingness that usually suffuses me. I am acutely aware of the smooth surface of the wall behind me, the feel of fabric and broken glass beneath my feet. But these perceptions are dim background noise in comparison to the *hatred* I feel for the woman before me, neglecting a gift that I had been robbed of. The strain of holding my physical form weighs on me, burning up my anger like gasoline in a hungry fire. I know the moment the mother becomes aware of my presence. I hiss at her, my voice cold and inhuman, audible only to her.

"You have failed her!"

Her eyes widen and she begins to scream with primal terror, pointing behind the officer to my corner. I fade back into the shadows, dizzy with exertion and numb once again, as he attempts to calm her.

"It's just the drugs! There's no one there – you're safe."

The blond officer repeats his words over and over as the paramedics finally arrive. The mother is quickly sedated, her body strapped to a gurney and wheeled out to the waiting ambulance. I watch her go without a trace of pity or remorse for her state. With any luck, this will be a turning point for her.

I follow the blond officer back to the kitchen, where his partner stands in the middle of the room with his back to the door. The child is crying again, distressed by the sound of her mother screaming and the strangers all around her. Feeling guilty for my part in that, I float up behind the dark-haired officer to stroke the child's tear-stained cheek. She reaches out for me again, seeking the comfort of familiarity, but I can only shake my head. I sing softly to her instead – an old lullaby I used to sing my own girls long ago. She quiets, tucking her little face against the officer's shoulder. He rubs her back soothingly as he confers with his partner, both men oblivious to my presence.

"Social's on the way. About 15 minutes."

The blond nods in acknowledgement, running a hand through his hair with a tired sigh as the younger officer continues, "I found something while you were in the other room. Take a look."

He motions to the kitchen table, where the changing supplies and empty bottle sit discarded. "Someone fed and changed her recently. Probably the same person who made the call. What did they say to the operator?"

"Nothing – it was dead air. Most likely a concerned neighbour who didn't want to get too involved."

The blond combs through the baby bag as he responds, searching for supplies as I had. The social worker would want to take whatever was available when she arrived.

"Should we knock on some doors? Ask around and see if we can find out who made the call?" the younger officer inquires, gently rocking the baby like someone who's used to holding one. The blond shakes his head.

"No point. This is the kind of building where people mind their own business. We're lucky anyone even cared enough to call. Without them, this poor little girl probably would've died of neglect."

Though it's a horrible thought, I feel validated by the older officer's opinion. My actions had been necessary, no matter how heart-wrenching it is to see the little one so distressed. *At least she's a little calmer now,* I think to myself, watching her lie passively against the man's shoulder. The younger officer looks disturbed by his partner's comment.

"Have you been to this building before? Is it known to be this… shady?"

The blond nods as he begins packing what little supplies remain into the bag.

"Many times. The worst one was about nine years back, when I was a rookie. I'd only been on the force for about a year when we got the call. Domestic disturbance, shots fired."

He sighs heavily, a look of weariness on his face. My throat is tight with grief as I listen to him recount an event that I still relive almost every night.

"We arrived on scene and came up to the third floor. I remember how fast my heart was beating as we made our way down the hall, to the last apartment on the left – 3A. There was a pool of blood leaking out from under the door. As soon as I saw it, I knew that whatever was inside would haunt me until the day I died."

He shakes his head as he rises, his gaze distant. He leaves the bag on the floor next to him and leans back against the counter, crossing his arms over his chest. His partner is silent, waiting for him to continue. In his arms, the baby's eyes are beginning to drift closed again, lulled by the officer's rocking and the silence of the house.

I watch the blond man from the kitchen doorway, my body bound to the present but my mind trapped in the past with his. Unbidden, I find myself recalling the loudness of the final gunshot, the coppery smell of Marcus' blood filling the air. *Or was it my own? There was so much blood…* The officer takes a moment to compose himself and when he speaks again, his voice is thick with emotion.

"Two deceased when we arrived. A big, ugly bastard, almost blocking the front door, and a woman – late twenties, working girl. The kids were hers. Best we could figure, she got into an argument with her pimp and her shot her. Right in front of her daughters. They were hiding in their bedroom when we got there. Fuckin' awful."

"Jesus. And the pimp - how did he die?"

The younger officer lays his hand on the back of the little girl's head, as if his touch could shield her from my past. The blond sighs and shakes his head, uncrossing his arms to rest them on either side of him, gripping the edge of the counter. Without meaning to, I find myself drawing closer to the older officer, wanting to watch his face as he remembers that night. *As we remember that night.*

"I wish I knew. The coroner could never figure it out. He said the mother would have been dead instantly so she couldn't have killed him. It definitely wasn't self-inflicted, so that leaves the girls or a third person in the house. But we didn't find any prints except his and those girls were so young I doubt they could have even lifted the gun, let alone taken it from him and shot him."

"Did they see anything? Another person in the house?" his partner presses, his expression curious. Another head shake.

"Nope. In fact, they said it was their mommy. That she protected them. They insisted she was still in the apartment and cried for her the whole time I carried them out."

A look of bewilderment and sadness paints his face as he stares off into the second bedroom, no doubt reliving the moment as I am. *Such heartbroken sobs.* Even the memory of them is enough to make my chest ache in a way that feels almost human again.

There's a heavy silence as he finishes his story. I stand in front of him, ghostly tears pouring down my cheeks to evaporate before they hit the ground. I can see the burden of every case he's worked etched in his very being – in the lines on his brow, the greying at his temples, the weariness in his eyes. I know better than anyone that there are some experiences that never truly leave you, just as you never really leave them.

"What happened to them? The girls, I mean," the younger officer asks from behind me, his tone subdued. I suck in a redundant breath and hold it, unexpected hope blossoming at the question. Though I've always known they must have ended up in a foster home, I don't know the specifics of what had become of my children after the blond officer took them away. I tried to find out where they went and if they were doing alright, but to no avail. My spirit is bound to this building – a prisoner of circumstance, even in death. I accepted the eternal uncertainty long ago and tried to take comfort in the knowledge that I had protected them from Marcus, even if I wasn't able to protect myself. *But now...*

"They went into the system. Got adopted by a nice family just outside the city. The oldest one is in high school now. She's doing good. Straight A's, great soccer player – a real bright future. The younger one is going into middle school soon. She's an artist and loves to draw. I still visit them every year on the anniversary. They're good kids. Strong in spite of their rough start, or maybe because of it. Hell, I don't know. What I can say is that their mother would have been proud."

He gives the younger man a bittersweet smile over my invisible head and I know the expression is mirrored on my own face. His words fill me with a joy I haven't experienced in almost a decade. Though it's a poor substitute for being in my daughter's lives, the news is a precious gift. *I am so proud of them. Always have been.*

On impulse, I reach out and wrap my phantom arms around him, pressing my face against his broad chest. He can't feel my touch any more than I can feel him in this intangible state, but his heartbeat is a steady thump in my ear, comforting after years of my own non-existent functions.

"Thank you for watching over them," I whisper to him, for his ears alone. He stiffens and I know he hears me. His eyes dart around the room nervously but before he can react further, the spell is broken by the sound of footsteps in the outer hallway. The social worker is here for the baby. *It's just as well* – this venture has taxed my reserves far beyond their normal limits and I'll need a long rest to recover.

As the apartment is once again filled with activity, I make my way back to the front door. From across the living room, I can see the older officer looking around surreptitiously, his expression perplexed. The younger officer speaks to the social worker in low tones, explaining the situation as he continues to rhythmically shift his weight back and forth.

With a final wave to the baby sleepily watching me over the cop's shoulder, I step back into the hallway and return to my home. For the first time since my murder, I think I'm going to have a restful sleep.

A View from a Hill

M.R. James

HOW PLEASANT IT can be, alone in a first-class railway carriage, on the first day of a holiday that is to be fairly long, to dawdle through a bit of English country that is unfamiliar, stopping at every station. You have a map open on your knee, and you pick out the villages that lie to right and left by their church towers. You marvel at the complete stillness that attends your stoppage at the stations, broken only by a footstep crunching the gravel. Yet perhaps that is best experienced after sundown, and the traveller I have in mind was making his leisurely progress on a sunny afternoon in the latter half of June.

He was in the depths of the country. I need not particularize further than to say that if you divided the map of England into four quarters, he would have been found in the south-western of them.

He was a man of academic pursuits, and his term was just over. He was on his way to meet a new friend, older than himself. The two of them had met first on an official inquiry in town, had found that they had many tastes and habits in common, liked each other, and the result was an invitation from Squire Richards to Mr. Fanshawe which was now taking effect.

The journey ended about five o'clock. Fanshawe was told by a cheerful country porter that the car from the Hall had been up to the station and left a message that something had to be fetched from half a mile farther on, and would the gentleman please to wait a few minutes till it came back? "But I see," continued the porter, "as you've got your bysticle, and very like you'd find it pleasanter to ride up to the 'All yourself. Straight up the road 'ere, and then first turn to the left – it ain't above two mile – and I'll see as your things is put in the car for you. You'll excuse me mentioning it, only I thought it were a nice evening for a ride. Yes, sir, very seasonable weather for the haymakers: let me see, I have your bike ticket. Thank you, sir; much obliged: you can't miss your road, etc., etc."

The two miles to the Hall were just what was needed, after the day in the train, to dispel somnolence and impart a wish for tea. The Hall, when sighted, also promised just what was needed in the way of a quiet resting-place after days of sitting on committees and college-meetings. It was neither excitingly old nor depressingly new. Plastered walls, sash-windows, old trees, smooth lawns, were the features which Fanshawe noticed as he came up the drive. Squire Richards, a burly man of sixty odd, was awaiting him in the porch with evident pleasure.

"Tea first," he said, "or would you like a longer drink? No? All right, tea's ready in the garden. Come along, they'll put your machine away. I always have tea under the lime-tree by the stream on a day like this."

Nor could you ask for a better place. Midsummer afternoon, shade and scent of a vast lime-tree, cool, swirling water within five yards. It was long before either of them suggested a move. But about six, Mr. Richards sat up, knocked out his pipe, and said: "Look here, it's cool enough now to think of a stroll, if you're inclined? All right: then what I suggest is that we walk up the park and get on to the hill-side, where we can look over the country. We'll have a map, and I'll show you where things are; and you can go off on your machine, or we can take the car, according as you want exercise or not. If you're ready, we can start now and be back well before eight, taking it very easy."

"I'm ready. I should like my stick, though, and have you got any field-glasses? I lent mine to a man a week ago, and he's gone off Lord knows where and taken them with him."

Mr. Richards pondered. "Yes," he said, "I have, but they're not things I use myself, and I don't know whether the ones I have will suit you. They're old-fashioned, and about twice as heavy as they make 'em now. You're welcome to have them, but I won't carry them. By the way, what do you want to drink after dinner?"

Protestations that anything would do were overruled, and a satisfactory settlement was reached on the way to the front hall, where Mr. Fanshawe found his stick, and Mr. Richards, after thoughtful pinching of his lower lip, resorted to a drawer in the hall-table, extracted a key, crossed to a cupboard in the panelling, opened it, took a box from the shelf, and put it on the table. "The glasses are in there," he said, "and there's some dodge of opening it, but I've forgotten what it is. You try." Mr. Fanshawe accordingly tried. There was no keyhole, and the box was solid, heavy and smooth: it seemed obvious that some part of it would have to be pressed before anything could happen. "The corners," said he to himself, "are the likely places; and infernally sharp corners they are too," he added, as he put his thumb in his mouth after exerting force on a lower corner.

"What's the matter?" said the Squire.

"Why, your disgusting Borgia box has scratched me, drat it," said Fanshawe. The Squire chuckled unfeelingly. "Well, you've got it open, anyway," he said.

"So I have! Well, I don't begrudge a drop of blood in a good cause, and here are the glasses. They are pretty heavy, as you said, but I think I'm equal to carrying them."

"Ready?" said the Squire. "Come on then; we go out by the garden."

So they did, and passed out into the park, which sloped decidedly upwards to the hill which, as Fanshawe had seen from the train, dominated the country. It was a spur of a larger range that lay behind. On the way, the Squire, who was great on earthworks, pointed out various spots where he detected or imagined traces of war-ditches and the like. "And here," he said, stopping on a more or less level plot with a ring of large trees, "is Baxter's Roman villa." "Baxter?" said Mr. Fanshawe.

"I forgot; you don't know about him. He was the old chap I got those glasses from. I believe he made them. He was an old watch-maker down in the village, a great antiquary. My father gave him leave to grub about where he liked; and when he made a find he used to lend him a man or two to help him with the digging. He got a surprising lot of things together, and when he died – I dare say it's ten or fifteen years ago – I bought the whole lot and gave them to the town museum. We'll run in one of these days, and look over them. The glasses came to me with the rest, but of course I kept them. If you look at them, you'll see they're more or less amateur work – the body of them; naturally the lenses weren't his making."

"Yes, I see they are just the sort of thing that a clever workman in a different line of business might turn out. But I don't see why he made them so heavy. And did Baxter actually find a Roman villa here?"

"Yes, there's a pavement turfed over, where we're standing: it was too rough and plain to be worth taking up, but of course there are drawings of it: and the small things and pottery that turned up were quite good of their kind. An ingenious chap, old Baxter: he seemed to have a quite out-of-the-way instinct for these things. He was invaluable to our archaeologists. He used to shut up his shop for days at a time, and wander off over the district, marking down places, where he scented anything, on the ordnance map; and he kept a book with fuller notes of the places. Since his death, a good many of them have been sampled, and there's always been something to justify him."

"What a good man!" said Mr. Fanshawe.

"Good?" said the Squire, pulling up brusquely.

"I meant useful to have about the place," said Mr. Fanshawe. "But was he a villain?"

"I don't know about that either," said the Squire; "but all I can say is, if he was good, he wasn't lucky. And he wasn't liked: I didn't like him," he added, after a moment.

"Oh?" said Fanshawe interrogatively.

"No, I didn't; but that's enough about Baxter: besides, this is the stiffest bit, and I don't want to talk and walk as well."

Indeed it was hot, climbing a slippery grass slope that evening. "I told you I should take you the short way," panted the Squire, "and I wish I hadn't. However, a bath won't do us any harm when we get back. Here we are, and there's the seat."

A small clump of old Scotch firs crowned the top of the hill; and, at the edge of it, commanding the cream of the view, was a wide and solid seat, on which the two disposed themselves, and wiped their brows, and regained breath.

"Now, then," said the Squire, as soon as he was in a condition to talk connectedly, "this is where your glasses come in. But you'd better take a general look round first. My word! I've never seen the view look better."

Writing as I am now with a winter wind flapping against dark windows and a rushing, tumbling sea within a hundred yards, I find it hard to summon up the feelings and words which will put my reader in possession of the June evening and the lovely English landscape of which the Squire was speaking.

Across a broad level plain they looked upon ranges of great hills, whose uplands – some green, some furred with woods – caught the light of a sun, westering but not yet low. And all the plain was fertile, though the river which traversed it was nowhere seen. There were copses, green wheat, hedges and pasture-land: the little compact white moving cloud marked the evening train. Then the eye picked out red farms and grey houses, and nearer home scattered cottages, and then the Hall, nestled under the hill. The smoke of chimneys was very blue and straight. There was a smell of hay in the air: there were wild roses on bushes hard by. It was the acme of summer.

After some minutes of silent contemplation, the Squire began to point out the leading features, the hills and valleys, and told where the towns and villages lay. "Now," he said, "with the glasses you'll be able to pick out Fulnaker Abbey. Take a line across that big green field, then over the wood beyond it, then over the farm on the knoll."

"Yes, yes," said Fanshawe. "I've got it. What a fine tower!"

"You must have got the wrong direction," said the Squire; "there's not much of a tower about there that I remember, unless it's Oldbourne Church that you've got hold of. And if you call that a fine tower, you're easily pleased."

"Well, I do call it a fine tower," said Fanshawe, the glasses still at his eyes, "whether it's Oldbourne or any other. And it must belong to a largish church; it looks to me like a central tower – four big pinnacles at the corners, and four smaller ones between. I must certainly go over there. How far is it?"

"Oldbourne's about nine miles, or less," said the Squire. "It's a long time since I've been there, but I don't remember thinking much of it. Now I'll show you another thing."

Fanshawe had lowered the glasses, and was still gazing in the Oldbourne direction. "No," he said, "I can't make out anything with the naked eye. What was it you were going to show me?"

"A good deal more to the left – it oughtn't to be difficult to find. Do you see a rather sudden knob of a hill with a thick wood on top of it? It's in a dead line with that single tree on the top of the big ridge."

"I do," said Fanshawe, "and I believe I could tell you without much difficulty what it's called."

"Could you now?" said the Squire. "Say on."

"Why, Gallows Hill," was the answer.

"How did you guess that?"

"Well, if you don't want it guessed, you shouldn't put up a dummy gibbet and a man hanging on it."

"What's that?" said the Squire abruptly. "There's nothing on that hill but wood."

"On the contrary," said Fanshawe, "there's a largish expanse of grass on the top and your dummy gibbet in the middle; and I thought there was something on it when I looked first. But I see there's nothing – or is there? I can't be sure."

"Nonsense, nonsense, Fanshawe, there's no such thing as a dummy gibbet, or any other sort, on that hill. And it's thick wood – a fairly young plantation. I was in it myself not a year ago. Hand me the glasses, though I don't suppose I can see anything." After a pause: "No, I thought not: they won't show a thing."

Meanwhile Fanshawe was scanning the hill – it might be only two or three miles away. "Well, it's very odd," he said, "it does look exactly like a wood without the glass." He took it again. "That is one of the oddest effects. The gibbet is perfectly plain, and the grass field, and there even seem to be people on it, and carts, or a cart, with men in it. And yet when I take the glass away, there's nothing. It must be something in the way this afternoon light falls: I shall come up earlier in the day when the sun's full on it."

"Did you say you saw people and a cart on that hill?" said the Squire incredulously. "What should they be doing there at this time of day, even if the trees have been felled? Do talk sense – look again."

"Well, I certainly thought I saw them. Yes, I should say there were a few, just clearing off. And now – by Jove, it does look like something hanging on the gibbet. But these glasses are so beastly heavy I can't hold them steady for long. Anyhow, you can take it from me there's no wood. And if you'll show me the road on the map, I'll go there tomorrow."

The Squire remained brooding for some little time. At last he rose and said, "Well, I suppose that will be the best way to settle it. And now we'd better be getting back. Bath and dinner is my idea." And on the way back he was not very communicative.

They returned through the garden, and went into the front hall to leave sticks, etc., in their due place. And here they found the aged butler Patten evidently in a state of some anxiety. "Beg pardon, Master Henry," he began at once, "but someone's been up to mischief here, I'm much afraid." He pointed to the open box which had contained the glasses.

"Nothing worse than that, Patten?" said the Squire. "Mayn't I take out my own glasses and lend them to a friend? Bought with my own money, you recollect? At old Baxter's sale, eh?"

Patten bowed, unconvinced. "Oh, very well, Master Henry, as long as you know who it was. Only I thought proper to name it, for I didn't think that box'd been off its shelf since you first put it there; and, if you'll excuse me, after what happened…". The voice was lowered, and the rest was not audible to Fanshawe. The Squire replied with a few words and a gruff laugh, and called on Fanshawe to come and be shown his room. And I do not think that anything else happened that night which bears on my story.

Except, perhaps, the sensation which invaded Fanshawe in the small hours that something had been let out which ought not to have been let out. It came into his dreams. He was walking in a garden which he seemed half to know, and stopped in front of a rockery made of old wrought stones, pieces of window tracery from a church, and even bits of figures. One of these moved his curiosity: it seemed to be a sculptured capital with scenes carved on it. He felt he must pull it out, and worked away, and, with an ease that surprised him, moved the stones that obscured it aside, and pulled out the block. As he did so, a tin label fell down by his feet with a little clatter. He picked it up and read on it: "On no account move this stone. Yours sincerely, J. Patten." As often happens in dreams, he felt that this injunction was of extreme importance; and with an anxiety that amounted to anguish he looked to see if the stone had really been shifted. Indeed it had; in fact, he could not see it anywhere. The removal had disclosed the mouth of a burrow, and he bent down to look into it. Something stirred in the blackness, and then, to his intense horror, a hand emerged – a clean right hand in a neat cuff and coatsleeve, just in the attitude of a hand that means to shake yours. He wondered whether it would not be rude to let it alone. But, as he looked at it, it began to grow hairy and dirty and thin, and also to change its pose and stretch out as if to take hold of his leg. At that he dropped all thought of politeness, decided to run, screamed and woke himself up.

This was the dream he remembered; but it seemed to him (as, again, it often does) that there had been others of the same import before, but not so insistent. He lay awake for some little time, fixing the details of the last dream in his mind, and wondering in particular what the figures had been which he had seen or half seen on the carved capital. Something quite incongruous, he felt sure; but that was the most he could recall.

Whether because of the dream, or because it was the first day of his holiday, he did not get up very early; nor did he at once plunge into the exploration of the country. He spent a morning, half lazy, half instructive, in looking over the volumes of the County Archaeological Society's transactions, in which were many contributions from Mr. Baxter on finds of flint implements, Roman sites, ruins of monastic establishments – in fact, most departments of archaeology. They were written in an odd, pompous, only half-educated style. If the man had had more early schooling, thought Fanshawe, he would have been a very distinguished antiquary; or he might have been (he thus qualified his opinion a little later), but for a certain love of opposition and controversy, and, yes, a patronizing tone as of one possessing superior knowledge, which left an unpleasant taste. He might have been a very respectable artist. There was an imaginary restoration and elevation of a priory church which was very well conceived. A fine pinnacled central tower was a conspicuous feature of this; it reminded Fanshawe of that which he had seen from the hill, and which the Squire had told him must be Oldbourne. But it was not Oldbourne; it was Fulnaker Priory. "Oh, well," he said to himself, "I suppose Oldbourne Church may have been built by Fulnaker monks, and Baxter has copied Oldbourne tower. Anything about it in the letterpress? Ah, I see it was published after his death – found among his papers."

After lunch the Squire asked Fanshawe what he meant to do.

"Well," said Fanshawe, "I think I shall go out on my bike about four as far as Oldbourne and back by Gallows Hill. That ought to be a round of about fifteen miles, oughtn't it?"

"About that," said the Squire, "and you'll pass Lambsfield and Wanstone, both of which are worth looking at. There's a little glass at Lambsfield and the stone at Wanstone."

"Good," said Fanshawe, "I'll get tea somewhere, and may I take the glasses? I'll strap them on my bike, on the carrier."

"Of course, if you like," said the Squire. "I really ought to have some better ones. If I go into the town today, I'll see if I can pick up some."

"Why should you trouble to do that if you can't use them yourself?" said Fanshawe.

"Oh, I don't know; one ought to have a decent pair; and – well, old Patten doesn't think those are fit to use."

"Is he a judge?"

"He's got some tale: I don't know: something about old Baxter. I've promised to let him tell me about it. It seems very much on his mind since last night."

"Why that? Did he have a nightmare like me?"

"He had something: he was looking an old man this morning, and he said he hadn't closed an eye."

"Well, let him save up his tale till I come back."

"Very well, I will if I can. Look here, are you going to be late? If you get a puncture eight miles off and have to walk home, what then? I don't trust these bicycles: I shall tell them to give us cold things to eat."

"I shan't mind that, whether I'm late or early. But I've got things to mend punctures with. And now I'm off."

* * *

It was just as well that the Squire had made that arrangement about a cold supper, Fanshawe thought, and not for the first time, as he wheeled his bicycle up the drive about nine o'clock. So also the Squire thought and said, several times, as he met him in the hall, rather pleased at the confirmation of his want of faith in bicycles than sympathetic with his hot, weary, thirsty, and indeed haggard, friend. In fact, the kindest thing he found to say was: "You'll want a long drink tonight? Cider-cup do? All right. Hear that, Patten? Cider-cup, iced, lots of it." Then to Fanshawe, "Don't be all night over your bath."

By half-past nine they were at dinner, and Fanshawe was reporting progress, if progress it might be called.

"I got to Lambsfield very smoothly, and saw the glass. It is very interesting stuff, but there's a lot of lettering I couldn't read."

"Not with glasses?" said the Squire.

"Those glasses of yours are no manner of use inside a church – or inside anywhere, I suppose, for that matter. But the only places I took 'em into were churches."

"H'm! Well, go on," said the Squire.

"However, I took some sort of a photograph of the window, and I dare say an enlargement would show what I want. Then Wanstone; I should think that stone was a very out-of-the-way thing, only I don't know about that class of antiquities. Has anybody opened the mound it stands on?"

"Baxter wanted to, but the farmer wouldn't let him."

"Oh, well, I should think it would be worth doing. Anyhow, the next thing was Fulnaker and Oldbourne. You know, it's very odd about that tower I saw from the hill. Oldbourne Church is nothing like it, and of course there's nothing over thirty feet high at Fulnaker, though you can see it had a central tower. I didn't tell you, did I? that Baxter's fancy drawing of Fulnaker shows a tower exactly like the one I saw."

"So you thought, I dare say," put in the Squire.

"No, it wasn't a case of thinking. The picture actually reminded me of what I'd seen, and I made sure it was Oldbourne, well before I looked at the title."

"Well, Baxter had a very fair idea of architecture. I dare say what's left made it easy for him to draw the right sort of tower."

"That may be it, of course, but I'm doubtful if even a professional could have got it so exactly right. There's absolutely nothing left at Fulnaker but the bases of the piers which supported it. However, that isn't the oddest thing."

"What about Gallows Hill?" said the Squire. "Here, Patten, listen to this. I told you what Mr. Fanshawe said he saw from the hill."

"Yes, Master Henry, you did; and I can't say I was so much surprised, considering."

"All right, all right. You keep that till afterwards. We want to hear what Mr. Fanshawe saw today. Go on, Fanshawe. You turned to come back by Ackford and Thorfield, I suppose?"

"Yes, and I looked into both the churches. Then I got to the turning which goes to the top of Gallows Hill; I saw that if I wheeled my machine over the field at the top of the hill I could join the home road on this side. It was about half-past six when I got to the top of the hill, and there was a gate on my right, where it ought to be, leading into the belt of plantation."

"You hear that, Patten? A belt, he says."

"So I thought it was – a belt. But it wasn't. You were quite right, and I was hopelessly wrong. I cannot understand it. The whole top is planted quite thick. Well, I went on into this wood, wheeling and dragging my bike, expecting every minute to come to a clearing, and then my misfortunes began. Thorns, I suppose; first I realized that the front tyre was slack, then the back. I couldn't stop to do more than try to find the punctures and mark them; but even that was hopeless. So I ploughed on, and the farther I went, the less I liked the place."

"Not much poaching in that cover, eh, Patten?" said the Squire.

"No, indeed, Master Henry: there's very few cares to go—"

"No, I know: never mind that now. Go on, Fanshawe."

"I don't blame anybody for not caring to go there. I know I had all the fancies one least likes: steps crackling over twigs behind me, indistinct people stepping behind trees in front of me, yes, and even a hand laid on my shoulder. I pulled up very sharp at that and looked round, but there really was no branch or bush that could have done it. Then, when I was just about at the middle of the plot, I was convinced that there was someone looking down on me from above—and not with any pleasant intent. I stopped again, or at least slackened my pace, to look up. And as I did, down I came, and barked my shins abominably on, what do you think? a block of stone with a big square hole in the top of it. And within a few paces there were two others just like it. The three were set in a triangle. Now, do you make out what they were put there for?"

"I think I can," said the Squire, who was now very grave and absorbed in the story. "Sit down, Patten."

It was time, for the old man was supporting himself by one hand, and leaning heavily on it. He dropped into a chair, and said in a very tremulous voice, "You didn't go between them stones, did you, sir?"

"I did not," said Fanshawe, emphatically. "I dare say I was an ass, but as soon as it dawned on me where I was, I just shouldered my machine and did my best to run. It seemed to me as if I was in an unholy evil sort of graveyard, and I was most profoundly thankful that it was one of the longest days and still sunlight. Well, I had a horrid run, even if it was only a few hundred yards. Everything caught on everything: handles and spokes and carrier and pedals—caught in them viciously, or I fancied so. I fell over at least five times. At last I saw the hedge, and I couldn't trouble to hunt for the gate."

"There is no gate on my side," the Squire interpolated.

"Just as well I didn't waste time, then. I dropped the machine over somehow and went into the road pretty near head-first; some branch or something got my ankle at the last moment. Anyhow, there I was out of the wood, and seldom more thankful or more generally sore. Then came the job of mending my punctures. I had a good outfit and I'm not at all bad at the business; but this was an absolutely hopeless case. It was seven when I got out of the wood, and I spent fifty minutes over one tyre. As fast as I found a hole and put on a patch, and blew it up, it went flat again. So I made up my mind to walk. That hill isn't three miles away, is it?"

"Not more across country, but nearer six by road."

"I thought it must be. I thought I couldn't have taken well over the hour over less than five miles, even leading a bike. Well, there's my story: where's yours and Patten's?"

"Mine? I've no story," said the Squire. "But you weren't very far out when you thought you were in a graveyard. There must be a good few of them up there, Patten, don't you think? They left 'em there when they fell to bits, I fancy."

Patten nodded, too much interested to speak. "Don't," said Fanshawe.

"Now then, Patten," said the Squire, "you've heard what sort of a time Mr. Fanshawe's been having. What do you make of it? Anything to do with Mr. Baxter? Fill yourself a glass of port, and tell us."

"Ah, that done me good, Master Henry," said Patten, after absorbing what was before him. "If you really wish to know what were in my thoughts, my answer would be clear in the affirmative. Yes," he went on, warming to his work, "I should say as Mr. Fanshawe's experience of today were very largely doo to the person you named. And I think, Master Henry, as I have some title to speak, in view of me 'aving been many years on speaking terms with him, and swore in to be jury on the Coroner's inquest near this time ten years ago, you being then, if you carry your mind back, Master Henry, travelling abroad, and no one 'ere to represent the family."

"Inquest?" said Fanshawe. "An inquest on Mr. Baxter, was there?"

"Yes, sir, on – on that very person. The facts as led up to that occurrence was these. The deceased was, as you may have gathered, a very peculiar individual in 'is 'abits – in my idear, at least, but all must speak as they find. He lived very much to himself, without neither chick nor child, as the saying is. And how he passed away his time was what very few could orfer a guess at."

"He lived unknown, and few could know when Baxter ceased to be," said the Squire to his pipe.

"I beg pardon, Master Henry, I was just coming to that. But when I say how he passed away his time – to be sure we know 'ow intent he was in rummaging and ransacking out all the 'istry of the neighbourhood and the number of things he'd managed to collect together – well, it was spoke of for miles round as Baxter's Museum, and many a time when he might be in the mood, and I might have an hour to spare, have he showed me his pieces of pots and what not, going back by his account to the times of the ancient Romans. However, you know more about that than what I do, Master Henry: only what I was a-going to say was this, as know what he might and interesting as he might be in his talk, there was something about the man – well, for one thing, no one ever remember to see him in church nor yet chapel at service-time. And that made talk. Our rector he never come in the house but once. 'Never ask me what the man said'; that was all anybody could ever get out of him. Then how did he spend his nights, particularly about this season of the year? Time and again the labouring men'd meet him coming back as they went out to their work, and he'd pass 'em by without a word, looking, they says, like someone straight out of the asylum. They see the whites of his eyes all round. He'd have a fish-basket with him, that they noticed, and he always come the same road. And the talk got to be that he'd made himself some business, and that not the best kind – well, not so far from where you was at seven o'clock this evening, sir.

"Well, now, after such a night as that, Mr. Baxter he'd shut up the shop, and the old lady that did for him had orders not to come in; and knowing what she did about his language, she took care to obey them orders. But one day it so happened, about three o'clock in the afternoon, the house being shut up as I said, there come a most fearful to-do inside, and smoke out of the windows, and Baxter crying out seemingly in an agony. So the man as lived next door he run round to the back premises and burst the door in, and several others come too. Well, he tell me he never in all his life smelt such a fearful – well, odour, as what there was in that kitchen-place. It seem as if Baxter had been boiling something in a pot and overset it on his leg. There he laid on the floor, trying to keep back the cries, but it was more than he could manage, and when he seen the people come in – oh, he was in a nice condition: if his tongue warn't blistered worse than his leg it warn't his fault. Well, they picked him up, and got him into a chair, and run for the medical man, and one of 'em was going to pick up the pot, and Baxter, he screams out to let it alone. So he did, but he couldn't see as there was anything in the pot but a few old brown bones. Then they says 'Dr. Lawrence'll be here in a minute, Mr. Baxter; he'll soon put you to rights.' And then he was off again. He must be got up to his room, he couldn't have the doctor come in there and see all that mess – they must throw a cloth over it – anything – the tablecloth out of the parlour; well, so they did. But that must have been poisonous stuff in that pot, for it was pretty near on two months afore Baxter were about agin. Beg pardon, Master Henry, was you going to say something?"

"Yes, I was," said the Squire. "I wonder you haven't told me all this before. However, I was going to say I remember old Lawrence telling me he'd attended Baxter. He was a queer card, he said. Lawrence was up in the bedroom one day, and picked up a little mask covered with black velvet, and put it on in fun and went to look at himself in the glass. He hadn't time for a proper look, for old Baxter shouted out to him from the bed: 'Put it down, you fool! Do you want to look through a dead man's eyes?' and it startled him so that he did put it down, and then he asked Baxter what he meant. And Baxter insisted on him handing it over, and said the man he bought it from was dead, or some such nonsense. But Lawrence felt it as he handed it over, and he declared he was sure it was made out of the front of a skull. He bought a distilling apparatus at Baxter's sale, he told me, but he could never use it: it seemed to taint everything, however much he cleaned it. But go on, Patten."

"Yes, Master Henry, I'm nearly done now, and time, too, for I don't know what they'll think about me in the servants' 'all. Well, this business of the scalding was some few years before Mr. Baxter was took, and he got about again, and went on just as he'd used. And one of the last jobs he done was finishing up them actual glasses what you took out last night. You see he'd made the body of them some long time, and got the pieces of glass for them, but there was somethink wanted to finish 'em, whatever it was, I don't know, but I picked up the frame one day, and I says: 'Mr. Baxter, why don't you make a job of this?' And he says, 'Ah, when I've done that, you'll hear news, you will: there's going to be no such pair of glasses as mine when they're filled and sealed,' and there he stopped, and I says: 'Why, Mr. Baxter, you talk as if they was wine bottles: filled and sealed – why, where's the necessity for that?' 'Did I say filled and sealed?' he says. 'O, well, I was suiting my conversation to my company.' Well, then come round this time of year, and one fine evening, I was passing his shop on my way home, and he was standing on the step, very pleased with hisself, and he says: 'All right and tight now: my best bit of work's finished, and I'll be out with 'em tomorrow.' 'What, finished them glasses?' I says, 'might I have a look at them ?' 'No, no,' he says, 'I've put 'em to bed for tonight, and when I do show 'em you, you'll have to pay for peepin', so I tell you.' And that, gentlemen, were the last words I heard that man say.

"That were the 17th of June, and just a week after, there was a funny thing happened, and it was doo to that as we brought in 'unsound mind' at the inquest, for barring that, no one as knew Baxter in business could anyways have laid that against him. But George Williams, as lived in the next house, and do now, he was woke up that same night with a stumbling and tumbling about in Mr. Baxter's premises, and he got out o' bed, and went to the front window on the street to see if there was any rough customers about. And it being a very light night, he could make sure as there was not. Then he stood and listened, and he hear Mr. Baxter coming down his front stair one step after another very slow, and he got the idear as it was like someone bein' pushed or pulled down and holdin' on to everythin' he could. Next thing he hear the street door come open, and out come Mr. Baxter into the street in his day-clothes, 'at and all, with his arms straight down by his sides, and talking to hisself, and shakin' his head from one side to the other, and walking in that peculiar way that he appeared to be going as it were against his own will. George Williams put up the window, and hear him say: 'O mercy, gentlemen!' and then he shut up sudden as if, he said, someone clapped his hand over his mouth, and Mr. Baxter threw his head back, and his hat fell off. And Williams see his face looking something pitiful, so as he couldn't keep from calling out to him: 'Why, Mr. Baxter, ain't you well?' and he was goin' to offer to fetch Dr. Lawrence to him, only he heard the answer: ''Tis best you mind your own business. Put in your head.' But whether it were Mr. Baxter said it so hoarse-like and faint, he never could be sure. Still there weren't no one but him in the street, and yet Williams was that upset by the way he spoke that he shrank back from the window and went and sat on the bed. And he heard Mr. Baxter's step go on and up the road, and after a minute or more he couldn't help but look out once more and he see him going along the same curious way as before. And one thing he recollected was that Mr. Baxter never stopped to pick up his 'at when it fell off, and yet there it was on his head. Well, Master Henry, that was the last anybody see of Mr. Baxter, leastways for a week or more. There was a lot of people said he was called off on business, or made off because he'd got into some scrape, but he was well known for miles round, and none of the railway-people nor the public-house people hadn't seen him; and then ponds was looked into and nothink found; and at last one evening Fakes the keeper come down from over the hill to the village, and he says he seen the Gallows Hill planting black with birds, and that were a funny thing, because he never see no sign of a creature there in his time. So they looked at each other a bit, and first one says: 'I'm game to go up,' and another says: 'So am I, if you are,' and half a dozen of 'em set out in the evening time, and took Dr. Lawrence with them, and you know, Master Henry, there he was between them three stones with his neck broke."

Useless to imagine the talk which this story set going. It is not remembered. But before Patten left them, he said to Fanshawe: "Excuse me, sir, but did I understand as you took out them glasses with you today? I thought you did; and might I ask, did you make use of them at all?"

"Yes. Only to look at something in a church."

"Oh, indeed, you took 'em into the church, did you, sir?"

"Yes, I did; it was Lambsfield church. By the way, I left them strapped on to my bicycle, I'm afraid, in the stable-yard."

"No matter for that, sir. I can bring them in the first thing tomorrow, and perhaps you'll be so good as to look at 'em then."

Accordingly, before breakfast, after a tranquil and well-earned sleep, Fanshawe took the glasses into the garden and directed them to a distant hill. He lowered them instantly, and looked at top and bottom, worked the screws, tried them again and yet again, shrugged his shoulders and replaced them on the hall-table.

"Patten," he said, "they're absolutely useless. I can't see a thing: it's as if someone had stuck a black wafer over the lens."

"Spoilt my glasses, have you?" said the Squire. "Thank you: the only ones I've got."

"You try them yourself," said Fanshawe, "I've done nothing to them."

So after breakfast the Squire took them out to the terrace and stood on the steps. After a few ineffectual attempts, "Lord, how heavy they are!" he said impatiently, and in the same instant dropped them on to the stones, and the lens splintered and the barrel cracked: a little pool of liquid formed on the stone slab. It was inky black, and the odour that rose from it is not to be described.

"Filled and sealed, eh?" said the Squire. "If I could bring myself to touch it, I dare say we should find the seal. So that's what came of his boiling and distilling, is it? Old Ghoul!"

"What in the world do you mean?"

"Don't you see, my good man? Remember what he said to the doctor about looking through dead men's eyes? Well, this was another way of it. But they didn't like having their bones boiled, I take it, and the end of it was they carried him off whither he would not. Well, I'll get a spade, and we'll bury this thing decently."

As they smoothed the turf over it, the Squire, handing the spade to Patten, who had been a reverential spectator, remarked to Fanshawe: "It's almost a pity you took that thing into the church: you might have seen more than you did. Baxter had them for a week, I make out, but I don't see that he did much in the time."

"I'm not sure," said Fanshawe, "there is that picture of Fulnaker Priory Church."

What Have You Brought Me?

Dylan Kingsley

NIX SAT NEARLY alone, his skin the colours of the stones beneath him and those beneath the water around him. His hair was the falling stream along his shoulders and down his back, coming near to forming a puddle below him in all the hues of creamy froth churned with peat. Leaning back and stretching himself long, he found the cup and ring hollows in his perch with his palms and pressed his weight into them, feeling the tingle of their empty circles travel no further than his wrists. Through the low hanging branches the sky stretched endlessly above, the moon lost in a puddle of her own. He gave her a smile and then called to the frogs who had leapt from their pads when he had first emerged naked and shedding water.

"Come here, loves," he beckoned, his voice a lulling roar of the wind against the cliffs and the salt air of his brackish cousins, the whistle of his breath between tongue and teeth a caress in their own language.

They came, what was graceful beneath the water now scrambling up and inelegantly sliding down the ladder of his legs, hefting weight that knew itself to be lighter, and hopping, at long last, into place. As each one found sure footing, he stretched out a rewarding finger with a nail tinged the slate-green of algae, stroking soft throats and smooth skin as delicately as the ripples they'd left behind. As the frogs settled beside him and upon him, beneath the eddies river fish nibbled at his stretched and wiggling toes while the guppies swam between them. He hadn't worn this skin in longer than their memory, and even he had forgotten the sensation of nip and tickle unhampered by hoof. He could hardly deny them their curiosity.

"Come now," he said to colony of amphibians, looking at them in turn, each a glistening gem of jade and agate and gold, and each precious, before reaching for the branch beside his thigh, "we don't have all night." They sang agreement in chorus while he, with nails sharper than flint or steel, whittled the wood into an ornate and flexible strip and smoothed the burrs with palms of sandpaper and silk.

"Decide amongst yourselves," he reminded them absently as he lifted the bow to his eye and to the heavens to check its arch and symmetry. Satisfied with his work and patient while the frogs debated, he plucked strands of his hair, one at a time, lengths that stretched from his sternum to the longest of his fingers, most so transparent that their only colour came from the moonlight and a few tinted like the depths and the shallows: deep auburn and ginger and champagne. Once plucked he strung them together, tying them into a neat knot at one end of the bow and spitting to hold it in place, before looking again to the frogs.

Out of the mass a single one waited beside his knee, perfect in form, in function, in hue.

"Aren't you lovely," he said to her, gently extending his palm for her penultimate perch.

"Thank you," he told her gathered companions.

"Thank you," he told her. She was a noble sacrifice, wrapping webbed toes around the bow's end and swallowing the loose strands of his hair until it was pulled taught and straight, breathing her last with the scent of all the waters of all the pools she would never know wafting from him and into her.

Out of the shallows and the reeds that wove themselves around his fingers he drew his fiddle, letting it drain against his chin as he checked the bow and the tuning. Eyes closed, he tested the hollow reverberations of each string and all nine together. The stream fell silent as he bowed, no melody just yet, instead a heartbeat of the rivers and rain and deep waters. A heartbeat that grew slower and slower until it stretched without breaking from one note to the next. And from that constant thrum a tune arose.

He played a lonely and melancholy air, one that escaped beyond the burbling water to touch each bobbing eye, each trembling wing, each slick scale. And then he sent it loose, tethering it to him with rhythm as it carried itself away, away from water and beyond tree, towards every tooth and every beak, every claw and foot that was cushioned by moss and soft earth. And each one quaked and fell silent, retreating into their dens and to their branches to wait out the long night.

In town his lament carried on curling tendrils of fog that rose from the ground to dim every crackling fire, making the air grow heavy with the scent of mud, of earth and iron and blood, and touching toes and fingers with the cold and damp of time spent too long submerged. Blankets pulled tighter. Arms clung and bodies shivered beside each other. All doors were barred save one.

She had waited for the fiddle, but now as she cracked the door open and peered beyond, as her eyes failed and the orange of safety within was swallowed by the purple of night outwith, as her ears filled with the heartbeat and the lilting melody, she hesitated. She'd grown up with the tales and with the warnings that came with them, after all. But what she risked by going seemed less than what she risked by staying.

The nixie will swallow you whole only to devour you later. He will fill your lungs with water, bind your ankles in reeds. He will pull you into the depths and never let you go. He is beautiful. And always hungry, always alone. He will give a boon for a price if only you can follow his song.

Not all the tales could be true, could they? None that she'd known had seen him. None that she knew had tried. Only one had been lost to the bog in all her memory and she'd been but a child. A child chasing wisps, turning her ankle, falling into dark water and unable to find the bank. Perhaps she wouldn't even find him. Perhaps she would spend her night chasing nothing more than the song of the wind through the trees. Perhaps he was nothing more than a legend of sharp teeth and moonlight. Perhaps he would have nothing to give.

Out into the night she went and his song wrapped around her, led her unstumbling through the forest, keeping her shoes unsodden on paths that were not swollen with ground water. Out of town and through the woods, towards him and the creek that flowed over rock and cliff like his hair over his shoulders, as wild as mane and tail. Towards the hungry water that had tasted the earth and salt of all the flesh that had ever been.

And there she found him where he sat naked in the midst of the pool, lily pads brushing his ankles, his fiddle pressed between chin and shoulder, his bow flashing like the lightning in the sky.

"Hello," he said, as the last notes died in the currents below and the heavens above. "What have you brought me? What do you desire?"

* * *

Ranghild had found her way by ear alone through the dark, but here, with him, beneath the moon and by the water, the light turned silver and bright enough to cast shadows that seemed even deeper than the ones beneath the trees. Here, like all the riches ever lost to waves and pools and wishes, precious metal glistened on his skin, through his hair, in his eyes. He was beautiful. But it was an uneasy beauty, one that seemed to lie above an undercurrent of peril. Despite his smile and for a moment only, she was possessed by fear that pursuing his call had been a mistake. But need had overcome her terror then and need remained now, reminding her that she'd been the one who chose to follow.

"Of course," he agreed. "You *could* have chosen not to come."

There was something in his voice that reminded her of her eels trapped within woven baskets, their skin slipping against one another's. It shouldn't have been comforting, a voice that sleek, a voice that smooth and soft and wet, but it was.

"Do you read thoughts?" she asked.

His laughter twinkled like starlight and he tipped his head to his fiddle, dancing his long nails across the stings in accompaniment. "I could. I do. I read many things." When he lifted his gaze, she knew it read her.

She didn't care for it.

"Then tell me what I have brought you," she said, setting her jaw. "Tell me what it is I want in return."

He blinked impossibly long and creamy lashes over eyes that shifted silver to blue and then to brown, and something in his flesh trembled, like the quivering muscles of the workhorses trying to shake loose a briar. After a moment he frowned. Somehow it made his face no less beautiful.

"All you offer me is darkness," he said quietly. "And that is all you want in return."

She was, for a moment, unsure if he spoke in metaphor or reality. It could be either.

It was both.

He moved like a storm approaching, his sudden proximity a crack of thunder making her shoulders jump and her heart race. He leaned so close that she could feel the water off him, nearly the water of him. Though after a moment he retreated without touching her. Instead, he pointed his shimmering bow towards her with its glistening gem of a frog securing the hair as though waiting for her to take it.

What difference a single jewel would make. It was worth more, she thought, than anything she'd ever seen before.

"It's worth more than gold," he said. "It's worth a life."

"That is what I offered," she said, her narrowing eyes calming the dread in her chest.

He snapped his bow back to his fiddle. However, dulling the strings with his grip, it made only a hollow thump. Like a drumbeat. Like a heartbeat. Like the strike of palm against sodden skirts while singing toiling songs at the water. "This," he hissed above it, "is not what you've come for. And *that* is not yours to offer. Do not waste my time."

She would not let herself be intimidated by the flash of his eyes or the straight line of his lips. "I was the only one to come to you," she told him plainly. "The only one to lay to bed without cotton in my ears and my door unbarred. What else would you spend your time on besides me?"

Silence was filled with the roar of the waterfall, drowning out even her breath. She expected at any moment for him to retreat to the river, to slip beneath it, until nothing of him remained except the tendrils of his hair, floating inconspicuously enough to ensnare.

He did not retreat.

Though his brows remained low, the light in his eyes glittering amidst shadow, he smiled.

"Let us barter then," he said, offering his bow once more. Was she deceiving herself, or did he seem pleased? "Do you play?"

"I sing," she said.

"Good enough," his said, his smile growing and again shifting the pools of light and dark that played about his features, turning silver and moonlight into peat and moss. "Come now," he said. "Let me hear it."

She didn't know how to sing without work. She didn't know how to find rhythm without her body moving to regulate it, and so she took a step closer to the water, drawing up her skirts and tying them high about her hips. Tucking the ends in the folds between her legs, she drew nearer. He watched in silence as she slipped off her shoes and waded in, the water sharp and cold and familiar, her feet finding purchase on the slick rocks beneath. Confident and summoning defiance, she met his gaze.

He made no sign of challenge. He waited. He watched, his smile settling into something softer, as if behind it there was a glimmer of uncertainty or a tumult of consideration. She could feel him near, feel his attention like the water lapping at her calves. She remembered the child lost to the bog, imagined how the cold must have settled into her bones. She knew she was only footsteps away from the same fate. And still, she began with certainty.

She bent her knees and leaned low, plunging her hand beneath the water and drawing out a pebble, tucking it neatly away like mussel, cockle, or snail before reaching for another. Her body became rhythm, her hand sliding beneath the water, time. Low. Her voice started low. Low like her hands in the water. Low like the curve of her back. Low like the black ends of her hair over her shoulder already twisting into wet ribbon. A low song. Song in the metre of labour, in the sound of her work and her mother's work and her mother's before her.

At first she sang alone, both call and answer, but soon the frogs joined in, deep bass and twinkling soprano. And then, so did he.

She called and strings responded. Low and echoing her refrain. Now as she lifted her hands to drop the pebbles into her skirt, she slapped her thigh. Now as she sang, she lifted her voice higher. His fiddle followed, looping around hers until it began to lead. And when she took up the answering, his voice joined hers. Low and high at once, too many notes for one throat, for one man.

The exquisiteness of the harmonizing chorus within him lifted her eyes from her task, though hair and lashes shielded the directness of her gaze. He was beautiful still. More beautiful perhaps, fiddle beneath his chin, his body moving in the time she had set. Beautiful. And yet, he was not a man, she reminded herself. He did not know labour despite learning the song. He wore man skin and man body, but she'd seen the hoof prints in the mud; she'd watched him glisten and shift like a spirit. He *still* glistened and shifted, as if his body bent light itself in its attempt to return to water. Whatever he appeared now, he merely appeared. Beautiful. Haunting. With sharp, sharp teeth and a kiss to fill her lungs with water.

Her voice stalled in a lilt, her fingers trembled with the chill, the last vibrations of string and voice and their complementing chirps and croaks fell silent.

"Will you devour me?" she asked, her back still bent and a single river-stone held between thumb and forefinger.

Again, his laughter was music, different from what they had made together, and different still from the laughter he had given her earlier. Knowing. It seemed knowing and thoughtful and mischievous all at once. Like his voices, so many contradictions should not layer so gloriously upon one another. And yet they did.

"What have you brought me?" he asked. "What do you desire?"

She thought of her husband, slumbering with rags in his ears and bruises on his knuckles. Of how she'd wished, this time and all the times that might come after, he'd not come home. She thought of a lifetime spent in her bed with her ears stuffed full, her eyes squeezed shut, and her bruises awake with every movement. She thought of the feather weight of the nixie's bow, of the price it might receive and the cost she'd been willing to pay. It had been a small desire, but the expense – a life not hers to give – had been a boon in and of itself. She shouldn't have thought to trick the nixie into giving her both freedom and the means to do something with it. Now, before him, she knew him to be more than that. She should have known it before she came.

She thought past the answer and deeper – to the root of those desires. To all the chances she might have and all the ones she never would in coming away from it – and she looked at the nixie, slender and as shifting as the water, as sea and pond, river and bog. As dangerous as all of them. As beautiful as all of them. She thought of all the few glimpses she'd seen of him and how he stood before her now, naked, unblemished and unashamed, wearing man skin that was as much his as it wasn't. She thought of the twice she'd heard the sound of his playing, both accompanying, though one lured through the forest and towards him and the other toiled sorrowfully alongside her.

"Can you play something that is not temptation, that is not labour?" she asked him.

He remained silent a moment, his fiddle resting against his hip, his bow against the other, both of their ends touching water and splitting it into rivulets that reformed as if never broken.

There was a single croak in the silence, a rumble that sounded like laughter. His gaze, thrown only briefly over his shoulder, silenced it, though when his attention returned to her, he was again smiling.

"I never have before," he said.

Strange that he admitted to it with a smile. Strange that her lips returned it before she was aware and able to stop it. She tucked a strand of her hair behind her ear, dripping fingers weaving his water through from scalp to tip. His body changed slightly, though not as she'd seen it before. His fingers tightened around the neck of his fiddle, his chin sunk to his chest, his eyes to the water beneath him.

And then his smile, like the glow came from within instead of upon. "But I will," he said.

"At what price?" she asked.

"None that is not mine to pay," he said simply.

Again, he lifted his bow. This was no tone poem or work song. He slid bow across string and down and then up, and then down and then up, chopping the air around him with dance. Spinning, spinning. It pulled at her again. Beneath the water and against the stones, her toes curled and uncurled in time. And then up onto toe and then back down again, she felt herself buoyant, lighter. She no longer worried about slipping, falling, drowning in his water. She no longer feared the lash of his hair binding wrist and ankle and trapping her beneath. She danced. And he with his bow and fiddle, with her. When she cried out with a woot that made an O of her lips to urge him on, he complied, spinning them faster and faster. And, when at last his song wound to an end, she was breathless and sodden from her skirts to her armpits.

"I was not sure I had it in me," he grinned his sharp teeth and crossed his arm across his chest, as though within a man's heart beat, as though if she were to press her hand to the spot she'd feel it settling within him.

She doubled over with laughter and he joined her, clapping his hands together with a sound that darted like a splash.

Hysteria, her husband would have said. Hypothermia, it could be. She thought it was neither.

"Do I offer darkness now?" she asked, her words still chasing after her racing breath and only catching them with mirth.

"No."

She chuckled and then attempted to catch it behind her hand. "Is that your magic?" she asked. "This… *lightness*."

"No," he said simply. "It is you."

He still smiled, his skin still shimmered in the moonlight, his eyes still changed from auburn to amber to gold. He still smiled, but it was different now.

They stilled together, quieted together, merriment fading into solemnity.

She watched him as carefully as he watched her, though she no longer felt frightened by it, no longer had to push past terror to return his gaze.

"What have you brought me?" He moved closer, gliding through the water as though it were no more substantial than air. His voice was a quiet waterfall, endless, churning. Striking the pit of her and then continuing to race forward, over slick pebble and stone, to whirl with the fishes and sing with the frogs, to coat her tongue and spill into her lungs like breath. "What do you desire?"

The shiver of what had once been cold trembled now upon her instead of from within. The third time he called she responded with an answer she hadn't known before, but it was as true and deep as the sea.

"Very well," he said, so quick to affirm that her thoughts had barely found words and had yet to find her lips. "I accept."

Her teasing was warm and gentle. "I accept, as well."

"I had suspected you would," he returned. "Just as I presumed I might never, however much I might have longed for it. I am a lonely creature, after all. But you have…" He paused for a moment, flourishing his bow as he searched for the word. "Fire. Fire about you. Oil about you."

"Neither fire nor oil go well with water," she said, her expression straight and unyielding for all of a second before her own smile returned.

"I wouldn't know," he chuckled softly. "I suppose we'll just have to see."

He extended his bow for the third time to her, and this time she curled her fingers around it. Neither let go. He took a step back and she followed. Another, another. Until the water swirled around their shoulders. It no longer felt cold.

"It is not easy," he said quietly, almost gently, letting go of his fiddle and bow and reaching for her hands.

"Nothing ever is," she told him and laced her fingers with his.

The corner of his beautiful lips lifted. He nodded his chin into the water and she followed. Beneath its surface she could see his hooves glistening like pearls.

And her own, like volcanic glass.

Shrieking Willow

Amanda Cecelia Lang

THE LEGEND OF Shrieking Willow was old when my grandparents were young. Gran says Willow was a girl like any girl who ever died from a broken heart. At night, she walks the mountain where she fell to her brutal end, searching for the moonlit lover who left her to die alone, and shrieking at young couples who dare to be in love. Sometimes she is the silver mist that blows through the forest where the trees grow crooked like spine-bent girls. Sometimes she appears as a gauzy, shadow-mouthed specter high atop the cliff beside the Falls, or as a nude, fish-pale body shimmering on the surface of the water below. Some believe she was once a maiden of the native tribes or the wayward daughter of colonial settlers or even a nubile spirit of the Black Hills themselves. But no matter who tells her story, those lucky, happy couples who see Willow always agree on one thing.

If she shrieks at you and yours, it means your love will last forever.

I've waited my entire life to hear her scream.

* * *

Adam turns onto a slow dirt road. The desolate scent of pine breezes through the windows, and filigree traces of moonlight glide across my blindfold.

I know where he's taking me – and not just by the sweet-nervous way he lured me into the passenger seat or the inevitability of it all. It's the mountain's eerie roller-coaster gravity. Not everyone feels it, but I always do. It sweeps over me long before the road runs out. Heavy granite sinks into my bones, my stomach floats on eddies of vertigo, up is down, inside is out, fantasy is reality. We're finally doing this.

My senses buzz on overdrive by the time our tires crunch to a stop. Adam doublechecks my blindfold then guides me into the brisk open air. My feet feel dizzy, my first steps tangle on loose rock.

"Careful now." He steadies my hips and walks me forward. His hands tremble, and I wonder if it's from the possibilities of ghosts or our first full night alone together. "Have you guessed where we are?"

"I hope so," I say as the blindfold lifts.

A rocky dead end, darkness, trees. I've never been here after sunset. Up ahead, hanging from a split rail fence, a lantern burns against the evergreen night. Beyond that, a long white shadow floats between the branches, caught wide-eyed in the lamp-glow.

Boo.

A shiver of terror thrills through me. I clutch Adam's arm a split-second before bursting with delicious, nervous laughter.

"Gotcha," he says.

It's only cheesecloth hanging there, wavering in a slow breeze, cut in the shape of a bedsheet ghost.

"You put that there?" My heart swells. He must've driven up here earlier just to do it.

He shrugs, so full of tiny gestures they're second nature. "Just setting the mood. In case the real thing has the night off."

"Impossible." I stare into the murky dark trees. "She's out there. Probably watching us right now. Don't you think?"

"I think if anyone can make her jealous, it's us." He kisses my hand, concealing his skepticism like a gentleman. But really it doesn't matter what he believes. The legend of Willow is in my blood. My grandparents saw her when they were our age and they're the happiest couple I know. It's my favorite bedtime story. Gran says Willow appeared on the cliffs above their campsite, a smudge of white wind, shrieking at them to beat the choir. That's how she knew Granddad was her one and only.

Adam sweeps my curls behind my shoulders and his grin turns ever-serious. "You sure you're ready for this, Annalee?"

The lantern light carves his bookish features with fiery new angles. Usually so strait-laced, he stands before me, defiant and daring and a little wild, a hero from my own gothic romance. The cheesecloth Willow flutters behind him like sweet surrender and I wonder what other surprises he has waiting. I glide my arms around his strong shoulders and kiss him until our heartbeats turn primal.

"Never been so ready," I whisper against his lips.

"Me too."

As he pulls our overnight packs from the truck, a nervous warmth blossoms inside my chest. We've whispered about this night since freshman year. All the candy-flavored kisses in the back row of the Rialto, all those study dates with the bedroom door closed, so many sweet-scary moments where we climbed to the edge of *almost*...

Up ahead, the split rail fence stretches in both directions, and there's a sign: *Danger, Forgotten Falls, No Trespassing.*

The wind holds its breath in the forbidden land beyond, and moonlight pools in the jagged spaces above the treetops, ethereal and swirling. Water crashes in the distance, calling to us. I take an unsteady step forward.

"Think we'll get in trouble?"

"I think it's worth the risk." Adam hops the fence and offers his hand.

For a guilty split-second, the good girl inside me balks. My grandparents still think I'm spending the weekend marathoning rom-coms at my best friend's house – and I *was*, until Adam appeared at her window, throwing pebbles and holding a blindfold out to me. I never lie to them. I always follow the rules. But it's the summer before college and this night is long overdue. Besides, I think Gran would understand.

Adam and I exchange rebellious smiles, then I take his hand and cross over.

Before we get started, he doublechecks our gear and trades the electric lantern for a heavy-duty flashlight. The beam cuts a hole through the darkened forest, and Adam chuckles. "Sorry, not as romantic, but it gets tricky deeper in. We should watch our feet."

There's no path, only the distant watery murmur of the Falls. Adam takes the lead, and I trust every step. Even at the peak of spontaneity, he always has a plan. His flashlight washes out the ponderosas and quaking aspens we pass. The branches seem to reach for us, bright and wraithlike. Although the rocky ground has only the slightest incline, my equilibrium tilts and my stomach floats in giddy knots. That upside-down gravity again.

"Whoa, you feel that?" I steady myself against him. "Getting dizzy out here."

"Yeah, it's spooky." He kisses my forehead. "I think I'm love-drunk."

"You goof." I grab his hand and hold my arms out, walking an invisible tightrope. "You know what I mean. This mountain is... *off-balance*."

Over the years, everyone from physicists to geologists to paranormal investigators have studied this area and its mysterious gut-bending qualities. They all have their pet theories.

Optical illusions, electromagnetism, even vortexes. Of course, Gran says it's Willow's forsaken heart that hangs heavy in the air here, wetting the stones and twisting the trees.

As we weave between branches, I try to sense invisible eyes on us. Has Willow noticed Adam's strong silhouette? Does she see how he sweeps me up like wings in a fairytale? It's not just his eagle scout confidence, it's his purity, his earnest chivalry. Every day with him is a waking adventure, every small moment the next best moment of my life.

Love-drunk indeed.

I yank Adam to a stop, silencing our footsteps, and turn an ear to the cool night, searching for a jealous murmur.

"What?" Adam says. "Do you hear something?"

The night holds silent. Fills with the pounding in my chest. I press his hand against the front of my jacket. "Can you feel my heart?"

"Always." He bows like a knight and I giggle. Exactly the kind of romantic cheese that makes our friends roll their eyes.

But I live for this. I'll never get enough.

We continue on. Slowly, the air turns heavy with the promise of wet earth. The tumbling thunder of the Falls echoes around us, louder and louder. We're close.

Up ahead, Adam's light brushes the skeletal white arm of something crooked and abnormal. I gasp, delighted, and aim his hand in that direction. "One of her trees!"

The aspen stands bent at an extreme angle and the top branches skew sideways, the sparse leaves twitching like fingers.

I flutter my hand, teasing a wave. "Why hello, you sad lonely thing."

"Just wait." Adam chuckles.

We pass dozens more, each tree bent and bowing into the landscape at random, crooked angles. Aspens, ponderosas, white spruce. I've seen these same trees in the daylight, of course, but that doesn't stop the gooseflesh from prickling the length of my neck. Not axe-cracked or staked down, they grow like this on their own. To me they've always seemed like tragic, forgotten dolls, leaning outward, reaching for something that will never be theirs. Looking at them too long makes me feel as if I'm tumbling off the edge of the sky.

"This place is amazing in the dark," I say. "Feels like the entire forest is float— "

"*Shhh.*" Adam presses his finger against my lips. "Look."

He clicks the flashlight off. The shadows are immediate. My eyes strain against the expanding jagged darkness. Then I see it.

Something glowing up ahead.

A pathway of lanterns.

They flicker inside a misty silver gloom, leading the way like will-o'-the-wisps.

"Adam?" I don't have to glance sideways to feel him grinning.

I grab his hand – or does he grab mine? We race each other forward, passing lantern after lantern until we burst from the tree line into open air. My blood rushes like I'm falling, even with a meadow firmly underfoot and Forgotten Falls rising above us. The waterfall reflects the moonlight and pulls my attention to the high cliffs, to the place where the river seems to pour from the sky. I brace myself against Adam, but Willow isn't up there. No lovely, wispy-white shadow glaring down at us from the edge, not even an after-image of all my daydreams.

Not yet.

"Night is young," Adam whispers in my ear, reading my mind.

I turn and take it all in. We stand knee-deep in wild grass and pink fireweed. The meadow reaches all the way to the murky shore. Nearby, more lanterns illuminate a campsite with a stone firepit and a two-person tent. It's perfect.

"You did all this?" I say.

"Well, not *all* this." He admires the view.

The power of the place rushes through me like water. This is it, this is where they say she died. Beneath the Falls, down where the jagged boulders ring the edge of the waterline like teeth in a jawbone. Willow and her lover used to swim right here. They'd run naked and dive from the cliffs – feel the gorgeous thrill of air and euphoria on their skin as they fell! No one knows if that long-ago girl stumbled or was pushed or simply leapt that final time – only that a luckier fall would've landed her safely, deep in the reflecting pool.

"Come out, come out," Adam calls.

The air feels playful but heavy. A ridiculously earnest part of me longs for this. Willow only unleashes her jealousy upon couples who outshine the love she lost. Her voice is the inverse of a curse. I believe in her like I believe in heaven and happily ever after. I *want* her to be true.

The full moon glows bright enough to see by as we bring our little campsite to life. Adam ignites the kindling in the firepit. Humming songs from old movies, I collect the electric lamps from the trees and arrange them around the meadow like set-pieces in a dream. All the while we trade soft kisses and keep our eyes on the cliffside.

I catch myself smiling slyly, a little cruelly. Are you watching, Willow? Is your envy turning you green?

By the time our campfire burns hot and crackling, the suspense has me ready to burst. I grab the flashlight. "What are we waiting for?"

"What do you mean?"

"Let's climb to the top." I aim the beam at the craggy edges that ladder up the cliffside. I hear stories all the time about people climbing up there and living to tell about it. Looks easy. "Don't you want to see what it's like where Willow fell?"

"Annalee, no!" Adam sounds genuinely horrified.

"Imagine the story we'd have."

"No way. I promised your granddad we wouldn't go up there."

Well, *that* stops me. I swing the light his way. "You what?"

He shields his eyes and his smile turns bashful. "I might've asked your grandparents' permission to take you up here."

Laughter, sweet nerdy relief, bubbles from me – so much for our rebellious streak. "You asked for their blessing?"

"Who do you think packed your sleeping bag? Your grandma called me *an honorable young gentleman.*"

Sounds like Gran alright. Sappy and perfectly romantic. She and Granddad met in kindergarten, just like Adam and me. They started dating as freshmen in high school, just like Adam and me. They were accepted to the same university, just like Adam and me. And of course, they only have eyes for each other. Gran invites Adam to supper so often, I'm convinced she only wants to moon at us over the pot roast and reminiscence about young love. And who can blame her? Young love makes a girl feel daring and electric and wild.

I return my light to the cliff and trace the water to the bottom. "People do it all the time. Jump. The water's deep enough."

"Doesn't matter how deep it is if we break our necks climbing rocks in the dark." Adam squeezes my hand. "Besides, I might know another way up there. But not until morning."

"You promise?"

"Have I ever let you down?"

That's enough for me.

As a back-up adventure, we slip off our hiking boots and tiptoe to the shore. The rippling water around my ankles is an icy, exhilarating shock. I shiver. I can't stop smiling. A shapeless silver mist hangs over the water where the pool catches the Falls. Even in the shallow end, the spray caresses my face. It should be deafening, but it sinks into the background as if I've always heard it. I marvel at the tranquility, the floating stillness.

Is this the breath before the scream?

"Now what?" Adam wraps his arms around me and scans the rocky cliffside.

"I don't know." I bite my lip. It's funny actually, I always imagined us being here would be enough. "The way Gran tells it, Willow just suddenly appeared."

"And started shrieking *to beat the choir*," Adam says. He's heard Gran's story nearly as many times as I have. "Your granddad thinks it was the wind howling down the cliffs."

"Granddad has no imagination." I stare out at the water, scanning the boulders for a smudge of ethereal white wind. "Which rock do you think broke her back?"

Adam sucks in a breath. "Christ, Annalee, that's grim."

"It's what they say happened."

"They also say her man watched from the shore then left her to die."

"You really don't believe it?"

He darkens. "I don't believe anyone could abandon someone they love like that."

"Maybe he didn't love her. Maybe he had someone better waiting at home. Or he just got bored with her…" I lean over and search my moonlit reflection, hoping to find Willow's sunken fish-pale face staring back, pining and abandoned. It's only me there, cherub cheeks, loose blonde curls.

I look eerily beautiful.

Where *is* that ghost? I glare at the cliffs then whirl on Adam and embrace him like he just slayed his first dragon. I drag my damsel fingers through his thick, windswept hair and exaggerate every slow, lusty kiss, putting on a show, brandishing him like a weapon. All's fair, right? By the time we stop, our skin is on fire.

"You see that?" I shout to the sky, liking the way my voice cracks and echoes against the cliffside. "He's all mine!"

Adam chuckles. "Be careful. A woman scorned…"

I brace for icy fingers to reach from the water and curl around my ankles, but after several minutes, my feet only turn numb. Willow's a no-show.

"The campfire's getting low," Adam says at last, a sudden shyness adding gravity to his voice. And I agree.

It's time.

We cross the meadow hand in hand. As we reach the campsite a new kind of nervousness pulses through me, altogether achy and wonderful.

After Adam tends the fire, we sit together and warm our feet with our shoulders wrapped in an oversized sleeping bag. We have a magical view of the Falls, but all I see is Adam.

"Are you disappointed?" he says.

Am I? Maybe. I was hoping we'd have a story to tell our grandkids one day, but… "I'm not here for a campfire tale." I brush my lips against him, across his mouth, his jawline, his throat. He tastes like first kisses and dizzy mountain air. I don't need a ghost to tell me what I already know. I slide my hand down and undo his top button.

He pulls back, holding me in a solemn burning gaze. “Are you sure?”

“Feel my heartbeat.” I press his open palm to my chest. My entire ribcage thunders like the Falls. “Never been so sure.”

By the light of the campfire, beneath a blazing sky of stars, this moment is inevitable. A rustle of clothing, then we are bare and warm and trembling inside the sleeping bag. We’ve never done this before, but it feels like we’ve been waiting all our lives.

A gentle sting, then sweet.

I gasp and Adam goes very still, concern and firelight flickering across his face.

“I’m fine,” I whisper and fall into the sweetness.

He moves slowly, shyly, hungrily, kissing me deeper as I tighten my arms around him. I never want to let go. I close my eyes and let his body unlock me, let my spirit loosen from my flesh until I am *his*. Completely, wholly, intertwined. I want to whimper, I want to cry out, I want to exhale our love and hear it echo. The mountain tilts with us until we’re floating, tumbling deliciously. The wind stirs, cool fingers in my hair. If I open my eyes while gravity is still spinning, I’m certain I’ll catch something watching us from the trees, spine-bent and misty and reaching. I smile wickedly. And for a quick, icy heartbeat I sense the piercing jealousy of a thousand shrieking ghosts.

Then Adam whispers my name and I’m back with him and it’s just the two of us.

Always.

* * *

Cool fingers snake across my shoulders and I wake to darkness.

My exposed skin prickles, but it’s not just the cold – I sense immediately that I’m alone.

“Adam?” I sit up. My head feels loose, my mind swoons, the darkness fills my eyes. I press a hand to my temple and my fingertips brush a band of cotton.

He blindfolded me?

Slowly, I pull the cloth from my eyes.

Darkness still. Where are the stars? My spirit feels turned around, disconnected. Unfelt wind rustles a thin nylon ceiling above my head – the tent?

I wrap my arms across my naked chest. I remember Adam holding me inside the sleeping bag, my nude body tender and exhausted. We fell asleep next to the fire, beneath the open sky. Sometime during the night, we must’ve crawled inside the tent. But I don’t remember waking up.

“Adam?” I say it louder this time and my fingers curl around the blindfold.

Why isn’t he answering me? I grope around the gritty empty floor for my clothing. My hand brushes the scattered lumps of my boots and a jacket. I pull them on quickly then unzip the door.

In the chilly open air, my exposed legs tremble and my body aches in delicate new ways. My footsteps sound unnatural, scraping and dull. I approach the cold ashes in the firepit. It’s not like Adam to let the fire burn out. Our sleeping bag sits nearby, a flattened forgotten husk.

I’m suddenly desperate for the light, but the lanterns I placed around the campsite are missing. This isn’t funny, though I can’t quite form the words. An icy hollowness spreads inside me. Why would Adam do this? Why would he leave me alone, naked and blindfolded? After everything we just gave to each other.

The meadow becomes slow-moving shadows. Wild grass sways like seaweed at the murkiest depths. The stars have gone impossibly black, and the moon hides behind the smoky grey arm of a cloud. Without the lunar reflection, the Falls disappear into the cliffside like a phantom lover slipping back into the night. My eyes slide to the top where they say a heartbroken girl fell to her doom. I don't want to look.

There's no one up there.

The emptiness is disorienting; it continues to gut me.

"Adam, please…" I turn in a small circle, tightening my arms around myself. All color has abandoned the night. A soft breeze rattles the tent, creating the illusion of unseen hands groping for the exit. That's *not* Adam. I slink backward into the tall grass while gravity sucks at the meat in my chest. Where *is* he? The promise we made to each other is still raw upon me. I can still *feel* him.

"Adam!" This time I scream it. My voice ricochets off the cliffs. "Answer me!"

Nothing. *Nothing.*

A branch snaps behind me, splitting the night.

I turn to face the trees.

And I see her in the light of a single lantern.

Willow.

I don't know how I missed her before. She must've been floating there this whole time. A white shadow against the murky evergreens.

A sting of sweet relief bleeds through me.

It's Adam's cheesecloth ghost.

The gauzy spirit ripples like a flag, waving to me from the trees. In the dim, I can just make out another light deeper in the forest, and another beyond that. The message is clear: *follow me…*

"Anywhere." I race to the tree line. The flashlight hangs beside the lantern. With a growing smile, I unhook it and aim the beam between the branches.

Movement, deeper in. A flash of Adam's naked chest blurs through my light. Is he crazy, with the chill in the air? Of course, all *I'm* wearing is boots and a jacket.

I don't waste another second. I chase after him, drunk on the memory of his touch and the tumbling gravity of the mountain. My quick breath echoes the crunching rhythm of his footsteps. I catch washed-out glimpses of him in my flashlight, pale shoulders and arms slipping behind a white spruce.

"Adam!" My voice ricochets. I can't tell if he calls back. I can barely tell sky from ground. I reach the first lantern. It hangs from a crooked ponderosa. The malformed trunk bows at the waist, sinking deeper even as I watch. Trick of the light, but the drifting sight of it slows me.

A twig snaps. Adam again – almost twenty trees ahead. A bright flash of eyes and grinning teeth. I bolt after him. My flashlight dances jagged lines across the forest. I follow the path of the lanterns, each one suspended from trees with glowing skeletal branches. My legs beat with upside-down adrenaline. The balmy oils of my earlier unease turn to exhilaration. But he's too fast, dashing through the trees ahead.

"Will you wait?" I cry.

The gap between us starts to shrink, closer and closer, until I pass the final lantern. Adam vanishes.

I stop cold and sweep the forest with my light.

Nothing moves ahead. The air is utter silence. I realize I've lost the sound of the Falls. The woods can disorient fast, I know that, but I should still be able to hear the water. I turn around, head spinning. The forest behind me is featureless. The lanterns have gone dark.

"Hello?"

A branch cracks immediately behind me, loud as thunder and intimately close. It could be the sound of my own spine snapping, it's so close. I lurch out of my flesh and pivot with my light. How did he sneak up so fast?

"You goof…" But the words wither on my lips.

The trees are bent.

Every last one.

The massive trunks bow away from me at brutal aberrant angles, every treetop reaching, every branch stretching for a single distant point in the forest:

Adam.

There in the center of the treefall, holding a single flickering lantern, waiting for me. The boy I've known all my life, the only boy I'll ever love.

"Oh, Adam, the trees…"

I stagger toward him – but something slithers around his waist.

I stop cold. To my very marrow, I freeze.

Hideous female hands stroke his torso.

Fingers like water-bloated worms crawl around his hips and his stomach. Muddy and slimy, they glide upward and fondle his naked chest.

Adam tilts his head at me.

His lips curve upward in carnal pleasure as the rest of the creature appears like mist behind him. Her ethereal, malformed torso slumps sideways, boneless and waterlogged. Jagged knobs of spinal cord protrude from her ragged flesh, and her endless, murky hair hangs like a midnight waterfall. Her arms cling tighter around Adam, hideously, horribly long, branches bound in bruised flesh, they snap and pop like twigs underfoot. She doesn't let go – and he doesn't struggle.

He just stands there with that gruesome sideways smile.

The thing that is Willow glares at me, and it's rage not jealousy that gathers in those empty, fish-eaten eyes. Her mouth unhinges and she sucks the nightmare wind into her wheezing rib-punctured lungs, inhaling the misty gloom deeper and deeper.

Preparing to shriek.

And it's strange – all those starry-eyed years listening to ghost stories. It never occurred to me to be afraid.

For a weightless second, my vision doubles, my spirit tumbles, and I see myself from her angle. Me, a blood-drained husk with limp blonde curls and horrified moon eyes, rooted in place by the deity I once worshipped. I never should've tempted her.

She caresses the top button of Adam's jeans.

"Get away from him," I cry, breaking the spell.

I stagger forward, but my vision tumbles again and I collapse over my own tangled feet, slamming the ground with my lungs. I gasp, try to breathe, try to see past the sudden prickling darkness. My hands fumble across pine needles, groping, grasping for the flashlight. I find the handle and aim the beam forward.

Nothing's there.

Nobody's there.

The trees are normal, tall and upright.

Pushing up onto my knees, I want to laugh but can barely breathe. I press a hand against my pounding head. Was that even *real*? A legend-induced hallucination? Those slimy hands caressing Adam's chest; his savage, euphoric grin – the after-images sear my vision. Shuddering to my feet, I try to blink them away.

"Annalee!" Adam's voice echoes from impossibly far away, sending a flock of sleeping birds full feather into the sky.

"I'm here!" I pivot toward the sound with a sob of manic relief. I can't believe it.

The lanterns are there.

They line the woods, showing the way back to him.

I can hear the Falls again. My knees wobble, liquid bones, but I rush toward the lights and the sound of Adam calling. When I break through the trees, he's there waiting.

He tilts his head, taking me in: scratched legs and pale lingering horror. He holds a hand out to me. "Told you I knew another way to the top."

As he says it, the mountain flips upside down, my stomach plunges, and I stagger backward with a gasp.

The Falls are magnificent and nearby.

But we're not at the bottom any longer.

We stand on the cliff, high above the meadow in the place where the river leaves the sky. Two final lanterns mark the edge, lights on a runway.

It's the second most amazing thing I've seen all night.

"Adam, she's out there, I saw, I..." I almost tell him everything. How Willow broke the trees, how she was horrible and muddy and had her hands all over him – and the insidiously enthusiastic way he *let* her. But the story withers on my lips, I breathe it back in. That *wasn't* Adam. Whatever hideous illusion that was back there between the trees, it won't be part of our legend.

What's real is right in front of me, standing tall and cherished on the edge. Flesh and blood and the other half of my soul.

We haven't been this close since we fell asleep, skin to skin beside the campfire. We lock eyes and an ambrosial shyness overtakes me. We're different now, yet still the same. My body burns with sweet-raw memories. And as I approach him, my blood beats for our next adventure.

We walk between the lanterns and peer down the welcoming arm of the river. We contemplate the drop into the moonlit pool below. It's going to be deep. And cold. But this is Adam, after all. Even at the height of spontaneity, he has a plan.

"What do you think, Annalee?" His words whisper chills through me. I can't believe we're standing here even as I know it's inevitable. "Are you ready?"

I take his hand – or does he take mine?

We back away from the edge, giving ourselves a running start.

Hand in hand, we rush and fly and soar over the side.

Gravity returns and yanks us straight down. Falling plummeting loving, it all happens in a slow-motion heartbeat. The air rushes past us, lifting my hair, and I hear my voice on the wind, and I see the meadow and our campsite below.

The campfire still burns.

The lamps still dot the tall grass.

And Adam's strong form is still there in the sleeping bag.

Even as I feel his hand tighten around mine. Slimy and wormy and cold.

I jerk sideways but there's no time to scream. A bloated muddy creature with whipping dark hair plummets beside me. She yanks me close, embraces me from behind. Her gangly, fish-pale arms squeeze my waist and we break against the rock.

Our spines split with the crack of a thousand trees.

I crush her and she slams through me as my spirit tears loose from my fibers.

In the dizzy black seconds that follow, my body slides limply off the rock. Blood and spirit, I seep into the water, dying as Willow once died. My tragedy will twist the trees. With the last of myself, I turn my head toward the shore. I try to call for Adam, but my voice chokes on sorrow and mist.

And yet someone shouts his name, *someone* does.

Floating beneath the Falls, I hear my voice echo against the cliffside. A heartbeat later, Adam's flashlight zigzags across my face, and he splashes through the water.

"Annalee, are you insane? Did you jump?"

He wades closer, and raw terror darkens his voice – of course it does. I can feel the split-branch nightmare of my spine protruding from my back.

But Adam's expression softens. His sudden relief disorients me. "You're okay, just breathe, I'm here. You knocked the air from yourself, that's all. My God, what were you thinking jumping alone like that?"

He guides me upright and walks me from the water, wet glistening legs and sagging blonde curls. Only…

Only the mountain is upside down and misty and I witness all this from outside myself. My body walks with Adam, possessed, lovely, upright, even as my spirit bobs here on the water.

No no no *no!*

I twist and writhe until my feet sink into the muddy shallows. As I attempt to stand upright my torso slumps sideways and my arms stretch outward like branches.

I reach for Adam.

He leads the girl that is not me from the shore and into the firelight. His voice is lush with concern as he drapes her in a sleeping bag. "Are you warm enough, Annalee?"

"Oh, yes." She smiles wickedly and presses his hand against her nude chest. "Feel my heartbeat."

He leans in to kiss her – and I reach and reach but cannot touch him! My mouth unhinges and the wind rushes from me, a gale force of hollowing despair.

I shriek.

And far, far away, Adam breaks their kiss just long enough to gasp. "*Shhh*. Did you hear that?"

The Story of Sidi-Nouman

from the One Thousand and One Nights

Andrew and Nora Lang

THE CALIPH, Haroun-al-Raschid, was much pleased with the tale of the blind man and the dervish, and when it was finished he turned to the young man who had ill-treated his horse, and inquired his name also. The young man replied that he was called Sidi-Nouman.

"Sidi-Nouman," observed the Caliph, "I have seen horses broken all my life long, and have even broken them myself, but I have never seen any horse broken in such a barbarous manner as by you yesterday. Every one who looked on was indignant, and blamed you loudly. As for myself, I was so angry that I was very nearly disclosing who I was, and putting a stop to it at once. Still, you have not the air of a cruel man, and I would gladly believe that you did not act in this way without some reason. As I am told that it was not the first time, and indeed that every day you are to be seen flogging and spurring your horse, I wish to come to the bottom of the matter. But tell me the whole truth, and conceal nothing."

Sidi-Nouman changed colour as he heard these words, and his manner grew confused; but he saw plainly that there was no help for it. So he prostrated himself before the throne of the Caliph and tried to obey, but the words stuck in his throat, and he remained silent.

The Caliph, accustomed though he was to instant obedience, guessed something of what was passing in the young man's mind, and sought to put him at his ease. "Sidi-Nouman," he said, "do not think of me as the Caliph, but merely as a friend who would like to hear your story. If there is anything in it that you are afraid may offend me, take courage, for I pardon you beforehand. Speak then openly and without fear, as to one who knows and loves you."

Reassured by the kindness of the Caliph, Sidi-Nouman at length began his tale.

"Commander of the Faithful," said he, "dazzled though I am by the lustre of your Highness' presence, I will do my best to satisfy your wishes. I am by no means perfect, but I am not naturally cruel, neither do I take pleasure in breaking the law. I admit that the treatment of my horse is calculated to give your Highness a bad opinion of me, and to set an evil example to others; yet I have not chastised it without reason, and I have hopes that I shall be judged more worthy of pity than punishment."

Commander of the Faithful, I will not trouble to describe my birth; it is not of sufficient distinction to deserve your Highness' attention. My ancestors were careful people, and I inherited enough money to enable me to live comfortably, though without show.

Having therefore a modest fortune, the only thing wanting to my happiness was a wife who could return my affection, but this blessing I was not destined to get; for on the very day after my marriage, my bride began to try my patience in every way that was most hard to bear.

Now, seeing that the customs of our land oblige us to marry without ever beholding the person with whom we are to pass our lives, a man has of course no right to complain as long as his wife is not absolutely repulsive, or is not positively deformed. And whatever defects her body may have, pleasant ways and good behaviour will go far to remedy them.

The first time I saw my wife unveiled, when she had been brought to my house with the usual ceremonies, I was enchanted to find that I had not been deceived in regard to the account that had been given me of her beauty. I began my married life in high spirits, and the best hopes of happiness.

The following day a grand dinner was served to us but as my wife did not appear, I ordered a servant to call her. Still she did not come, and I waited impatiently for some time. At last she entered the room, and she took our places at the table, and plates of rice were set before us.

I ate mine, as was natural, with a spoon, but great was my surprise to notice that my wife, instead of doing the same, drew from her pocket a little case, from which she selected a long pin, and by the help of this pin conveyed her rice grain by grain to her mouth.

"Amina," I exclaimed in astonishment, "is that the way you eat rice at home? And did you do it because your appetite was so small, or did you wish to count the grains so that you might never eat more than a certain number? If it was from economy, and you are anxious to teach me not to be wasteful, you have no cause for alarm. We shall never ruin ourselves in that way! Our fortune is large enough for all our needs, therefore, dear Amina, do not seek to check yourself, but eat as much as you desire, as I do!"

In reply to my affectionate words, I expected a cheerful answer; yet Amina said nothing at all, but continued to pick her rice as before, only at longer and longer intervals. And, instead of trying the other dishes, all she did was to put every now and then a crumb, of bread into her mouth, that would not have made a meal for a sparrow.

I felt provoked by her obstinacy, but to excuse her to myself as far as I could, I suggested that perhaps she had never been used to eat in the company of men, and that her family might have taught her that she ought to behave prudently and discreetly in the presence of her husband. Likewise that she might either have dined already or intend to do so in her own apartments. So I took no further notice, and when I had finished left the room, secretly much vexed at her strange conduct.

The same thing occurred at supper, and all through the next day, whenever we ate together. It was quite clear that no woman could live upon two or three bread-crumbs and a few grains of rice, and I determined to find out how and when she got food. I pretended not to pay attention to anything she did, in the hope that little by little she would get accustomed to me, and become more friendly; but I soon saw that my expectations were quite vain.

One night I was lying with my eyes closed, and to, all appearance sound asleep, when Amina arose softly, and dressed herself without making the slightest sound. I could not imagine what she was going to do, and as my curiosity was great I made up my mind to follow her. When she was fully dressed, she stole quietly from the room.

The instant she had let the curtain fall behind her, I flung a garment on my shoulders and a pair of slippers on my feet. Looking from a lattice which opened into the court, I saw her in the act of passing through the street door, which she carefully left open.

It was bright moonlight, so I easily managed to keep her in sight, till she entered a cemetery not far from the house. There I hid myself under the shadow of the wall, and crouched down cautiously; and hardly was I concealed, when I saw my wife approaching in company with a ghoul – one of those demons which, as your Highness is aware, wander about the country making their lairs in deserted buildings and springing out upon unwary travellers whose flesh they eat. If no live being goes their way, they then betake themselves to the cemeteries, and feed upon the dead bodies.

I was nearly struck dumb with horror on seeing my wife with this hideous female ghoul. They passed by me without noticing me, began to dig up a corpse which had been buried that day, and then sat down on the edge of the grave, to enjoy their frightful repast, talking quietly and cheerfully all the while, though I was too far off to hear what they said. When they had finished, they threw back the body into the grave, and heaped back the earth upon it. I made no effort to disturb them, and returned quickly to the house, when I took care to leave the door open, as I had previously found it. Then I got back into bed, and pretended to sleep soundly.

A short time after Amina entered as quietly as she had gone out. She undressed and stole into bed, congratulating herself apparently on the cleverness with which she had managed her expedition.

As may be guessed, after such a scene it was long before I could close my eyes, and at the first sound which called the faithful to prayer, I put on my clothes and went to the mosque. But even prayer did not restore peace to my troubled spirit, and I could not face my wife until I had made up my mind what future course I should pursue in regard to her. I therefore spent the morning roaming about from one garden to another, turning over various plans for compelling my wife to give up her horrible ways; I thought of using violence to make her submit, but felt reluctant to be unkind to her. Besides, I had an instinct that gentle means had the best chance of success; so, a little soothed, I turned towards home, which I reached about the hour of dinner.

As soon as I appeared, Amina ordered dinner to be served, and we sat down together. As usual, she persisted in only picking a few grains of rice, and I resolved to speak to her at once of what lay so heavily on my heart.

"Amina," I said, as quietly as possible, "you must have guessed the surprise I felt, when the day after our marriage you declined to eat anything but a few morsels of rice, and altogether behaved in such a manner that most husbands would have been deeply wounded. However I had patience with you, and only tried to tempt your appetite by the choicest dishes I could invent, but all to no purpose. Still, Amina, it seems to me that there be some among them as sweet to the taste as the flesh of a corpse?"

I had no sooner uttered these words than Amina, who instantly understood that I had followed her to the grave-yard, was seized with a passion beyond any that I have ever witnessed. Her face became purple, her eyes looked as if they would start from her head, and she positively foamed with rage.

I watched her with terror, wondering what would happen next, but little thinking what would be the end of her fury. She seized a vessel of water that stood at hand, and plunging her hand in it, murmured some words I failed to catch. Then, sprinkling it on my face, she cried madly:

"Wretch, receive the reward of your prying, and become a dog."

The words were not out of her mouth when, without feeling conscious that any change was passing over me, I suddenly knew that I had ceased to be a man. In the greatness of the shock and surprise – for I had no idea that Amina was a magician – I never dreamed of running away, and stood rooted to the spot, while Amina grasped a stick and began to beat me. Indeed her blows were so heavy, that I only wonder they did not kill me at once. However they succeeded in rousing me from my stupor, and I dashed into the court-yard, followed closely by Amina, who made frantic dives at me, which I was not quick enough to dodge. At last she got tired of pursuing me, or else a new trick entered into her head, which would give me speedy and painful death; she opened the gate leading into the street, intending to crush me as I passed through. Dog though I was, I saw through her design, and stung into presence of mind by the greatness of the danger, I timed my movements so well that I contrived to rush through, and only the tip of my tail received a squeeze as she banged the gate.

I was safe, but my tail hurt me horribly, and I yelped and howled so loud all along the streets, that the other dogs came and attacked me, which made matters no better. In order to avoid them, I took refuge in a cookshop, where tongues and sheep's heads were sold.

At first the owner showed me great kindness, and drove away the other dogs that were still at my heels, while I crept into the darkest corner. But though I was safe for the moment, I was not destined to remain long under his protection, for he was one of those who hold all dogs to be unclean, and that all the washing in the world will hardly purify you from their contact. So after my enemies had gone to seek other prey, he tried to lure me from my corner in order to force me into the street. But I refused to come out of my hole, and spent the night in sleep, which I sorely needed, after the pain inflicted on me by Amina.

I have no wish to weary your Highness by dwelling on the sad thoughts which accompanied my change of shape, but it may interest you to hear that the next morning my host went out early to do his marketing, and returned laden with the sheep's heads, and tongues and trotters that formed his stock in trade for the day. The smell of meat attracted various hungry dogs in the neighbourhood, and they gathered round the door begging for some bits. I stole out of my corner, and stood with them.

In spite of his objection to dogs, as unclean animals, my protector was a kind-hearted man, and knowing I had eaten nothing since yesterday, he threw me bigger and better bits than those which fell to the share of the other dogs. When I had finished, I tried to go back into the shop, but this he would not allow, and stood so firmly at the entrance with a stout stick, that I was forced to give it up, and seek some other home.

A few paces further on was a baker's shop, which seemed to have a gay and merry man for a master. At that moment he was having his breakfast, and though I gave no signs of hunger, he at once threw me a piece of bread. Before gobbling it up, as most dogs are in the habit of doing, I bowed my head and wagged my tail, in token of thanks, and he understood, and smiled pleasantly. I really did not want the bread at all, but felt it would be ungracious to refuse, so I ate it slowly, in order that he might see that I only did it out of politeness. He understood this also, and seemed quite willing to let me stay in his shop, so I sat down, with my face to the door, to show that I only asked his protection. This he gave me, and indeed encouraged me to come into the house itself, giving me a corner where I might sleep, without being in anybody's way.

The kindness heaped on me by this excellent man was far greater than I could ever have expected. He was always affectionate in his manner of treating me, and I shared his breakfast, dinner and supper, while, on my side, I gave him all the gratitude and attachment to which he had a right.

I sat with my eyes fixed on him, and he never left the house without having me at his heels; and if it ever happened that when he was preparing to go out I was asleep, and did not notice, he would call "Rufus, Rufus," for that was the name he gave me.

Some weeks passed in this way, when one day a woman came in to buy bread. In paying for it, she laid down several pieces of money, one of which was bad. The baker perceived this, and declined to take it, demanding another in its place. The woman, for her part, refused to take it back, declaring it was perfectly good, but the baker would have nothing to do with it. "It is really such a bad imitation," he exclaimed at last, "that even my dog would not be taken in. Here Rufus! Rufus!" and hearing his voice, I jumped on to the counter. The baker threw down the money before me, and said, "Find out if there is a bad coin." I looked at each in turn, and then laid my paw on the false one, glancing at the same time at my master, so as to point it out.

The baker, who had of course been only in joke, was exceedingly surprised at my cleverness, and the woman, who was at last convinced that the man spoke the truth, produced another piece of money in its place. When she had gone, my master was so pleased that he told all the neighbours what I had done, and made a great deal more of it than there really was.

The neighbours, very naturally, declined to believe his story, and tried me several times with all the bad money they could collect together, but I never failed to stand the test triumphantly.

Soon, the shop was filled from morning till night, with people who on the pretence of buying bread came to see if I was as clever as I was reported to be. The baker drove a roaring trade, and admitted that I was worth my weight in gold to him.

Of course there were plenty who envied him his large custom, and many was the pitfall set for me, so that he never dared to let me out of his sight. One day a woman, who had not been in the shop before, came to ask for bread, like the rest. As usual, I was lying on the counter, and she threw down six coins before me, one of which was false. I detected it at once, and put my paw on it, looking as I did so at the woman. "Yes," she said, nodding her head. "You are quite right, that is the one." She stood gazing at me attentively for some time, then paid for the bread, and left the shop, making a sign for me to follow her secretly.

Now my thoughts were always running on some means of shaking off the spell laid on me, and noticing the way in which this woman had looked at me, the idea entered my head that perhaps she might have guessed what had happened, and in this I was not deceived. However I let her go on a little way, and merely stood at the door watching her. She turned, and seeing that I was quite still, she again beckoned to me.

The baker all this while was busy with his oven, and had forgotten all about me, so I stole out softly, and ran after the woman.

When we came to her house, which was some distance off, she opened the door and then said to me, "Come in, come in; you will never be sorry that you followed me." When I had entered she fastened the door, and took me into a large room, where a beautiful girl was working at a piece of embroidery. "My daughter," exclaimed my guide, "I have brought you the famous dog belonging to the baker which can tell good money from bad. You know that when I first heard of him, I told you I was sure he must be really a man, changed into a dog by magic. Today I went to the baker's, to prove for myself the truth of the story, and persuaded the dog to follow me here. Now what do you say?"

"You are right, mother," replied the girl, and rising she dipped her hand into a vessel of water. Then sprinkling it over me she said, "If you were born dog, remain dog; but if you were born man, by virtue of this water resume your proper form." In one moment the spell was broken. The dog's shape vanished as if it had never been, and it was a man who stood before her.

Overcome with gratitude at my deliverance, I flung myself at her feet, and kissed the hem of her garment. "How can I thank you for your goodness towards a stranger, and for what you have done? Henceforth I am your slave. Deal with me as you will!"

Then, in order to explain how I came to be changed into a dog, I told her my whole story, and finished with rendering the mother the thanks due to her for the happiness she had brought me.

"Sidi-Nouman," returned the daughter, "say no more about the obligation you are under to us. The knowledge that we have been of service to you is ample payment. Let us speak of Amina, your wife, with whom I was acquainted before her marriage. I was aware that she was a magician, and she knew too that I had studied the same art, under the same mistress. We met often going to the same baths, but we did not like each other, and never sought to become friends. As to what concerns you, it is not enough to have broken your spell, she must be punished for her wickedness. Remain for a moment with my mother, I beg," she added hastily, "I will return shortly."

Left alone with the mother, I again expressed the gratitude I felt, to her as well as to her daughter.

"My daughter," she answered, "is, as you see, as accomplished a magician as Amina herself, but you would be astonished at the amount of good she does by her knowledge. That is why I have never interfered, otherwise I should have put a stop to it long ago." As she spoke, her daughter entered with a small bottle in her hand.

"Sidi-Nouman," she said, "the books I have just consulted tell me that Amina is not home at present, but she should return at any moment. I have likewise found out by their means, that she pretends before the servants great uneasiness as to your absence. She has circulated a story that, while at dinner with her, you remembered some important business that had to be done at once, and left the house without shutting the door. By this means a dog had strayed in, which she was forced to get rid of by a stick. Go home then without delay, and await Amina's return in your room. When she comes in, go down to meet her, and in her surprise, she will try to run away. Then have this bottle ready, and dash the water it contains over her, saying boldly, "Receive the reward of your crimes." That is all I have to tell you."

Everything happened exactly as the young magician had foretold. I had not been in my house many minutes before Amina returned, and as she approached I stepped in front of her, with the water in my hand. She gave one loud cry, and turned to the door, but she was too late. I had already dashed the water in her face and spoken the magic words. Amina disappeared, and in her place stood the horse you saw me beating yesterday.

This, Commander of the Faithful, is my story, and may I venture to hope that, now you have heard the reason of my conduct, your Highness will not think this wicked woman too harshly treated?

"Sidi-Nouman," replied the Caliph, "your story is indeed a strange one, and there is no excuse to be offered for your wife. But, without condemning your treatment of her, I wish you to reflect how much she must suffer from being changed into an animal, and I hope you will let that punishment be enough. I do not order you to insist upon the young magician finding the means to restore your wife to her human shape, because I know that when once women such as she begin to work evil they never leave off, and I should only bring down on your head a vengeance far worse than the one you have undergone already."

Squire Toby's Will

A Ghost Story

J. Sheridan Le Fanu

MANY PERSONS ACCUSTOMED to travel the old York and London road, in the days of stage-coaches, will remember passing, in the afternoon, say, of an autumn day, in their journey to the capital, about three miles south of the town of Applebury, and a mile and a half before you reach the old Angel Inn, a large black-and-white house, as those old-fashioned cage-work habitations are termed, dilapidated and weather-stained, with broad lattice windows glimmering all over in the evening sun with little diamond panes, and thrown into relief by a dense background of ancient elms. A wide avenue, now overgrown like a churchyard with grass and weeds, and flanked by double rows of the same dark trees, old and gigantic, with here and there a gap in their solemn files, and sometimes a fallen tree lying across on the avenue, leads up to the hall-door.

Looking up its sombre and lifeless avenue from the top of the London coach, as I have often done, you are struck with so many signs of desertion and decay, – the tufted grass sprouting in the chinks of the steps and window-stones, the smokeless chimneys over which the jackdaws are wheeling, the absence of human life and all its evidence, that you conclude at once that the place is uninhabited and abandoned to decay. The name of this ancient house is Gylingden Hall. Tall hedges and old timber quickly shroud the old place from view, and about a quarter of a mile further on you pass, embowered in melancholy trees, a small and ruinous Saxon chapel, which, time out of mind, has been the burying-place of the family of Marston, and partakes of the neglect and desolation which brood over their ancient dwelling-place.

The grand melancholy of the secluded valley of Gylingden, lonely as an enchanted forest, in which the crows returning to their roosts among the trees, and the straggling deer who peep from beneath their branches, seem to hold a wild and undisturbed dominion, heightens the forlorn aspect of Gylingden Hall.

Of late years repairs have been neglected, and here and there the roof is stripped, and "the stitch in time" has been wanting. At the side of the house exposed to the gales that sweep through the valley like a torrent through its channel, there is not a perfect window left, and the shutters but imperfectly exclude the rain. The ceilings and walls are mildewed and green with damp stains. Here and there, where the drip falls from the ceiling, the floors are rotting. On stormy nights, as the guard described, you can hear the doors clapping in the old house, as far away as old Gryston bridge, and the howl and sobbing of the wind through its empty galleries.

About seventy years ago died the old Squire, Toby Marston, famous in that part of the world for his hounds, his hospitality, and his vices. He had done kind things, and he had fought duels: he had given away money and he had horse-whipped people. He carried with him some blessings and a good many curses, and left behind him an amount of debts and charges upon the estates which appalled his two sons, who had no taste for business or accounts, and had never suspected, till that wicked, open-handed, and swearing old gentleman died, how very nearly he had run the estates into insolvency.

They met at Gylingden Hall. They had the will before them, and lawyers to interpret, and information without stint, as to the encumbrances with which the deceased had saddled them. The will was so framed as to set the two brothers instantly at deadly feud.

These brothers differed in some points; but in one material characteristic they resembled one another, and also their departed father. They never went into a quarrel by halves, and once in, they did not stick at trifles.

The elder, Scroope Marston, the more dangerous man of the two, had never been a favourite of the old Squire. He had no taste for the sports of the field and the pleasures of a rustic life. He was no athlete, and he certainly was not handsome. All this the Squire resented. The young man, who had no respect for him, and outgrew his fear of his violence as he came to manhood, retorted. This aversion, therefore, in the ill-conditioned old man grew into positive hatred. He used to wish that d——d pippin-squeezing, hump-backed rascal Scroope, out of the way of better men – meaning his younger son Charles; and in his cups would talk in a way which even the old and young fellows who followed his hounds, and drank his port, and could stand a reasonable amount of brutality, did not like.

Scroope Marston was slightly deformed, and he had the lean sallow face, piercing black eyes, and black lank hair, which sometimes accompany deformity.

"I'm no feyther o' that hog-backed creature. I'm no sire of hisn, d——n him! I'd as soon call that tongs son o' mine," the old man used to bawl, in allusion to his son's long, lank limbs: "Charlie's a man, but that's a jack-an-ape. He has no good-nature; there's nothing handy, nor manly, nor no one turn of a Marston in him."

And when he was pretty drunk, the old Squire used to swear he should never "sit at the head o' that board; nor frighten away folk from Gylingden Hall wi' his d——d hatchet-face – the black loon!"

"Handsome Charlie was the man for his money. He knew what a horse was, and could sit to his bottle; and the lasses were all clean *mad* about him. He was a Marston every inch of his six foot two."

Handsome Charlie and he, however, had also had a row or two. The old Squire was free with his horsewhip as with his tongue, and on occasion when neither weapon was quite practicable, had been known to give a fellow "a tap o' his knuckles." Handsome Charlie, however, thought there was a period at which personal chastisement should cease; and one night, when the port was flowing, there was some allusion to Marion Hayward, the miller's daughter, which for some reason the old gentleman did not like. Being "in liquor," and having clearer ideas about pugilism than self-government, he struck out, to the surprise of all present, at Handsome Charlie. The youth threw back his head scientifically, and nothing followed but the crash of a decanter on the floor. But the old Squire's blood was up, and he bounced from his chair. Up jumped Handsome Charlie, resolved to stand no nonsense. Drunken Squire Lilbourne, intending to mediate, fell flat on the floor, and cut his ear among the glasses. Handsome Charlie caught the thump which the old Squire discharged at him upon his open hand, and catching him by the cravat, swung him with his back to the wall. They said the old man never looked so purple, nor his eyes so goggle before; and then Handsome Charlie pinioned him tight to the wall by both arms.

"Well, I say – come, don't you talk no more nonsense o' that sort, and I won't lick you," croaked the old Squire. "You stopped that un clever, you did. Didn't he? Come, Charlie, man, gie us your hand, I say, and sit down again, lad." And so the battle ended; and I believe it was the last time the Squire raised his hand to Handsome Charlie.

But those days were over. Old Toby Marston lay cold and quiet enough now, under the drip of the mighty ash-tree within the Saxon ruin where so many of the old Marston race returned to dust, and were forgotten. The weather-stained top-boots and leather-breeches, the three-cornered cocked hat to which old gentlemen of that day still clung, and the well-known red waistcoat that reached below his hips, and the fierce pug face of the old Squire, were now but a picture of memory. And the brothers between whom he had planted an irreconcilable quarrel, were now in their new mourning suits, with the gloss still on, debating furiously across the table in the great oak parlour, which had so often resounded to the banter and coarse songs, the oaths and laughter of the congenial neighbours whom the old Squire of Gylingden Hall loved to assemble there.

These young gentlemen, who had grown up in Gylingden Hall, were not accustomed to bridle their tongues, nor, if need be, to hesitate about a blow. Neither had been at the old man's funeral. His death had been sudden. Having been helped to his bed in that hilarious and quarrelsome state which was induced by port and punch, he was found dead in the morning, – his head hanging over the side of the bed, and his face very black and swollen.

Now the Squire's will despoiled his eldest son of Gylingden, which had descended to the heir time out of mind. Scroope Marston was furious. His deep stern voice was heard inveighing against his dead father and living brother, and the heavy thumps on the table with which he enforced his stormy recriminations resounded through the large chamber. Then broke in Charles's rougher voice, and then came a quick alternation of short sentences, and then both voices together in growing loudness and anger, and at last, swelling the tumult, the expostulations of pacific and frightened lawyers, and at last a sudden break up of the conference. Scroope broke out of the room, his pale furious face showing whiter against his long black hair, his dark fierce eyes blazing, his hands clenched, and looking more ungainly and deformed than ever in the convulsions of his fury.

Very violent words must have passed between them; for Charlie, though he was the winning man, was almost as angry as Scroope. The elder brother was for holding possession of the house, and putting his rival to legal process to oust him. But his legal advisers were clearly against it. So, with a heart boiling over with gall, up he went to London, and found the firm who had managed his father's business fair and communicative enough. They looked into the settlements, and found that Gylingden was excepted. It was very odd, but so it was, specially excepted; so that the right of the old Squire to deal with it by his will could not be questioned.

Notwithstanding all this, Scroope, breathing vengeance and aggression, and quite willing to wreck himself provided he could run his brother down, assailed Handsome Charlie, and battered old Squire Toby's will in the Prerogative Court and also at common law, and the feud between the brothers was knit, and every month their exasperation was heightened.

Scroope was beaten, and defeat did not soften him. Charles might have forgiven hard words; but he had been himself worsted during the long campaign in some of those skirmishes, special motions, and so forth, that constitute the episodes of a legal epic like that in which the Marston brothers figured as opposing combatants; and the blight of law costs had touched him, too, with the usual effect upon the temper of a man of embarrassed means.

Years flew, and brought no healing on their wings. On the contrary, the deep corrosion of this hatred bit deeper by time. Neither brother married. But an accident of a different kind befell the younger, Charles Marston, which abridged his enjoyments very materially.

This was a bad fall from his hunter. There were severe fractures, and there was concussion of the brain. For some time it was thought that he could not recover. He disappointed these evil auguries, however. He did recover, but changed in two essential particulars. He had received an injury in his hip, which doomed him never more to sit in the saddle. And the rollicking animal spirits which hitherto had never failed him, had now taken flight for ever.

He had been for five days in a state of coma – absolute insensibility – and when he recovered consciousness he was haunted by an indescribable anxiety.

Tom Cooper, who had been butler in the palmy days of Gylingden Hall, under old Squire Toby, still maintained his post with old-fashioned fidelity, in these days of faded splendour and frugal housekeeping. Twenty years had passed since the death of his old master. He had grown lean, and stooped, and his face, dark with the peculiar brown of age, furrowed and gnarled, and his temper, except with his master, had waxed surly.

His master had visited Bath and Buxton, and came back, as he went, lame, and halting gloomily about with the aid of a stick. When the hunter was sold, the last tradition of the old life at Gylingden disappeared. The young Squire, as he was still called, excluded by his mischance from the hunting-field, dropped into a solitary way of life, and halted slowly and solitarily about the old place, seldom raising his eyes, and with an appearance of indescribable gloom.

Old Cooper could talk freely on occasion with his master; and one day he said, as he handed him his hat and stick in the hall:

"You should rouse yourself up a bit, Master Charles!"

"It's past rousing with me, old Cooper."

"It's just this, I'm thinking: there's something on your mind, and you won't tell no one. There's no good keeping it on your stomach. You'll be a deal lighter if you tell it. Come, now, what is it, Master Charlie?"

The Squire looked with his round grey eyes straight into Cooper's eyes. He felt that there was a sort of spell broken. It was like the old rule of the ghost who can't speak till it is spoken to. He looked earnestly into old Cooper's face for some seconds, and sighed deeply.

"It ain't the first good guess you've made in your day, old Cooper, and I'm glad you've spoke. It's bin on my mind, sure enough, ever since I had that fall. Come in here after me, and shut the door."

The Squire pushed open the door of the oak parlour, and looked round on the pictures abstractedly. He had not been there for some time, and, seating himself on the table, he looked again for a while in Cooper's face before he spoke.

"It's not a great deal, Cooper, but it troubles me, and I would not tell it to the parson nor the doctor; for, God knows what they'd say, though there's nothing to signify in it. But you were always true to the family, and I don't mind if I tell you."

"'Tis as safe with Cooper, Master Charles, as if 'twas locked in a chest, and sunk in a well."

"It's only this," said Charles Marston, looking down on the end of his stick, with which he was tracing lines and circles, "all the time I was lying like dead, as you thought, after that fall, I was with the old master." He raised his eyes to Cooper's again as he spoke, and with an awful oath he repeated – "I was with him, Cooper!"

"He was a good man, sir, in his way," repeated old Cooper, returning his gaze with awe." He was a good master to me, and a good father to you, and I hope he's happy. May God rest him!"

"Well," said Squire Charles, "it's only this: the whole of that time I was with him, or he was with me – I don't know which. The upshot is, we were together, and I thought I'd never get out of his hands again, and all the time he was bullying me about some one thing; and if it was to save my life, Tom Cooper, by —— from the time I waked I never could call to mind what it was; and I think I'd give that hand to know; and if you can think of anything it might be – for God's sake! don't be afraid, Tom Cooper, but speak it out, for he threatened me hard, and it was surely him."

Here ensued a silence.

"And what did you think it might be yourself, Master Charles?" said Cooper.

"I han't thought of aught that's likely. I'll never hit on't – *never*. I thought it might happen he knew something about that d—— hump-backed villain, Scroope, that swore before Lawyer Gingham I made away with a paper of settlements – me and father; and, as I hope to be saved, Tom Cooper, there never was a bigger lie! I'd a had the law of him for them identical words, and cast him for more than he's worth; only Lawyer Gingham never goes into nothing for me since money grew scarce in Gylingden; and I can't change my lawyer, I owe him such a hatful of money. But he did, he swore he'd hang me yet for it. He said it in them identical words – he'd never rest till he *banged* me for it, and I think it was, like enough, something about *that*, the old master was troubled; but it's enough to drive a man mad. I *can't* bring it to mind – I can't remember a word he said, only he threatened awful, and looked – Lord a mercy on us! – frightful bad."

"There's no need he should. May the Lord a-mercy on him!" said the old butler.

"No, of course; and you're not to tell a soul, Cooper – not a living soul, mind, that I said he looked bad, nor nothing about it."

"God forbid!" said old Cooper, shaking his head. "But I was thinking, sir, it might ha' been about the slight that's bin so long put on him by having no stone over him, and never a scratch o' a chisel to say who he is."

"Ay! Well, I didn't think o' that. Put on your hat, old Cooper, and come down wi' me; for I'll look after that, at any rate."

There is a bye-path leading by a turnstile to the park, and thence to the picturesque old burying-place, which lies in a nook by the roadside, embowered in ancient trees. It was a fine autumnal sunset, and melancholy lights and long shadows spread their peculiar effects over the landscape as "Handsome Charlie" and the old butler made their way slowly toward the place where Handsome Charlie was himself to lie at last.

"Which of the dogs made that howling all last night?" asked the Squire, when they had got on a little way.

"'Twas a strange dog, Master Charlie, in front of the house; ours was all in the yard – a white dog wi' a black head, he looked to be, and he was smelling round them mounting-steps the old master, God be wi' him! set up, the time his knee was bad. When the tyke got up a' top of them, howlin' up at the windows, I'd a liked to shy something at him."

"Hullo! Is that like him?" said the Squire, stopping short, and pointing with his stick at a dirty-white dog, with a large black head, which was scampering round them in a wide circle, half crouching with that air of uncertainty and deprecation which dogs so well know how to assume.

He whistled the dog up. He was a large, half-starved bull-dog.

"That fellow has made a long journey – thin as a whipping-post, and stained all over, and his claws worn to the stumps," said the Squire, musingly. "He isn't a bad dog, Cooper. My poor father liked a good bull-dog, and knew a cur from a good 'un."

The dog was looking up into the Squire's face with the peculiar grim visage of his kind, and the Squire was thinking irreverently how strong a likeness it presented to the character of his father's fierce pug features when he was clutching his horsewhip and swearing at a keeper.

"If I did right I'd shoot him. He'll worry the cattle, and kill our dogs," said the Squire. "Hey, Cooper? I'll tell the keeper to look after him. That fellow could pull down a sheep, and he shan't live on my mutton."

But the dog was not to be shaken off. He looked wistfully after the Squire, and after they had got a little way on, he followed timidly.

It was vain trying to drive him off. The dog ran round them in wide circles, like the infernal dog in "Faust"; only he left no track of thin flame behind him. These manœuvres were executed with a sort of beseeching air, which flattered and touched the object of this odd preference. So he called him up again, patted him, and then and there in a manner adopted him.

The dog now followed their steps dutifully, as if he had belonged to Handsome Charlie all his days. Cooper unlocked the little iron door, and the dog walked in close behind their heels, and followed them as they visited the roofless chapel.

The Marstons were lying under the floor of this little building in rows. There is not a vault. Each has his distinct grave enclosed in a lining of masonry. Each is surmounted by a stone kist, on the upper flag of which is enclosed his epitaph, except that of poor old Squire Toby. Over him was nothing but the grass and the line of masonry which indicate the site of the kist, whenever his family should afford him one like the rest.

"Well, it does look shabby. It's the elder brother's business; but if he won't, I'll see to it myself, and I'll take care, old boy, to cut sharp and deep in it, that the elder son having refused to lend a hand the stone was put there by the younger."

They strolled round this little burial-ground. The sun was now below the horizon, and the red metallic glow from the clouds, still illuminated by the departed sun, mingled luridly with the twilight. When Charlie peeped again into the little chapel, he saw the ugly dog stretched upon Squire Toby's grave, looking at least twice his natural length, and performing such antics as made the young Squire stare. If you have ever seen a cat stretched on the floor, with a bunch of Valerian, straining, writhing, rubbing its jaws in long-drawn caresses, and in the absorption of a sensual ecstasy, you have seen a phenomenon resembling that which Handsome Charlie witnessed on looking in.

The head of the brute looked so large, its body so long and thin, and its joints so ungainly and dislocated, that the Squire, with old Cooper beside him, looked on with a feeling of disgust and astonishment, which, in a moment or two more, brought the Squire's stick down upon him with a couple of heavy thumps. The beast awakened from his ecstasy, sprang to the head of the grave, and there on a sudden, thick and bandy as before, confronted the Squire, who stood at its foot, with a terrible grin, and eyes that glared with the peculiar green of canine fury.

The next moment the dog was crouching abjectly at the Squire's feet.

"Well, he's a rum 'un!" said old Cooper, looking hard at him.

"I like him," said the Squire.

"I don't," said Cooper.

"But he shan't come in here again," said the Squire.

"I shouldn't wonder if he was a witch," said old Cooper, who remembered more tales of witchcraft than are now current in that part of the world.

"He's a good dog," said the Squire, dreamily. "I remember the time I'd a given a handful for him – but I'll never be good for nothing again. Come along."

And he stooped down and patted him. So up jumped the dog and looked up in his face, as if watching for some sign, ever so slight, which he might obey.

Cooper did not like a bone in that dog's skin. He could not imagine what his master saw to admire in him. He kept him all night in the gun-room, and the dog accompanied him in his halting rambles about the place. The fonder his master grew of him, the less did Cooper and the other servants like him.

"He hasn't a point of a good dog about him," Cooper would growl. "I think Master Charlie be blind. And old Captain (an old red parrot, who sat chained to a perch in the oak parlour, and conversed with himself, and nibbled at his claws and bit his perch all day), – old Captain, the only living thing, except one or two of us, and the Squire himself, that remembers the old master, the minute he saw the dog, screeched as if he was struck, shakin' his feathers out quite wild, and drops down, poor old soul, a-hangin' by his foot, in a fit."

But there is no accounting for fancies, and the Squire was one of those dogged persons who persist more obstinately in their whims the more they are opposed. But Charles Marston's health suffered by his lameness. The transition from habitual and violent exercise to such a life as his privation now consigned him to, was never made without a risk to health; and a host of dyspeptic annoyances, the existence of which he had never dreamed of before, now beset him in sad earnest. Among these was the now not unfrequent troubling of his sleep with dreams and nightmares. In these his canine favourite invariably had a part and was generally a central, and sometimes a solitary figure. In these visions the dog seemed to stretch himself up the side of the Squire's bed, and in dilated proportions to sit at his feet, with a horrible likeness to the pug features of old Squire Toby, with his tricks of wagging his head and throwing up his chin; and then he would talk to him about Scroope, and tell him "all wasn't straight," and that he "must make it up wi' Scroope," that he, the old Squire, had "served him an ill turn," that "time was nigh up," and that "fair was fair," and he was "troubled where he was, about Scroope."

Then in his dream this semi-human brute would approach his face to his, crawling and crouching up his body, heavy as lead, till the face of the beast was laid on his, with the same odious caresses and stretchings and writhings which he had seen over the old Squire's grave. Then Charlie would wake up with a gasp and a howl, and start upright in the bed, bathed in a cold moisture, and fancy he saw something white sliding off the foot of the bed. Sometimes he thought it might be the curtain with white lining that slipped down, or the coverlet disturbed by his uneasy turnings; but he always fancied, at such moments, that he saw something white sliding hastily off the bed; and always when he had been visited by such dreams the dog next morning was more than usually caressing and servile, as if to obliterate, by a more than ordinary welcome, the sentiment of disgust which the horror of the night had left behind it.

The doctor half-satisfied the Squire that there was nothing in these dreams, which, in one shape or another, invariably attended forms of indigestion such as he was suffering from.

For a while, as if to corroborate this theory, the dog ceased altogether to figure in them. But at last there came a vision in which, more unpleasantly than before, he did resume his old place.

In his nightmare the room seemed all but dark; he heard what he knew to be the dog walking from the door round his bed slowly, to the side from which he always had come upon it. A portion of the room was uncarpeted, and he said he distinctly heard the peculiar tread of a dog, in which the faint clatter of the claws is audible. It was a light stealthy step, but at every tread the whole room shook heavily; he felt something place itself at the foot of his bed, and saw a pair of green eyes staring at him in the dark, from which he could not remove his own. Then he heard, as he thought, the old Squire Toby say – "The eleventh hour be passed, Charlie, and ye've done nothing – you and I 'a done Scroope a wrong!" and then came a good deal more, and then – "The time's nigh up, it's going to strike." And with a long low growl, the thing began to creep up upon his feet; the growl continued, and he saw the reflection of the up-turned green eyes upon the bed-clothes, as it began slowly to stretch itself up his body towards his face. With a loud scream, he waked. The light, which of late the Squire was accustomed to have in his bedroom, had accidentally gone out. He was afraid to get up, or even to look about the room for some time; so sure did he feel of seeing the green eyes in the dark fixed on him from some corner. He had hardly recovered from the first agony which nightmare leaves behind it, and was beginning to collect his thoughts, when he heard the clock strike twelve. And he bethought him of the words "the eleventh hour be passed – time's nigh up – it's going to strike!" and he almost feared that he would hear the voice reopening the subject.

Next morning the Squire came down looking ill.

"Do you know a room, old Cooper," said he, "they used to call King Herod's Chamber?"

"Ay, sir; the story of King Herod was on the walls o't when I was a boy."

"There's a closet off it – is there?"

"I can't be sure o' that; but 'tisn't worth your looking at, now; the hangings was rotten, and took off the walls, before you was born; and there's nou't there but some old broken things and lumber. I seed them put there myself by poor Twinks; he was blind of an eye, and footman afterwards. You'll remember Twinks? He died here, about the time o' the great snow. There was a deal o' work to bury him, poor fellow!"

"Get the key, old Cooper; I'll look at the room," said the Squire.

"And what the devil can you want to look at it for?" said Cooper, with the old-world privilege of a rustic butler.

"And what the devil's that to you? But I don't mind if I tell you. I don't want that dog in the gun-room, and I'll put him somewhere else; and I don't care if I put him there."

"A bull-dog in a bedroom! Oons, sir! the folks 'ill say you're clean mad!"

"Well, let them; get you the key, and let us look at the room."

"You'd shoot him if you did right, Master Charlie. You never heard what a noise he kept up all last night in the gun-room, walking to and fro growling like a tiger in a show; and, say what you like, the dog's not worth his feed; he hasn't a point of a dog; he's a bad dog."

"I know a dog better than you – and he's a good dog!" said the Squire, testily.

"If you was a judge of a dog you'd hang that 'un," said Cooper.

"I'm not a-going to hang him, so there's an end. Go you, and get the key; and don't be talking, mind, when you go down. I may change my mind."

Now this freak of visiting King Herod's room had, in truth, a totally different object from that pretended by the Squire. The voice in his nightmare had uttered a particular direction, which haunted him, and would give him no peace until he had tested it. So far from liking that dog today, he was beginning to regard it with a horrible suspicion; and if old Cooper had not stirred his obstinate temper by seeming to dictate, I dare say he would have got rid of that inmate effectually before evening.

Up to the third storey, long disused, he and old Cooper mounted. At the end of a dusty gallery, the room lay. The old tapestry, from which the spacious chamber had taken its name, had long given place to modern paper, and this was mildewed, and in some places hanging from the walls. A thick mantle of dust lay over the floor. Some broken chairs and boards, thick with dust, lay, along with other lumber, piled together at one end of the room.

They entered the closet, which was quite empty. The Squire looked round, and you could hardly have said whether he was relieved or disappointed.

"No furniture here," said the Squire, and looked through the dusty window. "Did you say anything to me lately – I don't mean this morning – about this room, or the closet – or anything – I forget—"

"Lor' bless you! Not I. I han't been thinkin' o' this room this forty year."

"Is there any sort of old furniture called a *buffet* – do you remember?" asked the Squire.

"A buffet? why, yes – to be sure – there was a buffet, sure enough, in this closet, now you bring it to my mind," said Cooper. "But it's papered over."

"And what is it?"

"A little cupboard in the wall," answered the old man.

"Ho – I see – and there's such a thing here, is there, under the paper? Show me whereabouts it was."

"Well – I think it was somewhere about here," answered he, rapping his knuckles along the wall opposite the window. "Ay, there it is," he added, as the hollow sound of a wooden door was returned to his knock.

The Squire pulled the loose paper from the wall, and disclosed the doors of a small press, about two feet square, fixed in the wall.

"The very thing for my buckles and pistols, and the rest of my gimcracks," said the Squire. "Come away, we'll leave the dog where he is. Have you the key of that little press?"

No, he had not. The old master had emptied and locked it up, and desired that it should be papered over, and that was the history of it.

Down came the Squire, and took a strong turn-screw from his gun-case; and quietly he reascended to King Herod's room, and, with little trouble, forced the door of the small press in the closet wall. There were in it some letters and cancelled leases, and also a parchment deed which he took to the window and read with much agitation. It was a supplemental deed executed about a fortnight after the others, and previously to his father's marriage, placing Gylingden under strict settlement to the elder son, in what is called "tail male." Handsome Charlie, in his fraternal litigation, had acquired a smattering of technical knowledge, and he perfectly well knew that the effect of this would be not only to transfer the house and lands to his brother Scroope, but to leave him at the mercy of that exasperated brother, who might recover from him personally every guinea he had ever received by way of rent, from the date of his father's death.

It was a dismal, clouded day, with something threatening in its aspect, and the darkness, where he stood, was made deeper by the top of one of the huge old trees overhanging the window.

In a state of awful confusion he attempted to think over his position. He placed the deed in his pocket, and nearly made up his mind to destroy it. A short time ago he would not have hesitated for a moment under such circumstances; but now his health and his nerves were shattered, and he was under a supernatural alarm which the strange discovery of this deed had powerfully confirmed.

In this state of profound agitation he heard a sniffing at the closet-door, and then an impatient scratch and a long low growl. He screwed his courage up, and, not knowing what to expect, threw the door open and saw the dog, not in his dream-shape, but wriggling with joy, and crouching and fawning with eager submission; and then wandering about the closet, the brute growled awfully into the corners of it, and seemed in an unappeasable agitation.

Then the dog returned and fawned and crouched again at his feet.

After the first moment was over, the sensations of abhorrence and fear began to subside, and he almost reproached himself for requiting the affection of this poor friendless brute with the antipathy which he had really done nothing to earn.

The dog pattered after him down the stairs. Oddly enough, the sight of this animal, after the first revulsion, reassured him; it was, in his eyes, so attached, so good-natured, and palpably so mere a dog.

By the hour of evening the Squire had resolved on a middle course; he would not inform his brother of his discovery, nor yet would he destroy the deed. He would never marry. He was past that time. He would leave a letter, explaining the discovery of the deed, addressed to the only surviving trustee – who had probably forgotten everything about it – and having seen out his own tenure, he would provide that all should be set right after his death. Was not that fair? at all events it quite satisfied what he called his conscience, and he thought it a devilish good compromise for his brother; and he went out, towards sunset, to take his usual walk.

Returning in the darkening twilight, the dog, as usual attending him, began to grow frisky and wild, at first scampering round him in great circles, as before, nearly at the top of his speed, his great head between his paws as he raced. Gradually more excited grew the pace and narrower his circuit, louder and fiercer his continuous growl, and the Squire stopped and grasped his stick hard, for the lurid eyes and grin of the brute threatened an attack. Turning round and round as the excited brute encircled him, and striking vainly at him with his stick, he grew at last so tired that he almost despaired of keeping him longer at bay; when on a sudden the dog stopped short and crawled up to his feet wriggling and crouching submissively.

Nothing could be more apologetic and abject; and when the Squire dealt him two heavy thumps with his stick, the dog whimpered only, and writhed and licked his feet. The Squire sat down on a prostrate tree; and his dumb companion, recovering his wonted spirits immediately, began to sniff and nuzzle among the roots. The Squire felt in his breast-pocket for the deed – it was safe; and again he pondered, in this loneliest of spots, on the question whether he should preserve it for restoration after his death to his brother, or destroy it forthwith. He began rather to lean toward the latter solution, when the long low growl of the dog not far off startled him.

He was sitting in a melancholy grove of old trees, that slants gently westward. Exactly the same odd effect of light I have before described – a faint red glow reflected downward from the upper sky, after the sun had set, now gave to the growing darkness a lurid uncertainty. This grove, which lies in a gentle hollow, owing to its circumscribed horizon on all but one side, has a peculiar character of loneliness.

He got up and peeped over a sort of barrier, accidentally formed of the trunks of felled trees laid one over the other, and saw the dog straining up the other side of it, and hideously stretched out, his ugly head looking in consequence twice the natural size. His dream was coming over him again. And now between the trunks the brute's ungainly head was thrust, and the long neck came straining through, and the body, twining after it like a huge white lizard; and as it came striving and twisting through, it growled and glared as if it would devour him.

As swiftly as his lameness would allow, the Squire hurried from this solitary spot towards the house. What thoughts exactly passed through his mind as he did so, I am sure he could not have told. But when the dog came up with him it seemed appeased, and even in high good-humour, and no longer resembled the brute that haunted his dreams.

That night, near ten o'clock, the Squire, a good deal agitated, sent for the keeper, and told him that he believed the dog was mad, and that he must shoot him. He might shoot the dog in the gun-room, where he was – a grain of shot or two in the wainscot did not matter, and the dog must not have a chance of getting out.

The Squire gave the gamekeeper his double-barrelled gun, loaded with heavy shot. He did not go with him beyond the hall. He placed his hand on the keeper's arm; the keeper said his hand trembled, and that he looked "as white as curds."

"Listen a bit!" said the Squire under his breath.

They heard the dog in a state of high excitement in the room – growling ominously, jumping on the window-stool and down again, and running round the room.

"You'll need to be sharp, mind – don't give him a chance – slip in edgeways, d'ye see? and give him both barrels!"

"Not the first mad dog I've knocked over, sir," said the man, looking very serious as he cocked the gun.

As the keeper opened the door, the dog had sprung into the empty grate. He said he "never see sich a stark, staring devil." The beast made a twist round, as if, he thought, to jump up the chimney – "but that wasn't to be done at no price," – and he made a yell – not like a dog – like a man caught in a mill-crank, and before he could spring at the keeper, he fired one barrel into him. The dog leaped towards him, and rolled over, receiving the second barrel in his head, as he lay snorting at the keeper's feet!

"I never seed the like; I never heard a screech like that!" said the keeper, recoiling. "It makes a fellow feel queer."

"Quite dead?" asked the Squire.

"Not a stir in him, sir," said the man, pulling him along the floor by the neck.

"Throw him outside the hall-door now," said the Squire;" and mind you pitch him outside the gate tonight – old Cooper says he's a witch," and the pale Squire smiled, "so he shan't lie in Gylingden."

Never was man more relieved than the Squire, and he slept better for a week after this than he had done for many weeks before.

It behoves us all to act promptly on our good resolutions. There is a determined gravitation towards evil, which, if left to itself, will bear down first intentions. If at one moment of superstitious fear, the Squire had made up his mind to a great sacrifice, and resolved in the matter of that deed so strangely recovered, to act honestly by his brother, that resolution very soon gave place to the compromise with fraud, which so conveniently postponed the restitution to the period when further enjoyment on his part was impossible. Then came more tidings of Scroope's violent and minatory language, with always the same burthen – that he would leave no stone unturned to show that there had existed a deed which Charles had either secreted or destroyed, and that he would never rest till he had hanged him.

This of course was wild talk. At first it had only enraged him; but, with his recent guilty knowledge and suppression, had come fear. His danger was the existence of the deed, and little by little he brought himself to a resolution to destroy it. There were many falterings and recoils before he could bring himself to commit this crime. At length, however, he did it, and got rid of the custody of that which at any time might become the instrument of disgrace and ruin. There was relief in this, but also the new and terrible sense of actual guilt.

He had got pretty well rid of his supernatural qualms. It was a different kind of trouble that agitated him now.

But this night, he imagined, he was awakened by a violent shaking of his bed. He could see, in the very imperfect light, two figures at the foot of it, holding each a bed-post. One of these he half-fancied was his brother Scroope, but the other was the old Squire – of that he was sure – and he fancied that they had shaken him up from his sleep. Squire Toby was talking as Charlie wakened, and he heard him say:

"Put out of our own house by you! It won't hold for long. We'll come in together, friendly, and stay. Forewarned, wi' yer eyes open, ye did it; and now Scroope'll hang you! We'll hang you together! Look at me, you devil's limb."

And the old Squire tremblingly stretched his face, torn with shot and bloody, and growing every moment more and more into the likeness of the dog, and began to stretch himself out and climb the bed over the foot-board; and he saw the figure at the other side, little more than a black shadow, begin also to scale the bed; and there was instantly a dreadful confusion and uproar in the room, and such a gabbling and laughing; he could not catch the words; but, with a scream, he woke, and found himself standing on the floor. The phantoms and the clamour were gone, but a crash and ringing of fragments was in his ears. The great china bowl, from which for generations the Marstons of Gylingden had been baptized, had fallen from the mantelpiece, and was smashed on the hearth-stone.

"I've bin dreamin' all night about Mr. Scroope, and I wouldn't wonder, old Cooper, if he was dead," said the Squire, when he came down in the morning.

"God forbid! I was adreamed about him, too, sir: I dreamed he was dammin' and sinkin' about a hole was burnt in his coat, and the old master, God be wi' him! said – quite plain – I'd 'a swore 'twas himself – 'Cooper, get up, ye d——d land-loupin' thief, and lend a hand to hang him – for he's a daft cur, and no dog o' mine.' 'Twas the dog shot over night, I do suppose, as was runnin' in my old head. I thought old master gied me a punch wi' his knuckles, and says I, wakenin' up, 'At yer service, sir'; and for a while I couldn't get it out o' my head, master was in the room still."

Letters from town soon convinced the Squire that his brother Scroope, so far from being dead, was particularly active; and Charlie's attorney wrote to say, in serious alarm, that he had heard, accidentally, that he intended setting up a case, of a supplementary deed of settlement, of which he had secondary evidence, which would give him Gylingden. And at this menace Handsome Charlie snapped his fingers, and wrote courageously to his attorney; abiding what might follow with, however, a secret foreboding.

Scroope threatened loudly now, and swore after his bitter fashion, and reiterated his old promise of hanging that cheat at last. In the midst of these menaces and preparations, however, a sudden peace proclaimed itself: Scroope died, without time even to make provisions for a posthumous attack upon his brother. It was one of those cases of disease of the heart in which death is as sudden as by a bullet.

Charlie's exultation was undisguised. It was shocking. Not, of course, altogether malignant. For there was the expansion consequent on the removal of a secret fear. There was also the comic piece of luck, that only the day before Scroope had destroyed his old will, which left to a stranger every farthing he possessed, intending in a day or two to execute another to the same person, charged with the express condition of prosecuting the suit against Charlie.

The result was, that all his possessions went unconditionally to his brother Charles as his heir. Here were grounds for abundance of savage elation. But there was also the deep-seated hatred of half a life of mutual and persistent agression and revilings; and Handsome Charlie was capable of nursing a grudge, and enjoying a revenge with his whole heart.

He would gladly have prevented his brother's being buried in the old Gylingden chapel, where he wished to lie; but his lawyers doubted his power, and he was not quite proof against the scandal which would attend his turning back the funeral, which would, he knew, be attended by some of the country gentry and others, with an hereditary regard for the Marstons.

But he warned his servants that not one of them were to attend it; promising, with oaths and curses not to be disregarded, that any one of them who did so, should find the door shut in his face on his return.

I don't think, with the exception of old Cooper, that the servants cared for this prohibition, except as it baulked a curiosity always strong in the solitude of the country. Cooper was very much vexed that the eldest son of the old Squire should be buried in the old family chapel, and no sign of decent respect from Gylingden Hall. He asked his master, whether he would not, at least, have some wine and refreshments in the oak parlour, in case any of the country gentlemen who paid this respect to the old family should come up to the house? But the Squire only swore at him, told him to mind his own business, and ordered him to say, if such a thing happened, that he was out, and no preparations made, and, in fact, to send them away as they came. Cooper expostulated stoutly, and the Squire grew angrier; and after a tempestuous scene, took his hat and stick and walked out, just as the funeral descending the valley from the direction of the "Old Angel Inn" came in sight.

Old Cooper prowled about disconsolately, and counted the carriages as well as he could from the gate. When the funeral was over, and they began to drive away, he returned to the hall, the door of which lay open, and as usual deserted. Before he reached it quite, a mourning coach drove up, and two gentlemen in black cloaks, and with crapes to their hats, got out, and without looking to the right or the left, went up the steps into the house. Cooper followed them slowly. The carriage had, he supposed, gone round to the yard, for, when he reached the door, it was no longer there.

So he followed the two mourners into the house. In the hall he found a fellow-servant, who said he had seen two gentlemen, in black cloaks, pass through the hall, and go up the stairs without removing their hats, or asking leave of anyone. This was very odd, old Cooper thought, and a great liberty; so up-stairs he went to make them out.

But he could not find them then, nor ever. And from that hour the house was troubled.

In a little time there was not one of the servants who had not something to tell. Steps and voices followed them sometimes in the passages, and tittering whispers, always minatory, scared them at corners of the galleries, or from dark recesses; so that they would return panic-stricken to be rebuked by thin Mrs. Beckett, who looked on such stories as worse than idle. But Mrs. Beckett herself, a short time after, took a very different view of the matter.

She had herself begun to hear these voices, and with this formidable aggravation, that they came always when she was at her prayers, which she had been punctual in saying all her life, and utterly interrupted them. She was scared at such moments by dropping words and sentences, which grew, as she persisted, into threats and blasphemies.

These voices were not always in the room. They called, as she fancied, through the walls, very thick in that old house, from the neighbouring apartments, sometimes on one side, sometimes on the other; sometimes they seemed to holloa from distant lobbies, and came muffled, but threateningly, through the long panelled passages. As they approached they grew furious, as if several voices were speaking together. Whenever, as I said, this worthy woman applied herself to her devotions, these horrible sentences came hurrying towards the door, and, in panic, she would start from her knees, and all then would subside except the thumping of her heart against her stays, and the dreadful tremors of her nerves.

What these voices said, Mrs. Beckett never could quite remember one minute after they had ceased speaking; one sentence chased another away; gibe and menace and impious denunciation, each hideously articulate, were lost as soon as heard. And this added to the effect of these terrifying mockeries and invectives, that she could not, by any effort, retain their exact import, although their horrible character remained vividly present to her mind.

For a long time the Squire seemed to be the only person in the house absolutely unconscious of these annoyances. Mrs. Beckett had twice made up her mind within the week to leave. A prudent woman, however, who has been comfortable for more than twenty years in a place, thinks oftener than twice before she leaves it. She and old Cooper were the only servants in the house who remembered the good old housekeeping in Squire Toby's day. The others were few, and such as could hardly be accounted regular servants. Meg Dobbs, who acted as housemaid, would not sleep in the house, but walked home, in trepidation, to her father's, at the gate-house, under the escort of her little brother, every night. Old Mrs. Beckett, who was high and mighty with the make-shift servants of fallen Gylingden, let herself down all at once, and made Mrs. Kymes and the kitchenmaid move their beds into her large and faded room, and there, very frankly, shared her nightly terrors with them.

Old Cooper was testy and captious about these stories. He was already uncomfortable enough by reason of the entrance of the two muffled figures into the house, about which there could be no mistake. His own eyes had seen them. He refused to credit the stories of the women, and affected to think that the two mourners might have left the house and driven away, on finding no one to receive them.

Old Cooper was summoned at night to the oak parlour, where the Squire was smoking.

"I say, Cooper," said the Squire, looking pale and angry, "what for ha' you been frightenin' they crazy women wi' your plaguy stories? d—— me, if you see ghosts here it's no place for you, and it's time you should pack. I won't be left without servants. Here has been old Beckett, wi' the cook and the kitchenmaid, as white as pipe-clay, all in a row, to tell me I must have a parson to sleep among them, and preach down the devil! Upon my soul, you're a wise old body, filling their heads wi' maggots! and Meg goes down to the lodge every night, afeared to lie in the house – all your doing, wi' your old wives' stories, – ye withered old Tom o' Bedlam!"

"I'm not to blame, Master Charles. 'Tisn't along o' no stories o' mine, for I'm never done tellin' 'em it's all vanity and vapours. Mrs. Beckett 'ill tell you that, and there's been many a wry word betwixt us on the head o't. Whate'er I may *think*," said old Cooper, significantly, and looking askance, with the sternness of fear in the Squire's face.

The Squire averted his eyes, and muttered angrily to himself, and turned away to knock the ashes out of his pipe on the hob, and then turning suddenly round upon Cooper again, he spoke, with a pale face, but not quite so angrily as before.

"I know you're no fool, old Cooper, when you like. Suppose there was such a thing as a ghost here, don't you see, it ain't to them snipe-headed women it 'id go to tell its story. What ails you, man, that you should think aught about it, but just what *I* think? You had a good headpiece o' yer own once, Cooper, don't be you clappin' a goosecap over it, as my poor father used to say; d——it, old boy, you mustn't let 'em be fools, settin' one another wild wi' their blether, and makin' the folk talk what they shouldn't, about Gylingden and the family. I don't think ye'd like that, old Cooper, I'm sure ye wouldn't. The women has gone out o' the kitchen, make up a bit o' fire, and get your pipe. I'll go to you, when I finish this one, and we'll smoke a bit together, and a glass o' brandy and water."

Down went the old butler, not altogether unused to such condescensions in that disorderly and lonely household; and let not those who can choose their company, be too hard on the Squire who couldn't.

When he had got things tidy, as he said, he sat down in that big old kitchen, with his feet on the fender, the kitchen candle burning in a great brass candlestick, which stood on the deal table at his elbow, with the brandy bottle and tumblers beside it, and Cooper's pipe also in readiness. And these preparations completed, the old butler, who had remembered other generations and better times, fell into rumination, and so, gradually, into a deep sleep.

Old Cooper was half awakened by some one laughing low, near his head. He was dreaming of old times in the Hall, and fancied one of "the young gentlemen" going to play him a trick, and he mumbled something in his sleep, from which he was awakened by a stern deep voice, saying, "You wern't at the funeral; I might take your life, I'll take your ear." At the same moment, the side of his head received a violent push, and he started to his feet. The fire had gone down, and he was chilled. The candle was expiring in the socket, and threw on the white wall long shadows, that danced up and down from the ceiling to the ground, and their black outlines he fancied resembled the two men in cloaks, whom he remembered with a profound horror.

He took the candle, with all the haste he could, getting along the passage, on whose walls the same dance of black shadows was continued, very anxious to reach his room before the light should go out. He was startled half out of his wits by the sudden clang of his master's bell, close over his head, ringing furiously.

"Ha, ha! There it goes – yes, sure enough," said Cooper, reassuring himself with the sound of his own voice, as he hastened on, hearing more and more distinct every moment the same furious ringing. "He's fell asleep, like me; that's it, and his lights is out, I lay you fifty——"

When he turned the handle of the door of the oak parlour, the Squire wildly called, "Who's *there*?" in the tone of a man who expects a robber.

"It's me, old Cooper, all right, Master Charlie, you didn't come to the kitchen after all, sir."

"I'm very bad, Cooper; I don't know how I've been. Did you meet anything?" asked the Squire.

"No," said Cooper.

They stared on one another.

"Come here – stay here! Don't you leave me! Look round the room, and say is all right; and gie us your hand, old Cooper, for I must hold it." The Squire's was damp and cold, and trembled very much. It was not very far from day-break now.

After a time he spoke again: "I'a done many a thing I shouldn't; I'm not fit to go, and wi' God's blessin' I'll look to it – why shouldn't I? I'm as lame as old Billy – I'll never be able to do any good no more, and I'll give over drinking, and marry, as I ought to 'a done long ago – none o' yer fine ladies, but a good homely wench; there's Farmer Crump's youngest daughter, a good lass, and discreet. What for shouldn't I take her? She'd take care o' me, and wouldn't bring a head full o' romances here, and mantua-makers' trumpery, and I'll talk with the parson, and I'll do what's fair wi' everyone; and mind, I said I'm sorry for many a thing I 'a done."

A wild cold dawn had by this time broken. The Squire, Cooper said, looked "awful bad," as he got his hat and stick, and sallied out for a walk, instead of going to his bed, as Cooper besought him, looking so wild and distracted, that it was plain his object was simply to escape from the house. It was twelve o'clock when the Squire walked into the kitchen, where he was sure of finding some of the servants, looking as if ten years had passed over him since yesterday. He pulled a stool by the fire, without speaking a word, and sat down. Cooper had sent to Applebury for the doctor, who had just arrived, but the Squire would not go to him. "If he wants to see me, he may come here," he muttered as often as Cooper urged him. So the doctor did come, charily enough, and found the Squire very much worse than he had expected.

The Squire resisted the order to get to his bed. But the doctor insisted under a threat of death, at which his patient quailed.

"Well, I'll do what you say – only this – you must let old Cooper and Dick Keeper stay wi' me. I mustn't be left alone, and they must keep awake o' nights; and stay a while, do *you*. When I get round a bit, I'll go and live in a town. It's dull livin' here, now that I can't do nou't, as I used, and I'll live a better life, mind ye; ye heard me say that, and I don't care who laughs, and I'll talk wi' the parson. I like 'em to laugh, hang 'em, it's a sign I'm doin' right, at last."

The doctor sent a couple of nurses from the County Hospital, not choosing to trust his patient to the management he had selected, and he went down himself to Gylingden to meet them in the evening. Old Cooper was ordered to occupy the dressing-room, and sit up at night, which satisfied the Squire, who was in a strangely excited state, very low, and threatened, the doctor said, with fever.

The clergyman came, an old, gentle, "book-learned" man, and talked and prayed with him late that evening. After he had gone the Squire called the nurses to his bedside, and said:

"There's a fellow sometimes comes; you'll never mind him. He looks in at the door and beckons, – a thin, hump-backed chap in mourning, wi' black gloves on; ye'll know him by his lean face, as brown as the wainscot: don't ye mind his smilin'. You don't go out to him, nor ask him in; he won't say nout; and if he grows anger'd and looks awry at ye, don't ye be afeared, for he can't hurt ye, and he'll grow tired waitin', and go away; and for God's sake mind ye don't ask him in, nor go out after him!"

The nurses put their heads together when this was over, and held afterwards a whispering conference with old Cooper. "Law bless ye! – no, there's no madman in the house," he protested; "not a soul but what ye saw, – it's just a trifle o' the fever in his head – no more."

The Squire grew worse as the night wore on. He was heavy and delirious, talking of all sorts of things – of wine, and dogs, and lawyers; and then he began to talk, as it were, to his brother Scroope. As he did so, Mrs. Oliver, the nurse, who was sitting up alone with him, heard, as she thought, a hand softly laid on the door-handle outside, and a stealthy attempt to turn it. "Lord bless us! who's there?" she cried, and her heart jumped into her mouth, as she thought of the hump-backed man in black, who was to put in his head smiling and beckoning – "Mr. Cooper! sir! are you there?" she cried. "Come here, Mr. Cooper, please – do, sir, quick!"

Old Cooper, called up from his doze by the fire, stumbled in from the dressing-room, and Mrs. Oliver seized him tightly as he emerged.

"The man with the hump has been atryin' the door, Mr. Cooper, as sure as I am here." The Squire was moaning and mumbling in his fever, understanding nothing, as she spoke. "No, no! Mrs. Oliver, ma'am, it's impossible, for there's no sich man in the house: what is Master Charlie sayin'?"

"He's saying *Scroope* every minute, whatever he means by that, and – and – hisht! – listen – there's the handle again," and, with a loud scream, she added – "Look at his head and neck in at the door!" and in her tremour she strained old Cooper in an agonizing embrace.

The candle was flaring, and there was a wavering shadow at the door that looked like the head of a man with a long neck, and a longish sharp nose, peeping in and drawing back.

"Don't be a d—— fool, ma'am!" cried Cooper, very white, and shaking her with all his might. "It's only the candle, I tell you – nothing in life but that. Don't you see?" and he raised the light; "and I'm sure there was no one at the door, and I'll try, if you let me go."

The other nurse was asleep on a sofa, and Mrs. Oliver called her up in a panic, for company, as old Cooper opened the door. There was no one near it, but at the angle of the gallery was a shadow resembling that which he had seen in the room. He raised the candle a little, and it seemed to beckon with a long hand as the head drew back. "Shadow from the candle!" exclaimed Cooper aloud, resolved not to yield to Mrs. Oliver's panic; and, candle in hand, he walked to the corner. There was nothing. He could not forbear peeping down the long gallery from this point, and as he moved the light, he saw precisely the same sort of shadow, a little further down, and as he advanced the same withdrawal, and beckon. "Gammon!" said he; "it is nout but the candle." And on he went, growing half angry and half frightened at the persistency with which this ugly shadow – a literal shadow he was sure it was – presented itself. As he drew near the point where it now appeared, it seemed to collect itself, and nearly dissolve in the central panel of an old carved cabinet which he was now approaching.

In the centre panel of this is a sort of boss carved into a wolf's head. The light fell oddly upon this, and the fugitive shadow seemed to be breaking up, and re-arranging itself as oddly. The eye-ball gleamed with a point of reflected light, which glittered also upon the grinning mouth, and he saw the long, sharp nose of Scroope Marston, and his fierce eye looking at him, he thought, with a steadfast meaning.

Old Cooper stood gazing upon this sight, unable to move, till he saw the face, and the figure that belonged to it, begin gradually to emerge from the wood. At the same time he heard voices approaching rapidly up a side gallery, and Cooper, with a loud "Lord a-mercy on us!" turned and ran back again, pursued by a sound that seemed to shake the old house like a mighty gust of wind.

Into his master's room burst old Cooper, half wild with fear, and clapped the door and turned the key in a twinkling, looking as if he had been pursued by murderers.

"Did you hear it?" whispered Cooper, now standing near the dressing-room door. They all listened, but not a sound from without disturbed the utter stillness of night. "God bless us! I doubt it's my old head that's gone crazy!" exclaimed Cooper.

He would tell them nothing but that he was himself "an old fool," to be frightened by their talk, and that "the rattle of a window, or the dropping o' a pin" was enough to scare him now; and so he helped himself through that night with brandy, and sat up talking by his master's fire.

The Squire recovered slowly from his brain fever, but not perfectly. A very little thing, the doctor said, would suffice to upset him. He was not yet sufficiently strong to remove for change of scene and air, which were necessary for his complete restoration.

Cooper slept in the dressing-room, and was now his only nightly attendant. The ways of the invalid were odd: he liked, half sitting up in his bed, to smoke his churchwarden o' nights, and made old Cooper smoke, for company, at the fireside. As the Squire and his humble friend indulged in it, smoking is a taciturn pleasure, and it was not until the Master of Gylingden had finished his third pipe that he essayed conversation, and when he did, the subject was not such as Cooper would have chosen.

"I say, old Cooper, look in my face, and don't be afeared to speak out," said the Squire, looking at him with a steady, cunning smile; "you know all this time, as well as I do, who's in the house. You needn't deny – hey? – Scroope and my father?"

"Don't you be talking like that, Charlie," said old Cooper, rather sternly and frightened, after a long silence; still looking in his face, which did not change.

"What's the good o' shammin', Cooper? Scroope's took the hearin' o' yer right ear – you know he did. He's looking angry. He's nigh took my life wi' this fever. But he's not done wi' me yet, and he looks awful wicked. Ye saw him – ye know ye did."

Cooper was awfully frightened, and the odd smile on the Squire's lips frightened him still more. He dropped his pipe, and stood gazing in silence at his master, and feeling as if he were in a dream.

"If ye think so, ye should not be smiling like that," said Cooper, grimly.

"I'm tired, Cooper, and it's as well to smile as t'other thing; so I'll even smile while I can. You know what they mean to do wi' me. That's all I wanted to say. Now, lad, go on wi' yer pipe – I'm goin' asleep."

So the Squire turned over in his bed, and lay down serenely, with his head on the pillow. Old Cooper looked at him, and glanced at the door, and then half-filled his tumbler with brandy, and drank it off, and felt better, and got to his bed in the dressing-room.

In the dead of night he was suddenly awakened by the Squire, who was standing, in his dressing-gown and slippers, by his bed.

"I've brought you a bit o' a present. I got the rents o' Hazelden yesterday, and ye'll keep that for yourself – it's a fifty – and give t' other to Nelly Carwell, tomorrow; I'll sleep the sounder; and I saw Scroope since; he's not such a bad 'un after all, old fellow! He's got a crape over his face – for I told him I couldn't bear it; and I'd do many a thing for him now. I never could stand shilly-shally. Good-night, old Cooper!"

And the Squire laid his trembling hand kindly on the old man's shoulder, and returned to his own room. "I don't half like how he is. Doctor don't come half often enough. I don't like that queer smile o' his, and his hand was as cold as death. I hope in God his brain's not a-turnin'!"

With these reflections, he turned to the pleasanter subject of his present, and at last fell asleep.

In the morning, when he went into the Squire's room, the Squire had left his bed. "Never mind; he'll come back, like a bad shillin'," thought old Cooper, preparing the room as usual. But he did not return. Then began an uneasiness, succeeded by a panic, when it began to be plain that the Squire was not in the house. What had become of him? None of his clothes, but his dressing-gown and slippers, were missing. Had he left the house, in his present sickly state, in that garb? and, if so, could he be in his right senses; and was there a chance of his surviving a cold, damp night, so passed, in the open air?

Tom Edwards was up to the house, and told them, that, walking a mile or so that morning, at four o'clock – there being no moon – along with Farmer Nokes, who was driving his cart to market, in the dark, three men walked, in front of the horse, not twenty yards before them, all the way from near Gylingden Lodge to the burial-ground, the gate of which was opened for them from within, and the three men entered, and the gate was shut. Tom Edwards thought they were gone in to make preparation for a funeral of some member of the Marston family. But the occurrence seemed to Cooper, who knew there was no such thing, horribly ominous.

He now commenced a careful search, and at last bethought him of the lonely upper storey, and King Herod's chamber. He saw nothing changed there, but the closet door was shut, and, dark as was the morning, something, like a large white knot sticking out over the door, caught his eye.

The door resisted his efforts to open it for a time; some great weight forced it down against the floor; at length, however, it did yield a little, and a heavy crash, shaking the whole floor, and sending an echo flying through all the silent corridors, with a sound like receding laughter, half stunned him.

When he pushed open the door, his master was lying dead upon the floor. His cravat was drawn halter-wise tight round his throat, and had done its work well. The body was cold, and had been long dead.

In due course the coroner held his inquest, and the jury pronounced, "that the deceased, Charles Marston, had died by his own hand, in a state of temporary insanity." But old Cooper had his own opinion about the Squire's death, though his lips were sealed, and he never spoke about it. He went and lived for the residue of his days in York, where there are still people who remember him, a taciturn and surly old man, who attended church regularly, and also drank a little, and was known to have saved some money.

The Shabah

Fiona Lehn

OCTOBER 5: How I love the heat and vastness of the desert! The sky sits so low here – have you noticed, Ray? Sometimes I feel I can almost touch it if I stretch far enough – but no, of course I can't. This morning, a streak of electric blue, the exact shade of the panel cells, etched itself into the shallow white firmament above. It dissolved into the sun as Omar's truck disappeared into the horizon.

My training finished, he packed up and nodded in the curt way that indicates as much respect as he can impart to a woman – PhD or no – and now I am alone. Alone! I almost danced through my morning duties, the panels creaking as they tracked the sun, the breeze tickling my leg hairs with hot kisses under this floppy uniform dress thing I must wear here.

Now with Omar gone, and you and the baby safely sequestered in the city of Milh, I feel nearly overcome by emotion. Late this morning, a sandbus flying the United Desert Nations flag cruised beyond the northern edge of the panel array, enroute to Milh. Children and tourists covered its upper deck, pointing and snapping pictures. The desert breeze delivered their chiming voices and laughter to my ears. I waved and shouted a standing invitation. I knew they couldn't hear me, but I felt so free, so giddy and light. Was I like this before? Before the fall of the Americas, and the squalor of the Midwestern Heap? Or even before my doctorate? I can't remember. All I know is, this feels like paradise. I lost faith several times during the past three years. I wouldn't have made it without you, always the steady one in situations where logic holds no purchase. I'm counting the days until my three-month probation period ends and you and Kyla can come visit. I mourn all those we left behind, and at the same time, I celebrate, for we are alive!

Kiss tiny Kyla toes and fingers for me. Kisses to you too – Macey *xox*

* * *

October 9: I dreamt of you and Kyla last night. We were in the Heap, waiting for the sun to cook cans of beans we'd scavenged from a collapsed building in the outer realm. Kyla was no longer a baby, and you and I were old. She was guarding us, not the other way around. I guess that means I miss you both dreadfully, but the dream was not as disturbing as what I have to tell you now.

It's hard for me to say this, so I will spit it out: I suspect a being haunts this panel field. I can imagine you laughing and getting out that old de Maupassant scary storybook you found in some burnt-out library in the Heap, but please don't tease me. I didn't leap to that conclusion immediately, as you can imagine. Logic led me.

Early morning, three days ago, as I inspected the panels, immersed in their orchestra of hums and creaks, I felt distinctly as though I were being watched. I saw no one amidst the panel array, and later, when I returned to the control tent to check the monitor, infrared detected no creature in the thirty-acre zone. I reached for my cup of water and found it empty. I dipped the cup into the urn outside the tent flap door. Also empty. I checked the urn for cracks and found it undamaged. I'd filled it just an hour before; so, where did the water go? I don't know. I suppose my attention could have lapsed somehow, but the water hadn't evaporated or leaked out of the urn during my training period here with Omar, when there were two of us drinking water and my attention was more divided than it is now.

Before I could refill the urn, the panel alarm sounded, indicating a malfunction in the array's western quadrant. I checked the meter: suspended dust in the air measured between 150 and 200 parts per million – about normal. Out in the field I found not a speck on the array – as I expected, since I had washed that quadrant the night before. Still, the control panel had reported a significant drop in solar absorption. There are batteries, and a backup generator, so the sectors of Milh serviced by Omar's company wouldn't brown out if I couldn't get those few panels back online, yet the incident set off a series of desperate thoughts: if I couldn't fix the panels, Omar could fire me, he could send us back to the Heap, and I'd have to win the contest again to get us out – could I do that? I began to panic.

Then I remembered logic and examined the area more closely. Something was missing. Remember the heat waves that rose off the ramshackle roofs of the Heap in summer? The entire panel array generates a similar shimmer from mid-morning to late afternoon, but in the airspace above seven panels in the center section of row 135, I perceived only plain, still air. As I drew closer I saw that a kind of hazy film covered those panels. When I spit on them, the droplets disappeared. When I sprinkled sand on the panels, the haze dispersed. I blinked. Still clear. I wiped the sand off the panels and the alarm shut off. Back in the control tent, I found absorption levels had returned to normal.

All during that time, and since then, I felt and feel watched. Observed. Studied. Much like I felt in the Heap when vermin hid nearby. I grabbed the M16 Omar had left, checked the magazine and noted two cartridges. I chambered one and strode around the array, hoping to scare something up, but I saw nothing. You know me, I do not fear solitude, so I can't believe that loneliness has gripped my mind and twisted it in some maddened way. Yet how can I explain these feelings? And how can I rid myself of them?

The desert wind, the slosh of water spilling over the side of the bucket at the well, the sporadic hum of the 2HP motors as they crank the panels in imperceivable increments to angle towards the sun – these are all relatively new languages to me. I am not fluent. I must translate in my head: wind, water, sun, panels – they all mean survival. Mine, yours, Kyla's, the Milhians'. The sanity of the panel guardian cannot come into question – mine least of all – or we get deported back to the hopelessness of the Heap.

I must remember what brought us here and regain my focus: you and Kyla. Write me soon and tell me all about our little darling. How much has she grown, I wonder? What is she exploring and learning today? The only consolation I have for missing this part of her life is the knowledge that I got her, and you, out of the Heap and into Milh. Cover her little toes and fingers with kisses for me. I feel better now, having written this all down and out of my system. Fear works one up into a frenzy, I suppose. Maybe this is all a delayed angst resulting from what we've gone through. Yes, perhaps so. Feeling better already. I don't think I should send this. Instead, I'll go check the alarm panel for faulty wiring.

* * *

October 11: I cannot account for today's occurrences in any logical way. The solar absorption alarm sounded first on the south line, then the east. Each time I traveled to the low-absorption area, it shifted. I say "it" because I now have no doubt that some being exists here with me in the panel array field.

How do I know? I've seen nothing that I can prove. I've heard, smelled, tasted, touched – again, nothing. That's not altogether true. The problem is that any small inkling of perception those overrated five senses may possess regarding things out of the ordinary, the mind can and does explain away. For example, I hear the pitch of the tracking panel rods shift in a Doppler-esque manner when the being moves between the rods and me, but my mind will call it the wind. I see tufts of sand dancing along on the breeze stop mid-dance, as though hitting a wall, and fall to the ground. My mind calls that a "fickle breeze" instead of "a breeze running into an invisible being." And when the being absorbs some water from the urn, or from my own cup, I see that water is missing but my mind intercedes: maybe I didn't remember the water levels accurately? Or maybe the absorption level alarm reacted to a granule of sand. Yes, these common senses can so easily be invalidated, and thus discounted by the mind.

A true logician would stop there, I know, but I'm discovering that I possess valid tools of assessment other than those overrated five. I can sense the being's presence with my… tight muscles, my quickened heart and lungs, my troubled sleep. I do, Ray. I know it's here.

* * *

October 13: You've often said I make things harder than they need to be. Do you think that's what's happening here? At last, with all of our troubles and worries about escaping the Heap allayed, and my training of panel care and controls here passed with flying colors, all I must do now is watch over the panel field in a sunny paradise. Anyone with solid window washing technique and half my brains could easily manage it, and who can shoot, of course, but Omar didn't test me on that. He said that since I won the contest, that was proof enough for him. But now, yet another impediment stands between me and my satisfaction. Have I somehow manifested this ghost with my imagination, so I could continue to struggle?

* * *

October 14: I didn't dream of you or Kyla last night, or the night before. Now, if I sleep, I dream of starvation, thirst, a kind of famine. Not like the wild famine of the Heap, more as if I'm experiencing an agonizing, slow depletion of all nourishment. Including air. Then I cannot breathe, and I start to gasp. I find myself on the sandy floor of the control tent in my tousled bedding, awake and alone. But not alone, for my thoughts are no longer my own. This space is not my own. Is my life my own? Was it ever? Do we only feel control or ownership of our lives when we can deny the presence of powers or beings greater than ourselves?

All that time in the Heap, I felt tired, but never afraid. Now, I know fear. Somehow this being has infiltrated even my innermost core with it. Fear of the unknown. The unseen. I believe it exists, though I cannot define it. Cannot draw it, or study it. So how do I learn its weaknesses, to escape it, or fight it? It seems I must remove my philosopher's cap, don the cloak of humanity, and return to a primal existence. But at the root of all, what other existence, really, is there?

To survive the atrocities of the Heap, you and I did things we would not have believed ourselves capable of. To make a better life for ourselves, and then for Kyla when she came along. And now, surrounded by acres of panels generating energy for hundreds of thousands, I find that we, people, can immerse ourselves in technology to make our lives easier and distance us from the mystery and desperation of life and death, but we still must and will fight to survive. Or perish.

* * *

October 15: Planning was always your strength, not mine, but I remember you saying, "Start with what you know." That's the same with logic, but I've been so preoccupied with fear that I lost focus. What do I know? I know this being absorbs water and solar energy, and all creatures require some sort of sustenance. When sustenance disappears, they move on, right? So, I cleaned Omar's M16 – crap that it is. These guns jammed on the militia in the Americas more often than they worked. I'm wishing now more than ever that Omar hadn't found and confiscated the pistol I'd brought with me. The M16 is cleaned, in any case. I've dumped the water urn and locked the lid over the well. I shut down the panels this morning too – let the region's power rely on the batteries. No one will know. No one but me, and the being.

It's here in the tent now. Its energy vibrates sometimes. It mostly feels like frenetic pressure changes thumping in my ears. I will ignore it and keep typing. I will focus on you and Kyla. Her kinky black hair, the sweet smell of her, the feel of her soft pudgy fingers on my face, tugging on my nose. The pressure fluctuations in my ears are growing stronger. I imagine her wide, shining eyes, taking in the world around her. The air around me is so dense it won't fit in my lungs.

* * *

October 16: Remember our motto back in the Heap – if you can't avoid a death fight, make sure you win, right? I lost, Ray. The beast smothered me until I passed out. When I awoke, it smothered me again. The next time I awoke, I lay still, face up on the sandy floor of the tent. My ears pulsated. It hovered around me so close I felt it inside my lungs, like the stench of the waste trenches downwind of the Heap. It must have sensed that I was awake, for the rate of pulsation in my ears increased and the air densified. My lungs shrank. I couldn't reach the gun a metre away. It took all my strength to roll over on to my belly and hide my face in my hands.

"You win!" I cried, as darkness enveloped my consciousness. "Let me breathe."

When I woke again, my ears thumped slowly. I switched on the panels, uncovered the well and, when I had enough strength, I emptied the urn and refilled it with water. Battle lost.

* * *

October 17: Cell pirates attacked tonight, and with them, rats moving in a swarm. Nothing like the anarchic vermin back home, these responded to vocal commands. The infrared scanner picked them up as they approached the north edge of the array, so I had time to hit the button. The panel covers slid into place, locking with ten thousand clacks. But I didn't touch the pod controls. Regulations strictly reserve the guardian storm pod "for sandstorms only". I must defend against cell pirates, not hide.

I grabbed the M16 and tapped Omar's code into the ammo crate keypad, my eye tracking the invaders on the infra-red monitor all the while. The keypad screen read "invalid code". I tried again, sure I had entered the code correctly. Invalid again. Then I remembered, when I had asked Omar for the code to the crate, he gave me a look bordering on disdain and said, "Solar cell pirates are rare. We used to have a whole defensive unit out here to protect the array, but there is little need now."

"Rare?" I said. "They come. You know they do. That's why you hired me."

"You were a mistake," he said. "Pray they stay away. Women mustn't wield weapons."

He knew full well that I could shoot the head off a baby mouse at 20 yards in the dark. After all, he had hired through the Heap's rat shoot contest because he wanted the best sharp shooter to protect his panel field. I said as much to him and he just shrugged. I bet he had never suspected a woman would win the contest, that he would be trapped into a contract his faith didn't allow him to honor. Sure, his company got credits from the World Poverty Organization for hiring from the Heap, and he got a sharp shooter for next to nothing, but he was trapped into the contract, until my death, at least. So he did what most people do when confronted by contradictions between their desires and their beliefs. He set me up, and walked away.

There was no time for anger. Along with the M16, I took the tranq gun reserved for use on the precious stray camels and horses that wandered into the array. It was calibrated for short distances but better than nothing. With my infrared goggles on, I went out hunting pirates. Can you picture the headlines? "Philosopher from Midwest Heap Now Fighting Solar Cell Pirates." Yes, but headlines like that aren't so unusual these days, I suppose – it takes less logic than luck to get a job, any job.

The cell pirates entered the north quadrant and their rats scurried onto the panels, using teeth and claws on the covers. I counted eight men and twenty rats in all. They couldn't pry the covers off without damaging the cells, their booty, yet they didn't give up. Leaving the rats to work on the panels, the men headed towards the central inverters, the control tent, and me. Tripped up by my uniform, I fell to the ground and took a shot from there. The M16 failed to fire. Yanking the charging handle back, I ejected the round and let go, chambering the second cartridge. I pulled the trigger and the firearm jammed. "No wonder the Americas fell," I muttered, tossing the useless gun into the sand. I let two tranq darts fly, one after the other. Both fell short. I cursed. The pirates crouched out of range, visible only as infrared blobs underneath the central zone panels.

I checked my shoulder and saw another gang approaching behind me. I let fly another two darts and hit the lead rat and pirate. They fell limp into the sand, but it was over. I had a few more darts – nowhere near enough. The pirates grabbed and propelled me towards the tent. Several had entered before my captors and me. From the entrance, I saw one pirate collapse, hands to ears. The others dropped me and fled, their fallen leader in their arms, their rats close around them in a protective swarm. The pirates shouted a single word as they ran, a word which rang out and echoed across the panel field: "*Shabah*!"

They had a name for this being. Existence confirmed. Fear validated. Situation worse, for not only do I fear this creature, but I feel a kind of gratitude towards it. While I had failed in my duty to defend the panel field, the *shabah* had driven the pirates away. It had saved me. In so doing, it saved you and Kyla. How can I destroy one to whom I'm beholden? And if I can't destroy it, then how can I escape?

* * *

October 21: The *shabah* prowls the panel field, lying across the panels, sucking heat, sucking energy, sucking my confidence and freedom. I can sometimes make out its form now, like a pale shadow, for its mass increases as time goes on. When it enters the control tent, the main board sparks and sizzles, the hair on my arms raises, sulfur burns inside my nostrils and I taste metal. My ears no longer pulsate – they ring.

It's growing so powerful, Ray, but the monster does have a weakness. Sometimes, when it hovers too close to me, I fling a handful of sand at it. The shadow disperses for a brief moment then. I think that sand could be used as a weapon against it, if I could fling enough sand, hard enough. A handful does next to nothing, causes more problems than the small act of rebellion is worth, for soon the monster returns and flutters about, as if agitated. It will keep me awake all night, or smother me time and again until I can't see or think straight.

I stoop when I walk, as if hunching under the low sky can protect me, or hide me. The desert, once expansive and warm, now feels like a box, a suffocatingly hot box with a closed lid and lock to which I have no key. If I run away, you and Kyla will be lost. And really, where can one run to escape the invisible? Yet if I stay, I will be lost. The monster saved me from the pirates, but only to protect its own interests. I feel no benevolence from this creature. I fear it will do away with me once it gains enough mass and learns how to tap the well on its own, or sucks it dry and moves on.

* * *

October 29: I keep holding my breath, Ray. I get lost in my thoughts for several minutes or hours – I don't know for how long – but when I return to the present moment, my chest is tight, my breath caught within. I force myself to ex- and inhale.

Sometimes I think I brought this upon me. I was so proud of Kyla, of you and I, so happy we'd escaped the Heap. I remember the sandbus that day and how gleefully I sent out that invitation across the desert. Do you think happiness and freedom attract fear and domination? Do you think some universal balance will counter any enjoyment of life with equal amounts of terror?

I feel like I have lived with this *shabah* for ever now. Am I still your mate if I live so intimately with another creature? With its eyes always upon me – if it has eyes; it feels like it does – with its presence ever close. It follows my every move, my tasks, my thoughts. I try to imagine you and Kyla, and I feel only a disconnection where once I felt a golden-braided tether. As if you don't belong to me anymore. As if I've lost my belonging.

Remember when I supposed something haunted the panel field? The ghost is now me. The creature drains me of myself, creating a vessel belonging not to me but to it. I move to the far reaches of the panel field and it follows. I fill the water urn and the monster drains it as soon as I have filled it, before I even take a drink for myself. If only I could render myself invisible! Perhaps then I'd have a chance.

* * *

November 1: Remember that time when the Top of the Heap gang broke into our refuge, guns a-blazing, and fell into the pit of toxic muck we'd dug as a trap? Their screams railed through the dilapidated walls of the Heap for hours, but only vermin came to end their suffering. Last night's sandstorm provided me with a similar opportunity. When the storm warning sounded, I was in the tent with the *shabah* hovering, agitated. Its sulfur odour clung to me. My ears pulsed without respite. I hit the button, the covers slid across the cells outside and locked into position. I lowered the control board and main computer into its underground safe crate and secured the hatch over the top, per protocol. I leapt out of the tent and zipped up the door flap, capturing the *shabah* inside. Then I pulled up the tent anchors around its base. When the storm hit full force, the tent would be swept away with the monster inside, and carry it far off, into the sea. That was plan B.

Plan A involved more risk, but promised a bigger prize. I pulled the tent zipper open one inch, a gap big enough for the *shabah* to squeeze itself through. It would need time to funnel through the tiny gap, time I needed to get to the guardian storm pod. Driven by a delirious idea of hope, I plunged into the raging wind towards the edge of the west quadrant. Sand stung my face, legs and hands though the storm had a kilometer to travel before reaching the panel field. I pushed on, eyes tearing and feet tripped up by the uniform dress whipping between my legs. My mind gnawed on formulas, calculating the amount of time the *shabah* would need to get through the gap in the control tent's zipper door, measuring each grueling step against estimations of the monster's size and current viscosity, and the strength of the wind. The wind that would whip the empty tent away and attack the exposed and vulnerable *shabab*. How much sand-blasting could the monster endure before it died? Would the storm be enough?

Finally I glimpsed the guardian storm pod, a beige clamshell at the end of the panel row, 1.5 meters high and about two meters wide. My fingers brushed over the "For Sandstorms Only" sign and fumbled with the pod's hatch controls. I imagined I smelled sulfur and held my breath. The hatch burst open. I jumped in, yanked down the hatch, and sealed it shut. Then I waited.

Within seconds, the storm arrived. Or was it the *shabab*? The pod shook and trembled as though an army beat upon it. I thought I heard a desperate keening and told myself it was the wild wind howling as it whipped through the panel array, sand filling every gap, then sweeping away. At some point I came to believe the pod was impenetrable even to a *shabab*. I let myself believe that my plan was more than future music. A great sense of relief washed over me. I felt alone again. Alone! And so, at last, I slept.

I awoke with images of you and Kyla in my head. I could picture your faces, smell your skin, hear your laughter, and her little sounds. It felt like a reunion, not like the desperate fantasy I'd tried and failed to concoct these past weeks. The sensations lingered in my mind as I explored the pod, careful not to disrupt my newly recovered connection to you and Kyla, and to me. Extending down into the desert floor some 3–4 metres, the pod anchors into rock and contains supplies and equipment a panel guardian might need during a protracted storm. I have water, oxygen, and computer link and could live here comfortably for a week, perhaps more. I found uniform trousers, like the ones Omar wore, and at last traded in the cumbersome uniform dress. And I found my pistol – the one Omar had confiscated – and my ammo, hidden in a case of food packs. I cleaned and loaded the pistol, powered up the computer and opened my private file. I thought that finishing this letter to you would help me formulate a Plan C.

Hours ago, the storm traveled on. My pistol in hand, wearing clothing that enables me to move about freely, I feel more like myself. Perhaps I am already free, but what if I climb out of the pod and into a very angry *shabab*? I fear the monster's retailation. I fear living again under its power. All that time in the Heap, Ray, I was tired, but not afraid. Why? Simply because I could see my enemies? And smell and hear them? Or because I knew exactly how to kill them?

I could rig this pod so it looked like an accident. I know what you're thinking – me too – Kyla with no mother, you with no me. But I have to consider every angle. My death in the line of duty would bring you and Kyla a comfortable living. Then again, if they discovered that I'd committed suicide, you both would be punished, worse than life in the Heap. I can't risk that. It would be a shameful sacrifice anyway.

I must leave this sanctuary and face whatever lies outside. If the *shabab* lives, well, I'll think of something. And I'll chant our Heap death fight motto like a mantra to keep the fear at bay. I will send this, all of this, to you now. Perhaps I should have done so earlier, but I didn't want to worry you. Don't worry now. I didn't survive the hell of the Heap to die in paradise. Kiss tiny Kyla toes and fingers for me. Kisses to you too – Macey *xox*

Pickman's Model

H.P. Lovecraft

YOU NEEDN'T THINK I'm crazy, Eliot – plenty of others have queerer prejudices than this. Why don't you laugh at Oliver's grandfather, who won't ride in a motor? If I don't like that damned subway, it's my own business; and we got here more quickly anyhow in the taxi. We'd have had to walk up the hill from Park Street if we'd taken the car.

I know I'm more nervous than I was when you saw me last year, but you don't need to hold a clinic over it. There's plenty of reason, God knows, and I fancy I'm lucky to be sane at all. Why the third degree? You didn't use to be so inquisitive.

Well, if you must hear it, I don't know why you shouldn't. Maybe you ought to, anyhow, for you kept writing me like a grieved parent when you heard I'd begun to cut the Art Club and keep away from Pickman. Now that he's disappeared I go around to the club once in a while, but my nerves aren't what they were.

No, I don't know what's become of Pickman, and I don't like to guess. You might have surmised I had some inside information when I dropped him – and that's why I don't want to think where he's gone. Let the police find what they can – it won't be much, judging from the fact that they don't know yet of the old North End place he hired under the name of Peters. I'm not sure that I could find it again myself – not that I'd ever try, even in broad daylight! Yes, I do know, or am afraid I know, why he maintained it. I'm coming to that. And I think you'll understand before I'm through why I don't tell the police. They would ask me to guide them, but I couldn't go back there even if I knew the way. There was something there – and now I can't use the subway or (and you may as well have your laugh at this, too) go down into cellars any more.

I should think you'd have known I didn't drop Pickman for the same silly reasons that fussy old women like Dr. Reid or Joe Minot or Bosworth did. Morbid art doesn't shock me, and when a man has the genius Pickman had I feel it an honour to know him, no matter what direction his work takes. Boston never had a greater painter than Richard Upton Pickman. I said it at first and I say it still, and I never swerved an inch, either, when he shewed that "Ghoul Feeding". That, you remember, was when Minot cut him.

You know, it takes profound art and profound insight into Nature to turn out stuff like Pickman's. Any magazine-cover hack can splash paint around wildly and call it a nightmare or a Witches' Sabbath or a portrait of the devil, but only a great painter can make such a thing really scare or ring true. That's because only a real artist knows the actual anatomy of the terrible or the physiology of fear – the exact sort of lines and proportions that connect up with latent instincts or hereditary memories of fright, and the proper colour contrasts and lighting effects to stir the dormant sense of strangeness. I don't have to tell you why a Fuseli really brings a shiver while a cheap ghost-story frontispiece merely makes us laugh. There's something those fellows catch – beyond life – that they're able to make us catch for a second. Doré had it. Sime has it. Angarola of Chicago has it. And Pickman had it as no man ever had it before or – I hope to heaven – ever will again.

Don't ask me what it is they see. You know, in ordinary art, there's all the difference in the world between the vital, breathing things drawn from Nature or models and the artificial truck that commercial small fry reel off in a bare studio by rule. Well, I should say that the really weird artist has a kind of vision which makes models, or summons up what amounts to actual scenes from the spectral world he lives in. Anyhow, he manages to turn out results that differ from the pretender's mince-pie dreams in just about the same way that the life painter's results differ from the concoctions of a correspondence-school cartoonist. If I had ever seen what Pickman saw – but no! Here, let's have a drink before we get any deeper. Gad, I wouldn't be alive if I'd ever seen what that man – if he was a man – saw!

You recall that Pickman's forte was faces. I don't believe anybody since Goya could put so much of sheer hell into a set of features or a twist of expression. And before Goya you have to go back to the mediaeval chaps who did the gargoyles and chimaeras on Notre Dame and Mont Saint-Michel. They believed all sorts of things – and maybe they saw all sorts of things, too, for the Middle Ages had some curious phases. I remember your asking Pickman yourself once, the year before you went away, wherever in thunder he got such ideas and visions. Wasn't that a nasty laugh he gave you? It was partly because of that laugh that Reid dropped him. Reid, you know, had just taken up comparative pathology, and was full of pompous "inside stuff" about the biological or evolutionary significance of this or that mental or physical symptom. He said Pickman repelled him more and more every day, and almost frightened him toward the last – that the fellow's features and expression were slowly developing in a way he didn't like; in a way that wasn't human. He had a lot of talk about diet, and said Pickman must be abnormal and eccentric to the last degree. I suppose you told Reid, if you and he had any correspondence over it, that he'd let Pickman's paintings get on his nerves or harrow up his imagination. I know I told him that myself – then.

But keep in mind that I didn't drop Pickman for anything like this. On the contrary, my admiration for him kept growing; for that "Ghoul Feeding" was a tremendous achievement. As you know, the club wouldn't exhibit it, and the Museum of Fine Arts wouldn't accept it as a gift; and I can add that nobody would buy it, so Pickman had it right in his house till he went. Now his father has it in Salem – you know Pickman comes of old Salem stock, and had a witch ancestor hanged in 1692.

I got into the habit of calling on Pickman quite often, especially after I began making notes for a monograph on weird art. Probably it was his work which put the idea into my head, and anyhow, I found him a mine of data and suggestions when I came to develop it. He shewed me all the paintings and drawings he had about; including some pen-and-ink sketches that would, I verily believe, have got him kicked out of the club if many of the members had seen them. Before long I was pretty nearly a devotee, and would listen for hours like a schoolboy to art theories and philosophic speculations wild enough to qualify him for the Danvers asylum. My hero-worship, coupled with the fact that people generally were commencing to have less and less to do with him, made him get very confidential with me; and one evening he hinted that if I were fairly close-mouthed and none too squeamish, he might shew me something rather unusual – something a bit stronger than anything he had in the house.

"You know," he said, "there are things that won't do for Newbury Street – things that are out of place here, and that can't be conceived here, anyhow. It's my business to catch the overtones of the soul, and you won't find those in a parvenu set of artificial streets on made land. Back Bay isn't Boston – it isn't anything yet, because it's had no time to pick up memories and attract local spirits. If there are any ghosts here, they're the tame ghosts of a salt marsh and a shallow cove; and I want human ghosts – the ghosts of beings highly organised enough to have looked on hell and known the meaning of what they saw.

"The place for an artist to live is the North End. If any aesthete were sincere, he'd put up with the slums for the sake of the massed traditions. God, man! Don't you realise that places like that weren't merely *made*, but actually *grew*? Generation after generation lived and felt and died there, and in days when people weren't afraid to live and feel and die. Don't you know there was a mill on Copp's Hill in 1632, and that half the present streets were laid out by 1650? I can shew you houses that have stood two centuries and a half and more; houses that have witnessed what would make a modern house crumble into powder. What do moderns know of life and the forces behind it? You call the Salem witchcraft a delusion, but I'll wage my four-times-great-grandmother could have told you things. They hanged her on Gallows Hill, with Cotton Mather looking sanctimoniously on. Mather, damn him, was afraid somebody might succeed in kicking free of this accursed cage of monotony – I wish someone had laid a spell on him or sucked his blood in the night!

"I can shew you a house he lived in, and I can shew you another one he was afraid to enter in spite of all his fine bold talk. He knew things he didn't dare put into that stupid *Magnalia* or that puerile *Wonders of the Invisible World*. Look here, do you know the whole North End once had a set of tunnels that kept certain people in touch with each other's houses, and the burying-ground, and the sea? Let them prosecute and persecute above ground – things went on every day that they couldn't reach, and voices laughed at night that they couldn't place!

"Why, man, out of ten surviving houses built before 1700 and not moved since I'll wager that in eight I can shew you something queer in the cellar. There's hardly a month that you don't read of workmen finding bricked-up arches and wells leading nowhere in this or that old place as it comes down – you could see one near Henchman Street from the elevated last year. There were witches and what their spells summoned; pirates and what they brought in from the sea; smugglers; privateers – and I tell you, people knew how to live, and how to enlarge the bounds of life, in the old times! This wasn't the only world a bold and wise man could know – faugh! And to think of today in contrast, with such pale-pink brains that even a club of supposed artists gets shudders and convulsions if a picture goes beyond the feelings of a Beacon Street tea-table!

"The only saving grace of the present is that it's too damned stupid to question the past very closely. What do maps and records and guide-books really tell of the North End? Bah! At a guess I'll guarantee to lead you to thirty or forty alleys and networks of alleys north of Prince Street that aren't suspected by ten living beings outside of the foreigners that swarm them. And what do those Dagoes know of their meaning? No, Thurber, these ancient places are dreaming gorgeously and overflowing with wonder and terror and escapes from the commonplace, and yet there's not a living soul to understand or profit by them. Or rather, there's only one living soul – for I haven't been digging around in the past for nothing!

"See here, you're interested in this sort of thing. What if I told you that I've got another studio up there, where I can catch the night-spirit of antique horror and paint things that I couldn't even think of in Newbury Street? Naturally I don't tell those cursed old maids at the club – with Reid, damn him, whispering even as it is that I'm a sort of monster bound down the toboggan of reverse evolution. Yes, Thurber, I decided long ago that one must paint terror as well as beauty from life, so I did some exploring in places where I had reason to know terror lives.

"I've got a place that I don't believe three living Nordic men besides myself have ever seen. It isn't so very far from the elevated as distance goes, but it's centuries away as the soul goes.

I took it because of the queer old brick well in the cellar – one of the sort I told you about. The shack's almost tumbling down, so that nobody else would live there, and I'd hate to tell you how little I pay for it. The windows are boarded up, but I like that all the better, since I don't want daylight for what I do. I paint in the cellar, where the inspiration is thickest, but I've other rooms furnished on the ground floor. A Sicilian owns it, and I've hired it under the name of Peters.

"Now if you're game, I'll take you there tonight. I think you'd enjoy the pictures, for as I said, I've let myself go a bit there. It's no vast tour – I sometimes do it on foot, for I don't want to attract attention with a taxi in such a place. We can take the shuttle at the South Station for Battery Street, and after that the walk isn't much."

Well, Eliot, there wasn't much for me to do after that harangue but to keep myself from running instead of walking for the first vacant cab we could sight. We changed to the elevated at the South Station, and at about twelve o'clock had climbed down the steps at Battery Street and struck along the old waterfront past Constitution Wharf. I didn't keep track of the cross streets, and can't tell you yet which it was we turned up, but I know it wasn't Greenough Lane.

When we did turn, it was to climb through the deserted length of the oldest and dirtiest alley I ever saw in my life, with crumbling-looking gables, broken small-paned windows, and archaic chimneys that stood out half-disintegrated against the moonlit sky. I don't believe there were three houses in sight that hadn't been standing in Cotton Mather's time – certainly I glimpsed at least two with an overhang, and once I thought I saw a peaked roof-line of the almost forgotten pre-gambrel type, though antiquarians tell us there are none left in Boston.

From that alley, which had a dim light, we turned to the left into an equally silent and still narrower alley with no light at all; and in a minute made what I think was an obtuse-angled bend toward the right in the dark. Not long after this Pickman produced a flashlight and revealed an antediluvian ten-panelled door that looked damnably worm-eaten. Unlocking it, he ushered me into a barren hallway with what was once splendid dark-oak panelling – simple, of course, but thrillingly suggestive of the times of Andros and Phipps and the Witchcraft. Then he took me through a door on the left, lighted an oil lamp, and told me to make myself at home.

Now, Eliot, I'm what the man in the street would call fairly "hard-boiled", but I'll confess that what I saw on the walls of that room gave me a bad turn. They were his pictures, you know – the ones he couldn't paint or even shew in Newbury Street – and he was right when he said he had "let himself go". Here – have another drink – I need one anyhow!

There's no use in my trying to tell you what they were like, because the awful, the blasphemous horror, and the unbelievable loathsomeness and moral foetor came from simple touches quite beyond the power of words to classify. There was none of the exotic technique you see in Sidney Sime, none of the trans-Saturnian landscapes and lunar fungi that Clark Ashton Smith uses to freeze the blood. The backgrounds were mostly old churchyards, deep woods, cliffs by the sea, brick tunnels, ancient panelled rooms, or simple vaults of masonry. Copp's Hill Burying Ground, which could not be many blocks away from this very house, was a favourite scene.

The madness and monstrosity lay in the figures in the foreground – for Pickman's morbid art was preëminently one of daemoniac portraiture. These figures were seldom completely human, but often approached humanity in varying degree. Most of the bodies, while roughly bipedal, had a forward slumping, and a vaguely canine cast. The texture of the majority was a kind of unpleasant rubberiness. Ugh! I can see them now! Their occupations – well, don't ask me to be too precise. They were usually feeding – I won't say on what. They were sometimes shewn in groups in cemeteries or underground passages, and often appeared to be in battle over their prey – or rather, their treasure-trove. And what damnable expressiveness Pickman sometimes gave the sightless faces of this charnel booty! Occasionally the things were shewn leaping through open windows at night, or squatting on the chests of sleepers, worrying at their throats. One canvas shewed a ring of them baying about a hanged witch on Gallows Hill, whose dead face held a close kinship to theirs.

But don't get the idea that it was all this hideous business of theme and setting which struck me faint. I'm not a three-year-old kid, and I'd seen much like this before. It was the faces, Eliot, those accursed faces, that leered and slavered out of the canvas with the very breath of life! By God, man, I verily believe they were alive! That nauseous wizard had waked the fires of hell in pigment, and his brush had been a nightmare-spawning wand. Give me that decanter, Eliot!

There was one thing called "The Lesson" – heaven pity me, that I ever saw it! Listen – can you fancy a squatting circle of nameless dog-like things in a churchyard teaching a small child how to feed like themselves? The price of a changeling, I suppose – you know the old myth about how the weird people leave their spawn in cradles in exchange for the human babes they steal. Pickman was shewing what happens to those stolen babes – how they grow up – and then I began to see a hideous relationship in the faces of the human and non-human figures. He was, in all his gradations of morbidity between the frankly non-human and the degradedly human, establishing a sardonic linkage and evolution. The dog-things were developed from mortals!

And no sooner had I wondered what he made of their own young as left with mankind in the form of changelings, than my eye caught a picture embodying that very thought. It was that of an ancient Puritan interior – a heavily beamed room with lattice windows, a settle, and clumsy seventeenth-century furniture, with the family sitting about while the father read from the Scriptures. Every face but one shewed nobility and reverence, but that one reflected the mockery of the pit. It was that of a young man in years, and no doubt belonged to a supposed son of that pious father, but in essence it was the kin of the unclean things. It was their changeling – and in a spirit of supreme irony Pickman had given the features a very perceptible resemblance to his own.

By this time Pickman had lighted a lamp in an adjoining room and was politely holding open the door for me; asking me if I would care to see his "modern studies". I hadn't been able to give him much of my opinions – I was too speechless with fright and loathing – but I think he fully understood and felt highly complimented. And now I want to assure you again, Eliot, that I'm no mollycoddle to scream at anything which shews a bit of departure from the usual. I'm middle-aged and decently sophisticated, and I guess you saw enough of me in France to know I'm not easily knocked out. Remember, too, that I'd just about recovered my wind and gotten used to those frightful pictures which turned colonial New England into a kind of annex of hell. Well, in spite of all this, that next room forced a real scream out of me, and I had to clutch at the doorway to keep from keeling over. The other chamber had shewn a pack of ghouls and witches overrunning the world of our forefathers, but this one brought the horror right into our own daily life!

Gad, how that man could paint! There was a study called "Subway Accident", in which a flock of the vile things were clambering up from some unknown catacomb through a crack in the floor of the Boylston Street subway and attacking a crowd of people on the platform. Another shewed a dance on Copp's Hill among the tombs with the background of today. Then there were any number of cellar views, with monsters creeping in through holes and rifts in the masonry and grinning as they squatted behind barrels or furnaces and waited for their first victim to descend the stairs.

One disgusting canvas seemed to depict a vast cross-section of Beacon Hill, with ant-like armies of the mephitic monsters squeezing themselves through burrows that honeycombed the ground. Dances in the modern cemeteries were freely pictured, and another conception somehow shocked me more than all the rest – a scene in an unknown vault, where scores of the beasts crowded about one who held a well-known Boston guide-book and was evidently reading aloud. All were pointing to a certain passage, and every face seemed so distorted with epileptic and reverberant laughter that I almost thought I heard the fiendish echoes. The title of the picture was, "Holmes, Lowell, and Longfellow Lie Buried in Mount Auburn".

As I gradually steadied myself and got readjusted to this second room of deviltry and morbidity, I began to analyse some of the points in my sickening loathing. In the first place, I said to myself, these things repelled because of the utter inhumanity and callous cruelty they shewed in Pickman. The fellow must be a relentless enemy of all mankind to take such glee in the torture of brain and flesh and the degradation of the mortal tenement. In the second place, they terrified because of their very greatness. Their art was the art that convinced – when we saw the pictures we saw the daemons themselves and were afraid of them. And the queer part was, that Pickman got none of his power from the use of selectiveness or bizarrerie. Nothing was blurred, distorted, or conventionalised; outlines were sharp and life-like, and details were almost painfully defined. And the faces!

It was not any mere artist's interpretation that we saw; it was pandemonium itself, crystal clear in stark objectivity. That was it, by heaven! The man was not a fantaisiste or romanticist at all – he did not even try to give us the churning, prismatic ephemera of dreams, but coldly and sardonically reflected some stable, mechanistic, and well-established horror-world which he saw fully, brilliantly, squarely, and unfalteringly. God knows what that world can have been, or where he ever glimpsed the blasphemous shapes that loped and trotted and crawled through it; but whatever the baffling source of his images, one thing was plain. Pickman was in every sense – in conception and in execution – a thorough, painstaking, and almost scientific realist.

My host was now leading the way down cellar to his actual studio, and I braced myself for some hellish effects among the unfinished canvases. As we reached the bottom of the damp stairs he turned his flashlight to a corner of the large open space at hand, revealing the circular brick curb of what was evidently a great well in the earthen floor. We walked nearer, and I saw that it must be five feet across, with walls a good foot thick and some six inches above the ground level – solid work of the seventeenth century, or I was much mistaken. That, Pickman said, was the kind of thing he had been talking about – an aperture of the network of tunnels that used to undermine the hill. I noticed idly that it did not seem to be bricked up, and that a heavy disc of wood formed the apparent cover. Thinking of the things this well must have been connected with if Pickman's wild hints had not been mere rhetoric, I shivered slightly; then turned to follow him up a step and through a narrow door into a room of fair size, provided with a wooden floor and furnished as a studio. An acetylene gas outfit gave the light necessary for work.

The unfinished pictures on easels or propped against the walls were as ghastly as the finished ones upstairs, and shewed the painstaking methods of the artist. Scenes were blocked out with extreme care, and pencilled guide lines told of the minute exactitude which Pickman used in getting the right perspective and proportions. The man was great – I say it even now, knowing as much as I do. A large camera on a table excited my notice, and Pickman told me that he used it in taking scenes for backgrounds, so that he might paint them from photographs in the studio instead of carting his outfit around the town for this or that view. He thought a photograph quite as good as an actual scene or model for sustained work, and declared he employed them regularly.

There was something very disturbing about the nauseous sketches and half-finished monstrosities that leered around from every side of the room, and when Pickman suddenly unveiled a huge canvas on the side away from the light I could not for my life keep back a loud scream – the second I had emitted that night. It echoed and echoed through the dim vaultings of that ancient and nitrous cellar, and I had to choke back a flood of reaction that threatened to burst out as hysterical laughter. Merciful Creator! Eliot, but I don't know how much was real and how much was feverish fancy. It doesn't seem to me that earth can hold a dream like that!

It was a colossal and nameless blasphemy with glaring red eyes, and it held in bony claws a thing that had been a man, gnawing at the head as a child nibbles at a stick of candy. Its position was a kind of crouch, and as one looked one felt that at any moment it might drop its present prey and seek a juicier morsel. But damn it all, it wasn't even the fiendish subject that made it such an immortal fountain-head of all panic – not that, nor the dog face with its pointed ears, bloodshot eyes, flat nose, and drooling lips. It wasn't the scaly claws nor the mould-caked body nor the half-hooved feet – none of these, though any one of them might well have driven an excitable man to madness.

It was the technique, Eliot – the cursed, the impious, the unnatural technique! As I am a living being, I never elsewhere saw the actual breath of life so fused into a canvas. The monster was there – it glared and gnawed and gnawed and glared – and I knew that only a suspension of Nature's laws could ever let a man paint a thing like that without a model – without some glimpse of the nether world which no mortal unsold to the Fiend has ever had.

Pinned with a thumb-tack to a vacant part of the canvas was a piece of paper now badly curled up – probably, I thought, a photograph from which Pickman meant to paint a background as hideous as the nightmare it was to enhance. I reached out to uncurl and look at it, when suddenly I saw Pickman start as if shot. He had been listening with peculiar intensity ever since my shocked scream had waked unaccustomed echoes in the dark cellar, and now he seemed struck with a fright which, though not comparable to my own, had in it more of the physical than of the spiritual. He drew a revolver and motioned me to silence, then stepped out into the main cellar and closed the door behind him.

I think I was paralysed for an instant. Imitating Pickman's listening, I fancied I heard a faint scurrying sound somewhere, and a series of squeals or bleats in a direction I couldn't determine. I thought of huge rats and shuddered. Then there came a subdued sort of clatter which somehow set me all in gooseflesh – a furtive, groping kind of clatter, though I can't attempt to convey what I mean in words. It was like heavy wood falling on stone or brick – wood on brick – what did that make me think of?

It came again, and louder. There was a vibration as if the wood had fallen farther than it had fallen before. After that followed a sharp grating noise, a shouted gibberish from Pickman, and the deafening discharge of all six chambers of a revolver, fired spectacularly as a lion-tamer might fire in the air for effect. A muffled squeal or squawk, and a thud. Then more wood and brick grating, a pause, and the opening of the door – at which I'll confess I started violently. Pickman reappeared with his smoking weapon, cursing the bloated rats that infested the ancient well.

"The deuce knows what they eat, Thurber," he grinned, "for those archaic tunnels touched graveyard and witch-den and sea-coast. But whatever it is, they must have run short, for they were devilish anxious to get out. Your yelling stirred them up, I fancy. Better be cautious in these old places – our rodent friends are the one drawback, though I sometimes think they're a positive asset by way of atmosphere and colour."

Well, Eliot, that was the end of the night's adventure. Pickman had promised to shew me the place, and heaven knows he had done it. He led me out of that tangle of alleys in another direction, it seems, for when we sighted a lamp post we were in a half-familiar street with monotonous rows of mingled tenement blocks and old houses. Charter Street, it turned out to be, but I was too flustered to notice just where we hit it. We were too late for the elevated, and walked back downtown through Hanover Street. I remember that walk. We switched from Tremont up Beacon, and Pickman left me at the corner of Joy, where I turned off. I never spoke to him again.

Why did I drop him? Don't be impatient. Wait till I ring for coffee. We've had enough of the other stuff, but I for one need something. No – it wasn't the paintings I saw in that place; though I'll swear they were enough to get him ostracised in nine-tenths of the homes and clubs of Boston, and I guess you won't wonder now why I have to steer clear of subways and cellars. It was – something I found in my coat the next morning. You know, the curled-up paper tacked to that frightful canvas in the cellar; the thing I thought was a photograph of some scene he meant to use as a background for that monster. That last scare had come while I was reaching to uncurl it, and it seems I had vacantly crumpled it into my pocket. But here's the coffee – take it black, Eliot, if you're wise.

Yes, that paper was the reason I dropped Pickman; Richard Upton Pickman, the greatest artist I have ever known – and the foulest being that ever leaped the bounds of life into the pits of myth and madness. Eliot – old Reid was right. He wasn't strictly human. Either he was born in strange shadow, or he'd found a way to unlock the forbidden gate. It's all the same now, for he's gone – back into the fabulous darkness he loved to haunt. Here, let's have the chandelier going.

Don't ask me to explain or even conjecture about what I burned. Don't ask me, either, what lay behind that mole-like scrambling Pickman was so keen to pass off as rats. There are secrets, you know, which might have come down from old Salem times, and Cotton Mather tells even stranger things. You know how damned life-like Pickman's paintings were – how we all wondered where he got those faces.

Well – that paper wasn't a photograph of any background, after all. What it shewed was simply the monstrous being he was painting on that awful canvas. It was the model he was using – and its background was merely the wall of the cellar studio in minute detail. But by God, Eliot, it was a photograph from life.

The Dream-Quest of Unknown Kadath

H.P. Lovecraft

THREE TIMES RANDOLPH CARTER dreamed of the marvelous city, and three times was he snatched away while still he paused on the high terrace above it. All golden and lovely it blazed in the sunset, with walls, temples, colonnades and arched bridges of veined marble, silver-basined fountains of prismatic spray in broad squares and perfumed gardens, and wide streets marching between delicate trees and blossom-laden urns and ivory statues in gleaming rows; while on steep northward slopes climbed tiers of red roofs and old peaked gables harbouring little lanes of grassy cobbles. It was a fever of the gods, a fanfare of supernal trumpets and a clash of immortal cymbals. Mystery hung about it as clouds about a fabulous unvisited mountain; and as Carter stood breathless and expectant on that balustraded parapet there swept up to him the poignancy and suspense of almost-vanished memory, the pain of lost things and the maddening need to place again what once had been an awesome and momentous place.

He knew that for him its meaning must once have been supreme; though in what cycle or incarnation he had known it, or whether in dream or in waking, he could not tell. Vaguely it called up glimpses of a far forgotten first youth, when wonder and pleasure lay in all the mystery of days, and dawn and dusk alike strode forth prophetic to the eager sound of lutes and song, unclosing fiery gates toward further and surprising marvels. But each night as he stood on that high marble terrace with the curious urns and carven rail and looked off over that hushed sunset city of beauty and unearthly immanence he felt the bondage of dream's tyrannous gods; for in no wise could he leave that lofty spot, or descend the wide marmoreal flights flung endlessly down to where those streets of elder witchery lay outspread and beckoning.

When for the third time he awakened with those flights still undescended and those hushed sunset streets still untraversed, he prayed long and earnestly to the hidden gods of dream that brood capricious above the clouds on unknown Kadath, in the cold waste where no man treads. But the gods made no answer and shewed no relenting, nor did they give any favouring sign when he prayed to them in dream, and invoked them sacrificially through the bearded priests of Nasht and Kaman-Thah, whose cavern-temple with its pillar of flame lies not far from the gates of the waking world. It seemed, however, that his prayers must have been adversely heard, for after even the first of them he ceased wholly to behold the marvellous city; as if his three glimpses from afar had been mere accidents or oversights, and against some hidden plan or wish of the gods.

At length, sick with longing for those glittering sunset streets and cryptical hill lanes among ancient tiled roofs, nor able sleeping or waking to drive them from his mind, Carter resolved to go with bold entreaty whither no man had gone before, and dare the icy deserts through the dark to where unknown Kadath, veiled in cloud and crowned with unimagined stars, holds secret and nocturnal the onyx castle of the Great Ones.

In light slumber he descended the seventy steps to the cavern of flame and talked of this design to the bearded priests Nasht and Kaman-Thah. And the priests shook their pshent-bearing heads and vowed it would be the death of his soul. They pointed out that the Great Ones had shown already their wish, and that it is not agreeable to them to be harassed by insistent pleas. They reminded him, too, that not only had no man ever been to Kadath, but no man had ever suspected in what part of space it may lie; whether it be in the dreamlands around our own world, or in those surrounding some unguessed companion of Fomalhaut or Aldebaran. If in our dreamland, it might conceivably be reached, but only three human souls since time began had ever crossed and recrossed the black impious gulfs to other dreamlands, and of that three, two had come back quite mad. There were, in such voyages, incalculable local dangers; as well as that shocking final peril which gibbers unmentionably outside the ordered universe, where no dreams reach; that last amorphous blight of nethermost confusion which blasphemes and bubbles at the centre of all infinity – the boundless daemon sultan Azathoth, whose name no lips dare speak aloud, and who gnaws hungrily in inconceivable, unlighted chambers beyond time amidst the muffled, maddening beating of vile drums and the thin, monotonous whine of accursed flutes; to which detestable pounding and piping dance slowly, awkwardly, and absurdly the gigantic Ultimate gods, the blind, voiceless, tenebrous, mindless Other Gods whose soul and messenger is the crawling chaos Nyarlathotep.

Of these things was Carter warned by the priests Nasht and Kaman-Thah in the cavern of flame, but still he resolved to find the gods on unknown Kadath in the cold waste, wherever that might be, and to win from them the sight and remembrance and shelter of the marvellous sunset city. He knew that his journey would be strange and long, and that the Great Ones would be against it; but being old in the land of dream he counted on many useful memories and devices to aid him. So asking a formal blessing of the priests and thinking shrewdly on his course, he boldly descended the seven hundred steps to the Gate of Deeper Slumber and set out through the Enchanted Wood.

In the tunnels of that twisted wood, whose low prodigious oaks twine groping boughs and shine dim with the phosphorescence of strange fungi, dwell the furtive and secretive Zoogs; who know many obscure secrets of the dream world and a few of the waking world, since the wood at two places touches the lands of men, though it would be disastrous to say where. Certain unexplained rumours, events, and vanishments occur among men where the Zoogs have access, and it is well that they cannot travel far outside the world of dream. But over the nearer parts of the dream world they pass freely, flitting small and brown and unseen and bearing back piquant tales to beguile the hours around their hearths in the forest they love. Most of them live in burrows, but some inhabit the trunks of the great trees; and although they live mostly on fungi it is muttered that they have also a slight taste for meat, either physical or spiritual, for certainly many dreamers have entered that wood who have not come out. Carter, however, had no fear; for he was an old dreamer and had learnt their fluttering language and made many a treaty with them; having found through their help the splendid city of Celephaïs in Ooth-Nargai beyond the Tanarian Hills, where reigns half the year the great King Kuranes, a man he had known by another name in life. Kuranes was the one soul who had been to the star-gulfs and returned free from madness.

Threading now the low phosphorescent aisles between those gigantic trunks, Carter made fluttering sounds in the manner of the Zoogs, and listened now and then for responses. He remembered one particular village of the creatures was in the centre of the wood, where a circle of great mossy stones in what was once a clearing tells of older and more terrible dwellers long forgotten, and toward this spot he hastened. He traced his way by the grotesque fungi, which always seem better nourished as one approaches the dread circle where elder beings danced and sacrificed. Finally the great light of those thicker fungi revealed a sinister green and grey vastness pushing up through the roof of the forest and out of sight. This was the nearest of the great ring of stones, and Carter knew he was close to the Zoog village. Renewing his fluttering sound, he waited patiently; and was at last rewarded by an impression of many eyes watching him. It was the Zoogs, for one sees their weird eyes long before one can discern their small, slippery brown outlines.

Out they swarmed, from hidden burrow and honeycombed tree, till the whole dim-litten region was alive with them. Some of the wilder ones brushed Carter unpleasantly, and one even nipped loathsomely at his ear; but these lawless spirits were soon restrained by their elders. The Council of Sages, recognizing the visitor, offered a gourd of fermented sap from a haunted tree unlike the others, which had grown from a seed dropt down by someone on the moon; and as Carter drank it ceremoniously a very strange colloquy began. The Zoogs did not, unfortunately, know where the peak of Kadath lies, nor could they even say whether the cold waste is in our dream world or in another. Rumours of the Great Ones came equally from all points; and one might only say that they were likelier to be seen on high mountain peaks than in valleys, since on such peaks they dance reminiscently when the moon is above and the clouds beneath.

Then one very ancient Zoog recalled a thing unheard-of by the others; and said that in Ulthar, beyond the River Skai, there still lingered the last copy of those inconceivably old Pnakotic Manuscripts made by waking men in forgotten boreal kingdoms and borne into the land of dreams when the hairy cannibal Gnophkehs overcame many-templed Olathoë and slew all the heroes of the land of Lomar. Those manuscripts he said, told much of the gods, and besides, in Ulthar there were men who had seen the signs of the gods, and even one old priest who had scaled a great mountain to behold them dancing by moonlight. He had failed, though his companion had succeeded and perished namelessly.

So Randolph Carter thanked the Zoogs, who fluttered amicably and gave him another gourd of moon-tree wine to take with him, and set out through the phosphorescent wood for the other side, where the rushing Skai flows down from the slopes of Lerion, and Hatheg and Nir and Ulthar dot the plain. Behind him, furtive and unseen, crept several of the curious Zoogs; for they wished to learn what might befall him, and bear back the legend to their people. The vast oaks grew thicker as he pushed on beyond the village, and he looked sharply for a certain spot where they would thin somewhat, standing quite dead or dying among the unnaturally dense fungi and the rotting mould and mushy logs of their fallen brothers. There he would turn sharply aside, for at that spot a mighty slab of stone rests on the forest floor; and those who have dared approach it say that it bears an iron ring three feet wide. Remembering the archaic circle of great mossy rocks, and what it was possibly set up for, the Zoogs do not pause near that expansive slab with its huge ring; for they realise that all which is forgotten need not necessarily be dead, and they would not like to see the slab rise slowly and deliberately.

Carter detoured at the proper place, and heard behind him the frightened fluttering of some of the more timid Zoogs. He had known they would follow him, so he was not disturbed; for one grows accustomed to the anomalies of these prying creatures. It was twilight when he came to the edge of the wood, and the strengthening glow told him it was the twilight of morning. Over fertile plains rolling down to the Skai he saw the smoke of cottage chimneys, and on every hand were the hedges and ploughed fields and thatched roofs of a peaceful land. Once he stopped at a farmhouse well for a cup of water, and all the dogs barked affrightedly at the inconspicuous Zoogs that crept through the grass behind. At another house, where people were stirring, he asked questions about the gods, and whether they danced often upon Lerion; but the farmer and his wife would only make the Elder Sign and tell him the way to Nir and Ulthar.

At noon he walked through the one broad high street of Nir, which he had once visited and which marked his farthest former travels in this direction; and soon afterward he came to the great stone bridge across the Skai, into whose central piece the masons had sealed a living human sacrifice when they built it thirteen-hundred years before. Once on the other side, the frequent presence of cats (who all arched their backs at the trailing Zoogs) revealed the near neighborhood of Ulthar; for in Ulthar, according to an ancient and significant law, no man may kill a cat. Very pleasant were the suburbs of Ulthar, with their little green cottages and neatly fenced farms; and still pleasanter was the quaint town itself, with its old peaked roofs and overhanging upper stories and numberless chimney-pots and narrow hill streets where one can see old cobbles whenever the graceful cats afford space enough. Carter, the cats being somewhat dispersed by the half-seen Zoogs, picked his way directly to the modest Temple of the Elder Ones where the priests and old records were said to be; and once within that venerable circular tower of ivied stone – which crowns Ulthar's highest hill – he sought out the patriarch Atal, who had been up the forbidden peak Hatheg-Kla in the stony desert and had come down again alive.

Atal, seated on an ivory dais in a festooned shrine at the top of the temple, was fully three centuries old; but still very keen of mind and memory. From him Carter learned many things about the gods, but mainly that they are indeed only Earth's gods, ruling feebly our own dreamland and having no power or habitation elsewhere. They might, Atal said, heed a man's prayer if in good humour; but one must not think of climbing to their onyx stronghold atop Kadath in the cold waste. It was lucky that no man knew where Kadath towers, for the fruits of ascending it would be very grave. Atal's companion Barzai the Wise had been drawn screaming into the sky for climbing merely the known peak of Hatheg-Kla. With unknown Kadath, if ever found, matters would be much worse; for although Earth's gods may sometimes be surpassed by a wise mortal, they are protected by the Other Gods from Outside, whom it is better not to discuss. At least twice in the world's history the Other Gods set their seal upon Earth's primal granite; once in antediluvian times, as guessed from a drawing in those parts of the Pnakotic Manuscripts too ancient to be read, and once on Hatheg-Kla when Barzai the Wise tried to see Earth's gods dancing by moonlight. So, Atal said, it would be much better to let all gods alone except in tactful prayers.

Carter, though disappointed by Atal's discouraging advice and by the meagre help to be found in the Pnakotic Manuscripts and the Seven Cryptical Books of Hsan, did not wholly despair. First he questioned the old priest about that marvellous sunset city seen from the railed terrace, thinking that perhaps he might find it without the gods' aid; but Atal could tell him nothing. Probably, Atal said, the place belonged to his especial dream world and not to the general land of vision that many know; and conceivably it might be on another planet. In that case Earth's gods could not guide him if they would. But this was not likely, since the stopping of the dreams shewed pretty clearly that it was something the Great Ones wished to hide from him.

Then Carter did a wicked thing, offering his guileless host so many draughts of the moon-wine which the Zoogs had given him that the old man became irresponsibly talkative. Robbed of his reserve, poor Atal babbled freely of forbidden things; telling of a great image reported by travellers as carved on the solid rock of the mountain Ngranek, on the isle of Oriab in the Southern Sea, and hinting that it may be a likeness which Earth's gods once wrought of their own features in the days when they danced by moonlight on that mountain. And he hiccoughed likewise that the features of that image are very strange, so that one might easily recognize them, and that they are sure signs of the authentic race of the gods.

Now the use of all this in finding the gods became at once apparent to Carter. It is known that in disguise the younger among the Great Ones often espouse the daughters of men, so that around the borders of the cold waste wherein stands Kadath the peasants must all bear their blood. This being so, the way to find that waste must be to see the stone face on Ngranek and mark the features; then, having noted them with care, to search for such features among living men. Where they are plainest and thickest, there must the gods dwell nearest; and whatever stony waste lies back of the villages in that place must be that wherein stands Kadath.

Much of the Great Ones might be learnt in such regions, and those with their blood might inherit little memories very useful to a seeker. They might not know their parentage, for the gods so dislike to be known among men that none can be found who has seen their faces wittingly; a thing which Carter realized even as he sought to scale Kadath. But they would have queer lofty thoughts misunderstood by their fellows, and would sing of far places and gardens so unlike any known even in the dreamland that common folk would call them fools; and from all this one could perhaps learn old secrets of Kadath, or gain hints of the marvellous sunset city which the gods held secret. And more, one might in certain cases seize some well-loved child of a god as hostage; or even capture some young god himself, disguised and dwelling amongst men with a comely peasant maiden as his bride.

Atal, however, did not know how to find Ngranek on its isle of Oriab; and recommended that Carter follow the singing Skai under its bridges down to the Southern Sea; where no burgess of Ulthar has ever been, but whence the merchants come in boats or with long caravans of mules and two-wheeled carts. There is a great city there, Dylath-Leen, but in Ulthar its reputation is bad because of the black three-banked galleys that sail to it with rubies from no clearly named shore. The traders that come from those galleys to deal with the jewellers are human, or nearly so, but the rowers are never beheld; and it is not thought wholesome in Ulthar that merchants should trade with black ships from unknown places whose rowers cannot be exhibited.

By the time he had given this information Atal was very drowsy, and Carter laid him gently on a couch of inlaid ebony and gathered his long beard decorously on his chest. As he turned to go, he observed that no suppressed fluttering followed him, and wondered why the Zoogs had become so lax in their curious pursuit. Then he noticed all the sleek complacent cats of Ulthar licking their chops with unusual gusto, and recalled the spitting and caterwauling he had faintly heard, in lower parts of the temple while absorbed in the old priest's conversation. He recalled, too, the evilly hungry way in which an especially impudent young Zoog had regarded a small black kitten in the cobbled street outside. And because he loved nothing on earth more than small black kittens, he stooped and petted the sleek cats of Ulthar as they licked their chops, and did not mourn because those inquisitive Zoogs would escort him no farther.

It was sunset now, so Carter stopped at an ancient inn on a steep little street overlooking the lower town. And as he went out on the balcony of his room and gazed down at the sea of red tiled roofs and cobbled ways and the pleasant fields beyond, all mellow and magical in the slanted light, he swore that Ulthar would be a very likely place to dwell in always, were not the memory of a greater sunset city ever goading one onward toward unknown perils. Then twilight fell, and the pink walls of the plastered gables turned violet and mystic, and little yellow lights floated up one by one from old lattice windows. And sweet bells pealed in the temple tower above, and the first star winked softly above the meadows across the Skai. With the night came song, and Carter nodded as the lutanists praised ancient days from beyond the filigreed balconies and tesselated courts of simple Ulthar. And there might have been sweetness even in the voices of Ulthar's many cats, but that they were mostly heavy and silent from strange feasting. Some of them stole off to those cryptical realms which are known only to cats and which villagers say are on the moon's dark side, whither the cats leap from tall housetops, but one small black kitten crept upstairs and sprang in Carter's lap to purr and play, and curled up near his feet when he lay down at last on the little couch whose pillows were stuffed with fragrant, drowsy herbs.

In the morning Carter joined a caravan of merchants bound for Dylath-Leen with the spun wool of Ulthar and the cabbages of Ulthar's busy farms. And for six days they rode with tinkling bells on the smooth road beside the Skai; stopping some nights at the inns of little quaint fishing towns, and on other nights camping under the stars while snatches of boatmen's songs came from the placid river. The country was very beautiful, with green hedges and groves and picturesque peaked cottages and octagonal windmills.

On the seventh day a blur of smoke rose on the horizon ahead, and then the tall black towers of Dylath-Leen, which is built mostly of basalt. Dylath-Leen with its thin angular towers looks in the distance like a bit of the Giant's Causeway, and its streets are dark and uninviting. There are many dismal sea-taverns near the myriad wharves, and all the town is thronged with the strange seamen of every land on earth and of a few which are said to be not on earth. Carter questioned the oddly robed men of that city about the peak of Ngranek on the isle of Oriab, and found that they knew of it well. Ships came from Baharna on that island, one being due to return thither in only a month, and Ngranek is but two days' zebra-ride from that port. But few had seen the stone face of the god, because it is on a very difficult side of Ngranek, which overlooks only sheer crags and a valley of sinister lava. Once the gods were angered with men on that side, and spoke of the matter to the Other Gods.

It was hard to get this information from the traders and sailors in Dylath-Leen's sea taverns, because they mostly preferred to whisper of the black galleys. One of them was due in a week with rubies from its unknown shore, and the townsfolk dreaded to see it dock. The mouths of the men who came from it to trade were too wide, and the way their turbans were humped up in two points above their foreheads was in especially bad taste. And their shoes were the shortest and queerest ever seen in the Six Kingdoms. But worst of all was the matter of the unseen rowers. Those three banks of oars moved too briskly and accurately and vigorously to be comfortable, and it was not right for a ship to stay in port for weeks while the merchants traded, yet to give no glimpse of its crew. It was not fair to the tavern-keepers of Dylath-Leen, or to the grocers and butchers, either; for not a scrap of provisions was ever sent aboard. The merchants took only gold and stout black slaves from Parg across the river. That was all they ever took, those unpleasantly featured merchants and their unseen rowers; never anything from the butchers and grocers, but only gold and the fat black men of Parg whom they bought by the pound. And the odours from those galleys which the south wind blew in from the wharves are not to be described. Only by constantly smoking strong thagweed could even the hardiest denizen of the old sea-taverns bear them. Dylath-Leen would never have tolerated the black galleys had such rubies been obtainable elsewhere, but no mine in all Earth's dreamland was known to produce their like.

Of these things Dylath-Leen's cosmopolitan folk chiefly gossiped whilst Carter waited patiently for the ship from Baharna, which might bear him to the isle whereon carven Ngranek towers lofty and barren. Meanwhile he did not fail to seek through the haunts of far travellers for any tales they might have concerning Kadath in the cold waste or a marvellous city of marble walls and silver fountains seen below terraces in the sunset. Of these things, however, he learned nothing; though he once thought that a certain old slant-eyed merchant looked queerly intelligent when the cold waste was spoken of. This man was reputed to trade with the horrible stone villages on the icy desert plateau of Leng, which no healthy folk visit and whose evil fires are seen at night from afar. He was even rumoured to have dealt with that High-Priest Not To Be Described, which wears a yellow silken mask over its face and dwells all alone in a prehistoric stone monastery. That such a person might well have had nibbling traffick with such beings as may conceivably dwell in the cold waste was not to be doubted, but Carter soon found that it was no use questioning him.

Then the black galley slipped into the harbour past the basalt wale and the tall lighthouse, silent and alien, and with a strange stench that the south wind drove into the town. Uneasiness rustled through the taverns along that waterfront, and after a while the dark wide-mouthed merchants with humped turbans and short feet clumped stealthily ashore to seek the bazaars of the jewellers. Carter observed them closely, and disliked them more the longer he looked at them. Then he saw them drive the stout black men of Parg up the gangplank grunting and sweating into that singular galley, and wondered in what lands – or if in any lands at all – those fat pathetic creatures might be destined to serve.

And on the third evening of that galley's stay one of the uncomfortable merchants spoke to him, smirking sinfully and hinting of what he had heard in the taverns of Carter's quest. He appeared to have knowledge too secret for public telling; and although the sound of his voice was unbearably hateful, Carter felt that the lore of so far a traveller must not be overlooked. He bade him therefore be his guest in locked chambers above, and drew out the last of the Zoogs' moon-wine to loosen his tongue. The strange merchant drank heavily, but smirked unchanged by the draught. Then he drew forth a curious bottle with wine of his own, and Carter saw that the bottle was a single hollowed ruby, grotesquely carved in patterns too fabulous to be comprehended. He offered his wine to his host, and though Carter took only the least sip, he felt the dizziness of space and the fever of unimagined jungles. All the while the guest had been smiling more and more broadly, and as Carter slipped into blankness the last thing he saw was that dark odious face convulsed with evil laughter and something quite unspeakable where one of the two frontal puffs of that orange turban had become disarranged with the shakings of that epileptic mirth.

Carter next had consciousness amidst horrible odours beneath a tent-like awning on the deck of a ship, with the marvellous coasts of the Southern Sea flying by in unnatural swiftness. He was not chained, but three of the dark sardonic merchants stood grinning nearby, and the sight of those humps in their turbans made him almost as faint as did the stench that filtered up through the sinister hatches. He saw slip past him the glorious lands and cities of which a fellow-dreamer of earth – a lighthouse-keeper in ancient Kingsport – had often discoursed in the old days, and recognized the templed terraces of Zak, abode of forgotten dreams; the spires of infamous Thalarion, that daemon-city of a thousand wonders where the eidolon Lathi reigns; the charnel gardens of Zura, land of pleasures unattained, and the twin headlands of crystal, meeting above in a resplendent arch, which guard the harbour of Sona-Nyl, blessed land of fancy.

Past all these gorgeous lands the malodourous ship flew unwholesomely, urged by the abnormal strokes of those unseen rowers below. And before the day was done Carter saw that the steersman could have no other goal than the Basalt Pillars of the West, beyond which simple folk say splendid Cathuria lies, but which wise dreamers well know are the gates of a monstrous cataract wherein the oceans of earth's dreamland drop wholly to abysmal nothingness and shoot through the empty spaces toward other worlds and other stars and the awful voids outside the ordered universe where the daemon sultan Azathoth gnaws hungrily in chaos amid pounding and piping and the hellish dancing of the Other Gods, blind, voiceless, tenebrous, and mindless, with their soul and messenger Nyarlathotep.

Meanwhile the three sardonic merchants would give no word of their intent, though Carter well knew that they must be leagued with those who wished to hold him from his quest. It is understood in the land of dream that the Other Gods have many agents moving among men; and all these agents, whether wholly human or slightly less than human, are eager to work the will of those blind and mindless things in return for the favour of their hideous soul and messenger, the crawling chaos Nyarlathotep. So Carter inferred that the merchants of the humped turbans, hearing of his daring search for the Great Ones in their castle of Kadath, had decided to take him away and deliver him to Nyarlathotep for whatever nameless bounty might be offered for such a prize. What might be the land of those merchants in our known universe or in the eldritch spaces outside, Carter could not guess; nor could he imagine at what hellish trysting-place they would meet the crawling chaos to give him up and claim their reward. He knew, however, that no beings as nearly human as these would dare approach the ultimate nighted throne of the daemon Azathoth in the formless central void.

At the set of sun the merchants licked their excessively wide lips and glared hungrily, and one of them went below and returned from some hidden and offensive cabin with a pot and basket of plates. Then they squatted close together beneath the awning and ate the smoking meat that was passed around. But when they gave Carter a portion, he found something very terrible in the size and shape of it; so that he turned even paler than before and cast that portion into the sea when no eye was on him. And again he thought of those unseen rowers beneath, and of the suspicious nourishment from which their far too mechanical strength was derived.

It was dark when the galley passed betwixt the Basalt Pillars of the West and the sound of the ultimate cataract swelled portentous from ahead. And the spray of that cataract rose to obscure the stars, and the deck grew damp, and the vessel reeled in the surging current of the brink. Then with a queer whistle and plunge the leap was taken, and Carter felt the terrors of nightmare as earth fell away and the great boat shot silent and comet-like into planetary space. Never before had he known what shapeless black things lurk and caper and flounder all through the aether, leering and grinning at such voyagers as may pass, and sometimes feeling about with slimy paws when some moving object excites their curiosity. These are the nameless larvae of the Other Gods, and like them are blind and without mind, and possessed of singular hungers and thirsts.

But that offensive galley did not aim as far as Carter had feared, for he soon saw that the helmsman was steering a course directly for the moon. The moon was a crescent shining larger and larger as they approached it, and shewing its singular craters and peaks uncomfortably. The ship made for the edge, and it soon became clear that its destination was that secret and mysterious side which is always turned away from earth, and which no fully human person, save perhaps the dreamer Snireth-Ko, has ever beheld. The close aspect of the moon as the galley drew near proved very disturbing to Carter, and he did not like the size and shape of the ruins which crumbled here and there. The dead temples on the mountains were so placed that they could have glorified no suitable or wholesome gods, and in the symmetries of the broken columns there seemed to be some dark and inner meaning which did not invite solution. And what the structure and proportions of the olden worshippers could have been, Carter steadily refused to conjecture.

When the ship rounded the edge, and sailed over those lands unseen by man, there appeared in the queer landscape certain signs of life, and Carter saw many low, broad, round cottages in fields of grotesque whitish fungi. He noticed that these cottages had no windows, and thought that their shape suggested the huts of Esquimaux. Then he glimpsed the oily waves of a sluggish sea, and knew that the voyage was once more to be by water – or at least through some liquid. The galley struck the surface with a peculiar sound, and the odd elastic way the waves received it was very perplexing to Carter. They now slid along at great speed, once passing and hailing another galley of kindred form, but generally seeing nothing but that curious sea and a sky that was black and star-strewn even though the sun shone scorchingly in it.

There presently rose ahead the jagged hills of a leprous-looking coast, and Carter saw the thick unpleasant grey towers of a city. The way they leaned and bent, the manner in which they were clustered, and the fact that they had no windows at all, was very disturbing to the prisoner; and he bitterly mourned the folly which had made him sip the curious wine of that merchant with the humped turban. As the coast drew nearer, and the hideous stench of that city grew stronger, he saw upon the jagged hills many forests, some of whose trees he recognized as akin to that solitary moon-tree in the enchanted wood of earth, from whose sap the small brown Zoogs ferment their curious wine.

Carter could now distinguish moving figures on the noisome wharves ahead, and the better he saw them the worse he began to fear and detest them. For they were not men at all, or even approximately men, but great greyish-white slippery things which could expand and contract at will, and whose principal shape – though it often changed – was that of a sort of toad without any eyes, but with a curious vibrating mass of short pink tentacles on the end of its blunt, vague snout. These objects were waddling busily about the wharves, moving bales and crates and boxes with preternatural strength, and now and then hopping on or off some anchored galley with long oars in their forepaws. And now and then one would appear driving a herd of clumping slaves, which indeed were approximate human beings with wide mouths like those merchants who traded in Dylath-Leen; only these herds, being without turbans or shoes or clothing, did not seem so very human after all. Some of the slaves – the fatter ones, whom a sort of overseer would pinch experimentally – were unloaded from ships and nailed in crates which workers pushed into the low warehouses or loaded on great lumbering vans.

Once a van was hitched and driven off, and the, fabulous thing which drew it was such that Carter gasped, even after having seen the other monstrosities of that hateful place. Now and then a small herd of slaves dressed and turbaned like the dark merchants would be driven aboard a galley, followed by a great crew of the slippery toad-things as officers, navigators, and rowers. And Carter saw that the almost-human creatures were reserved for the more ignominious kinds of servitude which required no strength, such as steering and cooking, fetching and carrying, and bargaining with men on the earth or other planets where they traded. These creatures must have been convenient on earth, for they were truly not unlike men when dressed and carefully shod and turbaned, and could haggle in the shops of men without embarrassment or curious explanations. But most of them, unless lean or ill-favoured, were unclothed and packed in crates and drawn off in lumbering lorries by fabulous things. Occasionally other beings were unloaded and crated; some very like these semi-humans, some not so similar, and some not similar at all. And he wondered if any of the poor stout black men of Parg were left to be unloaded and crated and shipped inland in those obnoxious drays.

When the galley landed at a greasy-looking quay of spongy rock a nightmare horde of toad-things wiggled out of the hatches, and two of them seized Carter and dragged him ashore. The smell and aspect of that city are beyond telling, and Carter held only scattered images of the tiled streets and black doorways and endless precipices of grey vertical walls without windows. At length he was dragged within a low doorway and made to climb infinite steps in pitch blackness. It was, apparently, all one to the toad-things whether it were light or dark. The odour of the place was intolerable, and when Carter was locked into a chamber and left alone he scarcely had strength to crawl around and ascertain its form and dimensions. It was circular, and about twenty feet across.

From then on time ceased to exist. At intervals food was pushed in, but Carter would not touch it. What his fate would be, he did not know; but he felt that he was held for the coming of that frightful soul and messenger of infinity's Other Gods, the crawling chaos Nyarlathotep. Finally, after an unguessed span of hours or days, the great stone door swung wide again, and Carter was shoved down the stairs and out into the red-litten streets of that fearsome city. It was night on the moon, and all through the town were stationed slaves bearing torches.

In a detestable square a sort of procession was formed; ten of the toad-things and twenty-four almost human torch-bearers, eleven on either side, and one each before and behind. Carter was placed in the middle of the line; five toad-things ahead and five behind, and one almost-human torch-bearer on either side of him. Certain of the toad-things produced disgustingly carven flutes of ivory and made loathsome sounds. To that hellish piping the column advanced out of the tiled streets and into nighted plains of obscene fungi, soon commencing to climb one of the lower and more gradual hills that lay behind the city. That on some frightful slope or blasphemous plateau the crawling chaos waited, Carter could not doubt; and he wished that the suspense might soon be over. The whining of those impious flutes was shocking, and he would have given worlds for some even half-normal sound; but these toad-things had no voices, and the slaves did not talk.

Then through that star-specked darkness there did come a normal sound. It rolled from the higher hills, and from all the jagged peaks around it was caught up and echoed in a swelling pandaemoniac chorus. It was the midnight yell of the cat, and Carter knew at last that the old village folk were right when they made low guesses about the cryptical realms which are known only to cats, and to which the elders among cats repair by stealth nocturnally, springing from high housetops. Verily, it is to the moon's dark side that they go to leap and gambol on the hills and converse with ancient shadows, and here amidst that column of foetid things Carter heard their homely, friendly cry, and thought of the steep roofs and warm hearths and little lighted windows of home.

Now much of the speech of cats was known to Randolph Carter, and in this far terrible place he uttered the cry that was suitable. But that he need not have done, for even as his lips opened he heard the chorus wax and draw nearer, and saw swift shadows against the stars as small graceful shapes leaped from hill to hill in gathering legions. The call of the clan had been given, and before the foul procession had time even to be frightened a cloud of smothering fur and a phalanx of murderous claws were tidally and tempestuously upon it. The flutes stopped, and there were shrieks in the night. Dying almost-humans screamed, and cats spit and yowled and roared, but the toad-things made never a sound as their stinking green ichor oozed fatally upon that porous earth with the obscene fungi.

It was a stupendous sight while the torches lasted, and Carter had never before seen so many cats. Black, grey, and white; yellow, tiger, and mixed; common, Persian, and Manx; Thibetan, Angora, and Egyptian; all were there in the fury of battle, and there hovered over them some trace of that profound and inviolate sanctity which made their goddess great in the temples of Bubastis. They would leap seven strong at the throat of an almost-human or the pink tentacled snout of a toad-thing and drag it down savagely to the fungous plain, where myriads of their fellows would surge over it and into it with the frenzied claws and teeth of a divine battle-fury. Carter had seized a torch from a stricken slave, but was soon overborne by the surging waves of his loyal defenders. Then he lay in the utter blackness hearing the clangour of war and the shouts of the victors, and feeling the soft paws of his friends as they rushed to and fro over him in the fray.

At last awe and exhaustion closed his eyes, and when he opened them again it was upon a strange scene. The great shining disc of the earth, thirteen times greater than that of the moon as we see it, had risen with floods of weird light over the lunar landscape; and across all those leagues of wild plateau and ragged crest there squatted one endless sea of cats in orderly array. Circle on circle they reached, and two or three leaders out of the ranks were licking his face and purring to him consolingly. Of the dead slaves and toad-things there were not many signs, but Carter thought he saw one bone a little way off in the open space between him and the warriors.

Carter now spoke with the leaders in the soft language of cats, and learned that his ancient friendship with the species was well known and often spoken of in the places where cats congregate. He had not been unmarked in Ulthar when he passed through, and the sleek old cats had remembered how he petted them after they had attended to the hungry Zoogs who looked evilly at a small black kitten. And they recalled, too, how he had welcomed the very little kitten who came to see him at the inn, and how he had given it a saucer of rich cream in the morning before he left. The grandfather of that very little kitten was the leader of the army now assembled, for he had seen the evil procession from a far hill and recognized the prisoner as a sworn friend of his kind on earth and in the land of dream.

A yowl now came from the farther peak, and the old leader paused abruptly in his conversation. It was one of the army's outposts, stationed on the highest of the mountains to watch the one foe which Earth's cats fear; the very large and peculiar cats from Saturn, who for some reason have not been oblivious of the charm of our moon's dark side. They are leagued by treaty with the evil toad-things, and are notoriously hostile to our earthly cats; so that at this juncture a meeting would have been a somewhat grave matter.

After a brief consultation of generals, the cats rose and assumed a closer formation, crowding protectingly around Carter and preparing to take the great leap through space back to the housetops of our earth and its dreamland. The old field-marshal advised Carter to let himself be borne along smoothly and passively in the massed ranks of furry leapers, and told him how to spring when the rest sprang and land gracefully when the rest landed. He also offered to deposit him in any spot he desired, and Carter decided on the city of Dylath-Leen whence the black galley had set out; for he wished to sail thence for Oriab and the carven crest Ngranek, and also to warn the people of the city to have no more traffick with black galleys, if indeed that traffick could be tactfully and judiciously broken off. Then, upon a signal, the cats all leaped gracefully with their friend packed securely in their midst; while in a black cave on an unhallowed summit of the moon-mountains still vainly waited the crawling chaos Nyarlathotep.

The leap of the cats through space was very swift; and being surrounded by his companions Carter did not see this time the great black shapelessnesses that lurk and caper and flounder in the abyss. Before he fully realised what had happened he was back in his familiar room at the inn at Dylath-Leen, and the stealthy, friendly cats were pouring out of the window in streams. The old leader from Ulthar was the last to leave, and as Carter shook his paw he said he would be able to get home by cockcrow. When dawn came, Carter went downstairs and learned that a week had elapsed since his capture and leaving. There was still nearly a fortnight to wait for the ship bound toward Oriab, and during that time he said what he could against the black galleys and their infamous ways. Most of the townsfolk believed him; yet so fond were the jewellers of great rubies that none would wholly promise to cease trafficking with the wide-mouthed merchants. If aught of evil ever befalls Dylath-Leen through such traffick, it will not be his fault.

In about a week the desiderate ship put in by the black wale and tall lighthouse, and Carter was glad to see that she was a barque of wholesome men, with painted sides and yellow lateen sails and a grey captain in silken robes. Her cargo was the fragrant resin of Oriab's inner groves, and the delicate pottery baked by the artists of Baharna, and the strange little figures carved from Ngranek's ancient lava. For this they were paid in the wool of Ulthar and the iridescent textiles of Hatheg and the ivory that the black men carve across the river in Parg. Carter made arrangements with the captain to go to Baharna and was told that the voyage would take ten days. And during his week of waiting he talked much with that captain of Ngranek, and was told that very few had seen the carven face thereon; but that most travellers are content to learn its legends from old people and lava-gatherers and image-makers in Baharna and afterward say in their far homes that they have indeed beheld it. The captain was not even sure that any person now living had beheld that carven face, for the wrong side of Ngranek is very difficult and barren and sinister, and there are rumours of caves near the peak wherein dwell the night-gaunts. But the captain did not wish to say just what a night-gaunt might be like, since such cattle are known to haunt most persistently the dreams of those who think too often of them. Then Carter asked that captain about unknown Kadath in the cold waste, and the marvellous sunset city, but of these the good man could truly tell nothing.

Carter sailed out of Dylath-Leen one early morning when the tide turned, and saw the first rays of sunrise on the thin angular towers of that dismal basalt town. And for two days they sailed eastward in sight of green coasts, and saw often the pleasant fishing towns that climbed up steeply with their red roofs and chimney-pots from old dreaming wharves and beaches where nets lay drying. But on the third day they turned sharply south where the roll of water was stronger, and soon passed from sight of any land. On the fifth day the sailors were nervous, but the captain apologized for their fears, saying that the ship was about to pass over the weedy walls and broken columns of a sunken city too old for memory, and that when the water was clear one could see so many moving shadows in that deep place that simple folk disliked it. He admitted, moreover, that many ships had been lost in that part of the sea; having been hailed when quite close to it, but never seen again.

That night the moon was very bright, and one could see a great way down in the water. There was so little wind that the ship could not move much, and the ocean was very calm. Looking over the rail Carter saw many fathoms deep the dome of the great temple, and in front of it an avenue of unnatural sphinxes leading to what was once a public square. Dolphins sported merrily in and out of the ruins, and porpoises revelled clumsily here and there, sometimes coming to the surface and leaping clear out of the sea. As the ship drifted on a little the floor of the ocean rose in hills, and one could clearly mark the lines of ancient climbing streets and the washed-down walls of myriad little houses.

Then the suburbs appeared, and finally a great lone building on a hill, of simpler architecture than the other structures, and in much better repair. It was dark and low and covered four sides of a square, with a tower at each corner, a paved court in the centre, and small curious round windows all over it. Probably it was of basalt, though weeds draped the greater part; and such was its lonely and impressive place on that far hill that it may have been a temple or a monastery. Some phosphorescent fish inside it gave the small round windows an aspect of shining, and Carter did not blame the sailors much for their fears. Then by the watery moonlight he noticed an odd high monolith in the middle of that central court, and saw that something was tied to it. And when after getting a telescope from the captain's cabin he saw that that bound thing was a sailor in the silk robes of Oriab, head downward and without any eyes, he was glad that a rising breeze soon took the ship ahead to more healthy parts of the sea.

The next day they spoke with a ship with violet sails bound for Zar, in the land of forgotten dreams, with bulbs of strange coloured lilies for cargo. And on the evening of the eleventh day they came in sight of the isle of Oriab with Ngranek rising jagged and snow-crowned in the distance. Oriab is a very great isle, and its port of Baharna a mighty city. The wharves of Baharna are of porphyry, and the city rises in great stone terraces behind them, having streets of steps that are frequently arched over by buildings and the bridges between buildings. There is a great canal which goes under the whole city in a tunnel with granite gates and leads to the inland lake of Yath, on whose farther shore are the vast clay-brick ruins of a primal city whose name is not remembered. As the ship drew into the harbour at evening the twin beacons Thon and Thal gleamed a welcome, and in all the million windows of Baharna's terraces mellow lights peeped out quietly and gradually as the stars peep out overhead in the dusk, till that steep and climbing seaport became a glittering constellation hung between the stars of heaven and the reflections of those stars in the still harbour.

The captain, after landing, made Carter a guest in his own small house on the shores of Yath where the rear of the town slopes down to it; and his wife and servants brought strange toothsome foods for the traveller's delight. And in the days after that Carter asked for rumours and legends of Ngranek in all the taverns and public places where lava-gatherers and image-makers meet, but could find no one who had been up the higher slopes or seen the carven face. Ngranek was a hard mountain with only an accursed valley behind it, and besides, one could never depend on the certainty that night-gaunts are altogether fabulous.

When the captain sailed back to Dylath-Leen Carter took quarters in an ancient tavern opening on an alley of steps in the original part of the town, which is built of brick and resembles the ruins of Yath's farther shore. Here he laid his plans for the ascent of Ngranek, and correlated all that he had learned from the lava-gatherers about the roads thither. The keeper of the tavern was a very old man, and had heard so many legends that he was a great help. He even took Carter to an upper room in that ancient house and shewed him a crude picture which a traveller had scratched on the clay wall in the old days when men were bolder and less reluctant to visit Ngranek's higher slopes. The old tavern-keeper's great-grandfather had heard from his great-grandfather that the traveller who scratched that picture had climbed Ngranek and seen the carven face, here drawing it for others to behold, but Carter had very great doubts, since the large rough features on the wall were hasty and careless, and wholly overshadowed by a crowd of little companion shapes in the worst possible taste, with horns and wings and claws and curling tails.

At last, having gained all the information he was likely to gain in the taverns and public places of Baharna, Carter hired a zebra and set out one morning on the road by Yath's shore for those inland parts wherein towers stony Ngranek. On his right were rolling hills and pleasant orchards and neat little stone farmhouses, and he was much reminded of those fertile fields that flank the Skai. By evening he was near the nameless ancient ruins on Yath's farther shore, and though old lava-gatherers had warned him not to camp there at night, he tethered his zebra to a curious pillar before a crumbling wall and laid his blanket in a sheltered corner beneath some carvings whose meaning none could decipher. Around him he wrapped another blanket, for the nights are cold in Oriab; and when upon awaking once he thought he felt the wings of some insect brushing his face he covered his head altogether and slept in peace till roused by the magah birds in distant resin groves.

The sun had just come up over the great slope whereon leagues of primal brick foundations and worn walls and occasional cracked pillars and pedestals stretched down desolate to the shore of Yath, and Carter looked about for his tethered zebra. Great was his dismay to see that docile beast stretched prostrate beside the curious pillar to which it had been tied, and still greater was he vexed on finding that the steed was quite dead, with its blood all sucked away through a singular wound in its throat. His pack had been disturbed, and several shiny knick-knacks taken away, and all round on the dusty soil were great webbed footprints for which he could not in any way account. The legends and warnings of lava-gatherers occurred to him, and he thought of what had brushed his face in the night. Then he shouldered his pack and strode on toward Ngranek, though not without a shiver when he saw close to him as the highway passed through the ruins a great gaping arch low in the wall of an old temple, with steps leading down into darkness farther than he could peer.

His course now lay uphill through wilder and partly wooded country, and he saw only the huts of charcoal-burners and the camp of those who gathered resin from the groves. The whole air was fragrant with balsam, and all the magah birds sang blithely as they flashed their seven colours in the sun. Near sunset he came on a new camp of lava-gatherers returning with laden sacks from Ngranek's lower slopes; and here he also camped, listening to the songs and tales of the men, and overhearing what they whispered about a companion they had lost. He had climbed high to reach a mass of fine lava above him, and at nightfall did not return to his fellows. When they looked for him the next day they found only his turban, nor was there any sign on the crags below that he had fallen. They did not search any more, because the old man among them said it would be of no use. No one ever found what the night-gaunts took, though those beasts themselves were so uncertain as to be almost fabulous. Carter asked them if night-gaunts sucked blood and liked shiny things and left webbed footprints, but they all shook their heads negatively and seemed frightened at his making such an inquiry. When he saw how taciturn they had become he asked them no more, but went to sleep in his blanket.

The next day he rose with the lava-gatherers and exchanged farewells as they rode west and he rode east on a zebra he bought of them. Their older men gave him blessings and warnings, and told him he had better not climb too high on Ngranek, but while he thanked them heartily he was in no wise dissuaded. For still did he feel that he must find the gods on unknown Kadath; and win from them a way to that haunting and marvellous city in the sunset. By noon, after a long uphill ride, he came upon some abandoned brick villages of the hill-people who had once dwelt thus close to Ngranek and carved images from its smooth lava. Here they had dwelt till the days of the old tavern-keeper's grandfather, but about that time they felt that their presence was disliked. Their homes had crept even up the mountain's slope, and the higher they built the more people they would miss when the sun rose. At last they decided it would be better to leave altogether, since things were sometimes glimpsed in the darkness which no one could interpret favourably; so in the end all of them went down to the sea and dwelt in Baharna, inhabiting a very old quarter and teaching their sons the old art of image-making which to this day they carry on. It was from these children of the exiled hill-people that Carter had heard the best tales about Ngranek when searching through Baharna's ancient taverns.

All this time the great gaunt side of Ngranek was looming up higher and higher as Carter approached it. There were sparse trees on the lower slopes and feeble shrubs above them, and then the bare hideous rock rose spectral into the sky, to mix with frost and ice and eternal snow. Carter could see the rifts and ruggedness of that sombre stone, and did not welcome the prospect of climbing it. In places there were solid streams of lava, and scoriac heaps that littered slopes and ledges. Ninety aeons ago, before even the gods had danced upon its pointed peak, that mountain had spoken with fire and roared with the voices of the inner thunders. Now it towered all silent and sinister, bearing on the hidden side that secret titan image whereof rumour told. And there were caves in that mountain, which might be empty and alone with elder darkness, or might – if legend spoke truly – hold horrors of a form not to be surmised.

The ground sloped upward to the foot of Ngranek, thinly covered with scrub oaks and ash trees, and strewn with bits of rock, lava, and ancient cinder. There were the charred embers of many camps, where the lava-gatherers were wont to stop, and several rude altars which they had built either to propitiate the Great Ones or to ward off what they dreamed of in Ngranek's high passes and labyrinthine caves. At evening Carter reached the farthermost pile of embers and camped for the night, tethering his zebra to a sapling and wrapping himself well in his blankets before going to sleep. And all through the night a voonith howled distantly from the shore of some hidden pool, but Carter felt no fear of that amphibious terror, since he had been told with certainty that not one of them dares even approach the slope of Ngranek.

In the clear sunshine of morning Carter began the long ascent, taking his zebra as far as that useful beast could go, but tying it to a stunted ash tree when the floor of the thin wood became too steep. Thereafter he scrambled up alone; first through the forest with its ruins of old villages in overgrown clearings, and then over the tough grass where anaemic shrubs grew here and there. He regretted coming clear of the trees, since the slope was very precipitous and the whole thing rather dizzying. At length he began to discern all the countryside spread out beneath him whenever he looked about; the deserted huts of the image-makers, the groves of resin trees and the camps of those who gathered from them, the woods where prismatic magahs nest and sing, and even a hint very far away of the shores of Yath and of those forbidding ancient ruins whose name is forgotten. He found it best not to look around, and kept on climbing and climbing till the shrubs became very sparse and there was often nothing but the tough grass to cling to.

Then the soil became meagre, with great patches of bare rock cropping out, and now and then the nest of a condor in a crevice. Finally there was nothing at all but the bare rock, and had it not been very rough and weathered, he could scarcely have ascended farther. Knobs, ledges, and pinnacles, however, helped greatly; and it was cheering to see occasionally the sign of some lava-gatherer scratched clumsily in the friable stone, and know that wholesome human creatures had been there before him. After a certain height the presence of man was further shewn by handholds and footholds hewn where they were needed, and by little quarries and excavations where some choice vein or stream of lava had been found. In one place a narrow ledge had been chopped artificially to an especially rich deposit far to the right of the main line of ascent. Once or twice Carter dared to look around, and was almost stunned by the spread of landscape below. All the island betwixt him and the coast lay open to his sight, with Baharna's stone terraces and the smoke of its chimneys mystical in the distance. And beyond that the illimitable Southern Sea with all its curious secrets.

Thus far there had been much winding around the mountain, so that the farther and carven side was still hidden. Carter now saw a ledge running upward and to the left which seemed to head the way he wished, and this course he took in the hope that it might prove continuous. After ten minutes he saw it was indeed no cul-de-sac, but that it led steeply on in an arc which would, unless suddenly interrupted or deflected, bring him after a few hours' climbing to that unknown southern slope overlooking the desolate crags and the accursed valley of lava. As new country came into view below him he saw that it was bleaker and wilder than those seaward lands he had traversed. The mountain's side, too, was somewhat different; being here pierced by curious cracks and caves not found on the straighter route he had left. Some of these were above him and some beneath him, all opening on sheerly perpendicular cliffs and wholly unreachable by the feet of man. The air was very cold now, but so hard was the climbing that he did not mind it. Only the increasing rarity bothered him, and he thought that perhaps it was this which had turned the heads of other travellers and excited those absurd tales of night-gaunts whereby they explained the loss of such climbers as fell from these perilous paths. He was not much impressed by travellers' tales, but had a good curved scimitar in case of any trouble. All lesser thoughts were lost in the wish to see that carven face which might set him on the track of the gods atop unknown Kadath.

At last, in the fearsome iciness of upper space, he came round fully to the hidden side of Ngranek and saw in infinite gulfs below him the lesser crags and sterile abysses of lava which marked olden wrath of the Great Ones. There was unfolded, too, a vast expanse of country to the south; but it was a desert land without fair fields or cottage chimneys, and seemed to have no ending. No trace of the sea was visible on this side, for Oriab is a great island. Black caverns and odd crevices were still numerous on the sheer vertical cliffs, but none of them was accessible to a climber. There now loomed aloft a great beetling mass which hampered the upward view, and Carter was for a moment shaken with doubt lest it prove impassable. Poised in windy insecurity miles above earth, with only space and death on one side and only slippery walls of rock on the other, he knew for a moment the fear that makes men shun Ngranek's hidden side. He could not turn round, yet the sun was already low. If there were no way aloft, the night would find him crouching there still, and the dawn would not find him at all.

But there was a way, and he saw it in due season. Only a very expert dreamer could have used those imperceptible footholds, yet to Carter they were sufficient. Surmounting now the outward-hanging rock, he found the slope above much easier than that below, since a great glacier's melting had left a generous space with loam and ledges. To the left a precipice dropped straight from unknown heights to unknown depths, with a cave's dark mouth just out of reach above him. Elsewhere, however, the mountain slanted back strongly, and even gave him space to lean and rest.

He felt from the chill that he must be near the snow line, and looked up to see what glittering pinnacles might be shining in that late ruddy sunlight. Surely enough, there was the snow uncounted thousands of feet above, and below it a great beetling crag like that he had just climbed; hanging there forever in bold outline. And when he saw that crag he gasped and cried out aloud, and clutched at the jagged rock in awe; for the titan bulge had not stayed as earth's dawn had shaped it, but gleamed red and stupendous in the sunset with the carved and polished features of a god.

Stern and terrible shone that face that the sunset lit with fire. How vast it was no mind can ever measure, but Carter knew at once that man could never have fashioned it. It was a god chiselled by the hands of the gods, and it looked down haughty and majestic upon the seeker.

Rumour had said it was strange and not to be mistaken, and Carter saw that it was indeed so; for those long narrow eyes and long-lobed ears, and that thin nose and pointed chin, all spoke of a race that is not of men but of gods.

He clung overawed in that lofty and perilous eyrie, even though it was this which he had expected and come to find; for there is in a god's face more of marvel than prediction can tell, and when that face is vaster than a great temple and seen looking downward at sunset in the cryptic silences of that upper world from whose dark lava it was divinely hewn of old, the marvel is so strong that none may escape it.

Here, too, was the added marvel of recognition; for although he had planned to search all dreamland over for those whose likeness to this face might mark them as the god's children, he now knew that he need not do so. Certainly, the great face carven on that mountain was of no strange sort, but the kin of such as he had seen often in the taverns of the seaport Celephaïs which lies in Ooth-Nargai beyond the Tanarian Hills and is ruled over by that King Kuranes whom Carter once knew in waking life. Every year sailors with such a face came in dark ships from the north to trade their onyx for the carved jade and spun gold and little red singing birds of Celephaïs, and it was clear that these could be no others than the half-gods he sought. Where they dwelt, there must the cold waste lie close, and within it unknown Kadath and its onyx castle for the Great Ones. So to Celephaïs he must go, far distant from the isle of Oriab, and in such parts as would take him back to Dylath-Leen and up the Skai to the bridge by Nir, and again into the enchanted wood of the Zoogs, whence the way would bend northward through the garden lands by Oukranos to the gilded spires of Thran, where he might find a galleon bound over the Cerenarian Sea.

But dusk was now thick, and the great carven face looked down even sterner in shadow. Perched on that ledge night found the seeker; and in the blackness he might neither go down nor go up, but only stand and cling and shiver in that narrow place till the day came, praying to keep awake lest sleep loose his hold and send him down the dizzy miles of air to the crags and sharp rocks of the accursed valley. The stars came out, but save for them there was only black nothingness in his eyes; nothingness leagued with death, against whose beckoning he might do no more than cling to the rocks and lean back away from an unseen brink. The last thing of earth that he saw in the gloaming was a condor soaring close to the westward precipice beside him, and darting screaming away when it came near the cave whose mouth yawned just out of reach.

Suddenly, without a warning sound in the dark, Carter felt his curved scimitar drawn stealthily out of his belt by some unseen hand. Then he heard it clatter down over the rocks below. And between him and the Milky Way he thought he saw a very terrible outline of something noxiously thin and horned and tailed and bat-winged. Other things, too, had begun to blot out patches of stars west of him, as if a flock of vague entities were flapping thickly and silently out of that inaccessible cave in the face of the precipice. Then a sort of cold rubbery arm seized his neck and something else seized his feet, and he was lifted inconsiderately up and swung about in space. Another minute and the stars were gone, and Carter knew that the night-gaunts had got him.

They bore him breathless into that cliffside cavern and through monstrous labyrinths beyond. When he struggled, as at first he did by instinct, they tickled him with deliberation. They made no sound at all themselves, and even their membranous wings were silent. They were frightfully cold and damp and slippery, and their paws kneaded one detestably. Soon they were plunging hideously downward through inconceivable abysses in a whirling, giddying, sickening rush of dank, tomb-like air; and Carter felt they were shooting into the ultimate vortex of shrieking and daemonic madness. He screamed again and again, but whenever he did so the black paws tickled him with greater subtlety. Then he saw a sort of grey phosphorescence about, and guessed they were coming even to that inner world of subterrene horror of which dim legends tell, and which is litten only by the pale death-fire wherewith reeks the ghoulish air and the primal mists of the pits at earth's core.

At last far below him he saw faint lines of grey and ominous pinnacles which he knew must be the fabled Peaks of Throk. Awful and sinister they stand in the haunted disc of sunless and eternal depths; higher than man may reckon, and guarding terrible valleys where the Dholes crawl and burrow nastily. But Carter preferred to look at them than at his captors, which were indeed shocking and uncouth black things with smooth, oily, whale-like surfaces, unpleasant horns that curved inward toward each other, bat wings whose beating made no sound, ugly prehensile paws, and barbed tails that lashed needlessly and disquietingly. And worst of all, they never spoke or laughed, and never smiled because they had no faces at all to smile with, but only a suggestive blankness where a face ought to be. All they ever did was clutch and fly and tickle; that was the way of night-gaunts.

As the band flew lower the Peaks of Throk rose grey and towering on all sides, and one saw clearly that nothing lived on that austere and impressive granite of the endless twilight. At still lower levels the death-fires in the air gave out, and one met only the primal blackness of the void save aloft where the thin peaks stood out goblin-like. Soon the peaks were very far away, and nothing about but great rushing winds with the dankness of nethermost grottoes in them. Then in the end the night-gaunts landed on a floor of unseen things which felt like layers of bones, and left Carter all alone in that black valley. To bring him thither was the duty of the night-gaunts that guard Ngranek; and this done, they flapped away silently. When Carter tried to trace their flight he found he could not, since even the Peaks of Throk had faded out of sight. There was nothing anywhere but blackness and horror and silence and bones.

Now Carter knew from a certain source that he was in the vale of Pnoth, where crawl and burrow the enormous Dholes; but he did not know what to expect, because no one has ever seen a Dhole or even guessed what such a thing may be like. Dholes are known only by dim rumour, from the rustling they make amongst mountains of bones and the slimy touch they have when they wriggle past one. They cannot be seen because they creep only in the dark. Carter did not wish to meet a Dhole, so listened intently for any sound in the unknown depths of bones about him. Even in this fearsome place he had a plan and an objective, for whispers of Pnoth were not unknown to one with whom he had talked much in the old days. In brief, it seemed fairly likely that this was the spot into which all the ghouls of the waking world cast the refuse of their feastings; and that if he but had good luck he might stumble upon that mighty crag taller even than Throk's peaks which marks the edge of their domain. Showers of bones would tell him where to look, and once found he could call to a ghoul to let down a ladder; for strange to say, he had a very singular link with these terrible creatures.

A man he had known in Boston – a painter of strange pictures with a secret studio in an ancient and unhallowed alley near a graveyard – had actually made friends with the ghouls and had taught him to understand the simpler part of their disgusting meeping and glibbering. This man had vanished at last, and Carter was not sure but that he might find him now, and use for the first time in dreamland that far-away English of his dim waking life. In any case, he felt he could persuade a ghoul to guide him out of Pnoth; and it would be better to meet a ghoul, which one can see, than a Dhole, which one cannot see.

So Carter walked in the dark, and ran when he thought he heard something among the bones underfoot. Once he bumped into a stony slope, and knew it must be the base of one of

Throk's peaks. Then at last he heard a monstrous rattling and clatter which reached far up in the air, and became sure he had come nigh the crag of the ghouls. He was not sure he could be heard from this valley miles below, but realised that the inner world has strange laws. As he pondered he was struck by a flying bone so heavy that it must have been a skull, and therefore realising his nearness to the fateful crag he sent up as best he might that meeping cry which is the call of the ghoul.

Sound travels slowly, so it was some time before he heard an answering glibber. But it came at last, and before long he was told that a rope ladder would be lowered. The wait for this was very tense, since there was no telling what might not have been stirred up among those bones by his shouting. Indeed, it was not long before he actually did hear a vague rustling afar off. As this thoughtfully approached, he became more and more uncomfortable; for he did not wish to move away from the spot where the ladder would come. Finally the tension grew almost unbearable, and he was about to flee in panic when the thud of something on the newly heaped bones nearby drew his notice from the other sound. It was the ladder, and after a minute of groping he had it taut in his hands. But the other sound did not cease, and followed him even as he climbed. He had gone fully five feet from the ground when the rattling beneath waxed emphatic, and was a good ten feet up when something swayed the ladder from below. At a height which must have been fifteen or twenty feet he felt his whole side brushed by a great slippery length which grew alternately convex and concave with wriggling; and thereafter he climbed desperately to escape the unendurable nuzzling of that loathsome and overfed Dhole whose form no man might see.

For hours he climbed with aching and blistered hands, seeing again the grey death-fire and Throk's uncomfortable pinnacles. At last he discerned above him the projecting edge of the great crag of the ghouls, whose vertical side he could not glimpse; and hours later he saw a curious face peering over it as a gargoyle peers over a parapet of Notre Dame. This almost made him lose his hold through faintness, but a moment later he was himself again; for his vanished friend Richard Pickman had once introduced him to a ghoul, and he knew well their canine faces and slumping forms and unmentionable idiosyncrasies. So he had himself well under control when that hideous thing pulled him out of the dizzy emptiness over the edge of the crag, and did not scream at the partly consumed refuse heaped at one side or at the squatting circles of ghouls who gnawed and watched curiously.

He was now on a dim-litten plain whose sole topographical features were great boulders and the entrances of burrows. The ghouls were in general respectful, even if one did attempt to pinch him while several others eyed his leanness speculatively. Through patient glibbering he made inquiries regarding his vanished friend, and found he had become a ghoul of some prominence in abysses nearer the waking world. A greenish elderly ghoul offered to conduct him to Pickman's present habitation, so despite a natural loathing he followed the creature into a capacious burrow and crawled after him for hours in the blackness of rank mould. They emerged on a dim plain strewn with singular relics of earth – old gravestones, broken urns, and grotesque fragments of monuments – and Carter realised with some emotion that he was probably nearer the waking world than at any other time since he had gone down the seven hundred steps from the cavern of flame to the Gate of Deeper Slumber.

There, on a tombstone of 1768 stolen from the Granary Burying Ground in Boston, sat a ghoul which was once the artist Richard Upton Pickman. It was naked and rubbery, and had acquired so much of the ghoulish physiognomy that its human origin was already obscure. But it still remembered a little English, and was able to converse with Carter in grunts and monosyllables, helped out now and then by the glibbering of ghouls. When it learned that

Carter wished to get to the enchanted wood and from there to the city Celephaïs in Ooth-Nargai beyond the Tanarian Hills, it seemed rather doubtful; for these ghouls of the waking world do no business in the graveyards of upper dreamland (leaving that to the red-footed wamps that are spawned in dead cities), and many things intervene betwixt their gulf and the enchanted wood, including the terrible kingdom of the Gugs.

The Gugs, hairy and gigantic, once reared stone circles in that wood and made strange sacrifices to the Other Gods and the crawling chaos Nyarlathotep, until one night an abomination of theirs reached the ears of earth's gods and they were banished to caverns below. Only a great trap door of stone with an iron ring connects the abyss of the earth-ghouls with the enchanted wood, and this the Gugs are afraid to open because of a curse. That a mortal dreamer could traverse their cavern realm and leave by that door is inconceivable; for mortal dreamers were their former food, and they have legends of the toothsomeness of such dreamers even though banishment has restricted their diet to the ghasts, those repulsive beings which die in the light, and which live in the vaults of Zin and leap on long hind legs like kangaroos.

So the ghoul that was Pickman advised Carter either to leave the abyss at Sarkomand, that deserted city in the valley below Leng where black nitrous stairways guarded by winged diorite lions lead down from dreamland to the lower gulfs, or to return through a churchyard to the waking world and begin the quest anew down the seventy steps of light slumber to the cavern of flame and the seven hundred steps to the Gate of Deeper Slumber and the enchanted wood. This, however, did not suit the seeker; for he knew nothing of the way from Leng to Ooth-Nargai, and was likewise reluctant to awake lest he forget all he had so far gained in this dream. It was disastrous to his quest to forget the august and celestial faces of those seamen from the north who traded onyx in Celephaïs, and who, being the sons of gods, must point the way to the cold waste and Kadath where the Great Ones dwell.

After much persuasion the ghoul consented to guide his guest inside the great wall of the Gugs' kingdom. There was one chance that Carter might be able to steal through that twilight realm of circular stone towers at an hour when the giants would be all gorged and snoring indoors, and reach the central tower with the sign of Koth upon it, which has the stairs leading up to that stone trap door in the enchanted wood. Pickman even consented to lend three ghouls to help with a tombstone lever in raising the stone door; for of ghouls the Gugs are somewhat afraid, and they often flee from their own colossal graveyards when they see them feasting there.

He also advised Carter to disguise as a ghoul himself; shaving the beard he had allowed to grow (for ghouls have none), wallowing naked in the mould to get the correct surface, and loping in the usual slumping way, with his clothing carried in a bundle as if it were a choice morsel from a tomb. They would reach the city of Gugs – which is coterminous with the whole kingdom – through the proper burrows, emerging in a cemetery not far from the stair-containing Tower of Koth. They must beware, however, of a large cave near the cemetery; for this is the mouth of the vaults of Zin, and the vindictive ghasts are always on watch there murderously for those denizens of the upper abyss who hunt and prey on them. The ghasts try to come out when the Gugs sleep and they attack ghouls as readily as Gugs, for they cannot discriminate. They are very primitive, and eat one another. The Gugs have a sentry at a narrow in the vaults of Zin, but he is often drowsy and is sometimes surprised by a party of ghasts. Though ghasts cannot live in real light, they can endure the grey twilight of the abyss for hours.

So at length Carter crawled through endless burrows with three helpful ghouls bearing the slate gravestone of Col. Nepemiah Derby, obit 1719, from the Charter Street Burying Ground in Salem. When they came again into open twilight they were in a forest of vast lichened monoliths reaching nearly as high as the eye could see and forming the modest gravestones of the Gugs. On the right of the hole out of which they wriggled, and seen through aisles of monoliths, was a stupendous vista of cyclopean round towers mounting up illimitable into the grey air of inner earth. This was the great city of the Gugs, whose doorways are thirty feet high. Ghouls come here often, for a buried Gug will feed a community for almost a year, and even with the added peril it is better to burrow for Gugs than to bother with the graves of men. Carter now understood the occasional titan bones he had felt beneath him in the vale of Pnoth.

Straight ahead, and just outside the cemetery, rose a sheer perpendicular cliff at whose base an immense and forbidding cavern yawned. This the ghouls told Carter to avoid as much as possible, since it was the entrance to the unhallowed vaults of Zin where Gugs hunt ghasts in the darkness. And truly, that warning was soon well justified; for the moment a ghoul began to creep toward the towers to see if the hour of the Gugs' resting had been rightly timed, there glowed in the gloom of that great cavern's mouth first one pair of yellowish-red eyes and then another, implying that the Gugs were one sentry less, and that ghasts have indeed an excellent sharpness of smell. So the ghoul returned to the burrow and motioned his companions to be silent. It was best to leave the ghasts to their own devices, and there was a possibility that they might soon withdraw, since they must naturally be rather tired after coping with a Gug sentry in the black vaults. After a moment something about the size of a small horse hopped out into the grey twilight, and Carter turned sick at the aspect of that scabrous and unwholesome beast, whose face is so curiously human despite the absence of a nose, a forehead, and other important particulars.

Presently three other ghasts hopped out to join their fellow, and a ghoul glibbered softly at Carter that their absence of battle-scars was a bad sign. It proved that they had not fought the Gug sentry at all, but had merely slipped past him as he slept, so that their strength and savagery were still unimpaired and would remain so till they had found and disposed of a victim. It was very unpleasant to see those filthy and disproportioned animals which soon numbered about fifteen, grubbing about and making their kangaroo leaps in the grey twilight where titan towers and monoliths arose, but it was still more unpleasant when they spoke among themselves in the coughing gutturals of ghasts. And yet, horrible as they were, they were not so horrible as what presently came out of the cave after them with disconcerting suddenness.

It was a paw, fully two feet and a half across, and equipped with formidable talons. After it came another paw, and after that a great black-furred arm to which both of the paws were attached by short forearms. Then two pink eyes shone, and the head of the awakened Gug sentry, large as a barrel, wobbled into view. The eyes jutted two inches from each side, shaded by bony protuberances overgrown with coarse hairs. But the head was chiefly terrible because of the mouth. That mouth had great yellow fangs and ran from the top to the bottom of the head, opening vertically instead of horizontally.

But before that unfortunate Gug could emerge from the cave and rise to his full twenty feet, the vindictive ghasts were upon him. Carter feared for a moment that he would give an alarm and arouse all his kin, till a ghoul softly glibbered that Gugs have no voice but talk by means of facial expression. The battle which then ensued was truly a frightful one. From all sides the venomous ghasts rushed feverishly at the creeping Gug, nipping and tearing with their muzzles, and mauling murderously with their hard pointed hooves. All the time they coughed excitedly, screaming when the great vertical mouth of the Gug would occasionally bite into one of their number, so that the noise of the combat would surely have aroused the sleeping city had not the weakening of the sentry begun to transfer the action farther and farther within the cavern. As it was, the tumult soon receded altogether from sight in the blackness, with only occasional evil echoes to mark its continuance.

Then the most alert of the ghouls gave the signal for all to advance, and Carter followed the loping three out of the forest of monoliths and into the dark noisome streets of that awful city whose rounded towers of cyclopean stone soared up beyond the sight. Silently they shambled over that rough rock pavement, hearing with disgust the abominable muffled snortings from great black doorways which marked the slumber of the Gugs. Apprehensive of the ending of the rest hour, the ghouls set a somewhat rapid pace; but even so the journey was no brief one, for distances in that town of giants are on a great scale. At last, however, they came to a somewhat open space before a tower even vaster than the rest; above whose colossal doorway was fixed a monstrous symbol in bas-relief which made one shudder without knowing its meaning. This was the central tower with the sign of Koth, and those huge stone steps just visible through the dusk within were the beginning of the great flight leading to upper dreamland and the enchanted wood.

There now began a climb of interminable length in utter blackness: made almost impossible by the monstrous size of the steps, which were fashioned for Gugs, and were therefore nearly a yard high. Of their number Carter could form no just estimate, for he soon became so worn out that the tireless and elastic ghouls were forced to aid him. All through the endless climb there lurked the peril of detection and pursuit; for though no Gug dares lift the stone door to the forest because of the Great One's curse, there are no such restraints concerning the tower and the steps, and escaped ghasts are often chased, even to the very top. So sharp are the ears of Gugs, that the bare feet and hands of the climbers might readily be heard when the city awoke; and it would of course take but little time for the striding giants, accustomed from their ghast-hunts in the vaults of Zin to seeing without light, to overtake their smaller and slower quarry on those cyclopean steps. It was very depressing to reflect that the silent pursuing Gugs would not be heard at all, but would come very suddenly and shockingly in the dark upon the climbers. Nor could the traditional fear of Gugs for ghouls be depended upon in that peculiar place where the advantages lay so heavily with the Gugs. There was also some peril from the furtive and venomous ghasts, which frequently hopped up onto the tower during the sleep hour of the Gugs. If the Gugs slept long, and the ghasts returned soon from their deed in the cavern, the scent of the climbers might easily be picked up by those loathsome and ill-disposed things; in which case it would almost be better to be eaten by a Gug.

Then, after aeons of climbing, there came a cough from the darkness above; and matters assumed a very grave and unexpected turn. It was clear that a ghast, or perhaps even more, had strayed into that tower before the coming of Carter and his guides; and it was equally clear that this peril was very close. After a breathless second the leading ghoul pushed Carter to the wall and arranged his kinfolk in the best possible way, with the old slate tombstone raised for a crushing blow whenever the enemy might come in sight. Ghouls can see in the dark, so the party was not as badly off as Carter would have been alone. In another moment the clatter of hooves revealed the downward hopping of at least one beast, and the slab-bearing ghouls poised their weapon for a desperate blow. Presently two yellowish-red eyes flashed into view, and the panting of the ghast became audible above its clattering. As it hopped down to the step above the ghouls, they wielded the ancient gravestone with prodigious force, so that there was only a wheeze and a choking before the victim collapsed in a noxious heap. There seemed to be only this one animal, and after a moment of listening the ghouls tapped Carter as a signal to proceed again. As before, they were obliged to aid him; and he was glad to leave that place of carnage where the ghast's uncouth remains sprawled invisible in the blackness.

At last the ghouls brought their companion to a halt; and feeling above him, Carter realised that the great stone trap door was reached at last. To open so vast a thing completely was not to be thought of, but the ghouls hoped to get it up just enough to slip the gravestone under as a prop, and permit Carter to escape through the crack. They themselves planned to descend again and return through the city of the Gugs, since their elusiveness was great, and they did not know the way overland to spectral Sarkomand with its lion-guarded gate to the abyss.

Mighty was the straining of those three ghouls at the stone of the door above them, and Carter helped push with as much strength as he had. They judged the edge next the top of the staircase to be the right one, and to this they bent all the force of their disreputably nourished muscles. After a few moments a crack of light appeared; and Carter, to whom that task had been entrusted, slipped the end of the old gravestone in the aperture. There now ensued a mighty heaving; but progress was very slow, and they had of course to return to their first position every time they failed to turn the slab and prop the portal open.

Suddenly their desperation was magnified a thousand fold by a sound on the steps below them. It was only the thumping and rattling of the slain ghast's hooved body as it rolled down to lower levels; but of all the possible causes of that body's dislodgement and rolling, none was in the least reassuring. Therefore, knowing the ways of Gugs, the ghouls set to with something of a frenzy; and in a surprisingly short time had the door so high that they were able to hold it still whilst Carter turned the slab and left a generous opening. They now helped Carter through, letting him climb up to their rubbery shoulders and later guiding his feet as he clutched at the blessed soil of the upper dreamland outside. Another second and they were through themselves, knocking away the gravestone and closing the great trap-door while a panting became audible beneath. Because of the Great One's curse no Gug might ever emerge from that portal, so with a deep relief and sense of repose Carter lay quietly on the thick grotesque fungi of the enchanted wood while his guides squatted near in the manner that ghouls rest.

Weird as was that enchanted wood through which he had fared so long ago, it was verily a haven and a delight after those gulfs he had now left behind. There was no living denizen about, for Zoogs shun the mysterious door in fear and Carter at once consulted with his ghouls about their future course. To return through the tower they no longer dared, and the waking world did not appeal to them when they learned that they must pass the priests Nasht and Kaman-Thah in the cavern of flame. So at length they decided to return through Sarkomand and its gate of the abyss, though of how to get there they knew nothing. Carter recalled that it lies in the valley below Leng, and recalled likewise that he had seen in Dylath-Leen a sinister, slant-eyed old merchant reputed to trade on Leng, therefore he advised the ghouls to seek out Dylath-Leen, crossing the fields to Nir and the Skai and following the river to its mouth. This they at once resolved to do, and lost no time in loping off, since the thickening of the dusk promised a full night ahead for travel. And Carter shook the paws of those repulsive beasts, thanking them for their help and sending his gratitude to the beast which once was Pickman; but could not help sighing with pleasure when they left. For a ghoul is a ghoul, and at best an unpleasant companion for man. After that Carter sought a forest pool and cleansed himself of the mud of nether earth, thereupon reassuming the clothes he had so carefully carried.

It was now night in that redoubtable wood of monstrous trees, but because of the phosphorescence one might travel as well as by day; wherefore Carter set out upon the well-known route toward Celephaïs, in Ooth-Nargai beyond the Tanarian Hills. And as he went he thought of the zebra he had left tethered to an ash-tree on Ngranek in far-away Oriab so many aeons ago, and wondered if any lava-gatherers had fed and released it. And he wondered, too, if he would ever return to Baharna and pay for the zebra that was slain by night in those ancient ruins by Yath's shore, and if the old tavern-keeper would remember him. Such were the thoughts that came to him in the air of the regained upper dreamland.

But presently his progress was halted by a sound from a very large hollow tree. He had avoided the great circle of stones, since he did not care to speak with Zoogs just now; but it appeared from the singular fluttering in that huge tree that important councils were in session elsewhere. Upon drawing nearer he made out the accents of a tense and heated discussion; and before long became conscious of matters which he viewed with the greatest concern. For a war on the cats was under debate in that sovereign assembly of Zoogs. It all came from the loss of the party which had sneaked after Carter to Ulthar, and which the cats had justly punished for unsuitable intentions. The matter had long rankled; and now, or at least within a month, the marshalled Zoogs were about to strike the whole feline tribe in a series of surprise attacks, taking individual cats or groups of cats unawares, and giving not even the myriad cats of Ulthar a proper chance to drill and mobilise. This was the plan of the Zoogs, and Carter saw that he must foil it before leaving upon his mighty quest.

Very quietly therefore did Randolph Carter steal to the edge of the wood and send the cry of the cat over the starlit fields. And a great grimalkin in a nearby cottage took up the burden and relayed it across leagues of rolling meadow to warriors large and small, black, grey, tiger, white, yellow, and mixed, and it echoed through Nir and beyond the Skai even into Ulthar, and Ulthar's numerous cats called in chorus and fell into a line of march. It was fortunate that the moon was not up, so that all the cats were on earth. Swiftly and silently leaping, they sprang from every hearth and housetop and poured in a great furry sea across the plains to the edge of the wood. Carter was there to greet them, and the sight of shapely, wholesome cats was indeed good for his eyes after the things he had seen and walked with in the abyss. He was glad to see his venerable friend and one-time rescuer at the head of Ulthar's detachment, a collar of rank around his sleek neck, and whiskers bristling at a martial angle. Better still, as a sub-lieutenant in that army was a brisk young fellow who proved to be none other than the very little kitten at the inn to whom Carter had given a saucer of rich cream on that long-vanished morning in Ulthar. He was a strapping and promising cat now, and purred as he shook hands with his friend. His grandfather said he was doing very well in the army, and that he might well expect a captaincy after one more campaign.

Carter now outlined the peril of the cat tribe, and was rewarded by deep-throated purrs of gratitude from all sides. Consulting with the generals, he prepared a plan of instant action which involved marching at once upon the Zoog council and other known strongholds of Zoogs; forestalling their surprise attacks and forcing them to terms before the mobilization of their army of invasion. Thereupon without a moment's loss that great ocean of cats flooded the enchanted wood and surged around the council tree and the great stone circle. Flutterings rose to panic pitch as the enemy saw the newcomers and there was very little resistance among the furtive and curious brown Zoogs. They saw that they were beaten in advance, and turned from thoughts of vengeance to thoughts of present self-preservation.

Half the cats now seated themselves in a circular formation with the captured Zoogs in the centre, leaving open a lane down which were marched the additional captives rounded up by the other cats in other parts of the wood. Terms were discussed at length, Carter acting as interpreter, and it was decided that the Zoogs might remain a free tribe on condition of rendering to the cats a large tribute of grouse, quail, and pheasants from the less fabulous parts of the forest. Twelve young Zoogs of noble families were taken as hostages to be kept in the Temple of Cats at Ulthar, and the victors made it plain that any disappearances of cats on the borders of the Zoog domain would be followed by consequences highly disastrous to Zoogs. These matters disposed of, the assembled cats broke ranks and permitted the Zoogs to slink off one by one to their respective homes, which they hastened to do with many a sullen backward glance.

The old cat general now offered Carter an escort through the forest to whatever border he wished to reach, deeming it likely that the Zoogs would harbour dire resentment against him for the frustration of their warlike enterprise. This offer he welcomed with gratitude; not only for the safety it afforded, but because he liked the graceful companionship of cats. So in the midst of a pleasant and playful regiment, relaxed after the successful performance of its duty, Randolph Carter walked with dignity through that enchanted and phosphorescent wood of titan trees, talking of his quest with the old general and his grandson whilst others of the band indulged in fantastic gambols or chased fallen leaves that the wind drove among the fungi of that primeval floor. And the old cat said that he had heard much of unknown Kadath in the cold waste, but did not know where it was. As for the marvellous sunset city, he had not even heard of that, but would gladly relay to Carter anything he might later learn.

He gave the seeker some passwords of great value among the cats of dreamland, and commended him especially to the old chief of the cats in Celephaïs, whither he was bound. That old cat, already slightly known to Carter, was a dignified Maltese; and would prove highly influential in any transaction. It was dawn when they came to the proper edge of the wood, and Carter bade his friends a reluctant farewell. The young sub-lieutenant he had met as a small kitten would have followed him had not the old general forbidden it, but that austere patriarch insisted that the path of duty lay with the tribe and the army. So Carter set out alone over the golden fields that stretched mysterious beside a willow-fringed river, and the cats went back into the wood.

Well did the traveller know those garden lands that lie betwixt the wood and the Cerenerian Sea, and blithely did he follow the singing river Oukranos that marked his course. The sun rose higher over gentle slopes of grove and lawn, and heightened the colours of the thousand flowers that starred each knoll and dangle. A blessed haze lies upon all this region, wherein is held a little more of the sunlight than other places hold, and a little more of the summer's humming music of birds and bees; so that men walk through it as through a faery place, and feel greater joy and wonder than they ever afterward remember.

By noon Carter reached the jasper terraces of Kiran which slope down to the river's edge and bear that temple of loveliness wherein the King of Ilek-Vad comes from his far realm on the twilight sea once a year in a golden palanquin to pray to the god of Oukranos, who sang to him in youth when he dwelt in a cottage by its banks. All of jasper is that temple, and covering an acre of ground with its walls and courts, its seven pinnacled towers, and its inner shrine where the river enters through hidden channels and the god sings softly in the night. Many times the moon hears strange music as it shines on those courts and terraces and pinnacles, but whether that music be the song of the god or the chant of the cryptical priests, none but the King of Ilek-Vad may say; for only he had entered the temple or seen the priests. Now, in the drowsiness of day, that carven and delicate fane was silent, and Carter heard only the murmur of the great stream and the hum of the birds and bees as he walked onward under the enchanted sun.

All that afternoon the pilgrim wandered on through perfumed meadows and in the lee of gentle riverward hills bearing peaceful thatched cottages and the shrines of amiable gods carven from jasper or chrysoberyl. Sometimes he walked close to the bank of Oukranos and whistled to the sprightly and iridescent fish of that crystal stream, and at other times he paused amidst the whispering rushes and gazed at the great dark wood on the farther side, whose trees came down clear to the water's edge. In former dreams he had seen quaint lumbering buopoths come shyly out of that wood to drink, but now he could not glimpse any. Once in a while he paused to watch a carnivorous fish catch a fishing bird, which it lured to the water by showing its tempting scales in the sun, and grasped by the beak with its enormous mouth as the winged hunter sought to dart down upon it.

Toward evening he mounted a low grassy rise and saw before him flaming in the sunset the thousand gilded spires of Thran. Lofty beyond belief are the alabaster walls of that incredible city, sloping inward toward the top and wrought in one solid piece by what means no man knows, for they are more ancient than memory. Yet lofty as they are with their hundred gates and two hundred turrets, the clustered towers within, all white beneath their golden spires, are loftier still; so that men on the plain around see them soaring into the sky, sometimes shining clear, sometimes caught at the top in tangles of cloud and mist, and sometimes clouded lower down with their utmost pinnacles blazing free above the vapours. And where Thran's gates open on the river are great wharves of marble, with ornate galleons of fragrant cedar and calamander riding gently at anchor, and strange bearded sailors sitting on casks and bales with the hieroglyphs of far places. Landward beyond the walls lies the farm country, where small white cottages dream between little hills, and narrow roads with many stone bridges wind gracefully among streams and gardens.

Down through this verdant land Carter walked at evening, and saw twilight float up from the river to the marvellous golden spires of Thran. And just at the hour of dusk he came to the southern gate, and was stopped by a red-robed sentry till he had told three dreams beyond belief, and proved himself a dreamer worthy to walk up Thran's steep mysterious streets and linger in the bazaars where the wares of the ornate galleons were sold. Then into that incredible city he walked; through a wall so thick that the gate was a tunnel, and thereafter amidst curved and undulant ways winding deep and narrow between the heavenward towers. Lights shone through grated and balconied windows, and,the sound of lutes and pipes stole timid from inner courts where marble fountains bubbled. Carter knew his way, and edged down through darker streets to the river, where at an old sea tavern he found the captains and seamen he had known in myriad other dreams. There he bought his passage to Celephaïs on a great green galleon, and there he stopped for the night after speaking gravely to the venerable cat of that inn, who blinked dozing before an enormous hearth and dreamed of old wars and forgotten gods.

In the morning Carter boarded the galleon bound for Celephaïs, and sat in the prow as the ropes were cast off and the long sail down to the Cerenerian Sea began. For many leagues the banks were much as they were above Thran, with now and then a curious temple rising on the farther hills toward the right, and a drowsy village on the shore, with steep red roofs and nets spread in the sun. Mindful of his search, Carter questioned all the mariners closely about those whom they had met in the taverns of Celephaïs, asking the names and ways of the strange men with long, narrow eyes, long-lobed ears, thin noses, and pointed chins who came in dark ships from the north and traded onyx for the carved jade and spun gold and little red singing birds of Celephaïs. Of these men the sailors knew not much, save that they talked but seldom and spread a kind of awe about them.

Their land, very far away, was called Inquanok, and not many people cared to go thither because it was a cold twilight land, and said to be close to unpleasant Leng; although high impassable mountains towered on the side where Leng was thought to lie, so that none might say whether this evil plateau with its horrible stone villages and unmentionable monastery were really there, or whether the rumour were only a fear that timid people felt in the night when those formidable barrier peaks loomed black against a rising moon. Certainly, men reached Leng from very different oceans. Of other boundaries of Inquanok those sailors had no notion, nor had they heard of the cold waste and unknown Kadath save from vague unplaced report. And of the marvellous sunset city which Carter sought they knew nothing at all. So the traveller asked no more of far things, but bided his time till he might talk with those strange men from cold and twilight Inquanok who are the seed of such gods as carved their features on Ngranek.

Late in the day the galleon reached those bends of the river which traverse the perfumed jungles of Kled. Here Carter wished he might disembark, for in those tropic tangles sleep wondrous palaces of ivory, lone and unbroken, where once dwelt fabulous monarchs of a land whose name is forgotten. Spells of the Elder Ones keep those places unharmed and undecayed, for it is written that there may one day be need of them again; and elephant caravans have glimpsed them from afar by moonlight, though none dares approach them closely because of the guardians to which their wholeness is due. But the ship swept on, and dusk hushed the hum of the day, and the first stars above blinked answers to the early fireflies on the banks as that jungle fell far behind, leaving only its fragrance as a memory that it had been. And all through the night that galleon floated on past mysteries unseen and unsuspected. Once a lookout reported fires on the hills to the east, but the sleepy captain said they had better not be looked at too much, since it was highly uncertain just who or what had lit them.

In the morning the river had broadened out greatly, and Carter saw by the houses along the banks that they were close to the vast trading city of Hlanith on the Cerenerian Sea. Here the walls are of rugged granite, and the houses peakedly fantastic with beamed and plastered gables. The men of Hlanith are more like those of the waking world than any others in dreamland; so that the city is not sought except for barter, but is prized for the solid work of its artisans. The wharves of Hlanith are of oak, and there the galleon made fast while the captain traded in the taverns. Carter also went ashore, and looked curiously upon the rutted streets where wooden ox-carts lumbered and feverish merchants cried their wares vacuously in the bazaars. The sea-taverns were all close to the wharves on cobbled lanes salted with the spray of high tides, and seemed exceedingly ancient with their low black-beamed ceilings and casements of greenish bull's-eye panes. Ancient sailors in those taverns talked much of distant ports, and told many stories of the curious men from twilight Inquanok, but had little to add to what the seamen of the galleon had told. Then at last, after much unloading and loading, the ship set sail once more over the sunset sea, and the high walls and gables of Hlanith grew less as the last golden light of day lent them a wonder and beauty beyond any that men had given them.

Two nights and two days the galleon sailed over the Cerenerian Sea, sighting no land and speaking but one other vessel. Then near sunset of the second day there loomed up ahead the snowy peak of Aran with its gingko-trees swaying on the lower slope, and Carter knew that they were come to the land of Ooth-Nargai and the marvellous city of Celephaïs. Swiftly there came into sight the glittering minarets of that fabulous town, and the untarnished marble walls with their bronze statues, and the great stone bridge where Naraxa joins the sea. Then rose the gentle hills behind the town, with their groves and gardens of asphodels and the small shrines and cottages upon them; and far in the background the purple ridge of the

Tanarians, potent and mystical, behind which lay forbidden ways into the waking world and toward other regions of dream.

The harbour was full of painted galleys, some of which were from the marble cloud-city of Serannian, that lies in ethereal space beyond where the sea meets the sky, and some of which were from more substantial parts of dreamland. Among these the steersman threaded his way up to the spice-fragrant wharves, where the galleon made fast in the dusk as the city's million lights began to twinkle out over the water. Ever new seemed this deathless city of vision, for here time has no power to tarnish or destroy. As it has always been is still the turquoise of Nath-Horthath, and the eighty orchid-wreathed priests are the same who builded it ten thousand years ago. Shining still is the bronze of the great gates, nor are the onyx pavements ever worn or broken. And the great bronze statues on the walls look down on merchants and camel drivers older than fable, yet without one grey hair in their forked beards.

Carter did not once seek out the temple or the palace or the citadel, but stayed by the seaward wall among traders and sailors. And when it was too late for rumours and legends he sought out an ancient tavern he knew well, and rested with dreams of the gods on unknown Kadath whom he sought. The next day he searched all along the quays for some of the strange mariners of Inquanok, but was told that none were now in port, their galley not being due from the north for full two weeks. He found, however, one Thorabonian sailor who had been to Inquanok and had worked in the onyx quarries of that twilight place; and this sailor said there was certainly a desert to the north of the peopled region, which everybody seemed to fear and shun. The Thorabonian opined that this desert led around the utmost rim of impassable peaks into Leng's horrible plateau, and that this was why men feared it; though he admitted there were other vague tales of evil presences and nameless sentinels. Whether or not this could be the fabled waste wherein unknown Kadath stands he did not know; but it seemed unlikely that those presences and sentinels, if indeed they existed, were stationed for naught.

On the following day Carter walked up the Street of the Pillars to the turquoise temple and talked with the High-Priest. Though Nath-Horthath is chiefly worshipped in Celephaïs, all the Great Ones are mentioned in diurnal prayers; and the priest was reasonably versed in their moods. Like Atal in distant Ulthar, he strongly advised against any attempts to see them; declaring that they are testy and capricious, and subject to strange protection from the mindless Other Gods from Outside, whose soul and messenger is the crawling chaos Nyarlathotep. Their jealous hiding of the marvellous sunset city shewed clearly that they did not wish Carter to reach it, and it was doubtful how they would regard a guest whose object was to see them and plead before them. No man had ever found Kadath in the past, and it might be just as well if none ever found it in the future. Such rumours as were told about that onyx castle of the Great Ones were not by any means reassuring.

Having thanked the orchid-crowned High-Priest, Carter left the temple and sought out the bazaar of the sheep-butchers, where the old chief of Celephaïs' cats dwelt sleek and contented. That grey and dignified being was sunning himself on the onyx pavement, and extended a languid paw as his caller approached. But when Carter repeated the passwords and introductions furnished him by the old cat general of Ulthar, the furry patriarch became very cordial and communicative; and told much of the secret lore known to cats on the seaward slopes of Ooth-Nargai. Best of all, he repeated several things told him furtively by the timid waterfront cats of Celephaïs about the men of Inquanok, on whose dark ships no cat will go.

It seems that these men have an aura not of earth about them, though that is not the reason why no cat will sail on their ships. The reason for this is that Inquanok holds shadows which no cat can endure, so that in all that cold twilight realm there is never a cheering purr or a homely mew. Whether it be because of things wafted over the impassable peaks from hypothetical Leng, or because of things filtering down from the chilly desert to the north, none may say; but it remains a fact that in that far land there broods a hint of outer space which cats do not like, and to which they are more sensitive than men. Therefore they will not go on the dark ships that seek the basalt quays of Inquanok.

The old chief of the cats also told him where to find his friend King Kuranes, who in Carter's latter dreams had reigned alternately in the rose-crystal Palace of the Seventy Delights at Celephaïs and in the turreted cloud-castle of sky-floating Serannian. It seemed that he could no more find content in those places, but had formed a mighty longing for the English cliffs and downlands of his boyhood; where in little dreaming villages England's old songs hover at evening behind lattice windows, and where grey church towers peep lovely through the verdure of distant valleys. He could not go back to these things in the waking world because his body was dead; but he had done the next best thing and dreamed a small tract of such countryside in the region east of the city where meadows roll gracefully up from the sea-cliffs to the foot of the Tanarian Hills. There he dwelt in a grey Gothic manor-house of stone looking on the sea, and tried to think it was ancient Trevor Towers, where he was born and where thirteen generations of his forefathers had first seen the light. And on the coast nearby he had built a little Cornish fishing village with steep cobbled ways, settling therein such people as had the most English faces, and seeking ever to teach them the dear remembered accents of old Cornwall fishers. And in a valley not far off he had reared a great Norman Abbey whose tower he could see from his window, placing around it in the churchyard grey stones with the names of his ancestors carved thereon, and with a moss somewhat like Old England's moss. For though Kuranes was a monarch in the land of dream, with all imagined pomps and marvels, splendours and beauties, ecstasies and delights, novelties and excitements at his command, he would gladly have resigned forever the whole of his power and luxury and freedom for one blessed day as a simple boy in that pure and quiet England, that ancient, beloved England which had moulded his being and of which he must always be immutably a part.

So when Carter bade that old grey chief of the cats adieu, he did not seek the terraced palace of rose crystal but walked out the eastern gate and across the daisied fields toward a peaked gable which he glimpsed through the oaks of a park sloping up to the sea-cliffs. And in time he came to a great hedge and a gate with a little brick lodge, and when he rang the bell there hobbled to admit him no robed and annointed lackey of the palace, but a small stubby old man in a smock who spoke as best he could in the quaint tones of far Cornwall. And Carter walked up the shady path between trees as near as possible to England's trees, and climbed the terraces among gardens set out as in Queen Anne's time. At the door, flanked by stone cats in the old way, he was met by a whiskered butler in suitable livery; and was presently taken to the library where Kuranes, Lord of Ooth-Nargai and the Sky around Serannian, sat pensive in a chair by the window looking on his little sea-coast village and wishing that his old nurse would come in and scold him because he was not ready for that hateful lawn-party at the vicar's, with the carriage waiting and his mother nearly out of patience.

Kuranes, clad in a dressing gown of the sort favoured by London tailors in his youth, rose eagerly to meet his guest; for the sight of an Anglo-Saxon from the waking world was very dear to him, even if it was a Saxon from Boston, Massachusetts, instead of from Cornwall. And for long they talked of old times, having much to say because both were old dreamers and well versed in the wonders of incredible places. Kuranes, indeed, had been out beyond the stars in the ultimate void, and was said to be the only one who had ever returned sane from such a voyage.

At length Carter brought up the subject of his quest, and asked of his host those questions he had asked of so many others. Kuranes did not know where Kadath was, or the marvellous sunset city; but he did know that the Great Ones were very dangerous creatures to seek out, and that the Other Gods had strange ways of protecting them from impertinent curiosity. He had learned much of the Other Gods in distant parts of space, especially in that region where form does not exist, and coloured gases study the innermost secrets. The violet gas S'ngac had told him terrible things of the crawling chaos Nyarlathotep, and had warned him never to approach the central void where the daemon sultan Azathoth gnaws hungrily in the dark. Altogether, it was not well to meddle with the Elder Ones; and if they persistently denied all access to the marvellous sunset city, it were better not to seek that city.

Kuranes furthermore doubted whether his guest would profit aught by coming to the city even were he to gain it. He himself had dreamed and yearned long years for lovely Celephaïs and the land of Ooth-Nargai, and for the freedom and colour and high experience of life devoid of its chains, and conventions, and stupidities. But now that he was come into that city and that land, and was the king thereof, he found the freedom and the vividness all too soon worn out, and monotonous for want of linkage with anything firm in his feelings and memories. He was a king in Ooth-Nargai, but found no meaning therein, and drooped always for the old familiar things of England that had shaped his youth. All his kingdom would he give for the sound of Cornish church bells over the downs, and all the thousand minarets of Celephaïs for the steep homely roofs of the village near his home. So he told his guest that the unknown sunset city might not hold quite that content he sought, and that perhaps it had better remain a glorious and half-remembered dream. For he had visited Carter often in the old waking days, and knew well the lovely New England slopes that had given him birth.

At the last, he was very certain, the seeker would long only for the early remembered scenes; the glow of Beacon Hill at evening, the tall steeples and winding hill streets of quaint Kingsport, the hoary gambrel roofs of ancient and witch-haunted Arkham, and the blessed meads and valleys where stone walls rambled and white farmhouse gables peeped out from bowers of verdure. These things he told Randolph Carter, but still the seeker held to his purpose. And in the end they parted each with his own conviction, and Carter went back through the bronze gate into Celephaïs and down the Street of Pillars to the old sea-wall, where he talked more with the mariners of far ports and waited for the dark ship from cold and twilight Inquanok, whose strange-faced sailors and onyx-traders had in them the blood of the Great Ones.

One starlit evening when the Pharos shone splendid over the harbour the longed-for ship put in, and strange-faced sailors and traders appeared one by one and group by group in the ancient taverns along the sea wall. It was very exciting to see again those living faces so like the godlike features of Ngranek, but Carter did not hasten to speak with the silent seamen. He did not know how much of pride and secrecy and dim supernal memory might fill those children of the Great Ones, and was sure it would not be wise to tell them of his quest or ask too closely of that cold desert stretching north of their twilight land. They talked little with the other folk in those ancient sea taverns; but would gather in groups in remote corners and sing among themselves the haunting airs of unknown places, or chant long tales to one another in accents alien to the rest of dreamland. And so rare and moving were those airs and tales that one might guess their wonders from the faces of those who listened, even though the words came to common ears only as strange cadence and obscure melody.

For a week the strange seamen lingered in the taverns and traded in the bazaars of Celephaïs, and before they sailed Carter had taken passage on their dark ship, telling them that he was an old onyx miner and wishful to work in their quarries. That ship was very lovely and cunningly wrought, being of teakwood with ebony fittings and traceries of gold, and the cabin in which the traveller lodged had hangings of silk and velvet. One morning at the turn of the tide the sails were raised and the anchor lifted, and as Carter stood on the high stern he saw the sunrise-blazing walls and bronze statues and golden minarets of ageless Celephaïs sink into the distance, and the snowy peak of Mount Man grow smaller and smaller. By noon there was nothing in sight save the gentle blue of the Cerenerian Sea, with one painted galley afar off bound for that realm of Serannian where the sea meets the sky.

And the night came with gorgeous stars, and the dark ship steered for Charles' Wain and the Little Bear as they swung slowly round the pole. And the sailors sang strange songs of unknown places, and they stole off one by one to the forecastle while the wistful watchers murmured old chants and leaned over the rail to glimpse the luminous fish playing in bowers beneath the sea. Carter went to sleep at midnight, and rose in the glow of a young morning, marking that the sun seemed farther south than was its wont. And all through that second day he made progress in knowing the men of the ship, getting them little by little to talk of their cold twilight land, of their exquisite onyx city, and of their fear of the high and impassable peaks beyond which Leng was said to be. They told him how sorry they were that no cats would stay in the land of Inquanok, and how they thought the hidden nearness of Leng was to blame for it. Only of the stony desert to the north they would not talk. There was something disquieting about that desert, and it was thought expedient not to admit its existence.

On later days they talked of the quarries in which Carter said he was going to work. There were many of them, for all the city of Inquanok was builded of onyx, whilst great polished blocks of it were traded in Rinar, Ogrothan, and Celephaïs and at home with the merchants of Thraa, Ilarnek, and Kadatheron, for the beautiful wares of those fabulous ports. And far to the north, almost in the cold desert whose existence the men of Inquanok did not care to admit, there was an unused quarry greater than all the rest; from which had been hewn in forgotten times such prodigious lumps and blocks that the sight of their chiselled vacancies struck terror to all who beheld. Who had mined those incredible blocks, and whither they had been transported, no man might say; but it was thought best not to trouble that quarry, around which such inhuman memories might conceivably cling. So it was left all alone in the twilight, with only the raven and the rumoured Shantak-bird to brood on its immensities. When Carter heard of this quarry he was moved to deep thought, for he knew from old tales that the Great Ones' castle atop unknown Kadath is of onyx.

Each day the sun wheeled lower and lower in the sky, and the mists overhead grew thicker and thicker. And in two weeks there was not any sunlight at all, but only a weird grey twilight shining through a dome of eternal cloud by day, and a cold starless phosphorescence from the under side of that cloud by night. On the twentieth day a great jagged rock in the sea was sighted from afar, the first land glimpsed since Aran's snowy peak had dwindled behind the ship. Carter asked the captain the name of that rock, but was told that it had no name and had never been sought by any vessel because of the sounds that came from it at night. And when, after dark, a dull and ceaseless howling arose from that jagged granite place, the traveller was glad that no stop had been made, and that the rock had no name. The seamen prayed and chanted till the noise was out of earshot, and Carter dreamed terrible dreams within dreams in the small hours.

Two mornings after that there loomed far ahead and to the east a line of great grey peaks whose tops were lost in the changeless clouds of that twilight world. And at the sight of them the sailors sang glad songs, and some knelt down on the deck to pray, so that Carter knew they were come to the land of Inquanok and would soon be moored to the basalt quays of the great town bearing that land's name. Toward noon a dark coastline appeared, and before three o'clock there stood out against the north the bulbous domes and fantastic spires of the onyx city. Rare and curious did that archaic city rise above its walls and quays, all of delicate black with scrolls, flutings, and arabesques of inlaid gold. Tall and many-windowed were the houses, and carved on every side with flowers and patterns whose dark symmetries dazzled the eye with a beauty more poignant than light. Some ended in swelling domes that tapered to a point, others in terraced pyramids whereon rose clustered minarets displaying every phase of strangeness and imagination. The walls were low, and pierced by frequent gates, each under a great arch rising high above the general level and capped by the head of a god chiselled with that same skill displayed in the monstrous face on distant Ngranek. On a hill in the centre rose a sixteen-angled tower greater than all the rest and bearing a high pinnacled belfry resting on a flattened dome. This, the seamen said, was the Temple of the Elder Ones, and was ruled by an old High-Priest sad with inner secrets.

At intervals the clang of a strange bell shivered over the onyx city, answered each time by a peal of mystic music made up of horns, viols, and chanting voices. And from a row of tripods on a gallery round the high dome of the temple there burst flares of flame at certain moments; for the priests and people of that city were wise in the primal mysteries, and faithful in keeping the rhythms of the Great Ones as set forth in scrolls older than the Pnakotic Manuscripts. As the ship rode past the great basalt breakwater into the harbour the lesser noises of the city grew manifest, and Carter saw the slaves, sailors, and merchants on the docks. The sailors and merchants were of the strange-faced race of the gods, but the slaves were squat, slant-eyed folk said by rumour to have drifted somehow across or around the impassable peaks from the valleys beyond Leng. The wharves reached wide outside the city wall and bore upon them all manner of merchandise from the galleys anchored there, while at one end were great piles of onyx both carved and uncarved awaiting shipment to the far markets of Rinar, Ograthan and Celephaïs.

It was not yet evening when the dark ship anchored beside a jutting quay of stone, and all the sailors and traders filed ashore and through the arched gate into the city. The streets of that city were paved with onyx and some of them were wide and straight whilst others were crooked and narrow. The houses near the water were lower than the rest, and bore above their curiously arched doorways certain signs of gold said to be in honour of the respective small gods that favoured each. The captain of the ship took Carter to an old sea tavern where flocked the mariners of quaint countries, and promised that he would next day shew him the wonders of the twilight city, and lead him to the taverns of the onyx-miners by the northern wall. And evening fell, and little bronze lamps were lighted, and the sailors in that tavern sang songs of remote places. But when from its high tower the great bell shivered over the city, and the peal of the horns and viols and voices rose cryptical in answer thereto, all ceased their songs or tales and bowed silent till the last echo died away. For there is a wonder and a strangeness on the twilight city of Inquanok, and men fear to be lax in its rites lest a doom and a vengeance lurk unsuspectedly close.

Far in the shadows of that tavern Carter saw a squat form he did not like, for it was unmistakably that of the old slant-eyed merchant he had seen so long before in the taverns of Dylath-Leen, who was reputed to trade with the horrible stone villages of Leng which no healthy folk visit and whose evil fires are seen at night from afar, and even to have dealt with that High-Priest Not To Be Described, which wears a yellow silken mask over its face and dwells all alone in a prehistoric stone monastery. This man had seemed to shew a queer gleam of knowing when Carter asked the traders of Dylath-Leen about the cold waste and Kadath; and somehow his presence in dark and haunted Inquanok, so close to the wonders of the north, was not a reassuring thing. He slipped wholly out of sight before Carter could speak to him, and sailors later said that he had come with a yak caravan from some point not well determined, bearing the colossal and rich-flavoured eggs of the rumoured Shantak-bird to trade for the dextrous jade goblets that merchants brought from Ilarnek.

On the following morning the ship-captain led Carter through the onyx streets of Inquanok, dark under their twilight sky. The inlaid doors and figured house-fronts, carven balconies and crystal-paned oriels all gleamed with a sombre and polished loveliness; and now and then a plaza would open out with black pillars, colonnades, and the statues of curious beings both human and fabulous. Some of the vistas down long and unbending streets, or through side alleys and over bulbous domes, spires, and arabesqued roofs, were weird and beautiful beyond words; and nothing was more splendid than the massive heights of the great central Temple of the Elder Ones with its sixteen carven sides, its flattened dome, and its lofty pinnacled belfry, overtopping all else, and majestic whatever its foreground. And always to the east, far beyond the city walls and the leagues of pasture land, rose the gaunt grey sides of those topless and impassable peaks across which hideous Leng was said to lie.

The captain took Carter to the mighty temple, which is set with its walled garden in a great round plaza whence the streets go as spokes from a wheel's hub. The seven arched gates of that garden, each having over it a carven face like those on the city's gates, are always open, and the people roam reverently at will down the tiled paths and through the little lanes lined with grotesque termini and the shrines of modest gods. And there are fountains, pools, and basins there to reflect the frequent blaze of the tripods on the high balcony, all of onyx and having in them small luminous fish taken by divers from the lower bowers of ocean. When the deep clang from the temple belfry shivers over the garden and the city, and the answer of the horns and viols and voices peals out from the seven lodges by the garden gates, there issue from the seven doors of the temple long columns of masked and hooded priests in black, bearing at arm's length before them great golden bowls from which a curious steam rises. And all the seven columns strut peculiarly in single file, legs thrown far forward without bending the knees, down the walks that lead to the seven lodges, wherein they disappear and do not appear again. It is said that subterrene paths connect the lodges with the temple, and that the long files of priests return through them; nor is it unwhispered that deep flights of onyx steps go down to mysteries that are never told. But only a few are those who hint that the priests in the masked and hooded columns are not human beings.

Carter did not enter the temple, because none but the Veiled King is permitted to do that. But before he left the garden the hour of the bell came, and he heard the shivering clang deafeningly above him, and the wailing of the horns and viols and voices loud from the lodges by the gates. And down the seven great walks stalked the long files of bowl-bearing priests in their singular way, giving to the traveller a fear which human priests do not often give. When the last of them had vanished he left that garden, noting as he did so a spot on the pavement over which the bowls had passed. Even the ship-captain did not like that spot, and hurried him on toward the hill whereon the Veiled King's palace rises many-domed and marvellous.

The ways to the onyx palace are steep and narrow, all but the broad curving one where the king and his companions ride on yaks or in yak-drawn chariots. Carter and his guide climbed up an alley that was all steps, between inlaid walls bearing strange signs in gold, and under balconies and oriels whence sometimes floated soft strains of music or breaths of exotic fragrance. Always ahead loomed those titan walls, mighty buttresses, and clustered and bulbous domes for which the Veiled King's palace is famous; and at length they passed under a great black arch and emerged in the gardens of the monarch's pleasure. There Carter paused in faintness at so much beauty, for the onyx terraces and colonnaded walks, the gay parterres and delicate flowering trees espaliered to golden lattices, the brazen urns and tripods with cunning bas-reliefs, the pedestalled and almost breathing statues of veined black marble, the basalt-bottomed lagoon's tiled fountains with luminous fish, the tiny temples of iridescent singing birds atop carven columns, the marvellous scrollwork of the great bronze gates, and the blossoming vines trained along every inch of the polished walls all joined to form a sight whose loveliness was beyond reality, and half-fabulous even in the land of dreams. There it shimmered like a vision under that grey twilight sky, with the domed and fretted magnificence of the palace ahead, and the fantastic silhouette of the distant impassable peaks on the right. And ever the small birds and the fountains sang, while the perfume of rare blossoms spread like a veil over that incredible garden. No other human presence was there, and Carter was glad it was so. Then they turned and descended again the onyx alley of steps, for the palace itself no visitor may enter; and it is not well to look too long and steadily at the great central dome, since it is said to house the archaic father of all the rumoured Shantak-birds, and to send out queer dreams to the curious.

After that the captain took Carter to the north quarter of the town, near the Gate of the Caravans, where are the taverns of the yak-merchants and the onyx-miners. And there, in a low-ceiled inn of quarrymen, they said farewell; for business called the captain whilst Carter was eager to talk with miners about the north. There were many men in that inn, and the traveller was not long in speaking to some of them; saying that he was an old miner of onyx, and anxious to know somewhat of Inquanok's quarries. But all that he learned was not much more than he knew before, for the miners were timid and evasive about the cold desert to the north and the quarry that no man visits. They had fears of fabled emissaries from around the mountains where Leng is said to lie, and of evil presences and nameless sentinels far north among the scattered rocks. And they whispered also that the rumoured Shantak-birds are no wholesome things; it being indeed for the best that no man has ever truly seen one (for that fabled father of Shantaks in the king's dome is fed in the dark).

The next day, saying that he wished to look over all the various mines for himself and to visit the scattered farms and quaint onyx villages of Inquanok, Carter hired a yak and stuffed great leathern saddle-bags for a journey. Beyond the Gate of the Caravans the road lay straight betwixt tilled fields, with many odd farmhouses crowned by low domes. At some of these houses the seeker stopped to ask questions; once finding a host so austere and reticent, and so full of an unplaced majesty like to that in the huge features on Ngranek, that he felt certain he had come at last upon one of the Great Ones themselves, or upon one with full nine-tenths of their blood, dwelling amongst men. And to that austere and reticent cotter he was careful to speak very well of the gods, and to praise all the blessings they had ever accorded him.

That night Carter camped in a roadside meadow beneath a great lygath-tree to which he tied his yak, and in the morning resumed his northward pilgrimage. At about ten o'clock he reached the small-domed village of Urg, where traders rest and miners tell their tales, and paused in its taverns till noon. It is here that the great caravan road turns west toward Selarn, but Carter kept on north by the quarry road. All the afternoon he followed that rising road, which was somewhat narrower than the great highway, and which now led through a region with more rocks than tilled fields. And by evening the low hills on his left had risen into sizable black cliffs, so that he knew he was close to the mining country. All the while the great gaunt sides of the impassable mountains towered afar off at his right, and the farther he went, the worse tales he heard of them from the scattered farmers and traders and drivers of lumbering onyx-carts along the way.

On the second night he camped in the shadow of a large black crag, tethering his yak to a stake driven in the ground. He observed the greater phosphorescence of the clouds at this northerly point, and more than once thought he saw dark shapes outlined against them. And on the third morning he came in sight of the first onyx quarry, and greeted the men who there laboured with picks and chisels. Before evening he had passed eleven quarries; the land being here given over altogether to onyx cliffs and boulders, with no vegetation at all, but only great rocky fragments scattered about a floor of black earth, with the grey impassable peaks always rising gaunt and sinister on his right. The third night he spent in a camp of quarry men whose flickering fires cast weird reflections on the polished cliffs to the west. And they sang many songs and told many tales, shewing such strange knowledge of the olden days and the habits of gods that Carter could see they held many latent memories of their sires the Great Ones. They asked him whither he went, and cautioned him not to go too far to the north; but he replied that he was seeking new cliffs of onyx, and would take no more risks than were common among prospectors. In the morning he bade them adieu and rode on into the darkening north, where they had warned him he would find the feared and unvisited quarry whence hands older than men's hands had wrenched prodigious blocks. But he did not like it when, turning back to wave a last farewell, he thought he saw approaching the camp that squat and evasive old merchant with slanting eyes, whose conjectured traffick with Leng was the gossip of distant Dylath-Leen.

After two more quarries the inhabited part of Inquanok seemed to end, and the road narrowed to a steeply rising yak-path among forbidding black cliffs. Always on the right towered the gaunt and distant peaks, and as Carter climbed farther and farther into this untraversed realm he found it grew darker and colder. Soon he perceived that there were no prints of feet or hooves on the black path beneath, and realised that he was indeed come into strange and deserted ways of elder time. Once in a while a raven would croak far overhead, and now and then a flapping behind some vast rock would make him think uncomfortably of the rumoured Shantak-bird. But in the main he was alone with his shaggy steed, and it troubled him to observe that this excellent yak became more and more reluctant to advance, and more and more disposed to snort affrightedly at any small noise along the route.

The path now contracted between sable and glistening walls, and began to display an even greater steepness than before. It was a bad footing, and the yak often slipped on the stony fragments strewn thickly about. In two hours Carter saw ahead a definite crest, beyond which was nothing but dull grey sky, and blessed the prospect of a level or downward course. To reach this crest, however, was no easy task; for the way had grown nearly perpendicular, and was perilous with loose black gravel and small stones. Eventually Carter dismounted and led his dubious yak; pulling very hard when the animal balked or stumbled, and keeping his own footing as best he might. Then suddenly he came to the top and saw beyond, and gasped at what he saw.

The path indeed led straight ahead and slightly down, with the same lines of high natural walls as before; but on the left hand there opened out a monstrous space, vast acres in extent, where some archaic power had riven and rent the native cliffs of onyx in the form of a giant's quarry. Far back into the solid precipice ran that cyclopean gouge, and deep down within earth's bowels its lower delvings yawned. It was no quarry of man, and the concave sides were scarred with great squares, yards wide, which told of the size of the blocks once hewn by nameless hands and chisels. High over its jagged rim huge ravens flapped and croaked, and vague whirrings in the unseen depths told of bats or urhags or less mentionable presences haunting the endless blackness. There Carter stood in the narrow way amidst the twilight with the rocky path sloping down before him; tall onyx cliffs on his right that led on as far as he could see and tall cliffs on the left chopped off just ahead to make that terrible and unearthly quarry.

All at once the yak uttered a cry and burst from his control, leaping past him and darting on in a panic till it vanished down the narrow slope toward the north. Stones kicked by its flying hooves fell over the brink of the quarry and lost themselves in the dark without any sound of striking bottom; but Carter ignored the perils of that scanty path as he raced breathlessly after the flying steed. Soon the left-hand cliffs resumed their course, making the way once more a narrow lane; and still the traveller leaped on after the yak whose great wide prints told of its desperate flight.

Once he thought he heard the hoofbeats of the frightened beast, and doubled his speed from this encouragement. He was covering miles, and little by little the way was broadening in front till he knew he must soon emerge on the cold and dreaded desert to the north. The gaunt grey flanks of the distant impassable peaks were again visible above the right-hand crags, and ahead were the rocks and boulders of an open space which was clearly a foretaste of the dark and limitless plain. And once more those hoofbeats sounded in his ears, plainer than before, but this time giving terror instead of encouragement because he realised that they were not the frightened hoofbeats of his fleeing yak. The beats were ruthless and purposeful, and they were behind him.

Carter's pursuit of the yak became now a flight from an unseen thing, for though he dared not glance over his shoulder he felt that the presence behind him could be nothing wholesome or mentionable. His yak must have heard or felt it first, and he did not like to ask himself whether it had followed him from the haunts of men or had floundered up out of that black quarry pit. Meanwhile the cliffs had been left behind, so that the oncoming night fell over a great waste of sand and spectral rocks wherein all paths were lost. He could not see the hoofprints of his yak, but always from behind him there came that detestable clopping; mingled now and then with what he fancied were titanic flappings and whirrings. That he was losing ground seemed unhappily clear to him, and he knew he was hopelessly lost in this broken and blasted desert of meaningless rocks and untravelled sands. Only those remote and impassable peaks on the right gave him any sense of direction, and even they were less clear as the grey twilight waned and the sickly phosphorescence of the clouds took its place.

Then dim and misty in the darkling north before him he glimpsed a terrible thing. He had thought it for some moments a range of black mountains, but now he saw it was something more. The phosphorescence of the brooding clouds shewed it plainly, and even silhouetted parts of it as vapours glowed behind. How distant it was he could not tell, but it must have been very far. It was thousands of feet high, stretching in a great concave arc from the grey impassable peaks to the unimagined westward spaces, and had once indeed been a ridge of mighty onyx hills. But now these hills were hills no more, for some hand greater than man's had touched them. Silent they squatted there atop the world like wolves or ghouls, crowned with clouds and mists and guarding the secrets of the north forever. All in a great half circle they squatted, those dog-like mountains carven into monstrous watching statues, and their right hands were raised in menace against mankind.

It was only the flickering light of the clouds that made their mitred double heads seem to move, but as Carter stumbled on he saw arise from their shadowy caps great forms whose motions were no delusion. Winged and whirring, those forms grew larger each moment, and the traveller knew his stumbling was at an end. They were not any birds or bats known elsewhere on earth or in dreamland, for they were larger than elephants and had heads like a horse's. Carter knew that they must be the Shantak-birds of ill rumour, and wondered no more what evil guardians and nameless sentinels made men avoid the boreal rock desert. And as he stopped in final resignation he dared at last to look behind him, where indeed was trotting the squat slant-eyed trader of evil legend, grinning astride a lean yak and leading on a noxious horde of leering Shantaks to whose wings still clung the rime and nitre of the nether pits.

Trapped though he was by fabulous and hippocephalic winged nightmares that pressed around in great unholy circles, Randolph Carter did not lose consciousness. Lofty and horrible those titan gargoyles towered above him, while the slant-eyed merchant leaped down from his yak and stood grinning before the captive. Then the man motioned Carter to mount one of the repugnant Shantaks, helping him up as his judgement struggled with his loathing. It was hard work ascending, for the Shantak-bird has scales instead of feathers, and those scales are very slippery. Once he was seated, the slant-eyed man hopped up behind him, leaving the lean yak to be led away northward toward the ring of carven mountains by one of the incredible bird colossi.

There now followed a hideous whirl through frigid space, endlessly up and eastward toward the gaunt grey flanks of those impassable mountains beyond which Leng was said to be. Far above the clouds they flew, till at last there lay beneath them those fabled summits which the folk of Inquanok have never seen, and which lie always in high vortices of gleaming mist. Carter beheld them very plainly as they passed below, and saw upon their topmost peaks strange caves which made him think of those on Ngranek; but he did not question his captor about these things when he noticed that both the man and the horse-headed Shantak appeared oddly fearful of them, hurrying past nervously and shewing great tension until they were left far in the rear.

The Shantak now flew lower, revealing beneath the canopy of cloud a grey barren plain whereon at great distances shone little feeble fires. As they descended there appeared at intervals lone huts of granite and bleak stone villages whose tiny windows glowed with pallid light. And there came from those huts and villages a shrill droning of pipes and a nauseous rattle of crotala which proved at once that Inquanok's people are right in their geographic rumours. For travellers have heard such sounds before, and know that they float only from the cold desert plateau which healthy folk never visit; that haunted place of evil and mystery which is Leng.

Around the feeble fires dark forms were dancing, and Carter was curious as to what manner of beings they might be; for no healthy folk have ever been to Leng, and the place is known only by its fires and stone huts as seen from afar. Very slowly and awkwardly did those forms leap, and with an insane twisting and bending not good to behold; so that Carter did not wonder at the monstrous evil imputed to them by vague legend, or the fear in which all dreamland holds their abhorrent frozen plateau. As the Shantak flew lower, the repulsiveness of the dancers became tinged with a certain hellish familiarity; and the prisoner kept straining his eyes and racking his memory for clues to where he had seen such creatures before.

They leaped as though they had hooves instead of feet, and seemed to wear a sort of wig or headpiece with small horns. Of other clothing they had none, but most of them were quite furry. Behind they had dwarfish tails, and when they glanced upward he saw the excessive width of their mouths. Then he knew what they were, and that they did not wear any wigs or headpieces after all. For the cryptic folk of Leng were of one race with the uncomfortable merchants of the black galleys that traded rubies at Dylath-Leen; those not quite human merchants who are the slaves of the monstrous moon-things! They were indeed the same dark folk who had shanghaied Carter on their noisome galley so long ago, and whose kith he had seen driven in herds about the unclean wharves of that accursed lunar city, with the leaner ones toiling and the fatter ones taken away in crates for other needs of their polypous and amorphous masters. Now he saw where such ambiguous creatures came from, and shuddered at the thought that Leng must be known to these formless abominations from the moon.

But the Shantak flew on past the fires and the stone huts and the less than human dancers, and soared over sterile hills of grey granite and dim wastes of rock and ice and snow. Day came, and the phosphorescence of low clouds gave place to the misty twilight of that northern world, and still the vile bird winged meaningly through the cold and silence. At times the slant-eyed man talked with his steed in a hateful and guttural language, and the Shantak would answer with tittering tones that rasped like the scratching of ground glass. All this while the land was getting higher, and finally they came to a wind-swept table-land which seemed the very roof of a blasted and tenantless world. There, all alone in the hush and the dusk and the cold, rose the uncouth stones of a squat windowless building, around which a circle of crude monoliths stood. In all this arrangement there was nothing human, and Carter surmised from old tales that he was indeed come to that most dreadful and legendary of all places, the remote and prehistoric monastery wherein dwells uncompanioned the High-Priest Not To Be Described, which wears a yellow silken mask over its face and prays to the Other Gods and their crawling chaos Nyarlathotep.

The loathsome bird now settled to the ground, and the slant-eyed man hopped down and helped his captive alight. Of the purpose of his seizure Carter now felt very sure; for clearly the slant-eyed merchant was an agent of the darker powers, eager to drag before his masters a mortal whose presumption had aimed at the finding of unknown Kadath and the saying of a prayer before the faces of the Great Ones in their onyx castle. It seemed likely that this merchant had caused his former capture by the slaves of the moon-things in Dylath-Leen, and that he now meant to do what the rescuing cats had baffled; taking the victim to some dread rendezvous with monstrous Nyarlathotep and telling with what boldness the seeking of unknown Kadath had been tried. Leng and the cold waste north of Inquanok must be close to the Other Gods, and there the passes to Kadath are well guarded.

The slant-eyed man was small, but the great hippocephalic bird was there to see he was obeyed; so Carter followed where he led, and passed within the circle of standing rocks and into the low arched doorway of that windowless stone monastery. There were no lights inside, but the evil merchant lit a small clay lamp bearing morbid bas-reliefs and prodded his prisoner on through mazes of narrow winding corridors. On the walls of the corridors were painted frightful scenes older than history, and in a style unknown to the archaeologists of earth. After countless aeons their pigments were brilliant still, for the cold and dryness of hideous Leng keep alive many primal things. Carter saw them fleetingly in the rays of that dim and moving lamp, and shuddered at the tale they told.

Through those archaic frescoes Leng's annals stalked; and the horned, hooved, and wide-mouthed almost-humans danced evilly amidst forgotten cities. There were scenes of old wars, wherein Leng's almost-humans fought with the bloated purple spiders of the neighbouring vales; and there were scenes also of the coming of the black galleys from the moon, and of the submission of Leng's people to the polypous and amorphous blasphemies that hopped and floundered and wriggled out of them. Those slippery greyish-white blasphemies they worshipped as gods, nor ever complained when scores of their best and fatted males were taken away in the black galleys. The monstrous moon-beasts made their camp on a jagged isle in the sea, and Carter could tell from the frescoes that this was none other than the lone nameless rock he had seen when sailing to Inquanok; that grey accursed rock which Inquanok's seamen shun, and from which vile howlings reverberate all through the night.

And in those frescoes was shewn the great seaport and capital of the almost-humans; proud and pillared betwixt the cliffs and the basalt wharves, and wondrous with high fanes and carven places. Great gardens and columned streets led from the cliffs and from each of the six sphinx-crowned gates to a vast central plaza, and in that plaza was a pair of winged colossal lions guarding the top of a subterrene staircase. Again and again were those huge winged lions shewn, their mighty flanks of diorite glistening in the grey twilight of the day and the cloudy phosphorescence of the night. And as Carter stumbled past their frequent and repeated pictures it came to him at last what indeed they were, and what city it was that the almost-humans had ruled so anciently before the coming of the black galleys. There could be no mistake, for the legends of dreamland are generous and profuse. Indubitably that primal city was no less a place than storied Sarkomand, whose ruins had bleached for a million years before the first true human saw the light, and whose twin titan lions guard eternally the steps that lead down from dreamland to the Great Abyss.

Other views shewed the gaunt grey peaks dividing Leng from Inquanok, and the monstrous Shantak-birds that build nests on the ledges half way up. And they shewed likewise the curious caves near the very topmost pinnacles, and how even the boldest of the Shantaks fly screaming away from them. Carter had seen those caves when he passed over them, and had noticed their likeness to the caves on Ngranek. Now he knew that the likeness was more than a chance one, for in these pictures were shewn their fearsome denizens; and those bat-wings, curving horns, barbed tails, prehensile paws and rubbery bodies were not strange to him. He had met those silent, flitting and clutching creatures before; those mindless guardians of the Great Abyss whom even the Great Ones fear, and who own not Nyarlathotep but hoary Nodens as their lord. For they were the dreaded night-gaunts, who never laugh or smile because they have no faces, and who flop unendingly in the dark betwixt the Vale of Pnath and the passes to the outer world.

The slant-eyed merchant had now prodded Carter into a great domed space whose walls were carved in shocking bas-reliefs, and whose centre held a gaping circular pit surrounded by six malignly stained stone altars in a ring. There was no light in this vast evil-smelling crypt, and the small lamp of the sinister merchant shone so feebly that one could grasp details only little by little. At the farther end was a high stone dais reached by five steps; and there on a golden throne sat a lumpish figure robed in yellow silk figured with red and having a yellow silken mask over its face. To this being the slant-eyed man made certain signs with his hands, and the lurker in the dark replied by raising a disgustingly carven flute of ivory in silk-covered paws and blowing certain loathsome sounds from beneath its flowing yellow mask. This colloquy went on for some time, and to Carter there was something sickeningly familiar in the sound of that flute and the stench of the malodorous place. It made him think of a frightful red-litten city and of the revolting procession that once filed through it; of that, and of an awful climb through lunar countryside beyond, before the rescuing rush of earth's friendly cats. He knew that the creature on the dais was without doubt the High-Priest Not

To Be Described, of which legend whispers such fiendish and abnormal possibilities, but he feared to think just what that abhorred High-Priest might be.

Then the figured silk slipped a trifle from one of the greyish-white paws, and Carter knew what the noisome High-Priest was. And in that hideous second, stark fear drove him to something his reason would never have dared to attempt, for in all his shaken consciousness there was room only for one frantic will to escape from what squatted on that golden throne. He knew that hopeless labyrinths of stone lay betwixt him and the cold table-land outside, and that even on that table-land the noxious Shantak still waited; yet in spite of all this there was in his mind only the instant need to get away from that wriggling, silk-robed monstrosity.

The slant-eyed man had set the curious lamp upon one of the high and wickedly stained altar-stones by the pit, and had moved forward somewhat to talk to the High-Priest with his hands. Carter, hitherto wholly passive, now gave that man a terrific push with all the wild strength of fear, so that the victim toppled at once into that gaping well which rumour holds to reach down to the hellish Vaults of Zin where Gugs hunt ghasts in the dark. In almost the same second he seized the lamp from the altar and darted out into the frescoed labyrinths, racing this way and that as chance determined and trying not to think of the stealthy padding of shapeless paws on the stones behind him, or of the silent wrigglings and crawlings which must be going on back there in lightless corridors.

After a few moments he regretted his thoughtless haste, and wished he had tried to follow backward the frescoes he had passed on the way in. True, they were so confused and duplicated that they could not have done him much good, but he wished none the less he had made the attempt. Those he now saw were even more horrible than those he had seen then, and he knew he was not in the corridors leading outside. In time he became quite sure he was not followed, and slackened his pace somewhat; but scarce had he breathed in half relief when a new peril beset him. His lamp was waning, and he would soon be in pitch blackness with no means of sight or guidance.

When the light was all gone he groped slowly in the dark, and prayed to the Great Ones for such help as they might afford. At times he felt the stone floor sloping up or down, and once he stumbled over a step for which no reason seemed to exist. The farther he went the damper it seemed to be, and when he was able to feel a junction or the mouth of a side passage he always chose the way which sloped downward the least. He believed, though, that his general course was down; and the vault-like smell and incrustations on the greasy walls and floor alike warned him he was burrowing deep in Leng's unwholesome table-land. But there was not any warning of the thing which came at last; only the thing itself with its terror and shock and breath-taking chaos. One moment he was groping slowly over the slippery floor of an almost level place, and the next he was shooting dizzily downward in the dark through a burrow which must have been well-nigh vertical.

Of the length of that hideous sliding he could never be sure, but it seemed to take hours of delirious nausea and ecstatic frenzy. Then he realized he was still, with the phosphorescent clouds of a northern night shining sickly above him. All around were crumbling walls and broken columns, and the pavement on which he lay was pierced by straggling grass and wrenched asunder by frequent shrubs and roots. Behind him a basalt cliff rose topless and perpendicular; its dark side sculptured into repellent scenes, and pierced by an arched and carven entrance to the inner blacknesses out of which he had come. Ahead stretched double rows of pillars, and the fragments and pedestals of pillars, that spoke of a broad and bygone street; and from the urns and basins along the way he knew it had been a great street of gardens. Far off at its end the pillars spread to mark a vast round plaza, and in that open circle there loomed gigantic under the lurid night clouds a pair of monstrous things. Huge winged lions of diorite they were, with blackness and shadow between them. Full twenty feet they reared their grotesque and unbroken heads, and snarled derisive on the ruins around them. And Carter knew right well what they must be, for legend tells of only one such twain. They were the changeless guardians of the Great Abyss, and these dark ruins were in truth primordial Sarkomand.

Carter's first act was to close and barricade the archway in the cliff with fallen blocks and odd debris that lay around. He wished no follower from Leng's hateful monastery, for along the way ahead would lurk enough of other dangers. Of how to get from Sarkomand to the peopled parts of dreamland he knew nothing at all; nor could he gain much by descending to the grottoes of the ghouls, since he knew they were no better informed than he. The three ghouls which had helped him through the city of Gugs to the outer world had not known how to reach Sarkomand in their journey back, but had planned to ask old traders in Dylath-Leen. He did not like to think of going again to the subterrene world of Gugs and risking once more that hellish tower of Koth with its Cyclopean steps leading to the enchanted wood, yet he felt he might have to try this course if all else failed. Over Leng's plateau past the lone monastery he dared not go unaided; for the High-Priest's emissaries must be many, while at the journey's end there would no doubt be the Shantaks and perhaps other things to deal with. If he could get a boat he might sail back to Inquanok past the jagged and hideous rock in the sea, for the primal frescoes in the monastery labyrinth had shewn that this frightful place lies not far from Sarkomand's basalt quays. But to find a boat in this aeon-deserted city was no probable thing, and it did not appear likely that he could ever make one.

Such were the thoughts of Randolph Carter when a new impression began beating upon his mind. All this while there had stretched before him the great corpse-like width of fabled Sarkomand with its black broken pillars and crumbling sphinx-crowned gates and titan stones and monstrous winged lions against the sickly glow of those luminous night clouds. Now he saw far ahead and on the right a glow that no clouds could account for, and knew he was not alone in the silence of that dead city. The glow rose and fell fitfully, flickering with a greenish tinge which did not reassure the watcher. And when he crept closer, down the littered street and through some narrow gaps between tumbled walls, he perceived that it was a campfire near the wharves with many vague forms clustered darkly around it; and a lethal odour hanging heavily over all. Beyond was the oily lapping of the harbour water with a great ship riding at anchor, and Carter paused in stark terror when he saw that the ship was indeed one of the dreaded black galleys from the moon.

Then, just as he was about to creep back from that detestable flame, he saw a stirring among the vague dark forms and heard a peculiar and unmistakable sound. It was the frightened meeping of a ghoul, and in a moment it had swelled to a veritable chorus of anguish. Secure as he was in the shadow of monstrous ruins, Carter allowed his curiosity to conquer his fear, and crept forward again instead of retreating. Once in crossing an open street he wriggled worm-like on his stomach, and in another place he had to rise to his feet to avoid making a noise among heaps of fallen marble. But always he succeeded in avoiding discovery, so that in a short time he had found a spot behind a titan pillar where he could watch the whole green-litten scene of action. There around a hideous fire fed by the obnoxious stems of lunar fungi, there squatted a stinking circle of the toadlike moonbeasts and their almost-human slaves. Some of these slaves were heating curious iron spears in the leaping flames, and at intervals applying their white-hot points to three tightly trussed prisoners that lay writhing before the leaders of the party. From the motions of their tentacles Carter could see that the blunt-snouted moonbeasts were enjoying the spectacle hugely, and vast was his horror when he suddenly recognised the frantic meeping and knew that the tortured ghouls were none other than the faithful trio which had guided him safely from the abyss, and had thereafter set out from the enchanted wood to find Sarkomand and the gate to their native deeps.

The number of malodorous moonbeasts about that greenish fire was very great, and Carter saw that he could do nothing now to save his former allies. Of how the ghouls had been captured he could not guess; but fancied that the grey toadlike blasphemies had heard them inquire in Dylath-Leen concerning the way to Sarkomand and had not wished them to approach so closely the hateful plateau of Leng and the High-Priest Not To Be Described. For a moment he pondered on what he ought to do, and recalled how near he was to the gate of the ghouls' black kingdom. Clearly it was wisest to creep east to the plaza of twin lions and descend at once to the gulf, where assuredly he would meet no horrors worse than those above, and where he might soon find ghouls eager to rescue their brethren and perhaps to wipe out the moonbeasts from the black galley. It occurred to him that the portal, like other gates to the abyss, might be guarded by flocks of night-gaunts; but he did not fear these faceless creatures now. He had learned that they are bound by solemn treaties with the ghouls, and the ghoul which was Pickman had taught him how to glibber a password they understood.

So Carter began another silent crawl through the ruins, edging slowly toward the great central plaza and the winged lions. It was ticklish work, but the moonbeasts were pleasantly busy and did not hear the slight noises which he twice made by accident among the scattered stones. At last he reached the open space and picked his way among the stunted trees and vines that had grown up therein. The gigantic lions loomed terrible above him in the sickly glow of the phosphorescent night clouds, but he manfully persisted toward them and presently crept round to their faces, knowing it was on that side he would find the mighty darkness which they guard. Ten feet apart crouched the mocking-faced beasts of diorite, brooding on cyclopean pedestals whose sides were chiselled in fearsome bas-reliefs. Betwixt them was a tiled court with a central space which had once been railed with balusters of onyx. Midway in this space a black well opened, and Carter soon saw that he had indeed reached the yawning gulf whose crusted and mouldy stone steps lead down to the crypts of nightmare.

Terrible is the memory of that dark descent in which hours wore themselves away whilst Carter wound sightlessly round and round down a fathomless spiral of steep and slippery stairs. So worn and narrow were the steps, and so greasy with the ooze of inner earth, that the climber never quite knew when to expect a breathless fall and hurtling down to the ultimate pits; and he was likewise uncertain just when or how the guardian night-gaunts would suddenly pounce upon him, if indeed there were any stationed in this primeval passage. All about him was a stifling odour of nether gulfs, and he felt that the air of these choking depths was not made for mankind. In time he became very numb and somnolent, moving more from automatic impulse than from reasoned will; nor did he realize any change when he stopped moving altogether as something quietly seized him from behind. He was flying very rapidly through the air before a malevolent tickling told him that the rubbery night-gaunts had performed their duty.

Awaked to the fact that he was in the cold, damp clutch of the faceless flutterers, Carter remembered the password of the ghouls and glibbered it as loudly as he could amidst the wind and chaos of flight. Mindless though night-gaunts are said to be, the effect was instantaneous; for all tickling stopped at once, and the creatures hastened to shift their captive to a more comfortable position. Thus encouraged Carter ventured some explanations; telling of the seizure and torture of three ghouls by the moonbeasts, and of the need of assembling a party to rescue them. The night-gaunts, though inarticulate, seemed to understand what was said; and shewed greater haste and purpose in their flight. Suddenly the dense blackness gave place to the grey twilight of inner earth, and there opened up ahead one of those flat sterile plains on which ghouls love to squat and gnaw. Scattered tombstones and osseous fragments told of the denizens of that place; and as Carter gave a loud meep of urgent summons, a score of burrows emptied forth their leathery, dog-like tenants. The night-gaunts now flew low and set their passenger upon his feet, afterward withdrawing a little and forming a hunched semicircle on the ground while the ghouls greeted the newcomer.

Carter glibbered his message rapidly and explicitly to the grotesque company, and four of them at once departed through different burrows to spread the news to others and gather such troops as might be available for a rescue. After a long wait a ghoul of some importance appeared, and made significant signs to the night-gaunts, causing two of the latter to fly off into the dark. Thereafter there were constant accessions to the hunched flock of night-gaunts on the plain, till at length the slimy soil was fairly black with them. Meanwhile fresh ghouls crawled out of the burrows one by one, all glibbering excitedly and forming in crude battle array not far from the huddled night-gaunts. In time there appeared that proud and influential ghoul which was once the artist Richard Pickman of Boston, and to him Carter glibbered a very full account of what had occurred. The erstwhile Pickman, pleased to greet his ancient friend again, seemed very much impressed, and held a conference with other chiefs a little apart from the growing throng.

Finally, after scanning the ranks with care, the assembled chiefs all meeped in unison and began glibbering orders to the crowds of ghouls and night-gaunts. A large detachment of the horned flyers vanished at once, while the rest grouped themselves two by two on their knees with extended forelegs, awaiting the approach of the ghouls one by one. As each ghoul reached the pair of night-gaunts to which he was assigned, he was taken up and borne away into the blackness; till at last the whole throng had vanished save for Carter, Pickman, and the other chiefs, and a few pairs of night-gaunts. Pickman explained that night-gaunts are the advance guard and battle steeds of the ghouls, and that the army was issuing forth to Sarkomand to deal with the moonbeasts. Then Carter and the ghoulish chiefs approached the waiting bearers and were taken up by the damp, slippery paws. Another moment and all were whirling in wind and darkness; endlessly up, up, up to the gate of the winged lions and the spectral ruins of primal Sarkomand.

When, after a great interval, Carter saw again the sickly light of Sarkomand's nocturnal sky, it was to behold the great central plaza swarming with militant ghouls and night-gaunts. Day, he felt sure, must be almost due; but so strong was the army that no surprise of the enemy would be needed. The greenish flare near the wharves still glimmered faintly, though the absence of ghoulish meeping shewed that the torture of the prisoners was over for the nonce. Softly glibbering directions to their steeds and to the flock of riderless night-gaunts ahead, the ghouls presently rose in wide whirring columns and swept on over the bleak ruins toward the evil flame. Carter was now beside Pickman in the front rank of ghouls, and saw as they approached the noisome camp that the moonbeasts were totally unprepared. The three prisoners lay bound and inert beside the fire, while their toadlike captors slumped drowsily about in no certain order. The almost-human slaves were asleep, even the sentinels shirking a duty which in this realm must have seemed to them merely perfunctory.

The final swoop of the night-gaunts and mounted ghouls was very sudden, each of the greyish toadlike blasphemies and their almost-human slaves being seized by a group of night-gaunts before a sound was made. The moonbeasts, of course, were voiceless; and even the slaves had little chance to scream before rubbery paws choked them into silence. Horrible were the writhings of those great jellyfish abnormalities as the sardonic night-gaunts clutched them, but nothing availed against the strength of those black prehensile talons. When a moonbeast writhed too violently, a night-gaunt would seize and pull its quivering pink tentacles; which seemed to hurt so much that the victim would cease its struggles. Carter expected to see much slaughter, but found that the ghouls were far subtler in their plans. They glibbered certain simple orders to the night-gaunts which held the captives, trusting the rest to instinct; and soon the hapless creatures were borne silently away into the Great Abyss, to be distributed impartially amongst the Dholes, Gugs, ghasts and other dwellers in darkness whose modes of nourishment are not painless to their chosen victims. Meanwhile the three bound ghouls had been released and consoled by their conquering kinsfolk, whilst various parties searched the neighborhood for possible remaining moonbeasts, and boarded the evil-smelling black galley at the wharf to make sure that nothing had escaped the general defeat. Surely enough, the capture had been thorough, for not a sign of further life could the victors detect. Carter, anxious to preserve a means of access to the rest of dreamland, urged them not to sink the anchored galley; and this request was freely granted out of gratitude for his act in reporting the plight of the captured trio. On the ship were found some very curious objects and decorations, some of which Carter cast at once into the sea.

Ghouls and night-gaunts now formed themselves in separate groups, the former questioning their rescued fellows anent past happenings. It appeared that the three had followed Carter's directions and proceeded from the enchanted wood to Dylath-Leen by way of Nir and the Skai, stealing human clothes at a lonely farmhouse and loping as closely as possible in the fashion of a man's walk. In Dylath-Leen's taverns their grotesque ways and faces had aroused much comment; but they had persisted in asking the way to Sarkomand until at last an old traveller was able to tell them. Then they knew that only a ship for Lelag-Leng would serve their purpose, and prepared to wait patiently for such a vessel.

But evil spies had doubtless reported much; for shortly a black galley put into port, and the wide-mouthed ruby merchants invited the ghouls to drink with them in a tavern. Wine was produced from one of those sinister bottles grotesquely carven from a single ruby, and after that the ghouls found themselves prisoners on the black galley as Carter had found himself. This time, however, the unseen rowers steered not for the moon but for antique Sarkomand; bent evidently on taking their captives before the High-Priest Not To Be Described. They had touched at the jagged rock in the northern sea which Inquanok's mariners shun, and the ghouls had there seen for the first time the red masters of the ship; being sickened despite their own callousness by such extremes of malign shapelessness and fearsome odour. There, too, were witnessed the nameless pastimes of the toadlike resident garrison-such pastimes as give rise to the night-howlings which men fear. After that had come the landing at ruined Sarkomand and the beginning of the tortures, whose continuance the present rescue had prevented.

Future plans were next discussed, the three rescued ghouls suggesting a raid on the jagged rock and the extermination of the toadlike garrison there. To this, however, the night-gaunts objected; since the prospect of flying over water did not please them. Most of the ghouls favoured the design, but were at a loss how to follow it without the help of the winged night-gaunts. Thereupon Carter, seeing that they could not navigate the anchored galley, offered to teach them the use of the great banks of oars; to which proposal they eagerly assented. Grey day had now come, and under that leaden northern sky a picked detachment of ghouls filed into the noisome ship and took their seats on the rowers' benches. Carter found them fairly apt at learning, and before night had risked several experimental trips around the harbour. Not till three days later, however, did he deem it safe to attempt the voyage of conquest. Then, the rowers trained and the night-gaunts safely stowed in the forecastle, the party set sail at last; Pickman and the other chiefs gathering on deck and discussing modes of approach and procedure.

On the very first night the howlings from the rock were heard. Such was their timbre that all the galley's crew shook visibly; but most of all trembled the three rescued ghouls who knew precisely what those howlings meant. It was not thought best to attempt an attack by night, so the ship lay to under the phosphorescent clouds to wait for the dawn of a greyish day. When the light was ample and the howlings still the rowers resumed their strokes, and the galley drew closer and closer to that jagged rock whose granite pinnacles clawed fantastically at the dull sky. The sides of the rock were very steep; but on ledges here and there could be seen the bulging walls of queer windowless dwellings, and the low railings guarding travelled highroads. No ship of men had ever come so near the place, or at least, had never come so near and departed again; but Carter and the ghouls were void of fear and kept inflexibly on, rounding the eastern face of the rock and seeking the wharves which the rescued trio described as being on the southern side within a harbour formed of steep headlands.

The headlands were prolongations of the island proper, and came so closely together that only one ship at a time might pass between them. There seemed to be no watchers on the outside, so the galley was steered boldly through the flume-like strait and into the stagnant putrid harbour beyond. Here, however, all was bustle and activity; with several ships lying at anchor along a forbidding stone quay, and scores of almost-human slaves and moonbeasts by the waterfront handling crates and boxes or driving nameless and fabulous horrors hitched to lumbering lorries. There was a small stone town hewn out of the vertical cliff above the wharves, with the start of a winding road that spiralled out of sight toward higher ledges of the rock. Of what lay inside that prodigious peak of granite none might say, but the things one saw on the outside were far from encouraging.

At sight of the incoming galley the crowds on the wharves displayed much eagerness; those with eyes staring intently, and those without eyes wriggling their pink tentacles expectantly. They did not, of course, realize that the black ship had changed hands; for ghouls look much like the horned and hooved almost-humans, and the night-gaunts were all out of sight below. By this time the leaders had fully formed a plan; which was to loose the night-gaunts as soon as the wharf was touched, and then to sail directly away, leaving matters wholly to the instincts of those almost-mindless creatures. Marooned on the rock, the horned flyers would first of all seize whatever living things they found there, and afterward, quite helpless to think except in terms of the homing instinct, would forget their fear of water and fly swiftly back to the abyss; bearing their noisome prey to appropriate destinations in the dark, from which not much would emerge alive.

The ghoul that was Pickman now went below and gave the night-gaunts their simple instructions, while the ship drew very near to the ominous and malodorous wharves. Presently a fresh stir rose along the waterfront, and Carter saw that the motions of the galley had begun to excite suspicion. Evidently the steersman was not making for the right dock, and probably the watchers had noticed the difference between the hideous ghouls and the almost-human slaves whose places they were taking. Some silent alarm must have been given, for almost at once a horde of the mephitic moonbeasts began to pour from the little black doorways of the windowless houses and down the winding road at the right. A rain of curious javelins struck the galley as the prow hit the wharf felling two ghouls and slightly wounding another; but at this point all the hatches were thrown open to emit a black cloud of whirring night-gaunts which swarmed over the town like a flock of horned and cyclopean bats.

The jellyish moonbeasts had procured a great pole and were trying to push off the invading ship, but when the night-gaunts struck them they thought of such things no more. It was a very terrible spectacle to see those faceless and rubbery ticklers at their pastime, and tremendously impressive to watch the dense cloud of them spreading through the town and up the winding roadway to the reaches above. Sometimes a group of the black flutterers would drop a toadlike prisoner from aloft by mistake, and the manner in which the victim would burst was highly offensive to the sight and smell. When the last of the night-gaunts had left the galley the ghoulish leaders glibbered an order of withdrawal, and the rowers pulled quietly out of the harbour between the grey headlands while still the town was a chaos of battle and conquest.

The Pickman ghoul allowed several hours for the night-gaunts to make up their rudimentary minds and overcome their fear of flying over the sea, and kept the galley standing about a mile off the jagged rock while he waited, and dressed the wounds of the injured men. Night fell, and the grey twilight gave place to the sickly phosphorescence of low clouds, and all the while the leaders watched the high peaks of that accursed rock for signs of the night-gaunts' flight. Toward morning a black speck was seen hovering timidly over the top-most pinnacle, and shortly afterward the speck had become a swarm. Just before daybreak the swarm seemed to scatter, and within a quarter of an hour it had vanished wholly in the distance toward the northeast. Once or twice something seemed to fall from the thinning swarm into the sea; but Carter did not worry, since he knew from observation that the toadlike moonbeasts cannot swim. At length, when the ghouls were satisfied that all the night-gaunts had left for Sarkomand and the Great Abyss with their doomed burdens, the galley put back into the harbour betwixt the grey headlands; and all the hideous company landed and roamed curiously over the denuded rock with its towers and eyries and fortresses chiselled from the solid stone.

Frightful were the secrets uncovered in those evil and windowless crypts; for the remnants of unfinished pastimes were many, and in various stages of departure from their primal state. Carter put out of the way certain things which were after a fashion alive, and fled precipitately from a few other things about which he could not be very positive. The stench-filled houses were furnished mostly with grotesque stools and benches carven from moon-trees, and were painted inside with nameless and frantic designs. Countless weapons, implements, and ornaments lay about, including some large idols of solid ruby depicting singular beings not found on the earth. These latter did not, despite their material, invite either appropriation or long inspection; and Carter took the trouble to hammer five of them into very small pieces. The scattered spears and javelins he collected, and with Pickman's approval distributed among the ghouls. Such devices were new to the doglike lopers, but their relative simplicity made them easy to master after a few concise hints.

The upper parts of the rock held more temples than private homes, and in numerous hewn chambers were found terrible carven altars and doubtfully stained fonts and shrines for the worship of things more monstrous than the wild gods atop Kadath. From the rear of one great temple stretched a low black passage which Carter followed far into the rock with a torch till he came to a lightless domed hall of vast proportions, whose vaultings were covered with demoniac carvings and in whose centre yawned a foul and bottomless well like that in the hideous monastery of Leng where broods alone the High-Priest Not To Be Described. On the distant shadowy side, beyond the noisome well, he thought he discerned a small door of strangely wrought bronze; but for some reason he felt an unaccountable dread of opening it or even approaching it, and hastened back through the cavern to his unlovely allies as they shambled about with an ease and abandon he could scarcely feel. The ghouls had observed the unfinished pastimes of the moonbeasts, and had profited in their fashion. They had also found a hogshead of potent moon-wine, and were rolling it down to the wharves for removal and later use in diplomatic dealings, though the rescued trio, remembering its effect on them in Dylath-Leen, had warned their company to taste none of it. Of rubies from lunar mines there was a great store, both rough and polished, in one of the vaults near the water; but when the ghouls found they were not good to eat they lost all interest in them. Carter did not try to carry any away, since he knew too much about those which had mined them.

Suddenly there came an excited meeping from the sentries on the wharves, and all the loathsome foragers turned from their tasks to stare seaward and cluster round the waterfront. Betwixt the grey headlands a fresh black galley was rapidly advancing, and it would be but a moment before the almost-humans on deck would perceive the invasion of the town and give the alarm to the monstrous things below. Fortunately the ghouls still bore the spears and javelins which Carter had distributed amongst them; and at his command, sustained by the being that was Pickman, they now formed a line of battle and prepared to prevent the landing of the ship. Presently a burst of excitement on the galley told of the crew's discovery of the changed state of things, and the instant stoppage of the vessel proved that the superior numbers of the ghouls had been noted and taken into account. After a moment of hesitation the newcomers silently turned and passed out between the headlands again, but not for an instant did the ghouls imagine that the conflict was averted. Either the dark ship would seek reinforcements or the crew would try to land elsewhere on the island; hence a party of scouts was at once sent up toward the pinnacle to see what the enemy's course would be.

In a very few minutes the ghoul returned breathless to say that the moonbeasts and almost-humans were landing on the outside of the more easterly of the rugged grey headlands, and ascending by hidden paths and ledges which a goat could scarcely tread in safety. Almost immediately afterward the galley was sighted again through the flume-like strait, but only for a second. Then a few moments later, a second messenger panted down from aloft to say that another party was landing on the other headland; both being much more numerous than the size of the galley would seem to allow for. The ship itself, moving slowly with only one sparsely manned tier of oars, soon hove in sight betwixt the cliffs, and lay to in the foetid harbour as if to watch the coming fray and stand by for any possible use.

By this time Carter and Pickman had divided the ghouls into three parties, one to meet each of the two invading columns and one to remain in the town. The first two at once scrambled up the rocks in their respective directions, while the third was subdivided into a land party and a sea party. The sea party, commanded by Carter, boarded the anchored galley and rowed out to meet the under-manned galley of the newcomers; whereat the latter retreated through the strait to the open sea. Carter did not at once pursue it, for he knew he might be needed more acutely near the town.

Meanwhile the frightful detachments of the moonbeasts and almost-humans had lumbered up to the top of the headlands and were shockingly silhouetted on either side against the grey twilight sky. The thin hellish flutes of the invaders had now begun to whine, and the general effect of those hybrid, half-amorphous processions was as nauseating as the actual odour given off by the toadlike lunar blasphemies. Then the two parties of the ghouls swarmed into sight and joined the silhouetted panorama. Javelins began to fly from both sides, and the swelling meeps of the ghouls and the bestial howls of the almost-humans gradually joined the hellish whine of the flutes to form a frantick and indescribable chaos of daemon cacophony. Now and then bodies fell from the narrow ridges of the headlands into the sea outside or the harbour inside, in the latter case being sucked quickly under by certain submarine lurkers whose presence was indicated only by prodigious bubbles.

For half an hour this dual battle raged in the sky, till upon the west cliff the invaders were completely annihilated. On the east cliff, however, where the leader of the moonbeast party appeared to be present, the ghouls had not fared so well; and were slowly retreating to the slopes of the pinnacle proper. Pickman had quickly ordered reinforcements for this front from the party in the town, and these had helped greatly in the earlier stages of the combat. Then, when the western battle was over, the victorious survivors hastened across to the aid of their hard-pressed fellows; turning the tide and forcing the invaders back again along the narrow ridge of the headland. The almost-humans were by this time all slain, but the last of the toadlike horrors fought desperately with the great spears clutched in their powerful and disgusting paws. The time for javelins was now nearly past, and the fight became a hand-to-hand contest of what few spearmen could meet upon that narrow ridge.

As fury and recklessness increased, the number falling into the sea became very great. Those striking the harbour met nameless extinction from the unseen bubblers, but of those striking the open sea some were able to swim to the foot of the cliffs and land on tidal rocks, while the hovering galley of the enemy rescued several moonbeasts. The cliffs were unscalable except where the monsters had debarked, so that none of the ghouls on the rocks could rejoin their battle-line. Some were killed by javelins from the hostile galley or from the moonbeasts above, but a few survived to be rescued. When the security of the land parties seemed assured, Carter's galley sallied forth between the headlands and drove the hostile ship far out to sea; pausing to rescue such ghouls as were on the rocks or still swimming in the ocean. Several moonbeasts washed on rocks or reefs were speedily put out of the way.

Finally, the moonbeast galley being safely in the distance and the invading land army concentrated in one place, Carter landed a considerable force on the eastern headland in the enemy's rear; after which the fight was short-lived indeed. Attacked from both sides, the noisome flounderers were rapidly cut to pieces or pushed into the sea, till by evening the ghoulish chiefs agreed that the island was again clear of them. The hostile galley, meanwhile, had disappeared; and it was decided that the evil jagged rock had better be evacuated before any overwhelming horde of lunar horrors might be assembled and brought against the victors.

So by night Pickman and Carter assembled all the ghouls and counted them with care, finding that over a fourth had been lost in the day's battles. The wounded were placed on bunks in the galley, for Pickman always discouraged the old ghoulish custom of killing and eating one's own wounded, and the able-bodied troops were assigned to the oars or to such other places as they might most usefully fill. Under the low phosphorescent clouds of night the galley sailed, and Carter was not sorry to be departing from the island of unwholesome secrets, whose lightless domed hall with its bottomless well and repellent bronze door lingered restlessly in his fancy. Dawn found the ship in sight of Sarkomand's ruined quays of basalt, where a few night-gaunt sentries still waited, squatting like black horned gargoyles on the broken columns and crumbling sphinxes of that fearful city which lived and died before the years of man.

The ghouls made camp amongst the fallen stones of Sarkomand, despatching a messenger for enough night-gaunts to serve them as steeds. Pickman and the other chiefs were effusive in their gratitude for the aid Carter had lent them. Carter now began to feel that his plans were indeed maturing well, and that he would be able to command the help of these fearsome allies not only in quitting this part of dreamland, but in pursuing his ultimate quest for the gods atop unknown Kadath, and the marvellous sunset city they so strangely withheld from his slumbers. Accordingly he spoke of these things to the ghoulish leaders; telling what he knew of the cold waste wherein Kadath stands and of the monstrous Shantaks and the mountains carven into double-headed images which guard it. He spoke of the fear of Shantaks for night-gaunts, and of how the vast hippocephalic birds fly screaming from the black burrows high up on the gaunt grey peaks that divide Inquanok from hateful Leng. He spoke, too, of the things he had learned concerning night-gaunts from the frescoes in the windowless monastery of the High-Priest Not To Be Described; how even the Great Ones fear them, and how their ruler is not the crawling chaos Nyarlathotep at all, but hoary and immemorial Nodens, Lord of the Great Abyss.

All these things Carter glibbered to the assembled ghouls, and presently outlined that request which he had in mind and which he did not think extravagant considering the services he had so lately rendered the rubbery doglike lopers. He wished very much, he said, for the services of enough night-gaunts to bear him safely through the air past the realm of Shantaks and carven mountains, and up into the old waste beyond the returning tracks of any other mortal. He desired to fly to the onyx castle atop unknown Kadath in the cold waste to plead with the Great Ones for the sunset city they denied him, and felt sure that the night-gaunts could take him thither without trouble; high above the perils of the plain, and over the hideous double heads of those carven sentinel mountains that squat eternally in the grey dusk. For the horned and faceless creatures there could be no danger from aught of earth since the Great Ones themselves dread them. And even were unexpected things to come from the Other Gods, who are prone to oversee the affairs of earth's milder gods, the night-gaunts need not fear; for the outer hells are indifferent matters to such silent and slippery flyers as own not Nyarlathotep for their master, but bow only to potent and archaic Nodens.

A flock of ten or fifteen night-gaunts, Carter glibbered, would surely be enough to keep any combination of Shantaks at a distance, though perhaps it might be well to have some ghouls in the party to manage the creatures, their ways being better known to their ghoulish allies than to men. The party could land him at some convenient point within whatever walls that fabulous onyx citadel might have, waiting in the shadows for his return or his signal whilst he ventured inside the castle to give prayer to the gods of earth. If any ghouls chose to escort him into the throne-room of the Great Ones, he would be thankful, for their presence would add weight and importance to his plea. He would not, however, insist upon this but merely wished transportation to and from the castle atop unknown Kadath; the final journey being either to the marvellous sunset city itself, in case the gods proved favourable, or back to the earthward Gate of Deeper Slumber in the Enchanted Wood in case his prayers were fruitless.

Whilst Carter was speaking all the ghouls listened with great attention, and as the moments advanced the sky became black with clouds of those night-gaunts for which messengers had been sent. The winged steeds settled in a semicircle around the ghoulish army, waiting respectfully as the doglike chieftains considered the wish of the earthly traveller. The ghoul that was Pickman glibbered gravely with his fellows and in the end Carter was offered far more than he had at most expected. As he had aided the ghouls in their conquest of the moonbeasts, so would they aid him in his daring voyage to realms whence none had ever returned; lending him not merely a few of their allied night-gaunts, but their entire army as they encamped, veteran fighting ghouls and newly assembled night-gaunts alike, save only a small garrison for the captured black galley and such spoils as had come from the jagged rock in the sea. They would set out through the air whenever he might wish, and once arrived on Kadath a suitable train of ghouls would attend him in state as he placed his petition before earth's gods in their onyx castle.

Moved by a gratitude and satisfaction beyond words, Carter made plans with the ghoulish leaders for his audacious voyage. The army would fly high, they decided, over hideous Leng with its nameless monastery and wicked stone villages; stopping only at the vast grey peaks to confer with the Shantak-frightening night-gaunts whose burrows honeycombed their summits. They would then, according to what advice they might receive from those denizens, choose their final course; approaching unknown Kadath either through the desert of carven mountains north of Inquanok, or through the more northerly reaches of repulsive Leng itself. Doglike and soulless as they are, the ghouls and night-gaunts had no dread of what those untrodden deserts might reveal; nor did they feel any deterring awe at the thought of Kadath towering lone with its onyx castle of mystery.

About midday the ghouls and night-gaunts prepared for flight, each ghoul selecting a suitable pair of horned steeds to bear him. Carter was placed well up toward the head of the column beside Pickman, and in front of the whole a double line of riderless night-gaunts was provided as a vanguard. At a brisk meep from Pickman the whole shocking army rose in a nightmare cloud above the broken columns and crumbling sphinxes of primordial Sarkomand; higher and higher, till even the great basalt cliff behind the town was cleared, and the cold, sterile table-land of Leng's outskirts laid open to sight. Still higher flew the black host, till even this table-land grew small beneath them; and as they worked northward over the wind-swept plateau of horror Carter saw once again with a shudder the circle of crude monoliths and the squat windowless building which he knew held that frightful silken-masked blasphemy from whose clutches he had so narrowly escaped. This time no descent was made as the army swept batlike over the sterile landscape, passing the feeble fires of the unwholesome stone villages at a great altitude, and pausing not at all to mark the morbid twistings of the hooved, horned almost-humans that dance and pipe eternally therein. Once they saw a Shantak-bird flying low over the plain, but when it saw them it screamed noxiously and flapped off to the north in grotesque panic.

At dusk they reached the jagged grey peaks that form the barrier of Inquanok, and hovered about these strange caves near the summits which Carter recalled as so frightful to the Shantaks. At the insistent meeping of the ghoulish leaders there issued forth from each lofty burrow a stream of horned black flyers with which the ghouls and night-gaunts of the party conferred at length by means of ugly gestures. It soon became clear that the best course would be that over the cold waste north of Inquanok, for Leng's northward reaches are full of unseen pitfalls that even the night-gaunts dislike; abysmal influences centering in certain white hemispherical buildings on curious knolls, which common folklore associates unpleasantly with the Other Gods and their crawling chaos Nyarlathotep.

Of Kadath the flutterers of the peaks knew almost nothing, save that there must be some mighty marvel toward the north, over which the Shantaks and the carven mountains stand guard. They hinted at rumoured abnormalities of proportion in those trackless leagues beyond, and recalled vague whispers of a realm where night broods eternally; but of definite data they had nothing to give. So Carter and his party thanked them kindly; and, crossing the topmost granite pinnacles to the skies of Inquanok, dropped below the level of the phosphorescent night clouds and beheld in the distance those terrible squatting gargoyles that were mountains till some titan hand carved fright into their virgin rock.

There they squatted in a hellish half-circle, their legs on the desert sand and their mitres piercing the luminous clouds; sinister, wolflike, and double-headed, with faces of fury and right hands raised, dully and malignly watching the rim of man's world and guarding with horror the reaches of a cold northern world that is not man's. From their hideous laps rose evil Shantaks of elephantine bulk, but these all fled with insane titters as the vanguard of night-gaunts was sighted in the misty sky. Northward above those gargoyle mountains the army flew, and over leagues of dim desert where never a landmark rose. Less and less luminous grew the clouds, till at length Carter could see only blackness around him; but never did the winged steeds falter, bred as they were in earth's blackest crypts, and seeing not with any eyes, but with the whole dank surface of their slippery forms. On and on they flew, past winds of dubious scent and sounds of dubious import; ever in thickest darkness, and covering such prodigious spaces that Carter wondered whether or not they could still be within earth's dreamland.

Then suddenly the clouds thinned and the stars shone spectrally above. All below was still black, but those pallid beacons in the sky seemed alive with a meaning and directiveness they had never possessed elsewhere. It was not that the figures of the constellations were different, but that the same familiar shapes now revealed a significance they had formerly failed to make plain. Everything focussed toward the north; every curve and asterism of the glittering sky became part of a vast design whose function was to hurry first the eye and then the whole observer onward to some secret and terrible goal of convergence beyond the frozen waste that stretched endlessly ahead. Carter looked toward the east where the great ridge of barrier peaks had towered along all the length of Inquanok and saw against the stars a jagged silhouette which told of its continued presence. It was more broken now, with yawning clefts and fantastically erratic pinnacles; and Carter studied closely the suggestive turnings and inclinations of that grotesque outline, which seemed to share with the stars some subtle northward urge.

They were flying past at a tremendous speed, so that the watcher had to strain hard to catch details; when all at once he beheld just above the line of the topmost peaks a dark and moving object against the stars, whose course exactly paralleled that of his own bizarre party. The ghouls had likewise glimpsed it, for he heard their low glibbering all about him, and for a moment he fancied the object was a gigantic Shantak, of a size vastly greater than that of the average specimen. Soon, however, he saw that this theory would not hold; for the shape of the thing above the mountains was not that of any hippocephalic bird. Its outline against the stars, necessarily vague as it was, resembled rather some huge mitred head, or pair of heads infinitely magnified; and its rapid bobbing flight through the sky seemed most peculiarly a wingless one. Carter could not tell which side of the mountains it was on, but soon perceived that it had parts below the parts he had first seen, since it blotted out all the stars in places where the ridge was deeply cleft.

Then came a wide gap in the range, where the hideous reaches of transmontane Leng were joined to the cold waste on this side by a low pass through which the stars shone wanly. Carter watched this gap with intense care, knowing that he might see outlined against the sky beyond it the lower parts of the vast thing that flew undulantly above the pinnacles. The object had now floated ahead a trifle, and every eye of the party was fixed on the rift where it would presently appear in full-length silhouette. Gradually the huge thing above the peaks neared the gap, slightly slackening its speed as if conscious of having outdistanced the ghoulish army. For another minute suspense was keen, and then the brief instant of full silhouette and revelation came; bringing to the lips of the ghouls an awed and half-choked meep of cosmic fear, and to the soul of the traveller a chill that never wholly left it. For the mammoth bobbing shape that overtopped the ridge was only a head – a mitred double head – and below it in terrible vastness loped the frightful swollen body that bore it; the mountain-high monstrosity that walked in stealth and silence; the hyaena-like distortion of a giant anthropoid shape that trotted blackly against the sky, its repulsive pair of cone-capped heads reaching half way to the zenith.

Carter did not lose consciousness or even scream aloud, for he was an old dreamer; but he looked behind him in horror and shuddered when he saw that there were other monstrous heads silhouetted above the level of the peaks, bobbing along stealthily after the first one. And straight in the rear were three of the mighty mountain shapes seen full against the southern stars, tiptoeing wolflike and lumberingly, their tall mitres nodding thousands of feet in the aft. The carven mountains, then, had not stayed squatting in that rigid semicircle north of Inquanok, with right hands uplifted. They had duties to perform, and were not remiss. But it was horrible that they never spoke, and never even made a sound in walking.

Meanwhile the ghoul that was Pickman had glibbered an order to the night-gaunts, and the whole army soared higher into the air. Up toward the stars the grotesque column shot, till nothing stood out any longer against the sky; neither the grey granite ridge that was still nor the carven mitred mountains that walked. All was blackness beneath as the fluttering legion surged northward amidst rushing winds and invisible laughter in the aether, and never a Shantak or less mentionable entity rose from the haunted wastes to pursue them. The farther they went, the faster they flew, till soon their dizzying speed seemed to pass that of a rifle ball and approach that of a planet in its orbit. Carter wondered how with such speed the earth could still stretch beneath them, but knew that in the land of dream dimensions have strange properties. That they were in a realm of eternal night he felt certain, and he fancied that the constellations overhead had subtly emphasized their northward focus; gathering themselves up as it were to cast the flying army into the void of the boreal pole, as the folds of a bag are gathered up to cast out the last bits of substance therein.

Then he noticed with terror that the wings of the night-gaunts were not flapping any more. The horned and faceless steeds had folded their membranous appendages, and were resting quite passive in the chaos of wind that whirled and chuckled as it bore them on. A force not of earth had seized on the army, and ghouls and night-gaunts alike were powerless before a current which pulled madly and relentlessly into the north whence no mortal had ever returned. At length a lone pallid light was seen on the skyline ahead, thereafter rising steadily as they approached, and having beneath it a black mass that blotted out the stars. Carter saw that it must be some beacon on a mountain, for only a mountain could rise so vast as seen from so prodigious a height in the air.

Higher and higher rose the light and the blackness beneath it, till half the northern sky was obscured by the rugged conical mass. Lofty as the army was, that pale and sinister beacon rose above it, towering monstrous over all peaks and concernments of earth, and tasting the atomless aether where the cryptical moon and the mad planets reel. No mountain known of man was that which loomed before them. The high clouds far below were but a fringe for its foothills. The groping dizziness of topmost air was but a girdle for its loins. Scornful and spectral climbed that bridge betwixt earth and heaven, black in eternal night, and crowned with a pshent of unknown stars whose awful and significant outline grew every moment clearer. Ghouls meeped in wonder as they saw it, and Carter shivered in fear lest all the hurtling army be dashed to pieces on the unyielding onyx of that cyclopean cliff.

Higher and higher rose the light, till it mingled with the loftiest orbs of the zenith and winked down at the flyers with lurid mockery. All the north beneath it was blackness now; dread, stony blackness from infinite depths to infinite heights, with only that pale winking beacon perched unreachably at the top of all vision. Carter studied the light more closely, and saw at last what lines its inky background made against the stars. There were towers on that titan mountaintop; horrible domed towers in noxious and incalculable tiers and clusters beyond any dreamable workmanship of man; battlements and terraces of wonder and menace, all limned tiny and black and distant against the starry pshent that glowed malevolently at the uppermost rim of sight. Capping that most measureless of mountains was a castle beyond all mortal thought, and in it glowed the daemon-light. Then Randolph Carter knew that his quest was done, and that he saw above him the goal of all forbidden steps and audacious visions; the fabulous, the incredible home of the Great Ones atop unknown Kadath.

Even as he realised this thing, Carter noticed a change in the course of the helplessly wind-sucked party. They were rising abruptly now, and it was plain that the focus of their flight was the onyx castle where the pale light shone. So close was the great black mountain that its sides sped by them dizzily as they shot upward, and in the darkness they could discern nothing upon it. Vaster and vaster loomed the tenebrous towers of the nighted castle above, and Carter could see that it was well-nigh blasphemous in its immensity. Well might its stones have been quarried by nameless workmen in that horrible gulf rent out of the rock in the hill pass north of Inquanok, for such was its size that a man on its threshold stood even as an ant on the steps of earth's loftiest fortress. The pshent of unknown stars above the myriad domed turrets glowed with a sallow, sickly flare, so that a kind of twilight hung about the murky walls of slippery onyx. The pallid beacon was now seen to be a single shining window high up in one of the loftiest towers, and as the helpless army neared the top of the mountain Carter thought he detected unpleasant shadows flitting across the feebly luminous expanse. It was a strangely arched window, of a design wholly alien to earth.

The solid rock now gave place to the giant foundations of the monstrous castle, and it seemed that the speed of the party was somewhat abated. Vast walls shot up, and there was a glimpse of a great gate through which the voyagers were swept. All was night in the titan courtyard, and then came the deeper blackness of inmost things as a huge arched portal engulfed the column. Vortices of cold wind surged dankly through sightless labyrinths of onyx, and Carter could never tell what Cyclopean stairs and corridors lay silent along the route of his endless aerial twisting. Always upward led the terrible plunge in darkness, and never a sound, touch or glimpse broke the dense pall of mystery. Large as the army of ghouls and night-gaunts was, it was lost in the prodigious voids of that more than earthly castle. And when at last there suddenly dawned around him the lurid light of that single tower room whose lofty window had served as a beacon, it took Carter long to discern the far walls and high, distant ceiling, and to realize that he was indeed not again in the boundless air outside.

Randolph Carter had hoped to come into the throne-room of the Great Ones with poise and dignity, flanked and followed by impressive lines of ghouls in ceremonial order, and offering his prayer as a free and potent master among dreamers. He had known that the Great Ones themselves are not beyond a mortal's power to cope with, and had trusted to luck that the Other Gods and their crawling chaos Nyarlathotep would not happen to come to their aid at the crucial moment, as they had so often done before when men sought out earth's gods in their home or on their mountains. And with his hideous escort he had half hoped to defy even the Other Gods if need were, knowing as he did that ghouls have no masters, and that night-gaunts own not Nyarlathotep but only archaic Nodens for their lord. But now he saw that supernal Kadath in its cold waste is indeed girt with dark wonders and nameless sentinels, and that the Other Gods are of a surety vigilant in guarding the mild, feeble gods of earth. Void as they are of lordship over ghouls and night-gaunts, the mindless, shapeless blasphemies of outer space can yet control them when they must; so that it was not in state as a free and potent master of dreamers that Randolph Carter came into the Great Ones' throne-room with his ghouls. Swept and herded by nightmare tempests from the stars, and dogged by unseen horrors of the northern waste, all that army floated captive and helpless in the lurid light, dropping numbly to the onyx floor when by some voiceless order the winds of fright dissolved.

Before no golden dais had Randolph Carter come, nor was there any august circle of crowned and haloed beings with narrow eyes, long-lobed ears, thin nose, and pointed chin whose kinship to the carven face on Ngranek might stamp them as those to whom a dreamer might pray. Save for the one tower room the onyx castle atop Kadath was dark, and the masters were not there. Carter had come to unknown Kadath in the cold waste, but he had not found the gods. Yet still the lurid light glowed in that one tower room whose size was so little less than that of all outdoors, and whose distant walls and roof were so nearly lost to sight in thin, curling mists. Earth's gods were not there, it was true, but of subtler and less visible presences there could be no lack. Where the mild gods are absent, the Other Gods are not unrepresented; and certainly, the onyx castle of castles was far from tenantless. In what outrageous form or forms terror would next reveal itself Carter could by no means imagine. He felt that his visit had been expected, and wondered how close a watch had all along been kept upon him by the crawling chaos Nyarlathotep. It is Nyarlathotep, horror of infinite shapes and dread soul and messenger of the Other Gods, that the fungous moonbeasts serve; and Carter thought of the black galley that had vanished when the tide of battle turned against the toadlike abnormalities on the jagged rock in the sea.

Reflecting upon these things, he was staggering to his feet in the midst of his nightmare company when there rang without warning through that pale-litten and limitless chamber the hideous blast of a daemon trumpet. Three times pealed that frightful brazen scream, and when the echoes of the third blast had died chucklingly away Randolph Carter saw that he was alone. Whither, why and how the ghouls and night-gaunts had been snatched from sight was not for him to divine. He knew only that he was suddenly alone, and that whatever unseen powers lurked mockingly around him were no powers of earth's friendly dreamland. Presently from the chamber's uttermost reaches a new sound came. This, too, was a rhythmic trumpeting; but of a kind far removed from the three raucous blasts which had dissolved his goodly cohorts. In this low fanfare echoed all the wonder and melody of ethereal dream; exotic vistas of unimagined loveliness floating from each strange chord and subtly alien cadence. Odours of incense came to match the golden notes; and overhead a great light dawned, its colours changing in cycles unknown to earth's spectrum, and following the song of the trumpets in weird symphonic harmonies. Torches flared in the distance, and the beat of drums throbbed nearer amidst waves of tense expectancy.

Out of the thinning mists and the cloud of strange incense filed twin columns of giant black slaves with loin-cloths of iridescent silk. Upon their heads were strapped vast helmet-like torches of glittering metal, from which the fragrance of obscure balsams spread in fumous spirals. In their right hands were crystal wands whose tips were carven into leering chimaeras, while their left hands grasped long thin silver trumpets which they blew in turn. Armlets and anklets of gold they had, and between each pair of anklets stretched a golden chain that held its wearer to a sober gait. That they were true black men of earth's dreamland was at once apparent, but it seemed less likely that their rites and costumes were wholly things of our earth. Ten feet from Carter the columns stopped, and as they did so each trumpet flew abruptly to its bearer's thick lips. Wild and ecstatic was the blast that followed, and wilder still the cry that chorused just after from dark throats somehow made shrill by strange artifice.

Then down the wide lane betwixt the two columns a lone figure strode; a tall, slim figure with the young face of an antique Pharaoh, gay with prismatic robes and crowned with a golden pshent that glowed with inherent light. Close up to Carter strode that regal figure; whose proud carriage and swart features had in them the fascination of a dark god or fallen archangel, and around whose eyes there lurked the languid sparkle of capricious humour. It spoke, and in its mellow tones there rippled the wild music of Lethean streams.

"Randolph Carter," said the voice, "you have come to see the Great Ones whom it is unlawful for men to see. Watchers have spoken of this thing, and the Other Gods have grunted as they rolled and tumbled mindlessly to the sound of thin flutes in the black ultimate void where broods the daemon-sultan whose name no lips dare speak aloud.

"When Barzai the Wise climbed Hatheg-Kla to see the Greater Ones dance and howl above the clouds in the moonlight he never returned. The Other Gods were there, and they did what was expected. Zenig of Aphorat sought to reach unknown Kadath in the cold waste, and his skull is now set in a ring on the little finger of one whom I need not name.

"But you, Randolph Carter, have braved all things of earth's dreamland, and burn still with the flame of quest. You came not as one curious, but as one seeking his due, nor have you failed ever in reverence toward the mild gods of earth. Yet have these gods kept you from the marvellous sunset city of your dreams, and wholly through their own small covetousness; for verily, they craved the weird loveliness of that which your fancy had fashioned, and vowed that henceforward no other spot should be their abode.

"They are gone from their castle on unknown Kadath to dwell in your marvellous city. All through its palaces of veined marble they revel by day, and when the sun sets they go out in the perfumed gardens and watch the golden glory on temples and colonnades, arched bridges and silver-basined fountains, and wide streets with blossom-laden urns and ivory statues in gleaming rows. And when night comes they climb tall terraces in the dew, and sit on carved benches of porphyry scanning the stars, or lean over pale balustrades to gaze at the town's steep northward slopes, where one by one the little windows in old peaked gables shine softly out with the calm yellow light of homely candles.

"The gods love your marvellous city, and walk no more in the ways of the gods. They have forgotten the high places of earth, and the mountains that knew their youth. The earth has no longer any gods that are gods, and only the Other Ones from outer space hold sway on unremembered Kadath. Far away in a valley of your own childhood, Randolph Carter, play the heedless Great Ones. You have dreamed too well, O wise arch-dreamer, for you have drawn dream's gods away from the world of all men's visions to that which is wholly yours; having builded out of your boyhood's small fancies a city more lovely than all the phantoms that have gone before.

"It is not well that earth's gods leave their thrones for the spider to spin on, and their realm for the Others to sway in the dark manner of Others. Fain would the powers from outside bring chaos and horror to you, Randolph Carter, who are the cause of their upsetting, but that they know it is by you alone that the gods may be sent back to their world. In that half-waking dreamland which is yours, no power of uttermost night may pursue; and only you can send the selfish Great Ones gently out of your marvellous sunset city, back through the northern twilight to their wonted place atop unknown Kadath in the cold waste.

"So. Randolph Carter, in the name of the Other Gods I spare you and charge you to seek that sunset city which is yours, and to send thence the drowsy truant gods for whom the dream world waits. Not hard to find is that roseal fever of the gods, that fanfare of supernal trumpets and clash of immortal cymbals, that mystery whose place and meaning have haunted you through the halls of waking and the gulfs of dreaming, and tormented you with hints of vanished memory and the pain of lost things awesome and momentous. Not hard to find is that symbol and relic of your days of wonder, for truly, it is but the stable and eternal gem wherein all that wonder sparkles crystallised to light your evening path. Behold! It is not over unknown seas but back over well-known years that your quest must go; back to the bright strange things of infancy and the quick sun-drenched glimpses of magic that old scenes brought to wide young eyes.

"For know you, that your gold and marble city of wonder is only the sum of what you have seen and loved in youth. It is the glory of Boston's hillside roofs and western windows aflame with sunset, of the flower-fragrant Common and the great dome on the hill and the tangle of gables and chimneys in the violet valley where the many-bridged Charles flows drowsily. These things you saw, Randolph Carter, when your nurse first wheeled you out in the springtime, and they will be the last things you will ever see with eyes of memory and of love. And there is antique Salem with its brooding years, and spectral Marblehead scaling its rocky precipices into past centuries! And the glory of Salem's towers and spires seen afar from Marblehead's pastures across the harbour against the setting sun.

"There is Providence quaint and lordly on its seven hills over the blue harbour, with terraces of green leading up to steeples and citadels of living antiquity, and Newport climbing wraithlike from its dreaming breakwater. Arkham is there, with its moss-grown gambrel roofs and the rocky rolling meadows behind it; and antediluvian Kingsport hoary with stacked chimneys and deserted quays and overhanging gables, and the marvel of high cliffs and the milky-misted ocean with tolling buoys beyond.

"Cool vales in Concord, cobbled lanes in Portsmouth, twilight bends of rustic New Hampshire roads where giant elms half hide white farmhouse walls and creaking well-sweeps. Gloucester's salt wharves and Truro's windy willows. Vistas of distant steepled towns and hills beyond hills along the North Shore, hushed stony slopes and low ivied cottages in the lee of huge boulders in Rhode Island's back country. Scent of the sea and fragrance of the fields; spell of the dark woods and joy of the orchards and gardens at dawn. These, Randolph Carter, are your city; for they are yourself. New England bore you, and into your soul she poured a liquid loveliness which cannot die. This loveliness, moulded, crystallised, and polished by years of memory and dreaming, is your terraced wonder of elusive sunsets; and to find that marble parapet with curious urns and carven rail, and descend at last these endless balustraded steps to the city of broad squares and prismatic fountains, you need only to turn back to the thoughts and visions of your wistful boyhood.

"Look! through that window shine the stars of eternal night. Even now they are shining above the scenes you have known and cherished, drinking of their charm that they may shine more lovely over the gardens of dream. There is Antares – he is winking at this moment over the roofs of Tremont Street, and you could see him from your window on Beacon Hill. Out beyond those stars yawn the gulfs from whence my mindless masters have sent me. Some day you too may traverse them, but if you are wise you will beware such folly; for of those mortals who have been and returned, only one preserves a mind unshattered by the pounding, clawing horrors of the void. Terrors and blasphemies gnaw at one another for space, and there is more evil in the lesser ones than in the greater; even as you know from the deeds of those who sought to deliver you into my hands, whilst I myself harboured no wish to shatter you, and would indeed have helped you hither long ago had I not been elsewhere busy, and certain that you would yourself find the way. Shun then, the outer hells, and stick to the calm, lovely things of your youth. Seek out your marvellous city and drive thence the recreant Great Ones, sending them back gently to those scenes which are of their own youth, and which wait uneasy for their return.

"Easier even than the way of dim memory is the way I will prepare for you. See! There comes hither a monstrous Shantak, led by a slave who for your peace of mind had best keep invisible. Mount and be ready – there! Yogash the Black will help you on the scaly horror. Steer for that brightest star just south of the zenith – it is Vega, and in two hours will be just above the terrace of your sunset city. Steer for it only till you hear a far-off singing in the high aether. Higher than that lurks madness, so rein your Shantak when the first note lures. Look then back to earth, and you will see shining the deathless altar-flame of Ired-Naa from the sacred roof of a temple. That temple is in your desiderate sunset city, so steer for it before you heed the singing and are lost.

"When you draw nigh the city steer for the same high parapet whence of old you scanned the outspread glory, prodding the Shantak till he cry aloud. That cry the Great Ones will hear and know as they sit on their perfumed terraces, and there will come upon them such a homesickness that all of your city's wonders will not console them for the absence of Kadath's grim castle and the pshent of eternal stars that crowns it.

"Then must you land amongst them with the Shantak, and let them see and touch that noisome and hippocephalic bird; meanwhile discoursing to them of unknown Kadath, which you will so lately have left, and telling them how its boundless halls are lonely and unlighted, where of old they used to leap and revel in supernal radiance. And the Shantak will talk to them in the manner of Shantaks, but it will have no powers of persuasion beyond the recalling of elder days.

"Over and over must you speak to the wandering Great Ones of their home and youth, till at last they will weep and ask to be shewn the returning path they have forgotten. Thereat can you loose the waiting Shantak, sending him skyward with the homing cry of his kind; hearing which the Great Ones will prance and jump with antique mirth, and forthwith stride after the loathly bird in the fashion of gods, through the deep gulfs of heaven to Kadath's familiar towers and domes.

"Then will the marvellous sunset city be yours to cherish and inhabit forever, and once more will earth's gods rule the dreams of men from their accustomed seat. Go now – the casement is open and the stars await outside. Already your Shantak wheezes and titters with impatience. Steer for Vega through the night, but turn when the singing sounds. Forget not this warning, lest horrors unthinkable suck you into the gulf of shrieking and ululant madness. Remember the Other Gods; they are great and mindless and terrible, and lurk in the outer voids. They are good gods to shun.

"*Hei! Aa-shanta 'nygh!* You are off! Send back earth's gods to their haunts on unknown Kadath, and pray to all space that you may never meet me in my thousand other forms. Farewell, Randolph Carter, and beware; for *I am Nyarlathotep, the Crawling Chaos.*"

And Randolph Carter, gasping and dizzy on his hideous Shantak, shot screamingly into space toward the cold blue glare of boreal Vega; looking but once behind him at the clustered and chaotic turrets of the onyx nightmare wherein still glowed the lone lurid light of that window above the air and the clouds of earth's dreamland. Great polypous horrors slid darkly past, and unseen bat wings beat multitudinous around him, but still he clung to the unwholesome mane of that loathly and hippocephalic scaled bird. The stars danced mockingly, almost shifting now and then to form pale signs of doom that one might wonder one had not seen and feared before; and ever the winds of nether howled of vague blackness and loneliness beyond the cosmos.

Then through the glittering vault ahead there fell a hush of portent, and all the winds and horrors slunk away as night things slink away before the dawn. Trembling in waves that golden wisps of nebula made weirdly visible, there rose a timid hint of far-off melody, droning in faint chords that our own universe of stars knows not. And as that music grew, the Shantak raised its ears and plunged ahead, and Carter likewise bent to catch each lovely strain. It was a song, but not the song of any voice. Night and the spheres sang it, and it was old when space and Nyarlathotep and the Other Gods were born.

Faster flew the Shantak, and lower bent the rider, drunk with the marvels of strange gulfs, and whirling in the crystal coils of outer magic. Then came too late the warning of the evil one, the sardonic caution of the daemon legate who had bidden the seeker beware the madness of that song. Only to taunt had Nyarlathotep marked out the way to safety and the marvellous sunset city; only to mock had that black messenger revealed the secret of these truant gods whose steps he could so easily lead back at will. For madness and the void's wild vengeance are Nyarlathotep's only gifts to the presumptuous; and frantick though the rider strove to turn his disgusting steed, that leering, tittering Shantak coursed on impetuous and relentless, flapping its great slippery wings in malignant joy and headed for those unhallowed pits whither no dreams reach; that last amorphous blight of nether-most confusion where bubbles and blasphemes at infinity's centre the mindless daemon-sultan Azathoth, whose name no lips dare speak aloud.

Unswerving and obedient to the foul legate's orders, that hellish bird plunged onward through shoals of shapeless lurkers and caperers in darkness, and vacuous herds of drifting entities that pawed and groped and groped and pawed; the nameless larvae of the Other Gods, that are like them blind and without mind, and possessed of singular hungers and thirsts

Onward unswerving and relentless, and tittering hilariously to watch the chuckling and hysterics into which the siren song of night and the spheres had turned, that eldritch scaly monster bore its helpless rider; hurtling and shooting, cleaving the uttermost rim and spanning the outermost abysses; leaving behind the stars and the realms of matter, and darting meteor-like through stark formlessness toward those inconceivable, unlighted chambers beyond time wherein Azathoth gnaws shapeless and ravenous amidst the muffled, maddening beat of vile drums and the thin, monotonous whine of accursed flutes.

Onward – onward – through the screaming, cackling, and blackly populous gulfs – and then from some dim blessed distance there came an image and a thought to Randolph Carter the doomed. Too well had Nyarlathotep planned his mocking and his tantalising, for he had brought up that which no gusts of icy terror could quite efface. Home – New England – Beacon Hill – the waking world.

"For know you, that your gold and marble city of wonder is only the sum of what you have seen and loved in youth… the glory of Boston's hillside roofs and western windows aflame with sunset; of the flower-fragrant Common and the great dome on the hill and the tangle of gables and chimneys in the violet valley where the many-bridged Charles flows drowsily… this loveliness, moulded, crystallised, and polished by years of memory and dreaming, is your terraced wonder of elusive sunsets; and to find that marble parapet with curious urns and carven rail, and descend at last those endless balustraded steps to the city of broad squares and prismatic fountains, you need only to turn back to the thoughts and visions of your wistful boyhood."

Onward – onward – dizzily onward to ultimate doom through the blackness where sightless feelers pawed and slimy snouts jostled and nameless things tittered and tittered and tittered. But the image and the thought had come, and Randolph Carter knew clearly that he was dreaming and only dreaming, and that somewhere in the background the world of waking and the city of his infancy still lay. Words came again – "You need only turn back to the thoughts and visions of your wistful boyhood." Turn – turn – blackness on every side, but Randolph Carter could turn.

Thick though the rushing nightmare that clutched his senses, Randolph Carter could turn and move. He could move, and if he chose he could leap off the evil Shantak that bore him hurtlingly doomward at the orders of Nyarlathotep. He could leap off and dare those depths of night that yawned interminably down, those depths of fear whose terrors yet could not exceed the nameless doom that lurked waiting at chaos' core. He could turn and move and leap – he could – he would – he would – he would—.

Off that vast hippocephalic abomination leaped the doomed and desperate dreamer, and down through endless voids of sentient blackness he fell. Aeons reeled, universes died and were born again, stars became nebulae and nebulae became stars, and still Randolph Carter fell through those endless voids of sentient blackness.

Then in the slow creeping course of eternity the utmost cycle of the cosmos churned itself into another futile completion, and all things became again as they were unreckoned kalpas before. Matter and light were born anew as space once had known them; and comets, suns and worlds sprang flaming into life, though nothing survived to tell that they had been and gone, been and gone, always and always, back to no first beginning.

And there was a firmament again, and a wind, and a glare of purple light in the eyes of the falling dreamer. There were gods and presences and wills; beauty and evil, and the shrieking of noxious night robbed of its prey. For through the unknown ultimate cycle had lived a thought and a vision of a dreamer's boyhood, and now there were remade a waking world and an old cherished city to body and to justify these things. Out of the void S'ngac the violet gas had pointed the way, and archaic Nodens was bellowing his guidance from unhinted deeps.

Stars swelled to dawns, and dawns burst into fountains of gold, carmine, and purple, and still the dreamer fell. Cries rent the aether as ribbons of light beat back the fiends from outside. And hoary Nodens raised a howl of triumph when Nyarlathotep, close on his quarry, stopped baffled by a glare that seared his formless hunting-horrors to grey dust. Randolph Carter had indeed descended at last the wide marmoreal flights to his marvellous city, for he was come again to the fair New England world that had wrought him.

So to the organ chords of morning's myriad whistles, and dawn's blaze thrown dazzling through purple panes by the great gold dome of the State House on the hill, Randolph Carter leaped shoutingly awake within his Boston room. Birds sang in hidden gardens and the perfume of trellised vines came wistful from arbours his grandfather had reared. Beauty and light glowed from classic mantel and carven cornice and walls grotesquely figured, while a sleek black cat rose yawning from hearthside sleep that his master's start and shriek had disturbed. And vast infinities away, past the Gate of Deeper Slumber and the enchanted wood and the garden lands and the Cerenarian Sea and the twilight reaches of Inquanok, the crawling chaos Nyarlathotep strode brooding into the onyx castle atop unknown Kadath in the cold waste, and taunted insolently the mild gods of earth whom he had snatched abruptly from their scented revels in the marvellous sunset city.

Only Monsters

Samuel Marzioli

LINGKOD HEARD THE aswang stirring in the dark of early morning, its excited moans and jabber drifting up and down the basement stairs. When it finally burst into her room at sunrise, it didn't say a word, but from its ecstatic smile – the tip of its proboscis tongue pushing through its blackened teeth – she knew exactly what it wanted. After three months, the day had come. The hunger had returned. Time to hunt.

While the aswang adjusted its human skin before the bathroom mirror, Lingkod packed the van, racing to and from the supply closet, corralling ropes, zip ties, and various forms of bait. Afterward, they traveled south. As it sat behind the wheel – switching FM channels between news and OPM – she brooded in the cargo space, imagining the faces of dead girls she'd delivered to their fate.

The aswang never stalked the same place twice, preferred to pick its hunting grounds at random. Sometimes it started at the break of dawn, other times at dusk. Sometimes it chose a major highway leading to a local stop; other times, it diverted through back roads and side streets for hours and miles before deciding on its final destination.

"Ritual is predictable," it had told her on the last hunt. "Once we fall into a pattern, we give ourselves away, shine a spotlight on our darkness. That is why we must make unpredictability our ritual"

She had given it the same side-eyed, rage expression that she gave it now, prickling at the presumption that she could ever be an eager student and not the unwilling slave. The fact its litany of rules worked only bolstered her resentment. After all, while other members of its kind had faded into folklore and rural superstition, it still lived.

Hours on, the aswang turned into the parking lot of Greentown Mall, found an isolated spot with a clear view of the entrance. Already droves of teenage shoppers poured inside, their reckless glee and careless blather like chum in shark-infested waters.

"Choose," it said, the wet clicking of its tongue swimming in salivation.

Lingkod shook her head. "Please don't make me. I can't do it."

"Do not forget our bargain." It stiffened, muscles rippling beneath slender arms of liver spots and wrinkles, as if a reminder: though it bore the semblance of an old woman, a monster lived inside its skin. "Do as you are told or you will find yourself back upon my table."

She did. Like the coward she was, of course she did.

Alone, she strolled into the food court, staked out an empty table and waited. Before she could even think to choose, she had to let the aching in her heart pass, her voice calm, and the tremble in her hands steady. She had to peel the feeling side of her away, pretend she wasn't herself, pretend she was a passive gun pointed toward the crowd and not the eager hands that aimed it.

When she finally found that space of inner separation, she stood, took a breath, scanned around. She only needed one, and like the lion culling from the zebra herd, anyone would do.

* * *

Her name was Carla, a tiny girl with chocolate hair and horned rim glasses perched upon a button nose. Lingkod spun some tale about working publicity for an American music label trying to break into the Philippine market, and how she needed the opinions of "smart girls of sophisticated taste" to guide them. Flattery wasn't one of the aswang's many rules, but Lingkod's innovation, which made it so much worse.

"All you have to do is listen to a few CDs, tell me what you think and you can have whichever is your favorite."

Carla believed her. She didn't hesitate when Lingkod led her to the aswang's seedy van, even with what appeared to be a strange, old woman gawking from the driver's seat. If only Carla could have sensed the lie, retreated back to her house and waited for the hunt to end, the danger to pass. But she didn't. No one ever did and Lingkod had to relive the exact same horrors again and again.

On the long drive home, Lingkod held Carla's hand and coaxed out answers, patient as she waited through the stutters and the sobbing. Carla said she was seventeen. She had graduated from senior high that year, loved musicals and plays, and hoped one day to be a singer.

Lingkod never understood the reasons why she had to ask such questions, to collect such information. It didn't matter what they said, didn't keep them from being dragged into the dust and shadows of the basement lair, where the aswang shed its skin and cut those sad, young things apart. She could only guess it boosted the undoing, the way a cook might season meat to enhance its flavor.

Minutes before they pulled into the side yard and shut and chained the gate, Lingkod stroked Carla's hair, told her comforting lies in soft whispers. "Keep your eyes shut tight. It won't hurt. Just a few more hours and you'll be free."

Once the aswang carried Carla away, Lingkod lingered in the front yard, far from all the squelching and the screaming, staring past the iron spires of the fence into the neighborhood beyond. Her scars began to burn, an affliction of her mind, not body, but it hurt her all the same. Like so many times before, she imagined herself escaping from this prison, sprinting down the street and racing through distant roads and half-remembered trails to her parents' home in Gattaran. What she wouldn't give to make it real and yet she'd long since given up on such dangerous dreams.

Her family was her peace, her strength, her reason for enduring, but how could she ever face them after everything she'd done? If they ever knew, the shame alone would destroy her. Not to mention how the aswang would react if she ever dared return back home. She couldn't help envisioning the result of such a vengeful hunt, scores of bodies soaked in their own blood, wrapped in their own viscera, only this time with faces of the people that she knew and loved.

Besides, she had no hope of refuge. Evil had corrupted her, had sunk into her skin, rooted deep into her soul. Even if she hid someplace the aswang couldn't find her, where could she go to hide from herself?

* * *

Lingkod passed throughout the house, shutting windows, drawing curtains, locking doors. The aswang sat upon the kitchen floor, a deep bass hum inside its throat, the TV blaring news from the countertop beside it. A cigarillo dangled from its mouth as it shaped its latest project, hacking, slicing, carving pieces from a pile of banana stalks beside it. Somehow the stalks transformed as well, and through the combination of conversion and removal, something new emerged. Here the eyes, and nose, and mouth. There the breasts, the hips, and waist.

It joined the pieces all together using talahib grass strengthened by some viscid excretion from its tongue. Once assembled, it gazed upon its creation: a simplistic doll of human proportions, folk art at a glance, but for the twitching of its limbs and the pulsing of its chest. Lingkod headed for the entryway, couldn't bear to witness what would happen next, but the aswang's growl stopped her short.

"*Imitasyon*," it said, grinning, eyes shining with a dull, unnatural light.

Once it regurgitated Carla's blood, Lingkod bolted from the house. Before she slammed the door behind her, she heard a whisper lost inside the aswang's manic cackle. "I don't feel well." These would be the final words the family heard before the mimic "died" and they placed it in a coffin meant for Carla. A vile deception, dark magic at its worst, one of the many ways the aswang concealed the savagery of its crimes.

* * *

The aswang lounged upon the lowest basement step, watching Lingkod clean the floors around its carving table. From TV, it had learned the basics of forensic science and wouldn't let her rest until every scrap had been discarded and every drop and print had been scrubbed into oblivion. Lingkod tried not think about the meaning of her work. While the aswang had murdered Carla, she was covering the crime, circumventing any chance of justice. Morally, that made her as culpable as it was.

Soon, the aswang started reminiscing, the way it always did in the idle hours after an undoing. Same old stories told as new.

"From the moment I first saw you, I knew you would be good, but you've exceeded my expectations. I used to be afraid before the hunt, did you know that? A fear of townsfolk riled into mobs who would hunt me, corner me, cut off my head or cast me into a bonfire – the way so many of my sisters died."

A low and rolling chuckle and then it said, "Now I don't even need to hide anymore. No more debasing myself with painful transformations: a boar wallowing in the mud or a dog rolling in the dusty streets."

Lingkod knew exactly what it meant, recalled the day she found its journals stacked inside its closet, chronicling its many sins. Though ever cautious, it had obscured the truth of what it was and what it did through riddles and insinuations. While she couldn't puzzle out its age, she saw hints of countless centuries hidden in the text and could almost bet that if she cut into its stomach, she would find fragments of ancient Spanish invaders still trapped inside.

The entire time it spoke, she kept silent, biting on her cheek to distract herself with pain. When she stuffed a blood-soaked rag into the trash bag, the aswang paused and skimmed the tapered end of its proboscis on its lips.

"Things have changed," it said. "No more stalking inhabitants of isolated houses or cornering victims on vacant roads at night. The Philippines has become a civilized country and you are the final piece to my assimilation."

Condescending though it was, Lingkod could remember things far worse. Like the night it dragged her down into its lair and strapped her to its carving table. The hours it spent cutting into her, lapping at her blood, warning her that if she cried she might push it past the point of self-control and make it do something drastic.

It had lied, though. She'd screamed and begged for hours, but it had only smiled and continued with its work. Perhaps it had sensed her weakness. Perhaps it already knew that it could break her, bend her to its will, use her in the hunt. If only she'd been brave enough to die and prove it wrong.

* * *

The aswang called the months between the hunt a reprieve. In that time, it gave Lingkod free rein of its house, made no room private, not even its lair. It hadn't always been so "generous." Three years ago, in the early weeks of her captivity, it had locked her in her room with nothing but a bucket for necessities and fed her from a trough fixed to the inside of her door.

The change came slow, new freedoms added over time. Stockholm syndrome tactic, she guessed, meant to ingratiate itself to her. It had even shared the ritual of transformation some weeks back, something it had never done before.

"I once read that humans think we have baby chickens living in us, that that's what gives us power," it had said, eyes rolling up into the red veins of its sclera. "Can you believe that? Ridiculous, of course. We share our essence by planting an egg deep inside our chosen, fertilized with our own blood. It's painful. The chosen dies, but when she rises again, she rises into power..."

It scrutinized her reaction. Had it hoped she would show an interest? Ask it questions? Beg it to make her a partner, a true daughter of the hunt? In truth, she didn't care, wouldn't take its curse for all the power in the world, but even a monster can dream.

On the days she didn't hide inside her room – reading books, listening to music, or languishing in the thrall of depression sleep – she slipped on her tsinelas and went outside. Often, she would press up against the front yard fence, pray that someone would see her, recognize her, call for help. "Missing Girl Reunited With Her Family!" she imagined tomorrow's headline would read, with "Mythic Beast Slain By Police" in smaller letters underneath. No one ever did. The people on her street clung to their privacy. On the rare occasions a neighbor deigned to look her way, all they had to offer were friendly waves or smiles.

She did her best to forget the girl she was, but in the quiet introspection roused by all those lonely hours, she couldn't stop the memories from coming. What it felt like to smile. What it meant to be free. The last time she'd felt the overwhelming joy of both, she had just moved to Manila for university at 17.

"Work hard and make something of yourself," her parents had told her and she'd promised that she would. Now her words only called to mind the night the aswang took her and the irony her promise had become. She could still recall the moment in photographic details, how she'd strolled the dark streets to her dorm room after a party at a friend's house. The cargo van that edged on to the curbside. The unnatural glint of eyes piercing through the windshield. All that swirling, suffocating darkness drawing her in until the world spiraled like a vortex in the center of her vision and she blacked out.

Later, in its basement, how it sloughed its pseudo-skin, exposing the devastation of its true hide. Only then did she realize what it was: a corpse barely clinging to the fringe of life, a demonic miscreation birthed by sins and nightmares, surviving on the pain and blood of the innocent. In a word, aswang.

Now that she was its accomplice, what had she become?

Have I made you proud of me, Mom and Dad? she thought. *I've never worked harder in all my life.*

* * *

Three months passed before Lingkod heard the aswang crawling through the house at night, claws dragging on the carpet, its telltale moans and jabber trailing up and down the basement stairs. At the barest blush of morning, it charged into her room, slithered up beside her bed to shake her.

"Get the van ready," it said, beaming. "Today we hunt."

This time, it drove them to San Mateo and parked outside the entrance to a grade school minutes after classes had let out. Children raced in groups or pairs, some with parents leading the way or trailing behind them. But some walked alone.

"Why are we here?" Lingkod asked.

The aswang only grinned and licked its lips.

She tried pretending they had stalled along a detour, waiting for police to pass or for traffic to let up. But she could sense a change: the aswang's sudden dead-eye focus, the hunger prodding it into a quivering, drooling frenzy. Pupils narrowed, it raised its hands, fingers rising, falling, as if practicing the undoing on every child passing by.

As soon as the crowds thinned to stragglers, it followed alongside a girl in a pink skirt, with little hands latched on to her backpack straps and tiny legs that barely lugged her forward.

"No!" Lingkod shook her head. "You can't do this."

"You should be thanking me," the aswang said, then paused to drop a taunting chuckle. "You told me not to make you choose. You said it was too hard. This time, you won't have to."

"I'm sorry. I shouldn't have complained. Take me somewhere else so we can do this right."

"Too late. How will you ever learn if there are no consequences?"

The little girl directed her attention to a tree where two birds trilled upon its branches, until they flapped and hopped and obscured themselves within the canopy above. Whatever they did next Lingkod couldn't see, but the little girl tilted back her head and laughed. Her innocence – it shone bright as day, a kitten batting at a ball of yarn.

"I refuse," Lingkod said. "The second you pull up, I'll scream and scream and scream."

The aswang snarled, its tongue lolling, writhing on its lap before retreating into its mouth again. In the wedge of light streaming through the windshield, its eyes shone like glass marbles set within the sockets of a corpse. A chill flooded through Lingkod and she recoiled, imagining the beast behind its skin. Crying, trembling, she slid the cargo door aside.

* * *

Alone, she hurried down the street, slinking half as much from shame as stealth. Before she could try to coax the little girl into the van, she had to crush the inner voice screaming insults and self-loathing in her head. She had to suppress her emotions, let apathy reign free. Pretend she wasn't a conscious, living being, but a machine operating on the cold, brute logic of its program.

Lingkod approached the little girl not two blocks on, dropped upon one knee to make herself seem small and harmless. "Thank God I found you!"

When the little girl turned, Lingkod nearly hissed. That face. It reminded her of Leonora, her father's favorite niece, a cousin she rarely spoke to outside of funerals and weddings. The last time had been at their *lola*'s wake some six years back. Leonora had sat beside Lingkod when she introduced the brand new baby in her arms that looked so much like the twin of her. Same wide eyes and long lashes, same full lips, with a matching rose-red mole upon their cheeks. What could it mean that this girl had such features or that she couldn't have been much more than six?

Lingkod didn't have the heart to ask, couldn't stand the thought of knowing whether it was true. Instead, she launched into another tale, said she had been working reception at the local hospital when the paramedics brought a woman in who had been struck by a car, had a broken leg, internal bleeding. Before they could haul her in for treatment, she begged Lingkod to fetch her daughter so they could speak one last time in case her health got worse.

The little girl's eyes went wide, her mouth agape, a look of utter devastation, like her world had come undone.

"Actually," Lingkod said. She glanced back at the aswang's van, half a block away and coasting. Still far enough where it couldn't hear. "You can wait at home and your mother will return as soon as she can. In fact, she might be there already. We have… good doctors."

The little girl didn't move.

"Go home!"

The van pulled up beside them with a sudden shriek of brakes.

"I said run!"

But the little girl had turned her gaze upon the aswang as soon as it arrived. Lingkod could feel its hypnotizing stare, the breath-stealing, energy-draining, dizzying, confounding power of it. The little girl fell and Lingkod caught her even as the cargo door slid wide.

"Run?" the aswang asked and shook its head. "Bring her here before I remember there's room enough for two upon my table."

She did. Like the coward she was, of course she did.

* * *

Her name was Rosalinda. She was six, loved dogs and cats and cartoons, and wanted to be a superhero so she could run fast and finish all her mother's work so they could always be together. Selfless and imaginative. Not old enough to dream real dreams yet. Lingkod recited those same false comforts as she held Rosalinda's hand. "Keep your eyes shut tight. It won't hurt. You'll be home before you know it."

Once the aswang carried Rosalinda away, Lingkod squatted on the porch while picking through the details of Rosalinda's final words. How she wished real superheroes existed, some muscle mass in spandex with sufficient strength to rip the aswang's head off and send that ghoul in pieces to its grave. "Little Girl Rescued!" she imagined tomorrow's headline would read, with "Mythic Beast slain By Manila's Super Champion" in smaller letters underneath.

Nevertheless, she knew better than to hope in silly notions such as "Justice will prevail." In this world, evil thrived while goodness gasped and floundered. No one would ever stop the aswang. No one would ever save Rosalinda. Superheroes didn't exist, only monsters.

Once the aswang finished the undoing, it stepped outside the house, gazed into the setting sun and stretched its arms until they popped.

"I will savor this one," it said, the words dribbling from its mouth in strings of sputum. "After all, she's practically *family*."

A smirk before it plodded to the side yard and unchained the gate. Once the van's sputter faded to a distant wheeze, Lingkod ventured down the basement stairs, already shaking, already sobbing from the agony of realization. It shouldn't have mattered that the aswang had confirmed she and Rosalinda were related – a child is a child is a child – and yet it did. She'd assumed her obedience would keep her family safe, spare them from the aswang's rage, from the consequences of her actions. Now that its attention had shifted to them, it angered her as much as it terrified her as much as it tormented her.

After descending to the basement and finding Rosalinda alive, she finally understood the other part of what the aswang said: the undoing had barely started. Rosalinda lay strapped to the carving table, squealing from a dozen shallow cuts and bruises. At the sight of her, Lingkod's old wounds began to burn, white scars the size and shape of tiger stripes spread across her body, a permanent reminder of what the aswang had done.

She'd tried so hard to shirk the blame, to define herself as a victim when she had played the part of predator as well. Thirteen girls caught by her own hands. Thirteen girls all sacrificed upon the altar of an evil god so that she herself would be spared. How many more would have to suffer the same fate before she had the strength to renounce this servile life, before she found the courage to say, "This is wrong. I will not help you anymore!"

With that, she scrambled to the table, unbuckled Rosalinda's bonds and carried her up the stairs while speaking words of comfort – only now with strength, with conviction, because all of it was true.

"Don't be scared. It's over now. You're safe."

Lingkod set Rosalinda upon the porch, hurried back inside and wrote a message on a sheet of paper.

When she returned, she said, "Find somewhere busy and then wave your hands and scream. Make yourself visible, make yourself known, until someone has to pay attention." She stuffed the sheet into Rosalinda's hands and pointed in the direction of the closest street with a mass of stores and crowds of people. "Show them this note. It'll explain everything."

Rosalinda turned and fled. Lingkod watched her little cousin run, that little spark of hope within the dying of the light. How she envied her, but she knew she couldn't follow. Having lived so long in shadows, complicit with the evils there, only death could set her free. Hers. Or the aswang's.

* * *

As soon as the aswang found out what she'd done, the bargain they had struck would be void. She could still remember that moment, lying half-conscious on the carving table as the aswang loomed above her, its rancid stink and slaver spilling on her face.

"If you become my servant, you'll never have to fear again because I will protect you," it had said. "But betray me and I will cut you apart and scatter the pieces across the four corners of the earth so that not even God himself could put you back together."

Simple words boosted by a casual tone, because it wasn't given as a threat, but an incidental truth. Same as fire burns or water drowns, the nature of the aswang entailed suffering. Lingkod understand that better than ever and yet nothing could surpass the torment of these last few years, the toll of which had spread an emptiness inside her too vast for life to fill again. Since pain and death had lost their vigor, what could the aswang do?

She descended to the lair, a chamber buried deep below the house's foundation, a bulb smothered by black cloth filling it with somber, yellow light. In the far off corner lay the aswang's bed, a shallow pit of soil where it burrowed when it slept. The carving table stood within the lair's center, ancient and unholy, a vast hewn limestone block etched with shapes like runes, leather straps and buckles bolted to its sides.

The aswang's knives were arrayed by size and shape upon it, tools it used because claws could never be so delicate and precise. Lingkod examined the serpentine blade with a narrow hilt. She imagined herself shoving the business end into the aswang's heart, watching the gleam within its eyes flare in shock before it faded… faded… and finally snuffed out.

Another dream for the aswang to ruin? Perhaps. However, for the last three years she had been as much a ruthless monster as the aswang itself. While she acknowledged it, accepted it, she could no longer let it stand. So long as she had breath, she would fight with everything inside her, not for vengeance or absolution, but to rectify the blood on her own hands.

She would have to be quick, have to be cunning, don a disguise of tears and weakness to catch it by surprise. It didn't matter if she failed, though, only that she tried. Because one way or another, a monster died tonight.

The Jumper

S.R. Masters

I

'I KNOW I'M standing before Cambridge University's paragons of rationality,' Nick said, laughter murmuring through a largely undergraduate audience of scientists and philosophers, 'but in the coming weeks, maybe even by the end of this lecture, all of you will admit you believe in ghosts.'

Nick pointed to a cardboard box beside the lectern. He scanned the packed rows from the stage: plenty of smiles, some cautious frowns. One blue-haired young man wearing a silver crucifix necklace appeared particularly wary. At the back he spotted Thalia, sitting with other members of the philosophy faculty – come to see for themselves why this visiting fellow in his early thirties had made such a splash up at Durham.

From the box he retrieved a mustard jumper and held it across his chest, hands shaking. 'Who here is brave enough to come up and try on this fetching jumper? Come on, don't be shy. It's been washed.'

He waited, willing them, and to his relief hands began to rise. Ten or so. The last of his pre-lecture nerves settled.

'Good stuff. First though, in the spirit of honesty, I have to tell you something about this jumper. Sometimes, when people find out *whose* jumper this was, they change their minds. Not that it will affect *you* lot. Shouldn't matter who once wore a jumper, should it?'

He studied them, basking in the disquiet and anticipation.

'If you all drop your hands again – thank you. So, this jumper once belonged to Malcolm Steadman.' Recognition evinced on lit faces and in low whooshes of amused horror. Mr. Blue Hair looked positively disgusted. 'The West Midlands Ripper, who killed fifteen men, women, and children, during the late seventies and early eighties. Fifteen we know of, because there were likely others, too.'

He clicked the remote and a famous photograph of Steadman appeared behind him. 'Here he is wearing it.'

Groans. Grim laughter.

'Now,' he said, grinning, 'anyone still want to try it on?'

II

PACKING UP afterwards, he allowed himself a small smile. To think how nauseous he'd been at breakfast. How stressed. But no, elite university or otherwise, it always went the same way. As usual there'd been someone willing to do it. A single contrarian looking to rut. But Nick hadn't invited them on stage to wear the jumper – because by then he'd made his point. Once Steadman's name had been invoked, the other hands stayed down.

'Human beings,' he'd told them, 'can't help believing in the supernatural. From birth our brains hunt for patterns and meaning when presented with chaos. We see faces in clouds and croissants, plead for traffic lights to turn green when we're late. And yes, for no rational reason – is serial killing contagious? – we don't want to put on Malcolm Steadman's old yellow jumper.'

It had all gone wonderfully. So many had stayed to talk, craving more. Not Thalia though. He was excited to hear her thoughts, but now he'd have to wait until tonight.

Hearing shuffling behind him, Nick turned, startled. Mr. Blue Hair, notebook clutched to his chest, stood at the edge of the stage.

'I didn't know anyone was still here,' Nick said.

'Sorry. I wasn't going to say anything but… I felt compelled.'

'Oh. Right.'

'Is it really his jumper?'

'Does it matter?' Nick picked up the box. What was this all about?

Mr Blue Hair addressed his trainers. 'Did you know he was from around here?'

'Steadman? He grew up in a village near here, yes. But he left for the West Midlands in his late teens.'

'People here have long memories.' The man didn't look up. 'Do you not worry all this might… have consequences? Offend someone?'

Nick took a breath and shifted his weight. 'Are *you* from around here?'

Mr Blue Hair nodded. 'From Ely.'

Nick swallowed. 'Have *you* been offended then?'

'No, not me personally.' The boy rolled his eyes, and Nick felt both irritation and relief. 'It's just more… It's still a sensitive matter. People knew him.'

Nick nodded, unsure what he was missing, his gaze drawn to the boy's gleaming crucifix.

'I see what you're saying,' Nick said, 'thanks for bringing it up. I'll keep it in mind certainly. The Steadman stuff is really only in this first lecture, so hopefully we won't do too much damage.'

The boy made a non-committal humming sound. 'Well… I thought you'd appreciate the context.'

'Thanks.'

'Some people don't think he acted alone.'

Nick shook his head, losing patience. 'Do you think they're still around now and might take umbrage?'

The boy looked up now. 'I just mean… it's raw. That things like that don't go away.'

'Well… again, thanks. I have to run. We can pick this up another time, perhaps.' Nick marched to the rear door.

The boy's voice echoed behind him. 'I didn't know if you knew the history, that's all.'

III

AFTER A DAY of supervisions, he walked back to Broughton College in the dark, still rattled by the boy. Of course, Nick *had* known the history. Very well in fact, but he hadn't wanted to get into that. He'd grown up in nearby Barton, the small village where Steadman had been born. The monster had been dead by then, his ashes interred – much to the consternation of the media – in the grounds of the same church where Nick's own father would later be buried. One Halloween, he and three teenage friends had even held an inebriated and ineffectual séance in the overgrown corner of the graveyard where Steadman's ashes supposedly lay.

So yes, he knew the context, thank you. And if he wanted to take something back from the bugger, then that was his right.

In his flat at the rear of the Neo-Gothic main building, Nick showered, dressed and went to hang the jumper up. He'd bought it four years before in a Durham charity shop, having known the instant he saw it that he could recreate an old trick of his doctoral supervisor's and pass it off as Steadman's.

A strong musty smell wafted out of the wardrobe when he opened the doors. Nick recoiled. He reached for one of the wire hangers and immediately withdrew his hand. Another mustard jumper hung there already. He stared at it, smiled weakly, and brought it out to lay on the bed.

This was chunkier than Nick's prop, older, too. Across the surface tufted wool hung like a toxic cloud above a desert. The whole effect, down to the lattice pattern, was much closer to the real thing than Nick's.

He called Thalia, because she was the only person with a key to his room. She claimed ignorance, and he believed her – she wasn't the pranking sort. And a prank this definitely was, and a good one, too – although someone must have broken in, and that wasn't really on, was it?

So he reported the incident to the porters, and, after placing the jumper in a bag, left it outside in the corridor. A funny thing to do, but he *was* running late. It certainly wasn't because the jumper unnerved him a little bit. No, not that at all.

IV

THALIA WAS THE cleverest and poshest person he'd ever met, and in the half-light of the Italian restaurant, peering at him with her wide, dark eyes, he floated between a state of gratitude and one of being terrifyingly out of his depth.

'Is it worth calling the police?' she said. 'Prank or not, they broke in.'

'It's someone trying to prove a point, isn't it? Might just wear it to the next lecture. It was probably one of the kids from this morning.'

He told her about Mr. Blue Hair. About the strange things he'd said.

She nodded. 'Well, I suppose if you swim in the New Atheist pool you have to expect to be dive-bombed occasionally.'

'Well…' Nick said. 'I don't know if I'm in that club. My point, really, is that atheists and sceptics have no reason to be smug. That we actually all have these sorts of irrational beliefs—'

'Oh, I understood your lecture,' she said, smiling, 'but saying the beliefs are irrational… that's begging the question, somewhat.'

'I see,' he said, unable to hold back a grin, conscious of the mischief in her eyes.

'You play at humility, Nick, but really you're just an unbeliever in sheep's clothing.'

Nick sipped his wine and never broke eye contact. She really was wonderful.

'I'm on the fence,' he said. 'I'm saying our senses look for patterns, even when there aren't patterns. That's all.'

'But what if there *are* patterns?'

'But sometimes there aren't.'

'But what if sometimes there are when you thought there weren't? What if there *were* faces in the clouds? What if you *did* turn the traffic light green?'

He pictured the jumper again, spread out on his bed, revulsion snaking up his back.

'I suppose the real question,' she said, 'is whether *you* have had a supernatural experience.'

'Have you?'

'Don't change the subject.'

He looked away, considered lying, and gulped his remaining half-glass. Thalia leaned forward.

'Don't laugh,' he said, 'but after Dad died, I used to see him.'

'I can't tell if you're winding me up.' Thalia studied him.

'My bedroom overlooked the village church, and after he'd gone I would wake up in the night and sort of… sense him. I was only eleven, but… I'd pull back my curtains and see him there at the church gate, dressed in his suit, gesturing at me, like this, urging me to come down.'

He met her incredulous stare. 'You're being serious. Nick… I'm—' She put a hand over her mouth.

'He was in his late fifties, had a heart attack on the sofa, and I found him. The night before we'd had this silly argument. He was at Cambridge, too, a biologist, and he wouldn't let me read about the supernatural. I was fascinated: ghosts, aliens, psychic powers. Rot, he used to call it. He found this book under my bed that I'd taken out the library, said he was really disappointed, and I bit back. Told him he was a bully and closed minded. Anyway… he looked so crushed. I planned to apologise the next morning, but—'

He shrugged and looked away.

'Oh, Nick. Let's change the subject.'

'I don't know if I dreamed those things, or it was my developing mind's way of coping. A sort of hallucination, like night terrors or sleep paralysis… At the time it felt very real. And I wanted to go to him, and say sorry, but I knew it couldn't be him really. And… I thought he would be proud of me for knowing that. For being rational and *not* going.'

'How long did you experience it for?'

'It stopped after a month or so. I'd wake up, look, and he wouldn't be there. But I never forgot. It's why I ended up studying neuroscience and philosophy.'

For the first time since he'd known her, Thalia was lost for words. Eventually, she said, 'You never went down? Not even once?'

'No,' he said, surprised with how animated it sounded. 'No, he wasn't actually there, was he?'

V

THEY STUMBLED INTO Nick's flat, kissing, and were about to collapse on to his bed when he jerked back from Thalia. The jumper lay on the bed behind her.

Thalia turned, saw the jumper, and looked back at him. 'You've gone all pale.'

'No, it's just… I swore I put that outside. That's the prank one.'

'Oh, the little buggers.'

'No, I must have… made a mistake.' That was rubbish, and he knew it. But he didn't want to spoil the mood.

She picked it up, smelled it, and made a face. 'It's nasty. You should be using this one in your lectures. Gives me the creeps.'

'It's just a jumper, Thalia.'

She held it out to him. 'Go on then. Try it on.'

He tried concealing his revulsion with a smirk. Her smile was wicked. Was it possible *she* was behind the prank? No, she'd been with him all evening. It had to be that blue-haired kid. He took the jumper from her and threw it behind him on a chair.

'Out of the question,' he said, and laughing, they climbed on to the bed.

VI

SOMETHING WOKE him at four in the morning. He had been dreaming about Dad, had been trying to tell him how sorry he was, how important it was he knew that. There'd been something else, too, but it wouldn't come.

The dream lingered. He wanted to turn on a light. Instead, he reached for his phone and comfort scrolled. Beside him Thalia didn't stir. Calmer, he was about to return his phone to the side table, when instead he typed 'Malcolm Steadman' into the search bar. He found the photo with the yellow jumper.

The illumination blackened the rest of the room around the phone's edge and his world became Steadman's face. Horsey teeth. Squinting eyes. Greying, blond curls. Incredible no one saw what he was. It was right there in his expression. A murderer, yes, but also so much worse. He'd kept his victims for weeks. Remains were always found buried, hands bound behind their backs, alongside seemingly obscure objects. Knitting needles. Bunches of cellophane. Twisted wire coat hangers.

He zoomed in on the jumper. The fuzzy wool. The lattice pattern. He shivered. That one he'd thrown on the chair in the corner wasn't just a close facsimile, was it?

More than anything he wanted to turn on the phone's torch function, to check the jumper was still there. Yet he couldn't look away from Steadman. Because it felt like if he looked away—

Ridiculous—

—he had lost some contest. That Steadman was daring him to—

God, ridiculous. Utterly ridiculous.

He turned off the screen and put the phone down. He lay back, trying to slow his breathing.

Thirty seconds passed, and he couldn't help himself. He sat back up, turned on the torch, and held the phone up to the room.

The jumper wasn't on the chair. It lay on the floor about halfway between the bed and the chair, one sleeve stretched out towards him as if caught mid-crawl.

VII

THE NEXT MORNING he cycled to the out-of-town supermarket and dropped the jumper in the charity clothes bin. The relief he felt was likely just because he'd completed something from his job list, and nothing to do with last night.

The jumper had just fallen off the chair, that was all it was.

VIII

OVER THE NEXT few days, embarrassment began to smother Nick. Dad would be rolling in his grave if he knew some of the things he'd been thinking.

It had been a prank. A clever prank, that's all. This was why you didn't read rot – it turned you daft.

At night he pretended he couldn't hear the soft metallic clangs inside the cupboard. The wire hangers *were not* brushing against one another, end of.

But one morning he awoke with something furry pressed against his tongue and lips. He cried out, appalled, and a yellow sleeve fell to his lap when he sat up. He stared at the jumper spread over him, mouth momentarily agape. Then he ran to the toilet to throw up.

Later, standing before the mirror on the wardrobe door, he stared at his colourless face. This was getting silly. Whoever was pulling this prank wanted him scared, but he'd be damned if he was going to be. It would take more than knitwear to frighten Nick James.

Go on then. Try it on.

Thalia's voice in his mind. He laughed. Oh, he'd put it on if anyone was around to see it. But no, the culprit had fled, because they were the fearful one. He'd clearly unsettled them with his views. Well, whatever, Nick was done playing. This person had come in last night and put the jumper over his mouth. That was practically assault.

So he reported it to the porters. He reported it to the police. An email went out to all students in the college about acceptable conduct.

The police took the jumper. More because Nick insisted they keep it for evidence than any protocol. They seemed a bit stumped by it all, and were surprised the CCTV at both ends of the corridor hadn't caught anything.

This was an organised trickster, though. Someone with a plan and motivation. Nick didn't know how they'd gotten the thing back from that sealed charity bin, for example, but they had. It was definitely the same jumper, too, he'd stared at the stitching long enough to know.

Nick grew more and more certain the blue-haired boy was involved in some way. He'd not mentioned it to the police or porters, because he knew he needed substantial evidence, but it wouldn't hurt to ask the kid a few questions, would it?

IX

AT HIS REQUEST, the boy stayed behind after the next lecture, looking shrunken and fearful.

'Listen,' Nick said to him, 'why do I keep finding this in my room?' He opened up a plastic bag and showed him the jumper. This morning it had been on the floor again between the door and the bed, face down with the sleeves crossed behind it. Like it had been tied up.

'I don't know. Isn't it yours?'

'No, this is different. And it keeps… appearing.'

The boy looked at him with a different fear darkening his face. 'I tried telling you.'

'Sorry, what?'

'I told you not to do it.' He looked around, exasperated. 'People round here… People don't even say his name.'

Nick could feel the back of his shirt sticking to his skin. 'Yes they do. I'm from here, and his name is Malcolm Steadman. Now tell me,' he shook the bag, 'are you responsible for this?'

The boy shook his head sadly. 'You must know about him. About what he used to do. He didn't just kill them. He picked them out. He watched them, toyed with them, sometimes for years. He played games. Left things for them.'

'What are you saying?'

'He's marked you.'

'Rot. If you're trying to say that Malcolm Steadman—'

'If you come across a lion on your path you don't run. You stay still and hope they don't notice you. People round here, they know that. Nothing good ever happens if you run. The reason they've always thought he had a helper was because… things keep happening to people. Like he never went.'

Nick wanted to yell at this ridiculous, deranged young man. Yet, didn't he now remember that, growing up, no one *had* ever said his name. And if they did, they whispered it.

'I don't think I want to talk anymore, Mr. James.'

'Dr James.'

'Dr James, sorry.' The boy turned towards the exit. 'I'd burn it if I were you. And I'd pray.'

X

THERE WOULD be no praying. But he did burn the jumper, watching it drift up the chimney as smoke before Thalia let herself in and asked what he was up to.

It was good to have her here. And once they had finished two bottles of Merlot and climbed into bed, he could almost forget about Malcolm Steadman.

That was until three in the morning, when he was wrenched out of some awful dream, convinced that someone was inside his wardrobe. He tossed the bedclothes aside, turned on the lamp and went to look.

Only his prop jumper hung there.

He turned to retreat, but his entire body seized with cold on seeing Thalia. Her face was wrapped in *the* jumper. It rose and fell with her laboured breathing.

He ran to her, yelling, and yanked it away. But it was okay, because she was moving, was alive, and confused, but sitting up now, yes, *yes*, thank… God? Yes, *God*, why not?

She wanted to know what was happening, her concern rising the more awake she became and the more she watched him pacing and biting his nails.

'It's this *prank* again,' he said, 'I'm just so… stressed by it and—'

She was shaking her head, wide-eyed. 'It was on me, Jesus.'

Her expression darkened, and she took him in anew.

'No, Thalia, it wasn't me.'

'Then what? You burned that jumper tonight. I saw pieces of it in the grate.'

He couldn't lie. But dare he admit the truth? There had to be something he wasn't seeing.

For the longest time they looked at one another.

'It's not a prank, is it Nick?'

'It is. It has to be.'

'Nick? You're shaking.'

'I'm not.'

She bent down, picked up the jumper and thrust it at him. He lurched back with another gag-like yell.

'Why are you so scared of it?' Her voice wavered. 'Why was it on my bloody face?'

'I'm not scared of it.'

She shook her head, glaring at him. 'Put it on.'

He stared at her. 'What?'

'If you aren't scared of it, and you really believe it's a prank, put the bloody thing on. Otherwise… tell me what the hell is happening.'

For a while he kept staring, stunned. Oh, how stupid he'd been. How utterly, utterly stupid. Of course, he saw it now. 'Do you really think I'm that daft, Thalia? Some ignorant comprehensive-educated interloper, starting to get a little too big for his boots. Is this my Cambridge hazing?'

'What? No, what are you—?'

He grabbed the jumper, pulled it over his head. 'Happy?'

She stared at him. 'Nick…'

'Now, get out.'

XI

THE RUSE WAS up, and his foe had been vanquished. When the door slammed, and her sobs echoed in the hall, he knew that if there was any sort of heaven, which obviously there wasn't, Dad would be looking down on him, proud.

He turned to the mirror, for the longest time unable to look at his face. Just because… just because what if he did and he didn't see himself looking back?

Rot. Just rot.

When he did finally look, he saw the jumper was a perfect fit. He began to cry.

XII

LATER, HE SAT on a bench in the graveyard of Barton church. Dawn was close, but darkness still held sway.

He'd been to Dad's grave. Because really that was what all this had been about, hadn't it? Even though he'd put the jumper on, had won the day for rationality in exposing Thalia's prank… he hadn't, had he? Because there had been nothing rational about any of it. Nothing rational about these… obscenities he had tried so hard to deny. To pin on poor Thalia.

That blue-haired boy had been right. Nick had been marked. Something was coming for him. It was close, too. But he'd been unable to truly accept it until he'd put that jumper on. Felt the true force of whatever lay behind it when, just momentarily, he had hated Thalia so much that he'd considered pinning her down, choking her, breaking her. Another will acting on *his* body.

Once he had taken it off, burned the jumper all over again, he was himself again. But the jumper would be back. Near him. On him. In him.

Let it come. Because what all this meant, really, was… perhaps it wasn't all rot? And if it wasn't all rot, Dad might really have been down there at the church gates all those nights. And he'd missed his chance to say sorry, and to make things right.

Perhaps now he understood though, he might get another chance.

'Dad, I'm so sorry,' he said. 'I'm so, so sorry. And if you come again, I understand now. I won't turn my back.'

He waited. Behind him to his left, his father's last resting place. Behind him to his right, Steadman's. And after a while footsteps approached Nick from some indistinct point to his rear. At first he didn't turn, wanting to stretch his hope to the limit. In the end, though, he had to.

Afterlife on Mars

Bret Nelson

A DAY ON MARS is 37 minutes longer than a day on Earth, so the Resnik Habitat (in the Arcadia Planitia lowlands) runs on a variation of military time. The clocks go up to 24:37, then jump to 00:00. This unearthly period of extra moments is called the "terminus," and if weird things were going to happen at Resnik, you'd think that's when they would occur.

But they didn't. The first evidence of the haunting took place at 09:23 on a Tuesday.

* * *

Anna Seward filled in the last section of her Supplies Report, noting she'd be needing mung seeds. The Operations Meeting didn't start until 09:30, which gave the botanist just enough time to finish her tea. As she reached for her cup, the room went cold. A rush of air tossed some pages off her desk. Before the papers landed, all was still again. The gust reminded her of Waterfoot, an hour north of Belfast, where she grew up.

"That's trouble," she said, pressing *CONTROL* on the comm link over her desk. A few beeps later, the screen showed Ranjit Dara's station at the Control Center. The black hair on top of the Technology Director's head filled the view. He didn't look up from his Supplies Report.

"Hello, Anna," he said. "This can't wait six minutes for the meeting?"

"Is there trouble with the airflow? Anything different?"

He glanced to his left. "No. Everything shows nominal."

"Odd that," she said, picking up the pages. "Felt like a window blew open."

Ranjit smiled. "Really? Let's check on that. First, are you dead? Because an open window will kill you. Second, have you built a window that opens? Because the habitat doesn't have any windows that open."

"Ranjit, come on," she laughed. "These papers blew off my desk. What could do that?"

"Not sure. Is it still happening?"

"No, just one pop."

"The next time I'm in the logs, I'll look for your pop."

* * *

There were a total of five people living on Mars, and they were a few months into the second year of their permanent residency. That's 723 days and nights.

The Director, Charlotte Durand, kept the Operations Meeting to a lean fifteen minutes. Later she'd upload the reports and logs for Mars Control in Toulouse, France.

A building full of people in Toulouse would, in turn, use that data to update the *Resnik Habitat Operations Manual: A Complete Guide of Protocols and Procedures.* It was the largest text in history, and it continued to grow.

In 117 days, a dozen more people would arrive at Resnik. Mars' population would more than triple, and each of the five pioneers (they eschewed the word *martian*) wanted to be ready.

* * *

The next day, Wednesday, at 16:22, Toda Mitsuo worked in the Fabrication Center. She leaned into the monitor at the aerogel station and twisted the control stick. The magnification increased as the engineer tugged her microneedles. Three sections of material were knitted with monomolecular threads.

She heard footsteps enter and come to a stop behind her. Someone needed something. "Give me a second," she said. "This is tight work."

Whoever it was kept still. "Thanks for your patience," Toda said, finishing the row. The thread bonded properly, completing the join. She stretched her back as she turned her chair. "Good news, that filament is… "

She was alone.

Seconds passed, and Doctor Russell Tate came in and trotted to the metals printer.

"Hi, Toda," he said.

"Were you just in here?"

"No. You saw me come in, like one second ago. What's up?"

"… nothing."

* * *

Thursday at 08:47, Ranjit combed through the airflow logs, looking for Anna's "pop." But a question Tate asked during breakfast gnawed at him.

The habitat had glow conduits in every ceiling. The conduits held lengths of flexible stasis cord containing a steady chemiluminescence reaction. It put out 600 lumens per meter without consuming power, a constant source of light. They were held in louvered channels which could be opened or closed manually to control the brightness.

Which made Tate's question impossible.

"Why are my lights flickering?"

That can't happen, Ranjit thought, trying to focus on the task at hand.

Airflow showed normal. Yet, readings confirmed four temperature anomalies in the last few days. An eight-degree drop, just for a few seconds, then back to normal.

Can't happen.

His screen flashed a message. A cleaning bot was stuck in the Forward Mess.

* * *

At 14:27 that afternoon, Russell Tate sat next to Ranjit in the Control Center. They stared at the largest screen.

"Run it again, please," said Tate.

"Did you see it?" asked Ranjit. "Am I crazy?"

"I'm not that kind of doctor. I didn't take crazy-class at USC."

They watched video from the Forward Mess earlier that day. A cleaning bot patrolled the empty room. Its floor brushes turned slowly while the upper tendrils sanitized the tabletops.

"It happens 24 seconds in," said Ranjit.

A triangle of LEDs on the bot's stalk flashed red. It stopped and sounded a collision alarm, though nothing blocked its way. Next, the flashing LEDs went solid, indicating the bot was jammed between objects. After twelve seconds, the LEDs and alarm stopped altogether, and the bot resumed its work.

Tate sighed. "Is there another angle?"

"Yes, the water station camera." Ranjit clicked another file. "You saw the cup, right?"

Leaning forward, Tate said, "No, something else. But I'll watch for it."

The action played again from the new camera. This time, Tate saw a coffee cup on the table slide six inches on its own. The bot never touched it.

"Woah," said Tate. "Now I see the cup. And look here, on the floor."

"What is that?" asked Ranjit.

"A shadow."

"It's from the bot."

"No," said Tate, pointing. "This one, this is the bot's shadow. That other one, it's bigger. It moves independently."

"Camera fault?"

"It's on the other angle, too," said Tate. "That cup travelled at least twice its length and whatever is casting that shadow moves so the bot can go past it."

"So, we're crazy."

"Yup."

The comm link beeped and Charlotte Durand interrupted their review.

"I need everyone in the Meet Room. Now."

* * *

"Twelve minutes ago," said Durand, "my quarters went cold and completely dark. I was making my way to the control box when I bumped into someone. They gasped. I heard them gasp and felt them move away."

She looked to the other four pioneers around the Meet Room table. "The lighting returned. There was no one there. The cold stopped. I know a couple of you had things like this happen."

Ranjit was poking his tablet. "I see the temperature drop, but everything else shows normal."

"All right," said Durand. "Each of you needs to report what you've experienced. Everything please, no editing."

Each pioneer described an event. Anna's cold snap. The presence Toda felt. Tate's flickering lights.

Ranjit went last, using the media wall to display the video from the Forward Mess.

"And," Ranjit concluded, "that can't happen."

As the video looped, Durand scrutinized the cup. "We need more information."

"Anyone else been having nightmares?" asked Ranjit.

"Haven't slept right all week," said Toda.

"Yeah," said Tate. "Night terrors, like when I was a kid."

"When I was twelve," said Ranjit, "my cousin told me a story about a chudail. It's this awful girl ghost. He said her feet were backwards and her eyes were upside down, but she only looked like that at a distance. If she got close, she'd trick you and just look like a nice lady. Then she'd get you. It spooked me so bad. I used to check everyone's feet, to make sure they weren't backwards. I'd peek out my window and jump because I thought I saw her on the corner."

"Are we telling ghost stories?" asked Anna.

"It's not the story," said Ranjit. "That feeling, that pressure is back. Strong. When I look outside, it's like she's going to be there in the sand."

"Okay, I'm starting to freak out a little," said Toda.

Anna shook her head. "It's the isolation. At the psych briefings, they said we'd have bad dreams."

"It's Ted," said Russell Tate. "It must be Ted Abbott."

"I knew somebody was going to say it," said Anna. "Can we stop this? Something is wrong, a technical fault, and it's causing peculiarity with systems and people. We need some non-fiction troubleshooting."

"Anna's right," said Durand. "Everyone, go to your sections. Run diagnostics, gather data. We'll come back here in two hours and work the problems."

* * *

When the pioneers arrived at Resnik, they called out every action as a historical first. Ranjit Dara was the first person to curse in Hindi on Mars. Charlotte Durand was the first person to make popcorn on Mars.

Theodore Abbott was the first person to die there. A chemical engineer, Ted researched improvements in shielding material and air filters. After he fell dead at his workstation, everyone stopped calling out "firsts."

With less than ninety days on Mars, no one was ready for this. They followed the procedures spelled out in the manual. They pressure-crated Ted's body and he was picked up with other Earth-bound cargo. The automated freight ships came every forty days and thankfully the next one was just six days out.

They sent him off wearing his Sao Paulo Football Club hoodie.

He arrived on Earth five months later. The autopsy left no doubts about the cause of death, a *cerebral aneurysm*. A blood vessel ruptured in his brain, and he died in seconds.

Ted made one more journey after that. He was flown to Brazil and buried next to his parents in the Vila Nova Cachoeirinha Cemetery.

* * *

Anna Seward spent the next two hours making sure her plants' lighting, moisture, and feed systems were operating normally.

Doctor Tate analyzed the habitat's breathing mix. He kept himself busy enough to stave off a panic attack.

Ranjit Dara had run a complete system check earlier, so he spent most of the time piloting his drones on a cartography pass over Mawrth Vallis. It calmed him.

In her quarters, Toda Mitsuo reviewed video from the Fabrication Center yesterday. She scrubbed to the moment she thought she had company. There were no extra shadows or objects moving on their own, but with the sound at maximum she *did* hear footsteps among the audio artifacts.

When she heard herself say *Give me a second, this is tight work,* it was loud enough to startle her.

But there was something else on the track. A pale whisper.

"Sorry," it said. The word was there, tangled in the white noise.

Her comm link beeped. "Toda, it's Charlotte. Can you meet me in the Fabrication Center?"

"Call me when you get there and I'll join you," said Toda, "I don't want to be there alone."

* * *

Later, the pioneers gathered again in the Meet Room. Ranjit, Anna, and Russell had no new information to report. Toda shared her audio discoveries.

"Sounds like static to me," said Anna.

Charlotte Durand went next. "I've consulted the Operations Manual." She moved to the media wall and brought up the document. "And I found a section labeled *Unexplainable Phenomena*. There's a troubleshooter that starts with a checklist of occurrences, asking you to flag any that apply."

She navigated to the relevant page. "Several of our issues are here. I marked odd dreams, temperature shifts, moving objects, and unsteady lighting. Here's where that takes us."

She clicked *NEXT*, and the screen showed a single question:

Has there been a death amongst the crew? (Y/N)

"That's nuts," said Anna.

"I answered 'yes.' It gave me a procedure to run." Durand tossed a folder onto the table. "This is the hard copy, PN/027. There's two parts. Toda, can you take over?"

Toda moved to the media wall. "I've been in the Fabrication Center, because the first half is a build," She pulled up a schematic titled *PN/027-001 (Spectral Coherer)*. "It's simple," she said. "A rectangular box with a disc on top and a cone on the side. The materials are printing now. It shouldn't take long to construct it."

"How big is that?" asked Anna.

"Thirty centimeters from the base to the top of the disc."

"But what is it?" asked Ranjit.

"Not sure," said Toda. "The disc holds half a gram of carbon granules between two metal plates. A tiny lead hooks that to some basic circuits and a power cell inside the box."

"That's a microphone," said Tate. "An old microphone."

"Is the cone powered?" asked Anna.

"Nope," said Toda. "A plain, copper cone held with two screws."

"This 'coherer' must have a purpose. What does the manual say?" asked Tate.

"We can't use it until after dinner," said Durand. "The second half of the procedure happens at night. The device sits in the middle of a table while we hold hands and concentrate. Then one of us reads this page out loud. That box is going to power a seance."

* * *

Toda carried the finished device into the Rear Mess. She was a few minutes late and the others had already started dinner, but they were doing more arguing than eating.

"This feels silly," said Anna. "Like slumber party nonsense."

"It's in the manual," said Ranjit. "If it was nonsense, it wouldn't be there."

Toda put the device on a table far away from the food and drinks. "The contraption is built. Came together easy. I still don't know how it works."

She retrieved her food tray. "Lasagna, yes!"

"You don't know how it works because it doesn't do anything," said Anna. "Someone's having us on."

"I can't imagine it's a prank," said Toda, between bites. "But it's not supernatural, either. Maybe the manual has an error."

Durand walked a lap around the device. "But that entry is so detailed."

"I guess," said Toda, "But whatever is going on, I can't call it a ghost. Can any of you, with a straight face, say the Resnik Habitat is haunted?"

Silence. Then...

"The Resnik Habitat is haunted," said Ranjit. "That's hard to say, because we're too smart. We don't trust anything outside of facts. In school, I ridiculed anyone dumb enough to have a faith-based belief.

"Now I look at things like string theory and dark matter. They haven't been absolutely proven out, but I believe they're real. Is that faith?"

"I say run the procedure," said Tate. "It's there for a reason. Doctor Sollis, one of my teachers, he used to say that when science looks over the last ridge, when we finally know everything, we may learn that spirituality was waiting there all along. That could be right, or not. Maybe after tonight, I'll understand a little more."

Anna took her tray to the basin, then collected everyone else's and put those away as well.

"I'm scared," she said, starting the wash system. "I'm scared that the real fault will kill us while we waste time on this. But to be fiercely honest, there's part of me that's scared of Ted Abbott. Not because he's some phantom, but because if Ted's here, then everything I know to be true – isn't. What then?"

"Then that would be a discovery," said Durand. "And that is why we're on Mars in the first place. Protocol already determined our next action. Everyone needs to find a personal item that relates to Ted and bring it to the Meet Room. We are running this procedure."

* * *

They'd sent his things back home with his body, so finding "personal items" required some thought. But everyone managed to find something. One by one, they were placed on the Meet Room table in a circle around the spectral coherer.

"This work order still cracks me up," said Ranjit. It was a scrap of paper Ted left for him during their first week: *Nothing works. Please help.*

Tate brought a steri-bag with a swab inside. "This went up his nose."

"This is his pen," said Charlotte. "I never gave it back. Maybe that's why he's here."

Anna had printed out the Sao Paulo Football Club logo in green and pink. "These are the wrong colors. If I know Ted, he'll cross worlds to correct me."

"Does everyone remember the atomic sieve?" asked Toda. She'd found the prototype for Ted's dream project – a small aerogel filter to make the air on Mars breathable.

"There's oxygen everywhere," he'd say, "but it's stuck to carbon atoms, no good for lungs. I'll make a filter that strains out the carbon, like a sieve, but with atom-size holes." He envisioned filling the habitat with usable air by means of a simple pump. Or wearing a facemask that enabled free breathing on the planet's surface.

"It's still a remarkable concept," said Tate.

"Let's talk about it later," said Anna. "What's next?"

"We work the procedure," said Durand. "Make certain you've got no personal electronics. Then take your seats around the table and hold hands."

"What do we do with the gadget?" asked Ranjit.

"Nothing," said Durand. "It's not for us. Everyone needs to be quiet now. We're going to sit and be calm, then in a few minutes I'll read this out loud. Here we go."

All five closed their eyes and tried to be still. They listened to the ambient sounds of the fans and motors that made up the habitat's background noise.

But there was a new sound as well. At the center of the table, the coherer was humming. Toda let go of Anna's hand and reached for it, but the noise stopped. When she took Anna's hand again, the noise resumed. "How—"

Anna squeezed her hand and shushed her. Everyone settled again and Charlotte Durand read from her page.

"We are gathered for a single purpose," she said. "A presence walks this place, an entity attempting contact. You have been heard. Now we hope you will hear us. If you can, please give us a sign."

Minutes passed with no change. Durand repeated her words, adding one phrase. "Please join us."

The lights flickered. "That's nuts," said Anna.

"Are you with us?" asked Durand.

Hollow scratches and pops emanated from the cone on the coherer.

"That's not hooked up to anything," whispered Toda.

"Be quiet," whispered Ranjit. "Keep going, Charlotte."

"We hear you. Please tell us how we can help you."

A series of hisses, nearly words.

"Please say again," said Durand.

Echoed and thin, but a voice now. "Ignored," it said.

Charlotte scanned her pages for an appropriate reply. "We apologize. We didn't know you were here. Tell us, are you Ted Abbott?"

The coherer's hum pitched lower. "Once."

Ranjit fought the urge to run.

"Your body is in Sao Paulo, in the cemetery," said Durand. "You must go."

The voice was still a whisper, "Can't go."

"You don't belong here. You must go."

"Can't go outside."

"We can help you," said Durand. "The device through which you speak, it will show you the way. Take it with you and go."

The coherer slid one inch toward Durand. She repeated the words twice more. "Take it with you and go. Take it with you and go."

The lights were getting brighter. "Join me," she said to the others. All the pioneers chanted along.

"Take it with you and go. Take it with you and go."

The coherer shook, as did the other objects on the table.

"Take it with you and go. Take it with you and go."

The lights went out and a rush of air moved through the room.

Earth air. It smelled of grass and mud.

Then silence.

At last, Durand spoke. "Is everyone all right?"

The lights came back up, and everybody jumped. Ranjit's hand was on the control box. "That was me," he said. "But I didn't close the louvres, they did that on their own."

The spectral coherer was gone.

The Sao Paulo Football Club logo was red and black. The correct colors.

"This makes no sense," said Anna.

"If anyone would like to join me," said Toda, "I'm going to stay up very late and eat candy."

* * *

In the days that followed, no new incidents took place. Durand included a full report in her next upload for Toulouse. She never got any feedback. It was treated like any other update.

After two months without incident, everyone had settled back into their routines. Some of them invented theories about what the occurrences *really* were. Others accepted a slightly expanded view of the universe.

Their focus returned to preparing the habitat for more people.

One morning, Russell Tate found Toda hunched over the aerogel workstation, scrutinizing a familiar structure.

"What is that?" he asked.

"I'm taking a closer look at Ted's atomic sieve."

"Breathable air with a little mask. Is that really possible?"

"I remember you calling it a 'remarkable concept,' Russell," she said. "There are some bits I can't understand. Maybe I can build another one of those coherers and ask Ted about it."

You Can Never Go Home Again

Lena Ng

AS THE OLD man drew closer to the house, still at least a mile away, his horse's plodding gait a steady crunch on the gravel road, it was as though he were travelling back in time, when he was a young man coming home to his young wife.

His first wife.

Yuki.

She had loved him once, when he was poor and foolish. Maybe she would love him again, now that he had returned to an impoverished state. No longer foolish, however; time had taught him hard lessons of wisdom. Yuki had supported him when they were struggling; as he put in long hours at the business, she uncomplainingly cooked and served his meals when he returned late in the evening.

But when his business had finally flourished, he betrayed her. His first wife had an inner beauty which seemed to hold no value when he had the money to purchase the outer kind. He had abandoned her and the house for his mistress, who later became his trophy wife. How blind he had been! How ungrateful, how unworthy he was of this jewel among wives. Now that the business had crumbled, all that remained was a sick, old man, his greedy second wife having fled for more prosperous pastures. Alone and haunted by this loneliness, the old man had a spark of madness. Maybe he could go back. Maybe he could reverse the clock's hands and use the wisdom of age to correct the rashness of youth.

Devoted and doting, his first wife had always said he was her only family. Her father had warned her that if she married him, they – her parents – would never speak to her again. And they never did. Although now, after so many years had passed, they were likely dead.

Although she was plain, his former wife had one point of beauty – her long, lush, black hair. The old man wondered if she had kept it or if it had turned as grey as his own.

The old man and his horse plodded along the familiar road which was built in simpler times. Simpler times when he could be happy with a bowl of soup and rice instead of steak drenched in butter. Simpler days when he could enjoy ale instead of a glass of aged wine. Simpler nights when he could appreciate a woman with a warm smile and outstretched arms instead of a woman with black-rimmed eyes and red lips.

He tried to think back to their first, giddy days of marriage. The heady days of summer that chilled into autumn. Soon subsistence began to starve their love. He grew to resent the hopeful face who welcomed him without complaint when his work day stretched longer. Over time, passionate first love burned down to flickering warmth, before it smouldered to its final embers and sank into ashes.

But he had never doubted her devotion. I love you, she had said. I will always love you.

At the foot of his former property, his horse planted four stolid feet into the dirt and wouldn't budge. For all his coaxing and pulling and cajoling and tugging, he couldn't convince it to continue. The old man tied it up at the edge of the property and continued the rest of the journey on foot.

The stars winked in the sky and they were bright and full of hope. As he passed the burgeoning oak tree, the old man ran his fingers over the bark. The crickets chirped with the same songs as when he had the strength to lift Yuki and carry her over the threshold. The owls cooed the same lullabies they had fallen asleep to every night.

With each step, the old man felt his body growing stronger. His pace changed from slow and shuffling to eager and strong. His back straightened and it seemed as though the weight of those foolish years fell away. He looked down at his hands. By some trick of the moonlight, they were no longer the hands of an elderly man, curled by age and knobby, but the unlined, solid hands of his prime.

The outline of his former house appeared and his house was lit and bright. Through the large picture window, he saw the table set for two, candles giving the room a romantic glow, a bottle of wine anticipating a visitor. He would swear the house was unchanged from when he used to reside there. As the old man reached the door, a chill of doubt came over him. How would he explain his leaving? He had left without a word, without a note, just went to work one day and didn't go back. And worse, how would he explain his return? His closed hand hovered above the oak door.

Before he could knock, the door opened. The welcoming light of the hearth illuminated Yuki as she stood there in the doorway. How could he have ever thought her plain? Her skin glowed with youthful fire, her eyes alive with welcome, her hair as rich and dark as ever.

She threw herself into his arms. "Takashi," she murmured into his ear, "I waited for you. All these years, I've been waiting for you."

His words fell away. He touched her beautiful soft hair, lush and black as ever it was. He wrapped his arms around her and kissed her impatient lips. After many years apart, it was as though no time had passed and they were man and wife again. They fell asleep wrapped in each other's arms.

* * *

The grey morning light fell upon the man. A biting gust of wind drew shivers. As he awoke, the man coughed at the musty smell and waved his hand to clear the dust from the air. Did he leave the window open? As he looked around the room, he shot up from the bed. Patches of the morose sky peered in through the rotting roof. Huge holes riddled the walls of the bedroom, fallen in from decay. The floorboards, no longer clean and gleaming, but dull and covered in grime.

Overnight, his house had aged and had fallen into ruins.

The man looked to his wife. No one lay on her futon. The sheets were moth-eaten but undisturbed, as though she had not slept there.

"Yuki?" he cried. "Yuki!" Only the wind answered him. What had happened? As he left the bed, his heart started racing. Where was she? Why didn't she answer his call? "Yuki!"

Again, only the mournful wind.

He raced from room to room. No longer was the house warm and inviting. No longer was the house the same as that of his youth. The tatami mats had frayed and yellowed. Drafts blew through broken windows and torn shoji paper coverings fluttered and danced. Thick layers of dust covered cracked furniture in the sitting room. The hearth was filled with soot, the mantel stones broken and crumbled. Each room seemed to have aged and rotted.

And strangely, as he ran from each room, the old man could feel himself aging as well. His rich black hair mottled as he searched each room, the colour fading until it moved beyond grey and into pure white. Deep lines carved into his face. He felt his shoulders contract and his back stooped. His hands wrinkled and curled into claws. His vision grew blurry.

His pace slowed as his body weakened. The old man was hobbling by the time he reached the great room.

It was there that his mouth stretched wide in mute horror. For all his calling, his first wife could never answer, would never be able to answer. All creatures are silent in death. A mummified corpse hung from the rafters, lush black hair obscuring its skull.

The History of Gherib and His Brother Agib

from the One Thousand and One Nights

John Payne

THERE WAS ONCE of old time a mighty king called Kundemir, who had been a brave and doughty man of war in his day, but was grown very old and decrepit. It pleased God to vouchsafe him, in his extreme old age, a son, whom he named Agib, because of his beauty and grace, and committed to the midwives and nurses and handmaids and serving-women, and they reared him till he was seven years old, when his father gave him in charge to a priest of his own people and faith. The priest taught the boy the laws and tenets of their infidel faith and instructed him in philosophy and all manner of other knowledge, and it needed but three full-told years before he was proficient therein and his resolve waxed strong and his judgment sound; yea, and he became learned, eloquent and accomplished, consorting with the wise and disputing with the doctors of the law. When his father saw this of him, it pleased him and he taught him to ride and thrust with spears and smite with swords, till by the end of his twentieth year he was an accomplished cavalier, versed in all martial exercises and surpassing in all things all the folk of his day. But he grew up a stubborn tyrant and an arrogant devil, using to ride forth to the chase with a thousand horse and make raids upon the neighbouring lands, waylaying caravans and carrying off the daughters of kings and nobles; wherefore many were the complaints against him to his father, who cried out to five of his servants, saying, 'Seize me yonder dog and beat him!' So they seized the prince and binding his hands behind him, beat him till he lost his senses; after which the king imprisoned him in a chamber, where one might not know heaven from earth or length from breadth; and there he abode two days and a night. Then the Amirs went in to the King and kissing the earth before him, interceded with him for the prince, and he released him.

Agib dissembled with his father for ten days, at the end of which time he went in to him by night and smote off his head, as he slept. When the day rose, he mounted the throne and bade his men arm themselves in complete steel and stand before him and on his either hand with drawn swords. By and by, the Amirs and captains entered and finding their king slain and his son Agib seated on the throne, were confounded and knew not what to do. But Agib said to them, 'O folk, ye see what hath befallen your king. Whoso obeyeth me, I will entreat him with munificence, and whoso gainsayeth me, I will do with him even as I did with my father.' When they heard this, they feared lest he should do them a mischief; so they replied, 'Thou art our king and the son of our king;' and kissed the earth before him; whereupon he thanked them and rejoiced in them. Then he let bring money and apparel and clad them in sumptuous dresses of honour and showered largesse upon them, wherefore they loved him and obeyed him. In like manner he dealt with the governors of the provinces and the Sheikhs of the Bedouins, both tributary and independent, so that all the kingdom submitted to him and the folk obeyed him and he reigned and commanded and forbade.

He abode thus five months, till, one night, he had a vision in sleep and awoke trembling, nor did sleep visit him again till the morning. As soon as it was day, he mounted his throne and his officers stood before him, right and left. Then he called the astrologers and expounders of dreams and said to them, 'As I slept last night, my father appeared to me, with his yard uncovered, and there came forth of it a thing the bigness of a bee, which grew till it became as a mighty lion, with claws like daggers. As I lay, wondering and alarmed at this, behold, it ran upon me and smiting me with its claws, rent my belly in sunder; whereupon I awoke, affrighted and trembling. Expound to me the meaning of this dream.' The interpreters looked at one another and answered, after consideration, 'O mighty King, this dream points to a child born of thy father, between whom and thee shall be strife, and he shall get the better of thee: so be thou ware of him, by reason of this thy dream.' When Agib heard their words, he said, 'I have no brother whom I should fear; so this your speech is a lying one.' 'We tell thee but what we know,' answered they; but he was wroth with them and beat them.

Then he rose and going in to his father's palace, examined his concubines and found one of them seven months gone with child; whereupon he bade two of his slaves carry her to the seashore and drown her. So they took her forth to the seashore and were about to drown her, when they looked at her and seeing her to be of surpassing beauty and grace, said to each other, 'Why should we drown this damsel? Let us rather carry her to the forest and live with her there in rare dalliance.' So they took her and fared on with her nights and days, till they brought her to a distant forest, abounding in fruit trees and streams, where they thought to take their will of her; but each said, 'I will lie with her first.' And they fell out one with the other concerning this. As they were thus engaged, a company of blacks fell upon them, and they drew their swords and defended themselves; but the blacks slew them both in less than the twinkling of an eye. So the damsel abode alone and wandered about the forest, eating of its fruits and drinking of its waters, till in due time she gave birth to a boy, brown but clean-limbed and comely, whom she named Gherib, by reason of her strangerhood. Then she cut his navel and wrapping him in some of her own clothes, gave him suck, mournful at heart and sorrowing for the fair estate she had lost and full of fear for her loneliness.

One day, there came horsemen and footmen into the forest, with hounds and hawks and horses laden with storks and cranes and herons and young ostriches and divers and other waterfowl and hares and gazelles and wild oxen and lynxes and wolves and lions. Presently, they came upon the damsel, sitting suckling her child, and said to her, 'Art thou a mortal or a genie?' 'I am a mortal, O chief of the Arabs,' answered she. So they told their chief, whose name was Merdas, prince of the Benou Kehtan, and who had come forth to hunt that day with five hundred of his kinsmen and the nobles of his tribe, and he bade them bring her before him. They did so and she related to him her story, at which he marvelled. Then they took her and returned, hunting by the way, to their encampment, where the Amir appointed her a separate dwelling-place and five damsels to serve her; and he loved her with an exceeding love and went in to her and lay with her. She straightway conceived by him, and when her months were accomplished, she bore a male child and named him Sehim el Leil. He grew up with his brother Gherib among the nurses and throve and waxed upon the lap of the Amir Merdas; and the latter in due time committed the two boys to a doctor of the law, who instructed them in the things of their faith; after which he gave them in charge to a valiant cavalier of the Arabs, who taught them to smite with swords and thrust with spears and shoot with bows, till, by the time they reached the age of fifteen, they knew all that they needed and surpassed all the warriors of their tribe; for each of them would undertake a thousand horse.

Now Merdas had many enemies, and the men of his tribe were the bravest of all the Arabs, being all doughty cavaliers, none might warm himself at their fire. Amongst his neighbours was an Amir, by name Hissan ben Thabit, who was his friend; and he took to wife a noble lady of his tribe and bade all his friends to the wedding, amongst them Merdas, prince of the Benou Kehtan, who accepted his invitation and came with three hundred horsemen of his tribe, leaving other four hundred to guard the women. Hissan received him with honour and seated him in the highest room. Then came all the cavaliers to the bridal and he made them bride feasts and held high festival by reason of the marriage, after which the guests departed to their dwelling-places. When Merdas came in sight of his camp, he saw dead men lying and birds hovering over them right and left and his heart sank within him at the sight. Then he entered the camp and was met by Gherib, clad in complete mail, who gave him joy of his safe return. Quoth Merdas, 'What meanest this, O Gherib?' And Gherib answered, 'El Hemel ben Majid attacked us with five hundred horse.'

Now the reason of this was that the Amir Merdas had a daughter called Mehdiyeh, never saw eyes a fairer than she, and El Hemel, prince of the Benou Nebhan, heard of her charms; whereupon he took horse with five hundred of his men and rode to Merdas to demand her hand; but he refused and sent him away disappointed. So he abode his time, till Merdas was absent on his visit to Hissan, when he fell upon the camp of the Benou Kehtan with his braves and slew a number of their warriors, and the rest fled to the mountains. Now Gherib and his brother had ridden forth a-hunting with a hundred horse and returned not till midday, when they found that El Hemel had sacked the camp and carried off the women and children captives, and Mehdiyeh among them. When Gherib saw this, he lost his wits for rage and cried out to Sehim, saying, 'They have plundered our camp and carried off our women and children! Up and at the enemy, that we may deliver the captives!' So Gherib and Sehim and their hundred horse rushed upon the foe, and Gherib's wrath redoubled, and he reaped a harvest of heads, giving the warriors to drink of the cup of death, till he won to El Hemel and saw Mehdiyeh among the captives. Then he drove at the prince of the Benou Nebhan and transfixing him with his lance, hurled him from the saddle; nor was the time of the afternoon-prayer come before he had slain the most part of the foe and put the rest to the rout and rescued the captives; whereupon he returned to the camp in triumph, bearing El Hemel's head on the point of his lance and reciting the following verses:

I'm he whose might is known upon the battle-day: Earth's Jinn do quake to see my shadow in the way.
I have a sword, which when my right hand shakes on high, Death hastens from my left to plunge into the fray;
And eke a spear I have, whereon if any look, Like to the crescent moon they see its steel point ray.
Gherib I'm called, that am the champion of my tribe: What if my men be few! My heart knows not dismay.

Hardly had he made an end of this when up came Merdas, to whom he related all that had passed in his absence. So Merdas alighted and entered his pavilion, and the men stood about him. Then all the people of the tribe fell to praising Gherib and saying, 'But for Gherib, O our lord, not one of the tribe had been saved!' So Merdas thanked him and said, 'Thou hast well requited our pains in rearing thee, O Gherib!'

Now, when Gherib delivered Mehdiyeh from El Hemel, she smote him with the arrows of her glances and he fell into the toils of her love, wherefore his heart could not forget her and he became drowned in passion and love-longing. Sleep forsook him and he had no delight of meat or drink, but would spur his horse up to the mountain-tops, where he would spend the day in reciting verses and return at nightfall; and indeed the signs of love-liking and distraction were manifest upon him. He discovered his secret to one of his companions and it became noised abroad in the camp, till it reached the ears of Merdas, who thundered and lightened and rose and sat down and puffed and snorted and reviled the sun and the moon, saying, 'This is the reward of him who rears bastards! Except I kill Gherib, I shall be put to shame.'

Then he opened out his mind to one of the elders of his tribe and took counsel with him of killing Gherib. 'O Amir,' replied he, 'it was but yesterday that he freed thy daughter from captivity. If thou must needs kill him, let it be by the hand of another than thyself, so the folk may not misdoubt of thee.' Quoth Merdas, 'Advise me how I may compass his death, for I look to none but thee for this.' 'O Amir,' answered the other. 'wait till he goes forth to hunt, when do thou take a hundred horse and lie in wait for him in the caves, till he passes; then take him off his guard and fall upon him and cut him in pieces, so shalt thou be quit of his reproach.' 'This should serve,' said Merdas and chose out a hundred and fifty of his stoutest horsemen, whom he lessoned to his will. Then he watched Gherib till, one day. he went forth to hunt and rode far away amongst the hills and valleys; whereupon Merdas followed him with his men and lay in wait for him by the way against he should return from the chase; but, as they lay in ambush among the trees, there fell upon them five hundred Amalekites, who slew of them three-score and made fourscore and ten prisoners and pinioned Merdas.

Now the reason of this was that when Gherib put El Hemel and his men to the sword, the rest fled to their lord's brother and told him what had happened, whereat his gorge rose and he gathered together his Amalekites and choosing out five hundred cavaliers, each fifty cubits high, set out with them in quest of revenge for his brother. By the way he fell in with Merdas and his company and there happened between them what happened; after which he bade his men alight and rest, saying, 'O folk, the idols have given us an easy revenge; so guard ye Merdas and his men, till I carry them away and put them to death on the foulest wise.' When Merdas found himself a prisoner, he repented of what he had done and said, 'This is the reward of tyranny.' Then they lay down to sleep, and the enemy passed the night, rejoicing in their victory, whilst Merdas and his men despaired of life and made sure of death.

Meanwhile, Sehim el Leil, who had been wounded in the fight with El Hemel, went in to his sister Mehdiyeh and she rose to him and kissed his hands, saying, 'May thy hand never wither nor thine enemies have occasion to rejoice! But for thee and Gherib, we had not escaped captivity. But know, O my brother,' continued she, 'that thy father hath ridden forth with a hundred and fifty horse, purposing to kill Gherib; and thou knowest it would be foul wrong to kill him, for that it was he who saved your honour and rescued your goods.' When Sehim heard this, the light in his eyes became darkness and he donned his battle-harness and mounting, rode in quest of Gherib. He presently came up with him and found that he had taken great plenty of game; so he saluted him and said to him, 'O my brother, why didst thou go forth, without telling me?' 'By Allah,' replied Gherib, 'it was but that I saw thee wounded and thought to give thee rest.' Then said Sehim, 'O my brother, beware of my father!' and told him how Merdas was abroad with a hundred and fifty men, seeking to kill him. Quoth Gherib, 'Allah will make his treason to return on his own head.'

Then they set out, to return to the camp, but the night overtook them by the way and they rode on in the darkness, till they drew near the valley where the enemy lay and heard the neighing of horses; whereupon said Sehim, 'O my brother, my father and his men are ambushed in yonder valley; let us flee from it.' But Gherib dismounted and throwing his bridle to his brother, said to him, 'Stay here till I come back to thee.' Then he went on till he came in sight of the folk, when he saw that they were not of his tribe and heard them name Merdas and say, 'We will not kill him save in his own land.' Wherefore he knew that Merdas was their prisoner and said, 'As Mehdiyeh liveth, I will not depart hence till I have delivered her father, that she may not be troubled!' Then he sought till he came upon Merdas and found him bound with cords; so he sat down by his side and said to him, 'God deliver thee, O uncle, from these bonds and humiliation!' When Merdas saw Gherib, his reason fled and he said to him, 'O my son, I am at thy mercy: deliver me in right of my fosterage of thee!' Quoth Gherib, 'If I deliver thee, wilt thou give me Mehdiyeh?' 'O my son,' answered the Amir, 'by all that is sacred to me, she is thine to all time!' So he loosed him, saying, 'Make for the horses, for thy son Sehim is there:' and Merdas crept along till he came to his son, who rejoiced in him and gave him joy of his escape.

Meanwhile, Gherib unbound one after another of the prisoners, till he had freed the whole ninety and they were all far from the enemy. Then he sent them their arms and horses, saying to them, 'Scatter yourselves round about the enemy and cry out, "O sons of Kehtan!" And when they awake, do ye remove from them and encircle them.' So he waited till the last watch of the night, when he cried out, 'O sons of Kehtan!' and his men answered, saying, 'O sons of Kehtan!' as with one voice; and the mountains echoed their crying, so that it seemed to the enemy as though the whole tribe were upon them; wherefore they all snatched up their arms and fell upon one another with slaughter. Gherib and his men held aloof, and they fought with one another till daybreak, when Merdas and Gherib and their ninety warriors fell in upon them and killed some of them and put the rest to flight. Then they took the arms and horses of the dead and the fugitives and returned to the camp, whilst Merdas could hardly credit his deliverance.

When they reached the encampment, the folk all came to meet them and rejoiced in their safe return. Then they alighted and betook them to their tents; and all the youths of the tribe flocked to Gherib's tent and great and small saluted him and did him honour. When Merdas saw this, he was more jealous of Gherib than before and said to his kinsfolk, 'Verily, hatred of Gherib grows on my heart, and why but because I see these flocking about him! And tomorrow he will demand Mehdiyeh of me.' Quoth his confidant, 'O Amir, ask of him somewhat he cannot avail unto.' This pleased Merdas, and on the morrow, as he sat on his divan, with the Arabs about him, Gherib entered, followed by his men and surrounded by the youth of the tribe, and kissed the earth before Merdas, who rose to do him honour, making a show of joy in him and seating him beside himself.

Then said Gherib, 'O uncle, thou madest me a promise; do thou fulfil it.' 'O my son,' answered the Amir, 'she is thine to all time; but thou lackest good.' 'O uncle,' said Gherib, 'ask of me what thou wilt, and I will fall upon the Amirs of the Arabs in their dwellings and on the kings in their cities and bring thee wealth enough to cover the land from East to West.' 'O my son,' rejoined Merdas, 'I have sworn by all the idols that I would give Mehdiyeh to none but him who should take my wreak and do away my reproach.' 'O uncle,' said Gherib, 'tell me with which of the kings thou hast a feud, that I may go to him and break his throne over his head.' 'O my son,' replied Merdas, 'know that I once had a son, a champion of the champions, and he went forth one day to hunt with a hundred horse. They fared on from valley to valley, till they had wandered far away into the mountains and came to the Valley of Flowers and the Castle of Ham ben Shith ben Sheddad ben Kheled.

Now in this place dwells a black giant, seventy cubits high, who uses to pluck up trees by the roots and fight with them; and he came out upon my son and his men and slew them all, save three, who escaped and bore me the news. So I assembled my braves and went forth to fight the giant, but could not avail against him; wherefore I was baulked of my revenge and swore that I would not give my daughter in marriage but to him who should avenge me of my son.' 'O uncle,' said Gherib, 'I will go to the giant and avenge thy son on him with the help of God the Most High.' And Merdas answered, saying, 'O Gherib, if thou get the victory over him, thou wilt gain of him such booty of wealth and treasures as fires may not devour.' Quoth Gherib, 'Swear to me that thou wilt give me Mehdiyeh to wife, that I may go to seek my fortune with a heart at ease.' So Merdas swore this to him and took the elders of the tribe to witness; whereupon Gherib went away, rejoicing in the fulfilment of his hopes, and went in to his mother, to whom he related what had passed. 'O my son,' said she, 'know that Merdas hates thee and doth but send thee to this mountain, to bereave me of thee; so take me with thee and let us depart the tents of this tyrant.' But he answered, saying, 'O my mother, I will not depart hence till I have compassed my desire and overcome my enemy.'

Then he slept, till the morning arose with its light and shone, and hardly had he mounted his charger when his friends, the young men, came up to him, two hundred stout cavaliers, and cried out to him, saying, 'Take us with thee; we will help thee and keep thee company by the way.' And he rejoiced in them and said, 'God requite you for us with good! Come, my friends, let us go.' So they set out and fared on for two days, till the evening of the second day, when they halted at the foot of a high scarped bill and unbridled their horses. As for Gherib, he left the rest and fared on into the mountain, till he came to a cave, whence issued a light. So he entered and found, at the upper end of the cave, an old man, three hundred and forty years old, whose eyebrows hung down over his eyes and whose moustaches hid his mouth. His aspect filled Gherib with awe and veneration, and the hermit said to him, 'O my son, methinks thou art of the idolaters that worship stones in the stead of the All-powerful King, the Creator of Night and Day and the revolving sphere.' When Gherib heard his words, his nerves quivered and he said, 'O elder, where is this lord of whom thou speakest, that I may worship him and take my fill of his sight?' 'O my son,' replied the old man, 'this is the Supreme Lord, none in the world may look upon Him; He seeth and is not seen. He is the Most High of aspect and is present everywhere in His works. He it is who maketh all things to be and ordereth the march of time; He is the Creator of men and Jinn and sendeth the prophets to guide His creatures into the right way. Whoso obeyeth Him, He bringeth into Paradise, and whoso disobeyeth Him, He casteth into the fire.'

'And how, O uncle,' asked Gherib, 'doth he say who worships this mighty Lord who hath power over all?' 'O my son,' answered the old man, 'I am of the tribe of Aad, which were transgressors in the land and believed not in God. So He sent unto them a prophet named Houd, but they believed not in him and he destroyed them by means of a deadly wind; but I believed, I and some of my tribe, and we were saved from destruction. Moreover, I was present with the tribe of Themoud and saw what befell them with their prophet Salih. After Salih, God the Most High sent a prophet called Abraham the Friend to Nimrod son of Canaan, and there befell what befell between them. Then my companions died and I continued in this cave to serve God the Most High, Who provideth me without my taking thought.' 'O uncle,' quoth Gherib, 'what shall I say, that I may become of the servants of this mighty Lord? 'Say,' replied the old man, '"There is no god but God and Abraham is the Friend of God."'

So Gherib embraced the faith of submission with heart and tongue and the old man said to him, 'May the sweetness of submission and belief be stablished in thy heart!' Then he taught him somewhat of the ordinances and scriptures of Islam and said to him, 'What is thy name?' And he answered, 'My name is Gherib.' 'O Gherib,' said the old man, 'whither art thou bound?' So he told him all his history, till he came to the mention of the Ghoul of the Mountain, whereupon quoth the other, 'O Gherib, art thou mad that thou goest forth against the Ghoul of the Mountain alone?' 'O my lord,' replied Gherib, 'I have with me two hundred horse.' 'O Gherib,' rejoined the hermit, 'hadst thou ten thousand, yet shouldest thou not prevail against him, for his name is *The-Ghoul-who-eats-men-we-pray-God-for-safety*, and he is of the children of Ham. His father's name was Hindi, who peopled Hind and named it, and he left this son after him, whom he called Saadan the Ghoul. Now, even in his father's lifetime he was a cruel tyrant and an arrogant devil and had no other food than men's flesh. His father forbade him from this, but he would not be forbidden and redoubled in his frowardness, till Hindi banished him and drove him forth of Hind, after battle and sore travail. Then he came to this country and fortified himself therein, making his dwelling in this place, whence he uses to sally forth and waylay all that come and go. Moreover, he hath begotten five stout and warlike sons, each one of whom will do battle with a thousand braves, and be hath filled the valley with his booty of horses and camels and oxen and sheep, besides other treasure and goods. Wherefore I fear for thee from him; so do thou implore God the Most High to succour thee against him by the word of Unity, and when thou drivest at the infidels, say, "God is Most Great!" for this saying confoundeth those who misbelieve.'

Then he gave him a mace of steel, a hundred pounds in weight, with ten rings, which clashed like thunder, when the wielder brandished it, and a sword forged of a thunderbolt, three cubits long and three spans broad, wherewith if one smote a rock, it would cleave it in sunder. Moreover, he gave him a hauberk and target and a book and said to him, 'Return to thy people and expound Islam to them.' So Gherib left him, rejoicing in his newly-gained faith, and returned to his companions, who saluted him, saying, 'What made thee tarry thus?' Whereupon he told them all that had befallen him and expounded to them Islam, and they all embraced the faith of submission.

Next morning, Gherib mounted and rode to the hermit to bid him farewell, after which he set out to return to his camp. On his way, there met him a horseman armed cap-a-pie, so that only his eyes appeared, who made at him, saying, 'Put off what is on thee, O dog of the Arabs; or I will slay thee!' Therewith Gherib drove at him and there befell between them a battle such as would make a newborn child turn gray and melt the flinty rock with its terror; but presently the stranger did off his face-veil, and behold, it was Gherib's half-brother Sehim el Leil.

Now the manner of his coming thither was on this wise. When Gherib set out in quest of the Ghoul of the Mountain, Sehim was absent and on his return, not seeing his brother, he went in to his mother, whom he found weeping. So he asked the reason and she told him what had happened, whereupon, without allowing himself aught of rest, he donned his harness of war and mounting, pricked after Gherib, till he overtook him and there befell between them what befell. When, therefore, he discovered his face, Gherib knew him and saluted him, saying, 'What moved thee to do this?' Quoth Sehim, 'I had a mind to measure myself with thee in the field and make trial of my force in cutting and thrusting.' Then they rode on, till they drew near the valley, and on the way Gherib expounded Islam to Sehim, who embraced the faith.

Meanwhile, the Ghoul espied the dust of their horses' feet and said to his sons, 'O my sons, mount and fetch me yonder booty.' So the five took horse and made for the party. When Gherib saw the five giants approaching, he spurred towards them and cried out, saying, 'Who and what are ye and what do ye want?' Whereupon Felhoun, the eldest of the five, came out and said, 'Dismount and bind one another and we will drive you to our father, that he may roast some of you and boil other, for it is long since he hath tasted human flesh.' When Gherib heard this, he drove at Felhoun, shaking his mace, so that the rings resounded like the pealing thunder and the giant was confounded. Then he smote him a light blow with the mace between the shoulders, and he fell to the ground like a great palm tree; whereupon Sehim and some of his men fell upon him and bound him; then, putting a rope about his neck, they haled him along like a cow.

When his brothers saw him a prisoner, they rushed upon Gherib, who took three of them captive and the fifth fled back to his father, who said to him, 'What is behind thee and where are thy brothers?' Quoth he, 'A beardless youth, forty cubits high, hath taken them prisoner.' 'May the sun pour no blessing on you!' replied Saadan and going down from his hold, tore up a huge tree, with which he went in quest of Gherib and his folk on foot, for that no horse might carry him, because of the bigness of his body. His son followed him and they went on till they came up with Gherib and his company, when the Ghoul fell upon them, without word said, and killed five men with his club. Then he made at Sehim and struck at him with his club, but Sehim avoided the blow and it fell harmless; whereat Saadan was wroth and throwing down the weapon, sprang upon Sehim and caught him up as the merlin catches up the sparrow.

When Gherib saw his brother in the Ghoul's clutches, he cried out, saying, 'God is most Great! By the favour of Abraham the Friend, whom God bless and preserve!' And spurred his charger at Saadan, shaking his mace, till the rings resounded. Then he cried out again, 'God is most Great!' and smote the Ghoul full on the ribs with his mace, whereupon he fell to the ground, insensible, and loosed his hold of Sehim; nor did he come to himself before he was bound and shackled. When his son saw this, he turned and fled; but Gherib drove after him and smiting him with his mace between the shoulders, unhorsed him. So they bound him with his father and brothers and haltering them with ropes, haled them all six along like camels, till they reached the Ghoul's castle, which they found full of goods and treasures and things of price; and there they found also twelve hundred Persians, bound and shackled.

Gherib sat down on Saadan's chair, which had aforetime belonged to Sasa ben Shith ben Sheddad ben Aad, with Sehim on his right and his companions standing on his either hand, and sending for the Ghoul of the Mountain, said to him, 'How findest thou thyself, O accursed one?' 'O my lord,' answered Saadan, 'in the sorriest of plights for abasement and mortification; my sons and I, we are bound with ropes like camels.' Quoth Gherib, 'It is my will that you enter my faith, that is, the faith of Islam, and acknowledge the Unity of the All-knowing King, Creator of light and darkness and of all things,—there is no God but He, the Requiting King,—and confess the prophethood of Abraham the Friend, on whom be peace!' So the Ghoul and his sons made profession of Islam after the goodliest fashion, and Gherib bade loose their bonds, whereupon Saadan wept and would have kissed his feet, he and his sons: but Gherib forbade them and they stood with the rest.

Then said Gherib, 'Harkye, Saadan!' 'At thy service, O my lord!' answered he. Quoth Gherib, 'What are these captives?' 'O my lord,' replied the Ghoul, 'these are my booty from the land of the Persians and are not the only ones.' 'And who is with them?' asked Gherib. 'O my lord,' answered Saadan, 'there is with them the princess Fekhr Taj, daughter of King Sabour of Persia, and a hundred damsels like moons.' When Gherib heard this, he marvelled and said, 'How came ye by these?' 'O Amir,' replied Saadan, 'I went forth one day with my sons and five of my slaves in quest of booty, but finding no spoil in our way, we dispersed over deserts and plains and fared on, so haply we might happen on somewhat of prey and not return empty-handed, till we found ourselves in the land of the Persians. Presently, we espied a cloud of dust in the distance and sent one of our slaves to reconnoitre, who returned after awhile and said, "O my lord, this is the princess Fekhr Taj, daughter of Sabour, King of the Persians and Medes and Turcomans, who is on a journey, attended by two thousand horse." Quoth I, "Mayst thou be gladdened with good news! We could have no finer purchase than this." Then I and my sons fell upon the Persians and slew of them three hundred men and took the princess and twelve hundred cavaliers prisoners, together with all that was with her of treasure and riches, and brought them hither.'

Quoth Gherib, 'Hast thou offered any violence to the princess Fekhr Taj?' 'Not I,' replied Saadan, 'as thy head liveth, and by the virtue of the faith I have embraced!' 'It was well done of thee, O Saadan,' said Gherib; 'for her father is king of the world and he will surely despatch troops in quest of her and lay waste the dwellings of those who took her. And who-so looks not to the issue of events, Fate is no friend to him. But where is the damsel?' And Saadan, 'I have set apart a pavilion for her and her damsels.' Quoth Gherib, 'Show me her lodging,' and Saadan answered, 'I hear and obey.' So he carried him to the pavilion, where he found the princess mournful and cast down, weeping for her former estate of honour and delight. When Gherib saw her, he thought the moon was near him and magnified God the All-hearing and seeing. The princess also looked at him and saw him a princely cavalier, with valour shining from between his eyes and testifying for him and not against him; so she rose and kissed his hands, then threw herself at his feet, saying, 'O hero of the age, I cast myself on thy mercy; protect me from this Ghoul, for I fear lest he do away my maidenhead and after devour me. So take me to serve thine handmaids.' Quoth Gherib, 'Thou shalt be restored in safety to thy father and the seat of thy worship.' Whereupon she prayed that he might live long and have advancement in rank.

Then he caused unbind the Persians and turning to the princess, said to her, 'What brought thee forth of thy palace to the deserts and wastes, so that the highway-robbers made prize of thee?' 'O my lord,' answered she, 'my father and all the people of his realm are Magians, who worship the fire, and not the All-powerful King. Now in our country is a monastery called the Monastery of the Fire, whither every year the daughters of the Magians and worshippers of the Fire resort at the time of their festival, after which they return to their houses. So I and my damsels set out, as of wont, attended by two thousand horse, whom my father sent with me to guard me; but by the way this Ghoul fell upon us and killed some of us and taking the rest captive, imprisoned us in this hold. This, then, is what befell me, O valiant champion, whom God guard against the shifts of fortune!' And Gherib said, 'Fear not; for I will bring thee to thy palace and the seat of thy worship.' Wherefore she blessed him and kissed his hands and feet.

Then he went out from her, after having commanded to treat her with honour, and slept till morning, when he made the ablution and prayed a two-bow prayer, after the rite of our father Abraham the Friend (on whom be peace), whilst the Ghoul and his sons and Gherib's company did the like after him. Then he turned to the Ghoul and said to him, 'O Saadan, wilt thou not show me the Valley of Flowers?' 'I will well, O my lord,' answered he. So Gherib and his company and Fekhr Taj all rose and went forth, whilst Saadan commanded his slaves and slave-girls, (of whom he had a hundred and fifty female and a thousand male slaves, to pasture his sheep and oxen and camels) to slaughter and cook and make ready the morning-meal and bring it to them among the trees.

When they came to the valley, they found it beautiful passing measure, full of trees growing singly and in clusters and birds warbling on the branches. There sang the mocking-bird, trilling out her melodious notes, and the cushat filling with her warble the mansions of God's creation, and the nightingale, with her voice like that of a man, and the merle, that the tongue fails to describe, and the turtle, whose plaining maddens men for love, and the ringdove and the popinjay answering her with fluent tongue. There also were trees laden with all manner of fruits, of each two kinds, the pomegranate, sweet and sour, the almond-apricot, the camphor-apricot and the almond of Khorassan and the plum, with whose branches entwine the boughs of the myrobalan, and the orange, as it were a flaming cresset, and the shaddock, weighing down its branches, and the lemon, that cures lack of appetite, and the citron, sovereign against the jaundice, and the date, red and yellow, the handiwork of God the Most High. Of the like of this place saith the poet El Welhan:

When its birds sing in the dawn o'er its limpid lake, El Welhan yearns for its sight ere morning break.
For as it were Paradise 'tis with its fragrant gales And its fruits and its streams that run through its shady brake.

Gherib marvelled at the beauty of the place and bade them set up there the pavilion of Fekhr Taj, daughter of the Chosroës; so they pitched it among the trees and spread it with rich carpets. Then he sat down and the slaves brought food and they ate till they were satisfied; after which quoth Gherib, 'Harkye, Saadan!' 'At thy service, O my lord,' answered the Ghoul. 'Hast thou any wine?' asked Gherib, and Saadan replied, 'Yes, I have a cistern full of old wine.' 'Then,' said Gherib, 'bring us some of it.' So Saadan sent ten slaves, who returned with great plenty of wine, and they ate and drank and made merry. And Gherib bethought him of Mehdiyeh and recited the following verses:

I mind me of the happy days of union and delight, And all my heart's on fire with love and longing for thy sight.
By God, I did not leave thy side of my unfettered will, But by the strange and evil chance of Fate in my despite!
Peace be upon thee, O my love, a thousand times be peace! Whilst I, afar from thee, remain a sad and weary wight.

They abode there three days, eating and drinking and taking their pleasure in the valley, at the end of which time they returned to the castle. Then Gherib called Sehim and said to him, 'Take a hundred horse and go to thy father and mother and thy people, the Benou Kehtan, and bring them all to this place, here to pass the rest of their days, whilst I carry the Princess of Persia back to her father. As for thee, O Saadan,' continued Gherib, addressing the Ghoul, 'abide thou here with thy sons, till I return to thee.' 'And why,' asked Saadan, 'wilt thou not carry me with thee to the land of the Persians?' 'Because,' answered Gherib, 'thou stolest away King Sabour's daughter and if his eye fall on thee he will eat thy flesh and drink thy blood.' When the Ghoul heard this, he laughed a great laugh, as it were the pealing thunder, and said, 'O my lord, if the Persians and the Medes united against me, I would make them quaff the cup of death.' 'Doubtless it is as thou sayest,' rejoined Gherib; 'but abide thou here till I return to thee.' And the Ghoul answered, 'I hear and obey.' Then Sehim departed with his comrades of the Benou Kehtan for the dwelling-places of their tribe, and Gherib set out with Fekhr Taj and her company, intending for the cities of Sabour, King of the Persians.

Meanwhile, King Sabour abode awaiting his daughter's return from the Monastery of the Fire, and when the appointed time passed by and she came not, fires raged in his heart. Now he had forty viziers, whereof the wisest and chiefest was called Daidan: so he said to him, 'O vizier, the day of my daughter's return is past and I have no news of her; so do thou send a courier to the Monastery of the Fire to learn what is come of her.' 'I hear and obey,' replied Daidan, and summoning the chief of the couriers, despatched him forthright to the Monastery. When he reached it, he asked the monks of the princess, and they said, 'We have not seen her this year.' So the Courier returned to the city of Ishanir and told the vizier, who went in to the king and told him. When Sabour heard this, he was sore concerned and casting his crown on the ground, tore his beard and fell down in a swoon. They sprinkled water upon him, and presently he came to himself, weeping-eyed and mournful-hearted and repeated the words of the poet:

When in thine absence to mine aid patience and tears I call, Tears come obedient to my word, but patience not at all.
What if the days have parted us? Indeed, 'tis of their wont; For unto Fortune perfidy, alas! is natural.

Then he called ten of his captains and bade them take each a thousand horse and ride in different directions, in quest of his daughter. So they mounted forthright and departed; whilst the princess's mother clad herself and her women in black and strewed ashes and sat weeping and lamenting.

Meanwhile Gherib and the princess journeyed on ten days, and on the eleventh day, a cloud of dust appeared in the distance and rose to the confines of the sky; whereupon Gherib called the Amir of the Persians and bade him go and learn the cause thereof. 'I hear and obey,' replied he and pricked his charger, till he came within the cloud of dust, where he saw folk and enquired of them. Quoth they, 'We are of the Benou Hettal and are questing for plunder; our Amir is Semsam ben Jirah and we are five thousand horse.' The Persian returned in haste and told Gherib, who cried out to his men and to the Persians, saying, 'Don your arms!' They did as he bade them and presently up came the Arabs, shouting, 'Booty! Booty!' Quoth Gherib, 'God confound you, O dogs of Arabs!' Then he set spurs to his horse and drove at them in valiant wise, shouting, 'God is most great! Ho for the faith of Abraham the Friend, on whom be peace!' And there befell between them a sore battle and great was the clash of arms and the din of the mellay; nor did they leave fighting, till the day fled and the darkness came, when they drew off from one another.

Then Gherib numbered his men and found that five of the Benou Kehtan had fallen and three-and-seventy of the Persians; but of the Benou Hettal they had slain more than five hundred horse. As for Semsam, he alighted and sought neither food nor sleep, but said, 'In all my life I never met such a fighter as this youth! Anon he fights with the sword and anon with the mace: but tomorrow I will go forth and defy him to single combat and cut off these Arabs.' Now, when Gherib returned to his camp, the princess met him, weeping and affrighted for the terror of that which had befallen, and kissed his foot in the stirrup, saying, 'May thy hands never wither nor thine enemies rejoice, O champion of the age! Praised be God Who hath saved thee alive this day! Verily, I am in fear for thee from yonder Arabs.' When Gherib heard this, he smiled in her face and comforted her, saying, 'Fear not, O princess! Were this desert full of the enemy, yet would I scatter them, by the might of God the Most High.' She thanked him and prayed that he might be given the victory over his enemies; after which she returned to her women and Gherib went to his tent, where he cleansed himself of the blood of the infidels, and they lay on their arms that night.

Next morning, the two hosts mounted and sought the field. The first to prick into the plain was Gherib, who spurred his charger till he was near the infidels and cried out, 'Who is for jousting? Let no sluggard or weakling come out to me!' Whereupon there came out a buirdly giant of the lineage of the tribe of Aad, armed with an iron mace, twenty pounds in weight, and drove at Gherib, saying, 'O scum of the Arabs, take what cometh to thee and know that thy last hour is at hand!' So saying, he aimed a blow at Gherib, but he avoided it and the mace sank a cubit into the ground. Now the Bedouin was bent in twain with the blow; so Gherib smote him with his mace and clove his forehead in sunder; and he fell down dead and God hurried his soul to the fire. Then Gherib made his horse wheel and curvet before the foe and offered battle. So there came out to him a second and a third and a fourth and so on, till ten had come forth to him and he slew them all.

When the infidels saw his swashing blows and the slaughter he made, they hung back and forbore to go forth to him, whereupon Semsam looked at them and said, 'May God not bless you! I will go forth to him.' So he donned his battle-harness and spurring his charger into the midst of the field, cried out to Gherib, saying, 'Out on thee, O dog of the Arabs! what art thou that thou shouldst defy me in the open field and slay my men?' And Gherib answered, 'Up and take thy wreak for the slaughter of thy braves!' So Semsam ran at Gherib, who awaited him with a dilated breast and a heart well pleased, and they hewed at one another with maces, till the two hosts marvelled and every eye was fixed on them. Then they wheeled about in the field, and struck at each other; but Gherib avoided Semsam's stroke and dealt him a buffet that beat in his breast and cast him to the ground, dead; whereupon all his host set upon Gherib as one man, and he ran at them, crying out, 'God is most Great! He giveth help and victory and forsaketh those who reject the faith of Abraham the Friend, on whom be peace!'

When the infidels heard the name of the All-powerful King, the One, the Victorious, whom the sights comprehend not, but He comprehendeth all sights, they looked at one another and said, 'What is this saying that makes us tremble in every nerve and weakens our resolution and causes the life to fail in us? Never in our lives heard we aught goodlier than this saying! Let us leave fighting, that we may ask its meaning.' So they held their hands from the battle and dismounted; and their chiefs assembled and held counsel together, seeking to go to Gherib and saying, 'Let ten of us go to him!' So they chose out ten of their best, who set out for Gherib's camp. Now he and his people had alighted and returned to their tents, marvelling at the withdrawal of the infidels from the fight. Presently, the ten elders came up and seeking speech of Gherib, kissed the earth before him and wished him glory and long life. Quoth he to them, 'What made you leave fighting?' 'O my lord,' answered they, 'thou didst affright us with the words thou shoutedst out at us.' Then said Gherib, 'What calamity do ye worship?' 'We worship Wedd and Souwaa and Yeghouth,' answered they, 'lords of the tribe of Noah;' and Gherib, 'We serve none but God the Most High, Maker of all things and Provider of every living creature. He it is who created the heavens and the earth and stablished the mountains, who maketh water to well from the rocks and the trees to grow and feedeth the wild beasts in the deserts; for He is God, the One, the All-powerful.'

When they heard this, their bosoms expanded to the words of the faith of Unity and they said, 'Verily, this God is a great lord, compassionate and merciful. What shall we say, to become of those that submit themselves to Him?' Quoth Gherib, 'Say, "There is no god but God and Abraham is the Friend of God."' So the ten made sincere profession of the true faith and Gherib said to them, 'If the sweetness of Islam be indeed stablished in your hearts, go to your people and expound the faith to them; and if they profess, they shall be saved, but if they refuse, we will burn them with fire.' So they returned and expounded Islam to their people and set forth to them the way of truth and righteousness, and they embraced the faith of submission with heart and tongue.

Then they repaired on foot to Gherib's tent and kissing the earth before him, wished him power and advancement, saying, 'O our lord, we are become thy slaves; command us what thou wilt, for we hearken to thee and obey thee and will never leave thee, for God hath guided us into the right way at thy hands.' 'May God abundantly requite you!' answered he. 'Return to your dwellings and take your goods and your children and forego me to the Valley of Flowers and the castle of Sasa ben Shith, whilst I carry the princess Fekhr Taj, daughter of Sabour, King of the Persians, back to her father and return to you.' 'We hear and obey,' said they and straightway returned to their encampment, rejoicing in Islam, and expounding the faith to their wives and children, who became true believers. Then they dismantled their dwellings and set forth, with their goods and cattle, for the Valley of Flowers. Now Gherib had charged them, saying, 'If the Ghoul of the Mountain come out to you and offer to attack you, do ye call upon the name of God, the Creator of all things, and he will leave his hostile intent and receive you hospitably.' So, when they came in sight of the castle of Shith, Saadan and his sons sallied forth to them and would have fallen upon them; but they called aloud upon the name of God the Most High, and straightway he received them kindly and asked them of their case. They told him all that had passed between Gherib and themselves, whereupon he rejoiced in them and lodged them with him and loaded them with kindnesses.

Meanwhile, Gherib and his company fared on five days' journey towards the city of Isbanir, and on the sixth day, they saw in the distance a cloud of dust. So Gherib sent one of the Persians to learn the meaning of this and he went and returned, swiftlier than a bird in its flight, saying, 'O my lord, these be a thousand horse of our comrades, whom the King hath sent in quest of his daughter.' When Gherib heard this, he commanded his men to halt and pitch the tents. So they halted and waited till the new comers reached them, when they went to meet them and told Touman, their captain, that the princess was with them; whereupon he went in to Gherib and kissing the earth before him, enquired for her. Gherib sent him to her tent, and he entered and kissed her hands and feet and acquainted her with what had befallen her father and mother. She told him in return all that had befallen her and how Gherib had delivered her from the Ghoul of the Mountain, who would else have eaten her, adding, 'And indeed, it behoves my father to give him the half of his kingdom.' Then Touman returned to Gherib and kissed his hands and feet and thanked him for his good dealing, saying, 'With thy leave, O my lord, I will return to Isbanir and acquaint the King with the good news of his daughter's approach.' 'Go,' answered Gherib, 'and take of him the gift for glad tidings.'

So Touman returned with all diligence to Isbanir and entering the palace, kissed the earth before the King, who said to him, 'What is the news, O bringer of glad tidings?' Quoth Touman, 'I will not speak, till thou give me the reward for good news.' 'Tell me thy good news,' answered the King, 'and I will content thee.' So Touman said, 'O King, I bring thee the glad tidings of the return of the princess Fekhr Taj.' When Sabour heard his daughter's name, he fell down in a swoon and they sprinkled rosewater on him, till he recovered and said to Touman, 'Draw near to me and tell me all.' So he came forward and acquainted him with all that had befallen the princess; and Sabour beat hand upon hand, saying, 'Alas, unhappy Fekhr Taj!' And he bade give Touman ten thousand dinars and conferred on him the government of the city of Ispahan. Then he cried out to his Amirs, saying, 'Mount, all of you, and go forth to meet the princess Fekhr Taj!' Whilst the chief eunuch went in to the queen-mother and told her and all the harem the good news, whereat she rejoiced and gave him a dress of honour and a thousand dinars. Moreover, the people of the city heard of this and decorated the streets and houses.

Then the King and Touman took horse and rode till they fell in with Gherib, when Sabour dismounted and made some steps towards Gherib, who also dismounted and advanced to meet him; and they embraced and saluted each other, and Sabour bent over Gherib's hand and kissed it and thanked him for his favours. They pitched their tents in face of one another and Sabour went in to his daughter, who rose and embracing him, told him all that had befallen her and how Gherib had rescued her from the clutches of the Ghoul of the Mountain. 'By thy life, O princess of fair ones,' said the King, 'I will overwhelm him with gifts!' 'O my father,' rejoined she, 'make him thy son-in-law, that he may be to thee a help against thine enemies, for he is passing valiant.'

This she said because her heart was enamoured of Gherib. 'O my daughter,' answered her father, 'knowst thou not that King Khired Shah seeks thee in marriage and that he hath cast the brocade and given a hundred thousand dinars , and he is King of Shiraz and its dependencies and is lord of empire and horsemen and footmen?' 'O my father,' said the princess, 'I desire not that whereof thou speakest, and if thou constrain me to that I have no mind to, I will kill myself.' So Sabour left her and went in to Gherib, with whom he sat awhile and could not take his fill of looking upon him; and he said in himself, 'By Allah, my daughter is excusable if she love this Bedouin!' Then he called for food and they ate and passed the night together.

On the morrow, they took horse and rode till they arrived at the city of Isbanir and entered, stirrup to stirrup, and it was a great day for them. Fekhr Taj repaired to her palace and the abiding-place of her rank, where her mother and her women received her with cries of joy. As for King Sabour, he sat down on his throne and seated Gherib on his right hand, whilst the princes and viceroys and chamberlains and viziers and officers stood on either hand and gave him joy of the recovery of his daughter. Quoth Sabour, 'Whoso loveth me let him bestow a robe of honour on Gherib,' and there fell dresses of honour on him like rain. Then Gherib abode the King's guest ten days, at the end of which time he would have departed, but Sabour clad him in a dress of honour and swore by his faith that he should not depart for a month. Quoth Gherib, 'O King, I am plighted to one of the girls of the Arabs and I desire to go in to her.' 'Whether is the fairer,' asked the King, 'thy betrothed or Fekhr Taj?' 'O King of the age,' replied Gherib, 'what is the slave beside the lord?' And Sabour said, 'Fekhr Taj is become thy handmaid, for that thou didst rescue her from the clutches of the Ghoul, and she shall have none other husband than thee.'

Thereupon Gherib rose and kissed the earth, saying, 'O King of the age, thou art a king and I am but a poor man, and belike thou wilt ask a heavy dowry.' 'O my son,' replied the King, 'know that Khired Shah, lord of Shiraz, seeks her in marriage and hath appointed a hundred thousand dinars to her dower; but I have chosen thee before all men, that I may make thee the shield of my kingship and the sword of my vengeance.' Then he turned to his chief officers and said to them, 'Bear witness against me that I give my daughter Fekhr Taj in marriage to my son Gherib.' With that he joined hands with him and she became his wife. Then said Gherib, 'Appoint me a dower and I will bring it to thee, for I have in the Castle of Sasa wealth and treasures beyond count.' 'O my son,' answered Sabour, 'I want of thee neither gold nor treasure and I will take nothing for her dower save the head of Jemrcan, King of Desht and the city of Ahwaz.' 'O King of the age,' rejoined Gherib, 'I will fetch my people and go to thine enemy and lay waste his realm.' Quoth Sabour, 'May God requite thee with good!' and dismissed the assembly, thinking that, if Gherib went forth against Jemrcan, he would never return.

Next morning, the King mounted with Gherib and all his troops and rode forth to the tilting-ground, where he said to his men, 'Do ye tilt with spears and gladden my heart.' So the Persian cavaliers tilted, one against the other, and Gherib said, 'O King of the age, I have a mind to tilt with the horsemen of the Persians, but on one condition.' 'What is that?' asked the King. 'It is,' answered Gherib, 'that I shall don a light tunic and take a headless spear, with a pennon dipped in saffron, whilst the Persians tilt against me with sharp spears. If any conquer me, I will give myself to him; but, if I conquer him, I will mark him on the breast and he shall leave the lists.' Then the King cried to the commander of the troops to bring forward the champions of the Persians; so he chose out twelve hundred of his stoutest champions, and the King said to them, in the Persian tongue, 'Whoso slayeth this Bedouin may ask of me what he will.' So they strove with each other for the precedence and advanced upon Gherib and truth was distinguished from falsehood and jest from earnest. Quoth Gherib, 'I put my trust in God, the God of Abraham the Friend, Who hath power over all and from whom nothing is hidden, the One, the Almighty, whom the sight comprehendeth not!'

Then a giant of the Persian champions pricked out to him, but Gherib let him not stand long before him ere he marked him and filled his breast with saffron, and as he turned away, he smote him on the nape with his spear, and he fell to the ground and his pages carried him forth of the lists. Then a second champion came forth against him and he overcame him and marked him on the breast; and thus did he with champion after champion, till he had overcome them all and marked them on the breast; for God the Most High gave him the victory over them and they went forth of the lists. Then the servants set food before them and they ate and drank till Gherib's wits were dazed. By and by, he went out upon an occasion and would have returned, but lost his way and entered the palace of Fekhr Taj. When she saw him, her reason fled and she cried out to her women, saying, 'Go to your own places!' So they withdrew and she rose and kissed Gherib's hand, saying, 'Welcome to my lord, who delivered me from the Ghoul! Indeed I am thine handmaid for ever.' Then she drew him to her bed and embraced him, whereupon desire was hot upon him and he broke her seal and lay with her till the morning. Now the King thought that he had departed; but on the morrow he went in to him and Sabour rose to him and made him sit by his side.

Then entered the kings and kissing the earth, stood on either hand and fell to talking of Gherib's valour and saying, 'Extolled be He who gave him such prowess, and he so young in years!' As they were thus engaged, the King espied from the palace-windows the dust of horse approaching and cried out to his scouts, saying, 'Out on you! Go and bring me news of yonder dust!' So one of them took horse and riding off, returned after awhile and said, 'O King, this is the dust of a hundred horse, and the name of their chief is Sehim el Leil.' Quoth Gherib, 'O my lord, this is my brother, whom I had sent on an errand, and I will go forth to meet him.' So saying, he mounted, with his hundred men of the Benou Kehtan and a thousand Persians, and rode forth to meet his brother in great state, for greatness belongeth to God alone. When they came up with each other, they dismounted and embraced, and Gherib said to Sehim, 'O my brother, hast thou brought our tribe to the Castle of the Ghoul of the Mountain and the Valley of Flowers?' 'O my brother,' answered Sehim, 'when the perfidious dog Merdas heard that thou hadst mastered the Ghoul of the Mountain and his stronghold, he was sore chagrined and said, "Except I depart hence, Gherib will come and take my daughter Mehdiyeh without dower." So he took his daughter and his goods and set out with his tribe for Irak, where he entered the city of Cufa and put himself under the protection of King Agib, seeking to give him his daughter to wife.' When Gherib heard his brother's story, he well-nigh gave up the ghost for rage and said, 'By the virtue of the faith of submission, the faith of Abraham the Friend, and by the Supreme Lord, I will assuredly go to the land of Irak and make fierce war upon it.'

Then they returned to the city and going in to the King, kissed the earth before him. He rose to Gherib and saluted Sehim; after which the former told him what had happened and he put ten captains at his command, under each one's hand ten thousand horse of the stoutest of the Persians and the Arabs, who equipped themselves and were ready to depart at the end of three days. Then Gherib set out and journeyed till he reached the Castle of Sasa, where the Ghoul and his sons came forth to meet him and dismounting, kissed his feet in the stirrups. He told them all that had passed and the Ghoul said, 'O my lord, do thou abide in this castle, whilst I repair to Irak with my sons and servants and lay waste town and hamlet and bring thee all its defenders bound hand and foot.' But Gherib thanked him and said, 'O Saadan, we will all go.' So they all made ready and set out for Irak, leaving a thousand horse to guard the castle.

Meanwhile, Merdas arrived at the city of Cufa and going in to Agib, kissed the earth before him and wished him what is usually wished to kings. Then he made him a handsome present, saying, 'O my lord, I come to throw myself on thy protection.' Tell me who hath wronged thee,' answered Agib, 'that I may protect thee against him, though it were Sabour, King of the Persians and Turcomans and Medes.' 'O King,' replied Merdas, 'he who hath wronged me is none other than a youth whom I reared in my bosom. I found him in his mother's lap in a certain valley and took her to wife. She brought me a son, whom I named Sehim el Leil, and her own son, whose name was Gherib, grew up on my knees and became a consuming lightning and a great calamity, for he slew El Hemel, prince of the Benou Nebhan, and routed footmen and overcame horsemen. Now I have a daughter, who befits thee alone, and he sought her of me; so I required of him the head of the Ghoul of the Mountain wherefore he went to him and engaging him in single combat, made him prisoner and took the castle of Sasa ben Shith ben Sheddad ben Aad, wherein are the treasures of the ancients and the moderns, and the Ghoul is become one of his liegemen. Moreover, I hear that he is become a Muslim and goeth about, summoning the folk to his faith. He is now gone to carry the princess of Persia, whom he delivered from the Ghoul, back to her father, King Sabour, and will not return but with the treasures of the Persians.'

When Agib heard Merdas's story, he changed colour and was in ill case and made sure of destruction; then he said to Merdas, 'Is his mother with thee or with him?' 'She is with me,' answered Merdas; 'in my tents.' Quoth Agib, 'What is her name?' and Merdas said, 'Her name is Nusreh.' 'It is indeed she,' rejoined Agib and sent for her. When she came before him, he looked on her and knew her and said to her, 'O accursed woman, where are the two slaves I sent with thee?' 'They slew each other on my account,' replied she; whereupon he drew his sword and smote her and cut her in twain. Then they took her up and cast her out; but trouble entered into Agib's heart and he said to Merdas, 'Give me thy daughter to wife.' 'She is one of thine handmaids,' answered he; 'I give her to thee to wife, and I am thy slave.' Quoth Agib, 'I desire to look upon this whoreson, Gherib, that I may make an end of him and cause him taste all manner of torments.' Then he bade give Merdas, to his daughter's dowry, thirty thousand dinars and a hundred pieces of silk fringed and brocaded with gold and a hundred pieces of bordered stuffs and handkerchiefs and collars of gold. So he went forth with this splendid dowry and set himself to equip Mehdiyeh with all diligence.

Meanwhile, Gherib fared on till he came to El Jezireh, which is the first town of Irak and is a walled and fortified city, and here he called a halt. When the people of the city saw his army encamp before it, they shut the gates and manned the walls, then went to the king of the city, who was called Damigh for that he used to brain the champions in the open field, and told him. So he looked forth from the battlements of the palace and seeing an immense army of Persians encamped before the city, said to the citizens, 'O folk, what do yonder Persians want?' 'We know not,' answered they.

Now Damigh had among his officers a man called Sebulkifar, keen of wit and subtle as he were a flame of fire; so he called him and bade him go to the stranger host and find out who they were and what they wanted and return quickly. Accordingly, he sped like the wind to the Persian camp, where a company of Arabs met him and said to him, 'Who art thou and what dost thou want?' Quoth he, 'I am a messenger and an ambassador from the lord of the city to your chief.' So they took him and carried him through the lines of tents and standards, till they came to Gherib's pavilion and told him of the envoy. He bade them bring him in and they did so, whereupon he kissed the earth before Gherib and wished him length of days and honour. Quoth Gherib, 'What is thine errand?' and Sebulkifar answered, saying, 'I am an envoy from the lord of the city of Jezireh, Damigh, brother of King Kundemir, lord of the city of Cufa and the land of Irak.' When Gherib heard his father's name, the tears ran from his eyes and he looked at the messenger and said, 'What is thy name?' 'My name is Sebulkifar,' answered he. 'O Sebulkifar,' said Gherib, 'return to thy master and tell him that the commander of this host is called Gherib, son of Kundemir, King of Cufa, whom his son Agib slew, and he is come to avenge his father on the perfidious dog Agib.'

So Sebulkifar returned to the city, rejoicing, and told Damigh all he had heard. The latter thought himself in a dream and said to the messenger, 'O Sebulkifar, is this thou tellest me true?' 'As thy head liveth,' replied Sebulkifar, 'it is true.' Then Damigh took horse forthright with his chief officers and rode out to the camp, where Gherib met him and they embraced and saluted one another; after which Gherib carried him to his pavilion and they sat down on beds of estate. And Damigh rejoiced in Gherib, his brother's son, and turning to him, said, 'I also have yearned to avenge thy father, but could not avail against the dog thy brother; for that his troops are many and mine few.' 'O uncle,' replied Gherib, 'I am come to avenge my father and blot out our reproach and rid the realm of Agib.' Quoth Damigh, 'O son of my brother, thou hast two wreaks to take, that of thy father and that of thy mother.' 'And what ails my mother?' asked Gherib. Thy brother Agib hath slain her,' replied Damigh and told him what had befallen, whereupon Gherib's reason fled and he swooned away and came nigh upon death. No sooner did he come to himself than he cried out to the troops, saying, 'To horse!' But Damigh said to him, 'O son of my brother, wait till I make ready mine estate and mount with my men and fare with thee and at thy stirrup.' 'O uncle,' replied Gherib, 'I have no patience to wait; do thou equip thy troops and join me at Cufa.'

So Gherib mounted with his troops and rode, till he came to the town of Babel, whose folk took fright at him. Now there was in this town a king called Jemek, under whose hand were twenty thousand horsemen, and there gathered themselves together to him from the villages other fifty thousand horse, who pitched their tents under the walls of the city. Then Gherib wrote a letter and sent it to King Jemek by a messenger, who came up to the city-gate and cried out, saying, 'I am a messenger;' whereupon the keeper of the gate went in and told Jemek, who said, 'Bring him to me.' So the messenger entered and kissing the earth before the King, gave him the letter. Jemek opened it and read as follows: 'Praise be to God, the Lord of the Worlds and of all things, Who provideth all creatures and hath power over all! These from Gherib, son of Kundemir, lord of Irak and Cufa, to Jemek. As soon as this letter reaches thee, let not thy reply be other than to break thine idols and confess the unity of the All-knowing King, Creator of light and darkness and of all things, the All-powerful; and except thou do as I bid thee, I will make this day the blackest of thy days. Peace be on those who follow in the way of righteousness, fearing the issues of frowardness, and obey the Most High King, Lord of this world and the next, Him who saith to a thing, "Be;" and it is.'

When Jemek read this letter, his eyes rolled and his colour changed and he cried out to the messenger, saying, 'Go to thy lord and say to him, "Tomorrow, at daybreak there shall be battle and conflict and it shall appear who is the master."' So he returned and told Gherib, who bade his men make ready for battle, whilst Jemek pitched his tents in face of Gherib's camp and his troops poured forth like the swollen sea and passed the night in expectation of battle. As soon as it was day, the two hosts mounted and drew up in battle array and beat their drums and spurred their swift horses, filling the plains; and the champions came out.

The first who sallied forth to the field was the Ghoul of the Mountain, bearing on his shoulder a terrible big tree, and he cried out between the two hosts, saying, 'I am Saadan the Ghoul: who is for fighting, who is for jousting? Let no sluggard or weakling come forth to me.' And he called out to his slaves, saying, 'Out on you! Bring me firewood and fire, for I am hungry.'

So the slaves brought firewood and kindled a fire midmost the lists. Then there came out to him a man of the infidels, an Amalekite of the unbelieving Amalekites, bearing on his shoulder a mace as it were the mast of a ship, and drove at the Ghoul, saying, 'Woe to thee, O Saadan!' When the Ghoul heard this, be was angered and raising his club, aimed at the infidel a blow, that whistled through the air. The other met the stroke with his mace, but it beat down his guard and descending with its own weight and that of the mace upon his head, beat in his brain-pan, and he fell like a great palm tree; whereupon Saadan cried to his slaves, saying, 'Take this fat calf and roast him quickly.' So they hastened to skin the infidel and roasted him and brought him to the Ghoul, who ate his flesh and crunched his bones.

When the infidels saw how Saadan did with their fellow, their skins quaked and their colour changed and their hearts died within them and they said to one another, 'Whoso goeth out against this Ghoul, he eats him and cracks his bones and maketh him to lack the wind of the world.' Wherefore they quailed for fear of the Ghoul and his sons and turned to fly, making for the town; but Gherib cried out to his troops, saying, 'Up and after them!' So the Persians and the Arabs drove after the King of Babel and his host and smote them with the sword, till they slew of them twenty thousand or more. Moreover, the fugitives crowded together in the gate of the city and there they slew of them much people; and they could not win to shut the gate. So the Persians and the Arabs entered with them, fighting, and Saadan, taking a mace from one of the slain, fought his way through the foe and broke into the King's palace, where be met with Jemek and smote him with the mace, that he fell senseless to the ground. Then he fell upon those who were in the palace and pounded them into fragments, till those who were left cried out for quarter and Saadan said to them, 'Bind your king.' So they bound Jemek and took him up, and Saadan drove them before him like sheep and brought them before Gherib, after the most part of the people of the city had perished by the swords of the latter's host.

When Jemek came to himself, he found himself bound and heard Saadan say, 'I will sup tonight off this king Jemek;' whereupon he turned to Gherib and said to him, 'I throw myself on thy mercy.' 'Become a Muslim,' replied Gherib, 'and thou shalt be safe from the Ghoul and from the vengeance of the Living who ceaseth not.' So Jemek professed Islam with heart and tongue and Gherib commanded his bonds to be loosed. Then he expounded the faith to his people and they all became Muslims; after which Jemek returned to the city and despatched thence meat and drink to the camp before Babel, where they passed the night. On the morrow, Gherib gave the signal for departure and they fared on till they came to Meyya Farikin, which they found empty, for its people had heard what had befallen Babel and had fled to Cufa and told Agib. When the latter heard the news, his gorge rose and he assembled his fighting men and bade them make ready to do battle with his brother's host; after which he numbered them and found them thirty thousand horse and ten thousand foot. So he levied other fifty thousand horse and foot and taking horse with a mighty host, rode forward five days, till he came upon his brother's army encamped before Mosul and pitched his tent in face of theirs.

Then Gherib wrote a letter and said to his officers, 'Which of you will carry this letter to Agib?' Whereupon up sprang Sehim and said, 'O King of the age, I will carry thy letter and bring thee back an answer.' So Gherib gave him the letter and he repaired to the pavilion of Agib, who bade admit him and said to him, 'Whence comest thou?' 'From the King of the Arabs and the Persians,' answered Sehim, 'son-in-law of Chosroës, King of the world, who sendeth thee a letter; so do thou return him an answer.' 'Give me the letter,' said Agib. So Sehim gave him the letter and he tore it open and read as follows: 'In the name of God the Compassionate, the Merciful! Peace be on Abraham the Friend! As soon as this letter comes to thy hands, do thou confess the unity of the Bountiful King, Causer of causes and Mover of the clouds, and leave worshipping idols. If thou do this thing, thou art my brother and ruler over us and I will pardon thee the deaths of my father and mother, nor will I reproach thee with what thou hast done. But if thou obey not my commandment, behold, I will hasten to thee and cut off thy head and lay waste thy dominions. Verily, I give thee good counsel, and peace be on those who follow in the way of righteousness and obey the Most High King!'

When Agib read these words and knew the threat they contained, his eyes sank into his head and he gnashed his teeth for rage. Then he tore the letter in pieces and threw it away, which vexed Sehim and he cried out upon Agib, saying, 'God wither thy hand for that thou hast done!' With this Agib cried out to his men, saying, 'Seize yonder dog and cut him in pieces with your swords.' So they ran at Sehim; but he drew his sword and fell upon them and killed more than fifty of them; after which he cut his way out and won back, covered with blood, to Gherib, who said, 'What is this, O Sehim?' And he told him what had passed, whereat he grew livid for rage and crying, 'God is most great!' bade the drums beat to battle. So the fighting-men donned their hauberks and coats of strait-woven mail and girt themselves with their swords; the footmen drew out in battle-array, whilst the horsemen mounted and set their long lances in the rest and the champions pricked into the field. Agib and his men also took horse and the two hosts charged down upon each other. Then ruled the Judge of Battle, in whose ordinance is no unright, for a seal is on his lips and he speaketh not, and the blood ran down in streams and laced the earth with curious broidery; heads grew gray and the battle raged ever hotter and fiercer. Feet slipped and the valiant stood firm and pushed forward, whilst the faint-heart turned and fled, nor did they leave fighting till the day waned and the night came with the darkness. Then the drums beat the retreat and the two hosts drew apart and returned to their tents, where they passed the night.

Next morning, as soon as it was day, the drums beat to battle, and the warriors donned their harness of war and girt on their fair swords and mounting their stout horses, couched their brown lances and cried out, saying, 'Let there be no budging today!' And the two hosts drew out in battle-array, like the swollen sea. The first to open the chapter of war was Sehim, who spurred his charger between the two hosts and played with swords and spears and plied all manner of martial exercises, till the choicest wits were confounded. Then he cried out, saying, 'Who is for fighting? Who is for jousting? Let no sluggard or weakling come out!' Whereupon there pricked out to him a horseman of the infidels, as he were a flame of fire; but it was not long before Sehim pierced him with his lance and overthrew him. Then a second came forth and he slew him also, and a third and he rent him in sunder, and a fourth, and he did him to death; nor did they leave to come out to him and he to slay them, till he had done to death two hundred fighting-men. Then Agib cried to his men to charge, and the two hosts met with a mighty shock and great was the clash of arms and the roar of the battle. The shining swords rang out and the blood ran in streams and men's skulls were as shoes to the horses' feet, nor did they cease from sore smiting till the day waned and the night came with the darkness, when they drew apart and returning to their tents, passed the night there.

As soon as it was day, the two hosts mounted and sought the field; and the Muslims looked for Gherib to mount and ride behind the standards as was his wont, but he came not. So Sehim sent a servant to his brother's pavilion, who, finding him not, questioned the tent-keepers, but they answered, 'We know nothing of him.' Whereat he was greatly concerned and went forth and told the troops, who refused to give battle, saying, 'If Gherib be absent from us, his enemy will destroy us.' Now there was for Gherib's absence a cause that we will set out in due order, and it was thus. When Agib returned to his camp on the preceding night, he called one of his officers by name Siyyar and said to him, 'O Siyyar, I have kept thee in reserve for a day like this;

and now I bid thee go to Gherib's camp and show thy skill by bringing Gherib himself to me.' And Siyyar said, 'I hear and obey.' So he repaired to the enemy's camp and stealing into Gherib's pavilion, in the darkness of the night, when all the men had gone to rest, passed himself off for a servant and stood to serve Gherib, who presently, being athirst, called to him for water. So he brought him a flagon of water, drugged with henbane, whereof no sooner had Gherib drunk, than he fell down head foremost; whereupon Siyyar wrapped him in his cloak and carrying him to Agib's tent, threw him down at his feet. Quoth Agib, 'O Siyyar, what is this?' 'This is thy brother Gherib,' answered he; whereat Agib rejoiced and said, 'The blessing of the idols light upon thee! Loose him and wake him.'

So they made him smell to vinegar and he came to himself and opened his eyes; then, finding himself bound and in a tent other than his own, said, 'There is no power and no virtue save in God the Most High, the Supreme!' Then Agib cried out at him, saying, 'O dog, dost thou draw on me and seek to slay me and take on me thy wreak of thy father and mother? This very day I will send thee to them and rid the world of thee.' 'O dog of the infidels,' replied Gherib, 'thou shalt see against whom the wheels of fate shall revolve and who shall be overthrown of the Almighty King, Who knoweth what is in the hearts and Who shall leave thee in hell, tormented and confounded! Have pity on thyself and say with me, "There is no god but God and Abraham is the Friend of God!"' When Agib heard Gherib's words, he puffed and snorted and railed at his god of stone and called for the headsman and the carpet of blood; but his vizier, who was at heart a Muslim, though outwardly an infidel, rose and kissing the earth before him, said, 'O King, deal not hastily, but wait till we know the conquered from the conqueror. If we prove the victors, we shall be free to kill him, and if we be beaten, his being alive in our hands will be a strength to us.' And the Amirs said, 'The vizier says sooth.' So Agib bade lay Gherib in irons and chain him up in his own tent and appointed a thousand stout warriors to guard him.

Meanwhile Gherib's host, when they awoke and found not their chief, were as sheep without a shepherd; but Saadan the Ghoul cried out to them, saying, 'O folk, don your harness and trust to your Lord to defend you!' So the Arabs and the Persians donned their hauberks of iron and their strait-knit shirts of mail and mounting their horses, sallied forth to the field, with the chiefs and the ensigns in the van. Then pricked out the Ghoul of the Mountain, with a mace on his shoulder, two hundred pounds in weight, and advanced and retreated, saying, 'Ho, worshippers of idols, come ye out today, for it is a day of battle! Whoso knoweth me hath enough of my mischief and whoso knoweth me not, I will make myself known to him. I am Saadan, servant of King Gherib. Who is for jousting? Who is for fighting? Let no faint-heart or weakling come forth to me today.' And there came forth to him a champion of the infidels, as he were a flame of fire, and drove at him, but Saadan met him and dealt him a blow with his mace, which beat in his ribs and cast him lifeless to the earth. Then he called out to his sons and slaves, saying, 'Light the fire, and whoso falls of the infidels, do ye roast him well with fire and bring him to me, that I may make the morning meal of him.' So they kindled a fire amiddleward the field and laid the slain man therein, till he was cooked, when they brought him to Saadan, who gnawed his flesh and crunched his bones.

When the infidels saw this, they were sore affrighted, but Agib cried out to his men, saying, 'Out on you! Fall upon him and cut him in pieces with your swords!' So twenty thousand men ran at Saadan, whilst the footmen circled round him and rained darts and arrows upon him, so that he was wounded in four-and-twenty places and his blood ran down upon the earth, and he was alone. Then the host of the Muslims drove at the idolaters, calling for help upon the Lord of the World; and they ceased not from the battle till the day came to an end, when they drew apart. But the infidels had made Saadan prisoner, as he were a drunken man for loss of blood; and they bound him fast and set him by Gherib. When the latter saw the Ghoul a prisoner, he said, 'There is no force and no virtue but in God the Most High, the Supreme! O Saadan, what is this?' 'O my lord,' answered Saadan, 'it is God (exalted and glorified be He!) Who ordaineth misfortune and deliverance, and needs must this and that betide.' And Gherib said, 'Thou sayst sooth, O Saadan!' But Agib and his host passed the night in joy, and he said to his men, 'Tomorrow, we will fall upon the Muslims and leave not one of them alive.'

Meanwhile, the Muslims passed the night, dejected and weeping for their King and for Saadan; but Sehim said to them, 'O folk, be not concerned, for the relief of God the Most High is near.' Then he waited till midnight, when he disguised himself in the habit of a tent-keeper and repairing to Agib's camp, made his way between the tents, till he came to the King's pavilion, where he saw him seated on his throne, in the midst of his princes. So he entered and going up to the candles that burnt in the tent, snuffed them and sprinkled powdered henbane on the wicks; after which he withdrew and waited without the tent, till the smoke of the burning henbane reached Agib and his princes and they fell to the earth like dead men. Then he left them and went to the prison-tent, where he found Gherib and Saadan, guarded by a thousand men, who were drowsed with sleep. So he cried out at the guards, saying, 'Out on you! Sleep not; but watch your prisoners and light the cressets.'

Then he filled a cresset with firewood, on which he strewed henbane, and lighting it, went round about the tent with it, till the smoke of the henbane entered the nostrils of the guards, and they all fell asleep; when he entered the tent and finding Gherib and Saadan insensible for the smoke of the henbane, which had been wafted in upon them, aroused them by making them smell to a sponge full of vinegar he had with him. Then he loosed their bonds, and when they saw him, they blessed him and rejoiced in him. Then they went forth and took all the guards' arms, and Sehim bade them go to their own camp; after which he re-entered Agib's camp, and wrapping him in his cloak, lifted him up and made for the Muslim camp. And the Merciful Lord protected him, so that he reached Gherib's tent in safety and unrolled the mantle before him. Gherib looked and seeing Agib bound, cried out, 'God is Most Great! He giveth aid and victory!' And he blessed Sehim and bade him arouse Agib. So he made him smell to vinegar, mixed with frankincense, and he opened his eyes and finding himself bound and shackled, hung down his head. 'O accursed one,' quoth Sehim, 'lift thy head!' So he raised his eyes and found himself amongst Arabs and Persians and saw his brother seated on the throne of his state and the place of his power, wherefore he was silent and spake not. Then Gherib cried out and said, 'Strip me this dog!' So they stripped him and beat him with whips, till his body was weakened and his pride subdued, after which Gherib set over him a guard of a hundred cavaliers.

Presently, they heard shouts of 'There is no god but God!' and 'God is Most Great!' from the infidel camp. Now the reason of this was that King Damigh, Gherib's uncle, had set out from El Jezireh, with twenty thousand horse, ten days after his nephew, and on nearing the field of battle, had despatched one of his riders to get news. The scout was absent a whole day, after which he returned and told Damigh all that had passed. So he waited till the night, when he fell upon the infidels, crying out, 'God is Most Great!' and put them to the edge of the sword. When Gherib heard the crying aforesaid, he said to Sehim, 'Go and find out the cause of these shouts.' So Sehim repaired to the field of battle and questioned the camp followers, who told him that King Damigh had come up with twenty thousand men and fallen upon the idolaters by night, saying, 'By the virtue of Abraham the friend, I will not forsake my brother's son, but will do a brave man's part and beat back the infidels and please the Omnipotent King!'

So Sehim returned and told Gherib, who cried out to his men, saying, 'Don your arms and mount your horses and let us succour my uncle!' So they mounted and fell upon the infidels with the sharp sword. By the morning, they had killed nigh fifty thousand of them and made other thirty thousand prisoners, and the rest of Agib's army dispersed over the length and breadth of the land. Then the Muslims returned in triumph and Gherib rode out to meet his uncle, whom he saluted and thanked for his help. Quoth Damigh, 'I wonder if that dog Agib fell in this day's battle.' 'O uncle,' replied Gherib, 'have no care for him; know that he is with me in chains.' When Damigh heard this, he rejoiced mightily and the two kings dismounted and entered the pavilion, but found no Agib there; whereupon Gherib exclaimed, 'O glory of Abraham the Friend! What an evil end is this to a glorious day!' and he cried out to the tent-keepers, saying, 'Out on you! Where is my enemy?' Quoth they, 'When thou mountedst and we went with thee, thou didst not bid us guard him;' and Gherib exclaimed, 'There is no power and no virtue but in God the Most High, the Supreme!' But Damigh said to him, 'Hasten not nor be concerned, for where can he go, and we in pursuit of him?'

Now the manner of Agib's escape was on this wise. His man Siyyar, being in the camp in disguise, saw Gherib mount and ride forth, leaving Agib unguarded, and could hardly credit his eyes; so he waited awhile and presently crept to the tent and taking Agib, who was senseless for the pain of the beating, on his back, made off with him into the open country and fared on at the top of his speed all that night and next day, till he came to a spring of water, under an apple tree. There he set Agib down and washed his face, whereupon he opened his eyes and seeing Siyyar, said to him, 'O Siyyar, carry me to Cufa, that I may recover there and levy horsemen and soldiers, wherewith to overcome mine enemy: and know, O Siyyar, that I am anhungred.' So Siyyar went out to the desert and caught an ostrich-poult and brought it to his lord. Then he gathered firewood and striking a light, kindled a fire, by which he roasted the bird and fed Agib with its flesh and gave him to drink of the water of the spring, till his strength returned to him; after which he went to one of the Bedouin encampments, and stealing a horse thence, mounted Agib upon it and journeyed on with him till they drew near the city of Cufa. The governor of the city came out to meet and salute the King, whom he found weak with the beating his brother had inflicted on him; and Agib entered the city and calling his physicians, bade them heal him in less than than ten days' time. 'We hear and obey,' answered they and tended him till he became whole of the sickness that was upon him and of the beating. Then he commanded his viziers to write letters to all his vassals, and he wrote one-and-twenty letters and despatched them to the different governors, who assembled their troops and set out for Cufa by forced marches.

Meanwhile, Gherib, being troubled for Agib's escape, despatched a thousand horse in quest of him, who dispersed on all sides and sought him a day and a night, but found no trace of him; so they returned and told Gherib, who called for his brother Sehim, but found him not; whereat he was sore concerned, fearing for him from the vicissitudes of fortune. However, presently, Sehim entered and kissed the earth before Gherib, who rose, when he saw him, and said, 'Where hast thou been, O Sehim?' 'O King,' answered he, 'I have been to Cufa and find that the dog Agib hath made his way thither and is cured of his wounds. Moreover, he hath written letters to his vassals, who have brought him troops.' When Gherib heard this, he gave command to depart; so they struck the tents and marched for Cufa. When they came in sight of the city, they found it compassed about with a host like the swollen ocean, having neither beginning nor end. So Gherib encamped with his troops in face of the infidels and set up his standards, and the dark fell down upon the two hosts, whereupon they lighted fires and kept watch till daybreak. Then Gherib rose and making the ablution, prayed two inclinations, according to the rite of our father Abraham; after which he commanded the drums to sound the point of war. Accordingly, the drums beat to battle and the standards waved, whilst the fighting-men armed and mounted and sought the lists.

The first to open the chapter of war was King Damigh, who spurred his charger between the two armies and displayed himself and played with swords and spears, till both hosts were confounded and marvelled at him; after which he cried out, saying, 'Who is for jousting? Let no sluggard or weakling come out to me; for I am King Damigh, brother of King Kundemir.' Then there came forth a horseman of the infidels, as he were a flame of fire, and drove at Damigh, without word said; but the King received him with a lance-thrust in the breast, that the point issued from between his shoulders and God hurried his soul to the fire, and ill was the abiding-place . Then came forth a second and he slew him also, and a third, and they ceased not to come out to him and he to slay them, till he had made an end of six-and-seventy fighting-men.

Therewith the infidels hung back and would not encounter him; but Agib cried out to his men and said, 'Out on you, O folk! If ye all go forth against him, one after another, he will not leave one of you, sitting or standing. Charge on them, all at once, and sweep the earth clean of them and make their heads a pavement for your horses' hoofs!' So they waved the awe-striking standard and host fell upon host; the blood rained in streams upon the earth and the Judge of battle ruled, in whose ordinance is no unright. The valiant stood firm on his feet in the stead of war, whilst the faint-heart gave back and fled, thinking the day would never come to an end nor the night draw the curtains of the dusk; and they ceased not to battle and smite with swords, till the day waned and the night darkened with the shadows. Then the drums of the infidels beat the retreat, but Gherib, refusing to stay his arms, drove at the idolaters, and the believers in the unity of God followed him. How many heads and hands they sundered, how many necks and sinews they shore, how many knees and spines they crushed and how many grown men and youths they did to death! With the first peep of dawn the infidels broke and fled, and the Muslims followed them till noon and took over twenty thousand of them, whom they brought back bound.

Then Gherib sat down before the gate of Cufa and commanded a herald to proclaim pardon and safety to all who should leave the worship of idols and acknowledge the One All-knowing God, the Creator of mankind and of light and darkness. So proclamation was made as he bade in the streets of Cufa, and all that were therein embraced the true faith, great and small. Moreover, they all issued forth and made good their submission before King Gherib, who rejoiced in them with an exceeding joy and his breast expanded and he was glad. Then he enquired of Merdas and his daughter Mehdiyeh, and being told that be had taken up his abode behind the Red Mountain, called Sehim and said to him, 'Find out for me what is come of thy father.' Sehim tarried not, but mounting, set his brown spear in the rest and fared on till he reached the Red Mountain, where he sought for his father, but found no trace of him nor of his tribe; but in their stead he saw an elder of the Arabs, a very old man, broken with excess of years, and asked him of the folk and whither they were gone. 'O my son,' replied he, 'when Merdas heard of Gherib's descent upon Cufa, he was smitten with great fear and taking his daughter, set out with his slaves, male and female, and all his tribe, into the deserts, and I know not whither he is gone.' So Sehim returned to Gherib and told him what he had learnt, whereat he was greatly concerned. Then he sat down on his father's throne and opening his treasuries, distributed largesse to his braves. And he took up his abode in Cufa and sent out spies, to get news of Agib. Moreover, he summoned the grandees of the realm, who came and did him homage; as also did the townsfolk, and he bestowed on them sumptuous dresses of honour and commended the people to their care.

One day, he went out to hunt, with a hundred horse, and fared on till he came to a valley, abounding in trees and fruits and streams and birds. It was a pasturing-place for antelopes and gazelles, delightsome to the spirit, and the fragrance of its flowers brought repose from the languor of strife. It was a brilliant day; so they encamped in the valley and passed the night there. On the morrow, Gherib made the ablution and prayed the morning prayers, offering up praise and thanks to God the Most High; when, behold, there arose a great clamour and tumult in the meadows, and he bade Sehim go and see what was the matter. So Sehim mounted and rode till he saw horsemen carrying off women and children, captive and crying out, and plundered goods and haltered horses; whereupon he questioned the shepherds and they said, 'This is the harem of Merdas, Chief of the Benou Kehtan, and his goods and those of his tribe; for yesterday Jemrcan slew Merdas and made prize of his women and children and household stuff and those of his tribe. It is his wont to go a-raiding and waylay travellers, and he is a mighty man of war; neither Arabs nor kings can avail against him and he is the scourge of the land.'

When Sehim heard this, he returned to Gherib and told him the case, wherefore fire was added to his fire and his blood boiled to avenge himself and wipe out his reproach. So he rode after the robbers, till he overtook them and fell upon them, crying out and saying, 'God is Most Great! Down with the covetous oppressors, who deny Him!' And he slew in one onset one-and-twenty fighting men. Then he halted in mid-field, with no coward's heart, and cried out, saying, 'Where is Jemrcan? Let him come out to me, that I may make him quaff the cup of humiliation and rid the earth of him!' Hardly had he made an end of speaking, when out came Jemrcan,—a huge tall Amalekite, as he were a calamity of calamities or a piece of a mountain, cased in steel, and bearing a passing heavy club of China steel, wherewith if he smote a mountain, he crashed it,—and drove at Gherib like a fierce tyrant, without speech or salutation. Gherib met him like a hungry lion, and the brigand aimed a blow at his head with his club; but he evaded it and the club smote the earth and sank therein half a cubit deep. Then Gherib took his mace and smiting Jemrcan on the wrist, crushed his fingers and the club dropped from his grasp; whereupon Gherib bent down from his saddle and snatching it up, swiftlier than the blinding lightning, smote him therewith full on the ribs, and he fell to the earth like a huge palm tree. So Sehim took him and binding him, haled him off with a rope, and Gherib's men fell on those of Jemrcan and slew fifty of them and put the rest to flight; nor did they draw bridle till they reached their camp and raised their voices in clamour; whereupon all who were in the stronghold came out to meet them and they told them what had passed, and when they heard that their chief was a prisoner, they set out for the valley, vying with each other in their haste to deliver him.

Meanwhile King Gherib dismounted and called for Jemrcan, who humbled himself before him, saying, 'I throw myself on thy mercy, O champion of the age!' 'O dog of the Arabs,' replied Gherib, 'dost thou waylay the servants of God the Most High and fearest not the Lord of the Worlds?' 'O my lord,' said Jemrcan, 'and who is the Lord of the Worlds?' 'O dog,' rejoined Gherib, 'and what calamity dost thou worship?' 'O my lord,' answered the brigand, 'I worship a god made of dates kneaded with butter and honey, and whiles I eat him and make me another.' When Gherib heard this, he laughed, till he fell backward, and said, 'O unhappy wretch, there is none worship-worth save God the Most High, who created thee and all things and provideth all creatures, from whom nothing is hidden and who hath power over all.' Quoth Jemrcan, 'And where is this mighty god, that I may worship him?' 'O fellow,' answered Gherib, 'know that this god's name is Allah, and it is He who created the heavens and the earth and maketh the trees to grow and the waters to run. He created beasts and birds and Paradise and Hell-fire and secludeth Himself from all eyes, seeing and being seen of none. Extolled be His perfection! There is no god but He!' When Jemrcan heard these words, the ears of his heart were opened and his skin shuddered and he said, 'O my lord, what shall I say that I may become one of you and that this mighty Lord may accept of me?' 'Say,' replied Gherib, '"There is no god but God and Abraham the Friend is the Apostle of God!"' So he repeated the profession of the faith and was written of the people of felicity. Then said Gherib, 'Hast thou tasted the sweetness of Islam?' 'Yes,' answered the other; and Gherib said, 'Loose his bonds.' So they unbound him and he kissed the earth before Gherib and his feet.

At this moment they espied a great cloud of dust, that spread tilled it walled the world, and Gherib bade Sehim go and see what it was. So he went off, like a bird in full flight, and presently returning, said, 'O King of the age, it is the Benou Aamir, the comrades of Jemrcan.' Whereupon quoth Gherib to the latter, 'Ride out to thy people and expound to them Islam, and if they profess, they shall be saved; but, if they refuse, we will put them to the sword.' So Jemrcan mounted and spurring towards his tribesmen, cried out to them; and they knew him and dismounting, came up to him on foot and said, 'We rejoice in thy safety, O our lord!' 'O folk,' said he, 'whoso obeyeth me shall be saved; but whoso gainsayeth me, I will cut him in twain with this sabre.' And they made answer, saying, 'Command us what thou wilt, for we will not gainsay thy commandment.' Quoth he, 'Then say with me, "There is no god but God and Abraham is the Friend of God!"' 'O our lord,' asked they, 'whence hast thou these words?' And he told them what had befallen him, adding, 'O folk, know ye not that I am your chief and foremost among you in the field and stead of war, and yet a single man took me prisoner and made me quaff the cup of humiliation?'

When they heard his speech, they spoke the word of Unity, and Jemrcan led them to Gherib, at whose hands they affirmed their profession and wished him glory and victory, after they had kissed the earth before him. Gherib rejoiced in them and bade them return to their people and expound Islam to them; but they said, 'O our lord, we will never leave thee, whilst we live; but we will go and fetch our families and return to thee.' And Gherib said, 'Go, and join me at the city of Cufa.' So Jemrcan and his comrades returned to their camp and expounded Islam to their women and children, who all to a soul embraced the true faith, after which they dismantled their houses and struck their tents and set out for Cufa, driving before them their horses and sheep and camels.

Meanwhile Gherib returned to Cufa, where the horsemen met him and carried him into the city in state. He entered his palace and sat down on his throne, with his officers standing on either hand. Then the spies entered and informed him that his brother Agib had made his escape and taken refuge with Julned ben Kerker, the lord of the city of Oman and land of Yemen; whereupon Gherib bade his troops make ready to set out in three days' time. Then he expounded Islam to the thirty thousand men he had taken in the first battle and exhorted them to profess and take service with him. Twenty thousand embraced the faith, but the rest refused and he slew them. Then came Jemrcan and his tribe and kissed the earth before Gherib, who bestowed on him a splendid dress of honour and made him captain of his vanguard, saying, 'O Jemrcan, mount with the chiefs of thy kinsmen and twenty thousand horse and fare on before us to the land of Julned ben Kerker.' 'I hear and obey,' answered Jemrcan and set forward with his men, leaving the women and children of the tribe in Cufa.

Then Gherib passed in review the harem of Merdas and his eye lit upon Mehdiyeh, who was among the women, whereupon he fell down in a swoon. They sprinkled rosewater on his face, till he came to himself, when he embraced Mehdiyeh and carried her into a privy chamber, where he sat with her; and they lay together that night without lewdness. Next morning, he went out and sitting down on the throne of his kingship, invested his uncle Damigh with a dress of honour and appointed him his viceroy over all Irak, commending Mehdiyeh to his care, till he should return from his expedition against Agib; after which he set out for the land of Yemen with twenty thousand horse and ten thousand foot.

Now, when Agib and his defeated army came in sight of Oman, King Julned saw the dust of their approach and sent scouts to find out its meaning, who returned and told him that this was the dust of Agib, lord of Irak. And Julned wondered at his coming and said to his officers, 'Go forth and meet him.' So they went forth and met him and pitched tents for him at the gate of the city; and Agib sent in to Julned, weeping and mournful-hearted. Now Julned's wife was the daughter of Agib's father's brother, and he had children by her. So, when he saw his kinsman in this plight, he asked what ailed him and Agib told him all that had befallen him, saying, 'O King, Gherib commandeth the folk to worship the Lord of the Heavens and forbiddeth them from the service of idols and other gods.' When Julned heard this, he was mightily enraged and said, 'By the virtue of the light-giving sun, I will not leave one of thy brother's folk on life! But where didst thou leave them and how many men are they?' 'I left them in Cufa,' answered Agib; 'and they are fifty thousand horse.' Whereupon Julned called his Vizier Jawamerd, saying, 'Take seventy thousand horse and go to Cufa and bring me the Muslims alive, that I may torture them with all manner of tortures.'

So Jawamerd departed with his host and fared on seven days' journey towards Cufa, till he came to a valley abounding in trees and streams and fruits, where he called a halt and they rested till the middle of the night, when the Vizier gave the signal for departure and mounting, rode on before them till hard upon daybreak. A little before the dawn, he descended into a well-wooded valley, whose flowers were fragrant and whose birds warbled on the branches, as they swayed gracefully to and fro, and Satan blew into his sides and he recited the following verses:

I put my battle-harness on and don my dreadful arms, And here and there on every side I drive through the mellay;
I and my troops, we plunge into the seething sea of war And of my prowess and my might the captives lead away.
The doughtiest horsemen of the world do know me for a fear, A scourge and terror to my foes, my kinsmen's help and stay.
Lo, upon Gherib will I seize and drag him forth in chains! Then, with a joyful heart and proud, I'll homeward wend my way.

Hardly had he made an end of his verses when there came out upon him from among the trees a horseman of noble presence, clad in complete steel, who cried out to him, saying, 'Stand, O brigand of the Arabs! Put off thy clothes and lay down thine arms and dismount and begone!' When Jawamerd heard this, the light in his eyes became darkness and he drew his sabre and drove at Jemrcan, saying, 'O thief of the Arabs, wilt thou play the highwayman with me, who am captain of the host of Julned ben Kerker and am come to bring Gherib and his men bound?' When Jemrcan heard these words, he said, 'How grateful is this to my heart!' And made at Jawamerd, reciting the following verses:

I am the cavalier renowned for valour in the field: The foemen everywhere do dread my sabre and my spear.
I'm Jemrcan, whose whole delight is in the press of war, And all the champions of the world my lance-thrust know and fear.
Gherib my lord and sultan is, the high-priest of my faith, That is the lion of the fight, when hosts to strife draw near!
Devout and full of pious dread, a doughty chief is he; Midmost the tented field he slays his enemies like deer.
Despite the gods of unbelief, verses he chants and bids The folk to Abraham his faith, with clarion voice and clear.

Now Jemrcan had fared on with his men ten days' journey from Cufa and called a halt on the eleventh day till midnight, when he bade depart and rode on in advance, till he came to the valley aforesaid and heard Jawamerd reciting his braggart verses. So he drove at him, as he were a ravening lion, and smiting him with his sword, clove him in twain and waited till his captains came up, when he told them what had passed and said to them, 'Let each of you take five thousand men and disperse round about the valley, whilst I and the Benou Aamir fall upon the enemy's van, crying out and saying, "God is Most Great!" When ye hear our shouts, do ye charge them with the same cry and smite them with the sword.' 'We hear and obey,' answered they and turning back to their men, spread themselves about the sides of the valley in the fore-dawn twilight.

Presently up came the army of Yemen, like a flock of sheep, filling mountain and plain, and Jemrcan and the Benou Aamir fell upon them, shouting, 'God is Most Great!' Whereupon the Muslims in ambush in the valley cried out in answer and the hills and mountains echoed the cry and all things, green and dry, answered, saying, 'God is Most Great! He giveth aid and victory and forsaketh those who deny Him!' And the infidels were confounded and smote one another with the keen sabre, whilst the true believers fell upon them like flames of fire and nothing was seen but heads flying and blood spouting and faint-hearts giving back in dismay. By the time they could see each other's faces, two-thirds of the infidels had perished and God hastened their souls to the fire and ill was the abiding-place. The rest took to flight and dispersed about the deserts, whilst the Muslims pursued them, slaying and taking captive till midday, when they returned in triumph with seven thousand prisoners; and but six-and-twenty thousand of the infidels escaped and the most of them wounded.

Then the Muslims collected the arms and horses and tents and baggage of the enemy and despatched them to Cufa with an escort of a thousand horse; whilst Jemrcan and the rest of his force dismounted and expounded Islam to the prisoners, who made profession of the faith with heart and tongue; whereupon they released them and embraced them and rejoiced in them. Then Jemrcan made his troops rest a day and a night and set out with the dawn, intending for the city of Oman; whilst the thousand horse fared back to Cufa with the booty. When they reached the city, they went in to Gherib and told him what had passed, whereat he rejoiced and said to the Ghoul of the Mountain, 'Take horse and follow Jemrcan with twenty thousand men.' So Saadan and his sons mounted and set out for Oman with twenty thousand horse.

Meanwhile, the remains of the defeated army reached Oman and went in to Julned, weeping and crying, 'Woe!' and 'Ruin!' whereat he was amazed and said to them, 'What hath befallen you?' So they told him what had happened and he said, 'Out on you! How many men were they?' 'O King,' answered they, 'there were twenty standards, under each a thousand men.' When Julned heard this, he said, 'May the sun pour no blessing on you! Out on you! Shall twenty thousand overcome you, and you seventy thousand horse and Jawamerd equal to three thousand in the open field!' Then, in the excess of his rage and mortification, he drew his sword and cried out to those who were present, saying, 'Fall on them!' So the courtiers drew their swords upon the fugitives and slew them to the last man and cast them to the dogs. Then Julned cried out to his son (whose name was Courejan and than whom there was no doughtier cavalier in the army of his father, for he was wont to undertake three thousand horse, single-handed), saying, 'Take a hundred thousand horse and go to Irak and lay it waste altogether.' So Courejan and his host made haste to equip themselves and set out in battle array, with the prince at their head, glorying in himself and reciting the following verses:

I'm El Courejan, the first-born of renown! I vanquish the dwellers in desert and town.
How many a champion I've slain with my sword! Like an ox, to the earth I have stricken him down.
How many a host have I scattered abroad And their heads made like balls roll o'er desert and down!
Now for Irak I'm bound, for the enemies' land, Where my foes in the sea of their blood I will drown.
I will lead away Gherib in chains with his chiefs, So their fate to the wise for a warning be known!

They fared on twelve days' journey, till a great cloud of dust arose before them and covered the horizon and the country, and Courejan sent out scouts to reconnoitre, who returned and said to him, 'O King, this is the dust of the Muslims.' Whereat he was glad and said, 'Did ye count them?' And they answered, saying, 'We counted the standards, and they were twenty in number.' 'By my faith,' quoth the prince, 'I will not send one man-at-arms against them, but will go forth to them alone and strew their heads under the hoofs of the horses!'

Now this was the army of Jemrcan, who, espying the host of the infidels and seeing them as the swollen sea, called a halt; so his troops pitched the tents and set up the standards, calling upon the name of the All-wise Creator of light and darkness, Lord of all creatures, who seeth and is not seen, blessed and exalted be He! There is no god but He! The infidels also halted and pitched their tents, and Courejan said to them, 'Sleep upon your arms, for in the last watch of the night we will mount and trample yonder handful under our feet!' Now one of Jemrcan's spies was standing by and heard what Courejan purposed; so he returned and told his chief who said to his men, 'Arm yourselves and as soon it is dark, bring me all the camels and mules and hang all the bells and bangles and rattles ye have about their necks.' And they had with them more than twenty thousand camels and mules.

So they waited till the infidels were asleep, when Jemrcan commanded them to mount, and they took horse, committing themselves to God and seeking aid of the Lord of the Worlds. Then said Jemrcan, 'Goad the mules and camels with the points of your spears and drive them to the infidels' camp.' They did as he bade and the beasts rushed upon the enemy's camp, whilst the bells and bangles and rattles jangled and the Muslims followed at their heels, shouting, 'God is Most Great!' till all the hills and mountains resounded with the name of the Most High God, to whom belong glory and majesty! The cattle, hearing this terrible din, took fright and rushed upon the tents and trampled the folk, as they lay asleep; whereupon the idolaters started up in confusion and snatching up their arms, fell upon one another with smiting, till the most part of them were slain.

When the day broke, they looked at each other and found no Muslims slain, but saw them all on horseback, armed; wherefore they knew that this was a trick that had been played them, and Courejan cried out to the remnant of his folk, saying, 'O sons of whores, what we had a mind to do with them, that have they done with us and their craft hath gotten the better of ours.' And they were about to charge, when, behold, a cloud of dust appeared and the wind smote it, so that it rose and hung vaulted in the air and there, appeared beneath it the glint of helmets and gleam of hauberks and splendid warriors, armed with tempered swords and supple spears. When the infidels saw this, they held back from the battle and each army sent out scouts, to know the meaning of this dust, who returned with the news that it was an army of Muslims.

Now this was the host of the Ghoul of the Mountain, whom Gherib had despatched to Jemrcan's aid, and Saadan himself rode in their van. So the two hosts of the true believers joined company and rushing upon the infidels, like a flame of fire, plied them with the keen sword and the straight and quivering spear, whilst the day was darkened and eyes blinded for the much dust. The valiant stood fast and the coward fled and sought the deserts, whilst the blood flowed like a tide over the earth; nor did they cease from the battle till the day departed and the night came with the darkness. Then the Muslims drew apart from the infidels and returned to their tents, where they ate and slept, till the darkness fled and gave place to the smiling morn; when they prayed the morning-prayer and mounted to battle.

Now, when Courejan found the most part of his men wounded, for indeed two-thirds of their number had perished by sword and spear, he said to them, 'Tomorrow, I will go forth into the open field and play the champion in the stead of war.' So, as soon as the day broke and the morning appeared with its light and shone, the two hosts mounted and unsheathed their swords and couched their brown lances and cried out lustily and drew out in order of battle. The first to open the chapter of war was Courejan, who cried out, saying, 'Let no weakling come out to me today!' Whereupon there ran at him a captain of the Benou Aamir and the two drove at each other awhile, like two rains butting. Presently Courejan seized the Muslim by his coat of arms and tearing him from his saddle, threw him to the ground; where the infidels laid hands on him and bound him and bore him off to their tents; whilst Courejan wheeled about and curvetted and offered battle, till another captain came out, whom also he took prisoner; nor did he leave to do thus till he had made prize of seven captains before midday. Then Jemrcan gave such a cry, that the whole field resounded thereto and both armies heard it, and ran at Courejan with a heart on fire with anger, reciting the following verses:

Hark ye, I'm Jemrcan, the champion stout and wight; The terror of my stroke is feared of every knight.
I take the strengths by storm and leave the fortress-walls To mourn the loss of those that held them in their might.
Wherefore, O Courejan, quit thou the erring path; Turn from the froward ways and tread the road of right;
Confess to the one true God, who spread the heavens above, Who made the streams to flow and hills to stand upright;
For, if the slave embrace the true, the only faith, Hell's anguish shall he 'scape and win to heaven's delight.

When Courejan heard these words, he puffed and snorted and railed at the sun and the moon and drove at Jemrcan, repeating these verses:

I'm Courejan, the chief and champion of the age! Es Shera's lions flee my shadow in affright!
I take the forts by storm and snare the beasts of prey, And all the horsemen fear to meet me in the fight.
Wherefore, O Jemrcan, if thou believe me not, Up to the middle field and try with me thy might!

Jemrcan met him with a stout heart and they hewed at each other with swords and thrust with spears, till the two hosts lamented for them and great was the clamour between them: nor did they leave fighting till the time of afternoon-prayer was passed and the day began to wane. Then Jemrcan drove at Courejan and smiting him on the breast with his mace, cast him to the ground, as he were the trunk of a palm tree; and the Muslims bound him and haled him away with ropes like a camel.

When the idolaters saw their prince captive, a blind fury seized on them and they bore down upon the Muslims, thinking to rescue him; but the Muslim champions met them and left them prostrate on the earth, whilst the rest turned and sought safety in flight, with the sword clanking at their backs. The Muslims pursued them till they had scattered them over mountain and desert, when they returned to the spoil, good luck to it for a spoil! great store was there of horses and tents and so forth. Then Jemrcan went in to Courejan and expounded Islam to him, threatening him with death, except he embraced the faith; but he refused; so they cut off his head and sticking it on a spear, fared on towards Oman.

Meanwhile, the survivors of the routed host returned to Julned and made known to him the death of his son and the destruction of his army, whereupon he cast his crown to the earth and buffeting his face, till the blood spouted from his nostrils, fell down in a swoon. They sprinkled rosewater on his face, till he came to himself and cried to his Vizier, saying, 'Write letters to all my governors and bid them leave not a smiter with the sword nor a thruster with the spear nor a bender of the bow, but bring them all to me.' So he wrote letters and despatched them by runners to the governors, who levied their power and joined the King with an immense army, whose number was ninescore thousand men. Then they made ready tents and camels and swift horses and were about to depart, when up came Jemrcan and Saadan the Ghoul, with seventy thousand horse, as they were fierce lions, all clad in complete steel; which when Julned saw, he rejoiced and said, 'By the virtue of the light-giving Sun, I will not leave one of mine enemies alive, no, not one to carry the news, and I will lay waste the land of Irak, that I may take my wreak for my son, the havoc-making champion; nor shall my fire be quenched!'

Then he turned to Agib and said to him, 'O dog of Irak, it was thou that broughtest this calamity on us! But by the virtue of that which I worship, except I avenge me of mine enemy, I will put thee to death after the foulest fashion!' When Agib heard this, he was sore troubled and blamed himself; but he waited till nightfall, when he took those who were left to him of his suite apart from the camp and said to them, 'O my kinsmen, know that Julned and I are sore dismayed at the coming of the Muslims, and I know that he will not avail to protect me from my brother nor from any other; so meseems we should do well to make our escape, whilst all men sleep, and flee to King Yaarub ben Kehtan, for that he hath more soldiers and is stronger of kingship.' They fell in with his proposal and he bade them kindle fires at the doors of their tents and set out under cover of the night. So they did his bidding and departing, by daybreak were far away.

As soon as it was morning, the drums beat a point of war, and Julned mounted with two hundred and sixty thousand fighting-men, clad cap-a-pie in hauberks and cuirasses and strait-knit coats of mail, and drew out in order of battle. Then Jemrcan and Saadan rode out with forty thousand stalwart fighting-men, under each standard a thousand cavaliers, doughty champions, foremost in the fight. The two hosts drew out in battalia and bared their swords and couched their limber lances, for the drinking of the cup of death. The first to open the chapter of battle was Saadan, as he were a mountain of flint or a Marid of the Jinn. Then pricked out to him a champion of the infidels, and he slew him and casting him to the earth, cried out to his sons and servants, saying, 'Light the fire and roast me this dead man.' They did as he bade and brought him the roast, and he ate it and crunched the bones, whilst the infidels stood looking on from afar; and they cried out, saying, 'O light-giving Sun!' and were affrighted at Saadan.

Then Julned cried out to his men, saying, 'Slay me yonder foul beast!' Whereupon another captain of his host drove at the Ghoul; but he slew him, and he ceased not to slay horseman after horseman, till he had made an end of thirty men. with this the vile infidels held back and feared to face him, saying, 'Who shall cope with Jinn and Ghouls?' But Julned cried out, saying, 'Let a hundred horse charge him and bring him to me, alive or dead.' So a hundred horse ran at Saadan with swords and spears, and he met them with a heart firmer than flint, proclaiming the unity of the Requiting King, whom no one thing diverteth from another. Then he set on them, crying, 'God is Most Great!' and smote them with his sword and made their heads fly. In one onset he slew of them four-and-seventy and put the rest to flight.

Then Julned cried out to ten of his captains, having each a thousand men under his hand, and said to them, 'Shoot his horse with arrows, till it fall under him, and then lay hands on him.' So ten thousand horse drove at Saadan, who met them with a stout heart; and Jemrcan, seeing this, bore down upon the infidels with his Muslims, crying out, 'God is Most Great!' Before they could win to the Ghoul, the enemy had slain his horse and taken him prisoner; but they ceased not to charge the infidels, though they were amongst them as a white patch on a black bull, till the day grew dark and eyes were blinded, and the sharp sword clanged, whilst the valiant stood firm and destruction overtook the faint-heart; nor did they stint from the mellay till the dark fell down, when they drew apart, after there had been slain of the infidels men without number.

Then Jemrcan and his men returned to their tents, in great grief for Saadan, so that neither meat nor sleep was sweet to them, and they counted their host and found that less than a thousand of them had fallen. And Jemrcan said, 'O folk, tomorrow I will go forth into the lists and slay their champions and make prize of them and their families and ransom Saadan therewith, if it please the Requiting King, whom no one thing distracteth from another!' Wherefore their hearts were comforted and they separated to their tents, rejoicing.

Meanwhile, Julned entered his pavilion and sitting down on his bed of estate, with his grandees about him, called for Saadan and said to him, 'O raging dog and least of the Arabs and carrier of firewood, who was it slew my son Courejan, the champion of the age, slayer of heroes and caster down of warriors?' Quoth the Ghoul, 'Jemrcan slew him, captain of the host of King Gherib, prince of cavaliers, and I roasted and ate him, for I was anhungred.' When Julned heard this, his eyes started from his head for rage and he bade his swordbearer strike off Saadan's head. So he came forward in that intent, but Saadan stretched himself mightily and bursting his bonds, snatched the sword from the headsman and cut off his head. Then he made at Julned; but he cast himself down from the throne and fled; whilst Saadan fell on the bystanders and slew twenty of the King's chief officers, and the rest fled. Therewith great was the crying in the camp of the infidels and the Ghoul sallied forth of the pavilion and falling upon the troops, smote them with the sword, till they opened and left a lane for him to pass; nor did he cease to press forward, cutting at them right and left, till he won free of the tents and made for the Muslim camp. As soon as he was gone, the infidels and their King returned to their tents and Julned said to them, 'O folk, by the virtue of the light-giving sun and by the darkness of the night and the light of the day and the wandering stars, I thought not to have escaped death this day; for, had I fallen into yonder fellow's hands, he had eaten me, as I were a grain of wheat or a barley-corn.' 'O King,' answered they, 'never saw we any do the like of this Ghoul.' And he said, 'Tomorrow do ye all don your arms and mount and trample them under your horses' feet.'

Meanwhile the Muslims heard the shouts of the infidels and said to each other, 'Haply, some succour hath reached them;' but, as they stood wondering, up came Saadan. So they all rejoiced in him and gave him joy of his escape, and the gladdest of them all was Jemrcan, who said to them, 'Tomorrow, I will show you my fashion and what behoveth the like of me, for, by the virtue of Abraham the Friend I will slay them on the foulest wise and smite them with the edge of the sword, till all who have understanding are confounded at them. But I mean to attack the right and left wings; so, when ye see me drive at the King under the standards, do ye charge resolutely behind me, and with God is it to decree what shall betide!'

So the two hosts lay upon their arms till the day broke and the sun appeared to sight, when they mounted swiftlier than the twinkling of the eye. The raven of ill-omen croaked and the two hosts drew out in battalia and looked at each other with the evil eye. The first to open the chapter of war was Jemrcan, who wheeled and curvetted and offered battle; and Julned and his men were about to charge, when, behold a cloud of dust arose and spread till it covered the plains and obscured the day. Then the four winds smote it and it dispersed and there appeared beneath it cavaliers, black and white, and princely champions, with keen swords and piercing lances, and footmen who knew not fear, as they were lions. At this sight both armies left fighting and sent out scouts, who disappeared within the cloud of dust and returned after awhile with the news that the approaching host was one of Muslims, under the command of King Gherib. When the Muslims heard of the coming of their King, they rejoiced and spurring out to meet him, dismounted and kissed the earth before him and saluted him, whilst he welcomed them and rejoiced in their safety. Then they escorted him to their camp and pitched pavilions for him and set up standards; and Gherib sat down on his couch of estate, with his grandees about him, and they related to him all that had befallen.

Meanwhile, the infidels sought for Agib and finding him not among them nor in their tents, told Julned of this, whereat his gorge rose and he bit his fingers, saying, 'By the light-giving sun, he is a perfidious dog and hath fled into the deserts with his crew of rascals! But nought save hard fighting will serve us to repel these enemies; so fortify your resolves and harden your hearts and beware of the Muslims.' And Gherib also said to the Muslims, 'Fortify your hearts and strengthen your courage and seek aid of your Lord, beseeching Him to vouchsafe you the victory over your enemies.' 'O King,' answered they, 'thou shalt see what we will do in the field and the stead of war.'

So the two hosts slept till the day arose with its light and the sun shone out upon hill and plain, when Gherib prayed two inclinations, after the rite of Abraham the Friend (on whom be peace) and wrote a letter, which he despatched by his brother Sehim to the King of the infidels. When Sehim reached the enemies' camp, the guards asked him what he wanted and he replied, 'I want your ruler.' Quoth they, 'Wait till we consult him;' and he waited, whilst they went in to their King and told him of the coming of a messenger, and he said, 'Bring him to me.' So they brought Sehim before Julned, who said to him, 'Who hath sent thee?' Quoth he, 'King Gherib sends me, whom God hath made ruler over the Arabs and Persians; take his letter and return an answer thereto.' So Julned took the letter and opening it, read as follows: 'In the name of God the Compassionate, the Merciful, the Immemorial Lord, the Supreme, the One, the All-knowing, the Lord of Noah and Salih and Hood and Abraham and of all things! Peace be on him who followeth in the way of righteousness and feareth the issues of frowardness, who obeyeth the Almighty King and preferreth the next world to the present! O Julned, none is worthy of worship save God alone, the One, the Victorious, Creator of night and day and the revolving sphere, who sendeth the holy prophets and maketh the streams to flow and the trees to grow, who vaulted the heavens and spread out the earth like a carpet and feedeth the birds in their nests and the wild beasts in the deserts; for He is the All-powerful God, the Forgiving, the Long-suffering, the Protector, whom no eye comprehendeth and who maketh the night to return upon the day, He who sent down the apostles and the Scripture. Know, O Julned, that there is no faith but the faith of Abraham the Friend; so do thou embrace the faith of submission and send me the dog Agib, that I may take my wreak of my father and mother. So shalt thou be saved from the sharp sword in this world and from the fiery torment in the world to come. But, if thou refuse, look for destruction and the wasting of thy realm and the cutting off of thy traces.'

When Julned had read this letter, he said to Sehim, 'Tell thy Lord that Agib hath fled, he and his people, and I know not whither he is gone; but, as for Julned, he will not forswear his faith, and tomorrow, there shall be battle between us and the Sun shall give us the victory.' So Sehim returned to his brother with this answer and on the morrow the Muslims donned their arms and bestrode their stout horses, calling aloud on the name of the All-conquering King, Creator of bodies and souls, and magnifying Him. The drums beat to battle, till the earth trembled, and all the lordly warriors and doughty champions sought the field.

The first to open the chapter of battle was Jemrcan, who spurred his charger into the mid-field and played with sword and javelin, till the understanding were amazed; after which he cried out, saying, 'Who is for jousting, who is for fighting? Let no sluggard nor weakling come out to me today! I am he who slew Courejan ben Julned; who will come forth to avenge him?' When Julned heard the name of his son, he cried out to his men, saying, 'O sons of whores, bring me yonder horseman who slew my son, that I may eat his flesh and drink his blood.' So a hundred fighting men ran at Jemrcan; but he slew the most part of them and put their chief to flight; which when Julned saw, he cried out to his men, saying, 'Charge upon him, all at once.' So the two hosts drove at one another and met in the mid-field, like two seas clashing together. The Yemen sword and spear wrought havoc and breasts and bellies were cloven, whilst the two armies saw the angel of death face to face and the dust of the battle rose up to the confines of the sky. Ears were deaf and tongues mute and death came on from every side, whilst the valiant stood fast and the faint-heart turned to flee; and they ceased not from the battle till ended day, when the drums beat the retreat and the two hosts drew apart and returned, each to its tent.

Then Gherib sat down on the throne of his kingship and the place of his dominion, whilst his chief officers ranged themselves about him, and said, 'I am sore troubled for the flight of the dog Agib and I know not whither he is gone. Except I overtake him and take my wreak of him, I shall die of despite.' Whereupon Sehim came forward and kissing the earth before him, said, 'O King, I will go to the army of the infidels and find out what is come of the perfidious dog Agib.' 'Go,' answered Gherib, 'and learn the truth regarding the hog.' So Sehim disguised himself in the habit of the infidels and became as he were of them; then, making for the enemy's camp, he found them all asleep, drunken with war and battle, and only the guards awake. Presently he came to the King's pavilion, where he found Julned asleep and unattended; so he made him smell to powdered henbane, and he became as one dead. Then Sehim went out and took a mule and wrapping the King in the coverlet of his bed, laid him on her back; after which he threw a mat over him and led the mule to the Muslim camp.

When he came to Gherib's pavilion and would have entered, the guards knew him not and forbade him entrance, saying, 'Who art thou?' He laughed and uncovered his face, and they knew him and admitted him. When Gherib saw him, he said, 'What hast thou there, O Sehim?' 'O King,' answered he, 'this is Julned ben Kerker.' Then he uncovered him, and Gherib knew him and said, 'Arouse him, O Sehim.' So he made him smell to vinegar and frankincense; and he cast the henbane from his nostrils and opening his eyes, found himself among the Muslims; whereupon, 'What is this foul dream?' quoth he and closing his eyes again, would have slept; but Sehim dealt him a buffet, saying, 'Open thine eyes, O accursed one!' So he opened them and said, 'Where am I?' Quoth Sehim, 'Thou art in the presence of Gherib ben Kundemir, King of Irak.' When Julned heard this, he said, 'O King, I am at thy mercy. Know that I am not at fault, but that he who made us come forth to fight thee was thy brother, who embroiled us with thee and fled.' 'Knowest thou whither he is gone?' asked Gherib. 'No, by the light-giving sun,' replied Julned, 'I know not.'

Then Gherib bade lay him in bonds and set guards over him, whilst each captain returned to his own tent, and amongst the rest Jemrcan, who said to his men, 'O sons of my uncle, I purpose this night to do a deed wherewith I may whiten my face with King Gherib.' 'Do what pleases thee,' answered they; 'we hearken and obey thy commandment.' Quoth he, 'Arm yourselves and disperse about the infidels' camp, muffling your steps, so that the very ants shall not be ware of you; and when you hear me magnify God, do ye the like and cry out, saying, "God is Most Great!" and hold back and make for the gate of the city; and we seek aid from God the Most High.' So the folk armed themselves cap-a-pie and waited till midnight, when they dispersed about the enemy's camp and waited till Jemrcan smote his target with his sword and shouted, 'God is Most Great!' Whereupon they all cried out the like, till valley and mountain and hill and sands and ruins rang again with the noise. The infidels awoke in dismay and fell upon one another, and the sword went round amongst them; but the Muslims held aloof and made for the gate of the city, where they slew the warders and entering, made themselves masters of the town, with all that was therein of treasure and women and children.

Meanwhile, Gherib, hearing the noise and clamour of 'God is Most Great!' mounted with all his troops and sent Sehim on in advance. When the latter came near the field of battle, he saw that Jemrcan had fallen upon the infidels with the Benou Aamir by night and made them drink the cup of death. So he returned and told his brother, who called down blessings on Jemrcan. And the infidels ceased not to smite each other mightily with the sharp sword, till the day rose and lighted up the land, when Gherib cried out to his men, saying, 'Charge, O ye noble, and win the favour of the All-knowing King!' So the true believers fell upon the idolaters and plied them with the keen sword and the quivering spear, till they sought to take refuge in the city; but Jemrcan came forth upon them with his tribesmen. So they hemmed them in, as between two mountain-ranges, and slew an innumerable host of them, and the rest fled into the deserts; nor did the Muslims give over pursuing them with the sword, till they had scattered them abroad in the plains and stony wastes. Then they returned to the city of Oman and Gherib entered the palace of the King and sitting down on the throne of his kingship, with his lords and officers on his either hand, sent for Julned. They brought him in haste and Gherib expounded to him Islam; but he refused to embrace the faith; wherefore Gherib let crucify him on the gate of the city, and they shot at him with arrows, till he was like unto a hedgehog. Then Gherib bestowed a dress of honour upon Jemrcan and said to him, 'Thou shalt be lord and ruler over this city, and thine be it to loose and to bind therein, for it was thou didst conquer it with thy sword and thy men.' And Jernrcan kissed the King's feet and wished him abiding victory and glory and fair fortune. Moreover, Gherib opened Julned's treasuries and saw what was therein and gave largesse to his captains and standard-bearers and fighting-men, yea, even to the women and children; and thus did he ten days long.

After this, one night he dreamt an ill dream and awoke, troubled and affrighted. So he aroused his brother Sehim and said to him, 'I dreamt that we were in a wide valley, when there swooped down on us two birds of prey, with legs like lances, never in my life saw I greater than they, and we were in fear of them.' 'O King,' answered Sehim, 'this portends some great enemy; be on thy guard, therefore, against him.' Gherib slept not the rest of the night and when the day broke, he called for his courser and mounted. Quoth Sehim, 'Whither goest thou, my brother?' and Gherib answered, saying, 'I am heavy at heart this morning; so I mean to ride abroad ten days and lighten my breast.' Said Sehim, 'Take with thee a thousand men;' but Gherib replied, 'I will not go forth but with thee alone.' So the two brothers mounted and seeking the open country, fared on from valley to valley and from meadow to meadow, till they came to a valley abounding in sweet-smelling flowers and streams and trees laden with all manner eatable fruits, two of each kind. On the branches were birds warbling their various songs; the mocking-bird trilled out her sweet notes and the turtle filled the place with her voice. There sang the nightingale, whose chant arouses the sleeper, and the merle with its note like the human voice and the cushat and the ring-dove, whilst the popinjay answered them with its fluent tongue.

The valley pleased them and they ate of its fruits and drank of its waters, after which they sat under the shadow of the trees, till drowsiness overcame them and they slept, glory be to Him who sleepeth not! As they lay asleep, two fierce Marids swooped down on them and taking each one on his shoulders, flew up with them into the air, till they were above the clouds. Presently, Gherib and Sehim awoke and found themselves betwixt heaven and earth; so they looked at those who bore them and saw that they were two Marids, each as big as a great palm tree, with hair like horses' tails and claws like lions' claws; the head of the one was as that of a dog and that of the other as that of an ape. When they saw this, they exclaimed, 'There is no power and no virtue save in God the Most High, the Supreme!'

Now the reason of this was that a certain king of the kings of the Jinn, Muraash by name, had a son called Saaïc, who loved a damsel of the Jinn, named Nejmeh; and the twain used to foregather in the valley, in the guise of birds. Gherib and Sehim saw them thus and deeming them birds, shot at them with arrows and wounded Saaïc, whose blood flowed. Nejmeh mourned over him, then, fearing lest the like should befall herself, caught up her lover and flew with him to his father's palace, where she cast him down at the gate. The warders bore him in and laid him before the King, who, seeing the arrow sticking in his side, exclaimed, 'Alas, my son! Who hath done with thee this thing, that I may lay waste his abiding-place and hasten his destruction, though he were the greatest of the kings of the Jinn?' Thereupon Saaïc opened his eyes and said, 'O my father, it was a mortal that slew me in the Valley of Springs.' Hardly had he made an end of these words, when his soul departed; whereupon his father buffeted his face, till the blood streamed from his mouth, and cried out to two Marids, saying: 'Go to the Valley of Springs and bring me all who are therein.' So they betook themselves to the valley in question, where they found Gherib and Sehim asleep and snatching them up, carried them to their King, whom they saw seated on the throne of his kingship, as he were a huge mountain, with four heads on his body, the first that of a lion, the second that of an elephant, the third that of a panther and the fourth that of a lynx. The Marids set them down before Muraash and said to him, 'These are they whom we found in the Valley of Springs.'

Muraash looked at them with wrathful eyes and puffed and snorted and blew sparks from his nostrils, so that all who stood by feared him. Then said he, 'O dogs of mankind, ye have slain my son and kindled fire in my heart.' 'Who is thy son,' asked Gherib, 'and who hath seen him?' Quoth Muraash, 'Were ye not in the Valley of Springs and did ye not see my son there, in the guise of a bird, and did ye not shoot at him with arrows, that he died?' 'I know not who slew him,' replied Garib; 'and by the virtue of the Great God, the One, the Immemorial, who knoweth all things, and of Abraham the Friend, we saw no bird, neither slew we bird nor beast!'

Now Muraash worshipped the Fire, not the All-powerful King; so, when he heard Gherib swear by God and His greatness and by Abraham the Friend, he knew that he was a Muslim and cried out to his people, saying, 'Bring me my mistress.' Accordingly they brought a brasier of gold and setting it before him, kindled therein fire and cast on drugs, whereupon there arose therefrom green and blue and yellow flames and the King and all who were present prostrated themselves before the brasier, whilst Gherib and Sehim ceased not to magnify God and attest His greatness and omnipotence. Presently, Muraash raised his head and seeing the two princes standing, said to them, 'O dogs, why do ye not prostrate yourselves?' 'Out on thee, O accursed one!' replied Gherib. 'Prostration befits not, save to the Worshipful King, who bringeth forth all creatures into being from nothingness and maketh water to well from the barren rock, Him who inclineth the heart of the father unto his newborn child and who may not be described as sitting or standing, the God of Noah and Salih and Houd and Abraham the Friend, who created Paradise and Hell-fire and trees and fruit, for He is God, the One, the All-powerful.'

When Muraash heard this, his eyes started from his head and he cried out to his guards, saying, 'Bind these two dogs and sacrifice them to my mistress.' So they bound them and were about to cast them into the fire, when, behold, one of the merlons of the parapet fell down upon the brasier and broke it and did out the fire, which became ashes flying in the air. Then said Gherib, 'God is Most Great! He giveth aid and victory and forsaketh those who deny Him and worship the Fire, not the Almighty King!' Quoth Muraash, 'Thou art a sorcerer and hast bewitched my mistress, so that this thing hath befallen her.' 'O madman,' answered Gherib, 'if the fire had soul or movement, it would ward off from itself that which doth it hurt.' When Muraash heard this, he roared and bellowed and reviled the Fire, saying, 'By my faith, I will not kill you save by the fire!'

Then he cast them into prison and calling a hundred Marids, bade them bring much firewood and set fire thereto. So they brought great plenty of wood and made a huge fire, which flamed up mightily till the morning, when Muraash mounted an elephant, bearing on its back a throne of gold set with jewels, and the tribes of the Jinn gathered about him, in their various kinds. Then they brought in Gherib and Sehim, who, seeing the flaming of the fire, sought help of the One God, the All-conquering Creator of and day, Him who is mickle of might, whom no sight comprehendeth, but who comprehendeth all sights, for He is the Subtle, the All-knowing; and they ceased not to solicit Him, till, behold, a cloud arose from West to East and pouring down showers of rain, like the swollen sea, quenched the fire.

When the King saw this, he was affrighted, he and his troops, and entered the palace, where he turned to his Vizier and grandees and said to them, 'How say ye of these two men?' 'O King,' answered they, 'were they not in the right, this thing had not befallen the fire; wherefore we say that they speak sooth.' 'Indeed,' rejoined Muraash, 'the truth hath been shown forth to me, ay, and the manifest way, and I am certified that the worship of the fire is false; for, were it mistress, it had warded off from itself the rain that quenched it and the stone that broke its brasier and beat it into ashes. Wherefore I believe in Him Who created the fire and the light and the shade and the heat. And ye, what say ye?' 'O King,' answered they, 'we also hear and follow and obey.'

So the King called for Gherib and Sehim and embraced them and kissed them between the eyes; whereupon the bystanders all crowded to kiss their hands and heads. Then Muraash sat down on the throne of his kingship and seating Gherib on his right and Sehim on his left hand, said to them, 'O mortals, what shall we say, that we may become Muslims?' 'Say,' answered Gherib, '"There is no god but God, and Abraham is the Friend of God!"' So the King and his folk professed Islam with heart and tongue, and Gherib abode with them awhile, teaching them the ritual of prayer. But presently he called to mind his people and sighed, whereupon quoth Muraash, 'Verily, trouble is past and gone and joy and gladness are come.' 'O King,' said Gherib, 'I have many enemies and I fear for my people from them.' Then he related to him his history from first to last, and Muraash said, 'O King of men, I will send one who shall bring thee news of thy people, for I will not let thee go till I have had my fill of gazing on thy face.' Then he called two stout Marids, by name Kailjan and Courjan, and bade them repair to Yemen and bring him news of Gherib's army. They replied, 'We hear and obey,' and departed.

Meanwhile, when the captains of the Muslims arose in the morning and rode to Gherib's palace, to do their service to him, the servants told them that the King had ridden forth with his brother at point of day. So they made for the valleys and mountains and followed the track of the princes, till they came to the Valley of Springs, where they found their arms cast down and their horses grazing and said, 'By the glory of Abraham the Friend, the King is missing from this place!' Then they dispersed and sought in the valley and the mountains three days, but found no trace of them; whereupon they raised lamentations and despatched couriers to all the cities and strengths and fortresses, to seek news of their King. Accordingly, the couriers dispersed hither and thither and sought everywhere for Gherib, but found no trace of him.

Now, when the news came to Agib by his spies that his brother was missing, he rejoiced and going in to King Yaarub ben Kehtan, sought aid of him. He granted him the help he sought and gave him two hundred thousand Amalekites, with whom he set out for Yemen and sat down before the city of Oman. Jemrcan and Saadan sallied forth and gave him battle, and there were slain of the Muslims much people, wherefore the true believers retired into the city and shut the gates and manned the walls. At this juncture the two Marids arrived and seeing the Muslims beleaguered, waited till the night, when they fell upon the infidels and plied them with sharp swords of the swords of the Jinn, each twelve cubits long, if a man smote therewith a rock, he would cleave it in sunder. They attacked the idolaters, shouting, 'God is Most Great! He giveth aid and victory and forsaketh those who deny the faith of Abraham the Friend!' whilst fire issued from their mouths and nostrils, and they made great slaughter amongst them. Thereupon the infidels ran out of their tents and seeing these strange things, were confounded and their flesh shuddered and their reason fled. So they snatched up their arms and fell on each other, whilst the Marids shore off their heads, as a reaper cuts grain, crying, 'God is Most Great! We are the henchmen of King Gherib, the friend of Muraash, King of the Jinn!' The sword ceased not to go round amongst them till the night was half spent, when the misbelievers, imagining that the mountains were all Afrits, loaded their tents and treasure and baggage upon camels and made off; and the first to fly was Agib. The Marids ceased not from the pursuit, till they had driven them far away into the hills and deserts; and but fifty thousand infidels of two hundred thousand escaped with their lives and made for their own land, wounded and discomfited.

Meanwhile, the Muslims gathered together, marvelling at this that had betided the infidels and fearing the tribesmen of the Jinn; but presently the latter returned and said to them, 'O host of the Muslims, your lord King Gherib and his brother Sehim salute you; they are the guests of Muraash, King of the Jinn, and will be with you anon.' When Gherib's men knew that he was safe and well, they rejoiced greatly and said to the Marids, 'May God rejoice you with good news, O noble spirits!' So Courjan and Kailjan returned to Muraash and Gherib and acquainted them with that which had happened, whereat Gherib's heart was set at ease and he said, 'May God abundantly requite you!'

Then said King Muraash, 'O my brother, I have a mind to show thee our country and the city of Japhet son of Noah, on whom be peace!' 'O King,' replied Gherib, 'do what seemeth good to thee.' So he called for horses and mounting, he and Gherib and Sehim, set out with a thousand Marids, as they were a piece of a mountain cut endlong. They fared on, diverting themselves with the sight of valleys and mountains, till they came to the city of Japhet son of Noah (on whom be peace), where the townsfolk all, great and small, came forth to meet King Muraash and brought them into the city in great state. Then Muraash went up to the palace of Japhet son of Noah and sat down on the throne of his kingship, which was of alabaster, ten stages high, hung with all manner coloured silks and trellised with wands of gold. The people of the city stood before him and he said to them, 'O descendants of Japhet, what did your fathers and grandfathers worship?' Quoth they, 'We found them worshipping the fire and followed their example, as thou well knowest.' 'O folk,' rejoined Muraash, 'it hath been manifested to us that the fire is but one of the creatures of God the Most High, Creator of all things; and when we knew this, we submitted ourselves to God, the One, the All-powerful Maker of night and day and the revolving sphere, whom no sight comprehendeth, but who comprehendeth all sights, for He is the Subtle, the All-wise. So do ye likewise, and ye shall be saved from the wrath of the Almighty and from the fiery torment in the world to come.' And they embraced Islam with heart and tongue.

Then Muraash took Gherib by the hand and showed him the palace and its ordinance and all the marvels it contained, till they came to the armoury, wherein were the arms of Japhet son of Noah. Here Gherib saw a sword hanging to a peg of gold and said, 'O King, whose sword is that?' Quoth Muraash, 'It is the sword of Japhet son of Noah, wherewith he was wont to do battle against men and Jinn. The sage Jerdoun forged it and graved on its back names of might. It is named El Mahic, for that it never descends upon a man, but it annihilates him, nor upon a genie, but it crushes him; and if one smote therewith a mountain, it would overthrow it.' When Gherib heard tell of the virtues of the sword, he said, 'I desire to look on this sword;' and Muraash said, 'As thou wilt.' So Gherib put out his hand and taking the sword, drew it from its sheath; whereupon it flashed and death crept and glittered on its edge; and it was twelve spans long and three broad. Now Gherib wished to take it, and Muraash said, 'If thou canst wield it, take it.' 'It is well,' answered Gherib, and took it up, and it was in his hand as a staff; wherefore all who were present, men and Jinn, marvelled and said, 'Well done, O prince of cavaliers!' Then said Muraash, 'Lay thy hand on this treasure, that the Kings of the earth sigh for in vain, and mount, that I may show thee the city.'

Then they took horse and rode forth the palace, with Jinn and men attending them on foot, and passed through the streets and thoroughfares of the town, threading their way through ranks of palaces and deserted mansions and gilded doorways, till they issued from the gates and entered gardens full of fruit-laden trees and running waters and birds speaking and celebrating the praises of Him to whom belong power and eternity; nor did they cease to take their pleasance in the land till nightfall, when they returned to the palace of Japhet son of Noah and they brought them the table of food. So they ate and Gherib turned to the King of the Jinn and said to him, 'O King, I would fain return to my people and my troops; for I know not their plight after me.' 'By Allah, O my brother,' answered Muraash, 'I will not part with thee for a full month, till I have had my fill of thy sight.'

Gherib could not say him nay, so he abode with him in the city of Japhet, eating and drinking and making merry, till the month was up, when Muraash clad him and Sehim in dresses of honour of gold-inwoven silk and set on Gherib's head a crown jewelled with pearls and diamonds of inestimable value. Moreover, he gave him great store of presents of emeralds and balass rubies and diamonds and other jewels and ingots of gold and silver and ambergris and musk and brocaded silks and other rarities and things of price. All these he made up into loads for him and calling five hundred Marids, said to them, 'Make ready to set out on the morrow, that we may bring King Gherib and Sehim back to their own country.' And they answered, saying, 'We hear and obey.' So they passed the night in the city, purposing to depart on the morrow, but, next morning, as they were about to set forth, they espied a great host advancing upon the city, with horses neighing and drums beating and trumpets sounding, to the number of threescore and ten thousand Marids, flying and diving, under a king called Bercan, and the earth was filled with them.

Now this Bercan was lord of the City of Cornelian and the Castle of Gold and under his rule were five strongholds, in each five hundred thousand Marids; and he and his people worshipped the fire, not the Omnipotent King. He was the son of Muraash's father's brother and the cause of his coming was on this wise. It chanced that there was among the subjects of King Muraash a misbelieving Marid, who professed Islam hypocritically, and he stole away from his people and made for the Valley of Cornelian, where he went in to King Bercan and kissing the earth before him, wished him abiding glory and fair fortune. Then he told him of Muraash's conversion to Islam, and Bercan said, 'How came he to forsake his faith?' So the rebel told him what had passed and Bercan snorted and puffed and railed at the sun and the moon and the sparkling fire, saying, 'By the virtue of my faith, I will surely slay my cousin and his people and this mortal, nor will I leave one of them on life!' Then he cried out to the tribes of the Jinn and choosing of them seventy thousand Marids, set out and fared on till he came to the city of Japhet and encamped before its gates. When Muraash saw this, he despatched a Marid to learn what the stranger host wanted, bidding him return in haste. So the messenger repaired to Bercan's camp, where the Marids hastened to meet him and said to him, 'Who art thou?' Quoth he, 'I bear a message from King Muraash;' whereupon they carried him in to Bercan, before whom he prostrated himself saying, 'O my lord, my master hath sent me to thee, to know what brings thee hither.' 'Return to thy lord,' replied Bercan, 'and say to him, "This is thy cousin Bercan, who is come to salute thee."' So the messenger returned and told Muraash, who said to Gherib, 'Abide here whilst I go and salute my cousin and return to thee.' Then he mounted and rode to Bercan's camp.

Now this was a trick of Bercan, to bring Muraash out and seize upon him, and he said to his Marids, who were about him, 'When ye see me embrace my cousin, lay hold of him and bind his hands behind him.' And they answered, saying, 'We hear and obey.' So, when Muraash came up and entered Bercan's pavilion, the latter rose to him and embraced him, whereupon the Jinn fell upon Muraash and seized him and bound him. He looked at Bercan and said, 'What manner of thing is this?' Quoth Bercan, 'O dog of the Jinn, wilt thou leave the faith of thy fathers and grandfathers and enter a faith thou knowest not?' 'O son of my uncle,' rejoined Muraash, 'indeed I have found the faith of Abraham the Friend to be the true faith and all other than it vain.' 'And who told thee of this?' asked Bercan. 'Gherib, King of Irak,' answered Muraash, 'whom I hold in the highest honour.' 'By the fire and the light and the shade and the heat,' cried Bercan, 'I will slay both thee and him!' And he cast him into prison.

Now, when Muraash's henchman saw what had befallen his lord, he fled back to the city and told the King's men, who cried out and mounted. Quoth Gherib, 'What is to do?' And they told him what had passed, whereupon he cried out to Sehim, saying, 'Saddle me one of the chargers that King Muraash gave me.' 'O my brother,' said Sehim, 'wilt thou do battle with the Jinn?' 'Yes,' answered Gherib; 'I will fight them with the sword of Japhet son of Noah, seeking help of the God of Abraham the Friend, (on whom be peace,) for He is Lord and Creator of all things. So Sehim saddled him a sorrel horse of the horses of the Jinn, as he were a castle, and he armed and mounting, rode out with the tribes of the Jinn, armed cap-a-pie. Then Bercan and his host mounted also and the two hosts drew out in battalia in face of one another. The first to open the chapter of war was Gherib, who spurred his charger into the mid-field and drew the enchanted sword, whence issued a glittering light, that dazzled the eyes of all the Jinn and struck terror to their heart. Then he played with the sword, till their wits were amazed, and cried out, saying, 'God is Most Great! I am Gherib, King of Irak. There is no faith save the faith of Abraham the Friend!'

When Bercan heard Gherib's words, he said, 'This is he who seduced my cousin from his faith; so, by the virtue of my faith, I will not sit down on my throne till I have cut off the head of this Gherib and made an end of his life and forced my cousin and his people back to their faith: and whoso baulketh me, I will destroy him.' Then he mounted a paper-white elephant, as he were a tower plastered with gypsum, and goaded him with a pike of steel, whereupon the elephant trumpeted and made for the middle of the field. When Bercan drew near Gherib, he cried out to him, saying, 'O dog of mankind, what made thee come into our land, to debauch my cousin and his people and pervert them from one faith to another? Know that this day is the last of thy worldly days.' And Gherib answered, saying, 'Avaunt, O vilest of the Jinn!' Therewith Bercan drew a javelin and poising it in his hand, cast it at Gherib; but it missed him. So he threw a second javelin at him; but Gherib caught it in mid-air and hurled it at the elephant. It smote him on the flank and came out on the other side, whereupon the beast fell down dead and Bercan was cast to the ground, like a great palm tree. Before he could stir, Gherib smote him with the sword of Japhet flatlings on the nape of the neck, and he fell down in a swoon; whereupon the Marids swooped down on him and bound him.

When Bercan's people saw their king a prisoner, they drove at the others, seeking to rescue him, but Gherib and the true-believing Jinn fell upon them and bravo for Gherib! indeed that day he pleased God who answereth prayer and slaked his vengeance with the enchanted sword! Whomsoever he smote, he clove him in sunder and before his soul could depart, he became a heap of ashes in the fire; whilst the two hosts of the Jinn cast flames of fire at one another, till the battlefield was wrapped in smoke. And Gherib tourneyed right and left among the infidels and they gave way before him, till he came to King Bercan's pavilion, with Kailjan and Courjan on his either hand, and cried out to them, saying, 'Loose your lord!' So they unbound Muraash and broke his fetters and he said to them, 'Bring me my arms and my winged horse.' Now he had two flying horses, one of which he gave to Gherib and the other he mounted himself, after he had donned his battle-harness. Then he and Gherib fell upon the enemy, flying through the air on their winged horses, and the true-believing Jinn followed them, shouting, 'God is Most Great!' till the earth and hills and valleys and mountains answered them. The infidels fled before them and they returned, after having slain more than thirty thousand Marids and Satans, to the city of Japhet, where the two kings sat down on their beds of estate and sought for Bercan, but found him not; for, whilst they were diverted from him by stress of battle, an Afrit of his servants made his way to him and loosing him, carried him to his folk, of whom he found part slain and the rest in full flight. So he flew up with the King into the air and set him down in the City of Cornelian and Castle of Gold, where Bercan seated himself on the throne of his kingship. Presently, those of his people who had escaped from the battle came in to him and gave him joy of his safety; and he said, 'O folk, where is safety? My army is slain and they took me prisoner and have rent in pieces my repute among the tribes of the Jinn.' 'O King,' answered they, 'it is ever thus that kings still smite and are smitten.' Quoth he, 'Needs must I take my revenge and wipe out my reproach, else shall I be for ever dishonoured among the tribes of the Jinn.' Then he wrote letters to the governors of his fortresses, who came to him with three hundred and twenty thousand fierce Marids and Satans; and he bade them make ready to set out in three days' time.

Meanwhile, when Muraash discovered Bercan's escape, it was grievous to him and he said, 'Had we set a hundred Marids to guard him, he had not fled; but whither shall he go from us?' Then said he to Gherib, 'Know, O my brother, that Bercan is perfidious and will never rest from avenging himself on us, but will assuredly assemble his clans and return upon us; wherefore I am minded to forestall him and fall on him, on the heels of his defeat, whilst he is yet weak by reason thereof.' 'This is well seen,' replied Gherib; and Muraash said, 'O my brother, let the Marids bear thee back to thine own country and leave me to fight the battles of the Faith against the infidels, that I may be lightened of the burden of my sins.' 'By the virtue of the Clement, the Bountiful, the Protector,' answered Gherib, 'I will not go hence till I do to death all the misbelieving Jinn and God hasten their souls to the fire and evil shall be the abiding-place and none shall be saved but those who worship God the One, the Victorious! But do thou send Sehim back to the city of Oman, so haply he may be healed of his sickness.' For Sehim was sick. So Muraash bade the Marids take up Sehim and the treasures and bear them to the city of Oman; and they took them and made for the land of men.

Then Muraash wrote letters to all his governors and captains of fortresses and they came to him with eight-score thousand men. So they made them ready and departed for the City of Cornelian. In one day, they marched a year's journey and halted in a valley, where they encamped and passed the night. Next morning, as they were about to set forth, the vanguard of Bercan's army appeared, whereupon the Jinn cried out and the two hosts met and fell upon each other in that valley, that the earth trembled with the shock. Then there befell a sore strife and the battle swayed to and fro with a mighty clamour. Jest gave place to earnest and there was an end of parley, whilst long lives were cut short and trouble and confusion befell the unbelievers; for Gherib charged them, proclaiming the Unity of God, the Worshipful, the Exalted, and shore through necks and made heads roll in the dust; nor did the dark betide before nigh seventy thousand of the infidels were slain, and of the true believers over ten thousand Marids had fallen. Then the drums beat the retreat, and the two hosts drew apart. So Gherib and Muraash returned to their tents, after they had wiped their arms, and the evening meal being set before them, they ate and gave each other joy of their safety. As for Bercan, he returned to his tent, grieving for the slaughter of his champions, and said to his officers, 'If we abide here and do battle thus with them, we shall be cut off to the last man in three days' time.' Quoth they, 'And how shall we do, O King?' 'We will fall upon them under cover of the night,' said Bercan, 'whilst they sleep, and not one of them shall be left to tell the tale. So take your arms and when I give the word of command, fall on your enemies as one man.'

Now there was amongst them a Marid named Jendel whose heart inclined to Islam; so, when he heard the infidels' plot, he stole away from them and going in to King Muraash and King Gherib, told them what Bercan had devised; whereupon Muraash turned to Gherib and said to him, 'O my brother, what shall we do?' Quoth Gherib, 'Tonight we will fall upon the infidels and chase them into the mountains and deserts, if it be the will of the Omnipotent King.' Then he summoned the captains of the Jinn and said to them, 'Arm yourselves, you and your men, and as soon as it is dark, steal out of your tents on foot and hide among the mountains; and when ye see the enemy engaged among the tents, do ye fall upon them from all quarters. Strengthen your hearts and put your faith in your Lord, and ye shall conquer; and behold, I am with you!' So, as soon as it was dark, the infidels attacked the camp, invoking the aid of the light and the fire; but, when they came among the tents, the Muslims fell upon them, calling for help on the Lord of the Worlds and saying, 'O Most Merciful of those that show mercy, O Creator of all created things!' till they left them like mown grass, cut down and dead. By the morning the most part of the unbelievers were bodies without souls and the rest made for the marshes and deserts, whilst Gherib and Muraash returned in triumph and making prize of the enemy's baggage, rested till the morrow, when they set out for the City of Cornelian.

As for Bercan, when he saw that the battle had turned against him and that the most part of his men were slain, he fled with the remnant of his folk to his capital city, where he entered his palace and assembling his tribes, said to them, 'O folk, whoso hath aught of price, let him take it and follow me to the Mountain Caf, to the Blue King, lord of the Parti-coloured Palace; for he it is who shall avenge us.' So they took their women and children and goods and made for the Mountain Caf. Presently Muraash and Gherib arrived at the City of Cornelian and found the gates open and none left to give them news; whereupon they entered and Muraash took Gherib, that he might show him the city, whose walls were builded of emeralds and its gates of red cornelian, with nails of silver, and the roofs of its houses and mansions ceiled with aloes and sandalwood. So they took their pleasance in its streets and alleys, till they came to the palace of gold and entering, passed through seven vestibules, till they came to a building, whose walls were of royal balass rubies and its pavement of emerald and jacinth. The two kings were astounded at the goodliness of the place and fared on from vestibule to vestibule, till they came to the inner court of the palace, wherein they saw four estrades, each different from the others, and in the midst a fountain of red gold, compassed about with golden lions, from whose mouths issued water. The estrade at the upper end was hung and carpeted with brocaded silks of various colours and thereon stood two thrones of red gold, inlaid with pearls and jewels. So Muraash and Gherib sat down on the thrones and held high state in the palace of gold. Then said Gherib to Muraash, 'What thinkest thou to do?' And Muraash answered, saying, 'O King of men, I have despatched a hundred horse to learn where Bercan is, that we may pursue him.'

Then they abode three days in the palace, till the scouts returned with the news that Bercan had fled to the Mountain Caf and thrown himself on the protection of the Blue King; whereupon quoth Muraash to Gherib, 'What sayst thou, O my brother?' And Gherib answered, saying, 'Except we attack them, they will attack us.' So they made ready for departure and after three days, they were about to set out with their troops, when the Marids, who had carried Sehim back to Oman, returned and kissed the earth before Gherib. He questioned them of his people and they answered, saying, 'After the last battle, thy brother Agib fled to the King of Hind and sought his protection. The King granted his prayer and writing letters to all his governors, levied an army as it were the swollen sea, having neither beginning nor end, with which he purposes to invade Irak and lay it waste.' When Gherib heard this, he said, 'Perish the unbelievers! Verily, God the Most High shall give the victory to Islam and I will show them cutting and thrusting.' 'O King of men,' said Muraash, 'by the virtue of the Mighty Name, I must needs go with thee to thy kingdom and destroy thine enemies and bring thee to thy desire.' Gherib thanked him and they rested till the morrow, when they set out, intending for the City of Alabaster and the Parti-coloured Palace.

Now this city was builded of alabaster and stones by Baric ben Fakia, father of the Jinn, and he built also the Parti-coloured Palace, which was so named for that the ordinance of its building was one brick of gold and one of silver, nor was there its like in all the world. When they came within half a day's journey of the city, they halted to rest, and Muraash sent out a scout to reconnoitre, who returned and said, 'O King, in the City of Alabaster are tribesmen of the Jinn in number as the leaves of the trees or as the drops of rain.' So Muraash said to Gherib, 'How shall we do, O King of men?' 'O King,' answered he, 'divide your men into four bodies and encompass the camp of the infidels with them; then, in the middle of the night, let them cry out, saying, "God is Most Great!" and hold aloof and watch what happens among the tribes of the Jinn.' So Muraash did as Gherib counselled and the troops waited till midnight, when they cried out, saying, 'God is Most Great! Ho for the Faith of Abraham the Friend, on whom be peace!' The unbelievers awoke in affright and snatching up their arms, fell upon each other till the morning, when the most part of them were dead men and but few remained. Then Gherib cried out to the true believers, saying, 'Up and at the remnant of the infidels! Behold, I am with you, and God is your helper!' So the Muslims drove at the enemy and Gherib drew his sword El Mahic and fell upon the foe, cutting off noses and sending heads flying. Presently he came up with Bercan and smote him and bereft him of life and he fell down, drenched in his blood. On like wise he did with the Blue King, and by the forenoon not one of the infidels was left alive to tell the tale.

Then Gherib and Muraash entered the Parti-coloured Palace and found its walls builded of alternate courses of gold and silver, with sills of crystal and keystones of emerald. In its midst was a fountain adorned with bells and pendants and figures of birds and beasts vomiting forth water, and thereby an estrade furnished with gold-brocaded silks, with borders of gold embroidered with jewels and they found the treasures of the palace past count or description. Then they entered the inner court, where they found a magnificent seraglio and Gherib saw, among the Blue King's women, a girl clad in a dress worth a thousand dinars, never had he beheld a goodlier. About her were a hundred slave-girls, holding up her skirts with hooks of gold, and she was in their midst as the moon among stars. When he saw her, his reason was confounded and he said to one of the waiting-women, 'Who is yonder damsel?' Quoth they, 'This is the Blue King's daughter, Morning Star.' Then Gherib turned to Muraash and said to him, 'O King of the Jinn, I have a mind to take yonder damsel to wife.' Quoth Muraash, 'The palace and all that therein is are the prize of thy right hand; for, hadst thou not devised a stratagem to destroy the Blue King and Bercan, they had cut us off to the last man wherefore the treasure is thy treasure and the people thy slaves.' Gherib thanked him for his fair speech and going up to the girl, gazed steadfastly upon her and loved her with an exceeding love, forgetting Fekhr Taj and Mehdiyeh.

Now her mother was the King's daughter of China, whom the Blue King had carried off from her palace and deflowered, and she conceived by him and bore this girl, whom he named Morning Star, by reason of her beauty and grace for she was the princess of the fair. Her mother died when she was a babe of forty days, and the nurses and eunuchs reared her, till she reached the age of seventeen; but she hated her father and rejoiced in his death. So Gherib put his hand in hers and went in to her that night and found her a virgin. Then he pulled down the Parti-coloured Palace and divided the spoil with the true-believing Jinn, and there fell to his share one-and-twenty thousand bricks of gold and silver and money and treasure beyond count. Then Muraash took Gherib and showed him the Mountain Caf and all its marvels; after which they returned to Bercan's fortress and dismantled it and shared the spoil thereof.

Then they returned to Muraash's capital, where they abode five days, at the end of which time Gherib sought to go to his own country and Muraash said, 'O King of men, I will ride at thy stirrup and bring thee to thine own land.' 'Nay, by the virtue of Abraham the Friend,' answered Gherib; 'I will not suffer thee to weary thyself thus nor will I take any of the Jinn save Kailjan and Courjan.' Quoth the King, 'Take with thee ten thousand horsemen of the Jinn, to serve thee;' but Gherib said, 'I will take only as I said to thee.' So Muraash bade a thousand Marids take him up and carry him to his native land, with his share of the spoil; and he commanded Kailjan and Courjan to follow him and obey him; and they answered, 'We hear and obey.' Then said Gherib to the Marids, 'Do ye carry the treasure and Morning Star;' for he himself thought to ride his flying charger. But Muraash said to him, 'O my brother, this horse will live only in our clime, and if it come upon the earth, it will die but I have in my stables a sea-horse, whose like is not found in Irak, no, nor in all the world.' So he caused bring forth the horse, and when Gherib saw it, it interposed between him and his reason. Then they bound it and Kailjan took it on his shoulders and Courjan took what he could carry. And Muraash embraced Gherib and wept for parting from him, saying, 'O my brother, if aught befall thee, to which thou art unable, send for me and I will come to thine aid with an army that may avail to lay waste the whole earth and all that is thereon.' Gherib thanked him for his courtesy and kindness and his zeal for the True Faith and took leave of him; whereupon the Marids set out with Gherib and his goods and after traversing fifty years' journey in two days and a night, alighted near the city of Oman and halted to rest.

Then Gherib sent out Kailjan, to learn news of his people, and he returned and said, 'O King, thy city is beleaguered by a host of infidels, as they were the swollen sea, and thy people are fighting them. The drums beat to battle and Jemrcan goeth forth to them in the field.' When Gherib heard this, he cried out, saying, 'God is Most Great!' and said to Kailjan, 'Saddle me the horse and bring me my arms; for today the valiant shall be known from the coward in the stead of war and battle.' So Kailjan brought him all he sought and Gherib armed and girding on El Mahic, mounted the sea-horse and made toward the armies. Quoth Kailjan and Courjan to him, 'Set thy heart at ease and let us go to the infidels and scatter them abroad in the wastes and deserts till, by the help of God the Most High, the All-powerful, we leave not a soul of them on life, no, not a blower of the fire.' But Gherib said, 'By the virtue of Abraham the Friend, I will not let you fight them without me!'

Now the manner of the coming of that great host was on this wise. When Agib fled from the field, after Yaarub's army had been put to the rout by Kailjan and Courjan, he said to his people, 'If we return to Yaarub ben Kehtan, he will say to us, "But for you, my son and my people had not been slain;" and he will put us to death, even to the last man. Wherefore, methinks we were better go to Terkenan, King of Hind, and beseech him to avenge us.' 'Come, let us go thither,' answered they; 'and the blessing of the Fire attend thee!' So they fared on days and nights till they reached King Terkenan's capital city and Agib went in to him and kissed the earth before him. Then he wished him what men use to wish to kings and said to him, 'O King, do thou protect me, so may the sparkling fire and the night with its thick darkness protect and defend thee!' Terkenan looked at Agib and said, 'Who art thou and what dost thou want?' 'I am Agib, King of Irak,' replied he; 'my brother hath usurped my throne and gotten the mastery of the land and the people have submitted themselves to him. Moreover, he has embraced the faith of Islam and ceases not to chase me from country to country; and behold, I am come to seek protection of thee and thy power.' When Terkenan heard Agib's words, he rose and sat down and said, 'By the virtue of the Fire, I will assuredly avenge thee and will let none serve other than my mistress the Fire!' And he cried out to his son, saying, 'O my son, make ready to go to Irak and lay it waste and bind all who serve aught but the Fire and punish them and make an example of them; yet slay them not, but bring them to me, that I may ply them with various tortures and make them taste the bitterness of humiliation and leave them a warning to all who will take warning in this time.' Then he chose out to accompany him fourscore thousand fighting-men on horseback and the like number on giraffes, beside ten thousand lephants, bearing on their backs turrets of sandalwood, trellised with network of gold and railed and plated with gold and silver and guarded with shields of gold and emerald, and store of warchariots, in each eight men fighting with all kinds of weapons.

Now the prince's name was Raadshah and he was the champion of his time, having no peer for prowess. So he and his army equipped them in ten days' time, then set out, as they were a bank of clouds, and fared on two months' journey, till they came to Oman and encompased it, to the joy of Agib, who thought himself assured of victory. So Jemrcan and Saadan and all their fighting-men sallied forth into the field, whilst the drums beat to battle and the horses neighed. At this moment up came King Gherib, who spurred his charger and entered among the infidels, waiting to see who should come forth and open the chapter of war. Then came out Saadan the Ghoul and offered battle, whereupon there issued forth to him one of the champions of Hind;

but Saadan scarce let him take his stand in front of him ere he smote him to the earth with his mace and crushed his bones; and so did he with a second and a third, till he had slain thirty fighting-men. Then there pricked out to him an Indian cavalier, by name Bettash el Acran, uncle to King Terkenan and the doughtiest champion of his time, reckoned worth five thousand horse in battle, and cried out to Saadan, saying, 'O thief of the Arabs, what art thou that thou shouldst slay the Kings of Hind and their champions and capture their horsemen? But today is the last of thy worldly days.' When Saadan heard this, his eyes waxed bloodshot and he drove at Bettash and aimed a stroke at him with his club; but he evaded it and the force of the blow bore Saadan to the earth; and before he could recover himself, the Indians bound him and haled him off to their tents.

When Jemrcan saw his comrade a prisoner, he cried out, saying, 'Ho for the faith of Abraham the Friend!' and clapping spurs to his horse, ran at Bettash. They wheeled and feinted awhile, till Bettash drove at Jemrcan and catching him by his coat of arms, tore him from his saddle and threw him to the ground; whereupon the Indians bound him and dragged him away to their tents. And Bettash ceased not to overcome all who came out to him, till he had made prisoners of four-and-twenty captains of the Muslims, whereat the latter were sore dismayed. When Gherib saw what had befallen his men, he drew from beneath his knee a mace of gold, six-score pounds in weight, which had belonged to King Bercan, and set spurs to his sea-horse, which bore him like the wind into the middle of the field. Then he drove at Bettash, crying out, 'God is Most Great! he giveth aid and victory and forsaketh those who reject the faith of Abraham the Friend!' and smote him with the mace, whereupon he fell to the ground and Gherib, turning to the Muslims, saw his brother Sehim and said to him, 'Bind this dog.' When Sehim heard his brother's words, he ran to Bettash and bound him fast and bore him off, whilst the Muslims wondered who this cavalier could be and the Indians said to one another, 'Who is this horseman that came out from amongst us and hath taken our chief prisoner?'

Meanwhile Gherib continued to offer battle and there came out to him a captain of the Indians, whom he felled to the earth with his mace, and Kailjan and Courjan bound him and delivered him to Sehim; nor did Gherib leave to do thus, till he had taken prisoner two-and-fifty of the doughtiest captains of the army of Hind. Then the day came to an end and the drums beat the retreat; whereupon Gherib left the field and rode towards the Muslim camp. The first to meet him was his brother Sehim, who kissed his feet in the stirrups and said, 'May thy hand never wither, O champion of the age! Tell us who thou art among the braves.' So Gherib raised his vizor and Sehim knew him and cried out, saying, 'This is your king and your lord Gherib, who is come back from the land of the Jinn!' When the Muslims heard Gherib's name, they threw themselves off their horses' backs and crowding about him, kissed his feet in the stirrups and saluted him, rejoicing in his safe return. Then they carried him into the city of Oman, where he entered his palace and sat down on the throne of his kingship, whilst his officers stood around him, in the utmost joy. Food was set on and they ate, after which Gherib related to them all that had befallen him with the Jinn in the Mountain Caf, and they marvelled thereat exceedingly and praised God for his safety. Then he dismissed them to their sleeping-places; so they withdrew to their several lodgings, and when none abode with him but Kailjan and Courjan, who never left him, he said to them, 'Can ye carry me to Cufa, that I may take my pleasure in my harem, and bring me back before the end of the night?' 'O our lord,' answered they, 'this thou askest is easy.'

Now the distance between Cufa and Oman is threescore days' journey for a diligent horseman, and Kailjan said to Courjan, 'I will carry him going and thou coming back.' So he took up Gherib and flew off with him, in company with Courjan; nor was an hour past before they set him down at the gate of his palace in Cufa. He went in to his uncle Damigh, who rose to him and saluted him; after which quoth Gherib, 'How is it with my wives Morning Star and Mehdiyeh?' And Damigh answered, saying, 'They are both well and in good case.' Then the eunuch went in and acquainted the women of the harem with Gherib's coming, whereat they rejoiced and raised cries of joy and gave him the reward for good news. Presently in came Gherib, and they rose and saluting him, conversed with him, till Damigh entered, when Gherib related to them all that had befallen him in the land of the Jinn, whereat they all marvelled. Then he lay with Morning Star till near daybreak, when he took leave of his uncle and wives and mounted Courjan's back, nor was the darkness dispelled before the two Marids set him down in the city of Oman. Then he and his men armed and he bade open the gates, when, behold, up came a horseman from the host of the Indians, with Jemrcan and Saadan and the rest of the captives, whom he had delivered, and committed them to Gherib. The Muslims rejoiced in their safety and the drums beat a point of war, whilst the two hosts drew out in battle array.

The first to open the chapter of war was Gherib, who drove his charger between the two ranks and drawing his sword El Mahic, cried out, saying, 'Whoso knoweth me hath enough of my prowess and whoso knoweth me not, I will make myself known to him. I am Gherib, King of Irak and Yemen, brother of Agib.' When Raadshah beard this, he cried out to his guards, saying, 'Bring me Agib.' So they brought him and Raadshah said to him, 'Thou knowest that this quarrel is thy quarrel and thou art the cause of all this slaughter. Now yonder stands thy brother Gherib amiddleward the field; go thou out to him and bring him to me prisoner, that I may set him on a camel, face to tail, and make a show of him and carry him to the land of Hind.' 'O King,' answered Agib, 'send out to him other than I, for I am in ill case this morning.' But Raadshah puffed and snorted and said, 'By the virtue of the sparkling fire and the light and shade and heat, except thou go out to thy brother and bring him to me in haste, I will cut off thy head and make an end of thee.' So Agib took courage and spurring his horse up to his brother in midfield, said to him, 'O dog of the Arabs and vilest of all who smite upon tent-pegs, wilt thou contend with kings? Take what cometh to thee and receive the tidings of thy death.' When Gherib heard this, he said to him, 'Who art thou among the kings?' And Agib answered, saying, 'I am thy brother, and today is the last of thy worldly days.'

When Gherib was assured that he was indeed his brother Agib, be cried out and said, 'Ho, to avenge my father and mother!' Then giving his sword to Kailjan, he drove at Agib and smote him with his mace a swashing blow, that all but beat in his ribs, and seizing him by the neck-rings, tore him from the saddle and cast him to the ground; whereupon the Marids fell on him and binding him fast, dragged him off, abject and humiliated; whilst Gherib rejoiced in the capture of his enemy and repeated the following verses of the poet:

I have won to my wish and the end of affrays: Unto Thee, O my Lord, be the thanks and the praise!
I grew up, uncared for and abject and poor; But God hath vouchsafed me the aim of my ways.
I have conquered the lands, I have mastered the folk: But for Thee, I were nothing, O Ancient of Days!

When Raadshah saw how Agib fared with his brother, he called for his charger and donning his harness and coat of arms, mounted and pricked out into the field. As soon as he drew near Gherib, he cried out to him, saying, 'O vilest of Bedouin faggot-bearers, who art thou, that thou shouldst capture kings and warriors? Dismount and put thy hands behind thy back and kiss my feet and set my warriors free and go with me in chains to my kingdom, that I may pardon thee and make thee an elder in our country, so mayst thou eat a morsel of bread there.' When Gherib heard this, he laughed till he fell backward and answered, saying, 'O raging dog and scurvy wolf, thou shalt soon see against whom the shifts of Fate will turn!' Then he cried out to Sehim to bring him the prisoners; so he brought them, and Gherib smote off their heads; whereupon Raadshah drove at him, with the onslaught of a lordly champion and a fierce warrior, and they wheeled and feinted and hewed at each other till nightfall, when the drums beat the retreat and the two Kings returned, each to his own place, where his people gave him joy of his safety. And the Muslims said to Gherib, 'O King, it is not of thy wont to prolong a fight.' 'O folk,' answered he, 'I have done battle with many kings and champions; but never saw I a sturdier swordsman than this one. Had I chosen to draw El Mahic upon him, I had crushed his bones and made an end of his days: but I went about with him, thinking to take him prisoner and give him part in Islam.'

Meanwhile, Raadshah returned to his pavilion, where his chiefs came in to him and asked him of his adversary, and he said, 'By the sparkling fire, never in my life saw I the like of yonder warrior! But tomorrow I will take him prisoner and lead him away, abject and humbled.' Then they slept till daybreak, when the drums beat to battle and the fighting-men girt on their scimitars and mounting their stout horses, raised their war-cries and drew out into the field, filling all the hills and plains and wide places. The first to open the chapter of battle was the prince of cavaliers and the lion of war, King Gherib, who drove his steed between the two hosts and spurred to and fro, crying, 'Who is for jousting, who is for fighting? Let no sluggard nor weakling come out to me today!' Before he had made an end of speaking, out came Raadshah, riding on an elephant, as he were a vast tower, in a howdah girthed with silken bands; and between the elephant's ears sat the driver, bearing in his hand a hook, wherewith he goaded the beast and directed him right and left. When the elephant drew near Gherib's horse, the latter, seeing a creature it had never before set eyes on, took fright; wherefore Gherib dismounted and gave the horse to Kailjan. Then he drew El Mahic and advanced to meet Raadshah on foot.

Now it was Raadshah's wont, when he found himself overmatched, to mount an elephant, taking with him an engine called the noose, which was in the shape of a net, narrow at top and wide at bottom, with a running cord of silk passed through rings along its edges. With this he would attack horsemen and casting the net over them, draw the running noose and pull the rider off his horse and make him prisoner; and thus had he conquered many cavaliers. So, when Gherib came up to him, he raised his hand and casting the net over him, pulled him on to the back of the elephant and cried out to the latter to return to the Indian camp. But Kailjan and Courjan, who had not left Gherib, laid hold of the elephant and falling upon Raadshah, bound him with a rope of palm-fibres, whilst Gherib strove with the net, till he rent it in sunder. Thereupon the two armies drove at each other and met with a shock like two seas crashing or two mountains smiting together, whilst the dust rose to the confines of the sky and all eyes were blinded. The battle waxed fierce and the blood ran in streams, nor did they cease to wage war lustily with push of pike and stroke of sword, till the day departed and the night brought on the darkness, when the drums beat the retreat and the two hosts drew asunder.

Now the Muslims were hard pushed that day by reason of the riders on elephants and giraffes, and many of them were slain and most of the rest wounded. This was grievous to Gherib, who commanded the wounded to be cared for and turning to his chief officers, asked them what they counselled. 'O King,' answered they, 'it is but the elephants and giraffes that irk us; were we but quit of them, we should overcome the enemy.' Quoth Kailjan and Courjan, 'We two will draw our swords and fall on them and slay the most part of them.' But there came forward a man of Oman, who had been privy counsellor to Julned, and said, 'O King, I will be surety for the army, if thou wilt but hearken to me and follow my counsel.' And Gherib turned to his captains and said to them, 'Obey this wise man in whatsoever he shall say to you.' And they answered, saying, 'We hear and obey.' So he chose out ten captains and said to them, 'How many men have ye under your hands?' And they replied, 'Ten thousand fighting-men.' Then he carried them into the armoury and armed five thousand with crossbows and taught them to shoot therewith.

As soon as it was day, the Indians came out to the field, armed cap-a-pie, with the elephants and giraffes in their van; whereupon Gherib and his men mounted and the drums beat and both hosts drew out in battle array. Then the counsellor cried out to the archers and arque-busiers to shoot, and they plied the elephants and giraffes with shafts and bullets. The arrows and the lead entered the beasts' flanks, and they roared out and turning upon their own ranks, trampled them with their feet. Then the Muslims charged the misbelievers and set on them right and left, whilst the elephants and giraffes trampled them and drove them into the hills and deserts. Moreover, the Muslims followed hard upon them with the keen-edged sword and but few of the giraffes and elephants escaped.

Then Gherib and his folk returned, rejoicing in their victory; and on the morrow they divided the spoil and rested five days; after which King Gherib sat down on his throne and sending for his brother Agib, said to him, 'O dog, how hast thou assembled the kings against us! But He who hath power over all things hath given us the victory over thee. Wherefore do thou embrace Islam and thou shalt be saved, and I will forbear to avenge my father and mother on thee. Moreover, I will make thee King again as thou wast and will myself be under thy hand.' But Agib said, 'I will not leave my faith.' So Gherib bade lay him in irons and appointed a hundred stalwart slaves to guard him; after which he turned to Raadshah and said to him. 'How sayst thou of the faith of Islam?' 'O my lord,' answered Raadshah, 'I will enter thy faith, for, were it not a true faith and a goodly, thou hadst not carried it over us. So put forth thy hand and I will testify that there is no god but God and that Abraham the Friend is His apostle.' At this Gherib rejoiced and said to him, 'Is thy heart indeed stablished in the sweetness of the Faith?' And he answered, saying, 'Yes, O my lord!' Then said Gherib, 'O Raadshah, wilt thou go to thy country and thy kingdom?' 'O my lord,' replied he, 'my father will put me to death, for that I have left his faith.' Quoth Gherib, 'I will go with thee and make thee King of the country and constrain the folk to obey thee, by the help of God the Bountiful, the Beneficent.' And Raadshah kissed his hands and feet. Then Gherib rewarded the counsellor, who had been the cause of the rout of the infidels, and gave him great riches; after which be turned to Kailjan and Courjan and said to them, 'O chiefs of the Jinn, it is my will that ye carry me, together with Raadshah and Jemrcan and Saadan, to the land of Hind.' 'We hear and obey,' answered they. So Courjan took up Jemrcan and Saadan, whilst Kailjan took Gherib and Raadshah, and flew on with them from sundown till the end of the night, when they set them down on the terrace of King Terkenan's palace at Cashmere.

Now news was come to Terkenan of the rout of his army and that his son, whereat he was sore troubled and slept not neither took delight in aught. As he sat in his harem, pondering his case, behold, Gherib and his company descended the stairways of the palace and came in to him; and when he saw his son and those who were with him, he was confounded and fear took him of the Marids. Then Raadshah turned to him and said, 'How long wilt thou persist in thy frowardness, O traitor and worshipper of the Fire? Woe to thee! Leave worshipping the fire and serve the Magnanimous King, Creator of night and day, whom no sight attaineth.' When Terkenan heard his son's speech, he cast at him an iron mace he had by him; but he avoided it and it fell upon a buttress of the palace and smote out three stones. Then said the King, 'O dog, thou hast destroyed my troops and forsaken thy faith and comest now to make me do likewise!'

With this Gherib stepped up to him and dealt him a buffet on the neck, that knocked him down; whereupon the Marids bound him fast and all the women fled.

Then Gherib sat down on the throne and said to Raadshah, 'Do thou justice upon thy father.' So Raadshah turned to him and said, 'O perverse old man, become a Muslim and thou shalt be saved from the fire and the wrath of the Almighty.' And Terkenan said, 'I will die in my own faith.' Whereupon Gherib drew El Mahic and smote him therewith, and he fell to the earth in two pieces, and God hurried his soul to the fire and ill was the abiding-place. Then Gherib bade hang his body over the gate of the palace and they hung one-half on the right hand and the other on the left and waited till day, when Gherib caused Raadshah don the royal habit and sit down on his father's throne, with himself on his right hand and Jemrcan and Saadan and the Marids standing right and left; and he said to Kailjan and Courjan, 'Whoso entereth of the princes and officers, seize him and bind him, and let not a single captain escape you.' And they answered, saying, 'We hear and obey.'

Presently, the officers made for the palace, to do their service to the King, and the first to appear was the chief captain, who, seeing Terkenan's dead body cut in half and banging on either side the gate, was seized with horror and amazement. Then Kailjan laid hold of him by the collar and dragged him into the palace and bound him; and before sunrise they had bound three hundred and fifty captains and set them before Gherib, who said to them, 'Have you seen your King hanging at the palace-gate?' Quoth they, 'Who hath done this thing?' And he answered, 'I did it, by the help of God the Most High; and whoso gainsayeth me, I will do with him likewise.' Then said they, 'What is thy will with us?' 'I am Gherib, King of Irak,' answered he, 'he who slew your warriors; and now Raadshah has embraced the faith of submission and is become a mighty king and ruler over you. So do ye become true believers and all shall be well with you; but, if you refuse, you shall repent it.' So they pronounced the profession of the faith and were numbered of the people of felicity. Then said Gherib, 'Are your hearts indeed stablished in the sweetness of the Faith?' And they answered, 'Yes;' whereupon he bade release them and clad them in robes of honour, saying, 'Go to your people and expound Islam to them. Whosoever accepts the faith, spare him; but, if he refuse, slay him.' So they went out and assembling the men under their command, expounded Islam to them, and they all professed, except a few, whom they put to death; after which they returned and told Gherib, who praised God the Most High and glorified Him, saying, 'Praised be God who hath made this thing easy to us without strife!'

Then he abode in Cashmere forty days, till he had ordered the affairs of the country and cast down the shrines and temples of the Fire and built mosques and places of worship in their stead, whilst Raadshah made ready for him gifts and treasures beyond count and despatched them to Irak in ships. Then Gherib mounted on Kailjan's back and Jemrcan and Saadan on that of Courjan, after they had taken leave of Raadshah, and before daybreak they were in Oman, where their troops met them and saluted them and rejoiced in them. Then they set out for Cufa, where Gherib called for his brother Agib and commanded to crucify him on the city-gate and shoot at him with arrows. So Sehim brought hooks of iron and driving them into the tendons of Agib's heels, hung him over the gate; and they riddled him with arrows, till he was like a porcupine.

Then Gherib entered his palace and sitting down on the throne of his kingship, passed the day in ordering the affairs of the state. At nightfall he went in to his harem, where Morning Star came to meet him and embraced him and gave him joy, she and her women, of his safety. He lay the night with her and on the morrow, after he had washed and prayed the morning prayer, he sat down on his throne and commanded preparation to be made for his marriage with Mehdiyeh. So they slaughtered three thousand head of sheep and two thousand oxen and a thousand goats and five hundred camels and the like number of horses, beside four thousand fowls and great store of geese; never was such a wedding in Islam to that day. Then he went in to Mehdiyeh and did away her maidenhead and abode with her ten days; after which he committed the kingdom to his uncle Damigh, charging him to rule the people justly, and journeyed with his women and warriors, till he came to the ships laden with presents, which Raadshah had sent him, and divided the treasure among his troops. Then they fared on till they reached the city of Babel, where he bestowed on Sehim a dress of honour and appointed him Sultan of the city. He abode with him ten days, at the end of which time he sẹt out again and journeyed till he reached the castle of Saadan the Ghoul, where they rested five days.

Then said Gherib to Kailjan and Courjan, 'Go ye to Isbanir el Medaïn, to the palace of Chosroës, and find what is come of Fekhr Taj and bring me one of the King's kinsmen, who shall acquaint me with what has passed.' 'We hear and obey,' answered they and set out forthright for Isbanir. As they flew between heaven and earth, they caught sight of a mighty army, as it were the swollen sea, and Kailjan said to Courjan, 'Let us descend and see what is this army.' So they alighted and walking among the troops, found them Persians and questioned the soldiers whose men they were and whither they were bound; to which they made answer, saying, 'We are bound for Irak, to kill Gherib and all who are with him.' When the Marids heard this, they repaired to the pavilion of the Persian general, whose name was Rustem, and waited till the soldiers slept, when they took up Rustem, bed and all, and made for Gherib's camp. They arrived there by midnight and going to the door of the King's pavilion, said, 'Permission;' which when the latter heard, he sat up and said, 'Enter.' So they entered and set down the couch with Rustem asleep thereon. Quoth Gherib, 'Who is this?' and they answered, 'This is a Persian prince, whom we met coming with a great host, thinking to slay thee and thine; and we have brought him to thee, that he may tell thee what thou hast a mind to know.' 'Fetch me a hundred men,' said Gherib, and they fetched them; whereupon he made them draw their swords and stand at Rustem's head.

Then they awoke him and he opened his eyes and finding a vault of steel over his head, shut them again, saying, 'What is this foul dream?' But Kailjan pricked him with his sword-point and he sat up and said 'Where am I?' Quoth Sehim, 'Thou art in the presence of King Gherib, son-in-law of the King of the Persians. What is thy name and whither goest thou?' When Rustem heard Gherib's name, he bethought himself and said, 'Am I asleep or on wake?' Whereupon Sehim dealt him a buffet, saying, 'Why dost thou not answer?' And he raised his head and said, 'Who brought me from my tent out of the midst of my men?' Quoth Gherib, 'These two Marids brought thee.' So he looked at them and voided in his hose . Then the Marids fell upon him, baring their tusks and brandishing their swords, and said to him, 'Wilt thou not rise and kiss the earth before King Gherib?' and he trembled at them and was assured that he was not asleep; so he stood up and kissed the earth before Gherib, saying, 'The blessing of the Fire be on thee, O King, and long be thy life!' 'O dog of the Persians,' answered Gherib, 'fire is not worshipful, for that it is harmful and profiteth not save for food.' 'Who then is worshipful?' asked Rustem; and Gherib replied, saying, 'God alone is worshipworth, who made thee and formed thee and created the heavens and the earth.' Quoth the Persian, 'What shall I say, that I may become of the party of this Lord and enter thy faith?' 'Say,' rejoined Gherib, '"There is no god but God, and Abraham is the friend of God."' So Rustem pronounced the profession of the faith and was written of the people of felicity.

Then said he to Gherib, 'Know, O my lord, that thy father-in-law, King Sabour, seeks to kill thee and hath sent me with a hundred thousand men, charging me to spare none of you.' Quoth

Gherib, 'Is this my reward for having delivered his daughter from death and dishonour? God will requite him his evil intent. But what is thy name?' And the Persian answered, saying, 'My name is Rustem, general of Sabour.' Quoth Gherib, 'Thou shalt have the like rank in my army. But tell me, O Rustem, how is it with the princess Fekhr Taj?' 'May thy head live, O King of the age!' answered Rustem. 'What was the cause of her death?' asked Gherib; and Rustem said, 'O my lord, no sooner hadst thou left us, than one of the princess's women went in to King Sabour and said to him, "O my lord, didst thou give Gherib leave to lie with the princess my mistress?" "No, by the virtue of the fire!" answered he, and drawing his sword, went in to his daughter and said to her, "O filthy baggage, why didst thou suffer yonder Bedouin to lie with thee, without wedding or dower?" "O my father," answered she, "thou gavest him leave to lie with me." "Did he have to do with thee?" asked he. But she was silent and hung down her head. Then he cried out to the midwives and slave-girls, saying, "Bind this harlot's hands behind her and look at her privy parts!" So they did as he bade and said to him, "O King, she hath lost her maidenhead." Whereupon he ran at her and would have slain her, but her mother threw herself between them, saying, "O King, slay her not, lest thou be for ever dishonoured; but shut her in a cell till she die." So he cast her into prison till nightfall, when he called two of his officers and said to them, "Carry her afar off and cast her into the river Jihon and tell none." They did his commandment, and indeed her memory is forgotten and her time is past.'

When Gherib heard this, he said, 'By the virtue of Abraham the Friend, I will assuredly go to yonder dog and destroy him and lay waste his kingdom!' Then he sent letters to Jemrcan and to the governors of Mosul and Meyya Farikin and turning to Rustem, said to him, 'How many men hadst thou in thine army?' 'A hundred thousand Persian horse,' answered he. And Gherib said, 'Take ten thousand horse and go to thy people and occupy them with war.' So Rustem took ten thousand Arab horse and departed, saying in himself, 'I will do a thing that shall whiten my face with King Gherib.' So he fared on seven days, till there remained but half a day's journey between him and the Persian camp; when he divided his men into four troops and bade them attack the Persians from different sides and fall on them with the sword. So they rode on from eventide till midnight, when they came to the camp of the Persians, who were asleep in security, and fell upon them, shouting, 'God is Most Great!' Whereupon the Persians started up from sleep and their feet slipped and the sabre went round amongst them; for the All-knowing King was wroth with them, and Rustem wrought amongst them as fire in dry firewood, till, by the end of the night, the whole of the Persian host was slain or wounded or fled, and the Muslims made prize of their tents and baggage and horses and camels and treasure-chests. Then they alighted and rested in the tents of the beaten army, till Gherib came up and seeing what Rustem had done, invested him with a dress of honour and said to him, 'O Rustem, it was thou didst put the Persians to the rout; wherefore all the spoil is thine.' So he kissed Gherib's hand and thanked him, and they rested till the end of the day, when they set out for King Sabour's capitaL

Meanwhile, the survivors of the defeated army reached Isbanir and went in to Sabour, crying out and saying, 'Alas!' and 'Ruin!' and 'Woe worth the day!' Quoth he, 'What hath befallen you and who hath smitten you with his mischief?' So they told him all that had passed and how his general Rustem had embraced Islam and fallen upon them in the darkness of the night and routed them. When the King heard this, he cast his crown to the ground and said, 'There is no worth left to us!' Then he turned to his son Werd Shah and said to him, 'O my son, there is none for this affair but thou.' 'By thy life, O my father,' answered Werd Shah, 'I will assuredly bring Gherib and his chiefs of the people in chains and slay all who are with him.' Then he numbered his army and found it eleven score thousand men. So they slept, intending to set forth on the morrow; but, next morning, as they were about to depart, a cloud of dust arose and spread till it covered the lands and baffled the sharpest sight.

Now Sabour had mounted to take leave of his son, and when he saw this great dust, he despatched a runner to discover the cause thereof, who went and returned, saying, 'O my lord, Gherib and his men are upon you;' whereupon they unloaded their beasts and drew out in order of battle. When Gherib came up and saw the Persians drawn out in battalia, he cried out to his men, saying, 'Charge, and the blessing of God be upon you!' So they waved the standards and the Arabs and the Persians drove at each other and people fell upon people. The blood ran in streams and all souls saw death face to face; the brave advanced and pressed forward and the coward turned and fled and they ceased not from the battle till ended day, when the drums beat the retreat and the two hosts drew apart. Then Sabour commanded to pitch his camp before the city-gate, and Gherib set up his tents in front of theirs and every one went to his tent until the morning. As soon as it was day, the two hosts mounted their strong horses and couched their lances and donned their harness of war; then they raised their war-cries and drew out in battle-array, whilst all the lordly champions and the lions of war came forth.

The first to open the chapter of battle was Rustem, who spurred his charger into the mid-field and cried out, saying, 'God is Most Great! I am Rustem, chief of the champions of the Arabs and the Persians. Who is for jousting, who is for fighting? Let no sluggard or weakling come out to me today!' Then there came forth to him a champion of the Persians and there befell between them a sore battle, till Rustem smote his adversary with a mace he had with him, seventy pounds in weight, and beat his head down upon his breast, and he fell to the earth, dead and drowned in his blood. This was grievous to Sabour and he commanded his men to charge; so they drove at the Muslims, invoking the aid of the light-giving Sun, whilst the Muslims called for help upon the Magnanimous King. But the infidels outnumbered the true believers and made them drink the cup of death; which when Gherib saw, he drew his sword El Mahic and crying out , fell upon the Persians, with Kailjan and Courjan at his either stirrup; nor did he leave tourneying amongst them with the sword till he hewed his way to the standard-bearer and smote him on the head with the flat of his sword, whereupon he fell down in a swoon and the two Marids carried him off to their camp. When the Persians saw the standard fallen, they turned and fled towards the gates of the city; but the Muslims followed them with the sword and they crowded together to enter the city, so that they could not shut the gates and there died of them much people. Then Rustem and Saadan and Jemrcan and Sehim and Kailjan and Courjan and all the Muslim braves and the champions of the Faith of Unity fell upon the misbelieving Persians in the gates and the blood of the infidels ran in the streets like a tide, till they threw down their arms and harness and called out for quarter; whereupon the Muslims stayed their hands from the slaughter and drove them to their tents, as one drives a flock of sheep.

Meanwhile, Gherib returned to his pavilion, where he did off his harness and washed himself of the blood of the infidels; after which he donned his royal robes and sat down on his chair of estate. Then he called for the King of the Persians and said to him, 'O dog of the Persian; what moved thee to deal thus with thy daughter? How seest thou me unworthy to be her husband?' And Sabour answered, saying, 'O King, be not wroth with me for that which I did; for I repent me and came out to thee in battle but in my fear of thee.' When Gherib heard this, he bade throw him down and beat him. So they beat him, till he could no longer groan, and cast him among the prisoners. Then Gherib expounded Islam to the Persians and six-score thousand of them embraced the faith, and the rest he put to the sword. Moreover, all the townsfolk professed Islam and Gherib mounted and entered the city in great state.

Then he went into the King's palace and sitting down on his throne, gave gifts and largesse and distributed the booty and treasure among the Arabs and Persians, wherefore they loved him and wished him power and victory and length of days. But Fekhr Taj's mother remembered her daughter and raised the voice of mourning for her, and the palace was filled with crying and lamentation. Gherib heard this and entering the harem, asked the women what ailed them, whereupon the princess's mother came forward and said, 'O my lord, thy presence put me in mind of my daughter and how she would have joyed in thy coming, had she been alive.' Gherib wept for her and sitting down on his throne, called for Sabour, and they brought him, stumbling in his shackles. Quoth Gherib to him, 'O dog of the Persians, what didst thou with thy daughter?' 'I gave her to such an one and such an one,' answered the King, 'saying, "Drown her in the river Jihon."' So Gherib sent for the two men and said to them, 'Is what he saith true?' 'Yes, O King,' answered they; 'yet did we not drown her, but took pity on her and left her on the banks of the Jihon, saying, "Save thyself and do not return to the city, lest the King put thee to death and us with thee." This is all we know of her.' When Gherib heard this, he summoned the astrologers and said to them, 'Draw me a geomantic figure and find out what is come of Fekhr Taj and whether she is still in the chains of life or dead.' So they levelled a table of sand and drawing a geomantic figure, said, 'O King, the princess is alive and hath borne a male child; but she is with a tribe of the Jinn and will be absent from thee twenty years; look, therefore, how many years thou hast been absent.' So he reckoned up the years of his absence and found them eight years and said, 'There is no power and no virtue but in God the Most High, the Supreme!' Then he sent for all Sabour's governors of towns and strongholds and they came and did him homage.

One day after this, as he sat in his palace, a cloud of dust appeared in the distance and spread till it covered the whole country and darkened the horizon. So he despatched the two Marids to reconnoitre, and they went forth and snatching up a horseman of the advancing army, returned and set him down before Gherib, saying, 'Ask this fellow, for he is of the army.' Quoth Gherib, 'Whose army is this?' And the man answered, 'O King, it is the army of Khired Shah, King of Shiraz, who is come to do battle with thee.' Now the manner of Khired Shah's coming was on this wise. When Gherib defeated Sabour's army, as hath been related, and took the King himself, the latter's son fled, with a handful of his father's men, to Shiraz, where he went in to King Khired Shah and kissed the earth before him, whilst the tears ran down his cheeks. When the King saw him in this case, he said to him, 'Lift thy head, O youth, and tell me what makes thee weep.' 'O King,' answered the prince, 'a King of the Arabs, by name Gherib, hath fallen on us and taken the King my father prisoner and slain the Persians and made them drink the cup of death.' And he told him all that had befallen. Quoth Khired Shah, 'Is my wife well?' And the prince answered, saying, 'Gherib hath taken her.' 'As my head liveth,' cried the King, 'I will not leave a Bedouin or a Muslim on the face of the earth!' So he wrote letters to his governors, who levied their troops and joined him with an army of four-score and five thousand men. Then he opened his armouries and distributed arms and armour to the troops, after which he set out with them and journeyed till he came to Isbanir and encamped before the city-gate.

With this Kailjan and Courjan came in to Gherib and kissing his knee, said to him, 'O King, heal our hearts and give us this army to our share!' And he said, 'Up and at them!' So they flew up into the air and lighting down in the pavilion of the King of Shiraz, found him seated on his chair of estate, with the Prince of Persia sitting on his right hand, and about him his captains, with whom he was taking counsel for the slaughter of the Muslims. Kailjan caught up the Prince and Courjan the King and flew back with them to Gherib, who caused beat them, till they fainted. Then the Marids returned to the Shirazi camp and drawing their swords, which no mortal man might wield, fell upon the infidels, and God hurried their souls to the fire and evil was the abiding-place , whilst they saw nothing but two swords flashing and reaping men, as a husbandman reaps corn. So they forsook their tents and mounting their horses bare-backed, fled for their lives. The Marids pursued them two days and slew of them much people, after which they returned and kissed Gherib's hand. He thanked them for that which they had done and said to them, 'The spoil of the infidels is yours alone: none shall share with you therein.' So they called down blessings on him and going forth gathered the booty together and abode in their own place.

Meanwhile, the remains of the beaten army drew not bridle, till they reached the city of Shiraz and there lifted up the voice of weeping for those that had been slain of them. Now King Khired Shah had a brother by name Siran the Sorcerer, than whom there was no greater wizard in his day, and he lived apart from his brother in a certain stronghold, called the Castle of Fruits, in a place abounding in trees and streams and birds and flowers, half a day's journey from Shiraz. So the fugitives betook them thither and went in to Siran, weeping and crying out. Quoth he, 'O folk, what ails you to weep?' And they told him all that had happened, whereupon the light in his eyes became darkness and he said, 'By the virtue of my faith, I will slay Gherib and all his men and leave not one alive to tell the tale!' Then he pronounced certain magical words and summoned the Red King, who appeared and Siran said to him, 'Go to Isbanir and fall on Gherib, as he sits upon his throne.' 'I hear and obey,' answered the genie, and gathering his troops, repaired to Isbanir and set upon Gherib. When the latter saw him, he drew his sword El Mahic and he and Kailjan and Courjan fell upon the army of the Red King and slew of them five hundred and thirty and wounded the King himself grievously; whereupon he and his people fled and stayed not in their flight, till they reached the Castle of Fruits and went in to Siran, crying out and saying, 'Woe!' and 'Ruin!' And the Red King said to Siran, 'O sage, Gherib hath with him the enchanted sword of Japhet son of Noah, whomsoever he smites withal, he cuts him in sunder, and with him also are two Marids from the Mountain Caf, given him by King Muraash. He it is who slew the Blue King and Bercan, lord of the Cornelian City, and did to death much people of the Jinn.'

When Siran heard this, he dismissed the Red King and conjuring up a Marid, by name Zuazia, gave him a drachm of powdered henbane and said to him, 'Take the form of a sparrow and go to King Gherib's palace at Isbanir. Wait till he is asleep and there is none with him; then put the henbane up his nostrils and bring him to me.' 'I hear and obey,' answered the Marid and changing himself into a sparrow, flew to Isbanir, where he perched on a window of the palace and waited till all Gherib's attendants retired and the King himself slept. Then he flew down and going up to Gherib, blew the powdered henbane into his nostrils, till he lost his senses, whereupon he wrapped him in the coverlet of the bed and flew off with him, like the storm-wind, to the Castle of Fruits; where he arrived at midnight and laid his prize before Siran. The enchanter thanked him and would have put Gherib to death, as he lay senseless; but a man of his people withheld him, saying, 'O sage, if thou slay him, his friend King Muraash will fall on us with all his Jinn and lay waste our realm.' 'How then shall we do with him? asked Siran. 'Cast him into the Jihon,' answered the other, 'and he will be drowned and none will know who threw him in.' And Siran bade the Marid take Gherib and cast him into the Jihon. So he carried him down to the river-bank, but it was grievous to him to drown him, wherefore he made a raft of wood and binding it with cords, pushed it and Gherib thereon out into the current, which carried it away.

Meanwhile, when Gherib's people awoke in the morning and went in to do their service to their King, they found him not and seeing his rosary on the throne, awaited him awhile, but he came not. So they sought out the chamberlain and said to him, 'Go into the harem and look for the King; for it is not his wont to tarry till this time.' Accordingly, the chamberlain entered the harem and enquired for the King, but the women said, 'We have not seen him since yesterday.' So he returned and told the officers, who were confounded and said, 'Let us see if he have gone to take his pleasure in the gardens.' Then they went out and questioned the gardeners if they had seen the King, and they answered, 'No;' whereat they were sore concerned and searched all the gardens till the end of the day, when they returned, weeping. Moreover, the Marids sought for him all round the town, but returned after three days, without having come on any tidings of him. So the people donned black and made their complaint to the Lord of all Creatures, who doth what pleaseth Him.

Meanwhile, the current bore the raft along for five days, till it brought it to the salt sea, where the waves played with Gherib and his stomach, being troubled, threw up the henbane. Then he opened his eyes and finding himself in the midst of the sea, tossed about by the waves, said, 'There is no power and no virtue but in God the Most High, the Supreme! I wonder who hath done this thing with me!' Presently, as he lay, knowing not what to make of his case, he caught sight of a ship and signalled with his sleeve to the sailors, who came to him and took him up, saying, 'Who art thou and whence comest thou?' Quoth he, 'Do ye feed me and give me to drink, till I recover myself, and after I will tell you who I am.' So they brought him water and victual, and he ate and drank and God restored his reason to him. Then said he to them, 'O folk, what countrymen are ye and what is your faith?' 'We are from Kerej,' answered they, 'and worship an idol called Mincash.' 'Perdition to you and your idol!' cried Gherib. 'O dogs, none is worthy of worship save God who created all things, who saith to a thing "Be!" and it is.' When they heard this, they fell upon him in great wrath and would have seized him. Now he was unarmed, but whomsoever he struck, he smote down and deprived of life, till he had felled forty men, after which they overcame him by force of numbers and bound him fast, saying. 'We will not put him to death save in our own country, that we may show him to our King.'

Then they sailed on till they came to the city of Kerej, the builder whereof was a fierce Amalekite and set up at each gate of the city a magical figure of brass, which, whenever a stranger entered, blew a blast on a trumpet, that all in the city heard it and fell upon the stranger and slew him, except he embraced their faith. When Gherib entered the city, the brazen figure stationed at the gate blew such a terrible blast that the King was affrighted and going in to his idol, found fire and smoke issuing from its eyes and mouth and nostrils. Now a devil had entered the belly of the idol and speaking as with its tongue, said to the King of the city, 'O King, there is come to thy city one Gherib, King of Irak, who uses to bid the folk quit their faith and worship his Lord; wherefore, when they bring him before thee, look thou spare him not.' So the King went out and sat down on his throne; and presently, the sailors brought in Gherib, saying, 'O King, we found this youth shipwrecked in the midst of the sea, and he believeth not in our gods.' Then they told him all that had passed and the King said, 'Carry him to the house of the great idol and cut his throat before him, so haply he may look favourably upon us.' But the Vizier said, 'O King, it befits not to slaughter him thus, for he would die forthright; rather let us burn him with fire.'

So the King commanded to cast Gherib into prison and caused wood to be brought; and they made a great pyre and set fire to it, and it burnt till the morning. Then the King and the people of the city came forth and the King sent to fetch Gherib; but his men found him not; so they returned and told the King, who said, 'How made he his escape?' Quoth they, 'We found the doors locked and the chains and shackles cast down.' Whereat the King marvelled and said, 'Hath this fellow flown up to heaven or sunk into the earth?' And they said, 'We know not.' Then said the King, 'I will go and ask my god, and he will tell me whither he is gone.' So he rose and went in, to prostrate himself to his idol, but found it not and began to rub his eyes and say, 'Am I asleep or awake?' Then he turned to his Vizier and said to him, 'Where is my god and where is the prisoner? By my faith, O dog of Viziers, hadst thou not counselled me to burn him, I had slaughtered him; for it is he who hath stolen my god and fled; and needs must I be avenged of him!' Then he drew his sword and cut off the Vizier's head.

Now there was a strange cause for Gherib's escape, and it was on this wise. When they had shut him up in a cell adjoining the temple of the idol, he rose to pray, calling upon the name of God the Most High and seeking deliverance of Him, may He be exalted and glorified! The Marid who had charge of the idol and spoke in its name, heard him and fear gat hold upon his heart and he said, 'Confusion! Who is this that seeth me and whom I see not?' So he went in to Gherib and throwing himself at his feet, said to him, 'O my lord, what must I say that I may become of thy company and enter thy religion?' 'Say,' answered Gherib, '"There is no god but God, and Abraham is the Friend of God."' So the Marid pronounced the profession of the faith and was written of the people of felicity. Now his name was Zelzal, son of El Muzelzel, one of the chief of the Kings of the Jinn. Then he unbound Gherib and taking him and the idol, made for the upper air.

When the King's soldiers saw what had befallen, they renounced the worship of the idol and drawing their swords, slew the King; after which they fell on one another, and the sword went round amongst them three days, till there abode alive but two men, one of whom overcame the other and killed him. Then the boys attacked the survivor and slew him and fell to fighting amongst themselves, till they were all killed; and the women and girls fled to the hamlets and villages; wherefore the city became desert and none dwelt therein but the owl.

Meanwhile, the Marid Zelzal flew with Gherib towards his own country, the Islands of Camphor and the Castle of Crystal and the land of the Enchanted Calf, so called because its King, Muzelzel, had a pied calf which he clad in housings of gold brocade and worshipped as a god. One day, the King and his people went in to the calf and found him trembling; so the King said, 'O my god, what hath troubled thee?' Whereupon the Satan in the calf's belly cried out and said, 'O Muzelzel, thy son hath deserted to the faith of Abraham the Friend, at the hands of Gherib, King of Irak.' When the King heard this, he was confounded and going forth, sat down upon his throne. Then he summoned his grandees and told them what he had heard from the idol, whereat they marvelled and said, 'What shall we do, O King?' Quoth he, 'When my son comes and ye see me embrance him, do ye lay hold of him.' And they said, 'We hear and obey.'

After two days came Zelzal and Gherib, with the King's idol of Kerej, but no sooner had they entered the palace-gate than the Jinn seized on them and carried them before Muzelzel, who looked at his son with angry eyes and said to him, 'O dog of a genie, hast thou left thy faith and that of thy fathers and grandfathers?' Quoth Zelzal, 'I have embraced the true faith, and thou, do thou likewise and thou shalt be saved from the wrath of the Almighty King, Creator of Night and Day.' Therewith his father waxed wroth and said, 'O whoreson, dost thou affront me with these words?' Then he bade clap him in prison and turning to Gherib, said to him, 'O wretch of a mortal, how hast thou abused my son's wit and seduced him from his faith?' Quoth Gherib, 'Indeed, I have brought him out of error into the way of righteousness, out of Hell into Paradise and out of idolatry to the true faith.' Whereupon the King cried out to a Marid called Siyyar, saying, 'Take this dog and cast him into the Valley of Fire, that he may perish.'

Now this valley was situate in the desert quarter of the world and was so named by reason of the excess of its heat and the flaming of its fire, which was so fierce that none who fell therein could live an hour, but was destroyed; and it was compassed about by high and slippery mountains, wherein was no opening. So Siyyar took up Gherib and flew with him towards the

Valley of Fire, till he came within an hour's journey thereof, when, being aweary, he alighted in a valley full of trees and streams and fruits, and setting down Gherib, chained as he was, fell asleep for weariness. When Gherib saw that he slept and heard him snore, he strove with his bonds till he burst them; then, taking up a heavy stone, he cast it down on the Marid's head and crushed his bones, so that he died forthright. Then he fared on into the valley and found himself in a great island in mid-ocean, full of all fruits, that lips and tongue could desire. So he abode alone on the island, drinking of its waters and eating of its fruits and of fish that he caught, and days and years passed over him, till he had sojourned there seven years.

One day, as he sat, there came down on him from the air two Marids, each carrying a man; and they said to him, 'Who art thou, O fellow, and of which of the tribes art thou?' Now they took him for a genie, because his hair was grown long; and he replied, saying, 'I am no genie,' and told them all that had befallen him; whereupon they grieved for him and said, 'Abide here till we carry these two lambs to our king, that he may make the morning meal of the one and sup on the other, and after we will come back and carry thee to thine own country.' He thanked them and said, 'Where are the lambs?' Quoth they, 'These two mortals are the lambs.' And Gherib said, 'I crave the protection of the God of Abraham the Friend, the Lord of all creatures, who hath power over everything!' Then the Marids flew away and Gherib abode awaiting them two days, when one of them returned, bringing with him a suit of clothes, in which he clad him. Then he took him up and flew with him out of sight of earth, till Gherib heard the angels glorifying God in heaven, and a flaming arrow issued from amongst them and made for the Marid, who fled from it towards the earth. The arrow pursued him, till he came within a spear's cast of the earth, when Gherib leapt from his back, and the fiery shaft overtook the Marid, who became a heap of ashes.

As for Gherib, he fell into the sea and sank two fathoms deep, after which he came to the surface and swam for two days and two nights, till his strength failed him and he despaired of life. But, on the third day, he caught sight of a steep and mountainous island; so he made for it and landing, walked on inland, where he rested a day and a night, feeding on the fruits of the earth. Then he climbed to the mountain-top and descending the opposite slope, fared on two days till he came in sight of a walled and fortified city, abounding in trees and streams. So he made for it, but, when he reached the gate, the warders seized on him and carried him to their queen, whose name was Janshah. Now she was five hundred years old, and every man who entered the city, they brought to her and she lay with him; then, when he had done his work, she put him to death, and so had she slain many men. When she saw Gherib, he pleased her and she said to him, 'What is thy name and faith and whence comest thou?' Quoth he, 'My name is Gherib, King of Irak, and I am a Muslim.' 'Leave this faith,' said she, 'and enter mine and I will marry thee and make thee king.' But he looked at her with angry eyes and said, 'Thy faith perish with thee!' Quoth she, 'Dost thou blaspheme my idol, the which is of red cornelian, set with pearls and jewels?' And she cried out to her men, saying, 'Imprison him in the house of the idol; peradventure it will soften his heart.' So they shut him up in the temple and locking the doors upon him, went their way. As soon as they were gone, Gherib went up to the idol, which was of red cornelian, with collars of pearls and precious stones about its neck, and lifting it up, dashed it on the ground and broke it in pieces; after which he lay down and slept till daybreak.

Next morning, the Queen sat down on her bed of estate and said to her men, 'Bring me the prisoner.' So they opened the temple doors and entering, found the idol broken in pieces, whereupon they buffeted their faces, till the blood ran from the corners of their eyes. Then they made at Gherib, to seize him; but he smote one of them with his fist and killed him, and so did he with another and another, till he had slain five-and-twenty of them and the rest fled to Queen

Janshah, crying out. Quoth she, 'What is the matter?' And they said, 'The prisoner hath broken thine idol and slain thy men,' and told her all that had passed. When she heard this, she cast her crown to the ground and said, 'There is no worth left in idols!' Then she mounted with a thousand fighting-men and rode to the temple, where she found Gherib had gotten him a sword and come forth and was slaying men and overthrowing warriors. When she saw his prowess, her heart was drowned in the love of him and she said in herself, 'I have no need of the idol and care for nought but this Gherib, that he may lie in my bosom the rest of my life.' Then she bade her men hold aloof from Gherib, and going up to him, muttered certain magical words, whereupon his arm became benumbed and the sword dropped from his grasp. So they seized him and bound him, as he stood confounded and stupefied.

Then the Queen returned to her palace and seating herself on her throne, bade her people withdraw and leave Gherib with her. When they were alone, she said to him, 'O dog of the Arabs, wilt thou break my idol and slay my men?' 'O accursed woman,' answered he, 'had he been a god, he had defended himself!' Quoth she, 'Lie with me and I will forgive thee that which thou hast done.' But he replied, saying, 'I will do nought of this.' And she said, 'By the virtue of my faith, I will punish thee grievously!' So she took water and conjuring over it, sprinkled it upon him and he became an ape. And she used to feed and keep him in a closet, appointing one to care for him; and in this plight he abode two years. Then she called him to her one day and said to him, 'Wilt thou hearken to me?' And he signed to her with his head, as who should say, 'Yes.' So she rejoiced and freed him from the enchantment. Then she brought him food and he ate and toyed with her and kissed her, so that she trusted in him. When it was night, she lay down and said to him, 'Come, do thy business.' 'It is well,' answered he and mounting on her breast, seized her by the neck and broke it, nor did he arise from her till life had left her. Then, seeing an open cabinet, he went in and found there a sword of watered steel and a buckler of Chinese iron; so he armed himself cap-a-pie and waited till the day.

As soon as it was morning, he went forth and stood at the gate of the palace. When the Amirs came and would have gone in to do their service to the Queen, they found Gherib standing at the gate, clad in complete steel; and he said to them, 'O folk, leave the service of idols and worship the All-wise King, Creator of Night and Day, who giveth life to dry bones, for He made all things and hath dominion over all.' When they heard this, they ran at him, but he fell on them like a ravening lion and slew of them much people; but, when the night came, they overcame him by dint of numbers and would have taken him, when behold, there descended upon the infidels a thousand Marids, under the command of Zelzal, who plied them with the keen sabre and made them drink the cup of perdition, whilst God hurried their souls to the fire, till but few were left of the people of Janshah and the rest cried out for quarter and believed in the Requiting King, whom no one thing diverteth from another, the Destroyer of tyrants and Exterminator of the Chosroës, Lord of this world and the next.

Then Zelzal saluted Gherib and gave him joy of his safety; and Gherib said to him, 'How knewest thou of my plight?' 'O my lord,' answered Zelzal, 'my father kept me in prison two years, after which he released me, and I abode with him another year, till I was restored to favour with him, when I slew him and his subjects submitted to me. I ruled them for a year's space, till, one night, I lay down to sleep, having thee in my mind, and saw thee, in a dream, fighting against Janshah's people; wherefore I took these thousand Marids and came to thee.' And Gherib marvelled at this happy chance. Then he took Janshah's treasures and those of the slain and appointed a ruler over the city, after which the Marids took up Gherib and the treasure and he lay the same night in the palace of Crystal. He abode Zelzal's guest six months, at the end of which time he desired to depart; so Zelzal gave him rich presents and despatched three thousand Marids, who brought the spoils of the city of Kerej and added them to those of Janshah. Then Zelzal loaded forty thousand Marids with the treasure and himself taking up Gherib, flew with his host towards the city of Isbanir, where they arrived at midnight.

Gherib looked and seeing the city invested on all sides by a vast army, as it were the swollen sea, said to Zelzal, 'O my brother, how cometh the city thus beleaguered and what is this army?' Then he alighted on the roof of his palace and cried out, saying, 'Ho, Morning Star! Ho, Mehdiyeh!' Whereupon they started up from sleep in amazement and said, 'Who calleth us at this hour?' Quoth he, 'It is I, your lord, Gherib of the wondrous deeds.' When the princesses heard their lord's voice, they rejoiced and so did the eunuchs and women. Then Gherib went down to them and they threw themselves upon him and raised cries of joy, that all the palace rang again and the captains of the army awoke and said, 'What is to do?' So they made for the palace and said to the eunuchs, 'Hath one of the King's women given birth to a child?' 'No,' answered they; 'but rejoice, for King Gherib hath returned to you.' So they rejoiced, and Gherib came forth to his comrades, who threw themselves upon him and kissed his hands and feet, returning thanks to God the Most High. Then he sat down on his throne, with his officers about him, and questioned them of the beleaguering army. 'O King,' answered they, 'they sat down before the city three days ago, and we know not what they want; for we have had with them neither battle nor speech.'

Now the name of the commander of the besieging army was Murad Shah and he had with him a hundred thousand horse and three thousand foot, besides two hundred tribesmen of the Jinn; and the manner of his coming was on this wise. When the two men, whom Sabour had charged to drown his daughter Fekhr Taj, let her go, bidding her flee for her life, she went forth distracted, knowing not whither to go and saying, 'Where is thine eye, O Gherib, that thou mayst see my case?' and wandered on from place to place and country to country, till she came to a valley abounding in trees and streams, in whose midst stood a lofty and strong-builded castle, as it were one of the pavilions of Paradise. So she betook herself thither and entering the castle, found it hung and carpeted with stuffs of silk, and therein were a hundred beautiful damsels and great plenty of gold and silver vessels. When the damsels saw her, they came up to her and saluted her, deeming her of the damsels of the Jinn, and asked her of her case. Quoth she, 'I am the King's daughter of the Persians,' and told them all that had befallen her; which when they heard, they wept over her and condoled with her, saying, 'Take comfort and be of good cheer, for here shalt thou have meat and drink and raiment, and we all are thy handmaids.' She called down blessings on them and they brought her food, of which she ate till she was satisfied. Then said she to them, 'Who is the owner of this palace and lord over you?' Quoth they, 'King Selsal, son of Dal, is our master; he passes a night here once in every month and departs in the morning to rule over the tribes of the Jinn.'

So Fekhr Taj took up her abode with them and after five days she gave birth to a male child, as he were the moon. They cut the cord of his navel and anointing his eyes with kohl, named him Murad Shah, and he grew up in his mother's lap. After awhile came Selsal, riding on a paper-white elephant, as he were a tower plastered with gypsum, and attended by the troops of the Jinn. He entered the palace, where the hundred damsels met him and kissed the earth before him, and amongst them Fekhr Taj. When he saw her, he looked at her and said to the others, 'Who is yonder damsel?' And they answered, saying, 'She is the daughter of Sabour, King of the Persians and Turcomans and Medes.' Quoth he, 'Who brought her hither?' And they repeated to him her story; whereat he was moved to pity for her and said to her, 'Grieve not, but take patience till thy son be grown a man, when I will go to the land of the Persians and strike thy father's head from his shoulders and seat thy son on the throne in his stead.' So she rose and kissed his hands and blessed him.

Then she abode in the castle and her son grew up and was reared with the children of the King. They used to ride forth together a-hunting, and he became skilled in the chase of the wild beasts and of the ravening lions and ate of their flesh, till his heart became harder than the rock. When he reached the age of fifteen, his spirit waxed big in him and he said to Fekhr Taj, 'O my mother, who is my father?' 'O my son,' answered she, 'Gherib, King of Irak, is thy father and I am the King's daughter of the Persians,' and she told him her story. Quoth he, 'Did my grandfather indeed give orders to slay thee and my father Gherib?' And she answered, 'Yes.' Whereupon, 'By the claim thou hast on me for that thou rearedst me,' cried he, 'I will assuredly go to thy father's city and cut off his head and bring it to thee!' And she rejoiced in his speech.

Then he used to go a-riding with two hundred Marids till he grew to man's estate, when he fell to making raids and excursions in quest of plunder, till, one day, he attacked the city of Shiraz and took it and cut off the King's head, as he sat on his throne, and slew many of his troops, whereupon the rest, to the number of ten thousand horse, cried out for quarter and kissed his stirrups. He led them to Balkh, where he slew the King of the city and put his men to the rout and made himself master of the riches of the place. Thence he passed to Nourain, at the head of an army of thirty thousand horse, and the King of the city came out to him, with presents and tribute, and did him homage. Then he went on to Samarcand of the Persians and took the city, and after that to Akhlat and took that town also; nor was there any city he came to but he took it. On this wise he became at the head of a great army, and all the booty he made he divided among his soldiers, who loved him for his valour and munificence. At last he came to Isbanir el Medaïn and sat down before it, saying, 'Let us wait till the rest of my army come up, when I will seize on my grandfather and solace my mother's heart by striking off his head in her presence.' So he sent for her, and by reason of this, there was no battle for three days, at the end of which time Gherib and Zelzal arrived with the forty thousand Marids, laden with treasure. Presently came Fekhr Taj, and her son Murad Shah embraced her, saying, 'Abide in thy tent till I bring thy father to thee.' And she sought succour for him of the Lord of the Worlds, the Lord of the heavens and the earths.

Next morning, as soon as it was day, Murad Shah mounted and rode forth, with the two hundred Marids on his right hand and the kings of men on his left, whilst the drums beat a point of war. When Gherib heard this, he also took horse and calling his people to battle, rode out, with the Jinn on his right hand and the men on his left. Then came forth Murad Shah, armed cap-a-pie, and spurred his charger right and left, saying, 'O folk, let none come forth to me but your King. If he conquer me, he shall be lord of both armies, and if I conquer him, I will slay him, as I have slain others.' When Gherib heard his speech, he said, 'Avaunt, O dog of the Arabs!' And they drove at each other and thrust with spears, till they broke, then hewed at each other with swords, till the blades were notched; nor did they cease to advance and retreat and wheel and feint, till the day was half spent and their horses fell down under them, when they dismounted and gripped each other. Then Murad Shah lifted Gherib up and strove to dash him to the ground; but Gherib seized him by the ears and pulled them with his might, till it seemed to him as if the heavens were falling on the earth and he cried out, with his heart in his mouth, saying, 'I yield myself to thy mercy, O champion of the age!' So Gherib bound him, and the Marids his comrades would have charged and rescued him, but Gherib fell on them with a thousand Marids and was about to smite them down, when they cried out for quarter and threw down their arms.

Then Gherib returned to his pavilion, which was of green silk, embroidered with red gold and set with pearls and jewels, and seating himself on his throne, called for Murad Shah. So they brought him, shuffling in his fetters, and Gherib said to him, 'O dog of the Arabs, who art thou that thou shouldst ride forth and measure thyself against kings?' 'O my lord,' replied Murad Shah, 'reproach me not, for indeed I have excuse.' Quoth Gherib, 'What is thine excuse?' And he answered, saying, 'Know, O my lord, that I came out to avenge my mother and my father on Sabour, King of the Persians; for he would have slain them; but my mother escaped and I know not whether he killed my father or not.' 'By Allah! rejoined Gherib, 'thou art indeed excusable! But who were thy father and mother and what are their names?' Quoth Murad Shah, 'My father was Gherib, King of Irak, and my mother Fekhr Taj, daughter of King Sabour of Persia.' When Gherib heard this, he gave a great cry and fell down in a swoon. They sprinkled rosewater on him, till he came to himself, when he said to Murad Shah, 'Art thou indeed Gherib's son by Fekhr Taj?' And he answered, 'Yes.' Quoth Gherib, 'Thou art a champion, the son of a champion. Loose my son.' And Sehim and Kailjan went up to Murad Shah and loosed him.

Then Gherib embraced him and seating him beside himself, said to him, 'Where is thy mother?' 'She is with me in my tent,' answered Murad Shah; and Gherib said, 'Bring her to me.' So Murad Shah mounted and repaired to his camp, where his men met him, rejoicing in his safety, and asked him of his case; but he answered, saying, 'This is no time for questions.' Then he went in to his mother and told her what had passed; whereat she rejoiced with an exceeding joy. So he carried her to Gherib, and they embraced and rejoiced in each other. Then Fekhr Taj and Murad Shah embraced Islam and expounded the faith to their troops, who all made profession with heart and tongue. After this, Gherib sent for Sabour and his son Wird Shah and upbraided them for their evil dealing and expounded Islam to them; but they refused to profess. So he crucified them on the gate of the city and the people decorated the town and held high festival. Then Gherib crowned Murad Shah with the crown of the Chosroës and made him King of the Persians and Turcomans and Medes. Moreover, he made his uncle, King Damigh, King over Irak, and all peoples and lands submitted themselves to Gherib. Then he abode in his kingship, doing justice among his subjects, wherefore all the people loved him, and he and his wives and comrades ceased not from all delight and solace of life, till there came to them the Destroyer of Delights and Sunderer of Companies, and extolled be the perfection of Him whose glory endureth for ever and whose benefits embrace all His creatures! This is all that hath come down to us of the history of Gherib and Agib.

Words for the Dead

Sam W. Pisciotta

CONALL LEANED THE muskets against a birch and eased his son to the ground. By the time they had reached the boulder field, the moon had taken the sky, its light a pale echo of the sun. Too dark for Conall to check the wound, he reached down and snugged the bandage at his son's leg. Blood soaked the boy's pants, and the sticky fluid squelched between Conall's fingers as he cinched the cloth around Seamus's thigh. He hoped the bandage might staunch the bleeding until they reached their packs on the other side of the field. There, he could clean and re-dress the wound before they made the trek to the cabin. The boy needed proper care – the safety and warmth of a hearth, the attention of his mother – but moving Seamus had come with a cost. His condition had worsened.

Conall took a moment to steel his mettle. The trees to the east appeared as cutouts against the moonlit sky. Two years on, and the American frontier remained alien to him; its distances somehow longer, lonelier. Seamus moaned and Conall offered him small sips of water.

Conall cached the muskets beneath a wedge of granite. He didn't want to risk the extra weight and awkwardness of the guns as he carried Seamus over the boulders. Anyway, he was loath to look at the guns just now. His own musket had accidentally discharged during their hunt, and the ball had ripped through Seamus's leg. He nudged the boy to urge him awake.

"Ready, son?"

"Tired." The word puffed from Seamus like a blown seed.

"We need to move now." Seamus was a lean boy and, at twelve, just a head shorter than his father, big enough to make the haul back to the cabin a strain.

"Just leave me, Da," said Seamus. "I can't go no farther."

"Hey, hey! None of that now. Bear down and get yourself through this." Fear threatened to consume him, but he doused its fire, held it deep and hidden. If he were strong, Seamus would be strong. "Besides, you don't want to worry your mam. We need to go." Conall took his son's wrist and lugged him over his shoulder. Seamus screamed and the son's cry quaked through the father's heart. "Sorry, lad. It won't be long now."

Draped at his father's back, Seamus wilted and his breath grew ragged.

The boulder field skirted the base of the mountain they had hunted all day. Ahead lay thirty yards of tumbled rocks each the size of a sleeping wolfhound. His eyes strained to catch the moonlit edges of rock. Conall stepped on to the first boulder, keeping his center low. When he found his balance, he leaped to the next stone and then to a third. Several more hops took him deeper into the field, but when he stopped, he fought to keep his balance.

A fall in this jumble of stone would likely break his own leg, and then he'd never get Seamus home before the boy bled out. He slowed his mind, focused on the field ahead, then picked his path and took a step.

Just ahead, a dark shape the size of a grown man skulked on the boulders some twenty yards off – but it wasn't a man at all. At first, Conall thought it might be a bear, but its movements were unnatural. The shadow rose and dipped between the jumbled stone, and slithered as a great serpent in an arc around them.

Conall crouched and listened. Long gasps that ended in a scratchy moan. The black form panted and convulsed in the pallid light of moon and stars.

Conall glanced back to the muskets beneath the boulder. Too far away. Instead, he cried out. Shouted to drive the animal off.

It screeched and yawned and seemed to spit a string of words. *All the living know that they will die.* Clear as day, it mocked the Holy Writ.

He squatted and dropped Seamus from his shoulder to rest at his feet. He leaned in to check his son's breathing. From behind, the same dark voice hissed at his ear – *but the dead know nothing.*

Conall turned and lashed out with his fists at everything and nothing at all. And nothing at all was there. The creature had moved off a dozen paces, and its eyes gleamed in the wan light. He knew then what it was – a Sluagh, the fairy host of the dead.

The creature rose and winged past him, close enough to touch. Conall shielded his son and watched the Sluagh glide past. Its features were as delicate as those of a child, but beneath the pale and torn skin protruded the bone-hard beak of a bird, scissor-sharp below two sunken eyes; it was a nightmare caught between man and bird. And on its face an expression that chilled the heart with its twisted gospel: *You are powerless in the face of the darkness descending upon you.* When Conall's breath stilled with understanding, the Sluagh's smile widened to reveal rows of putrid teeth, teeth filed sharp on the souls of men.

He thought they had left such creatures behind when they made their way across the ocean to this new world. Before they left, he had buried such fairy lore with his youngest son back in Éire. But this thing had left its ancient mound, crossed the wide ocean to steal his eldest boy's soul.

Unnerved, Conall hunched across Seamus's flaccid body. This fiend would not take another son of his, not tonight. A seashell hung from a string around his son's neck, and the boy's mother wore the matching half – a memory of their home on Inis Cathaigh.

Conall pulled the necklace over Seamus's head and skipped across several boulders to place it on a flat ledge of stone. A sacrifice of a thing that had touched the boy. This was the old way, a sort of magic. Conall quick-stepped back to his son and addressed the Sluagh. He stirred the air with magic words, the most potent magic available to a son of Adam – a story true and from the heart.

"This boy," said Conall, shouting toward the Sluagh, "was born in Inis Cathaigh on a night filled with rain and heaven's light. He called out his arrival with the birth-cries of his mother, and pushed into this world on the joy of her tears."

The Sluagh split into smaller shadows resembling a conspiracy of ravens, each a lost soul so evil it couldn't burn in the fires of Hell. The flock took wing to close the distance; it swiped at Seamus, now unconscious from his pain. Conall bent as a shield, and the Sluagh flew back to reassemble on its perch in the rocks.

To weave a tale was an ancient way to pull the threads of Heaven. A proper story told from the heart could create a sort of net, a trap to hold the darkness within the web of words. If Conall could hold off the Sluagh long enough, he might get Seamus home to his mother. Máire would join him in the fight to heal the boy, but until then he'd have to fight alone. Conall spun his words.

"His name is Seamus Francis Griffin, born April 12th in the year of Our Lord seventeen-fifty-three." Conall caressed the boy's cheek. "He's a headstrong lad, and everyone says he's meant to be his own man."

The Sluagh lifted like fog above them. Leathery wings spread wide, its birdlike jaws snapping and grinding. Conall cradled his son. The beast would dive at any moment, but he continued to weave his tale, a memory from the heart.

"When we arrived in our new home, I took Seamus on his first hunt. He's a sensitive boy, and I knew it would be hard for him to bring down an animal. But a man must leave childish sentiment behind."

The Sluagh dropped with such speed that Conall fell back, leaving his son exposed. The sound of dark wings roiled the air, and the lights of heaven flickered. Seamus screamed. Talons clutched at the boy's breast, and beads of blood seeped into his muslin shirt. Conall thrashed his fists with panic, driving back the Sluagh.

He fought back with the magic of story. "When the moment came to drop the buck, Seamus froze. I took the shot for him. We tracked the deer half a mile before it dropped. When we found it in the brush, Seamus watched the animal draw its final breath. I noticed he was crying. He glanced at me as if I'd meant to judge him, so I turned away."

The veil around them thickened. Conall held his story true, for the truer the story, the more magic it held. "I wanted to comfort him, but I didn't. I couldn't."

Once again, the Sluagh sat at a distance. Waiting. Listening. Conall closed his eyes to the memory.

"I wanted to comfort him, but there is so little comfort in this world. It's a lesson best learned early." The Sluagh's wings beat at the night. "Brutal nature holds sovereignty over tenderness." The pain of withheld affection rose within him, but Conall knew the danger of tenderness. "This is Seamus Francis Griffin, destined to be a good man." Conall growled his words at the Sluagh. "So now I say, his soul does not belong to you."

The creature keened into the night, so loud and terrible it seemed to peel the stars from the sky. It curled and drifted as smoke across the boulders before settling at the far edge of the field. The necklace hadn't been taken, and Conall jumped over and snatched it off the rock. The magic of his story hadn't dispelled the nightmare. From across the field, the Sluagh's moan drifted on the breeze.

Despair filled his heart as he lifted Seamus into his arms. He leaped from boulder to boulder until he found himself at the opposite edge of the field. Their packs sat near the base of a forked birch. Conall jerked to a stop.

Next to the packs, in the moonlight as pale as bone's ash, stood his youngest son Fionn, come back from the dead.

The air rushed out of Conall's chest. His mind raced to catch hold of the solid world around him. His boy. Fionn. Standing beneath the tree as if he'd never died, like he'd been waiting for his Da and brother to come back from the hunt so that he could share a treasure he'd found. Conall fell to his knees, the weight of his older son now impossible to bear.

Fionn stood motionless beneath the tree, and moonlight lit the dead boy's face. Deeper still, pinpricks of starlight burned where Fionn's eyes once sat – his whole wan complexion eclipsed by a look of sorrow that tore at Conall's heart. Fionn. No more than six years on this earth the night he was taken.

The Sluagh had come that night as well, howling outside their cottage on Inis Cathaigh, called by the promise of death.

On the first night, Fionn complained of a headache, and his mother fed him tea made from feverfew. By morning he was vomiting and complaining of chill. By the third night, the pain had moved to his back, and the boy had no will to lift himself from his bed. By the fifth night, the Sluagh's cries filled the air around their home.

Fionn had fought the pox for over a week when the howls and moans from the menace began to pull at him. When the specter cried, the child would lapse into a torpor. Conall had tried the old magic on each night in succession. Story after story. But although his words were accurate, they lacked an inner truth. He knew his fault but couldn't summon the strength to break through the crust of his heart and reveal its core of tenderness and compassion. And then one morning while cutting wood for the hearth, Conall heard his wife scream out, a cry that tore the world in half.

After the clothing and bedding had been burnt, after their home had been emptied and cleaned, after their son had been laid in the ground, Conall had no will to stay in the family home. He used what little he'd saved to book passage to America.

Now here they were, and the Sluagh had come calling a second time. Fionn lifted his arm to point toward the tree line where the Sluagh rose and dipped above the ground.

It hadn't been satisfied with the sacrifice, and the story had failed to trap the Sluagh in magic. It was back for Seamus, and the boy began to talk and whimper in his sleep. When he looked again toward their packs beneath the tree, Fionn had vanished.

The Sluagh let out a mournful cry. Conall could bolt with Seamus the half-mile trek back to the cabin; he dreaded being outside with the creature and longed for the safety of home. But Seamus would die before they reached the farm. He had already lost a lot of blood, and the wound needed to be staunched and the bandages reset.

Conall glanced back at the creature waiting for his son. He picked up Seamus and carried him to the packs. He would take care of the leg before he tried for the cottage. He prayed that Máire would find her last son alive when he got there.

Conall leaned Seamus against a pack beneath the tree. The boy was half awake and groaning. By moonlight, Conall scratched at the ground and gathered kindling for a fire. He found twigs and larger branches a bit farther out, but he didn't want to leave his son alone with the Sluagh's wails growing louder.

Conall didn't notice the tremor in his hands until he tried to strike the flint on to his knife. Fionn had appeared so gaunt and hollow, and there seemed to be a longing there as well. A thread of shame stitched through the memory of him. Conall had failed to save his boy. He heaved a breath to calm himself, then sent sparks into the cattail char he'd pulled from his tinderbox; he blew an ember bright enough to bring into the kindling nest. Flames cracked upward through the dry twigs and pushed back at the night.

Conall searched the darkness past the fire for another glimpse of his youngest boy. If he could reach across the veil and take Fionn's hand, lead him back to the fire, could he find the strength to show him tenderness? Was it too much to ask for a second chance?

The spirit wailed, and a different sort of ember flared inside him. Searing and consuming. The Sluagh had taken Fionn and now it wanted Seamus.

Conall unwrapped the blood-soaked bandages, and dark fluid oozed from the boy's leg. Thankfully, the ball had passed through, but the flesh was torn and ragged. Too much blood had been lost trying to get Seamus back to the cabin. Conall cursed the decision to move his son at all. He should have let Seamus rest back in the glade, staunched the leg's bleeding, and let him sleep for the night. Instead, he'd panicked – afraid to be alone in the woods with his injured son, afraid that he wouldn't be able to do enough, that he wouldn't be father enough to save him.

Caring for the boys had always been Máire's job, she was infinitely tender and calm in the face of sickness and injury. She held an inner trust that if she gave a thing her full attention, all would work out right; it was a belief he'd never shared. And never understood. At the end of Fionn's life, Conall had felt sick that he had been right. Things hadn't turned out well. In the face of so much loss, it was easy to retreat further inside.

Conall was shaken from his cold thoughts by a whisper at his ear. *A locked heart is safest.* He pivoted toward the taunt. The Sluagh had closed the distance by half. It danced above the ground – a bow, a turn, a lightness that mocked the joy in men's hearts. *Dance to forget that the grave is waiting.* As the Sluagh's wails grew louder, Seamus began to thrash in his sleep, mumbling an incoherent cry for help. Before long, the creature would fight to rip his son from this earth, to carry his soul into the night.

Just behind the Sluagh, Fionn stepped out from the shadowed trees.

The sight of his dead son shook him a second time, and Conall rocked back on his heels as if he might increase the distance between that dark world and his own, between the land of the dead and this new world where he fought to hold on to his last child. Even at this distance, the whisper on Fionn's lips pierced the night, a whimper that begged for understanding. *Father*, he said, and *Father* he repeated.

"Son," Conall whispered back. And an avalanche of shame piled on to him. Fear had caused him to draw away from his youngest boy. Alive or dead, Fionn was his son. He deserved better. Had always deserved better. Conall's heart pounded against the hard shell built around it, a hardness passed down from his own father, the belief that strength and safety meant hiding your weakness. If the darkness knew what you most loved, it would surely come for it. And the weakness he most feared exposing was his love for his sons.

He'd learned to temper his sorrow and joy. It was a sort of leveling of the plowland, smoothing out the highs and lows, but the result was a wasteland that would never bear fruit. And Seamus was learning the lesson well, learning to face the darkness with a cold strength. And what good was it all? The darkness had found him anyway. One son dead and another one dying. He felt it keenly. His failure as a father of sons. And it was this failure to release the magic of words, the power of the heart, that had resulted in Fionn's death.

Father, Fionn repeated. And the shell encasing his heart split and cracked open.

A screech tore Conall from his murky thoughts. The Sluagh closed the distance, dipping and rising over the earth. The shade of night within it expanded and threatened to consume the entire world, and the howling revealed a hunger that nicked at Conall's bones.

Seamus cried in pain, his screams reaching a terrible crescendo. As the Sluagh weaved closer, the boy's distress increased. Seamus was fading.

Conall reached down into the shattered cauldron of his heart to dip into the magic there. He pulled out words, true and full of magic, and strung them together into the story of his son – not the living boy but the one he had already lost. Fionn.

"I want to tell you about my son Fionn Patrick Griffin, born on a November morning in the year of Our Lord, seventeen-fifty-seven, who came into this world on the joyful tears of his mother."

The Sluagh screeched and closed, clawing at them as it passed. Seamus lay unconscious, unable to fight back. Conall beat the air, waving his arms to push the creature back.

"I loved him from the first moment." He cried with urgency. "My sweat and blood. I gave my life to make his better. I thought the words unnecessary."

The Sluagh circled overhead, swirling the air into dark shadow.

"When Fionn lay dying in our home in Inis Cathaigh, I could barely sit in the same room with him. His wan complexion. The tears in his mother's eyes. And the pain was unbearable. I busied myself with the chores of life while his mother sat by our son. And I choked on that pain."

The Sluagh brushed against him with a cold grasp at Seamus. Conall closed his eyes and reached deeper.

"When at last I heard his mother's cry after Fionn had been taken, I left my wood splitting and walked behind the shed. I hid away and cried. Not letting my family see my pain, not allowing Máire or Seamus the chance to share the loss with me."

Sobs split him open, freeing the part of him that felt most human. "I was weak and too afraid to hold Fionn's hand as he stood at the edge." Conall took Seamus's hand in his own. "But I'm here now. And I'll walk Seamus into the dark as far as I'm allowed. And farther if he asks it of me."

The screams of the Sluagh filled the air. It strained against the words that bound it to the dark edge of the known world. Conall leaned toward Seamus, holding him close. The breeze rustled the leaves overhead, and a cricket chirped from the bushes behind him. A gentleness settled around them like the moonlight sprinkling the leaves on trees. Fionn had vanished, but Conall could feel him there, the warmth of him.

The Sluagh had stopped its keening and was nowhere in sight.

"Da. My leg." It was Seamus, drenched in the sweat from his fight.

Conall's tears fell as he pulled his son tighter. If he were strong enough to express his love, then his son would be strong too. Conall eased him back to the earth.

The magic had bought him time. Time to fight and time to heal. The cabin wasn't far, and Máire would hold their son again, but that could wait until the morning. Tonight, Conall would care for him.

Seamus reached for his father's hand, and the moonlight reached from the old world to the new. Conall smiled and reached back.

Tangled Tales of Jumbies and Silk Cotton Trees

Josephine Queen

WE WALK THROUGH the forest in the order we were born. Long-limbed Gwendolyn with her tightly braided hair strides ahead. Lily, who usually trails behind, slopes along in the middle, throwing glances back at me every few steps. It was Lily who found the piglet and brought all this trouble down on us. But Gwen made me carry it. It squeals and squeals like it thinks it's going to slaughter. Like it knows.

The trees grow close together this deep in the forest. Their roots huddle like elders at a church meeting, whispering secrets and making plans. I scratch at my arms where the biting bugs nip and shift the cloth sack that bounces at my hip. The weight of the piglet is strangely calming. Its grunts and cries intertwine with the language of the evening: the shushing of the leaves, the calling of the birds above the canopy, the scurrying and slithering of things unseen in the undergrowth. We'll walk backwards going home, so the jumbie can't follow us. But now we walk forwards – through the soup of the humid evening.

Lily slows, her short legs no match for the trek. Her yellow dress is sticking to her back. She looks at me again. I shrug. What am I to do? She brought the piglet into our home. There are no birthing sows for miles around. She should have known better.

* * *

The piglet had scuffled across the just-swept floor of the house, got under Mama's feet and stunk up the air in the kitchen. The cook-up rice bubbled in the pot on the stove, and Mama told the piglet it would be dinner if it got too close.

"Me nah tell you again. Get out." Mama shooed Lily and the piglet from the kitchen with her ladle.

Lily sat on our bed, shoulders heaving, whispering into the piglet's ear. I swear that creature looked at me with black eyes gleaming and a smile behind its snout.

Mama took ill that night. As the hot wind rolled in from the hills and shook the chimney stack, rustled the hen house and colored our dreams, a fever rolled in beneath Mama's skin. When we tried to wake her the next morning, her eyes twitched behind yellowed lids and sweat poured from her into the buckets we laid around her mattress.

The piglet foraged through the cassava; it ate leftover stew from the cook-pot and overturned jars of guava jelly and semolina; it sat on its haunches and smiled its wicked smile as Gwen hustled me out the door to fetch Aunty Aquiles.

There's no doctor in the village, the closest lives in the next town. Aunty Aquiles is the best thing we have. She uses nature to heal from a shack down by the canal. I didn't want to be the one to go. Aunty speaks Broke Broke English; her tongue wrapping around the local language like a lover, but spilling words I don't understand.

Gwendolyn pushed me out the door. "Tell her, Mama lossing away and she needs to come quick."

Aunty had walked to our home hunched over in her apron, a basket of remedies clasped in her hand. Her skin was the darkest brown, the lines on her face deep and twisted, a map of rivers and canyons, her eyes milky with memories.

Mama moaned from her fever dream. Aunty instructed Gwendolyn to boil water and my sister left the room. Aunty laid out sweetbroom and the candles of the carrion-crow bush; stems of black sage and jars of turmeric, the glass stained yellow; shards of lemongrass and leaves of a madar plant.

The piglet ran from the dark corner of our mother's room with a squeal. Aunty Aquiles threw up her hands, jars of herbs cracked open on the floor.

"Dat wutless pig got jumbie in it."

Jumbie. Every night, Gwendolyn would tell us tales as we huddled in our bed, listening to the rats scratching and the branches of the monkey-apple tree tap-tap-tapping at the door. *The jumbies,* she'd whisper, *are the spirits of evil people.* She told us about Baccoo and Ole Higue. We would imagine the elongated and twisted shadows that danced across the floor belonged to Moon Gazer and we'd hide beneath the covers.

Aunty Aquiles glared at Lily and me, looking deep into our eyes to discover which of us brought evil into the house. Gwendolyn came back into the room with a pot of hot water. Aunty pushed past her, through the curtain that divided Mama's room from the rest of the house.

"Me gaan fetch de Obeah man."

Aunty said something more to Gwendolyn that I couldn't unravel.

"What'd she say?" whispered Lily.

"She said we should leave salt on the doorstep after she takes the piglet outside."

I frowned. "Why? Pigs like salt, they..."

"Nah. The jumbie like to count. They can't come in the house until they count all the grains. It gives her time to find the Obeah man."

I'd heard tales of him – light-skinned, gold-toothed practitioner of Obeah – conjuring spirits, speaking in tongues and drifting between worlds. He lives in the corners and dark alleys of the village – we know to only walk in the sunlit spaces.

Squeals and shouts erupted from beyond the curtain, it sounded as if Aunty was wrestling with the piglet, pulling the evil from its heart. Lily grabbed my arm, her mouth open wide. I rushed to the window just as Aunty left the house and hustled down the road, waving her arms about her head as if insects were bothering her.

"She look fine," I said. But there was something odd about the way she moved – upright and stiff, not hunched and shuffling.

There was a snuffle at the curtain. Lily knelt and hugged the piglet. Gwendolyn pulled our sister up by the cuff of her dress.

"He has to go," Gwen said. "He's got jumbie and we have to take him to the silk cotton tree."

I shook my head. "Gwen, that's not right. Jumbies don't have anything to do with—"

"It's true. We have to sacrifice him on the roots of the silk cotton tree. The spirits will take it as a blessing and the jumbie will be sent screaming to the Underworld. It's where the roots go," Gwen said. "And the branches go up to Heaven." She raised her arms above her head, to mime branches reaching for the sky.

Gwendolyn arrived in the world seven minutes before Lily and thirteen minutes before me. She takes her eldest-sister duties seriously and learned to understand the patois of our elders before she could crawl. We send her to eavesdrop on stories and village gossip. But those tales sometimes get tangled up in each other.

Mama moaned from her bed. Her fever didn't care about the order of stories.

"Well, no matter. We need to get rid of the jumbie. Mama don't have time," I said.

We poured a mountain of salt on to the doorstep as we left. Gwendolyn pushed the piglet into a sack and handed it to me. We both ignored Lily's wails as we crossed over to the forest.

* * *

A bird screeches above us, and I startle. The world beneath the canopy is darkening. I feel the pull of night as the sun drifts to the horizon. The land will swallow the light soon enough. We will go home in the dark.

In the gathering shadows beneath the trees, I wish I could forget about the stories of jumbies.

The piglet has settled, seeming to accept its fate. Gwendolyn has Mama's chopping knife, she's using it to clear vines, but it will soon spill blood. Lily walks in silence, her head down. Occasionally she swipes at her face with one hand or the other.

"Are you sure this will work?" I call, thinking of Mama, caught in her sickness. I wonder if Aunty has found the Obeah man yet, if he has started his bargaining with the spirits to let Mama go.

"Yes, of course," says Gwendolyn. "Look."

The silk cotton towers above the other trees. Its roots lay across the forest floor like an old man's hands across a felt-covered table; veined and gnarled and reaching. I have to crane my neck to see where the trunk starts. I imagine the broiling pits that lie beneath the tree, the Underworld. I turn to Gwendolyn who is kneeling with the knife by her side. She places a piece of sugar cake and a bottle containing a splash of rum between the giant spades of the tree's roots. Lily sniffles beside her.

"They used to bury treasure under the trees," Gwendolyn says. "Then they'd kill and bury the slave they got to do the work, so he'd guard it. Now you have to leave gifts otherwise…" she slices her finger across her throat.

"If you kill the piglet will the jumbie leave?" I'm still not sure. The piglet, when I peer in at it, seems less somehow. I think of the sounds in the kitchen before Aunty Aquiles left. "It looks like… just a piglet," I say to myself.

"Bring it here."

I do as Gwendolyn says and we crouch together by the roots. Lily joins us, her face shiny with tears, but she squeezes her lips together, containing her grief.

"Alice." Gwendolyn is looking at me. She points at the sack. "The pig."

I open the sack and nudge the bottom of it to rouse the piglet. It snorts and trundles out of the sack and into the mud. I forget, for a second, that it's a wild animal, and watch stupidly as it bolts from us.

"Gyal! Why are you so backward tinking?" Gwendolyn's words fall into our elders' patois when her anger surfaces. She jumps up and chases the piglet through the trees. I'm a second behind her, scolding myself before she does for letting it slip away.

We run through brambles and spiderwebs, thorns grab at our bare arms and legs. The world beneath the canopy is darkening and I don't want to be out here when night washes over the forest.

Lily falls behind, she trips over roots and kicks at the undergrowth, waking snakes and spiders and spirits best left to rest. The twilit forest begins to come alive; monkeys howl, bats chirrup and squeak as they dive for insects between the trees, something chitters close by. It's a sound I don't recognize.

"Lily, hurry." But my sister trails with her head down. Gwendolyn looks over her shoulder as she pushes through the forest, frowning at us.

"You want Baccoo to get you? Come nah."

The light drains from the forest and darkness seeps into every crevice. Red dots blink in the gloom, like demon eyes marking our progress. The chittering sounds again, closer this time. It echoes as if whatever makes the sound surrounds us, a presence waiting to enshroud us completely. Lily catches up to me and takes hold of my hand. Hers is cold and damp.

"Alice," she whispers. "What is it?"

I hear rustling close by and imagine a large cat stalking us, its sleek body close to the ground, empty eyes following us.

"It's nothing. Hush nah." But I hold tight to her hand and we creep quietly through the forest, trying to be as silent as any predator.

We've gone deeper into the forest than we've ever gone before. The ground before us reflects the canopy and it takes me a second to understand we've reached the edge of a pool. The water is black and something bubbles from beneath the surface, sending the smell of decay into the humid evening. Things with mottled and oil-rainbowed scales arch their backs above the surface, before sliding down into the noxious water. Lily is still holding my hand and she squeezes my fingers painfully. A small, pale thing lies prone at the edge of the water. It's difficult to see in the gloom, but something glistens red in its center. Gwendolyn turns, wide-eyed, to me. She grabs my arm and pulls me away from the pool, but not before I've seen that it's the piglet we've been following. We turn and walk quickly back the way we came.

Red pinpricks blink from the shadows. I hear the chittering in the distance, then right by my ear, as if whatever makes it travels swift through the forest. The sound of teeth chattering comes from the canopy above and laughter bubbles from the trees. The forest feels larger somehow and filled with things that lurk just beyond our sight. But we can feel them; their hot breath, their hunger, their need. We come back around to the silk cotton tree, its branches cradle the moon. Something slithers and waits in the roots, its eyes glowing from the gloom.

"Show yourself." Gwendolyn's voice shakes.

The thing cackles and chortles and unwinds itself from the tree. It has long, many-jointed legs and its head is large. Yellow eyes gleam from its narrow face and the moonlight that struggles through the trees glints off razor-sharp teeth. The creature – a jumbie – clacks those teeth together and sniffs at the air, its nostrils flaring impossibly wide.

Its voice, when it speaks, is one of things that live underground with throats filled with grave dirt and maggots. "Mmm, me tink you gaan give me summa dat fine, fine spirit, nah?" It cocks its head at us, smiling. My skin sets to crawling and I'm rooted to the ground. The thing moves closer – slowly, slowly.

I point at the bottle that still sits between the spade-like roots of the silk cotton tree. "That's the only spirit we have."

"Nah. Me smell dat fine wine dat run in your veins." It sniffs at the air again, a tongue flickers out of its maw, impossibly long and gray.

Gwendolyn pulls at me. I take a step back, but the creature skitters forward, now just a few inches away. I smell rot on its hot breath. Suddenly Lily reaches into her dress pocket and pulls out a small bag. She throws it at the creature and its yellow eyes follow the bag's arc through the air. It lands on the leaf-strewn ground, rice grains spill from it. I bless Lily for her forethought. The jumbie slithers back to the tree, snatching up the bag as it goes, brushing the spilled rice grains into a pile. It folds its legs beneath itself and begins counting the grains.

We turn and run into the darkness, the night birds cry at our hurried passage. We touch the rough trunks of trees and follow the stars that blink beyond the canopy, finding our way through the shadows. We feel home before we see it and, instinctively, turn around and walk backwards to the edge of the trees. If the jumbie followed us, this will confuse it. As the trees thin, I peer over my shoulder. Our house sits by the side of the road, silhouetted against the moonlit sky. There are no lights in the windows. A figure hunches on the doorstep, passing something from one hand to the other.

"Gwen," I whisper. She stops beside me and turns.

"A jumbie," she says.

How did the jumbie get ahead of us? We left it counting rice grains below the silk cotton tree. Is this another? We stand beneath the broad limbs of the last trees of the forest, on the very edge of the road that twists and turns through the countryside. The figure on the doorstep pauses and sniffs the air. It turns its head and its face is caught in the light that pours from the moon. I gasp.

"Aunty!"

Gwendolyn slaps her hand across my mouth. "Shhh!"

It *is* Aunty. She is crouched on the threshold of our house, and she is counting grains of salt. I wonder about Mama, twisting in her sheets in her room, drenched in the sweat of sickness. It's up to us to find the Obeah man, now. We'll enter the dark corners and side alleys to bargain with him, but first we wait for sunrise, for the light to kiss the village and chase the jumbie from our door. And we pray to all the spirits in the roots of the silk cotton tree, hoping a sugar cake and a splash of rum will save Mama's life.

Walnut-Tree House

Charlotte Riddell (Mrs J. H. Riddell)

Chapter I
The New Owner

MANY YEARS AGO there stood at the corner of a street leading out of Upper Kennington Lane a great red brick house, covering a goodly area of ground, and surrounded by gardens magnificent in their proportions when considered in relation to the populous neighbourhood mentioned.

Originally a place of considerable pretention; a gentleman's seat in the country probably when Lambeth Marsh had not a shop in the whole of it; when Vauxhall Gardens were still in nubilus; when no South-Western Railway was planned or thought of; when London was comparatively a very small place, and its present suburbs were mere country villages – hamlets lying quite remote from the heart of the city.

Once, the house in question had been surrounded by a small park, and at that time there were fish-ponds in the grounds, and quite a stretch of meadow-land within the walls. Bit by bit, however, the park had been cut up into building ground and let off on building leases; the meadows were covered with bricks and mortar, shops were run up where cows once chewed the cud, and the roar and rumble of London traffic sounded about the old house and the deserted garden, formerly quiet and silent as though situated in some remote part of the country.

Many a time in the course of the generations that had come and gone, been born and buried, since the old house was built, the freehold it covered changed hands. On most estates of this kind round London there generally is a residence, which passes like a horse from buyer to buyer. When it has served one man's need it is put up for sale and bid for by another. When rows and rows of houses, and line after line of streets, have obliterated all the familiar marks, it is impossible to cultivate a sentiment as regards property; and it is unlikely that the descendants of the first possessors of Walnut-Tree House who had grown to be country folk and lived in great state, oblivious of business people, and entertaining a great contempt for trade, knew that in a very undesirable part of London there still stood the residence where the first successful man of their family went home each day from his counting-house over against St. Mildred's Church, in The Poultry.

One very wet evening, in an autumn the leaves of which have been dead and gone this many a year, Walnut-Tree House, standing grim and lonely in the mournful twilight, looked more than ordinarily desolate and deserted.

There was not a sign of life about it; the shutters were closed – the rusty iron gates were fast locked – the approach was choked up with grass and weeds – through no chink did the light of a single candle flicker. For seven years it had been given over to rats and mice and blackbeetles; for seven years no one had been found to live in it; for seven years it had remained empty, while its owner wore out existence in fits of moody dejection or of wild frenzy in the madhouse close at hand; and now that owner was dead and buried and forgotten, and the new owner was returning to take possession. This new owner had written to his lawyers, or rather he had written to the lawyers of his late relative, begging them to request the person in charge of the house to have rooms prepared for his arrival; and, when the train drew into the station at Waterloo, he was met by one of the clerks in Messrs Timpson and Co.'s office, who, picking out Mr. Stainton, delivered to that gentleman a letter from the firm, and said he would wait and hear if there were any message in reply.

Mr. Stainton read the letter – looked at the blank flyleaf – and then, turning back to the first words, read what his solicitors had to say all through once again, this time aloud.

"The house has stood empty for more than seven years," he said, half addressing the clerk and half speaking to himself. "Must be damp and uninhabitable; there is no one living on the premises. Under these circumstances we have been unable to comply with your directions, and can only recommend you to go to an hotel till we are able personally to discuss future arrangements."

"Humph," said the new owner, after he had finished. "I'll go and take a look at the place, anyhow. Is it far from here, do you know?" he asked, turning to the young man from Timpsons'.

"No, sir; not very far."

"Can you spare time to come over there with me?" continued Mr. Stainton. The young man believed that he could, adding, "If you want to go into the house we had better call for the key. It is at an estate agent's in the Westminster Bridge Road."

"I cannot say I have any great passion for hotels," remarked the new owner, as he took his seat in the cab.

"Indeed, sir?"

"No; either they don't suit me, or I don't suit them. I have led a wild sort of life: not much civilisation in the bush, or at the goldfields, I can tell you. Rooms full of furniture, houses where a fellow must keep to the one little corner he has hired, seem to choke me. Then I have not been well, and I can't stand noise and the trampling of feet. I had enough of that on board ship; and I used to lie awake at nights and think how pleasant it would be to have a big house all to myself, to do as I liked in."

"Yes, sir," agreed the clerk.

"You see, I have been used to roughing it, and I can get along very well for a night without servants."

"No doubt, sir."

"I suppose the house is in substantial repair – roof tight, and all that sort of thing?"

"I can't say, I am sure, sir."

"Well, if there is a dry corner where I can spread a rug, I shall sleep there tonight."

The clerk coughed. He looked out of the window, and then he looked at Messrs. Timpsons' client.

"I do not think—" he began, apologetically, and then stopped.

"You don't think what?" asked the other.

"You'll excuse me, sir, but I don't think – I really do not think, if I were you, I'd go to that house tonight."

"Why not?"

"Well, it has not been slept in for nearly seven years, and it must be blue mouldy with damp; and if you have been ill, that is all the more reason you should not run such a risk. And, besides—"

"Besides?" suggested Mr. Stainton. "Out with it! Like a postscript, no doubt, that 'besides' holds the marrow of the argument."

"The house has stood empty for years, sir, because – there is no use in making any secret of it – the place has a bad name."

"What sort of a bad name – unhealthy?"

"Oh, no!"

"Haunted?"

The clerk inclined his head. "You have hit it, sir," he said.

"And that is the reason no one has lived there?"

"We have been quite unable to let the house on that account."

"The sooner it gets unhaunted, then, the better," retorted Mr. Stainton. "I shall certainly stop there tonight. You are not disposed to stay and keep me company, I suppose?"

With a little gesture of dismay the clerk drew back. Certainly, this was one of the most unconventional of clients. The young man from Timpsons' did not at all know what to make of him.

"A rough sort of fellow," he said afterwards, when describing the new owner; "boorish; never mixed with good society, that sort of thing."

He did not in the least understand this rich man, who treated him as an equal, who objected to hotels, who didn't mind taking up his abode in a house where not even a drunken charwoman could be induced to stop, and who calmly asked a stranger on whom he had never set eyes before – a clerk in the respectable office of Timpson and Co., a young fellow anxious to rise in the world, careful as to his associates, particular about the whiteness of his shirts and the sit of his collar and the cut of his coats – to "rough" things with him in that dreadful old dungeon, where, perhaps, he might even be expected to light a fire.

Still, he did not wish to offend the new owner. Messrs. Timpson expected him to be a profitable client; and to that impartial firm the money of a boor would, he knew, seem as good as the money of a count.

"I am very sorry," he stammered; "should only have felt too much honoured; but the fact is – previous engagement—"

Mr. Stainton laughed.

"I understand," he said. "Adventures are quite as much out of your line as ghosts. And now tell me about this apparition. Does the 'old man' walk?"

"Not that I ever heard of," answered the other. "Is it, then, the miserable beggar who tried to do for himself?"

"It is not the late Mr. Stainton, I believe," said the young man, in tone which mildly suggested that reference to a client of Timpsons' as a "miserable beggar" might be considered bad taste.

"Then who on earth is it?" persisted Mr. Stainton.

"If you must know, sir, it is a child – a child who has driven every tenant in succession out of the house."

The new owner burst into a hearty laugh – a laugh which gave serious offence to Timpsons' clerk.

"That is too good a joke," said Mr. Stainton. "I do not know when I heard anything so delicious."

"It is a fact, whether it be delicious or not," retorted the young man, driven out of all his former propriety of voice and demeanour by the contemptuous ridicule this "digger" thought fit to cast on his story; "and I, for one, would not, after all I have heard about your house, pass a night in it – no, not if anybody offered me fifty pounds down."

"Make your mind easy, my friend," said the new owner, quietly. "I am not going to bid for your company. The child and I can manage, I'll be bound, to get on very comfortably by ourselves."

Chapter II
The Child

IT WAS LATER on in the same evening; Mr. Stainton had an hour previously taken possession of Walnut-Tree House, dismissed his cab, bidden Timpsons' clerk good evening, and, having ordered in wood and coals from the nearest greengrocer, besides various other necessary articles from various other tradesmen, he now stood by the front gate waiting the coming of the goods purchased.

As he waited, he looked up at the house, which in the uncertain light of the street lamps appeared gloomier and darker than had been the case even in the gathering twilight.

The long rows of shuttered windows, the silent solemnity of the great trees, remnants of a once goodly avenue that had served to give its name to Walnut-Tree House; the appalling silence of everything within the place, when contrasted with the noise of passing cabs and whistling street boys, and men trudging home with unfurled umbrellas and women scudding along with draggled petticoats, might well have impressed even an unimpressionable man, and Edgar Stainton, spite of his hard life and rough exterior, was impressionable and imaginative.

"It has an 'uncanny' look, certainly," he considered; "but is not so cheerless for a lonely man as the 'bush'; and though I am not over-tired, I fancy I shall sleep more soundly in my new home than I did many a night at the goldfields. When once I can get a good fire up I shall be all right. Now, I wonder when those coals are coming!"

As he turned once again towards the road, he beheld on its way the sack of fuel with which the nearest greengrocer said he thought he could – indeed, said he would – "oblige" him. A ton – half a ton – quarter of a ton, the greengrocer affirmed would be impossible until the next day; but a sack – yes – he would promise that. Bill should bring it round; and Bill was told to put his burden on the truck, and twelve bundles of wood, "and we'll make up the rest tomorrow," added Bill's master, with the air of one who has conferred a favour.

In the distance Mr. Stainton descried a very grimy Bill, and a very small boy, coming along with the truck leisurely, as though the load had been Herculean.

Through the rain he watched the pair advancing and greeted Bill with a glad voice of welcome.

"So you've come at last; that's right. Better late than never. Bring them this way. I'll have this small lot shot in the kitchen for the night."

"Begging your pardon, sir," answered Bill, "I don't think you will – that is to say, not by me. As I told our governor, I'll take 'em to the house as you've sold 'em to the house, but I won't set a foot inside it."

"Do you mean to say you are going to leave them out on the pavement?" asked Mr. Stainton.

"Well, sir, I don't mind taking them to the front door if it'll be a convenience."

"That will do. You are a brave lot of people in these parts I must say."

"As for that," retorted Bill, with sack on back and head bent forward, "I dare say we're as brave about here as where you come from."

"It is not impossible," retorted Mr. Stainton; "there are plenty of cowards over there too."

With a feint of being very much afraid, Bill, after he had shot his coals on the margin of the steps, retreated from the door, which stood partly open, and when the boy who brought up the wood was again out with the truck, said, putting his knuckles to his eyebrows:

"Beg pardon, sir, but I suppose you couldn't give us a drop of beer? Very wet night, sir."

"No, I could not," answered Mr. Stainton, very decidedly. "I shall have to shovel these coals into the house myself; and, as for the night, it is as wet for me as it is for you."

Nevertheless, as Bill shuffled along the short drive – shuffling wearily – like a man who, having nearly finished one day's hard work, was looking forward to beginning another hard day in the morning, the new owner relented.

"Here," he said, picking out a sixpence to give him, "it isn't your fault, I suppose, that you believe in old women's tales."

"Thank you kindly, sir," Bill answered; "I am sure I am extremely obliged; but if I was in your shoes I wouldn't stop in that house – you'll excuse me, sir, meaning no offence – but I wouldn't; indeed I wouldn't."

"It seems to have got a good name, at any rate," thought Mr. Stainton, while retracing his steps to the banned tenement. "Let us see what effect a fire will have in routing the shadows."

He entered the house, and, striking a match, lighted some candles he had brought in with him from a neighbouring oil-shop.

Years previously the gas company, weary of receiving no profit from the house, had taken away their meter and cut off their connections. The water supply was in the same case, as Mr. Stainton, going round the premises before it grew quite dark, had discovered.

Of almost all small articles of furniture easily broken by careless tenants, easily removed by charwomen, the place was perfectly bare; and as there were no portable candlesticks in which to place the lights the new tenant was forced to make his illumination by the help of some dingy mirrors provided with sconces, and to seek such articles as he needed by the help of a guttering mould candle stuck in the neck of a broken bottle. After an inspection of the ground-floor rooms he decided to take up his quarters for the night in one which had evidently served as a library.

In the centre of the apartment there was the table covered with leather. Around the walls were bookcases, still well filled with volumes, too uninviting to borrow, too valueless in the opinion of the ignorant to steal. In one corner stood a bureau, where the man, who for so many years had been dead even while living, kept his letters and papers.

The floor was bare. Once a Turkey carpet had been spread over the centre of the polished oak boards, but it lay in its wonted place no longer; between the windows hung a convex mirror, in which the face of any human being looked horrible and distorted; whilst over the mantle-shelf, indeed, forming a portion of it, was a long, narrow glass, bordered by a frame ornamented with a tracery of leaves and flowers. The ceiling was richly decorated, and, spite of the dust and dirt and neglect of years, all the appointments of the apartment he had selected gave Edgar Stainton the impression that it was a good thing to be the owner of such a mansion, even though it did chance to be situated as much out of the way of fashionable London as the diggings whence he had come.

"And there is not a creature but myself left to enjoy it all," he mused, as he sat looking into the blazing coals. "My poor mother, how she would have rejoiced tonight, had she lived to be the mistress of so large a place! And my father, what a harbour this would have seemed after the storms that buffeted him! Well, they are better off, I know; and yet I cannot help thinking how strange it all is – that I, who went away a mere beggar, should come home rich, to be made richer, and yet stand so utterly alone that in the length and breadth of England I have not a relative to welcome me or to say I wish you joy of your inheritance."

He had eaten his frugal supper, and now, pushing aside the table on which the remains of his repast were spread, he began walking slowly up and down the room, thinking over the past and forming plans for the future.

As he was buried in reflection, the fire began to die down without his noticing the fact; but a sudden feeling of chilliness at length causing him instinctively to look towards the hearth, he threw some wood into the grate, and, while the flames went blazing up the wide chimney, piled on coals as though he desired to set the house alight.

While he was so engaged there came a knock at the door of the room – a feeble, hesitating knock, which was repeated more than once before it attracted Mr. Stainton's attention.

When it did, being still busy with the fire, and forgetting he was alone in the house, he called out, "Come in."

Along the panels there stole a rustling sort of touch, as if someone were feeling uncertainly for the handle – a curious noise, as of a weak hand fumbling about the door in the dark; then, in a similar manner, the person seeking admittance tried to turn the lock.

"Come in, can't you?" repeated Mr. Stainton; but even as he spoke he remembered he was, or ought to be, the sole occupant of the mansion.

He was not alarmed; he was too much accustomed to solitude and danger for that; but he rose from his stooping position and instinctively seized his revolver, which he had chanced, while unpacking some of his effects, to place on the top of the bureau.

"Come in, whoever you are," he cried; but seeing the door remained closed, though the intruder was evidently making futile efforts to open it, he strode half-way across the room, and then stopped, amazed.

For suddenly the door opened, and there entered, shyly and timidly, a little child – a child with the saddest face mortal ever beheld; a child with wistful eyes and long, ill-kept hair; a child poorly dressed, wasted and worn, and with the mournfullest expression on its countenance that face of a child ever wore.

"What a hungry little beggar," thought Mr. Stainton. "Well, young one, and what do you want here?" he added, aloud.

The boy never answered, never took the slightest notice of his questioner, but simply walked slowly round the room, peering into all the corners, as if looking for something. Searching the embrasures of the windows, examining the recesses beside the fire-place, pausing on the hearth to glance under the library table, and finally, when the doorway was reached once more, turning to survey the contents of the apartment with an eager and yet hopeless scrutiny.

"What is it you want, my boy?" asked Mr. Stainton, glancing as he spoke at the child's poor thin legs, and short, shabby frock, and shoes wellnigh worn out, and arms bare and lean and unbeautiful. "Is it anything I can get for you?"

Not a word – not a whisper; only for reply a glance of the wistful brown eyes.

"Where do you come from, and who do you belong to?" persisted Mr. Stainton.

The child turned slowly away.

"Come, you shall not get off so easily as you seem to imagine," persisted the new owner, advancing towards his visitor. "You have no business to be here at all; and before you go you must tell me how you chance to be in this house, and what you expected to find in this room." He was close to the doorway by this time, and the child stood on the threshold, with its back towards him.

Mr. Stainton could see every detail of the boy's attire – his little plaid frock, which he had outgrown, the hooks which fastened it; the pinafore, soiled and crumpled, tied behind with strings broken and knotted; in one place the skirt had given from the body, and a piece of thin, poor flannel showed that the child's under habiliments matched in shabbiness his exterior garments.

"Poor little chap," thought Mr. Stainton. "I wonder if he would like something to eat. Are you hungry, my lad?"

The child turned and looked at him earnestly, but answered never a word.

"I wonder if he is dumb," marvelled Mr. Stainton; and, seeing he was moving away, put out a hand to detain him. But the child eluded his touch, and flitted out into the hall and up the wide staircase with swift, noiseless feet.

Only waiting to snatch a candle from one of the sconces, Mr. Stainton pursued as fast as he could follow.

Up the easy steps he ran at the top of his speed; but, fast as he went, the child went faster. Higher and higher he beheld the tiny creature mounting, then, still keeping the same distance between them, it turned when it reached the top storey and trotted along a narrow corridor with rooms opening off to right and left. At the extreme end of this passage a door stood ajar. Through this the child passed, Mr. Stainton still following.

"I have run you to earth at last," he said, entering and closing the door. "Why, where has the boy gone?" he added, holding the candle above his head and gazing round the dingy garret in which he found himself.

The room was quite empty. He examined it closely, but could find no possible outlet save the door, and a skylight which had evidently not been opened for years.

There was no furniture in the apartment, except a truckle bedstead, a rush-bottomed chair, and a rickety washstand. No wardrobe, or box or press where even a kitten might have lain concealed.

"It is very strange," muttered Mr. Stainton, as he turned away baffled. "Very strange!" he repeated, while he walked along the corridor. "I don't understand it at all," he decided, proceeding slowly down the topmost flight of stairs; but then all at once he stopped.

"IT IS THE CHILD!" he exclaimed aloud, and the sound of his own voice woke strange echoes through the silence of that desolate house. "IT IS THE CHILD!" And he descended the principal staircase very slowly, with bowed head, and his grave, thoughtful face graver and more thoughtful than ever.

Chapter III
Seeking for Information

IT WAS ENOUGH to make any man look grave; and as time went on the new owner of Walnut-Tree House found himself pondering continually as to what the mystery could be which attached to the child he had found in possession of his property, and who had already driven tenant after tenant out of the premises. Inclined at first to regard the clerk's story as a joke, and his own experience on the night of his arrival a delusion, it was impossible for him to continue incredulous when he found, even in broad daylight, that terrible child stealing down the staircase and entering the rooms, looking – looking, for something it never found.

Never after the first horror was over did Mr. Stainton think of leaving the house in consequence of that haunting presence which had kept the house tenantless. It would have been worse than useless, he felt. With the ocean stretching between, his spirit would still be in the old mansion at Lambeth – his mental vision would always be watching the child engaged in the weary search to which there seemed no end – that never appeared to produce any result.

At bed and at board he had company, or the expectation of it. No apartment in the building was secure from intrusion. It did not matter where he lay; it did not matter where he ate; between sleeping and waking, between breakfast and dinner, whenever the notion seized it, the child came gliding in, looking, looking, looking, and never finding; not lingering longer than was necessary to be certain the object of its search was absent, but wandering hither and thither, from garret to kitchen, from parlour to bed-chamber, in that quest which still seemed fresh as when first begun.

Mr. Stainton went to his solicitors as the most likely persons from whom to obtain information on the subject, and plunged at once into the matter. "Who is the child supposed to be, Mr. Timpson?" he asked, making no secret that he had seen it.

"Well, that is really very difficult to say," answered Mr. Timpson.

"There was a child once, I suppose – a real child – flesh and blood?"

Mr. Timpson took off his spectacles and wiped them.

"There were two; yes, certainly, in the time of Mr. Felix Stainton – a boy and a girl."

"In that house?"

"In that house. They survived him."

"And what became of them?"

"The girl was adopted by a relation of her father's, and the – boy – died."

"Oh the boy died, did he? Do you happen to know what he died of?"

"No; I really do not. There was nothing wrong about the affair, however, if that is what you are thinking of. There never was a hint of that sort."

Mr. Stainton sat silent for a minute; then he said:

"Mr. Timpson, I can't shake off the idea that somehow there has been foul play with regard to those children. Who were they?"

"Felix Stainton's grandchildren. His daughter made a low marriage, and he cast her adrift. After her death the two children were received at Walnut-Tree House on sufferance – fed and clothed, I believe, that was all; and when the old man died the heir-at-law permitted them to remain."

"Alfred Stainton?"

"Yes; the unhappy man who became insane. His uncle died intestate, and he consequently succeeded to everything but the personalty, which was very small, and of which these children had a share."

"There was never any suspicion you say, of foul play on the part of the late owner?"

"Dear, dear! No; quite the contrary."

"Then can you throw the least light on the mystery?"

"Not the least; I wish I could."

For all that, Mr. Stainton carried away an impression Mr. Timpson knew more of the matter than he cared to tell; and was confirmed in this opinion by a chance remark from Mr. Timpson's partner, whom he met in the street almost immediately after.

"Why can't you let the matter rest, Mr. Stainton?" asked the Co. with some irritation of manner when he heard the object of their client's visit. "What is the use of troubling your head about a child who has been lying in Lambeth Churchyard these dozen years? Take my advice, have the house pulled down and let or sell the ground for building. You ought to get a pot of money for it in that neighbourhood. If there were a wrong done it is too late to set it right now."

"What wrong do you refer to?" asked Mr. Stainton eagerly, thinking he had caught Timpson's partner napping. But that gentleman was too sharp for him.

"I remarked if there were a wrong done – not that there had been one," he answered; and then, without a pause, added, "We shall hope to hear from you that you have decided to follow our advice."

But Mr. Stainton shook his head.

"I will not pull down the old house just yet," he said, and walked slowly away.

"There is a mystery behind it all," he considered. "I must learn more about these children.

Perhaps some of the local tradespeople may recollect them."

But the local tradespeople for the most part were newcomers – or else had not supplied "the house."

"So far as ever I could understand," said one "family butcher," irascibly sharpening his knife as he spoke, "there was not much to supply. *That* custom was not worth speaking of. I hadn't it, so what I am saying is not said on my own account. A scrag end of neck of mutton – a bit of gravy beef – two pennyworth of sheep's liver – that was the sort of thing. Misers, sir, misers; the old gentleman bad, and the nephew worse. A bad business, first and last. But what else could be expected? When people as can afford to live on the fat of the land never have a sirloin inside their doors, why, worse must come of it. No, sir, I never set eyes on the children to my knowledge; I only knew there were children by hearing one of them was dead, and that it was the poorest funeral ever crossed a decent threshold."

"Poor little chap," thought Mr. Stainton, looking straight out into the street for a moment; then added, "lest the family misfortunes should descend to me, you had better send round a joint to Walnut-Tree House."

"Lor', sir, are you the gentleman as is living there? I beg your pardon, I am sure, but I have been so bothered with questions in regard of that house and those children that I forget my manners when I talk about them. A joint, sir – what would you please to have?"

The new owner told him; and while he counted out the money to pay for it Mr. Parker remarked:

"There is only one person I can think of sir, likely to be able to give any information about the matter."

"And that is?"

"Mr. Hennings, at the 'Pedlar's Dog.' He had some aquaintance with the old lady as was housekeeper both to Mr. Felix Stainton and the gentleman that went out of his mind."

Following the advice, the new owner repaired to the 'Pedlar's Dog,' where (having on his first arrival at Walnut-Tree House ordered some creature comforts from that well-known public) he experienced a better reception than had been accorded to him by Mr. Parker.

"Do I know Walnut-Tree House, sir?" said Mr. Hennings, repeating his visitor's question. "Well, yes, rather. Why, you might as well ask me, do I know the 'Pedlar's Dog.' As boy and man I can remember the old house for close on five-and-fifty years. I remember Mr. George Stainton; he used to wear a skull-cap and knee-breeches. There was an orchard then where Stainton Street is now, and his whole time was taken up in keeping the boys out of it. Many a time I have run from him."

"Did you ever see anything of the boy and girl who were there, after Mr. Alfred succeeded to the property – Felix Stainton's grandchildren, I mean?" asked the new owner, when a pause in Mr. Henning's reminiscences enabled him to take his part in the conversation.

"Well, sir, I may have seen the girl, but I can't bring it to my recollection; the boy I do remember, however. He came over here two or three times with Mrs. Toplis, who kept house for both Mr. Staintons, and I took notice of him, both because he looked so peaky and oldfashioned, and also on account of the talk about him."

"There was talk about him, then?"

"Bless you, yes, sir; as much talk while he was living as since he died. Everybody thought he ought to have been the heir."

"Why?" enquired the new owner.

"Because there was a will made leaving the place to him."

Here was information. Mr. Stainton's heart seemed to stand still for a second and then leap on with excitement.

"Who made the will?"

"The grandfather, Felix Stainton, to be sure; who else should make it?"

"I did not mean that. Was it not drawn out by a solicitor?"

"Oh! Yes – now I understand you, sir. The will was drawn right enough by Mr. Quinance, in the Lambeth Road, a very clever lawyer."

"Not by Timpson, then? How was that?"

"The old man took the notion of making it late one night, and so Mrs. Toplis sent to the nearest lawyer she knew of."

"Yes; and then?"

"Well, the will was made and signed and witnessed, and everything regular; and from that day to this no one knows what has become of it."

"How very strange."

"Yes, sir, it is more than strange – unaccountable. At first Mr. Quinance was suspected of having given it up to Mr. Alfred; but Mrs. Toplis and Quinance's clerk – he has succeeded to the business now – say that old Felix insisted upon keeping it himself. So, whether he destroyed it or the nephew got hold of it, Heaven only knows; for no man living does, I think."

"And the child – the boy, I mean?"

"If you want to hear all about him, sir, Mrs. Toplis is the one to tell you. If you have a mind to give a shilling to a poor old lady who always did try to keep herself respectable, and who, I will say, paid her way honourable as long as she had a sixpence to pay it honourable with, you cannot do better than go and see Mrs. Toplis, who will talk to you for hours about the time she lived at Walnut-Tree House."

And with this delicate hint that his minutes were more valuable than the hours of Mrs. Toplis, Mr. Hennings would have closed the interview, but that his visitor asked where he should be able to find the housekeeper.

"A thousand pardons!" he answered, with an air; "forgetting the very cream and marrow of it, wasn't I? Mrs. Toplis, sir, is to be found in Lambeth Workhouse – and a pity, too."

Edgar Stainton turned away, heart-sick. Was this all wealth had done for his people and those connected with them?

No man seemed to care to waste a moment in speaking about their affairs; no one had a good word for or kindly memory of them. The poorest creature he met in the streets might have been of more use in the world then they. The house they had lived in mentioned as if a curse rested on the place; themselves only recollected as leaving everything undone which it befitted their station to do. An old servant allowed to end her days in the workhouse!

"Heaven helping me," he thought, "I will not so misuse the wealth which has been given me."

The slight put upon his family tortured and made him wince, and the face of the dead boy who ought to have been the heir seemed, as he hurried along the streets, to pursue and look on him with a wistful reproach.

"If I cannot lay that child I shall go mad," he said, almost audibly, "as mad, perhaps, as Alfred Stainton." And then a terrible fear took possession of him. The horror of that which is worse than any death made for the moment this brave, bold man more timid than a woman.

"God preserve my senses," he prayed, and then, determinedly putting that phantom behind him, he went on to the Workhouse.

Chapter IV
Brother and Sister

MR. STAINTON HAD expected to find Mrs. Toplis a decrepit crone, bowed with age and racked with rheumatism, and it was therefore like a gleam of sunshine streaming across his path to behold a woman, elderly, certainly, but carrying her years with ease, ruddy cheeked, clear eyed, upright as a dart, who welcomed him with respectful enthusiasm.

"And so you are Mr. Edgar, the son of the dear old Captain," she said, after the first greetings and explanations were over, after she had wiped her eyes and uttered many ejaculations of astonishment and expressions of delight. "Eh! I remember him coming to the house just after he was married, and telling me about the sweet lady his wife. I never heard a gentleman so proud; he never seemed tired of saying the words, 'My wife'."

"She was a sweet lady," answered the new owner.

"And so the house has come to you, sir? Well, I wish you joy. I hope you may have peace, and health, and happiness, and prosperity in it. And I don't see why you should not – no, indeed, sir."

Edgar Stainton sat silent for a minute, thinking how he should best approach his subject.

"Mrs. Toplis," he began at last, plunging into the very middle of the difficulty, "I want you to tell me about it. I have come here on purpose to ask you what it all means."

The old woman covered her face with her hands, and he could see that she trembled violently.

"You need not be afraid to speak openly to me," he went on. "I am quite satisfied there was some great wrong done in the house, and I want to put it right, if it lies in my power to do so. I am a rich man. I was rich when the news of this inheritance reached me, and I would gladly give up the property tomorrow if I could only undo whatever may have been done amiss."

Mrs. Toplis shook her head.

"Ah, sir; you can't do that," she said. "Money can't bring back the dead to life; and, if it could, I doubt if even you could prove as good a friend to the poor child sleeping in the churchyard yonder as his Maker did when He took him out of this troublesome world. It was just soul rending to see the boy the last few months of his life. I can't bear to think of it, sir! Often at night I wake in a fright, fancying I still hear the patter, patter of his poor little feet upon the stair."

"Do you know, it is a curious thing, but he doesn't frighten me," said Mr. Stainton; "that is when I am in the house; although when I am away from it the recollection seems to dog every step I take."

"What?" cried Mrs. Toplis. "*Have you, then, seen him too?* There what am I talking about? I hope, sir, you will forgive my foolishness."

"I see him constantly," was the calm reply.

"I wonder what it means! – I wonder what it can mean!" exclaimed the housekeeper, wringing her hands in dire perplexity and dismay.

"I do not know," answered the new owner, philosophically; "but I want you to help me to find out. I suppose you remember the children coming there at first?"

"Well, sir – well, they were poor Miss Mary's son and daughter. She ran away, you know, with a Mr. Fenton – made a very poor match; but I believe he was kind to her. When they were brought to us, a shivering little pair, my master was for sending them here. Ay, and he would have done it, too, if somebody had not said he could be made to pay for their keep. You never saw brother and sister so fond of one another – never. They were twins. But, Lor'! the boy was more like a father to the little girl than aught else. He'd have kept an apple a month rather than eat it unless she had half; and the same with everything. I think it was seeing that – watching the love they had, he for her and she for him, coming upon them unsuspected, with their little arms round one another's necks, made the old gentleman alter his mind about leaving the place to Mr. Alfred; for he said to me, one day, thoughtful like, pointing to them, 'Wonderful fond, Toplis!' and I answered, 'Yes, sir; for all the world like the Babes in the Wood;' not thinking of how lonely that meant—

"Shortly afterwards he took to his bed; and while he was lying there, no doubt, better thoughts came to him, for he used to talk about his wife and Miss Mary, and the Captain, your father, sir, and ask if the children were gone to bed, and such like – things he never used to mention before.

"So when he made the will Mr. Quinance drew out I was not surprised – no, not a bit.

Though before that time he always spoke of Mr. Alfred as his heir, and treated him as such."

"That will never was found," suggested Mr. Stainton, anxious to get at another portion of the narrative.

"Never, sir; we hunted for it high and low. Perhaps I wronged him, but I always thought Mr. Alfred knew what became of it. After the old gentleman's death the children were treated shameful – shameful. I don't mean beaten, or that like; but half-starved and neglected. He would not buy them proper clothes, and he would not suffer them to wear decent things if anybody else bought them. It was just the same with their food. I durs'n't give them even a bit of bread and butter unless it was on the sly; and, indeed, there was not much to give in that house. He turned regular miser. Hoarding came into the family with Mrs. Lancelot Stainton, Mr. Alfred's great grandmother, and they went on from bad to worse, each one closer and nearer than the last, begging your pardon for saying so, sir; but it is the truth."

"I fear so, Mrs. Toplis," agreed the man, who certainly was neither close nor near.

"Well, sir, at last, when the little girl was about six years old, she fell sick, and we didn't think she would get over the illness. While she was about at her worst, Mrs. May, her father's sister, chanced to be stopping up in London, and, as Mr. Alfred refused to let a doctor inside his doors, she made no more ado but wrapped the child up in blankets, sent for a cab, and carried her off to her own lodgings. Mr. Alfred made no objection to that. All he said as she went through the hall was:

"'If you take her now, remember, you must keep her.'

"'Very well,' she replied, 'I will keep her.'"

"And the boy? the boy?" cried Mr. Stainton, in an agony of impatience.

"I am coming to him, sir, if you please. He just dwindled away after his sister and he were parted, and died in December, as she was taken away in the July."

"What did he die of?"

"A broken heart, sir. It seems a queer thing to say about a child; but if ever a heart was broken his was. At first he was always wandering about the house looking for her, but towards the end he used to go up to his room and stay there all by himself. At last I wrote to Mrs. May, but she was ill when the letter got to her, and when she did come up he was dead. My word, she talked to Mr. Alfred! I never heard any one person say so much to another. She declared he had first cheated the boy of his inheritance, and then starved him to death; but that was not true, the child broke his heart fretting after his sister."

"Yes; and when he was dead—"

"Sir, I don't like to speak of it, but as true as I am sitting here, the night he was put in his coffin he came pattering down just as usual, looking, looking for his sister. I went straight upstairs, and if I had not seen the little wasted body lying there still and quiet, I must have thought he had come back to life. We were never without him afterwards, never; that, and nothing else, drove Mr. Alfred mad. He used to think he was fighting the child and killing it.When the worst fits were on him he tried to trample it under foot or crush it up in a corner, and then he would sob and cry, and pray for it to be taken away. I have heard he recovered a little before he died, and said his uncle told him there was a will leaving all to the boy, but he never saw such a paper. Perhaps it was all talk, though, or that he was still raving?'

"You are quite positive there was no foul play as regards the child?" asked Mr. Stainton, sticking to that question pertinaciously.

"Certain, sir; I don't say but Mr. Alfred wished him dead. That is not murder, though."

"I am not clear about that," answered Mr. Stainton.

Chapter V
The Next Afternoon

MR. STAINTON was trying to work off some portion of his perplexities by pruning the grimy evergreens in front of Walnut-Tree House, and chopping away at the undergrowth of weeds and couch grass which had in the course of years matted together beneath the shrubs, when his attention was attracted to two ladies who stood outside the great iron gate looking up at the house.

"It seems to be occupied now," remarked the elder, turning to her companion. "I suppose the new owner is going to live here. It looks just as dingy as ever; but you do not remember it, Mary."

"I think I do," was the answer. "As I look the place grows familiar to me. I do recollect some of the rooms, I am sure just like a dream, as I remember Georgie. What I would give to have a peep inside."

At this juncture the new owner emerged from amongst the bushes, and, opening the gate, asked if the ladies would like to look over the place.

The elder hesitated; whilst the younger whispered, "Oh, aunt, pray do!"

"Thank you," said Mrs. May to the stranger, whom she believed to be a gardener; "but perhaps Mr. Stainton might object."

"No; he wouldn't, I know," declared the new owner. "You can go through the house if you wish. There is no one in it. Nobody lives there except myself."

"Taking charge, I suppose?" suggested Mrs. May blandly.

"Something of that sort," he answered.

"I do not think he is a caretaker," said the girl, as she and her relative passed into the old house together.

"What do you suppose he is, then?" asked her aunt.

"Mr. Stainton himself."

"Nonsense, child!" exclaimed Mrs. May, turning, nevertheless, to one of the windows, and casting a curious glance towards the new owner, who was now, his hands thrust deep in his pockets, walking idly up and down the drive.

After they had been all over the place, from hall to garret, with a peep into this room and a glance into that, Mrs. May found the man who puzzled her leaning against one of the pillars of the porch, waiting, apparently, for their reappearance.

"I am sure we are very much obliged to you," she began, with a hesitation in her manner.

"Pray do not mention it," he said.

"This young lady has sad associations connected with the house," May proceeded, still doubtfully feeling her way.

He turned his eyes towards the girl for a moment, and, though her veil was down, saw she had been weeping.

"I surmised as much," he replied. "She is Miss Fenton, is she not?"

"Yes, certainly," was the answer; "and you are—"

"Edgar Stainton," said the new owner, holding out his hand.

"I am all alone here," he went on, after the first explanations were over. "But I can manage to give you a cup of tea. Pray do come in, and let me feel I am not entirely alone in England."

Only too well pleased, Mrs. May complied, and ten minutes later the three were sitting round a fire, the blaze of which leapt and flickered upon the walls and over the ceiling, casting bright lights on the dingy mirrors and the dark oak shelves.

"It is all coming back to me now," said the girl softly, addressing her aunt. "Many an hour Georgie and I have sat on that hearth seeing pictures in the fire."

But she did not see something which was even then standing close beside her, and which the new owner had witnessed approach with a feeling of terror that precluded speech.

It was the child! The child searching about no longer for something it failed to find, but standing at the girl's side still and motionless, with its eyes fixed upon her face, and its poor, wasted figure nestling amongst the folds of her dress.

"Thank Heaven she does not see it!" he thought, and drew his breath, relieved.

No; she did not see it – though its wan cheek touched her shoulder, though its thin hand rested on her arm, though through the long conversation which followed it never moved from her side, nor turned its wistful eyes from her face.

When she went away – when she took her fresh young beauty out of the house it seemed to gladden and light up – the child followed her to the threshold; and then in an instant it vanished, and Mr. Stainton watched for its flitting up the staircase all in vain.

But later on in the evening, when he was sitting alone beside the fire, with his eyes bent on the glowing coals, and perhaps seeing pictures there, as Mary said she and her brother had done in their lonely childhood, he felt conscious, even without looking round, that the boy was there once again.

And when he fell to thinking of the long, long years during which the dead child had kept faithful and weary watch for his sister, searching through the empty rooms for one who never came, and then bethought him of the sister to whom her dead brother had become but the vaguest of memories, of the summers and winters during the course of which she had probably forgotten him altogether, he sighed deeply; and heard his sigh echoed behind him in the merest faintest whisper.

More, when he, thinking deeply about his newly found relative and trying to recall each feature in her face, each tone of her voice, found it impossible to dissociate the girl grown to womanhood from the child he had pictured to himself as wandering about the old house in company with her twin brother, their arms twined together, their thoughts one, their sorrows one, their poor pleasures one – he felt a touch on his hand, and knew the boy was beside him, looking with wistful eyes into the firelight, too.

But when he turned he saw that sadness clouded those eyes no longer. She was found; the lost had come again to meet a living friend on the once desolate hearth, and up and down the wide, desolate staircase those weary little feet pattered no longer.

The quest was over, the search ended; into the darksome corners of that dreary house the child's glance peered no longer.

She was come! Through years he had kept faithful watch for her, but the waiting was ended now.

That night Edgar Stainton slept soundly; and yet when morning dawned he knew that once in the darkness he wakened suddenly and was conscious of a small, childish hand smoothing his pillow and touching his brow.

Sweet were the dreams which visited his rest subsequently; sweet as ought to be the dreams of a man who had said to his own soul – and meant to hold fast by words he had spoken:

"As I deal by that orphan girl, so may God deal with me!"

Chapter VI
The Missing Will

ERE LONG THERE were changes in the old house. Once again Mrs. Toplis reigned there, but this time with servants under her – with maids she could scold and lads she could harass.

The larder was well plenished, the cellars sufficiently stocked; windows formerly closely shuttered now stood open to admit the air; and on the drive grass grew no longer – too many footsteps passed that way for weeds to flourish.

It was Christmas-time. The joints in the butchers' shops were gay with ribbons; the grocers' windows were tricked out to delight the eyes of the – children, young and old, who passed along. In Mr. May's house up the Clapham Road all was excitement, for the whole of the family – father, mother, grown-up sons and daughters – girls still in short frocks and boys in round jackets – were going to spend Christmas Eve with their newly-found cousin, whom they had adopted as a relation with a unanimity as rare as charming.

Cousin Mary also was going – Cousin Mary had got a new dress for the occasion, and was having her hair done up in a specially effective manner by Cissie May, when the toilette proceedings were interrupted by half a dozen young voices announcing:

"A gentleman in the parlour wants to see you, Mary. Pa says you are to make haste and come down immediately."

Obediently Mary made haste as bidden and descended to the parlour, to find there the clerk from Timpsons' who met Mr. Stainton on his arrival in London.

His business was simple, but important. Once again he was the bearer of a letter from Timpson and Co., this time announcing to Miss Fenton that the will of Mr. Felix Stainton had been found, and that under it she was entitled to the interest of ten thousand pounds, secured upon the houses in Stainton Street.

"Oh! aunt, Oh! uncle, how rich we shall be," cried the girl, running off to tell her cousins; but the uncle and aunt looked grave. They were wondering how this will might effect Edgar Stainton.

While they were still talking it over – after Timpsons' young man had taken his departure, Mr. Edgar Stainton himself arrived.

"Oh, it's all right!" he said, in answer to their questions. "I found the will in the room where Felix Stainton died. Walnut-Tree House and all the freeholds were left to the poor little chap who died, chargeable with Mary's ten thousand pounds, five hundred to Mrs. Toplis, and a few other legacies. Failing George, the property was to come to me. I have been to Quinance's successor, and found out the old man and Alfred had a grievous quarrel, and that in consequence he determined to cut him out altogether. Where is Mary? I want to wish her joy."

Mary was in the little conservatory, searching for a rose to put in her pretty brown hair. He went straight up to her, and said:

"Mary, dear, you have had one Christmas gift tonight, and I want you to take another with it."

"What is it, Cousin Edgar?" she asked; but when she looked in his face she must have guessed his meaning, for she drooped her head, and began pulling her sweet rose to pieces.

He took the flower, and with it her fingers.

"Will you have me, dear?" he asked. "I am but a rough fellow, I know; but I am true, and I love you dearly."

Somehow, she answered him as he wished, and all spent a very happy evening in the old house.

Once, when he was standing close beside her in the familiar room, hand clasped in hand, Edgar Stainton saw the child looking at them.

There was no sorrow or yearning in his eyes as he gazed – only a great peace, a calm which seemed to fill and light them with an exquisite beauty.

Oh Bury Me Not

Erica Ruppert

MY HUSBAND'S GONE. He killed himself as surely as if he'd strung himself up a noose in the barn rafters.

Harman came into the soddy one night at the beginning of November with a strange look on his face.

"There's someone out there," he said. He sounded strange, too.

"Who?" I said.

"Don't know. He's just standing out in the field, watching."

I opened the door and peered out into the dusk. The dog was past the barn, barking at something.

"I don't see anybody," I told him. "Are you sure it was somebody, and not a deer?"

"I know a deer," Harman said. "It was a man. Acting spooky. Just watching."

"So what are we going to do?"

The strange look on Harman's face was fear. He was scared. It made me scared, too.

"Bolt the door and wait for morning, I guess," he said.

We did, and in the morning two of the goats were gone, and the dog. The next night the sorrel pony was gone. We never heard anything but the wind.

But Harman knew he had to do something to stop the thieving. He knew something was waiting for him, hiding in the dark and the rustling grass. He told me he was going to wait in the barn, in the dark, in the empty stall, to meet whoever would come. But he thought since he had a plan, that it meant he had a chance.

They won't take another of the horses, he said. Not tonight.

So he went out, into the dark. With his rifle, and his plan.

That night was cold, with winter just starting to settle in over the plains. The first snow hadn't come yet but the frost surely had. The ground was getting hard beneath the long dead grass, and the wind never stopped blowing. At first I couldn't hear anything over the sigh of the wind. And I couldn't see Harman clearly, just what might have been his shadow crossing the yard. He didn't take a lantern that night, thinking he could sneak up on whoever was out there better without one.

Then I heard him holler curses, and then I heard the sharp clap of hooves on hard ground, and a scream like a baby's wail, trailing off into the sky.

And that was the last I heard of my husband.

I barred the door and shuttered the windows, and fed the fire all night. The soddy got too warm with everything buttoned up, but there was no way I was going to crack open anything or let the fire die. Especially not when I wasn't sure if the noise I heard above me was something walking around up on the roof. Dirt sifting down into the overhead canvas made a sound like falling snow, and it could have been stirred by the sharp wind and not the unsteady tapping of feet. But I wasn't going to risk being wrong about it.

When the sun came up I slept some, but by about nine I took the hand axe and went out into the yard. The barn was open, and the bay mare was gone, but the roan and the mule were still in their stalls. Harman's rifle lay before the barn door. He hadn't fired it. I picked it up.

I'm no tracker, but a wide swath of grass was flattened in a rough line heading west. I took the roan and the rifle and followed the trail.

It didn't take long to reach him. Maybe an hour.

Harman was in the middle of a stamped-down patch of grass, his arms and legs all splayed out like a broken toy. His face was turned up to the sky and his eyes were wide open.

As I walked up to him I swear his eyes rolled to follow me. And as much as I knew it was my imagination, I couldn't help but feel like he saw me coming to him.

The grass around him was brown and sticky with drying blood. As I got close I could see his body was all hollowed out, his belly opened up and his innards removed. I could see down to his wet red backbone.

I retched hard and spit bile, but I hadn't eaten anything to bring up. Just as well.

The roan was dancing at the edge of the flattened space, nervous and unhappy. I caught hold of her bridle and figured out what I would have to do.

I couldn't bring his body into town. Not in the state it was in, with all the meat missing. And especially not after I shot him a couple of times to make sure what was left of him stayed down.

I didn't trust the way his eyes still looked alive.

So I rode back home to get a spade and an old horse blanket, then went back up the valley about another mile past where Harman lay and dug a grave. Lucky the ground wasn't frozen too hard, yet, but it still took me a long while to cut through the turf with only the spade and the hand axe and longer still to dig a big enough hole. Then I rolled what was left of my husband into the blanket and dragged him up to his grave. I laid the turf back over it when I was done and scuffed the spilled dirt into the long grass to hide it.

I hoped the grave was deep enough, and far enough away. His bright eyes still scared me, even from underground.

Harman always said the prairie called to him. It's why we went as far as we did. He would have taken us out of reach of any human settlement if I'd let him.

He said he liked the loneliness of the wide plains. But we were never really alone out here. Not if you listened. The wind hid things in it, voices and songs and sighs that no human throat made. Harman said my imagination was too wild, that I needed to forget what I learned back East in Harrisburg. Especially what I learned about the value of railroads.

He didn't want to be too close to the railroad, even though that's where things were booming. He said it just made things dirty and loud, and he wanted quiet. So we got away from it.

Harman found us a piece of land far off from the nearest homestead, a good part of a day's ride from Ogallala, up north and west of the Platte. When we went to file our claim in the spring of '76 the land agent tried to talk us into moving to an abandoned parcel adjoining another homestead, so we would be close by our neighbors, to help and be helped. Building the community. He told us there was still plenty of good land near the river. Harman told the agent our parcel had its own water, and that he would plant trees in exchange for 320 acres, and that we would be back in five years.

We did plant trees – cottonwood, pine, sugar maple, cedar. They'd be good for lumber, in time. Until then they helped a little to break the wind that rolled over the long stretches of prairie like a lonely ghost.

Harman really wanted to go even further west, and northward. He said the town was going to grow too big for us, even this far out, and would swallow us up. But I said no, and stuck to it.

So we built our soddy nearly eight miles north and west of Ogallala, in a long shallow valley. I was pregnant then, and if we were going to have a family it wouldn't be so far from other people that no one would know if we all died.

And though Harman said the prairie called to him, he didn't want us to be buried out here.

He wanted to be buried back in the churchyard in Ogallala with all the other dead folk, where his bones would be safe. He always tried to tell me it was because he didn't want any wild Indians messing with our graves, but I understood he told me that because he was scared of something else, something spookier than just wild men.

I couldn't put a name on his fear, but I understood it.

I wasn't scared of any Indians, exactly, either. The Pawnees and Lakotas had given up their lands to the government and moved to the Indian territories years ago. But I never could shake the feeling that they had left some part of themselves behind. Like they still kept a watch out there in the wind and the long grass.

The baby did end up being buried out here, though, just by the biggest cottonwood. We named him Harman Junior, but he only lived a day.

There weren't any more after him. Just as well.

So a week or so after Harman died, I gathered myself and took stock of what I had here. It wasn't much. And I had the feeling I'd have to be here for a while. To make sure of things. Whatever had taken Harman still lingered. It couldn't be all my imagination.

I hitched up the mule and took the wagon into town. I was usually the one to go in when we needed anything. Harman preferred to stay away.

This time I needed cornmeal and flour, salt and a little sugar, from Mattie Willwright's general store. She had dried beans, and coffee, so I got those too. It would be enough to last a while, with what I had put away in the root cellar. I looked at the few bright bolts of cloth on the shelf above the counter. Maybe in the spring. If I made it through. I gave her my wedding band as payment.

"What am I going to do with that, Dorsey?" Mattie said, letting it lay on her open palm.

"Sell it. Or hold it, if you want," I said. "Until I can get you real cash. Harman's gone, so it might be a while."

She looked at me slantwise as she wrapped up my purchases.

"Gone where?"

I had practiced my lie on the slow ride in. "Farther west. He left about two weeks ago, said we were still too close to civilization. But I'm done traveling."

Mattie kept her head down.

"You know, Dorsey," she said to her hands. "Folks here did think Harman was odd." She took her time with the wrapping. "Maybe it's better you stay behind. Move into town for a while. See if he comes home."

"Maybe I will," I said. I was still lying.

Mattie handed me my packages.

"Don't wait for him too long," she said.

I nodded to her and brought my supplies out to the wagon. There was nowhere else in town I needed to stop, so even though it was after noon I headed back home.

The winter was hard.

I wished the dog was still alive. But he had been the first that the thing out there took.

It was lonely, by myself in the damp little soddy. I think I went a little bit crazy out there. I heard things in the wind, and I imagined things.

Like his eyes. Harman's eyes followed me, even though he was in his grave under the thick prairie sod. I could feel his eyes looking at me through the drafty windows, waiting to stare me down whenever I opened the door. Whenever I set foot on the prairie grass.

Eventually I went back to where I'd buried him. I had to see.

The sod was peeled back and the scratch I'd made for him was empty, nothing but a stain in the dirt where Harman had been. There was a scuffle of coyote prints along the side of the hole.

Where the coyotes had dragged him to, I didn't need to know. But now I did know he wasn't underground, anymore.

All those long nights, I stayed tucked in from the wind and the snow, waiting for the sun. I heard things whispering down the chimney, scratching around the door. Shadows where there shouldn't be.

Sometimes even in daylight I would look up from digging out and see something standing out in the deep snow in the field, watching me. Harman was right. It was no deer.

Sometimes it was closer than that. Sometimes from the corner of my eye it looked like it was right at the edge of the yard. If I tried to face it, to see it clear, it wasn't there anymore.

When the winter finally blew itself out and the prairie started to thaw the something revealed itself to me.

The mud around the house had dried to a hard cracked layer but the floor of the soddy was still soft and swampy in the back. I was going to get some more hay from the barn to lay down, but it was there in the yard when I opened the door. At first I thought, Oh, it's Harman come home. I was so lonely after that winter.

But it wasn't Harman.

Whatever it was hunkered in front of my house was as shaggy as a brown bear, but leaner. Longer. My hair stood up as a great fear took hold of me. Whatever it was, was more dangerous than any bear. It was smart. And hungry. I can't explain how I knew that, but I was as sure of its hunger as I was of my fear.

I dashed back inside and dragged the table over to the door to block it. The leaded glass windows we had carried with us from back home, that I was so proud of, made me feel naked with that thing outside. They were pretty, and useless. I did not dare open them to reach the shutters.

The thing's fur looked yellow in the weak sun, faded like straw. As it stood up and raised its lump of a head to me I could see that it was grass. Sod. It looked like a face made of sod and dirt. It looked like it was looking at me. But it couldn't have been. It had no eyes, just smears of mud.

And then it turned, and another face grinned at me from the back of its head. And Harman's eyes peered out from it, sharp and blue as glass.

I don't know how I didn't scream as the sod-thing with Harman's eyes rushed at me, faster than anything has any right to run. But even with my thoughts all burnt with fear I raised the rifle, which is always loaded and close at hand since Harman died. I fired four shots into it through my pretty windows, and hit it. The thing fell with a thud like a sack of dirt, its chest and belly blown clear through and its arms and legs thrown about like sticks. The head, the head with two faces, rolled a little distance on the hard dirt of the yard before it stopped with the sod face turned toward me.

It could still see me. I could feel it. But it couldn't do anything, blown apart like it was.

This time I burned it. Burying wasn't good enough.

I was alone out here for better than four months, and I paid mind to what went on. I knew the thing would haunt me wherever I went, if I tried to run off. That's why I stayed out here, going a little bit crazy. After the first snows came at the end of November, I couldn't have run off if I wanted to. I had just enough food to get by on, and enough cow chips to keep the stove going. I kept a path to the barn cleared, kept the roan and the mule and the last goat fed. Anyway, I made it.

And it's about time for me to give up my claim, here. Didn't make the five years. Barely made two.

But this was Harman's land more than it was ever mine.

All I have to do now is load the wagon with what I can lift. Whoever comes after me is welcome to whatever I can't.

I imagine that's why you're out here, isn't it? You and your blue eyes?

Too bad I didn't see you coming up the valley to get here.

Now, if you'll just take your hat off and turn around once for me, I won't have to shoot you down. You won't have to be buried out here on the empty prairie. Then we can both have what we want after all.

Xarus's Mirror

C.R. Serajeddini

WE ARRIVE AT the small sandstone house just as the glittering stars begin to fade in the light of dawn. The door creaks open to reveal Raf's red face. The old man stumbles back, eyes widening as he scans the vision before him. Can he see the horrors written on our faces, I wonder? Can he smell the bitter stink of death and blood and sweat?

"By God…" the old man rasps. "What happened to you?"

I follow his gaze to Uncle's weathered face. Uncle opens his mouth to speak, but then glances down at me and croaks, "Later."

Later when I am not there to listen, he means. As though I did not also watch our enemies punch a thousand holes through the bodies of the boys and men from our village, leaving the walls behind them sticky with blood. As though I did not also hear my mother's screams or breathe in the bitter smoke that chased us over the mountains.

Raf's wife, Hannah, is a hearty woman with a warm smile. Raf and Hannah do not speak as they light their samovar and prepare a tray of warm bread and sweet tea. When finally Hannah and Raf bring the food to us, I eat and drink until my belly hurts.

"You should get some rest, Mari," Uncle says when I have finished. "You look pale."

A small part of me, in the back of my mind, screams at him that I cannot rest. When I close my eyes, I see flames licking my home, men clad in black stepping out of them like demons rising from Jahannam. *How will I rest ever again?* But I have no will to fight Uncle, and no courage to scream at anyone.

Hannah leads me to a small room furnished with overlapping rugs. There is a bed on one side, draped in dusty knitted blankets and floral pillows. Pushed against the wall on the opposite side of the room is a single chest of drawers. Above this hangs an oval mirror, cheap polished copper, its frame dented and edged with green blossoms of rust. *An ugly piece for such a pretty room,* I think.

Peeling my eyes from the mirror, I thank Hannah for her hospitality, and she takes my face in both hands to plant a kiss on my forehead.

"I will close the door so you have peace, Mari," she says before she leaves.

She doesn't know. It's in silence that the dead scream loudest. I wait until Hannah's footsteps fade and reopen the door to a crack.

When I turn, my gaze locks on to the vision in the mirror. My eyes are bloodshot – yet still dry – and my long braid a tangled mess. I tease it open with my fingertips and brush through it as my mother would have done, but before I can finish, exhaustion wraps a shroud around me. I let my hands drop. Brushed hair or tangled, what difference does it make? I sink into the bed, afraid of what I will see if I close my eyes. But I have seen the sunrise twice since I last slept, and my mind soon slips into a dreamless void.

Harsh whispers lurch me awake. My movements are silent as I rise from the bed and shuffle towards the door. Sliding on to the rugs, I hug my knees to my chest and listen.

"They call us djinn," Uncle says. "Can you believe it? They say we are djinn. They call us abominations, Raf. I don't think they will stop this time… They mean to kill us all."

"This is what they always do," Hannah spits. "They kill the men. Take the women and the girls. Force them to marry. Give them children. In that way they erase our existence."

My blood curdles at her words. *They take the women and the girls.* I brush my cheeks with my fingertips, and for the first time since my world crumbled around me, I find them wet. I leap to my feet and shut the door, then I turn to the ugly mirror on the wall.

When I was a little girl, my mother told me of the legend of Xarus's Mirror. Xarus was a magus who lived in the time of the Medes. "He struggled with introspection," Mother would say. The story went that when Xarus came by a rough sheet of copper, he spent days polishing it until eventually he could see his reflection. Xarus realised that he was like the copper, that his soul would need much polishing until he could reflect on to the world only what was true, and clean, and good.

Xarus lived to a great age, and people from all sides of the mountain went to see him, from north to south, east to west. Even the old king of Persia sought Xarus's wisdom. And then came the moment in the story that transformed history into legend: The story says that when Xarus died his spirit remained in the mirror, and ever since, if one who is worthy looks into a mirror and reflects their truth, Xarus may grant them a single wish.

Nonsense, all of it. If only my mother had spent less time filling my head with fantasies, and more time teaching me to fight and hunt like they taught the boys. I blink back the memories of my mother's heart-shaped face, her green eyes, and I focus on the image in the mirror instead.

At thirteen years of age, the slight rise of my chest is still easy to hide with the right clothes, but my hair falls to the small of my back. *They take the girls. They say we are djinn.* I find myself wishing I *was* a djinn. Djinn are made of smokeless fire; they are swift, elusive, powerful. It is said that djinn can see us even when we cannot see them. They can change shape. I wish that I could change the way I look so that our enemies would never see me for what I am. "I wish I was a djinn," I whisper. Then, louder, "I wish I was a djinn." If I were, I could hide as a bird in the sky or a lizard in the sand and they would never find me.

But no matter how hard I wish, it is flesh and bone that stare back at me; brown hair, and pale skin – miserably human.

I will have to use another way to hide. Searching the drawers beneath the mirror, sliding them open and closed, I find that the bottom one is stuffed with silks and floral fabrics, threads, and yarn, and knitting needles.

And one pair of sewing scissors.

My heart sinks for only a moment, but I quickly remind myself that there are worse things in this world than a girl with no hair. I lift a fistful of dark curls. The blades of the shears glisten in the mirror. Setting my jaw, I cut close to my scalp. *Waste,* the scissors whisper with each pass. *Waste. Waste. Waste.*

Dark curls and strands fall around me like plucked feathers. They mix with my tears and cling to my cheeks and my neck, but I continue until the girl in the mirror resembles a boy.

Through the blur in my eyes, I envision the skin on that new boy's face cracking – like the face of a ceramic plate left too long in flames – and between the cracks, smokeless tongues of fire lick and stretch to crest the surface.

I squeeze my eyes shut against the vision, startled by its depth. When I open my eyes, the face in the mirror crumbles like dust to reveal a dark and sinuous monster beneath.

With a jolt, the scissors fall from my hand and clatter to the floor; a shrill scream escapes my lungs.

Uncle bursts in first, followed by the others. They stare at me, their mouths agape and their faces twisted in disgust. Uncle picks up the scissors and gives them to Hannah before kneeling before me and gripping my shoulders.

"Why are you screaming?" he asks.

My eyes stick to the mirror, which now reflects unadorned reality. I shake my head and pat my cheeks, my lips, my forehead. I want to tell Uncle what I saw, but my jaws are locked tight, and in my fear, I have forgotten my tongue.

Uncle does not remark about my hair. He wipes my face with a cloth, then sits beside me in silence. When he does, I rest my head on his shoulder, and he wraps a protective arm around me. We stay this way for what feels like hours.

"Uncle," I whisper when I remember how to speak. "I cut my hair bec—"

"Because you wanted to look like a boy," he says. "Because you don't want them to take you. Do you know what they do to the boys, Mari?"

"They execute them," I answer, trying desperately not to think of my father. My jaw tightens. "Death is better than the other option."

Uncle pulls away and turns to me sharply. "Do not speak that way, Mari. I won't let that happen. They will not find you – I'll make sure of it."

"How?"

His determined expression changes. His hard eyes soften around the edges, and he looks away from me, dropping his gaze to the colourful rugs instead.

My heart sinks. "You're going to go, aren't you?"

"Raf, some others, and I. We are assembling a large company. All of us are trained and strong. We will be armed—"

"No!"

"Mari—"

"You're going to leave me!"

"Raf's wife, she will be here with you, Mari." He takes my hand, squeezes it. "She will look after you, and I will come back when this is over. I promise."

My mouth is stuck dry, and dread has lodged in my throat. I am losing him, just as I lost the rest of my family. I will have no one. I do not want to know what it is like to be completely alone in the world.

"What if they come here?" I ask, clinging to his arm, desperate to find reason for him to stay. "Shouldn't you be here?"

"If they get here, then we have already lost, Mari. We will stop them before they come into the village. This is the only way. You must be brave."

I nod, despite the doubt in my heart. My uncle will become *peshmerga* – one who stands against death to protect others. To protect me. Perhaps to avenge his brother and the rest of our family. I wish that I could be brave like him. I wish more that he wouldn't go. The two of us could travel far away, perhaps even far enough to be safe. But truth stares at me like a clear reflection from a mirror, and it says that I can never run from what has happened to us.

"Take me with you," I whisper to Uncle, thinking back to the image in the mirror, the boy, the strong child who knows how to fight. My blood feels as though it's simmering beneath my skin, vibrating with caged energy. "Give me a rifle, too."

Uncle turns his face and studies me for a moment. He looks as though he is about to agree, but then his eyes soften and he sighs. "You are just a child, Mari. No. You will stay here. One day, you will grow into a young woman, and you will have children of your own. Then, you will understand why I must keep you safe."

I grit my teeth. *They take the women and the girls.* That is what they had done, back in the village. I hid, and I escaped. Uncle found me beneath my mother's bed, even as the flames devoured my home, the smoke burning my throat and my lungs…

I swallow hard and force the memory away. "When are you leaving?"

"Tonight," he says. "It is best to travel under the cover of darkness."

If Uncle were a djinn, I find myself thinking, *he could hide in the brightest light of day and yet remain unseen. If I were a djinn, I could go with him.*

* * *

"Come," Hannah calls. "Help me make bread."

It is the morning after Uncle, Raf, and the other men of the village left. The house smells of fresh naan cooking in a clay oven. Hannah uses a slender rod to roll out balls of dough until they are paper-thin and round. Her sleeves are turned up to her elbows and her cheeks pink with exertion, and she smiles despite our pathetic situation.

I sit on a wooden stool opposite her, and she slaps a ball of dough on the work surface in front of me. When I do not move, she stops and glances up. I can feel her gaze burning my bare head.

"You know," she says. "You should never be ashamed of being a woman."

"I didn't do it out of shame."

"No." She tilts her head, then nods. "You did it out of fear."

I snap my gaze to hers. "Aren't *you a*fraid? For your husband? For yourself?"

She sighs. "Fear is what our enemies want us to feel. Fear of being ourselves. Fear of living. Fear of being happy." Hannah shakes her head. "I choose not to be afraid, Mari, or else they win."

Now shame does burn my collar and my cheeks, and prickles my scalp until I wish I hadn't cut my hair. This woman who bakes bread, makes tea, and refuses fear – she is far braver than I am.

* * *

Xarus is nothing but a children's tale, I tell myself. The vision I saw in the mirror was brought on by terror and grief and a lack of sleep.

But what if Xarus *was r*eal? Even the greatest lies hold grains of truth. Running my hand against the bristly stubble on my head, I wonder if I should wish for it to regrow, but immediately the sound of my mother's screams rings in my ears. *They take the women and the girls.*

What good is bravery and long hair if I cannot protect myself? If I cannot protect others?

I stare hard into the eyes of the boyish face in the mirror. Perhaps if I believe in the legend of Xarus, as though it is the last hope in the world for me... "I wish to be a djinn." I whisper it at first. What would I do with such power? Protect, of course. No... it is not enough to protect. They would only commit their crimes elsewhere.

Had I the strength, I would hunt them down, as they hunt us. I would taste their blood and eat their sorrows for my own. Something inside of me catches fire, and I begin to shout.

"I wish to be a djinn! *I wish to be a djinn!* **I wish to be a djinn!**"

This time when the cracks run down my forehead and bifurcate across my face, I smile, despite the hammering in my chest and the burning of my skin.

* * *

I wake to gunfire.

A crash at the door. Screaming. A woman. *Hannah. S*econds later my door slams open and the man stands before me, one of the marauders, dressed as they had at my village in black clothing and a black turban. Uncle told me they dress this way so that they are harder to see in the night. But I see him. He snarls with yellowed teeth. Yet he does not lunge, does not even look at me. It comes to me in a flash.

He cannot see me.

My body has turned to vapour, invisible to his eyes. I am made of smokeless fire. I am a child of the shadows.

I have become a djinn.

"You," I call, and he spins, sweeping his rifle around the room.

"Where are you?" he shouts. "Come out." He smiles cruelly. "We won't hurt you."

The invisibility happened instinctively, and it makes me wonder what else I can do. I come out of the shadows and step back into the physical realm, my body reforming almost immediately.

"I can hurt you," I tell him.

His jaw turns slack and before he can squeeze the trigger, I touch his forehead and seep into his being.

There, I tear him apart, cell by cell.

For him, it is only moments of agony. For me, it seems as though hours pass. The whole world has slowed since I changed.

I seek Hannah and find her bound up and loaded on to the back of a truck with the other village women. Some are only children, barely four or five years old. Anger boils within me and sets my skin alight. Once this was only a metaphor, but now… I turn my hands over; flames have replaced my flesh, my clothes, my hair. Black and blue, dancing and shifting, ever-changing.

The truck driver startles when I suddenly appear next to him, and with a little help, his pounding heart convulses and stops. His eyes roll back inside his head, and his body falls limp. The swiftness of his demise bothers me; I wanted him to hurt.

I cut through the women's ropes, though I wish to do so unseen lest I scare the younger ones, and my body obeys by turning to mist. But I show the attackers no mercy as I jump from one to the other, undoing the very fabric of their existence. It's what they wanted to do to us. *I am like a mirror,* I muse. *I reflect only their intentions.*

I find another standing alone, his rifle held loosely in his hands. The next instant I appear before him. His eyes widen as I rip the scarf from his face – I want to see the agony on his bearded face.

But there is no beard, only a shadow, a wisp of one. His weapon slips from his fingers. "Please," he whimpers, his voice high pitched. "Mercy… please."

I stumble back, clutching the scarf between fiery fingers.

Mercy?

The boy lumbers up and stutters, "Thank you," but as he spins away I touch his shoulder and set him aflame. His screams sound inhuman, animalistic. He runs away, a torch blazing through the night.

Mercy. I spit. I gave him only what he asked for. Better to die than grow up like the rest of his people. If I end them all now, it will be a mercy for everyone.

The rest of his kin scream until their voices turn raw and blood gurgles in their throats. They beg their God for mercy, but they receive only mine. I bathe in their blood. It feeds my fury, and the more I kill, the more I feel the urge to kill again.

When the sun rises over the peaks of the mountains, the ground is littered with bodies clad in black and stained with red. The village is silent. Useless rifles lie scattered across the battlefield like forgotten toys.

It dawns on me that the nightmare is over. Our people are safe. Uncle can come home now, and if others like these men come, I can protect us, forever. My new body allows me speed unimaginable to a human and in moments I travel to the far edge of the village to seek my uncle and tell him this magnificent news.

I find his body in a ditch, bruised, bloodied, and lifeless.

My mind scrambles for solutions; I search my powers, my unfamiliar inhuman abilities. But there is nothing I can do to bring him back, I have no power to turn back time, to resurrect. Those are powers only granted to gods and angels, it seems. I am not all-powerful, almighty. I can destroy, but I cannot create, and this knowledge floods my mouth with the bitter taste of loss. I sit with my uncle's head cradled in my lap and weep until the sun burns through the morning mist and the sparrows in the distance begin to sing.

* * *

It is only right that I carry Uncle and Raf home. I arrive to find the villagers clearing the invaders' bodies and piling them up. They mean to take the carrion away and bury them respectfully.

When Hannah catches sight of Raf hoisted over my shoulder, she runs towards him. She claws at her husband's shirt, begging him to wake. When he does not, she buries her face in his matted hair, and cries until her voice turns raw.

"How did you manage to carry them all of this way, Mari?" Hannah sniffs and wipes at her eyes. "Where have you been all this time? How did you find them?"

She shakes her head and begins to cry again. I changed my form before they could see me, and I do not intend on revealing my true being now. All they would see is a monster.

"It's a miracle," Hannah says, nodding to herself. "Yes, it must be a miracle, my child. The Almighty sent you to me for a reason."

* * *

Hannah and I do not speak much in the days after the attack. I think she grieves for Raf.

I am grieving, too.

"Why don't you go and play with the children?" she asks. So I go outside. I try.

Walking around the village, I see boys and girls of my age playing and sharing secrets. I hate them. How can they laugh and play when there is such cruelty in the world? And then I hate myself for hating them. They are only children. But am I not also a child? I no longer feel like one. Yet when I go to spend time with the women, they send me away on small tasks, whisper amongst themselves. I do not belong with them either.

And then there is *her*. She stares back at me in the mirror, the djinn with rippling flames for skin. I only let her out at night, when I can be sure nobody is there. But when I do, the urge to fight, to scream, is too much.

Perhaps I can learn to control her. Perhaps I need to accept her as part of me now, and not a monster of legend. I trace the edges of the mirror with my fingertips, and remember Xarus. The magus who found solace in the mountains and polished copper to find himself.

* * *

I leave the village quietly. The children have not yet woken, and the shepherds have not yet left. Possessions mean nothing to me now, and even if they did, I brought none from my village when Uncle and I escaped.

Now, I have only the mirror.

Perhaps a century of polishing copper and staring at my reflection will cleanse the ugliness from within me. Perhaps it will help me find what I seek, whatever it is.

Three Years

Evelyn Teng

ON THE FIRST day of the Lunar New Year, Jessica drove to the cemetery for grave visits.

At least, she tried to. Her relatives widely joked that she was capable of getting lost in her own house, but even so, this was excessive. Though the grave visits had been an annual family event until the pandemic drove everyone to fearful seclusion, she found herself circling entire blocks, once – twice – three times – before finally pulling into an apartment parking lot and pulling up directions on her phone. Even technology seemed reluctant to behave. The GPS app creatively misinterpreted her, guiding her to cemeteries across Houston, or to cities named Houston in Alaska, Ohio, Canada, and Scotland; almost as if her phone were intentionally and spitefully changing her destination. Jessica had to laugh even through her exasperation.

Finally, she managed to find directions to the correct cemetery, in the correct Houston, Texas, the United States, the Earth, the Milky Way, the Universe.

Should have used a map in the first place, instead of relying on memory, she told herself as she backed out of the parking lot. And, now that she knew where she was, she felt supremely silly. She knew this neighborhood as intimately as she knew every nascent wrinkle on her thirty-year-old face. She'd attended Chinese school every weekend at the nearby community center, learning to read, write, and speak her parents' native tongue. With her eyes closed, in rain or dark, she should have been able to navigate this area blind.

But – and she could barely admit it to herself – even now, driving past familiar signs and shops, she was trying *not* to remember the neighborhood. The memories of her grandfather were too strong, and even years later, too painful.

Grandfather, of few words but expressive actions, never once telling Jessica he loved her but showing it in a million ways, which she hadn't recognized until too late.

Grandfather, buried far from where he'd grown up, in the city he'd learned to call home.

After far too many wrong turns, Jessica came at last to the cemetery in which her relatives were interred. A chaotic property, this, with its mausoleum styled after a Spanish villa, and its Chinese gateway overlooking the exit, and the life-size statues of Joseph, Mary, and Jesus battling sculptures of Chinese deities and seated Buddhas for height. The tombstones themselves bore more Chinese, Vietnamese, and Hispanic surnames than any others, a feature that made Jessica feel unjustifiably comfortable after having grown up alongside endless classmates named Smith and Johnson and Taylor. A familiar place, this cemetery, as familiar as the surrounding neighborhood.

As she wound her old Camry along the twisting paths, though, a chill seeped into her, making her shudder. Odd. It was only winter in Houston, which with the exception of one memorable February, shouldn't get cold enough to eat through a car's heater.

And she was lost again! This cemetery wasn't particularly large, and the graves she intended to visit were right beside a curving path, yet somehow she'd managed to find her way to the exit *twice*! Jessica scowled. Her sense of direction was terrible, but this was beyond ridiculous.

"Bother," she hissed after turning a corner and finding herself face-to-face for the third time with a six-foot-tall, eight-foot-wide stone slab bearing a Renaissance-looking etching of the twelve apostles. She screeched to a halt and hopped out of the car. At once the wind sucked the warmth out of her, right through three layers and a scarf, but she was too exasperated to care. She could see the family plot *right there*, in a direct line across path and grass and tombstones. Yet whenever she got behind the wheel, it seemed, the road twisted so that she ended up anywhere *but* her destination. It was as if – though she felt crazy for even thinking it – someone, or something, was reaching through an invisible dimension and twisting the road beneath her tires.

Fine. If she couldn't drive, she'd walk.

Popping open the trunk of her car, she hauled out everything she'd brought for the grave visit. A bulging canvas bag on each shoulder; her purse in her left hand; a metal bucket in her right. Fixing her eyes on the far-off gravestone, she set off.

At once Jessica knew she'd made the right choice. The world stayed steady around her – no more sliding around, or turning to find that she was somehow heading in the complete opposite direction – and her spirits lifted. A weak sun was breaking across the cemetery, too, its runny-yolk color spreading out in runnels of liquid gold. It really was a fabulous view, once you got past the idea of dead people. There was something wonderfully welcoming about the indiscriminate monuments. And the weather had finally gotten cold enough – and stayed cold long enough – for the trees to start turning red and gold at the edges. Really, anyone who chose to drive instead of walking in such weather was an unappreciative fool.

She was roughly a hundred yards from the family plot when someone pushed her hard on her left side.

The touch was cold – like a glacier – like liquid nitrogen – and she whirled around with a yelp as her left arm went numb. The air rushed trembling into her lungs as her eyes swept over lawns green-brown with winter's touch. Not a person in sight. She was alone, as she had been since driving through the gates.

Just my imagination, Jessica tried to tell herself, but the numbness of her left arm was too real to ignore. Shaking, she turned back towards the grave. It was still there, luckily. She'd half expected it to have slid off to the side the instant she took her eyes away. But she trekked on, and within a few minutes stood before the familiar gravestone, six feet tall and elegantly designed to resemble a doorframe. The center "door" slab was carved with only three names.

Her great-aunt, dead before Jessica was even born.

Her great-aunt's husband, who'd lingered decades after his wife's death and succumbed only recently to Alzheimer's disease.

Her grandfather.

There was plenty of space for subsequent names; and though Jessica found it morbid, she remembered, in years past, how her grandmother would hold on to her arm for support and point at the gravestone, saying that *here* was space for when she died, and *there* would be written the names of Jessica's other great-aunt and great-uncle, her grandmother's younger sister and other brother-in-law. Her grandmother never sounded eager or sad when she spoke thus. To her, it was as businesslike as deciding how many dumplings to make for the New Year's Eve dinner.

But for now, three names only. Three names she hadn't visited for the last three years, on her grandmother's orders. With the universal fear of burying her own children and the unquestioned obedience of a matriarch, her grandmother had ordered the whole family into strict quarantine. They could leave the house only for groceries, she declared, and if they still worked, were to push for work-from-home privileges as much as possible. Even the family celebrations that her grandmother cherished – Lunar New Year, the Mid-Autumn Festival, and yes, the yearly grave visits – were banned. The safety of the living nullified the demands of the dead, especially in the interest of keeping the dead at a minimum.

But Jessica, raised in American schools, surrounded now by American colleagues, beset year-round by advertisements for quintessentially American holidays, feared losing herself in the pitiless melting pot of the country more than she feared a cough. So, without telling her grandmother, without so much as hinting at her relatives, she'd *disobeyed*.

From her canvas bags, Jessica brought out four porcelain plates and laid them at the foot of the family plot. Then came oranges, arranged in a pyramid on one plate; red-bean buns, similarly stacked, on a second; and on the third, she upended a container of *ba bao fan*, that sweet, sticky studded dessert of steamed glutinous rice. Shop-bought, not homemade as it had been in prior years, for Jessica feared her grandmother guessing her intent.

Finally, on the last plate, she placed a Tupperware container of *kao fu*, a vegetarian dish of steamed wheat gluten, bamboo shoots, rehydrated shiitake and cloud-ear mushrooms, and peas, all soaked in a savory broth and fragrant with sesame oil. This one she'd made just last night. It had to be handmade, and it had to be her grandmother's recipe. Her grandmother's version of *kao fu* had been beloved by both her grandfather and her great-uncle.

The feast laid out, Jessica stood back – then blinked. It might have been the cold, dry air, which always caused skin problems when for nine out of twelve months Houston swam in a soup of car exhaust, pollen, and coastal humidity; but her eyes felt filmed over. Vague, wispy drifts swam across her vision, dulling the outlines of gravestone, grass, and trees alike. They even seemed to leach color from the sky itself.

And the more she looked, the less the drifting wisps seemed like fog, and the more they seemed like *people* – but people so uncertain, so inconstant, that just glimpsing them made Jessica feel as if she herself were floating away from her own body. With a mental wrench, she ripped herself back into the present.

Beset by the unshakeable sensation of being watched, Jessica prepared the rest of the grave-offering ritual. Three sticks of incense, lit with a utility lighter. Sudden, sideways winds gusted at Jessica from all sides, puffing out the pilot light. Grimly she hunched over and shielded the fire with her own body until the incense caught and trails of sweet smoke wreathed her head.

"Bow once," she whispered in her stilted, accented Chinese, and suited action to words, incense clasped in both hands. "Bow twice. Bow thrice." The brief, familiar, rote words faltered. Every syllable from her mouth seemed to draw the specters closer. Their eyes were clearer now, not smoke any longer but coals, singeing the fog of their bodies a burnt-wood color.

I should go – but tradition and ritual rooted Jessica to the spot. She would go, *after* she made the final offering. Swiftly, she tore open the packets of funeral money and scattered handfuls into the metal bucket. A quick caress with the utility lighter. The thin, crisp sheets curled into ash, white paper staining black and brown, gilt and red ink becoming indistinguishable from each other as the flames devoured them. She tossed in the remnants of her incense sticks as well, and the smoke that rose up stabbed thick and sharp through her nostrils.

The money flared and flickered in blue-edged tongues – died to smoldering clumps – and then there was nothing but ash, feathery and gray and warm.

That was it. The grave visit was over – and, even more than when she'd been a child and had thought this just a boring yearly ceremony, Jessica was relieved. She poked through the ash with the lighter to make sure no fire remained. How strange. The ashes gave off no heat. Or rather, she was so cold that the warmth barely touched her flesh. And the swirling figures of fog were stronger than ever now. At the corners of her vision, they looked like they were reaching for her—

They *were* reaching for her – and one more strongly than the others.

Ice crawled across her skin. She straightened up, looked at the ghost, and felt the ice sink into her pores, to pierce blood and bone and marrow. Unlike the vague, clawing things crowding on all sides and clouding her sight, this one appeared to be a real person, solid, with color to its cheeks and clothes. Still, she knew it was a ghost without a doubt.

Her grandfather had been dead for over a decade.

Jessica shook – not from cold or shock this time, but longing. She hadn't been young when her grandfather died. They'd had almost twenty years together, far longer than many people got. But that had made it hurt all the more. The memories of years, *decades* really, came roaring back to the forefront of her mind, and there were so many it was almost too much weight to bear.

And here he stood before her again, in not quite the flesh.

"Grandfather," she whispered. Her heart poured into her mouth everything she'd wished she'd said, all the sentiment and affection that she'd unthinkingly possessed as a child but hadn't had the introspection to express. What little reserve she possessed broke like a dam. She reached for her grandfather with both hands—

He took a step back.

Just one step; but it might as well have been a sword through the gut or a cudgel to the head. Jessica stopped in her tracks. Her heart was having trouble beating. Tears made fractal rainbows of her vision and broke her grandfather's figure into an indistinct shadow, layered with streaks of diamond brilliance.

"Grandfather," Jessica pleaded, but her arms remained outstretched and frozen. "Grandfather, I'm sorry. I didn't realize until – until later – I never told you that I—"

A creaking sigh drifted towards her. Blinking tears aside, she saw her grandfather's mouth move, and realized he was speaking.

"What? I'm sorry – I can't hear—"

Her grandfather shook his head. "You shouldn't have come. Leave."

Another blade in her belly, tearing her insides to bits. The tears came thick and fast now.

"I didn't mean to neglect you. I never forgot. But these last few years, everyone's been afraid to step outside – there's been a pandemic, and grandmother said—" Even as the words tumbled from her mouth, she recognized them for the excuses that they were, but hoped beyond hope that her grandfather would relent. He'd been so kind in life, getting up in the middle of the night whenever she slept over to make sure she was tucked in warm. She didn't know if death changed people, but surely it couldn't have turned him to hatred…

"Leave," her grandfather repeated.

"No!"

"Leave – or die."

Jessica scrambled to her feet. "Whatever I did, I'm sorry. I'll make it right. Just tell me how!"

Her grandfather *roared.*

And, as if obeying a command, the fog circling Jessica took shape, undefined mist condensing into distinct shapes. Men, women, toddlers, grandparents, aunts, uncles, siblings. They whirled into clarity, and the sight of them wrenched a scream from Jessica's lips, for one and all, they had the empty bellies and gaunt limbs of beings starved beyond recognition, beyond sentience, and the light of senseless, unthinking hunger glowed dark in the sunken pits of their eyes.

Starved ghosts, hungry ghosts, bereft of offerings and sustenance these three years, while the living humans huddled in their houses for fear of sickness. Jessica knew, in the same distant way she knew that carp swam up waterfalls to turn into dragons and Hou-Yi the Archer shot down shot down nine suns to prevent the earth from burning up, that people believed the spirits of their ancestors took sustenance from offerings. They ate the food, spent the funeral money, and thrived in the afterlife so long as their descendants continued to burn incense in their memories. Jessica, born in the United States, raised on myths of Paul Bunyan and the first Thanksgiving, understood the foundations of her relatives' beliefs with an outsider's clinical appreciation. She herself believed in such things as much as she believed in the Tooth Fairy.

Until now.

Because – and the realization tore through her with the force of one of Hou-Yi's arrows – just because she didn't believe in it *didn't mean it wasn't true.*

Cold hands snared her arms; cold sharpness sank into her back and shoulders and legs. She wrenched away with a cry, but the ghosts were relentless, clawing and gnawing at her with teeth that for three years had known no nourishment. No matter which way Jessica turned and flailed, more ghosts came at her on all sides. She drowned in ice as substantial as smoke.

But her grandfather still stood before her, unmoving. Desperation wringing her voice, she reached for him. "Grandfather, please—"

Her grandfather looked at her – and his eyes flared. Jessica's heart, already half-frozen by the greedy, grasping ghosts, shriveled to a leaden lump. This was it, then. Her penance for taking her grandfather for granted in life and neglecting him in the afterlife. Frozen tears rolled down her cheeks as her grandfather lunged—

—not *at* her, but *through* her.

He swept like a winter gale through her body, chilling her to the bone, and she shook so much she thought she might fall over. But there was howling in her ears. It came not from her own lips, but from the ones around her. And her shuddering heart thumped within her chest, because her grandfather flew at the encircling ghosts. Thin and starved, three years without offerings or incense, but his figure burned with a darkling fire, and a single sweep of his arms scattered the other ghosts like leaves on the wind. Jessica cowered back, fearing the heat of those flames and the fury in her grandfather's face. Never before had she seen her grandfather angered; never before had he shown her anything but smiles and patience. She saw it now, and the sight strangled the air in her lungs.

Left and right he flung those ghosts, with such force that they struck distant tombstones and broke apart – but reformed themselves almost immediately. As implacable as he was, the other ghosts were more implacable still. The cemetery teemed and boiled with them; they turned the ground white and the sky gray; they snatched at Jessica and chewed at her, ignoring her own blows, until her grandfather's spectral hands hurled them aside.

"Mine!" he thundered, and his voice quaked through Jessica's ears and drove her to her knees in agony. "She is *mine*! You cannot have my granddaughter!"

The wind rose to knives that pierced Jessica to the bone. Clouds swirled overhead, a tornado forming improbably from a clear winter's day, churned to a tempest by the whirl of her grandfather's arms and the wails of inrushing ghosts, all hungry for Jessica's living flesh. She crouched and cowered as the storm raged around her, whipping her hair into wild snarls and tearing the breath from her mouth. Her grandfather's bellows rose above all other sound—

And then, abruptly, everything went still.

Breath too loud and raspy in the silence, Jessica raised her head.

The cemetery looked the same as always, with its neat, chaotic monuments and clipped lawns – except it was layered in white. Soft tufts mounded at the bases of tombstones and drooped like Spanish moss from trees and fences. Whiteness lay in tender clouds along the curbs, shrouded the grass in whispering down, and drifted in shreds and flakes from a sky calming back to clarity. It was snow – such snow as Houston hadn't seen in years, perhaps decades – and like snow, the merest kiss of a flake on Jessica's cheek turned that spot numb and cold.

Amidst it all, in the one clear spot melted away by his dimming fire, was Jessica's grandfather.

Jessica straightened up.

A thousand thoughts and more stormed through her head. Everything she'd ever wished to say – everything she'd felt, but never had the words for – everything that had occurred to her only after the funeral, too late for him to hear, or so she'd thought—

A picture is worth a thousand words, the saying went; popularly attributed to Confucius, but the actual translation went, *Hearing something a hundred times can never be equal to seeing it once.*

So, instead of saying anything, Jessica walked up to her grandfather and hugged him.

He was cold, despite the flames still licking across his skin; colder than any of the other ghosts had been. But Jessica didn't feel it, for in that moment she was four again, zooming through her grandparents' living room as an airplane, arms outstretched while her grandfather held her up. She was nine again, learning how to play *weiqi* and *xiangqi*, those classic strategy board games, smug about defeating a five-time tournament champion and never realizing that he'd deliberately misplayed. She was twelve again, sitting at the dining-room table, wrapping dumplings while her grandmother cooked yet more dishes in the kitchen and her grandfather sat beside her, peeling shrimp into a large metal bowl and dropping their shells on to a spread of newspapers. She was fourteen again, traipsing around her grandparents' backyard, picking cucumbers off the wooden trellises and dropping them into the bucket her grandfather carried.

She was twenty again, in the hospital, reluctant to walk into the room and hear the ventilator that kept air in her grandfather's lungs. She *did not* want to see him like that, a shrunken caricature of his former strong self. Instead, she went home and baked cupcakes for the nurses, because she'd heard they took better care of patients if the family treated them nicely.

She was twenty again, unable to speak at the funeral.

She simply had no words.

Her grandfather took her hands and held them for a second – then pushed her away.

"Leave," he whispered.

"I don't want to," Jessica said. The words stuck in her throat. She clung to her grandfather's glacier-cold hands, even though her grip was so tight that her fingers sank into his ghost-flesh.

"Leave." The word quieter – and now she heard the harmonics she hadn't noticed before. Not telling her to leave and never come back, but to leave – to save herself – to take herself out of danger, so that she might return another time, when other humans had come with offerings and the ghosts were no longer hungry.

Slowly, Jessica turned around. Every step felt like a betrayal. But the snowy whiteness around her was stirring already, tumbling together and building up into tremulous shapes, like snowmen melting in reverse. Her trudge turned into a walk, then a trot, then a run. Tears pouring down her cheeks, she pelted for her car, plowing through ghosts reassembling themselves and ripping away from shaky, snatching fingers. Sobs ached in her throat and chest as she dove into the driver's seat, gunned the engine, and whirled back down the lane. There was no confusion now, no wrenching and twisting of directions. Her grandfather was no longer trying to redirect her away from the cemetery, but guiding her towards the exit.

At the gates, Jessica braked and turned around. Dangerous, she knew, for even now the ghosts roiled towards her over the grass and pavement; but her eyes swept the tombstones, seeking out one spot of color amidst the filmy shapes.

Almost clear across the cemetery, she saw her grandfather raise a hand. Then he knelt, picked up one of the oranges she'd offered, and took a bite.

Something within Jessica relaxed. Facing forward again, she eased the car out of the gates and melted back into Houston traffic. She left her grandfather behind.

But not forever, and not for long.

Ghost Festival in the Desert

Wen Wen Yang

"WOULD YOU LIKE another story?" I asked the white workers.

The Chinese men were watching me expectantly as I finished collecting the white men's empty bowls. The air still carried the sweet scent of hoisin sauce and beef. I had given them the meals with chopsticks sticking upright. The white men had laughed because they could not eat Chinese food with chopsticks. They still preferred my food to their white cooks' though.

The white men were varying shades of brown from the relentless dirt and unforgiving sun. Yellow light from the campfire flickered across the men's faces.

Charles killed a moth that ventured too close and wiped his hand against his pants. He picked at his teeth with a wooden splinter. "How about a game of poker?"

The men groaned, tired of losing their money. Charles had Crenshaw's favorite gun, an Army-issue 1860 Colt 44, and a stack of IOUs from Louis.

"Tell the talking pig one," said Patrick, leaning against his pack. The other men around the campfire grunted their agreement.

Crenshaw spat his tobacco, then replaced it with another pinch of chew.

Johnson snorted. "What about that hairy king one?" His eyes always lingered too long on me, as if he could see through my clothes and bindings.

I glanced at the tents where the other Chinese people slept while the white men stayed in the railroad cars. The latter still hung their windchimes while we had taken down anything that made noise. Hell, their railroad car doors were wide open to the night breeze. Idiots.

I took a sip of tea, then started to clean my knives. "I'll tell you a different one. It's a good ghost story."

The Chinese man washing the clothes sucked his teeth. If you were going to run a laundry, a "knight of the washtub" as they called it, you had to work through the night. He was about my height, his cue hanging down his back.

I had shorn my hair short like the white men. I told them it was to keep the lice off. After tonight, I will grow my hair back.

"It's about a man who came to this gilded country in search of his missing brother," I said.

The laundry man's hands slowed. The white men's clothes hung on the clothesline behind him, haunting in the full moon's brilliance.

"It was his older brother," I said. "The Chinese word for it is Gege."

Some men repeated the sound.

"Sounds like burping." Charles yawned and stretched like a cat.

I ignored him. "Gege had sent money home for his grandparents, parents, and younger siblings. Monthly letters."

"Shit," Charles spat. "He would have saved some money if he sent one a year."

"Until one day, his grandmother – we call her Nainai – started wailing. 'He's dead!' she cried. 'They killed him and hung him from the second story.'"

Charles shifted in his seat. "I don't like this one. Can't you tell the one about the wolf in the woods?"

"I'll tell that one after."

Charles draped his arm behind his head and started whistling. I did not tell him to stop. Let the ghosts come.

"Nainai was a wise woman." I rubbed at a stubborn spot on my smallest knife. "She knew how to bundle children up when they had fevers, where to hang mirrors to repel dangerous spirits, but her protection could not stretch across the ocean. So when the monthly letter from Gege didn't come, his younger brother, we call him Didi, came here, to the beautiful country."

"Was he looking for gold?" Patrick asked.

"Pfft, we'd already gotten it," answered Charles.

The men chuckled.

I nodded. "Yes, he couldn't pay the foreign miners' tax. He started working on the railroad like Gege before him. Though he was paid half of the white mens' wages, he started sending money home. Some men may have come to this beautiful country and never sent home a single coin. But first Gege and now Didi made sure his family had coal for warm nights and meals to fill their bellies."

"That's some good kids." Johnson rubbed his eyes.

"But what happened to the older brother?" Patrick insisted. "That isn't a full story, Cook. You can't let that be the end."

I set my knives aside and picked up a pair of scissors. I started cutting pages out of a tattered Bible I found a few miles back. "Do you remember what I told you about the Ghost Festival?"

"Yeah," Patrick chuckled. "Your god doesn't provide food, so you gotta feed your ghosts once a year."

"Piss poor god," said Charles.

"We haven't been welcomed to your god." I pointed toward the mountains. "When a minister opened a Sunday School for us up north, they burned down the church." I could feel the men growing tense. "Patrick is right. Good memory, sir. Maybe those men were just sending the church to the dead. For the Ghost Festival, you burn things for the dead to have, like paper houses and fake money."

I tossed the cut-out paper knives and irons, railroad spikes and axes into the fire. They collapsed into black smoke.

"Can't burn gold," Charles pointed out.

"No, no gold for the dead." I cut out a crude handgun from the onion skin pages. "During the first Ghost Festival here, Didi set out the food offering for Gege, trusting Nainai's dream. When the moon rose, Gege came through and told his brother what had happened."

The men leaned closer, their eyes focusing on me. Except Charles. He still stared at the stars.

"His boss had refused to pay him." I shook my head sadly.

The men nodded in sympathy.

"He had counted out how many men had died during the building of his section of the railroad." I held up nine fingers. "The cold, the gnawing hunger. One of his friends had died slowly, crushed under rocks. Gege heard the screaming, then the moaning. Then the silence."

The workers wiped calloused hands across their cheeks. Were the miners remembering the sound of the men's cries in the caves? Did we all cry in the same language: Cantonese, Mandarin, English?

I could have stopped there with this show of emotion. I could have.

I didn't.

"Gege didn't want to die in the desert. Not with his family depending on his wages. So he went to Los Angeles."

The men groaned. "Bad luck, that." Crenshaw spat his chew.

Good. They knew this part – remembered it.

"When the mob stormed the city's Chinese quarter, he was one of the unlucky ones. They strung him up with a clothesline."

The men twisted in their seats.

"Gege heard them before he saw them. The Chinese people had tried to barricade themselves inside. Foolishly, they thought they would be safe behind locked doors. Then he heard the sound of cracking wood, the windows bursting into shards. When the door gave in, they ran upstairs. There was a young boy in front of him. Gege outran him and left him to the mob.

"When Gege returned during the Ghost Festival, there were nail marks on his neck from where he tried to remove the noose." I had wept and pounded the ground with my fists. Had he cried for Mama, Baba?

"I heard they cut off one of their fingers to get a diamond ring." Patrick sucked his teeth.

"Where would a Chinamen get a diamond ring?" Charles shot Patrick a glare that could have burned paper. "It was probably glass."

"It's what I heard," Patrick protested. "They make more on laundry than some miners do."

A silence covered the white men like a heavy blanket of snow.

Did the mutilated Chinese bodies haunt these white men's dreams? Could they hear Gege's screams? Or hell, maybe they just needed to take a piss. I can't read minds.

They yawned, heads nodding against their will.

"What happened to the men who killed him, Cook?" shouted the laundry man. It was the first time I'd heard him raise his voice in front of the white men.

"All eight convictions were overturned." I called back. "Technicalities." The anti-coolie clubs – good old boys saving their men.

"So what did Didi do, Cook?" The laundry man wrung out the shirt. His biceps strained against his sleeves. "Did he go home?"

"Sadly, he had no money to get home. He decided to work in the mining towns. He thought maybe it would be safer than Los Angeles. Didi did the usual work." I burned paper bullets. "Laundry, herbal medicine, even cooking. He got really good at cooking."

I winked at the laundry man.

When the workers joked that we all knew each other, that we were all related, did they understand the consequences of that truth?

"And today is the Ghost Day, of the Ghost Month. My nainai told me it was dangerous to be outside in the dark."

The men were slow to react. The poison from their meal was starting to take effect. "What? What did you say, Cook?"

"Do you believe in ghosts?" I asked louder. "How many dead Chinese men are there for every mile of track?" I tossed the last bit of the paper weapons into the crackling fire. The embers danced upwards, lighting the faces of the ghosts approaching the campsite.

They had heard Charles's whistles calling them. They had seen the clothes hung up under the full moon's light. The white men had devoured the offerings meant for the ghosts, with upright chopsticks like joss sticks.

"Did you think you could run far enough from Los Angeles?" I shouted, my voice echoing against the rocks.

Legions of Chinese ghosts dotted the horizon with their wide brimmed hairs and cues hanging over one shoulder. The living Chinese men erupted from the tents, swinging their hammers and railroad spikes. I grabbed chopsticks from the empty bowls and snuck up behind wide-eyed Louis, then stabbed two chopsticks into his ears.

They remained there like bicycle handlebars.

I drove another pair of chopsticks up Patrick's nostrils. His blood flowed down my hand, dripping from my elbow.

Swinging his body aside, I ripped apart his nose. The chopsticks gave a squick as they left his brain.

I wiped them against my pants, leaving two red streaks. His body twitched.

Johnson came roaring at me, and I plunged the chopsticks into his eyes.

My hand found my cleaver. I danced around the fire and caught Crenshaw across the neck. The first two spurts were the largest sprays, but his hand interrupted the subsequent gushing. He fell to the ground, the blood slipping between his fingers. His gasps sounded wet.

One man tried to run. A ghost caught up with him, holding a newly acquired paper knife. It was strong enough to puncture him, right above the belly button. It smelled of shit.

Charles fired his gun at the approaching ghosts. Bam, bam, bam. The sound echoed in the camp. Bam, bam, bam. The bullets bounced off rocks and whizzed into sandy dirt.

I longed to trace my cleaver across his throat. He was the one my brother had heard breathing in his ear as the clothesline landed under his jaw. Charles had stood as close as a lover before dropping my brother over the balcony.

There was a chorus of white men's shouts as they emerged from their railcars. I watched the ghosts chase men down mineshafts. Their screams echoed up as they fell to the eighteen hells. The mines were not satisfied with this meager sacrifice. Gray shadows dragged a shrieking man down. He left a brown dust trail.

Charles tried to grab a ghost's long braid, but it was like grabbing clouds. He finally turned to run, then turned his gun on me.

The gun clicked empty just as an iron smashed into the side of his head. Charles's eyes rolled up into his head, and he fell forward. The laundry man behind him didn't even acknowledge me before he spun and crashed the iron into another white man's face.

The paper guns had paper bullets. They tore through the white men's flesh just the same as metal.

"What yellow evil is this?" one man shouted as he hefted his miner's pick against the invading ghosts. Two appeared under him and sunk him straight into the dirt. Sand swirled for long moments before it finally stilled.

The massacre could have lasted minutes or hours. But eventually, we realized that only the Chinese people remained. The desert filled with Mandarin, Cantonese, Hokkien, Shanghainese, and others I could not name.

I finally unclenched my fingers from the knife's handle. The blood had started to dry, and my fingers were sticky.

I searched the gray crowd for a familiar face – one that shared my father's broad nose, my mother's narrow eyes. A young ghostly man separated from the other ghosts and tipped his fedora to me. He looked the way I remembered, without the bruised neck and scratch marks. The offerings must have filled him out, as he no longer looked gaunt.

"Were you the little brother?" asked the laundry man beside me.

"Thank you for your help earlier," I said, ignoring his question.

"Hell, he'd be handsome if he wasn't dead," commented the laundry man.

"Careful. If you were a woman, I would offer you a ghost groom."

I scrutinized his face as it split with a smile, bright with crowded teeth. "I think I could be your sao zi." Older brother's wife?

I laughed. "How did I not guess it before?"

She snorted. "With your anger, you were too focused on the white men." The laundry woman held out her calloused hand. Dried blood was embedded in both our hands.

I shook hers, smiling. "Then, you would call me xiao gu zi." Husband's younger sister.

She laughed, surprising me with a fearless sound I had not heard in a very long time. We had been keeping the same secret from the men. When she finally released my hand – or I released hers – my cheeks were burning.

I spent the rest of the night telling Gege about my search for his killers in the past year. Each railroad station, miners' town, mile of track brought me closer and closer to this final revenge. Without the red mist clouding my vision, I kept catching the laundry woman's glances.

The ghost grinned at me, eyes crinkling. "Xie xie, mei mei." Thank you, little sister.

"There is enough money in these dead mens' pockets for a boat ride home," I told him. "I will tell Nainai that you are at peace, if she doesn't already know."

He looked over his shoulder at the laundress. "What about Old Gold Mountain? Maybe you can make some more money there. Our village always seemed too small for you." My brother grinned impishly. "Besides, who else will burn offerings for me here?"

We helped the ghosts loot the camp. The clothes and furniture fed the fire. We laughed as we furnished the ghosts' homes in the afterlife. The bonfire was loud in its hunger pangs.

When the sun started to rise, the ghosts stepped back into the darkness. After I cook everyone some breakfast, perhaps I will find enough for the boat fare home. Or enough for a home by the ocean for a cook and a laundress.

THE END

Biographies & Sources

Dr. Ahmed Al-Rawi
Foreword: Spirits & Ghouls Short Stories
Dr. Ahmed Al-Rawi is an Associate Professor at the School of Communication at Simon Fraser University, Canada. His research expertise is related to the study of folklore, popular culture, and communication with emphasis on the Middle East. Al-Rawi has published several academic studies that traced the historical origins of mythical creatures in Arabia like the ghoul, rukh, and dragon often using cross-cultural literary comparisons.

Stewart C. Baker
The Mother of Sands
(Originally Published in *Tales of Mystery, Suspense & Terror*, 2014)
Stewart C. Baker is an academic librarian and author of speculative fiction and poetry, along with the occasional piece of interactive fiction. His fiction has appeared in *Nature*, *Lightspeed*, and *Flash Fiction Online*, among other places, and his poetry has appeared in Fantasy, Asimov's, and numerous haiku magazines. Stewart was born in England, has lived in South Carolina, Japan, and Southern California, and now lives within the traditional homelands of the Luckiamute Band of Kalapuya in western Oregon, along with his family – although if anyone asks, he'll usually say he's from the Internet.

Mary Elizabeth Braddon
Good Lady Ducayne
(Originally Published in *The Strand Magazine*, 1896)
Mary Elizabeth Braddon (1835–1915) was born in London, England. During her lifetime, Braddon was a productive writer, producing over eighty novels. Her most notable novel, *Lady Audley's Secret* (1862), brought Braddon much recognition and fortune. In addition to her tales of intrigue, Braddon wrote a number of works on the supernatural, including, *Gerard, or, the World, the Flesh and the Devil*, 'The Cold Embrace' and 'At Chrighton Abbey'. Beyond her literary endeavours, Braddon founded the magazine *Belgravia* (1866), showcasing the latest serialized sensation novels, poems and travel narratives alongside essays on fashion, history and science.

Rebecca Brothers
The Widow Watcher of Wooten Creek
(First Publication)
Rebecca Brothers is a writer and teacher from Lexington, Kentucky. In her preteen years, she was an avid consumer of paranormal paperbacks, titles like *Christina's Ghost* and Richard Peck's *The Ghost Belonged to Me*, the kind of books that haunt you forever. She currently resides in Louisville with her husband and children, but still makes frequent trips to the mountains where her father was born. She writes novels and articles about her home in the bourbon and bluegrass state.

Ramsey Campbell
Holding the Light
(Originally Published by PS Publishing, 2011)
The Oxford Companion to English Literature describes Ramsey Campbell as 'Britain's most respected living horror writer'. He has been given more awards than any other writer in the field, including the Grand Master Award of the World Horror Convention, the Lifetime Achievement Award of the Horror Writers Association, the Living Legend Award of the International Horror Guild and the World Fantasy Lifetime Achievement Award. In 2015 he was made an Honorary Fellow of Liverpool John Moores University for outstanding services to literature. Among his novels available from Flame Tree Press are *Thirteen Days by Sunset Beach*, *The Wise Friend*, *Somebody's Voice*, *Fellstones*, *The Lonely Lands*, and his *Three Births of Daoloth* trilogy: *The Searching Dead*, *Born to the Dark* and *The Way of the Worm*.

Georgia Cook
They Come at Night
(First Publication)
Georgia Cook is an illustrator and writer from London. She has written for publications such as *Baffling* magazine, *Luna Station Quarterly*, and *Vastarien Lit*, as well as the Doctor Who range with Big Finish. She also frequently writes and narrates for horror anthology podcasts such as 'Creepy', 'The Other Stories', and 'The Night's End'. She can be found on Twitter @georgiacooked and on her website at georgiacookwriter.com.

Gina Easton
Once Upon a Graveyard
(First Publication)
Gina Easton is a former registered nurse. She has had over twenty-five short-stories (horror and fantasy) published in various magazines and anthologies. Her debut horror novel, *Black Jack*, was released in 2020 by World Castle Publishing. A second novel is currently in the publication process. It is a paranormal romance with elements of fantasy and magic. When not writing, Gina enjoys quality time with her husband and dog (both of whom are house-trained). She adores the mysterious and magical aspects of life. She lives in Toronto, Canada.

Amelia B. Edwards
Sister Johanna's Story
(Originally Published in *A Night on the Borders of the Black Forest*, 1890)
The Story of Salome
(Originally Published in *Tinsley's Christmas Annual*, 1867)
Amelia B. Edwards (1831–92) was born in London, England. Enjoying a rich and varied career as a writer, journalist and Egyptologist, Edwards was a precocious talent, as her first poem was published when she was only seven years old. Her most successful works included the short story 'The Phantom Coach' – one of her many ghost stories, and the novels *Barbara's History* and *Lord Brackenbury*, alongside her Egyptian travelogue *A Thousand Miles up the Nile*, which detailed her extensive 1873–74 voyage through the country.

Elizabeth Gaskell
The Poor Clare
(Originally Published in *Household Words*, 1856)
Victorian novelist Elizabeth Gaskell (1810–65) was born in London, England, and is widely known for her biography of her friend Charlotte Brontë. In a family of eight children, only Elizabeth and her brother John survived past childhood. Her mother's early death caused her to be raised by her aunt in Knutsford, Cheshire, a place that inspired her to later write her most famous work *Cranford*. Tragedy struck again when Gaskell's only son died, and it was then that she began to write. All the misfortune in her life led her to write her many gothic and horror tales.

Bruce Golden
The Devil of Avalon
(First Publication)
Bruce Golden's short stories have been published across more than two dozen countries and 40 anthologies. *New Myths* magazine said of his novel *Red Sky, Blue Moon*, 'With thematic echoes of *Dune*, *Dances with Wolves*, and *The Last Samurai*, it's an epic tale of adventure and arrogance, discovery and desire, courage and greed.' *Asimov's Science Fiction* described his novel *Evergreen*, 'If you can imagine Ursula Le Guin channeling H. Rider Haggard, you'll have the barest conception of this stirring book, which centers around a mysterious artifact and the people in its thrall.' His recent book *Monster Town*, a satirical send-up of old hard-boiled detective stories featuring movie monsters of the black & white era, has been stuck in TV series development hell for some years now. Read more at goldentales.tripod.com

Caye Gowyn
In Bleak December
(First Publication)
Caye Gowyn is from Louisiana but currently resides on Long Island, New York with her husband. From a young age, her mother, an author of sixteen novels, inspired her passion for words. She is working on completing her first book while also writing short stories, most of which focus on ghosts, the end of the world, or both. Outside of writing she is a photographer whose work has been featured in several exhibitions and publications, and she also holds a master's degree in history.

John Linwood Grant
The Smoke Market
(First Publication)
John Linwood Grant is a professional writer/editor from Yorkshire. He generally calls his work strange fictions, incorporating a range of weird, psychological and supernatural elements, and has had some eighty tales published in the last few years, including in award-winning anthologies. His second collection, *Where All is Night, and Starless* (2021, Trepidatio), was nominated for the Shirley Jackson Award. As an editor, he is responsible for the *Sherlock Holmes & the Occult Detectives* series (Belanger) and other anthologies, as well as the successful *Occult Detective Magazine.* He can be found regularly on Facebook, and at his eclectic website greydogtales.com/blog.

Rayne Hall
Nine Rings of Silver and One of Bronze
(*Originally Published in Fiends: Ten Tales of Demons*, 2015)
Rayne Hall lives in rural Bulgaria (Eastern Europe) where she writes practical non-fiction books and creepy gothic stories. She is the author of the Writer's Craft series (e.g. *Writing Gothic Fiction*, *Writing Scary Scenes*, *Writing Vivid Dialogue*, *Writing Deep Point of View*) and horror story collections (e.g. *The Bride's Curse: Bulgarian Gothic Ghost and Horror Stories*), and the editor of horror anthologies (e.g. *The Haunted Train: Creepy Tales from the Railways*, *Among the Headstones: Creepy Tales from the Graveyard*). She creates an organic food forest garden, explores spooky abandoned homes from Bulgaria's Communist period, and trains black cats. See more at *rayneball.com*.

Vanessa C. Hawkins
Two Trees
(Originally Published by Dark Dragon Publishing, 2019)
A life-long lover of horror, Vanessa wrote her first story when she was in grade five. It was titled 'Mutilated' and warranted a trip to the school guidance counsellor. With over a dozen publications under her belt, Vanessa is not only a proud mom, but a bestselling author. She was afforded second place in the David Adams Richards Prize last year, and honorable mentions in the WFNB writing competition for her novel *A Child to Cry Over*. She lives with her husband Brendon and daughter Bernie in Canada, and still hasn't gotten the dog she was promised seven years ago…

Jennifer Hudak
Atticat
(First Publication)
Jennifer Hudak is a speculative fiction writer fuelled mostly by tea. Her short stories can be found in publications such as *The Magazine of Fantasy & Science Fiction*, *Fantasy Magazine*, and *Drabblecast*. Her work has appeared on both *the Locus Magazine* and the SFWA recommended reading lists, and has been twice nominated for a Pushcart Prize. Originally from Boston, she now lives with her family in Upstate New York where she teaches yoga, knits pocket-sized animals, and misses the ocean. Find out more about her on her website: JenniferHudakWrites.com.

Brianna Ishii-McFaull
Apartment 3G
(Originally Published on Brianna's Personal Website in 2021, and Adapted for Audio by Thirteen Podcast in 2022)
Brianna Ishii-McFaull is a Canadian who sometimes writes stuff. A lifelong fan of horror, Brianna has a degree in physics that she uses exclusively for half-sober party trivia. When she's not writing, she can be found cleaning up after a very polite leopard gecko and two exceedingly disrespectful rabbits, or playing 'one more turn' of Civ VI. You can follow Brianna's work by visiting her website, briannaishiimcfaull.ca, or connecting with her on social media.

M.R. James
A View from a Hill
(Originally Published in *A Warning to the Curious, and Other Ghost Stories*, 1925)
Montague Rhodes James (1862–1936), whose works are regarded as being at the forefront of the ghost story genre, was born in Kent, England. James dispensed with the traditional, predictable techniques of ghost story construction, instead using realistic contemporary settings for his works. He was also a British medieval scholar, so his stories tended to incorporate antiquarian elements. His stories often reflect his childhood in Suffolk and his talented acting career, which both seem to have assisted in the build-up of tension and horror in his works.

Dylan Kingsley
What Have You Brought Me?
(First Publication)
Dylan Kingsley is a writer, a printmaker and sculptor, and a historian of The Long Eighteenth Century. In both his fiction and non-fiction, he uses the lens of intimacy to delve into the complexities and messiness of being human. His work was selected for *Apparition Literary Magazine's* January 2023 Flash Fiction Challenge. He currently lives in the White Mountains of northern New Hampshire with his partner, three black cats, and a rescue pug.

Amanda Cecelia Lang
Shrieking Willow
(Originally Published *Thirteen Podcast* by, May 2021)
Amanda Cecelia Lang is a horror author and aspiring recluse from Denver, Colorado. As a die-hard scary movie nerd, her favourite things are meta-slashers, 80s nostalgia, and the rise of a fierce final girl. Her stories currently haunt the dark corners of several podcasts, magazines, and anthologies, including *NoSleep*, *Uncharted*, *Dark Matter*, and *Mixtape: 1986*. Her short story 'The Clover Café' was recently long-listed for Ellen Datlow's Best Horror of the Year. You can stalk her work at amandacecelialang.com – just don't be surprised if she leaps out at you from the shadows.

Andrew and Nora Lang
The Story of Sidi Nouman
(Originally Published in *The Arabian Nights Entertainments*, 1898)
Scottish writer and critic Andrew Lang (1844–1912) was born and raised in Selkirk. In 1875 he married Leonora 'Nora' Blanche Alleyne (1851–1933), who would become his collaborator on many works. Although Lang worked variously as a historian, journalist, poet, and anthropologist, his greatest legacy has been his works on folklore, mythology, and religion. Among these are the *Fairy Books*, 25 volumes of folk and fairy tales published Lang published with his wife, including *The Arabian Nights Entertainments* (1898), their adaptation of the One Thousand Nights and a Night folk tales. While many volumes in the series list Lang alone as the editor, it was in fact Nora who translated and adapted these works. Lang later acknowledged his wife's significant contribution in the preface to *The Lilac Fairy Book (1910)*, crediting almost all of the series to 'the work of Mrs. Lang', and later volumes also listed her as an author.

J.Sheridan Le Fanu

Squire Toby's Will

(Originally Published in *Madam Crowl's Ghost and Other Tales of Mystery*, 1923)

The remarkable father of Victorian ghost stories Joseph Thomas Sheridan Le Fanu (1814–73) was born in Dublin, Ireland. His gothic tales and mystery novels led to him become a leading ghost story writer of the nineteenth century. Three oft-cited works of his are *Uncle Silas*, *Carmilla* and *The House by the Churchyard*, which all are assumed to have influenced Bram Stoker's *Dracula*. Le Fanu wrote his most successful and productive works after his wife's tragic death and he remained a relatively strong writer up until his own death.

Fiona Lehn

The Shabah

(First Publication)

Little is known about reclusive writer Fiona Lehn, but legends abound. Some claim she emerged from her mother's womb singing 'We Are the Champions', a half-written story clenched in her fists. Many believe she is serving life without parole for leading an Ottawa sit-in demanding that cloudberries be made one of the four food groups. Others assert that Lehn daily frolics with Sasquatch in glacier-fed slipstreams. All we really know is this: Lehn lives in Canada and has M.E. She writes songs and speculative stories, is a Writers of the Future winner, and has been published by Aqueduct Press. Discover more at fb.me/FiFiHermitage.

H.P. Lovecraft

Pickman's Model

(Originally Published in *Weird Tales*, 1927)

The Dream-Quest of Unknown Kadath

(Originally Published in *Arkham House*, 1943)

Master of weird fiction Howard Phillips Lovecraft (1890–1937) was born in Providence, Rhode Island. Featuring unknown and otherworldly creatures, his stories were one of the first to mix science fiction with horror. Plagued by nightmares from an early age, he was inspired to write his dark and strange fantasy tales; and the isolation he must have experienced from suffering frequent illnesses can be felt as a prominent theme in his work. Lovecraft inspired many other authors, and his most famous story 'The Call of Cthulhu' has gone on to influence many aspects of popular culture.

Samuel Marzioli

Only Monsters

(First Publication)

Samuel Marzioli is a Filipino-American author of dark fiction. He has work in numerous publications and podcasts, including *The Best of Apex Magazine*, Flame Tree's *Asian Ghost Short Stories*, *The Dread Machine*, and *LeVar Burton Reads*. 'Only Monsters' is a retelling of his story 'Servant of the Aswang'. Both are part of a series of unconnected works inspired by Filipino folklore, some of which appear in his debut collection *Hollow Skulls and Other Stories*. For more information, visit his blog marzioli.blogspot.com or follow him on Twitter (@marzioli).

S.R. Masters
The Jumper
(Originally Published in *Afraid of the Shadows*, 2021)
S R Masters grew up around Birmingham in the UK. After studying Philosophy at Cambridge University, he worked in public health. He currently lives in Oxford with his wife and children. His award-winning short fiction and novels have been published internationally. Labelled as 'a writer to watch' by *Publishers Weekly*, his novels include *The Killer You Know* (Sphere) and *The Trial (*Harper Collins).

Bret Nelson
Afterlife on Mars
(First Publication)
Bret Nelson is an Emmy Award-winning creator. You can find his short fiction in *Gabba Gabba Hey: An anthology of fiction inspired by the music of The Ramones* from Fahrenheit Press or *The Best of MetaStellar Year One*. When he's not writing stories, he directs TV shows and makes games. He has worked with Kermit the Frog, Buzz Lightyear, and Conan the Cimmerian. Right now, he's working on things he can't talk about (that's what the contracts say).

Lena Ng
You Can Never Go Home Again
(Originally Published in *Devolution Z: The Horror Magazine*, Issue #16, Jan 2017)
Lena Ng lives in Toronto, Canada. Her short stories have appeared in eighty publications including *Amazing Stories* and Flame Tree's *Asian Ghost Short Stories* and *Weird Horror*. Her stories have been performed for podcasts such as *Gallery of Curiosities*, *Utopia Science Fiction*, *Love Letters to Poe*, and *Horrifying Tales of Wonder*. *Under an Autumn Moon* is her short story collection. Her story 'You Can Never Go Home Again' was inspired by *onryou*, Japanese female ghosts who died after being wronged.

John Payne
The History of Gherib and His Brother Agib
(Originally Published in *The Book of the Thousand Nights and One Night*, 1882–4)
Devon-born poet, translator and scholar John Payne (1842–1916) is most remembered for his translations of Giovanni Boccacio's *Decameron*, *The Book of the Thousand Nights and One Night*, and the Diwan Hafez. He was a particularly ardent admirer Hafez, who he felt to be one of the greatest poets in the world, and his translation of the poetry of Francois Villon was considered the 'foundation' of the Villon Society. His own poetry is often grouped with that of the Pre-Raphaelite Brotherhood, with whom he associated.

Sam W. Pisciotta
Words for the Dead
(First Publication)
Sam W. Pisciotta lives in Colorado. After years of difficult training in daydreaming and doodling, he now calls himself a writer and visual artist. Thousands of cups of coffee and hours of contemplation have prepared him to pull worlds from the ether. Sam is a member of the SFWA, HWA, and Codex Writers. He holds a Master of Arts in Literary Studies from the University of Colorado. His fiction has appeared in or is forthcoming in *F&SF*, *Asimov's*,

Analog, *Factor Four Magazine*, and other fine publications. His award-winning artwork has been shown throughout Colorado. Follow him on Twitter @silo34 and silo34.com.

Josephine Queen
Tangled Tales of Jumbies and Silk Cotton Trees
(First Publication)
Josephine writes tales that tend towards the darker side of fiction. She is represented by Alyssa Eisner Henkin of Birch Path Literary and is currently working on a rewrite of a middle-grade fantasy novel. You can read her work *in Devil's Party Press Halloween Party 2019*, *The Siren's Call*, *72 Hours of Insanity* Volumes 8 and 11, *Fudoki Magazine*, *Little Old Lady Comedy*, and *Potato Soup Journal*. The inspiration for this story comes from tales of jumbies her Guyanese mother told her – often after the sun went down and things whispered from the shadows.

Charlotte Riddell (Mrs J. H. Riddell)
The Walnut-Tree House
(Originally Published in *Weird Stories*, 1882)
Charlotte Riddell (1832–1906) was born in County Antrim, Ireland. After the death of her father she moved with her mother to London in 1855. She is best known for her ghost stories with their atmospheric settings, which Riddell drew from her own experiences in Ireland and London. Riddell struggled to earn a living from her writing, despite being a highly popular author, and due to her poor circumstances became the first pensioner of the Society of Authors in 1901.

Erica Ruppert
Oh Bury Me Not
(First Publication)
Erica Ruppert, HWA, SFWA. lives in northern New Jersey with her husband and too many cats. Her novella *Sisters in Arms* was released in 2021. Her short stories have appeared in magazines including *Vastarien*, *Lamplight*, and *Nightmare*, on podcasts including *PodCastle*, and in multiple anthologies. Her collection *Imago and Other Transformations* will be released by Trepidatio Publishing in March 2023. When she is not writing, she runs, bakes, and gardens with more enthusiasm than skill.

C.R. Serajeddini
Xarus's Mirror
(First Publication)
C.R. Serajeddini is a British-Kurdish author of fantasy and science fiction. Inspired by her background, her work borrows from Kurdish history, and Mesopotamian and Persian mythology, often interwoven with fantastical and extra-terrestrial elements. Her writing has appeared – or is forthcoming – in several anthologies, ncluding *Immigrant Sci-Fi* and *Lost Atlantis* from Flame Tree Publishing, and *Gargantua* from Air & Nothingness Press. She's currently working on her first novel, a YA Space Fantasy featuring a kick-ass heroine. When she's not busy exploring imaginary worlds, she enjoys hiking the mountains and coast with her family and gazing up at the stars.

Evelyn Teng
Three Years
(First Publication)
Evelyn was born and raised in Houston, Texas. After earning a double major in English and Psychology at Texas A&M University, she worked at a number of jobs, including writing tutor, library

assistant, legal/technical writer, and contract writer for an aerospace company. Currently, she works for an immigration law firm. In her free time, she reads, writes, plays video games, and practises baking way too many cookies, which she happily shares with anyone who walks through her door.

Wen Wen Yang

Ghost Festival in the Desert

(Originally Published in *Blood in the Soil, Terror on the Wind*, 2022)

Wen Wen Yang is a first-generation Chinese American from the Bronx, New York. She graduated from Barnard College of Columbia University with a degree in English and creative writing. This story was inspired by the Los Angeles Chinese massacre of 1871. You can find her short fiction in *Fantasy Magazine*, *Zooscape*, *Fit for the Gods* and more. An up-to-date bibliography is on WenWenWrites.com. She listens to audiobooks at three times speed, talks almost as fast, and misses dependable public transportation.

FLAME TREE PUBLISHING
Epic, Dark, Thrilling & Gothic

New & Classic Writing

Flame Tree's Gothic Fantasy books offer a carefully curated series of new titles, each with combinations of original and classic writing:

*Chilling Horror • Chilling Ghost • Asian Ghost • Science Fiction • Murder Mayhem
Crime & Mystery • Swords & Steam • Dystopia Utopia • Supernatural Horror
Lost Worlds • Time Travel • Heroic Fantasy • Pirates & Ghosts • Agents & Spies
Endless Apocalypse • Alien Invasion • Robots & AI • Lost Souls • Haunted House
Cosy Crime • American Gothic • Urban Crime • Epic Fantasy • Detective Mysteries
Detective Thrillers • A Dying Planet • Footsteps in the Dark
Bodies in the Library • Strange Lands • Weird Horror • Lost Atlantis
Lovecraft Mythos • Terrifying Ghosts • Black Sci-Fi • Chilling Crime
Compelling Science Fiction • Christmas Gothic • First Peoples Shared Stories
Alternate History • Hidden Realms • Immigrant Sci-Fi • Spirits & Ghouls*

Also, new companion titles offer rich collections of classic fiction, myths and tales in the gothic fantasy tradition:

*Charles Dickens Supernatural • George Orwell Visions of Dystopia • H.G. Wells
Sherlock Holmes • Edgar Allan Poe • Bram Stoker Horror • Mary Shelley Horror
Lovecraft • M.R. James Ghost Stories • The Divine Comedy • The Age of Queen Victoria
Brothers Grimm Fairy Tales • Hans Christian Andersen Fairy Tales • Moby Dick
Alice's Adventures in Wonderland • King Arthur & The Knights of the Round Table
The Wonderful Wizard of Oz • Ramayana • The Odyssey and the Iliad • The Aeneid
Paradise Lost • The Decameron • One Thousand and One Arabian Nights
Persian Myths & Tales • African Myths & Tales • Celtic Myths & Tales
Greek Myths & Tales • Norse Myths & Tales • Chinese Myths & Tales
Japanese Myths & Tales • Native American Myths & Tales • Irish Fairy Tales
Heroes & Heroines Myths & Tales • Gods & Monsters Myths & Tales
Beasts & Creatures Myths & Tales • Witches, Wizards, Seers & Healers Myths & Tales*

Available from all good bookstores, worldwide, and online at
flametreepublishing.com

See our new fiction imprint
FLAME TREE PRESS | FICTION WITHOUT FRONTIERS
New and original writing in Horror, Crime, SF and Fantasy

And join our monthly newsletter with offers and more stories:
FLAME TREE FICTION NEWSLETTER
flametreepress.com

GOTHIC FANTASY